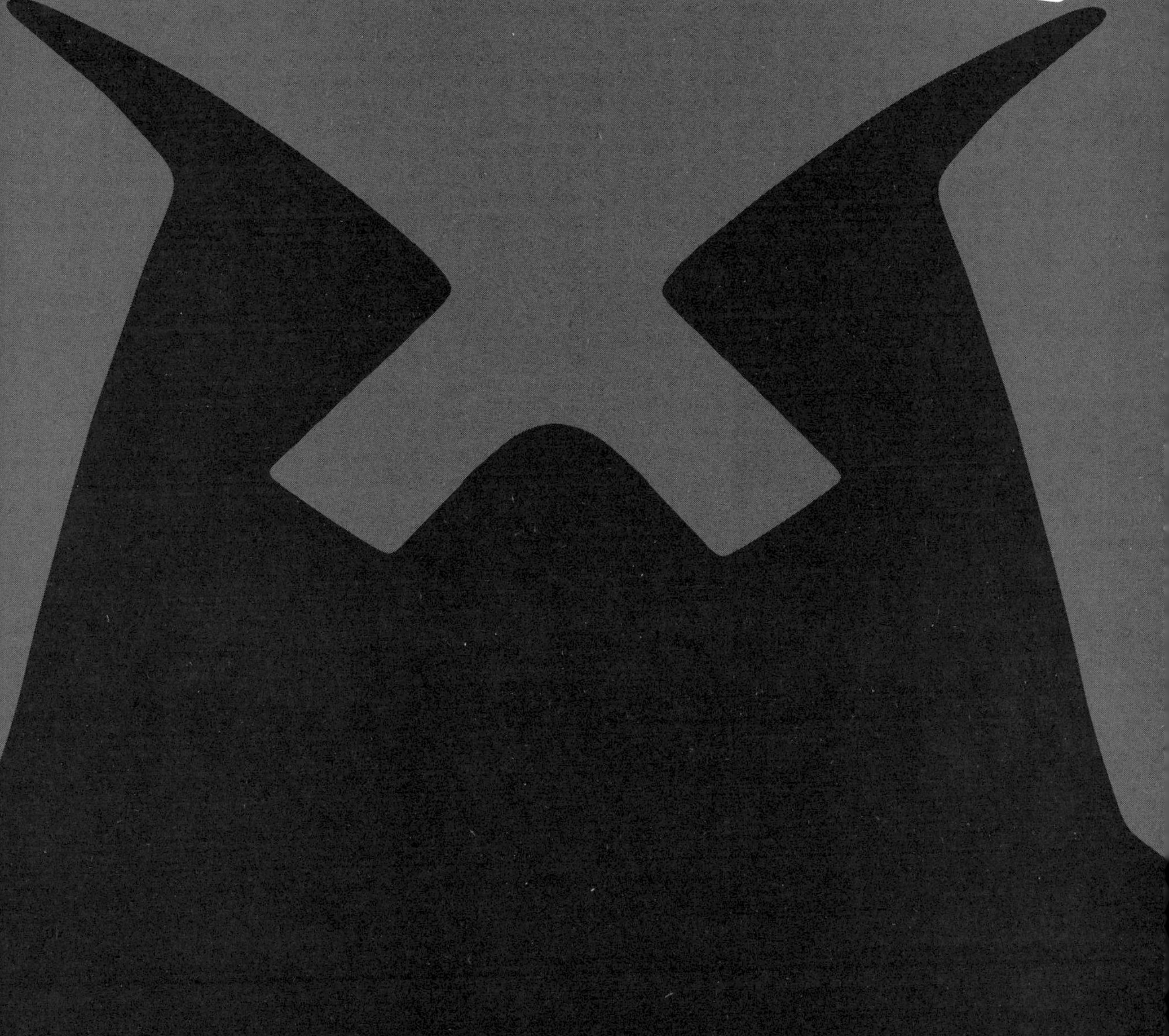

JUDGE DREDD
THE COMPLETE CASE FILES 02

JUDGE DREDD CREATED BY JOHN WAGNER AND CARLOS EZQUERRA

JUDGE DREDD
THE COMPLETE CASE FILES 02

PAT MILLS ★ JOHN WAGNER ★ CHRIS LOWDER
Writers

MIKE McMAHON ★ RON SMITH ★ DAVE GIBBONS ★ BRIAN BOLLAND
BRENDAN McCARTHY ★ BRETT EWINS ★ GARRY LEACH
Artists

TOM FRAME ★ JOHN ALDRICH ★ JACK POTTER ★ PETER KNIGHT ★ TOM KNIGHT ★ DAVE GIBBONS
Letterers

MIKE McMAHON
Cover Artist

Creative Director and CEO: Jason Kingsley
Chief Technical Officer: Chris Kingsley
2000 AD Editor in Chief: Matt Smith
Graphic Novels Editor: Keith Richardson
Graphic Design: Simon Parr & Luke Preece
Reprographics: Kathryn Symes

Original Commissioning Editor: Kelvin Gosnell

Published by Rebellion, Riverside House, Osney Mead, Oxford OX2 0ES, UK.
www.rebellion.co.uk

ISBN: 978-1-906735-99-9
Printed in the USA
10 9 8 7 6 5 4 3 2 1
1st Printing: December 2010

For information on other *2000 AD* graphic novels, or if you have any comments on this book, please email books@2000ADonline.com

To find out more about *2000 AD*, visit www.2000ADonline.com

THE GREAT FRIED FOOD FIASCO!

Welcome to *Case Files 02*, which features 'The Cursed Earth' saga; an early *Judge Dredd* epic written in parts by Pat Mills, John Wagner and Chris Lowder (credited as Jack Adrian), and featuring the stunning artwork of Brian Bolland and Mike McMahon.

Unfortunately parts 11-12 and 17-18 of the story have had to be omitted due to copyright infringement, but here is the synopsis to these stories, starting below.

Parts 11-12 of 'The Cursed Earth' appeared in Progs 71-72 respectively and were titled 'Battle of The Burger Barons' and 'Burger Law!' These two episodes were written by John Wagner and featured the art of Mike McMahon. In this part of the story Judge Dredd and the punk biker Spikes Harvey Rotten get caught up in the middle of a war between two burger barons, who were the descendants of original fast-food chain owners. Dredd and Spikes are captured by the Marauders and taken to MacDonald City where burgers and shakes are on everybody's menu and natural food is completely outlawed. They escape the sluggish burger-fed guards only to fall into the hands of the opposition, who have mistaken them for Marauders. The duo are sentenced to death by hanging, but luckily Judge Jack and the Land Raider come to our heroes' rescue at the last moment.

Parts 17-18 of 'The Cursed Earth' were published in Progs 77-78 and were titled 'Giants Aren't Gentlemen' and 'Soul Food'. Chris Lowder wrote these chapters and the art was provided by Brian Bolland. Dredd and his team come across a pre-Atomic War agricultural research station run by Dr Gribbon, who bears an uncanny resemblance to a well-known Southern fried chicken Colonel. Gribbon's experiments, based on recognizable characters from the 20th century, live within the station's confines. Dredd, Spikes and Judge Jack are captured but escape with a little extra help from tweak and a rebellious faction amongst Gribbon's creations. The station is finally destroyed along with all of it's inhabitants, leaving Dredd and his party free to continue their mission across the Cursed Earth...

Keith Richardson
Graphic Novels Editor

JUDGE DREDD

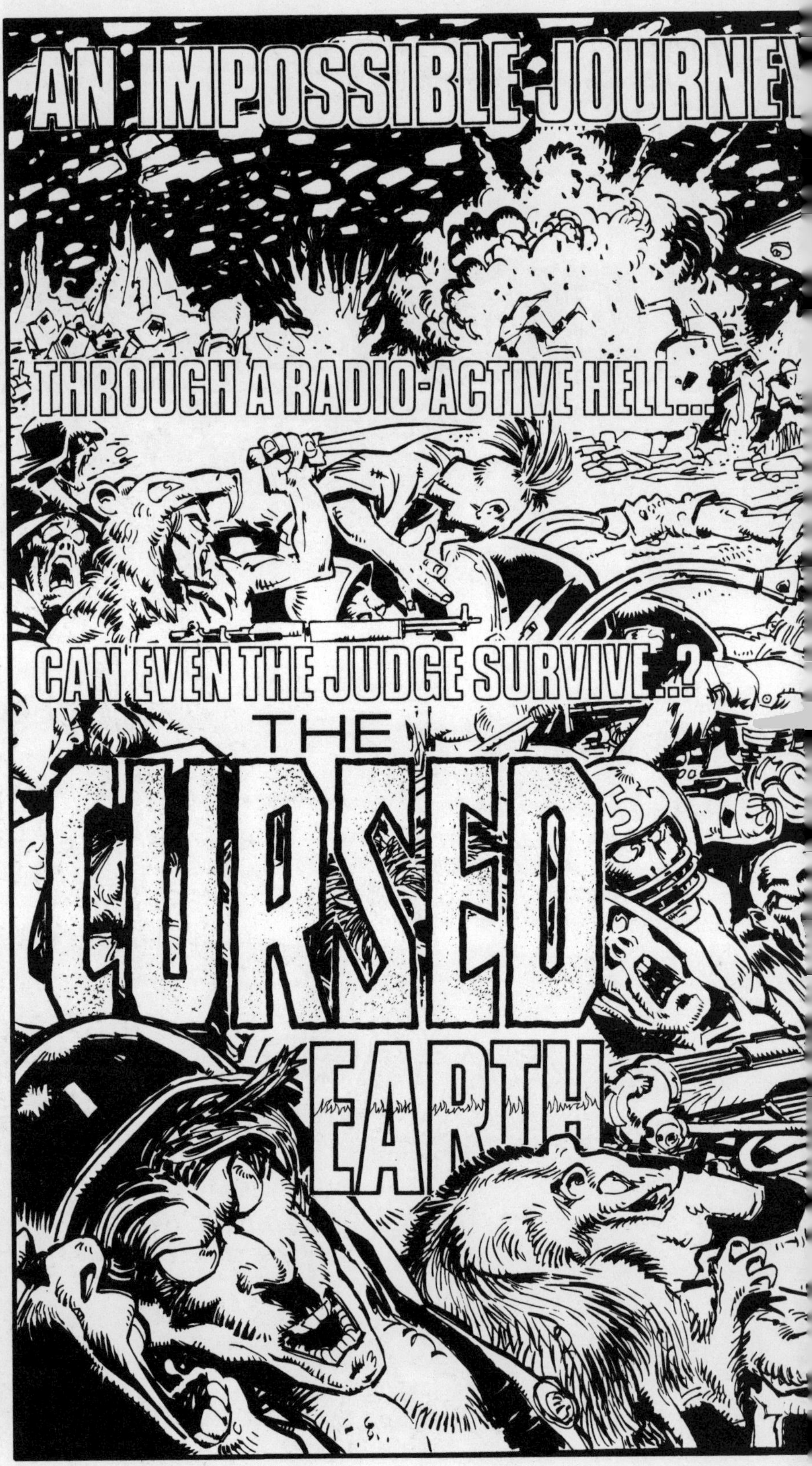
AN IMPOSSIBLE JOURNEY
THROUGH A RADIO-ACTIVE HELL...
CAN EVEN THE JUDGE SURVIVE..?
THE CURSED EARTH

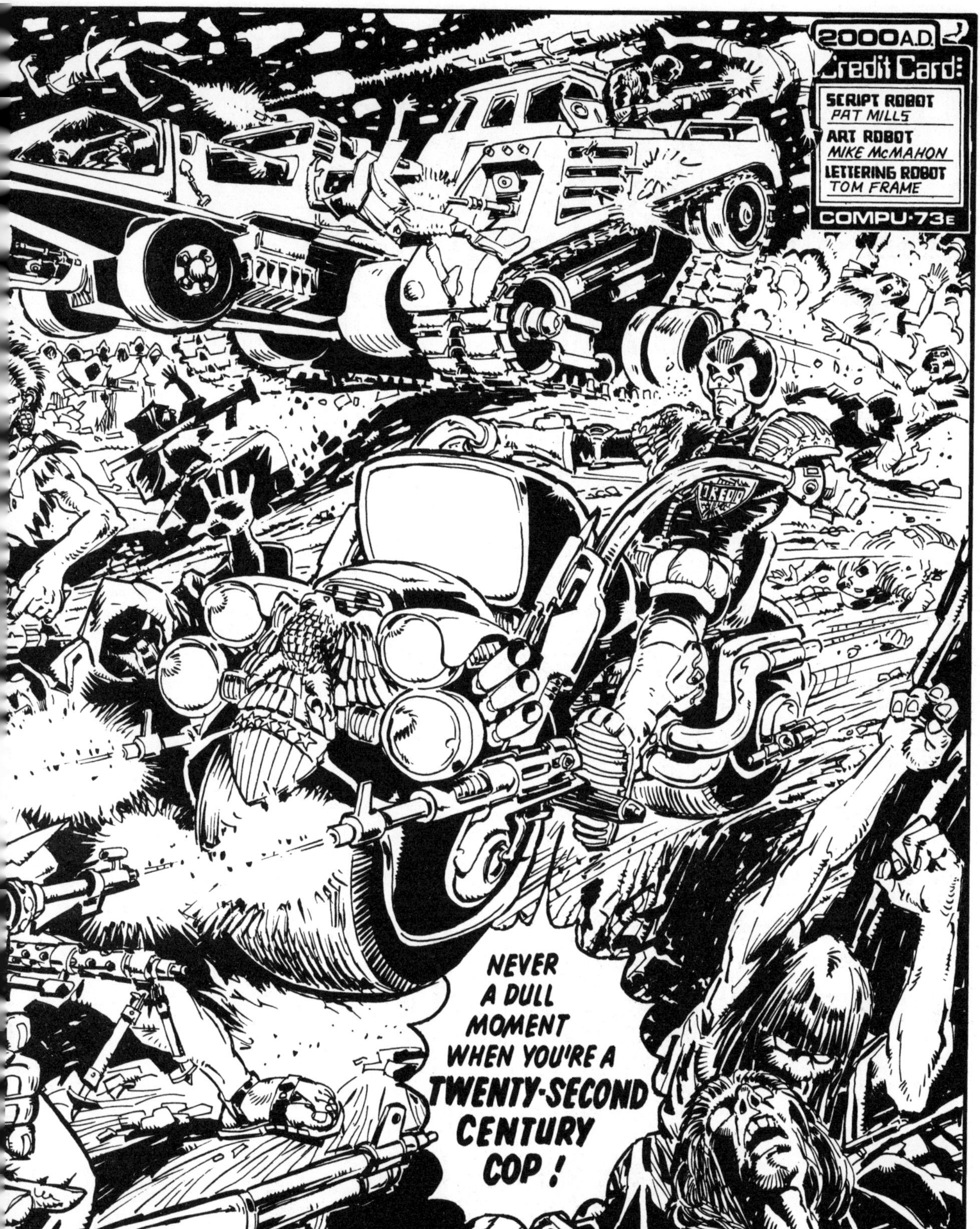
2000 A.D.
Credit Card:
SCRIPT ROBOT
PAT MILLS
ART ROBOT
MIKE McMAHON
LETTERING ROBOT
TOM FRAME
COMPU·73E
NEVER A DULL MOMENT WHEN YOU'RE A TWENTY-SECOND CENTURY COP!

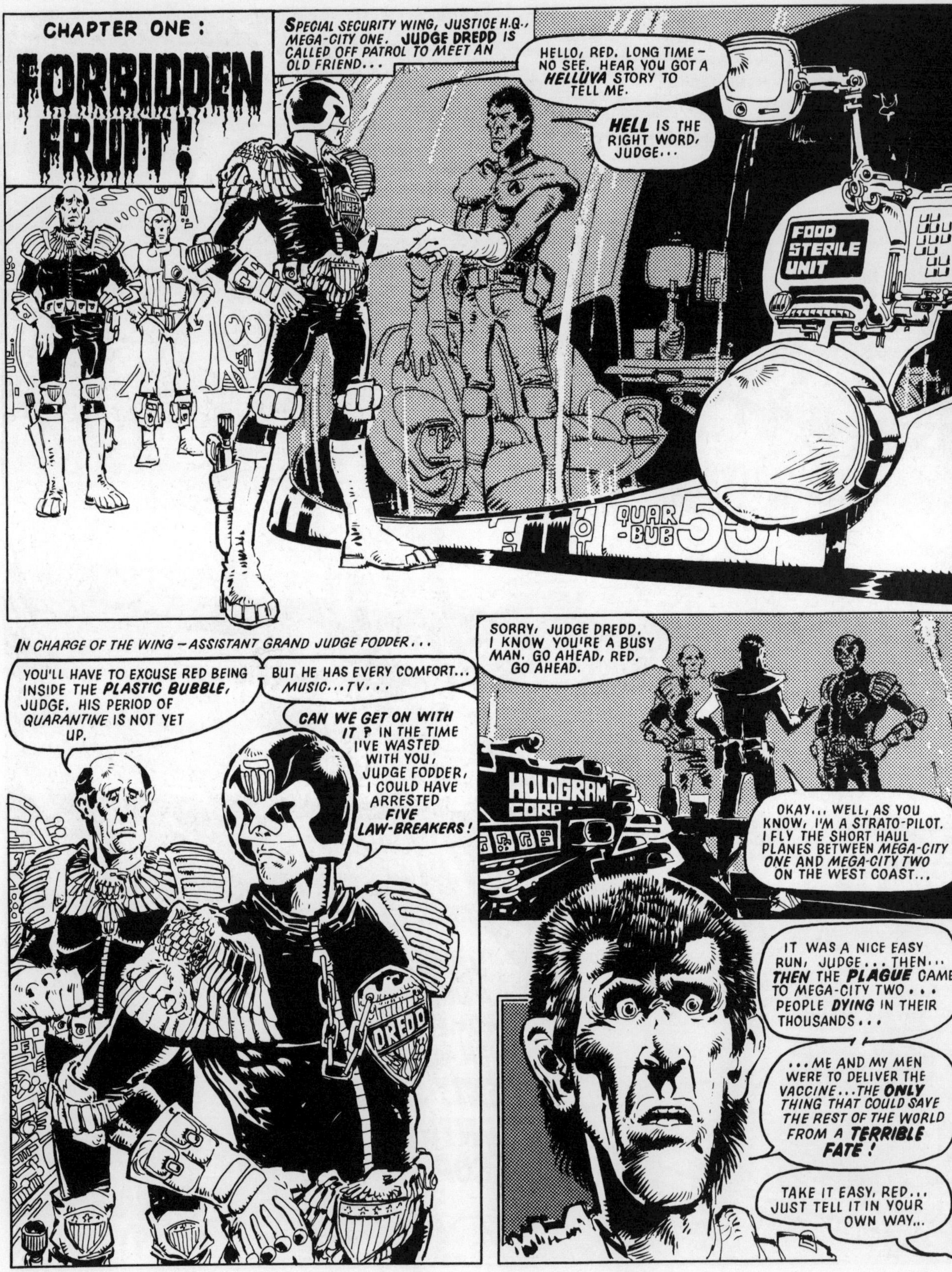
CHAPTER ONE :
FORBIDDEN FRUIT!
SPECIAL SECURITY WING, JUSTICE H.Q., MEGA-CITY ONE. JUDGE DREDD IS CALLED OFF PATROL TO MEET AN OLD FRIEND...
HELLO, RED. LONG TIME - NO SEE. HEAR YOU GOT A HELLUVA STORY TO TELL ME.
HELL IS THE RIGHT WORD, JUDGE...
FOOD STERILE UNIT
QUAR-BUB 55
IN CHARGE OF THE WING — ASSISTANT GRAND JUDGE FODDER...
YOU'LL HAVE TO EXCUSE RED BEING INSIDE THE PLASTIC BUBBLE, JUDGE. HIS PERIOD OF QUARANTINE IS NOT YET UP.
— BUT HE HAS EVERY COMFORT... MUSIC...TV...
CAN WE GET ON WITH IT ? IN THE TIME I'VE WASTED WITH YOU, JUDGE FODDER, I COULD HAVE ARRESTED FIVE LAW-BREAKERS!
DREDD
SORRY, JUDGE DREDD, I KNOW YOU'RE A BUSY MAN. GO AHEAD, RED. GO AHEAD.
HOLOGRAM CORP
OKAY... WELL, AS YOU KNOW, I'M A STRATO-PILOT. I FLY THE SHORT HAUL PLANES BETWEEN MEGA-CITY ONE AND MEGA-CITY TWO ON THE WEST COAST...
IT WAS A NICE EASY RUN, JUDGE... THEN... THEN THE PLAGUE CAME TO MEGA-CITY TWO... PEOPLE DYING IN THEIR THOUSANDS...
...ME AND MY MEN WERE TO DELIVER THE VACCINE...THE ONLY THING THAT COULD SAVE THE REST OF THE WORLD FROM A TERRIBLE FATE!
TAKE IT EASY, RED... JUST TELL IT IN YOUR OWN WAY...

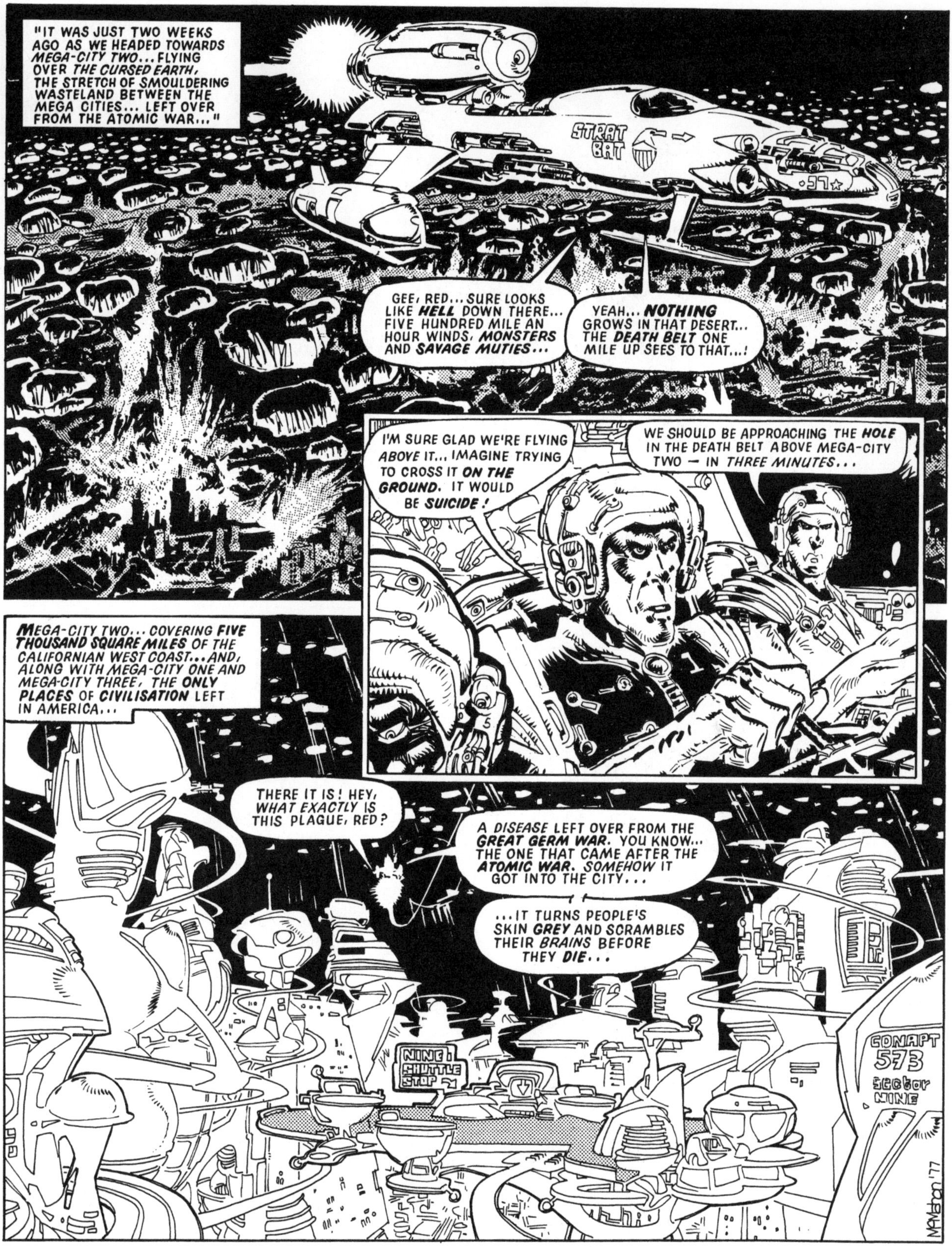
"IT WAS JUST TWO WEEKS AGO AS WE HEADED TOWARDS MEGA-CITY TWO... FLYING OVER THE CURSED EARTH, THE STRETCH OF SMOULDERING WASTELAND BETWEEN THE MEGA CITIES... LEFT OVER FROM THE ATOMIC WAR..."
STRAT BAT
GEE, RED... SURE LOOKS LIKE HELL DOWN THERE... FIVE HUNDRED MILE AN HOUR WINDS, MONSTERS AND SAVAGE MUTIES...
YEAH... NOTHING GROWS IN THAT DESERT... THE DEATH BELT ONE MILE UP SEES TO THAT...!
I'M SURE GLAD WE'RE FLYING ABOVE IT... IMAGINE TRYING TO CROSS IT ON THE GROUND. IT WOULD BE SUICIDE!
WE SHOULD BE APPROACHING THE HOLE IN THE DEATH BELT ABOVE MEGA-CITY TWO – IN THREE MINUTES...
MEGA-CITY TWO... COVERING FIVE THOUSAND SQUARE MILES OF THE CALIFORNIAN WEST COAST... AND, ALONG WITH MEGA-CITY ONE AND MEGA-CITY THREE, THE ONLY PLACES OF CIVILISATION LEFT IN AMERICA...
THERE IT IS! HEY, WHAT EXACTLY IS THIS PLAGUE, RED?
A DISEASE LEFT OVER FROM THE GREAT GERM WAR. YOU KNOW... THE ONE THAT CAME AFTER THE ATOMIC WAR. SOMEHOW IT GOT INTO THE CITY...
...IT TURNS PEOPLE'S SKIN GREY AND SCRAMBLES THEIR BRAINS BEFORE THEY DIE...
NINE SHUTTLE STOP
CONAPT 573 SECTOR NINE
McMahon '77

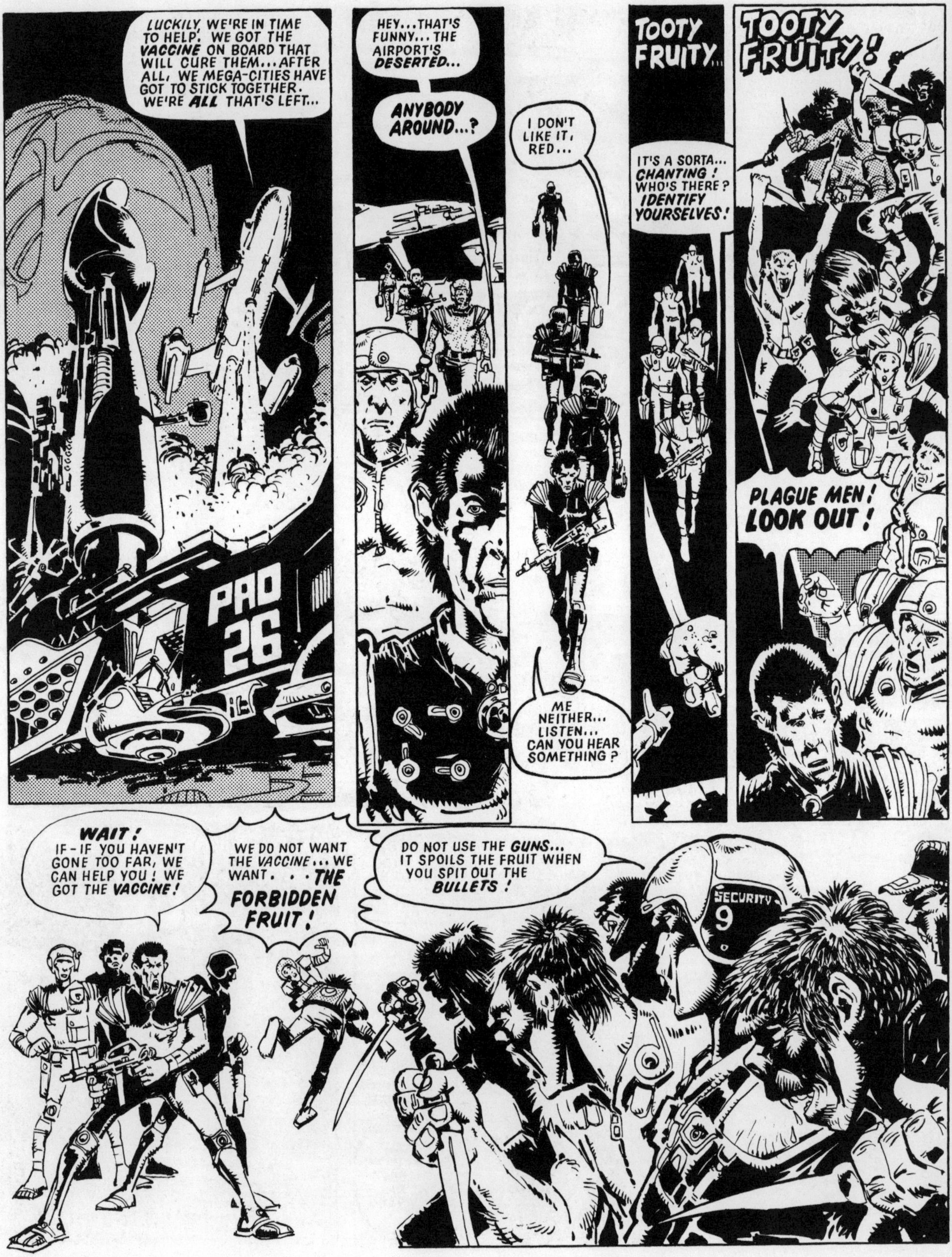
LUCKILY, WE'RE IN TIME TO HELP. WE GOT THE VACCINE ON BOARD THAT WILL CURE THEM... AFTER ALL, WE MEGA-CITIES HAVE GOT TO STICK TOGETHER. WE'RE ALL THAT'S LEFT...
PAD 26
HEY... THAT'S FUNNY... THE AIRPORT'S DESERTED...
ANYBODY AROUND...?
I DON'T LIKE IT, RED...
ME NEITHER... LISTEN... CAN YOU HEAR SOMETHING?
TOOTY FRUITY...
IT'S A SORTA... CHANTING! WHO'S THERE? IDENTIFY YOURSELVES!
TOOTY FRUITY!
PLAGUE MEN! LOOK OUT!
WAIT! IF - IF YOU HAVEN'T GONE TOO FAR, WE CAN HELP YOU! WE GOT THE VACCINE!
WE DO NOT WANT THE VACCINE... WE WANT. . . THE FORBIDDEN FRUIT!
DO NOT USE THE GUNS... IT SPOILS THE FRUIT WHEN YOU SPIT OUT THE BULLETS!
SECURITY 9

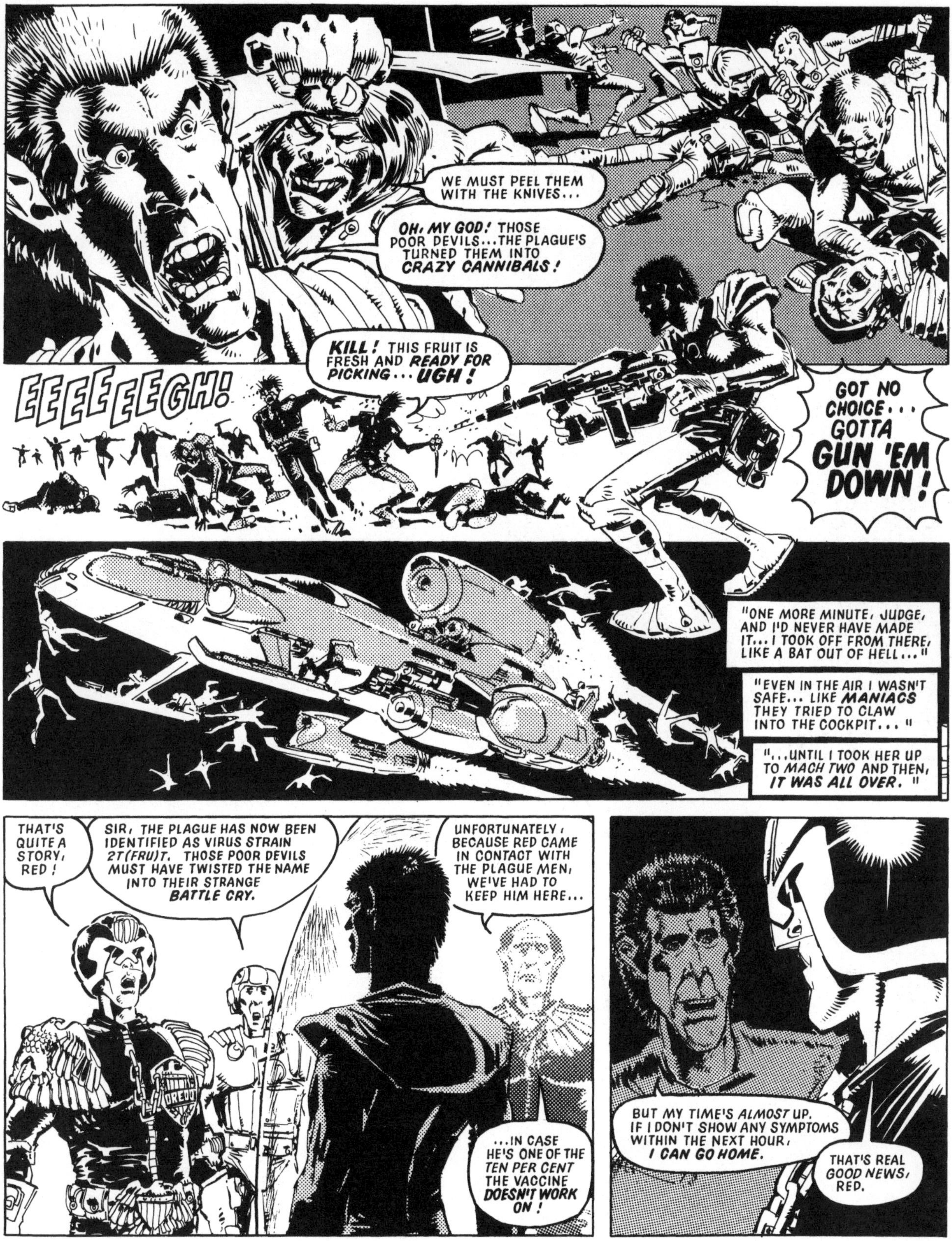

WE MUST PEEL THEM WITH THE KNIVES...
OH, MY GOD! THOSE POOR DEVILS...THE PLAGUE'S TURNED THEM INTO CRAZY CANNIBALS!
KILL! THIS FRUIT IS FRESH AND READY FOR PICKING...UGH!
EEEEEEGH!
GOT NO CHOICE... GOTTA GUN 'EM DOWN!
"ONE MORE MINUTE, JUDGE, AND I'D NEVER HAVE MADE IT... I TOOK OFF FROM THERE, LIKE A BAT OUT OF HELL..."
"EVEN IN THE AIR I WASN'T SAFE... LIKE MANIACS THEY TRIED TO CLAW INTO THE COCKPIT..."
"...UNTIL I TOOK HER UP TO MACH TWO AND THEN, IT WAS ALL OVER."
THAT'S QUITE A STORY, RED!
SIR, THE PLAGUE HAS NOW BEEN IDENTIFIED AS VIRUS STRAIN 2T(FRU)T. THOSE POOR DEVILS MUST HAVE TWISTED THE NAME INTO THEIR STRANGE BATTLE CRY.
UNFORTUNATELY, BECAUSE RED CAME IN CONTACT WITH THE PLAGUE MEN, WE'VE HAD TO KEEP HIM HERE...
...IN CASE HE'S ONE OF THE TEN PER CENT THE VACCINE DOESN'T WORK ON!
BUT MY TIME'S ALMOST UP. IF I DON'T SHOW ANY SYMPTOMS WITHIN THE NEXT HOUR, I CAN GO HOME.
THAT'S REAL GOOD NEWS, RED.

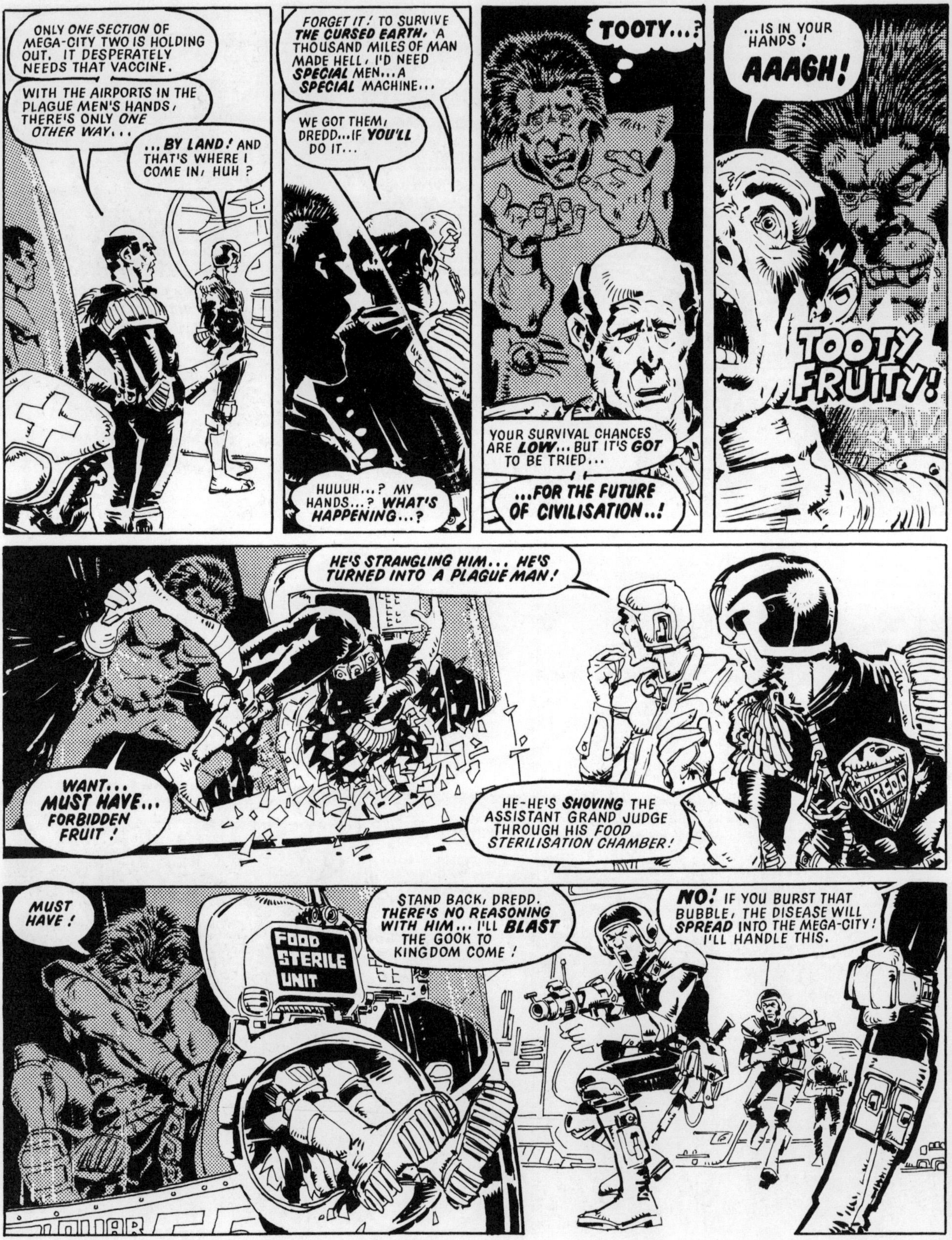
ONLY ONE SECTION OF MEGA-CITY TWO IS HOLDING OUT. IT DESPERATELY NEEDS THAT VACCINE.
WITH THE AIRPORTS IN THE PLAGUE MEN'S HANDS, THERE'S ONLY ONE OTHER WAY...
...BY LAND! AND THAT'S WHERE I COME IN, HUH ?
FORGET IT! TO SURVIVE THE CURSED EARTH, A THOUSAND MILES OF MAN MADE HELL, I'D NEED SPECIAL MEN...A SPECIAL MACHINE...
WE GOT THEM, DREDD...IF YOU'LL DO IT...
HUUUH...? MY HANDS...? WHAT'S HAPPENING...?
TOOTY...?
YOUR SURVIVAL CHANCES ARE LOW...BUT IT'S GOT TO BE TRIED...
...FOR THE FUTURE OF CIVILISATION..!
...IS IN YOUR HANDS!
AAAGH!
TOOTY FRUITY!
HE'S STRANGLING HIM... HE'S TURNED INTO A PLAGUE MAN!
WANT... MUST HAVE... FORBIDDEN FRUIT!
HE-HE'S SHOVING THE ASSISTANT GRAND JUDGE THROUGH HIS FOOD STERILISATION CHAMBER!
MUST HAVE!
FOOD STERILE UNIT
STAND BACK, DREDD. THERE'S NO REASONING WITH HIM... I'LL BLAST THE GOOK TO KINGDOM COME!
NO! IF YOU BURST THAT BUBBLE, THE DISEASE WILL SPREAD INTO THE MEGA-CITY! I'LL HANDLE THIS.

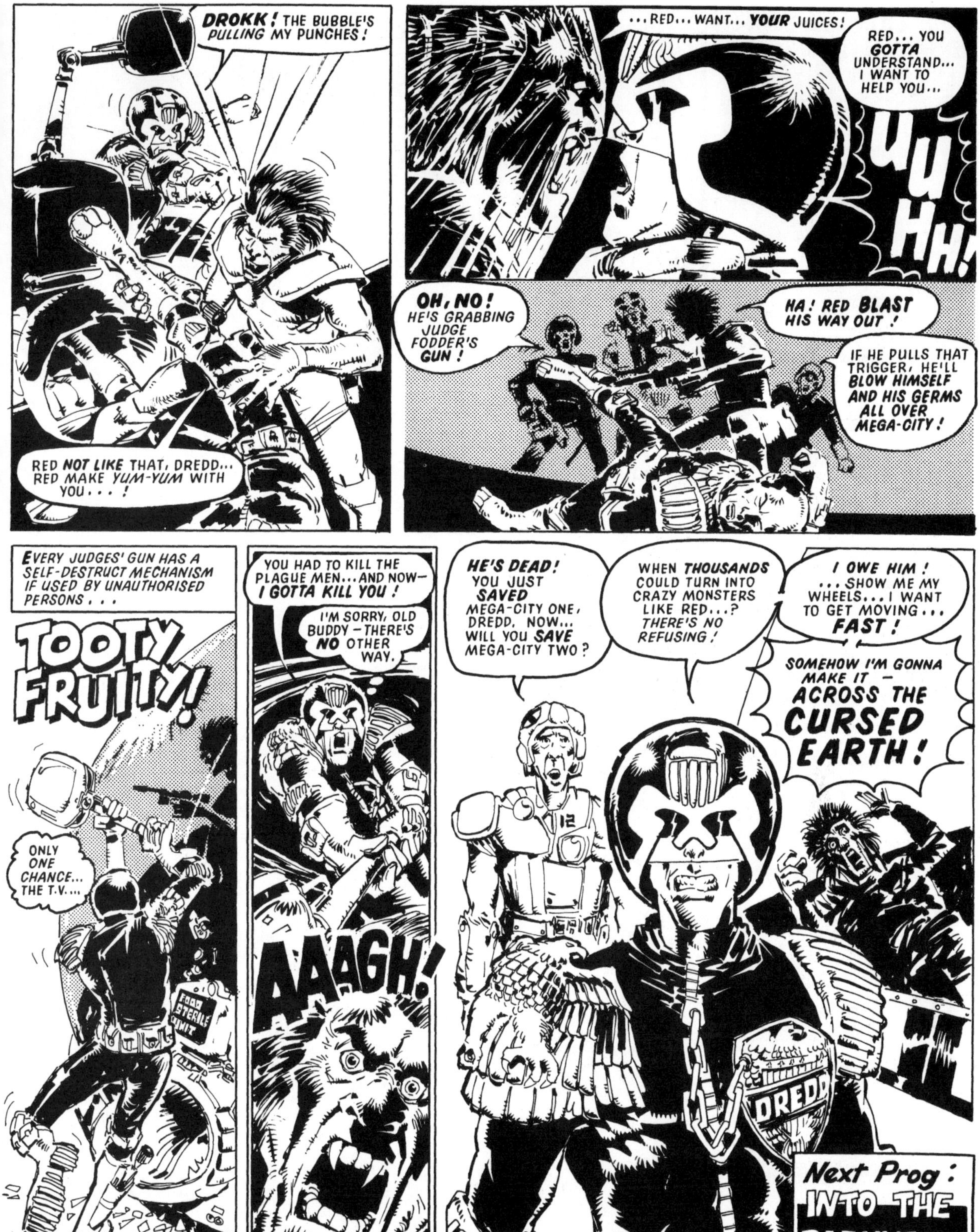

DROKK! THE BUBBLE'S PULLING MY PUNCHES!
RED NOT LIKE THAT, DREDD... RED MAKE YUM-YUM WITH YOU...!
...RED... WANT... YOUR JUICES!
RED... YOU GOTTA UNDERSTAND... I WANT TO HELP YOU...
UUHH!
OH, NO! HE'S GRABBING JUDGE FODDER'S GUN!
HA! RED BLAST HIS WAY OUT!
IF HE PULLS THAT TRIGGER, HE'LL BLOW HIMSELF AND HIS GERMS ALL OVER MEGA-CITY!
EVERY JUDGES' GUN HAS A SELF-DESTRUCT MECHANISM IF USED BY UNAUTHORISED PERSONS...
TOOTY FRUITY!
ONLY ONE CHANCE... THE T.V....
FOOD STERILE UNIT
YOU HAD TO KILL THE PLAGUE MEN... AND NOW— I GOTTA KILL YOU!
I'M SORRY, OLD BUDDY — THERE'S NO OTHER WAY.
AAAGH!
HE'S DEAD! YOU JUST SAVED MEGA-CITY ONE, DREDD. NOW... WILL YOU SAVE MEGA-CITY TWO?
WHEN THOUSANDS COULD TURN INTO CRAZY MONSTERS LIKE RED...? THERE'S NO REFUSING!
I OWE HIM! ...SHOW ME MY WHEELS... I WANT TO GET MOVING... FAST!
SOMEHOW I'M GONNA MAKE IT — ACROSS THE CURSED EARTH!
DREDD
Next Prog: INTO THE DARKNESS!

THE CURSED EARTH
CHAPTER TWO
INTO THE DARKNESS

JUDGE DREDD IS ABOUT TO BEGIN A *DESPERATE RESCUE MISSION* TO MEGA-CITY TWO, ACROSS THE ***CURSED EARTH*** — A STRETCH OF RADIOACTIVE WASTELAND LEFT OVER FROM THE ATOMIC WARS...

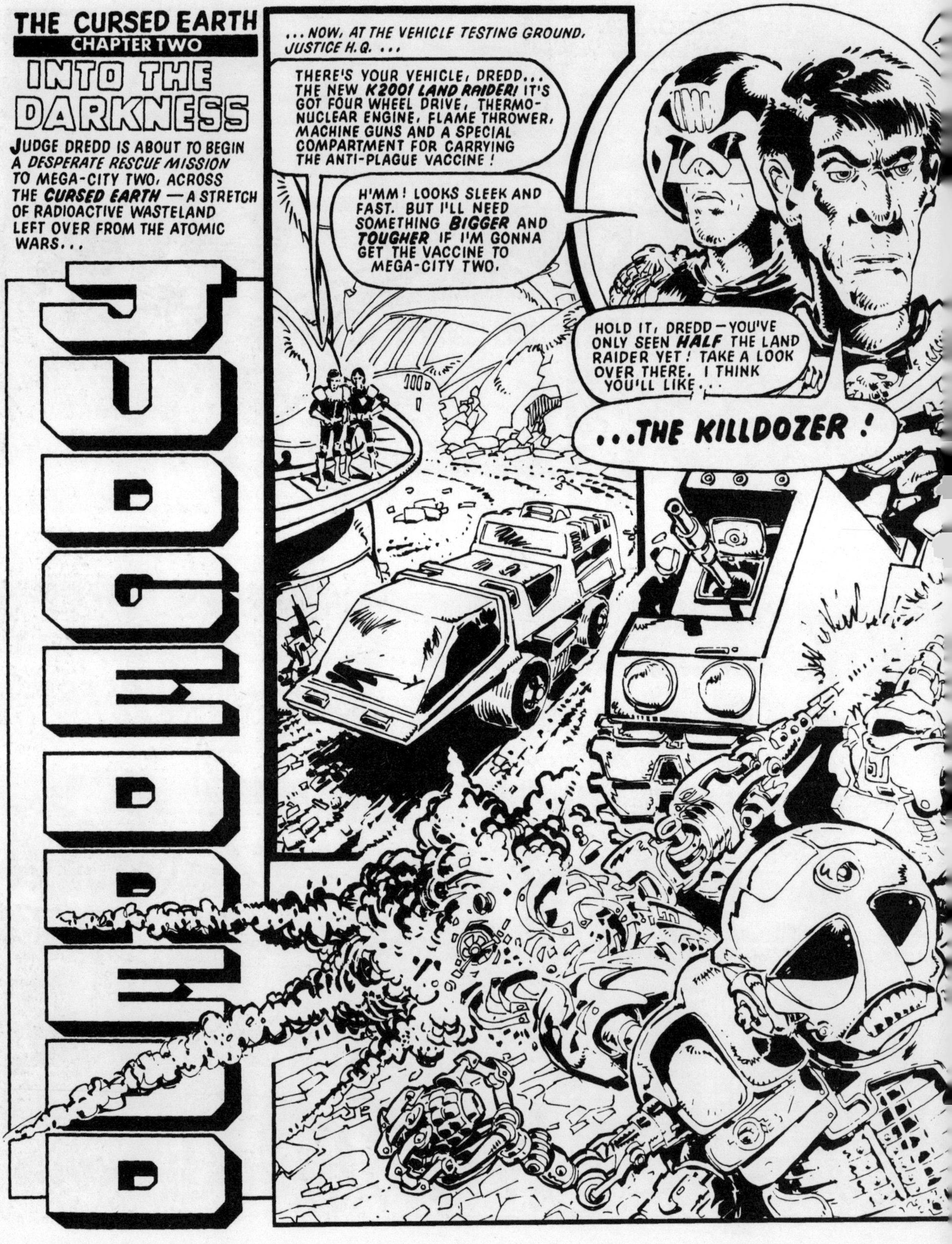

...NOW, AT THE VEHICLE TESTING GROUND, JUSTICE H.Q. ...
THERE'S YOUR VEHICLE, DREDD... THE NEW K2001 LAND RAIDER! IT'S GOT FOUR WHEEL DRIVE, THERMO-NUCLEAR ENGINE, FLAME THROWER, MACHINE GUNS AND A SPECIAL COMPARTMENT FOR CARRYING THE ANTI-PLAGUE VACCINE!
H'MM! LOOKS SLEEK AND FAST. BUT I'LL NEED SOMETHING BIGGER AND TOUGHER IF I'M GONNA GET THE VACCINE TO MEGA-CITY TWO.
HOLD IT, DREDD — YOU'VE ONLY SEEN HALF THE LAND RAIDER YET! TAKE A LOOK OVER THERE. I THINK YOU'LL LIKE...
...THE KILLDOZER!

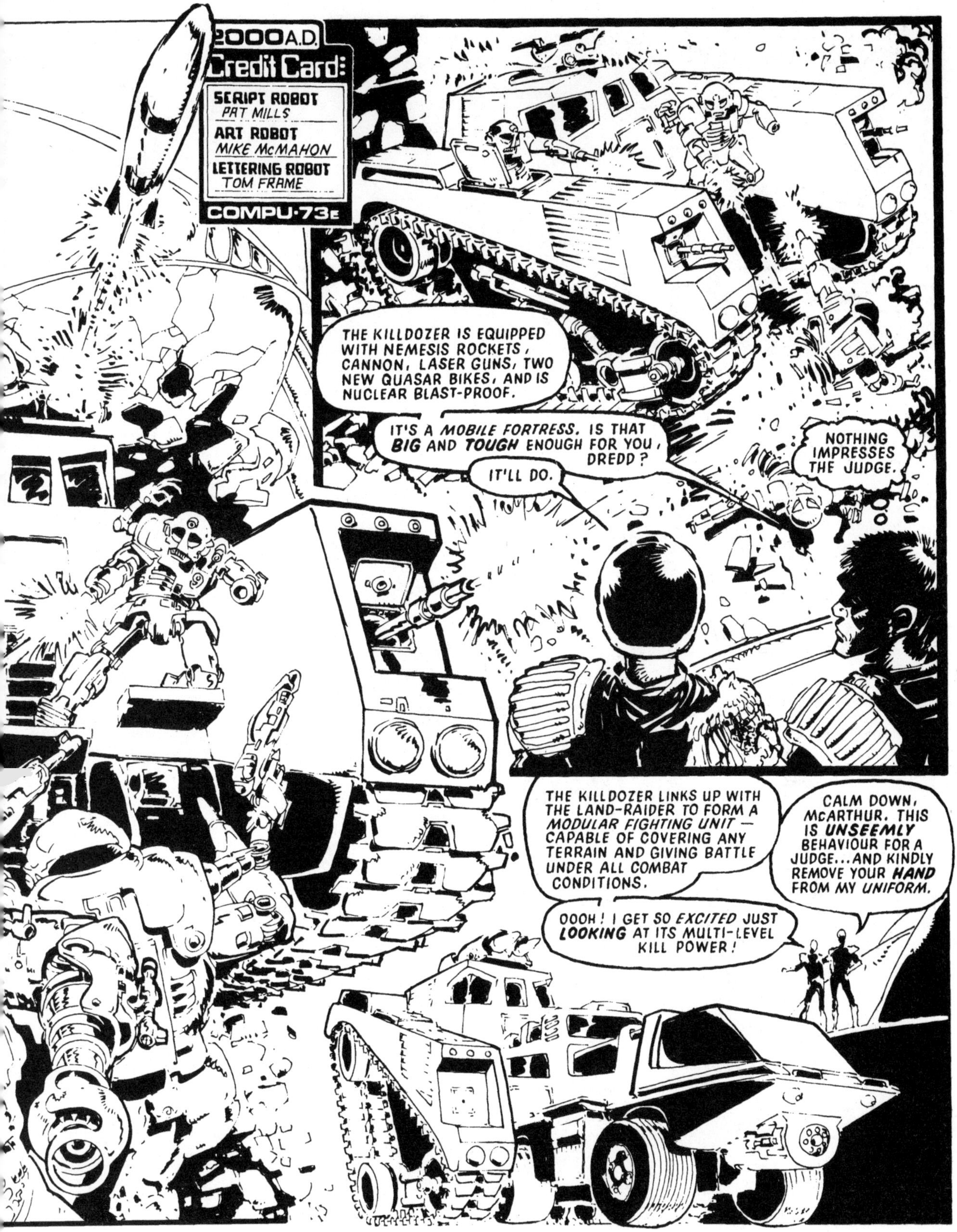
2000 A.D. Credit Card:
SCRIPT ROBOT PAT MILLS
ART ROBOT MIKE McMAHON
LETTERING ROBOT TOM FRAME
COMPU-73E
THE KILLDOZER IS EQUIPPED WITH NEMESIS ROCKETS, CANNON, LASER GUNS, TWO NEW QUASAR BIKES, AND IS NUCLEAR BLAST-PROOF.
IT'S A *MOBILE FORTRESS.* IS THAT **BIG** AND **TOUGH** ENOUGH FOR YOU, DREDD?
IT'LL DO.
NOTHING IMPRESSES THE JUDGE.
THE KILLDOZER LINKS UP WITH THE LAND-RAIDER TO FORM A *MODULAR FIGHTING UNIT* — CAPABLE OF COVERING ANY TERRAIN AND GIVING BATTLE UNDER ALL COMBAT CONDITIONS.
OOOH! I GET SO *EXCITED* JUST **LOOKING** AT ITS MULTI-LEVEL KILL POWER!
CALM DOWN, McARTHUR. THIS IS **UNSEEMLY** BEHAVIOUR FOR A JUDGE... AND KINDLY REMOVE YOUR **HAND** FROM MY *UNIFORM*.

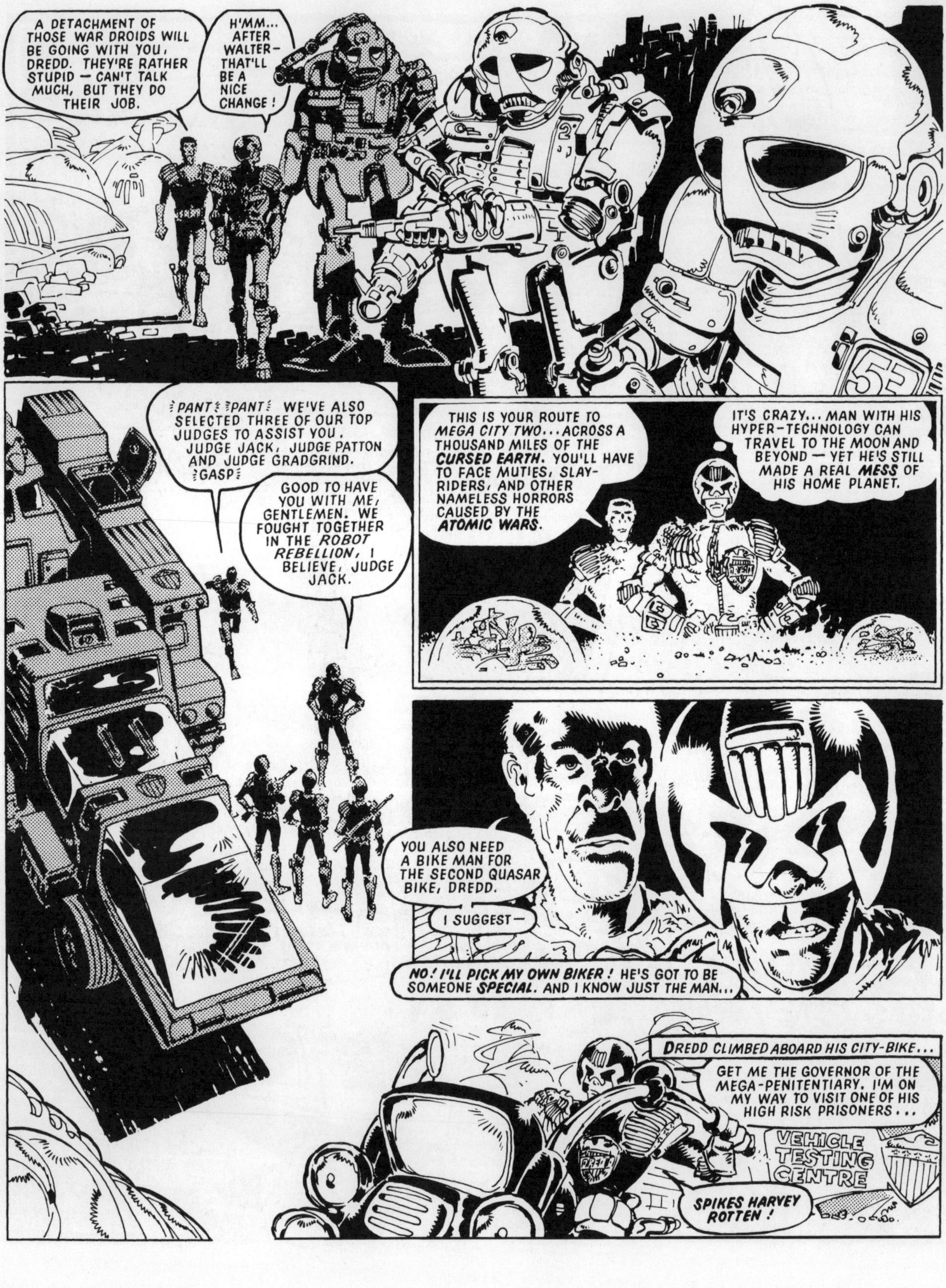
A DETACHMENT OF THOSE WAR DROIDS WILL BE GOING WITH YOU, DREDD. THEY'RE RATHER STUPID — CAN'T TALK MUCH, BUT THEY DO THEIR JOB.
H'MM... AFTER WALTER— THAT'LL BE A NICE CHANGE!
PANT PANT WE'VE ALSO SELECTED THREE OF OUR TOP JUDGES TO ASSIST YOU. JUDGE JACK, JUDGE PATTON AND JUDGE GRADGRIND. GASP
GOOD TO HAVE YOU WITH ME, GENTLEMEN. WE FOUGHT TOGETHER IN THE ROBOT REBELLION, I BELIEVE, JUDGE JACK.
THIS IS YOUR ROUTE TO MEGA CITY TWO... ACROSS A THOUSAND MILES OF THE CURSED EARTH. YOU'LL HAVE TO FACE MUTIES, SLAY-RIDERS, AND OTHER NAMELESS HORRORS CAUSED BY THE ATOMIC WARS.
IT'S CRAZY... MAN WITH HIS HYPER-TECHNOLOGY CAN TRAVEL TO THE MOON AND BEYOND — YET HE'S STILL MADE A REAL MESS OF HIS HOME PLANET.
YOU ALSO NEED A BIKE MAN FOR THE SECOND QUASAR BIKE, DREDD.
I SUGGEST—
NO! I'LL PICK MY OWN BIKER! HE'S GOT TO BE SOMEONE SPECIAL. AND I KNOW JUST THE MAN...
DREDD CLIMBED ABOARD HIS CITY-BIKE...
GET ME THE GOVERNOR OF THE MEGA-PENITENTIARY. I'M ON MY WAY TO VISIT ONE OF HIS HIGH RISK PRISONERS...
VEHICLE TESTING CENTRE
SPIKES HARVEY ROTTEN!

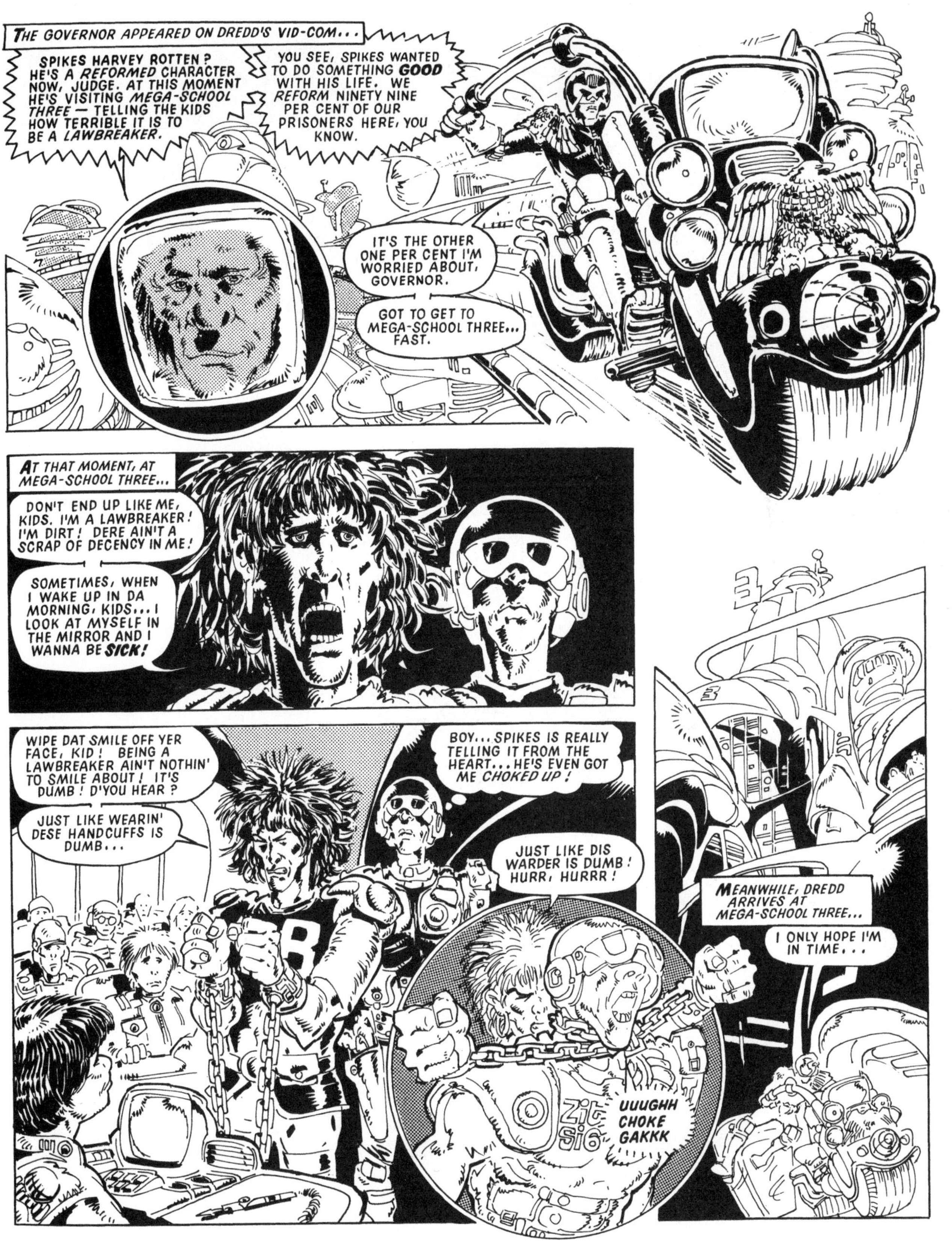
THE GOVERNOR APPEARED ON DREDD'S VID-COM...
SPIKES HARVEY ROTTEN? HE'S A REFORMED CHARACTER NOW, JUDGE. AT THIS MOMENT HE'S VISITING MEGA-SCHOOL THREE — TELLING THE KIDS HOW TERRIBLE IT IS TO BE A LAWBREAKER.
YOU SEE, SPIKES WANTED TO DO SOMETHING GOOD WITH HIS LIFE. WE REFORM NINETY NINE PER CENT OF OUR PRISONERS HERE, YOU KNOW.
IT'S THE OTHER ONE PER CENT I'M WORRIED ABOUT, GOVERNOR.
GOT TO GET TO MEGA-SCHOOL THREE... FAST.
AT THAT MOMENT, AT MEGA-SCHOOL THREE...
DON'T END UP LIKE ME, KIDS. I'M A LAWBREAKER! I'M DIRT! DERE AIN'T A SCRAP OF DECENCY IN ME!
SOMETIMES, WHEN I WAKE UP IN DA MORNING, KIDS... I LOOK AT MYSELF IN THE MIRROR AND I WANNA BE SICK!
WIPE DAT SMILE OFF YER FACE, KID! BEING A LAWBREAKER AIN'T NOTHIN' TO SMILE ABOUT! IT'S DUMB! D'YOU HEAR?
JUST LIKE WEARIN' DESE HANDCUFFS IS DUMB...
BOY... SPIKES IS REALLY TELLING IT FROM THE HEART... HE'S EVEN GOT ME CHOKED UP!
JUST LIKE DIS WARDER IS DUMB! HURR, HURRR!
UUUGHH CHOKE GAKKK
MEANWHILE, DREDD ARRIVES AT MEGA-SCHOOL THREE...
I ONLY HOPE I'M IN TIME...

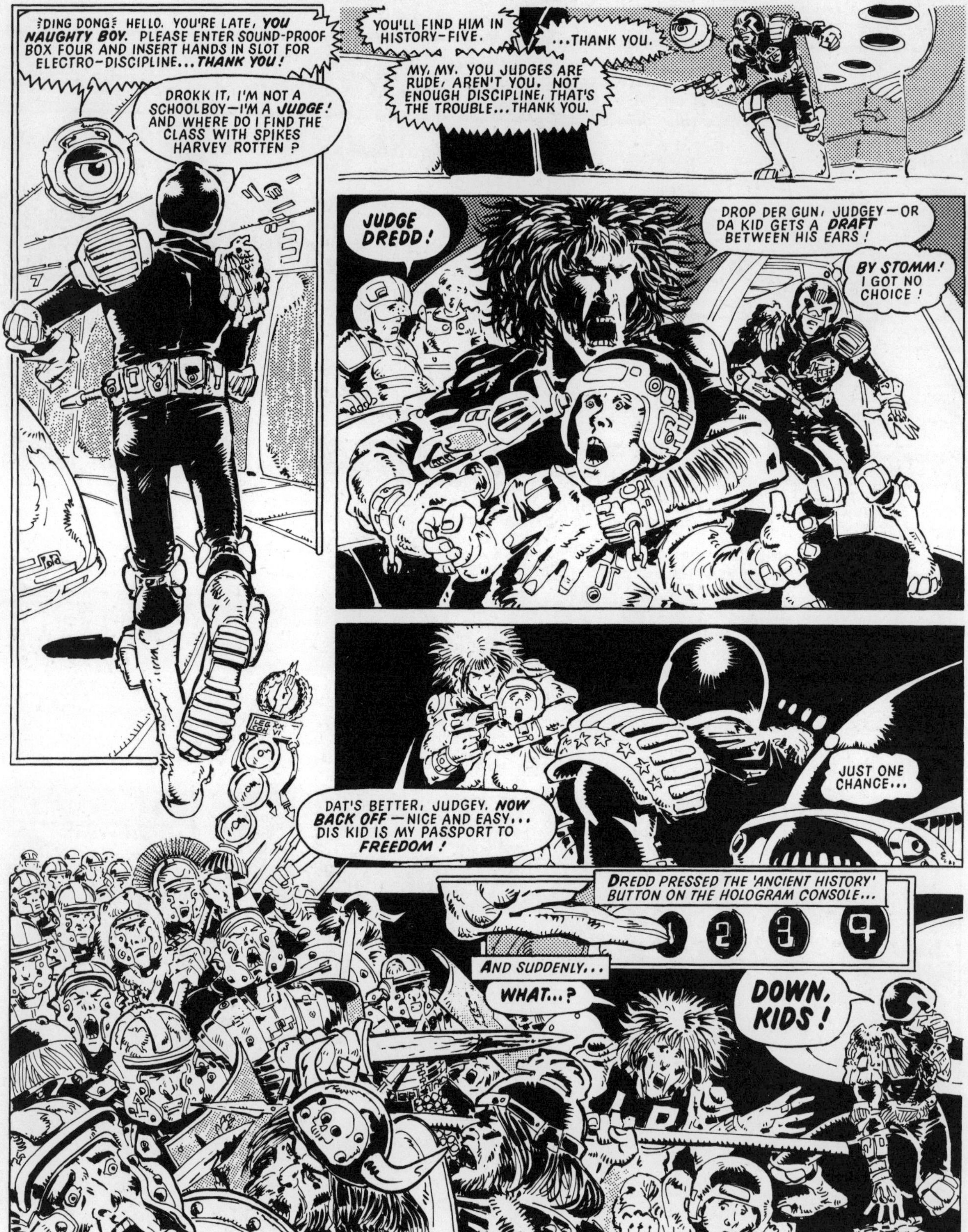

DING DONG! HELLO. YOU'RE LATE, YOU NAUGHTY BOY. PLEASE ENTER SOUND-PROOF BOX FOUR AND INSERT HANDS IN SLOT FOR ELECTRO-DISCIPLINE... THANK YOU!
DROKK IT, I'M NOT A SCHOOLBOY—I'M A JUDGE! AND WHERE DO I FIND THE CLASS WITH SPIKES HARVEY ROTTEN ?
YOU'LL FIND HIM IN HISTORY-FIVE.
...THANK YOU.
MY, MY. YOU JUDGES ARE RUDE, AREN'T YOU. NOT ENOUGH DISCIPLINE, THAT'S THE TROUBLE... THANK YOU.
JUDGE DREDD!
DROP DER GUN, JUDGEY—OR DA KID GETS A DRAFT BETWEEN HIS EARS!
BY STOMM! I GOT NO CHOICE!
DAT'S BETTER, JUDGEY. NOW BACK OFF—NICE AND EASY... DIS KID IS MY PASSPORT TO FREEDOM!
JUST ONE CHANCE...
DREDD PRESSED THE 'ANCIENT HISTORY' BUTTON ON THE HOLOGRAM CONSOLE...
AND SUDDENLY...
WHAT...?
DOWN, KIDS!

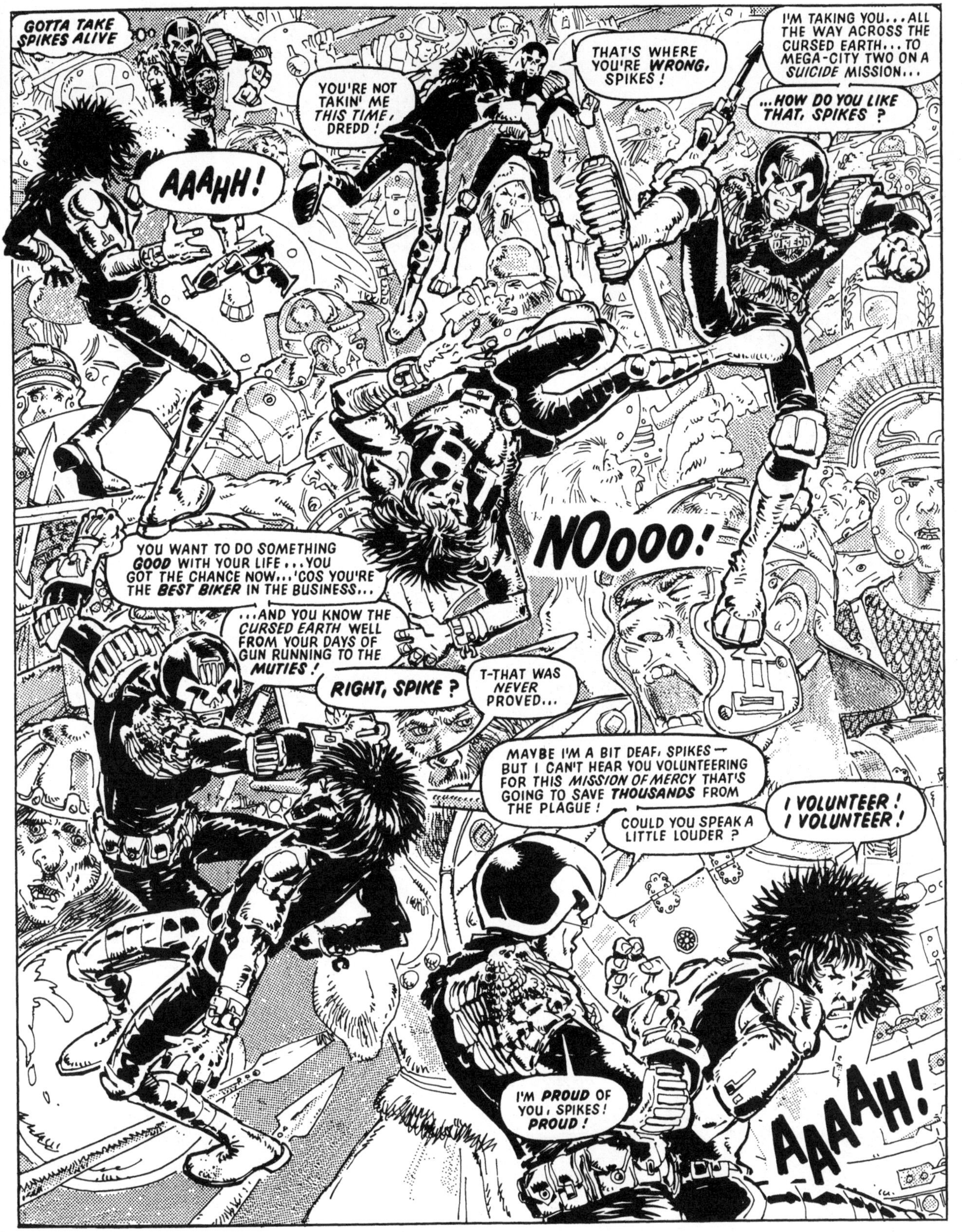
GOTTA TAKE SPIKES ALIVE
AAAHH!
YOU'RE NOT TAKIN' ME THIS TIME, DREDD!
THAT'S WHERE YOU'RE WRONG, SPIKES!
I'M TAKING YOU... ALL THE WAY ACROSS THE CURSED EARTH... TO MEGA-CITY TWO ON A SUICIDE MISSION...
...HOW DO YOU LIKE THAT, SPIKES?
NOOOO!
YOU WANT TO DO SOMETHING GOOD WITH YOUR LIFE... YOU GOT THE CHANCE NOW... 'COS YOU'RE THE BEST BIKER IN THE BUSINESS...
...AND YOU KNOW THE CURSED EARTH WELL FROM YOUR DAYS OF GUN RUNNING TO THE MUTIES!
RIGHT, SPIKE?
T-THAT WAS NEVER PROVED...
MAYBE I'M A BIT DEAF, SPIKES — BUT I CAN'T HEAR YOU VOLUNTEERING FOR THIS MISSION OF MERCY THAT'S GOING TO SAVE THOUSANDS FROM THE PLAGUE!
COULD YOU SPEAK A LITTLE LOUDER?
I VOLUNTEER! I VOLUNTEER!
I'M PROUD OF YOU, SPIKES! PROUD!
AAAAH!

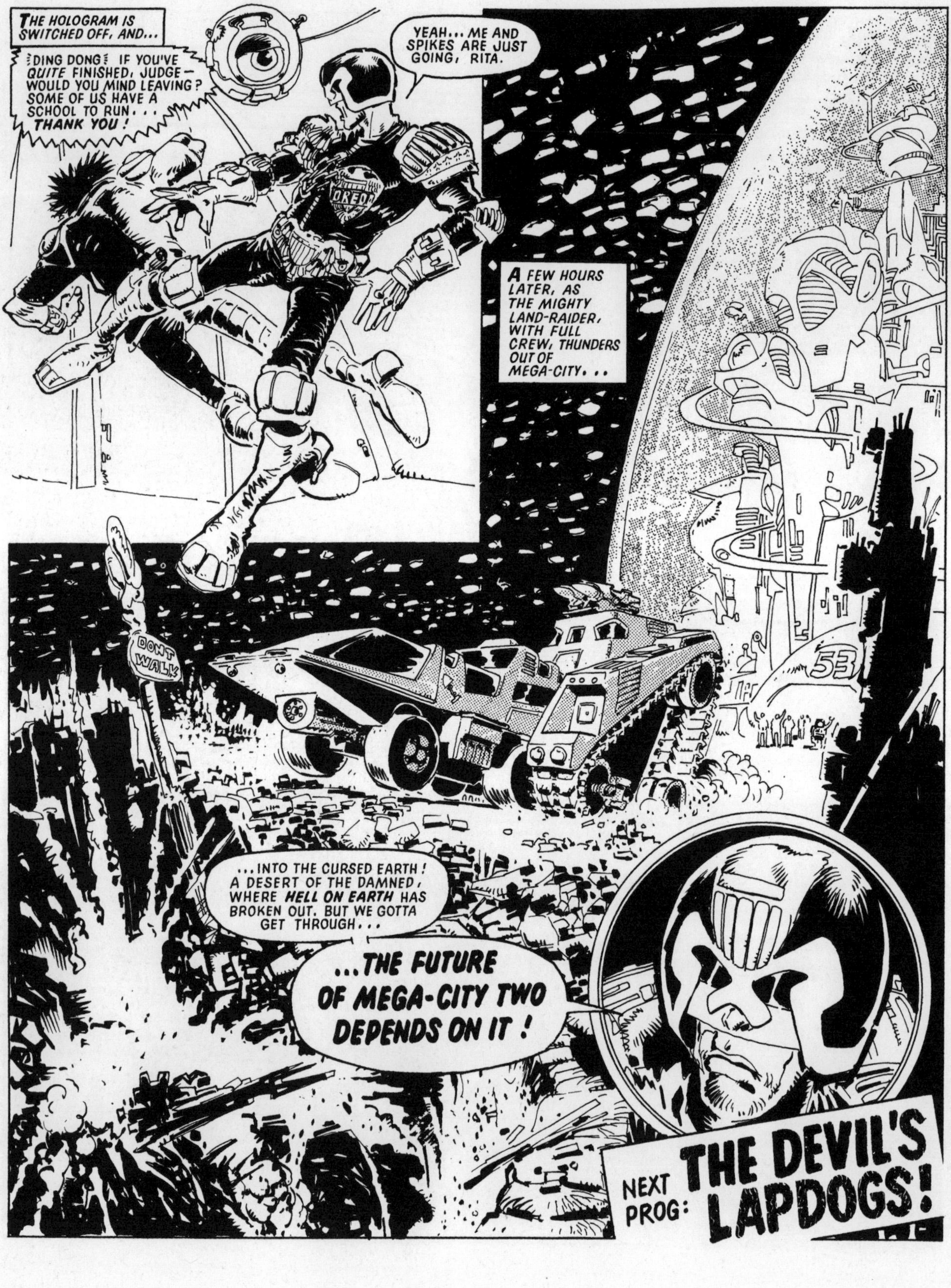

THE HOLOGRAM IS SWITCHED OFF, AND...
DING DONG IF YOU'VE QUITE FINISHED, JUDGE—WOULD YOU MIND LEAVING? SOME OF US HAVE A SCHOOL TO RUN... THANK YOU!
YEAH... ME AND SPIKES ARE JUST GOING, RITA.
DREDD
A FEW HOURS LATER, AS THE MIGHTY LAND-RAIDER, WITH FULL CREW, THUNDERS OUT OF MEGA-CITY...
DONT WALK
53
...INTO THE CURSED EARTH! A DESERT OF THE DAMNED, WHERE HELL ON EARTH HAS BROKEN OUT. BUT WE GOTTA GET THROUGH...
...THE FUTURE OF MEGA-CITY TWO DEPENDS ON IT!
NEXT PROG: THE DEVIL'S LAPDOGS!

THE CURSED EARTH.
CHAPTER 3:

THE DEVIL'S LAPDOGS

JUDGE DREDD

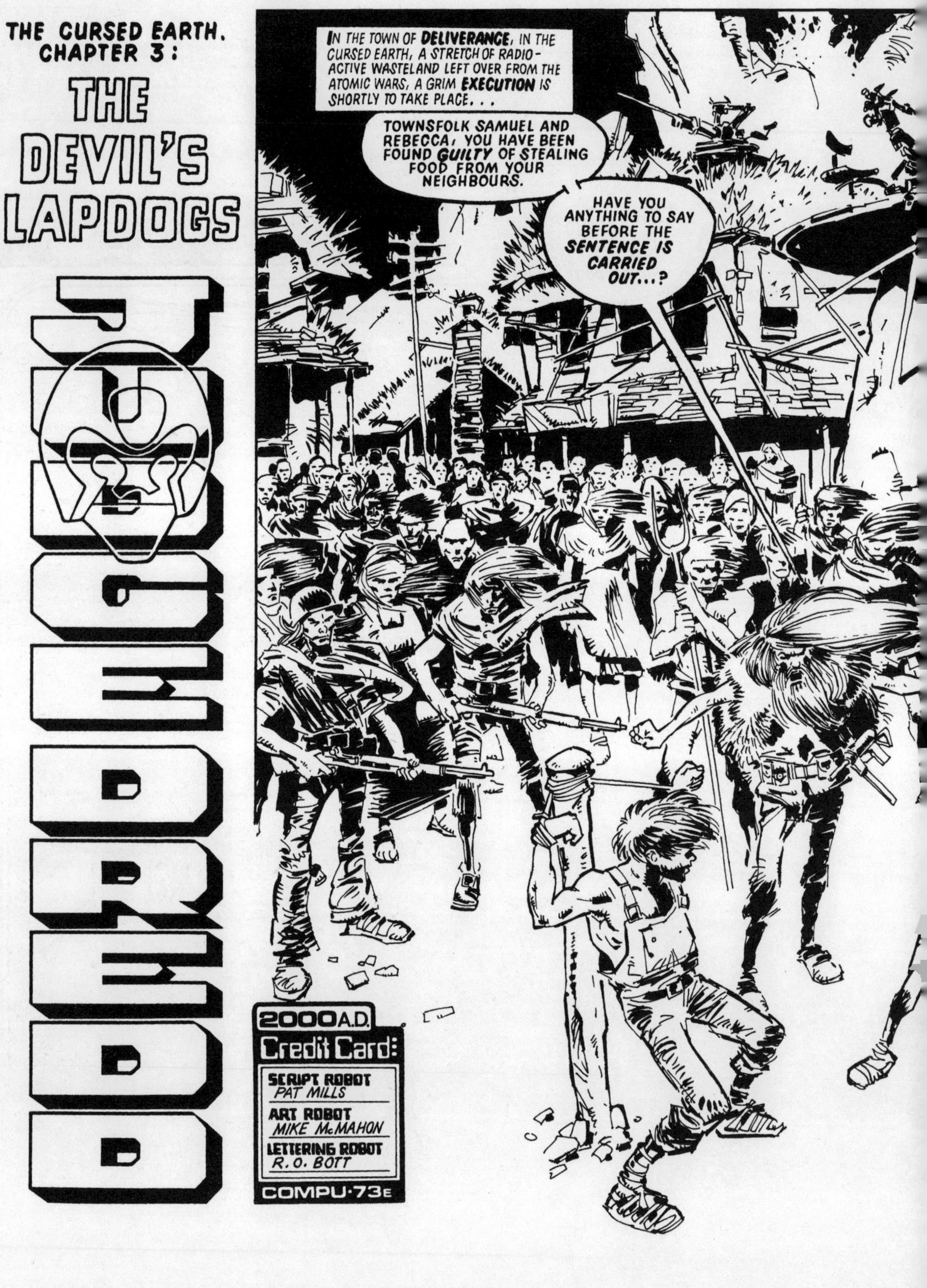
IN THE TOWN OF DELIVERANCE, IN THE CURSED EARTH, A STRETCH OF RADIO-ACTIVE WASTELAND LEFT OVER FROM THE ATOMIC WARS, A GRIM EXECUTION IS SHORTLY TO TAKE PLACE. . .
TOWNSFOLK SAMUEL AND REBECCA, YOU HAVE BEEN FOUND GUILTY OF STEALING FOOD FROM YOUR NEIGHBOURS.
HAVE YOU ANYTHING TO SAY BEFORE THE SENTENCE IS CARRIED OUT...?
2000 A.D. Credit Card:
SCRIPT ROBOT PAT MILLS
ART ROBOT MIKE McMAHON
LETTERING ROBOT R.O. BOTT
COMPU·73E

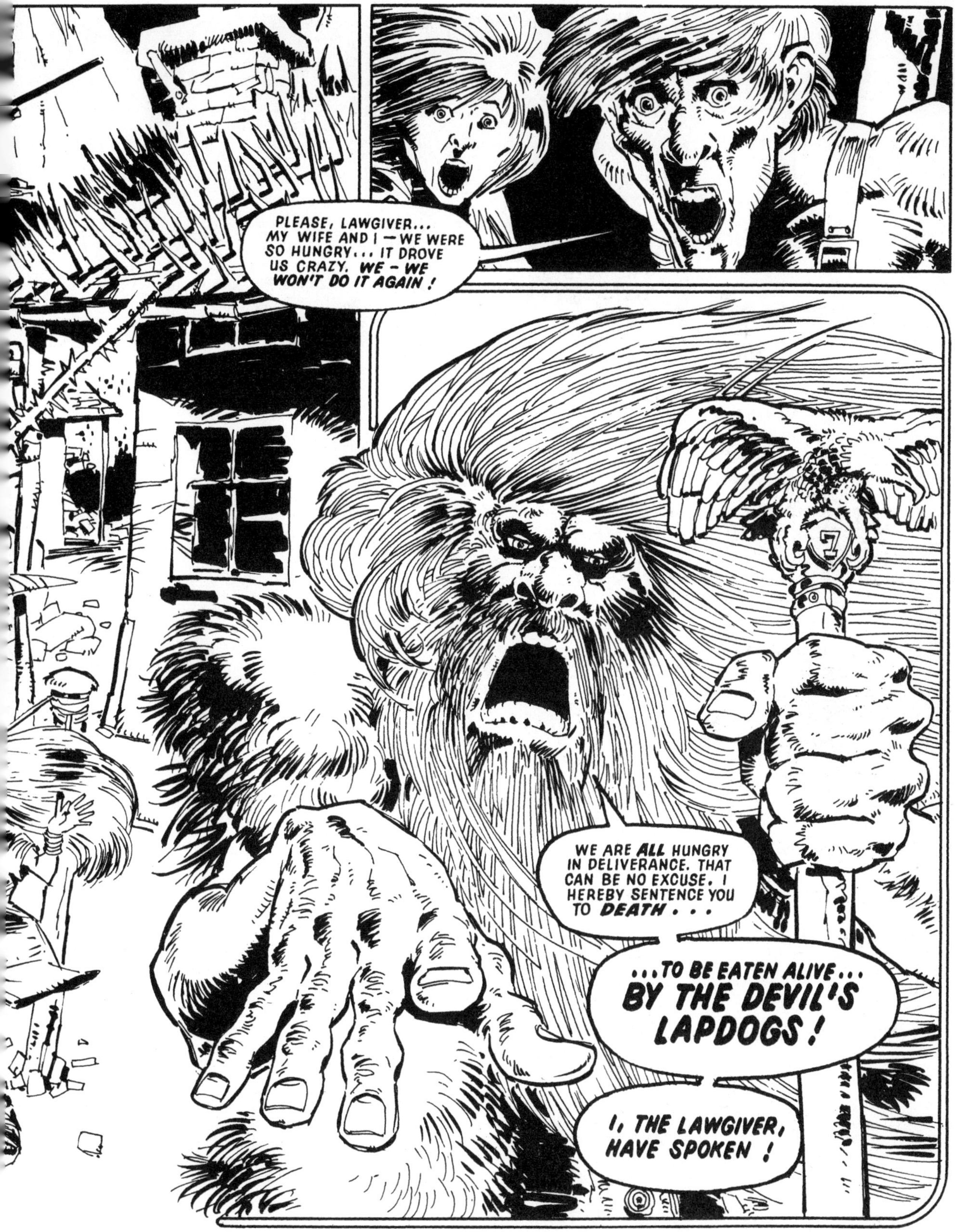
PLEASE, LAWGIVER... MY WIFE AND I — WE WERE SO HUNGRY... IT DROVE US CRAZY. WE - WE WON'T DO IT AGAIN!
WE ARE ALL HUNGRY IN DELIVERANCE. THAT CAN BE NO EXCUSE. I HEREBY SENTENCE YOU TO DEATH...
...TO BE EATEN ALIVE... BY THE DEVIL'S LAPDOGS!
I, THE LAWGIVER, HAVE SPOKEN!

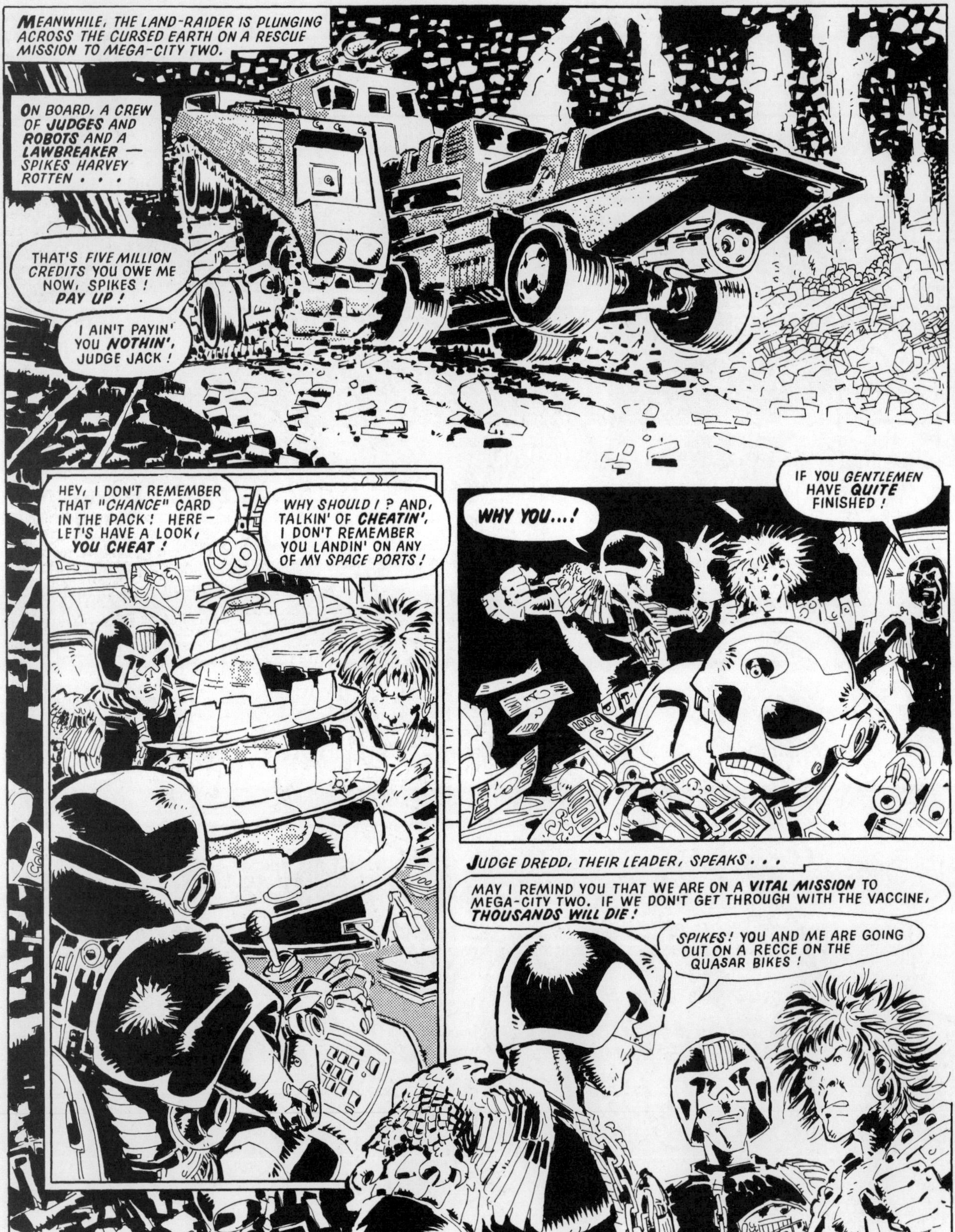
MEANWHILE, THE LAND-RAIDER IS PLUNGING ACROSS THE CURSED EARTH ON A RESCUE MISSION TO MEGA-CITY TWO.
ON BOARD, A CREW OF JUDGES AND ROBOTS AND A LAWBREAKER — SPIKES HARVEY ROTTEN . . .
THAT'S FIVE MILLION CREDITS YOU OWE ME NOW, SPIKES ! PAY UP !
I AIN'T PAYIN' YOU NOTHIN', JUDGE JACK !
HEY, I DON'T REMEMBER THAT "CHANCE" CARD IN THE PACK ! HERE— LET'S HAVE A LOOK, YOU CHEAT !
WHY SHOULD I ? AND, TALKIN' OF CHEATIN', I DON'T REMEMBER YOU LANDIN' ON ANY OF MY SPACE PORTS !
WHY YOU...!
IF YOU GENTLEMEN HAVE QUITE FINISHED !
JUDGE DREDD, THEIR LEADER, SPEAKS . . .
MAY I REMIND YOU THAT WE ARE ON A VITAL MISSION TO MEGA-CITY TWO. IF WE DON'T GET THROUGH WITH THE VACCINE, THOUSANDS WILL DIE !
SPIKES ! YOU AND ME ARE GOING OUT ON A RECCE ON THE QUASAR BIKES !

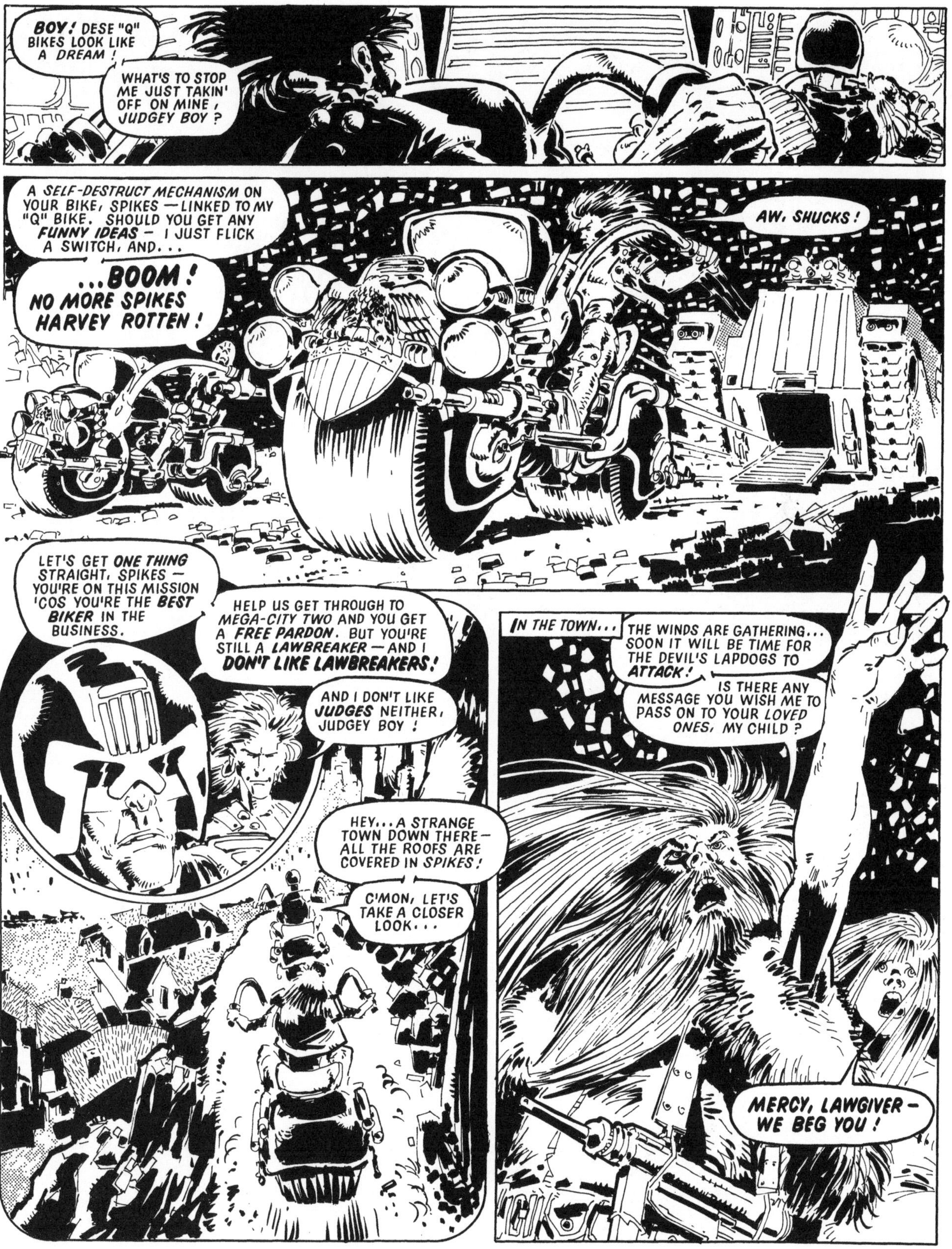
BOY! DESE "Q" BIKES LOOK LIKE A DREAM!
WHAT'S TO STOP ME JUST TAKIN' OFF ON MINE, JUDGEY BOY?
A SELF-DESTRUCT MECHANISM ON YOUR BIKE, SPIKES — LINKED TO MY "Q" BIKE. SHOULD YOU GET ANY FUNNY IDEAS — I JUST FLICK A SWITCH, AND...
...BOOM! NO MORE SPIKES HARVEY ROTTEN!
AW, SHUCKS!
LET'S GET ONE THING STRAIGHT, SPIKES — YOU'RE ON THIS MISSION 'COS YOU'RE THE BEST BIKER IN THE BUSINESS.
HELP US GET THROUGH TO MEGA-CITY TWO AND YOU GET A FREE PARDON. BUT YOU'RE STILL A LAWBREAKER — AND I DON'T LIKE LAWBREAKERS!
AND I DON'T LIKE JUDGES NEITHER, JUDGEY BOY!
HEY... A STRANGE TOWN DOWN THERE— ALL THE ROOFS ARE COVERED IN SPIKES!
C'MON, LET'S TAKE A CLOSER LOOK...
IN THE TOWN...
THE WINDS ARE GATHERING... SOON IT WILL BE TIME FOR THE DEVIL'S LAPDOGS TO ATTACK!
IS THERE ANY MESSAGE YOU WISH ME TO PASS ON TO YOUR LOVED ONES, MY CHILD?
MERCY, LAWGIVER— WE BEG YOU!

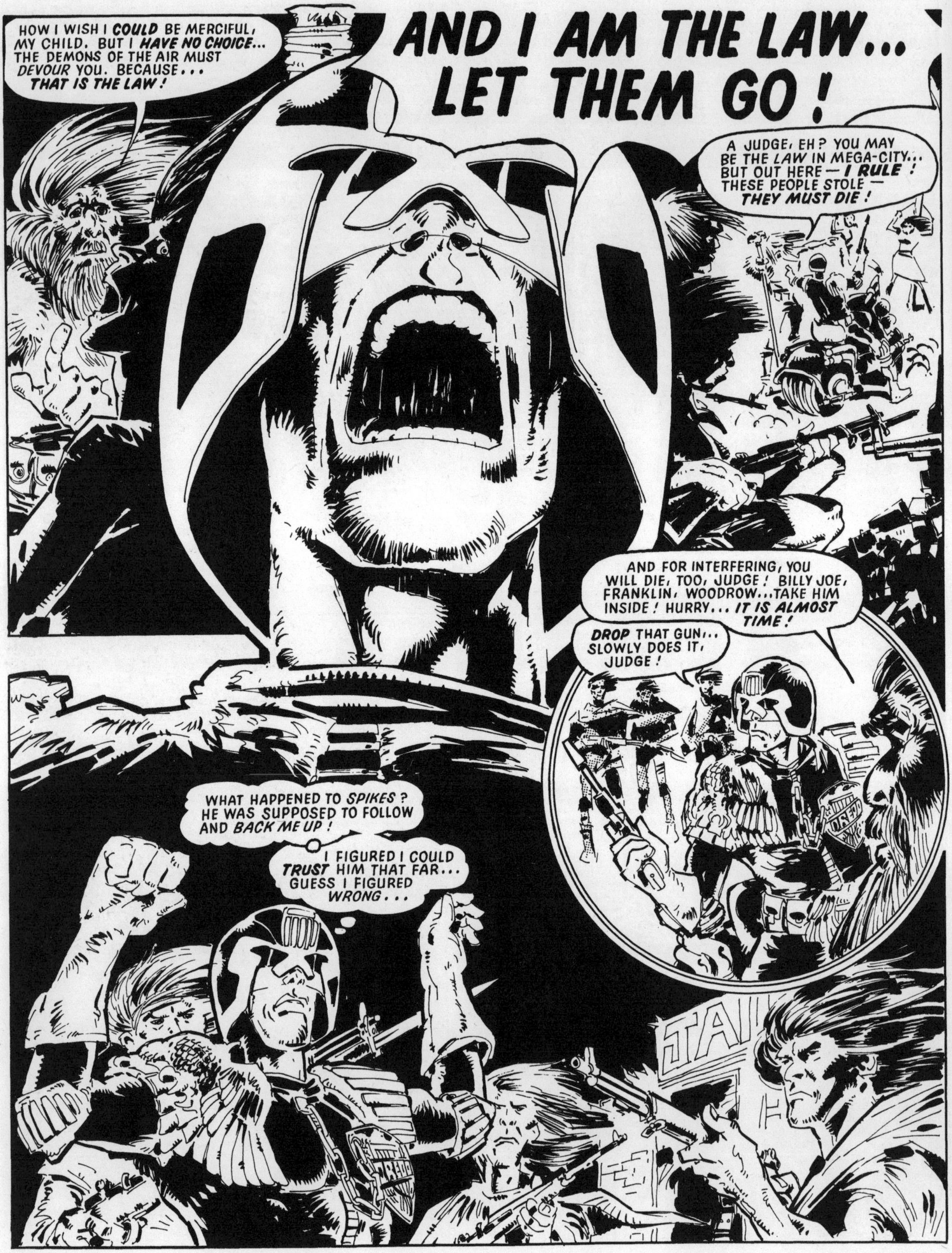
HOW I WISH I COULD BE MERCIFUL, MY CHILD. BUT I HAVE NO CHOICE... THE DEMONS OF THE AIR MUST DEVOUR YOU. BECAUSE... THAT IS THE LAW!
AND I AM THE LAW... LET THEM GO!
A JUDGE, EH? YOU MAY BE THE LAW IN MEGA-CITY... BUT OUT HERE — I RULE! THESE PEOPLE STOLE — THEY MUST DIE!
AND FOR INTERFERING, YOU WILL DIE, TOO, JUDGE! BILLY JOE, FRANKLIN, WOODROW... TAKE HIM INSIDE! HURRY... IT IS ALMOST TIME!
DROP THAT GUN... SLOWLY DOES IT, JUDGE!
WHAT HAPPENED TO SPIKES? HE WAS SUPPOSED TO FOLLOW AND BACK ME UP!
I FIGURED I COULD TRUST HIM THAT FAR... GUESS I FIGURED WRONG...

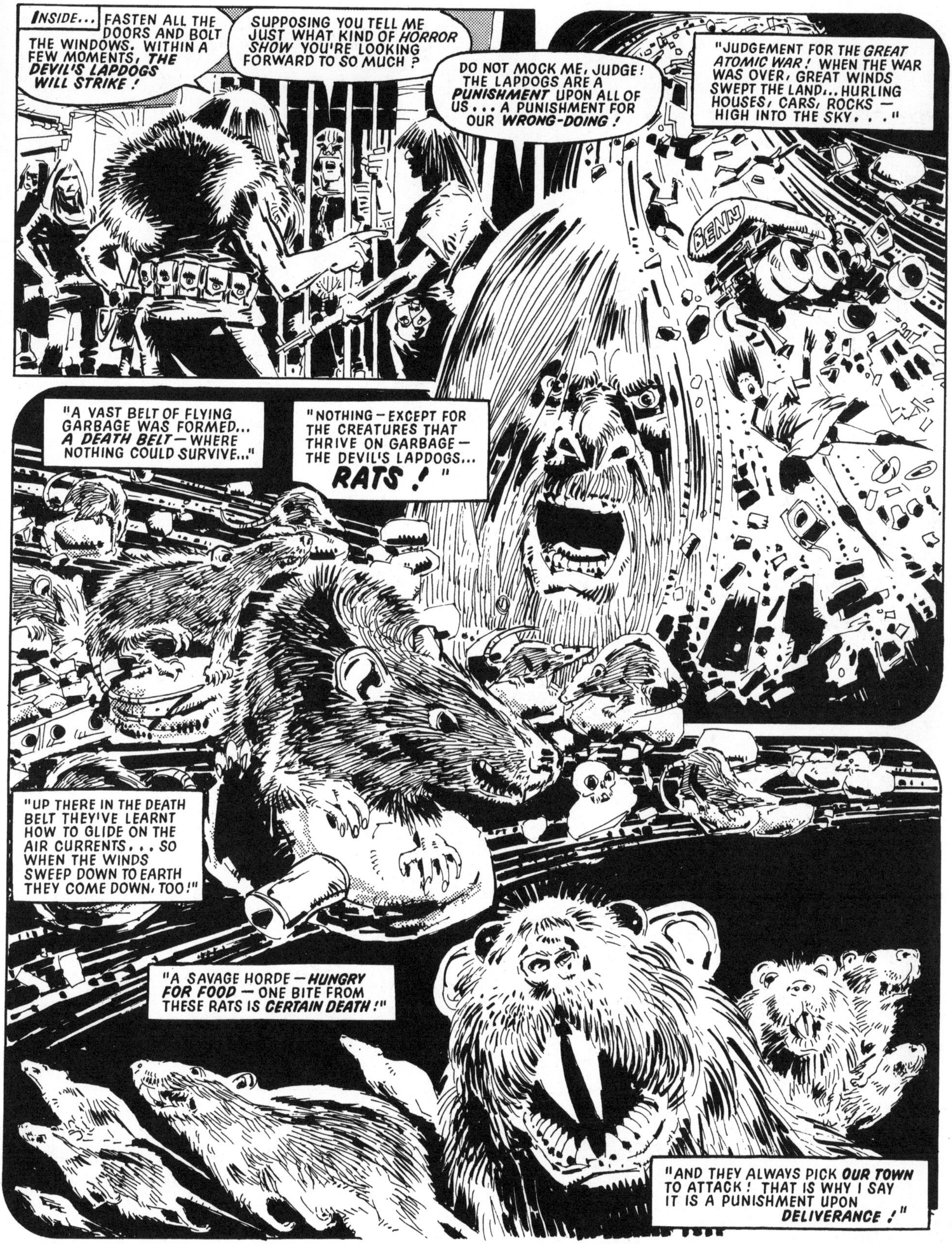
INSIDE...
FASTEN ALL THE DOORS AND BOLT THE WINDOWS. WITHIN A FEW MOMENTS, THE DEVIL'S LAPDOGS WILL STRIKE!
SUPPOSING YOU TELL ME JUST WHAT KIND OF HORROR SHOW YOU'RE LOOKING FORWARD TO SO MUCH?
DO NOT MOCK ME, JUDGE! THE LAPDOGS ARE A PUNISHMENT UPON ALL OF US... A PUNISHMENT FOR OUR WRONG-DOING!
"JUDGEMENT FOR THE GREAT ATOMIC WAR! WHEN THE WAR WAS OVER, GREAT WINDS SWEPT THE LAND... HURLING HOUSES, CARS, ROCKS — HIGH INTO THE SKY..."
"A VAST BELT OF FLYING GARBAGE WAS FORMED... A DEATH BELT — WHERE NOTHING COULD SURVIVE..."
"NOTHING — EXCEPT FOR THE CREATURES THAT THRIVE ON GARBAGE — THE DEVIL'S LAPDOGS... RATS!"
"UP THERE IN THE DEATH BELT THEY'VE LEARNT HOW TO GLIDE ON THE AIR CURRENTS... SO WHEN THE WINDS SWEEP DOWN TO EARTH THEY COME DOWN, TOO!"
"A SAVAGE HORDE — HUNGRY FOR FOOD — ONE BITE FROM THESE RATS IS CERTAIN DEATH!"
"AND THEY ALWAYS PICK OUR TOWN TO ATTACK! THAT IS WHY I SAY IT IS A PUNISHMENT UPON DELIVERANCE!"

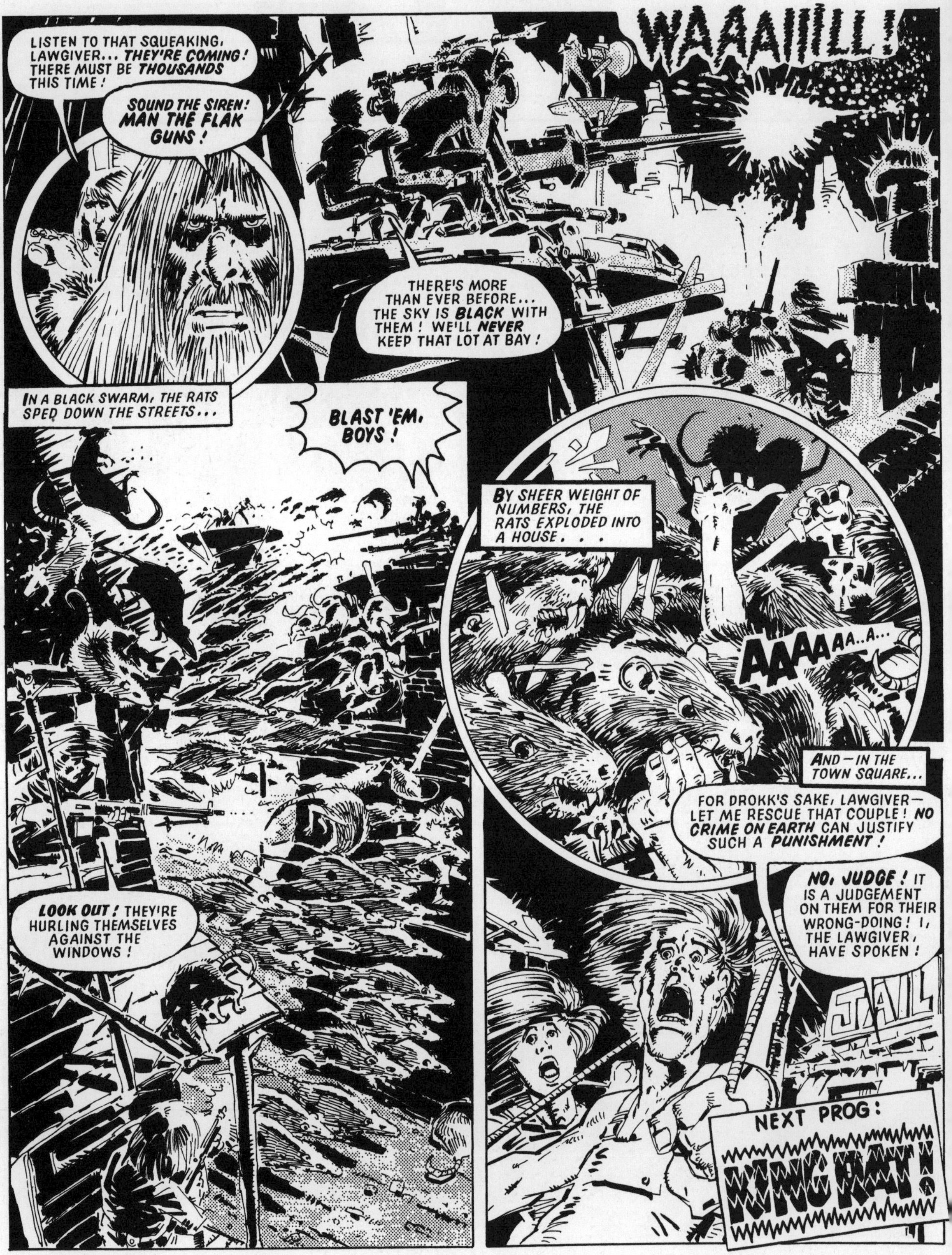
LISTEN TO THAT SQUEAKING, LAWGIVER... THEY'RE COMING! THERE MUST BE THOUSANDS THIS TIME!
SOUND THE SIREN! MAN THE FLAK GUNS!
WAAAIIILL!
THERE'S MORE THAN EVER BEFORE... THE SKY IS BLACK WITH THEM! WE'LL NEVER KEEP THAT LOT AT BAY!
IN A BLACK SWARM, THE RATS SPED DOWN THE STREETS...
BLAST 'EM, BOYS!
LOOK OUT! THEY'RE HURLING THEMSELVES AGAINST THE WINDOWS!
BY SHEER WEIGHT OF NUMBERS, THE RATS EXPLODED INTO A HOUSE...
AAAAAA..A...
AND—IN THE TOWN SQUARE...
FOR DROKK'S SAKE, LAWGIVER—LET ME RESCUE THAT COUPLE! NO CRIME ON EARTH CAN JUSTIFY SUCH A PUNISHMENT!
NO, JUDGE! IT IS A JUDGEMENT ON THEM FOR THEIR WRONG-DOING! I, THE LAWGIVER, HAVE SPOKEN!
JAIL
NEXT PROG:
KING RAT!

THE CURSED EARTH
CHAPTER 4.

THE TOWN OF DELIVERANCE, IN THE CURSED EARTH, IS IN TROUBLE... **BIG TROUBLE!** IT IS BEING ATTACKED BY A RAIN OF FLYING RATS—AND JUST ONE BITE FROM THE RATS IS... **CERTAIN DEATH!**

JUDGE DREDD

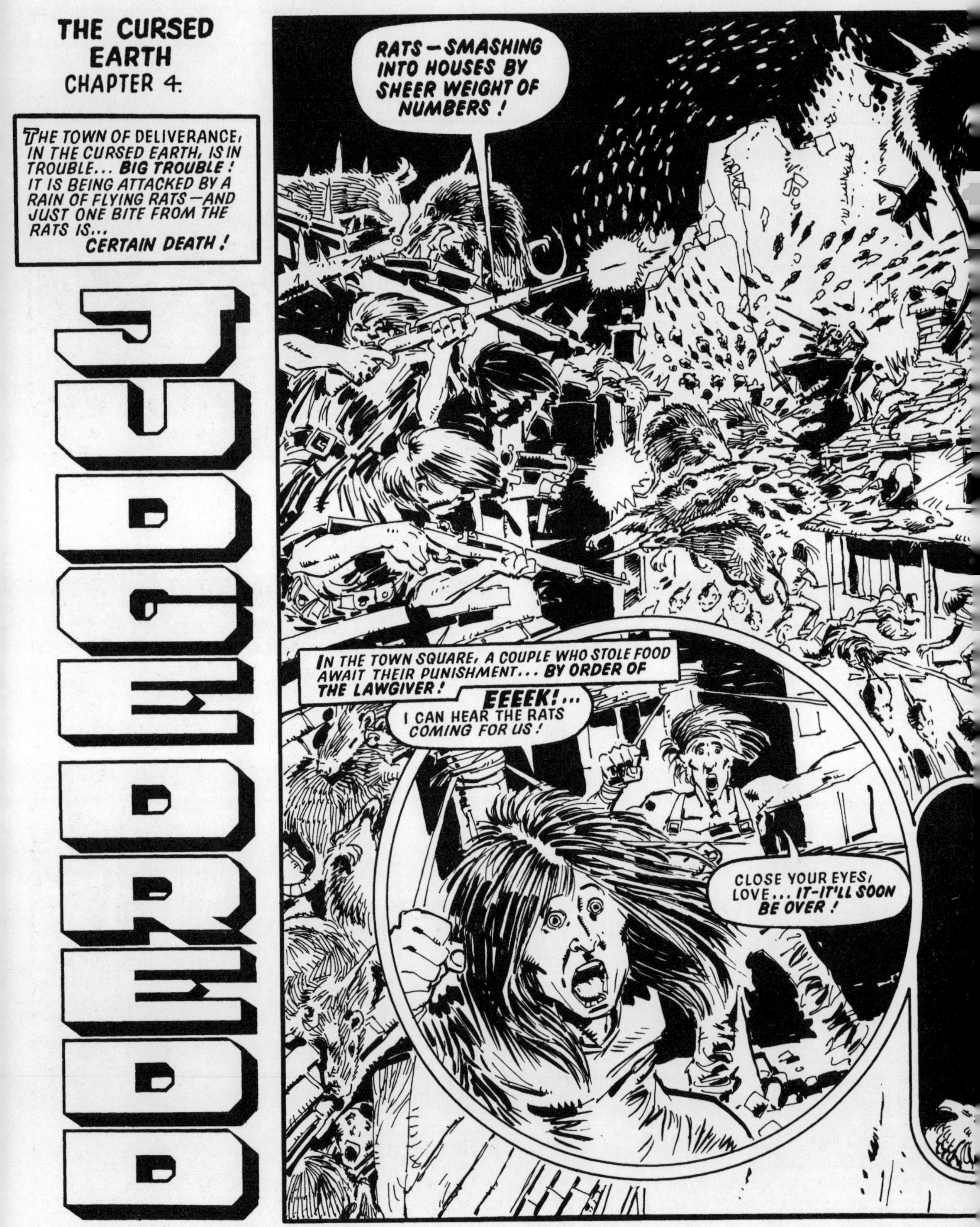
RATS—SMASHING INTO HOUSES BY SHEER WEIGHT OF NUMBERS!
IN THE TOWN SQUARE, A COUPLE WHO STOLE FOOD AWAIT THEIR PUNISHMENT... BY ORDER OF THE LAWGIVER!
EEEEK!... I CAN HEAR THE RATS COMING FOR US!
CLOSE YOUR EYES, LOVE... IT-IT'LL SOON BE OVER!

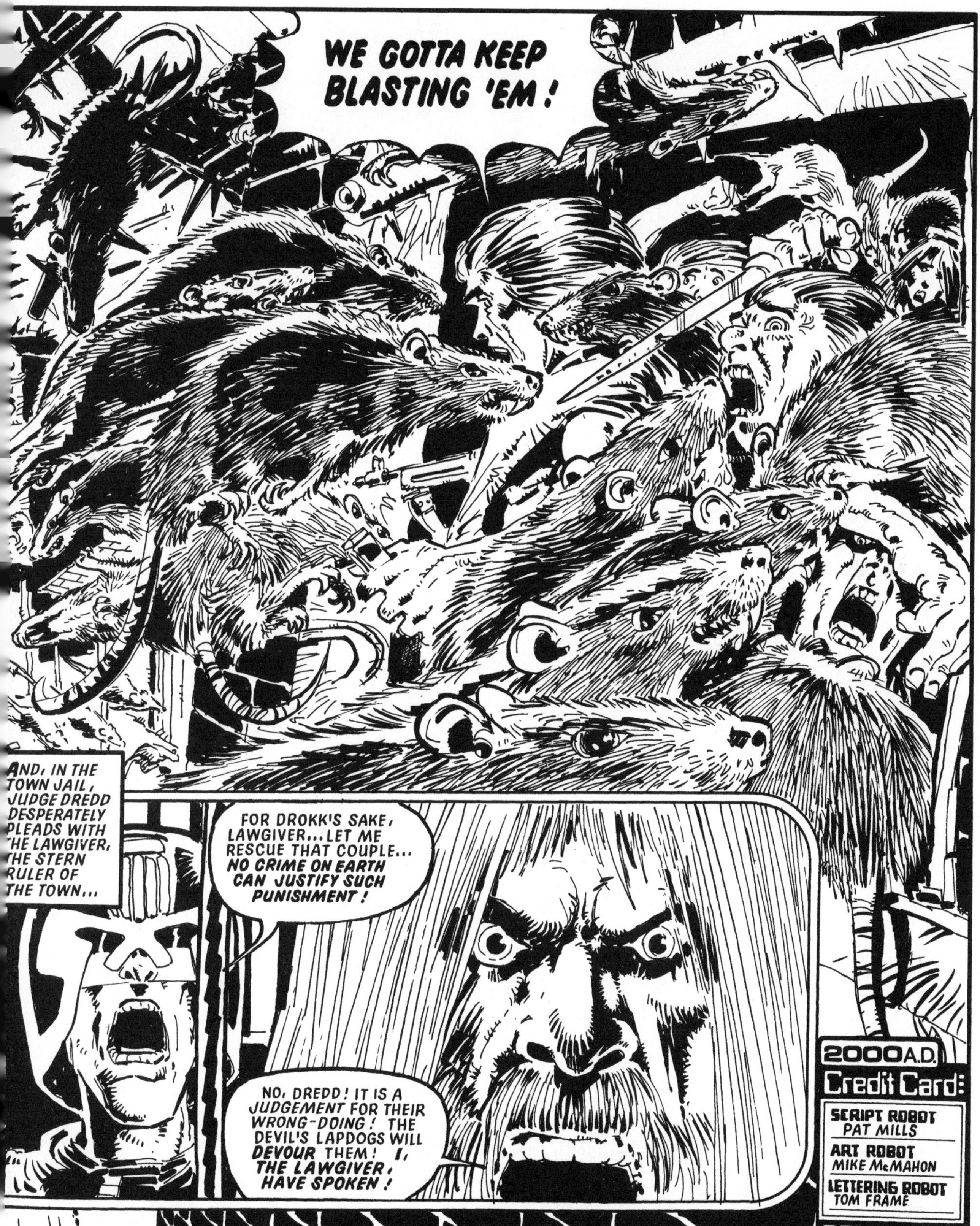

WE GOTTA KEEP BLASTING 'EM !
AND, IN THE TOWN JAIL, JUDGE DREDD DESPERATELY PLEADS WITH THE LAWGIVER, THE STERN RULER OF THE TOWN...
FOR DROKK'S SAKE, LAWGIVER... LET ME RESCUE THAT COUPLE... NO CRIME ON EARTH CAN JUSTIFY SUCH PUNISHMENT !
NO, DREDD! IT IS A JUDGEMENT FOR THEIR WRONG-DOING! THE DEVIL'S LAPDOGS WILL DEVOUR THEM! I, THE LAWGIVER, HAVE SPOKEN !
2000 A.D. Credit Card:
SCRIPT ROBOT PAT MILLS
ART ROBOT MIKE McMAHON
LETTERING ROBOT TOM FRAME
COMPU·73E

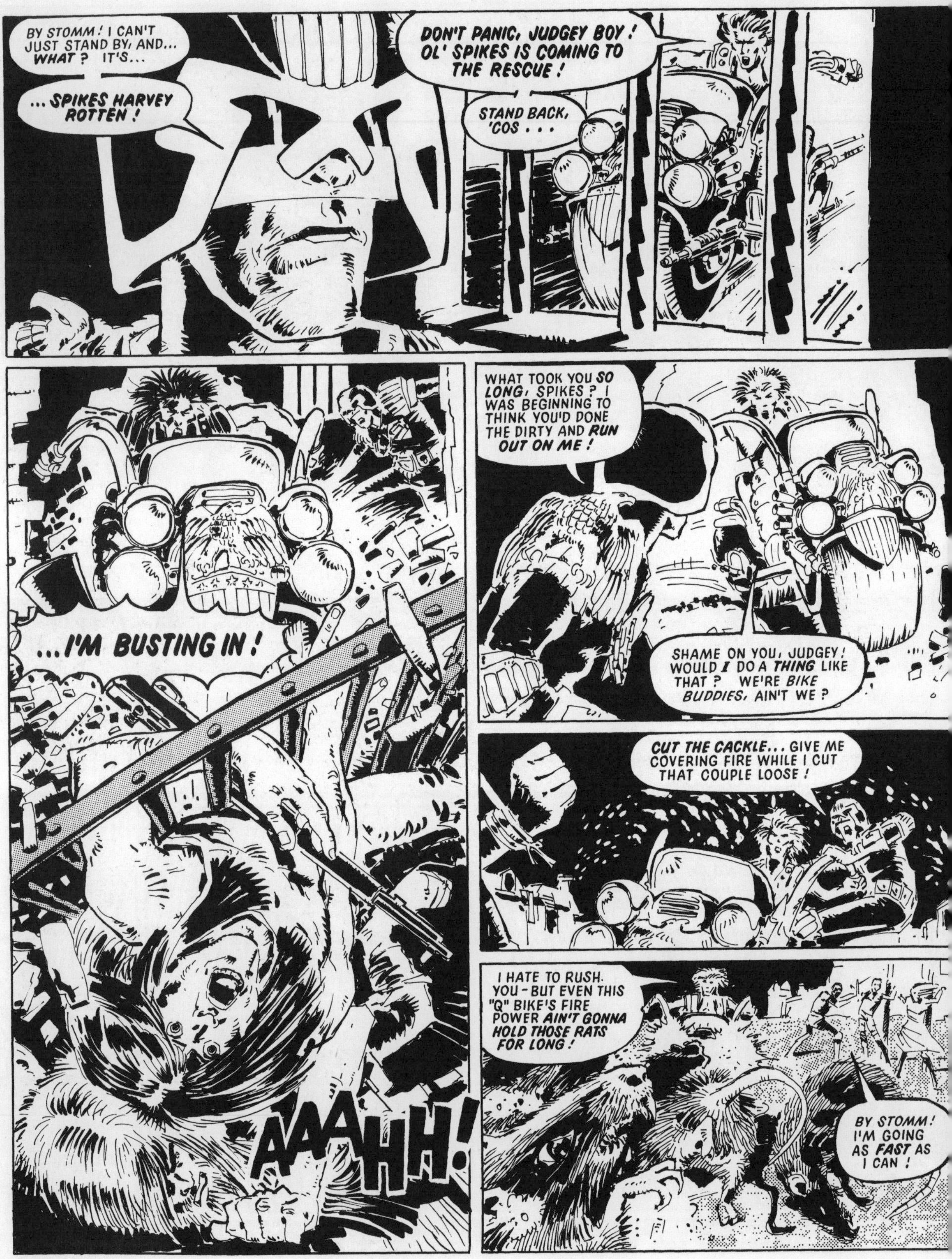

BY STOMM! I CAN'T JUST STAND BY, AND... WHAT? IT'S...
... SPIKES HARVEY ROTTEN!
DON'T PANIC, JUDGEY BOY! OL' SPIKES IS COMING TO THE RESCUE!
STAND BACK, 'COS . . .
... I'M BUSTING IN!
AAAHH!
WHAT TOOK YOU SO LONG, SPIKES? I WAS BEGINNING TO THINK YOU'D DONE THE DIRTY AND RUN OUT ON ME!
SHAME ON YOU, JUDGEY! WOULD I DO A THING LIKE THAT? WE'RE BIKE BUDDIES, AIN'T WE?
CUT THE CACKLE... GIVE ME COVERING FIRE WHILE I CUT THAT COUPLE LOOSE!
I HATE TO RUSH YOU - BUT EVEN THIS "Q" BIKE'S FIRE POWER AIN'T GONNA HOLD THOSE RATS FOR LONG!
BY STOMM! I'M GOING AS FAST AS I CAN!

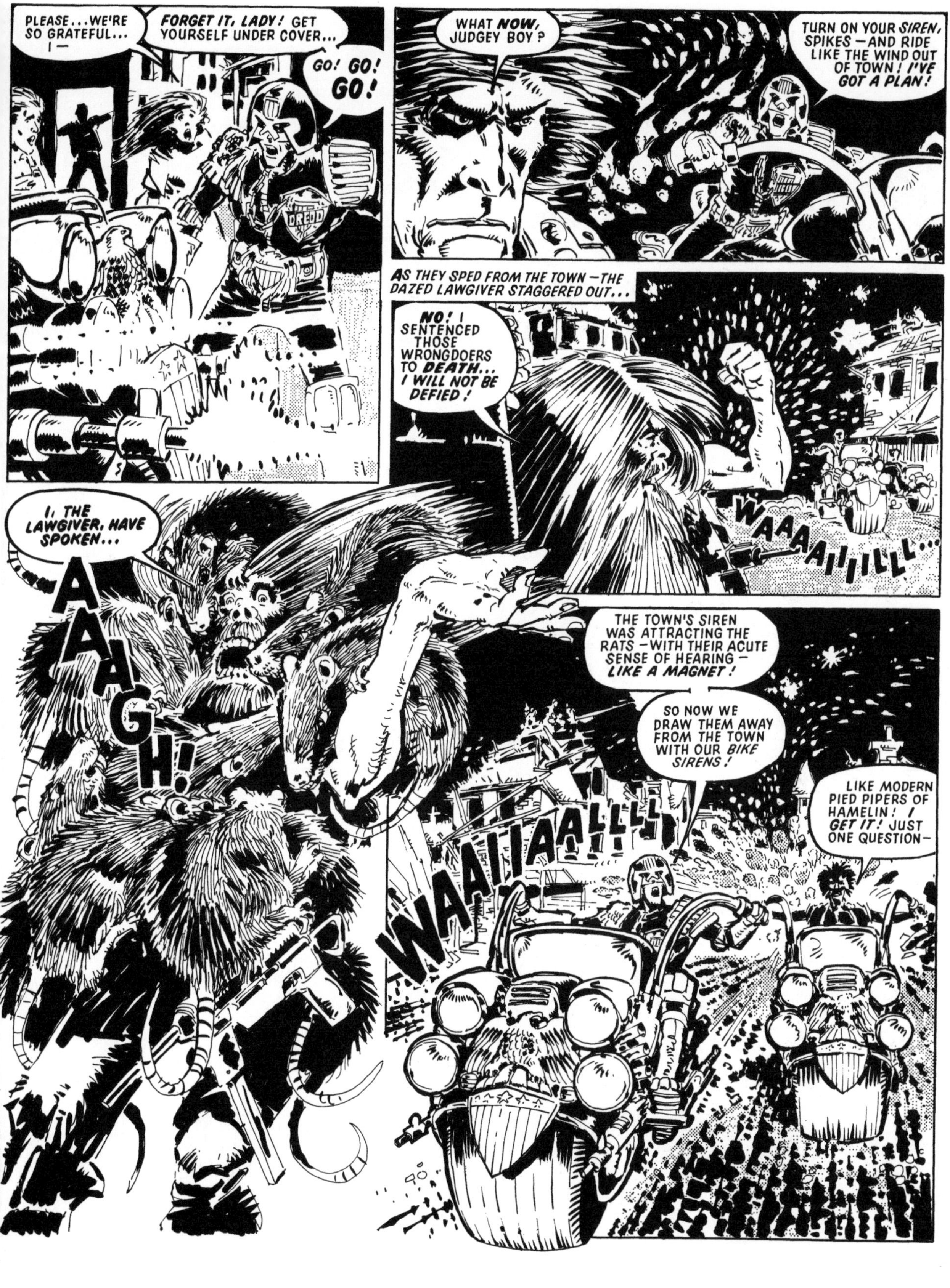
PLEASE... WE'RE SO GRATEFUL... I—
FORGET IT, LADY! GET YOURSELF UNDER COVER...
GO! GO! GO!
WHAT NOW, JUDGEY BOY?
TURN ON YOUR SIREN, SPIKES — AND RIDE LIKE THE WIND OUT OF TOWN! I'VE GOT A PLAN!
AS THEY SPED FROM THE TOWN — THE DAZED LAWGIVER STAGGERED OUT...
NO! I SENTENCED THOSE WRONGDOERS TO DEATH... I WILL NOT BE DEFIED!
WAAAAIIIILLL...
I, THE LAWGIVER, HAVE SPOKEN...
AAAGH!
THE TOWN'S SIREN WAS ATTRACTING THE RATS — WITH THEIR ACUTE SENSE OF HEARING — LIKE A MAGNET!
SO NOW WE DRAW THEM AWAY FROM THE TOWN WITH OUR BIKE SIRENS!
LIKE MODERN PIED PIPERS OF HAMELIN! I GET IT! JUST ONE QUESTION—
WAAIIIAALLLL

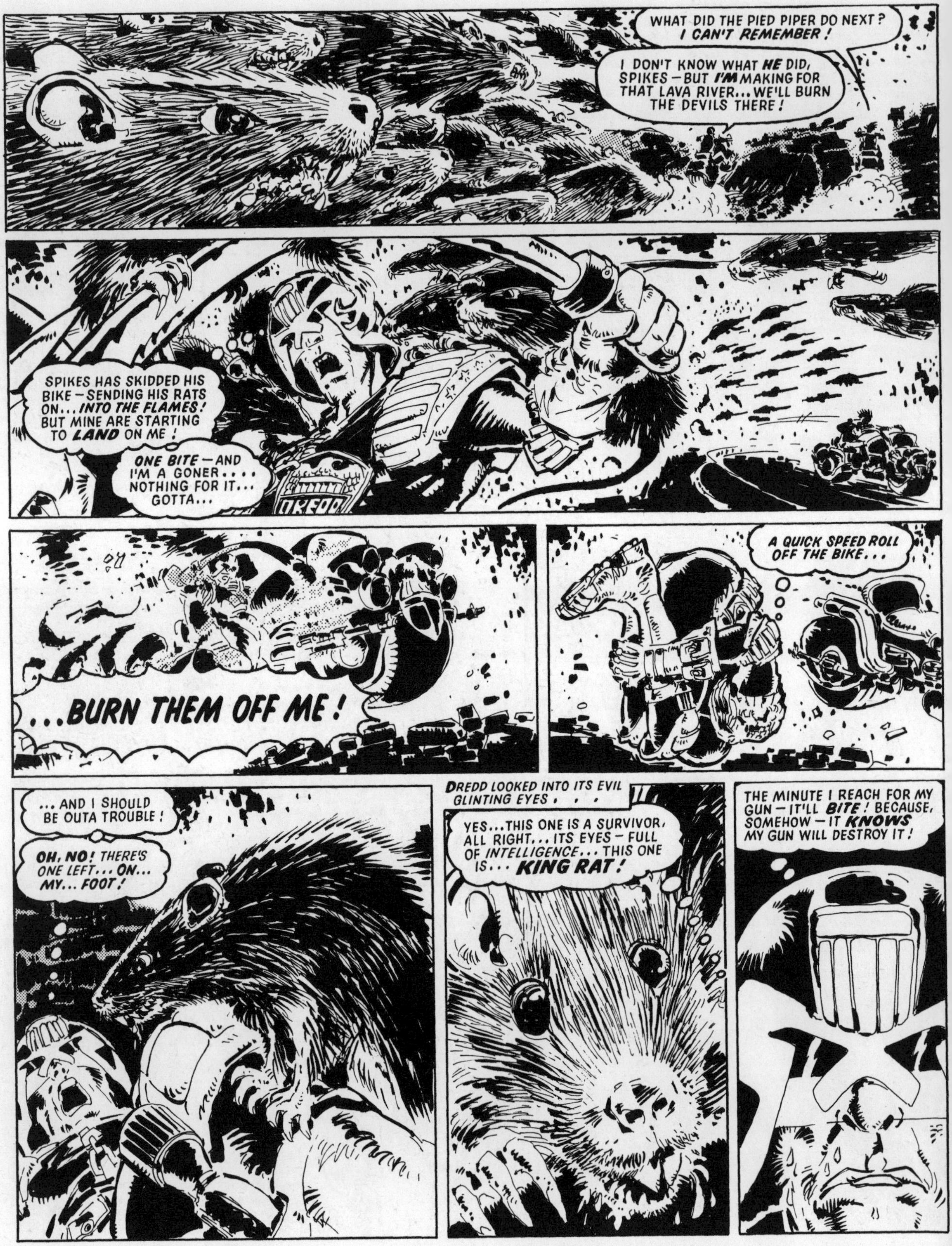

WHAT DID THE PIED PIPER DO NEXT? I CAN'T REMEMBER!
I DON'T KNOW WHAT HE DID, SPIKES — BUT I'M MAKING FOR THAT LAVA RIVER... WE'LL BURN THE DEVILS THERE!
SPIKES HAS SKIDDED HIS BIKE — SENDING HIS RATS ON... INTO THE FLAMES! BUT MINE ARE STARTING TO LAND ON ME!
ONE BITE — AND I'M A GONER.... NOTHING FOR IT... GOTTA...
...BURN THEM OFF ME!
A QUICK SPEED ROLL OFF THE BIKE...
... AND I SHOULD BE OUTA TROUBLE!
OH, NO! THERE'S ONE LEFT... ON... MY... FOOT!
DREDD LOOKED INTO ITS EVIL GLINTING EYES . . .
YES... THIS ONE IS A SURVIVOR, ALL RIGHT... ITS EYES — FULL OF INTELLIGENCE... THIS ONE IS... KING RAT!
THE MINUTE I REACH FOR MY GUN — IT'LL BITE! BECAUSE, SOMEHOW — IT KNOWS MY GUN WILL DESTROY IT!

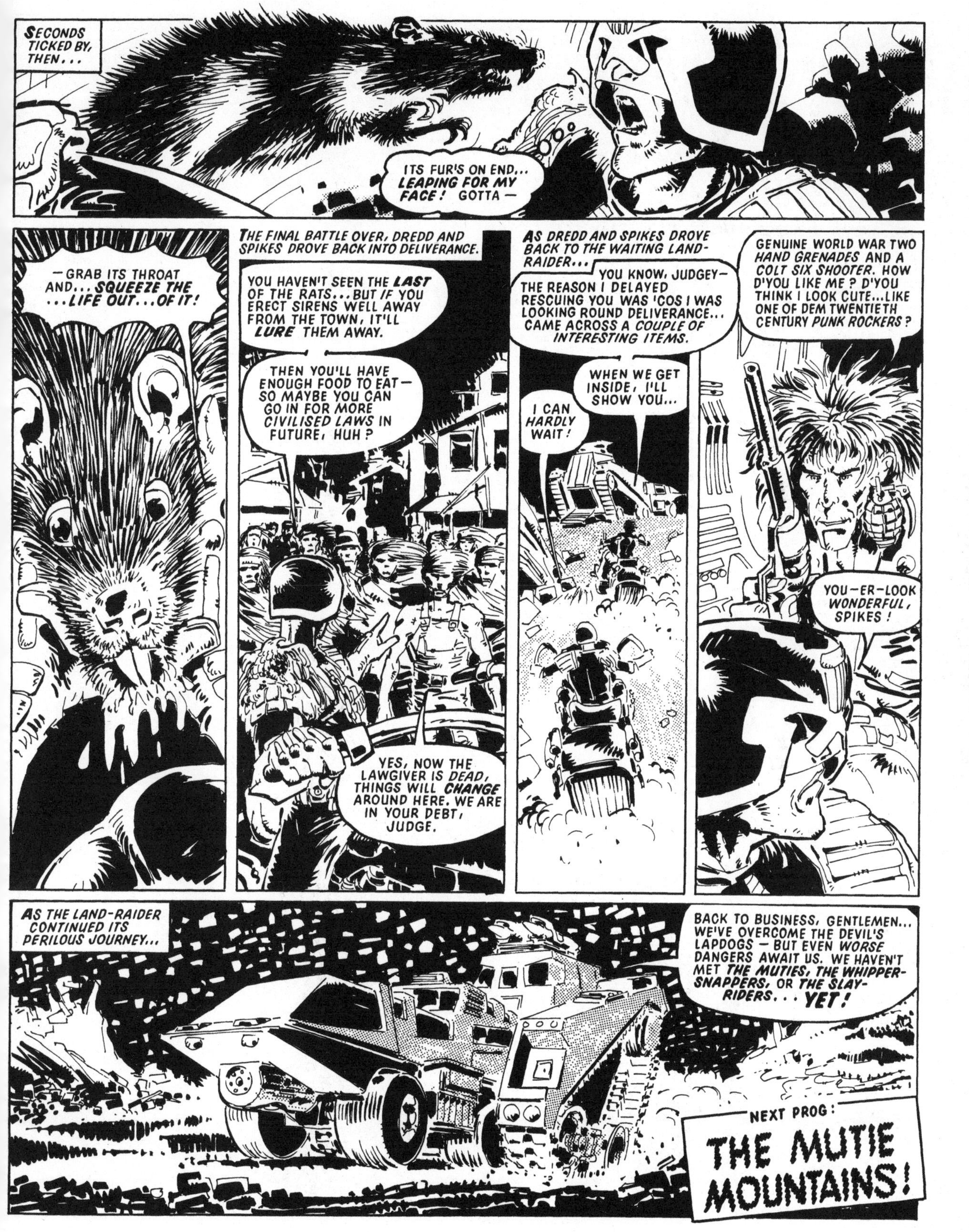
SECONDS TICKED BY, THEN...
ITS FUR'S ON END... LEAPING FOR MY FACE! GOTTA —
— GRAB ITS THROAT AND... SQUEEZE THE ...LIFE OUT...OF IT!
THE FINAL BATTLE OVER, DREDD AND SPIKES DROVE BACK INTO DELIVERANCE.
YOU HAVEN'T SEEN THE LAST OF THE RATS... BUT IF YOU ERECT SIRENS WELL AWAY FROM THE TOWN, IT'LL LURE THEM AWAY.
THEN YOU'LL HAVE ENOUGH FOOD TO EAT — SO MAYBE YOU CAN GO IN FOR MORE CIVILISED LAWS IN FUTURE, HUH?
YES, NOW THE LAWGIVER IS DEAD, THINGS WILL CHANGE AROUND HERE. WE ARE IN YOUR DEBT, JUDGE.
AS DREDD AND SPIKES DROVE BACK TO THE WAITING LAND-RAIDER...
YOU KNOW, JUDGEY — THE REASON I DELAYED RESCUING YOU WAS 'COS I WAS LOOKING ROUND DELIVERANCE... CAME ACROSS A COUPLE OF INTERESTING ITEMS.
WHEN WE GET INSIDE, I'LL SHOW YOU...
I CAN HARDLY WAIT!
GENUINE WORLD WAR TWO HAND GRENADES AND A COLT SIX SHOOTER. HOW D'YOU LIKE ME? D'YOU THINK I LOOK CUTE...LIKE ONE OF DEM TWENTIETH CENTURY PUNK ROCKERS?
YOU — ER — LOOK WONDERFUL, SPIKES!
AS THE LAND-RAIDER CONTINUED ITS PERILOUS JOURNEY...
BACK TO BUSINESS, GENTLEMEN... WE'VE OVERCOME THE DEVIL'S LAPDOGS — BUT EVEN WORSE DANGERS AWAIT US. WE HAVEN'T MET THE MUTIES, THE WHIPPER-SNAPPERS, OR THE SLAY-RIDERS... YET!
NEXT PROG:
THE MUTIE MOUNTAINS!

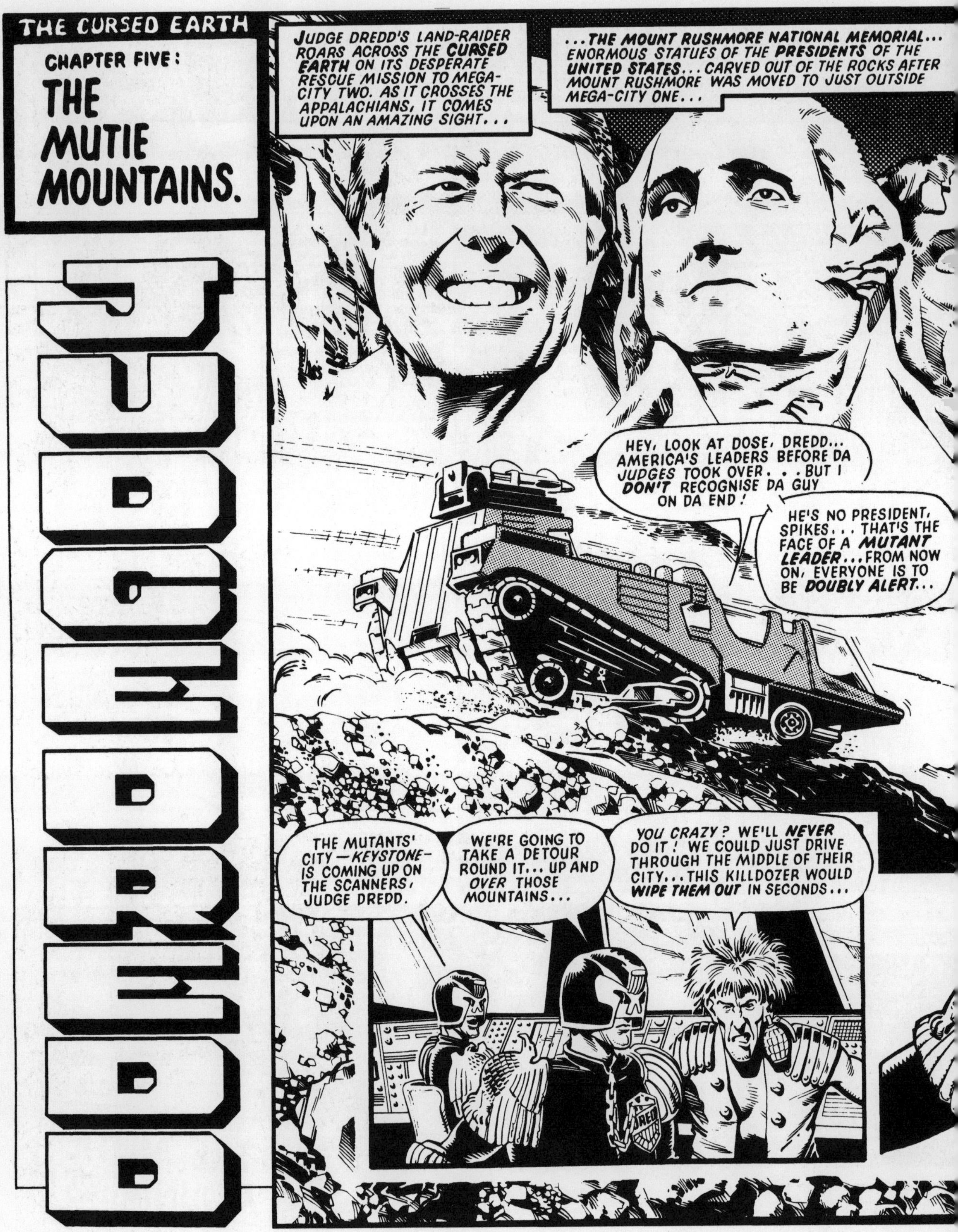
THE CURSED EARTH
CHAPTER FIVE: THE MUTIE MOUNTAINS.
JUDGE DREDD
JUDGE DREDD'S LAND-RAIDER ROARS ACROSS THE CURSED EARTH ON ITS DESPERATE RESCUE MISSION TO MEGA-CITY TWO. AS IT CROSSES THE APPALACHIANS, IT COMES UPON AN AMAZING SIGHT...
...THE MOUNT RUSHMORE NATIONAL MEMORIAL... ENORMOUS STATUES OF THE PRESIDENTS OF THE UNITED STATES... CARVED OUT OF THE ROCKS AFTER MOUNT RUSHMORE WAS MOVED TO JUST OUTSIDE MEGA-CITY ONE...
HEY, LOOK AT DOSE, DREDD... AMERICA'S LEADERS BEFORE DA JUDGES TOOK OVER... BUT I DON'T RECOGNISE DA GUY ON DA END!
HE'S NO PRESIDENT, SPIKES... THAT'S THE FACE OF A MUTANT LEADER... FROM NOW ON, EVERYONE IS TO BE DOUBLY ALERT...
THE MUTANTS' CITY—KEYSTONE—IS COMING UP ON THE SCANNERS, JUDGE DREDD.
WE'RE GOING TO TAKE A DETOUR ROUND IT... UP AND OVER THOSE MOUNTAINS...
YOU CRAZY? WE'LL NEVER DO IT! WE COULD JUST DRIVE THROUGH THE MIDDLE OF THEIR CITY... THIS KILLDOZER WOULD WIPE THEM OUT IN SECONDS...

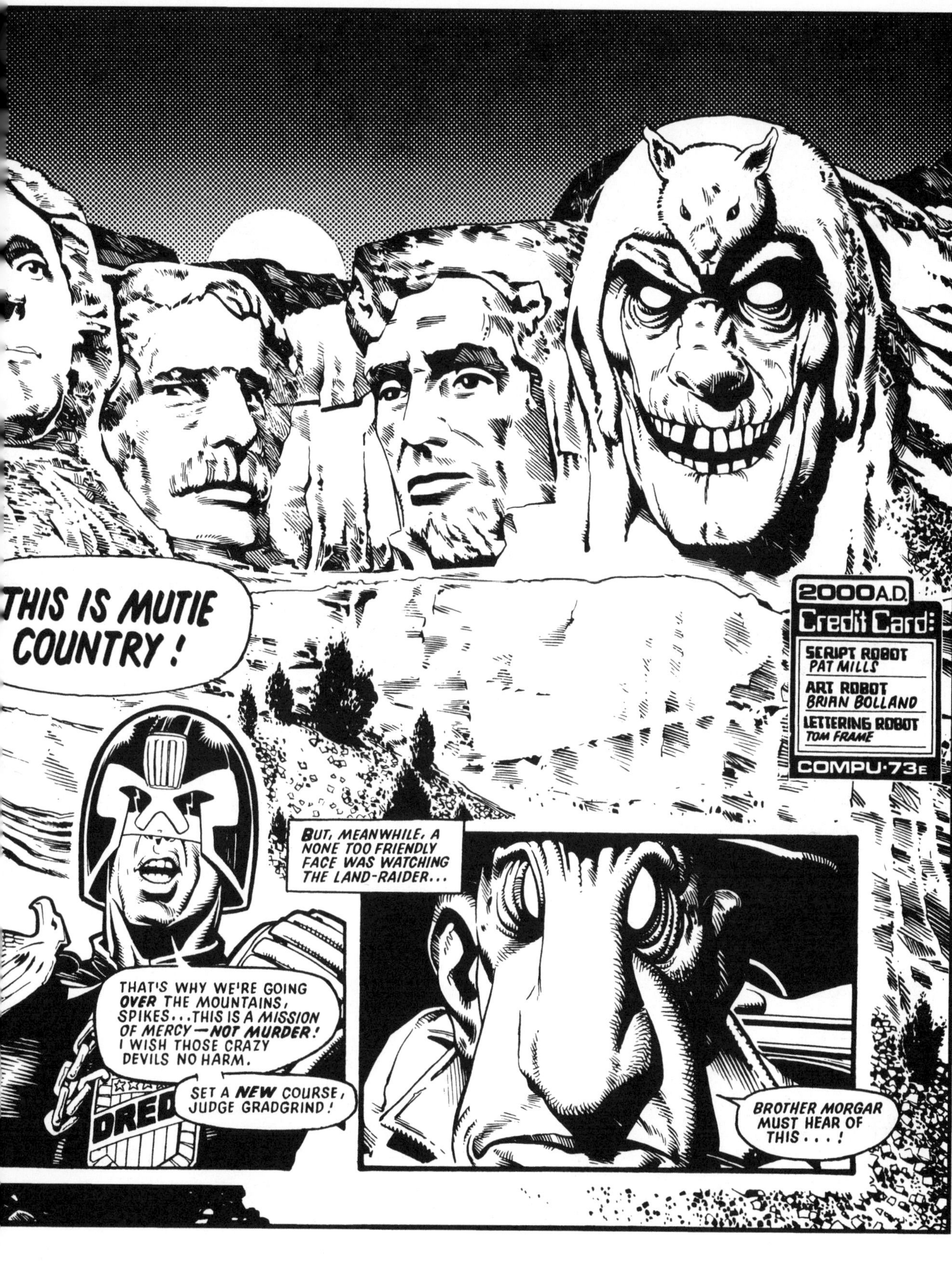
THIS IS MUTIE COUNTRY!
2000 A.D. Credit Card: SCRIPT ROBOT PAT MILLS ART ROBOT BRIAN BOLLAND LETTERING ROBOT TOM FRAME COMPU-73E
BUT, MEANWHILE, A NONE TOO FRIENDLY FACE WAS WATCHING THE LAND-RAIDER...
THAT'S WHY WE'RE GOING OVER THE MOUNTAINS, SPIKES...THIS IS A MISSION OF MERCY—NOT MURDER! I WISH THOSE CRAZY DEVILS NO HARM.
SET A NEW COURSE, JUDGE GRADGRIND!
DREDD
BROTHER MORGAR MUST HEAR OF THIS...!

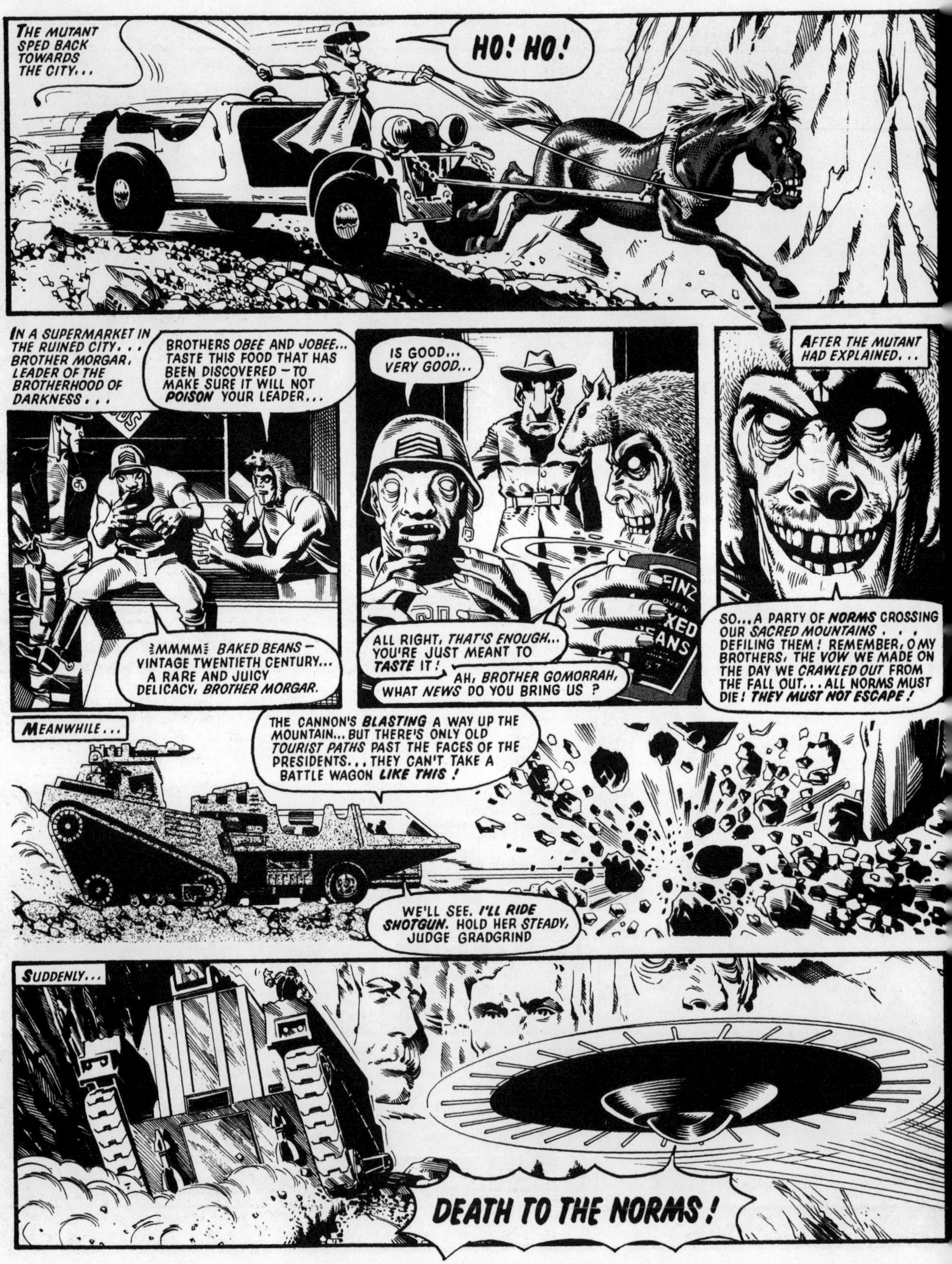
THE MUTANT SPED BACK TOWARDS THE CITY...
HO! HO!
IN A SUPERMARKET IN THE RUINED CITY... BROTHER MORGAR, LEADER OF THE BROTHERHOOD OF DARKNESS...
BROTHERS OBEE AND JOBEE... TASTE THIS FOOD THAT HAS BEEN DISCOVERED — TO MAKE SURE IT WILL NOT POISON YOUR LEADER...
MMMMM! BAKED BEANS — VINTAGE TWENTIETH CENTURY... A RARE AND JUICY DELICACY, BROTHER MORGAR.
IS GOOD... VERY GOOD...
ALL RIGHT, THAT'S ENOUGH... YOU'RE JUST MEANT TO TASTE IT!
AH, BROTHER GOMORRAH, WHAT NEWS DO YOU BRING US ?
AFTER THE MUTANT HAD EXPLAINED...
SO... A PARTY OF NORMS CROSSING OUR SACRED MOUNTAINS . . . DEFILING THEM! REMEMBER, O MY BROTHERS, THE VOW WE MADE ON THE DAY WE CRAWLED OUT FROM THE FALL OUT... ALL NORMS MUST DIE! THEY MUST NOT ESCAPE!
MEANWHILE...
THE CANNON'S BLASTING A WAY UP THE MOUNTAIN... BUT THERE'S ONLY OLD TOURIST PATHS PAST THE FACES OF THE PRESIDENTS... THEY CAN'T TAKE A BATTLE WAGON LIKE THIS!
WE'LL SEE. I'LL RIDE SHOTGUN. HOLD HER STEADY, JUDGE GRADGRIND
SUDDENLY...
DEATH TO THE NORMS!

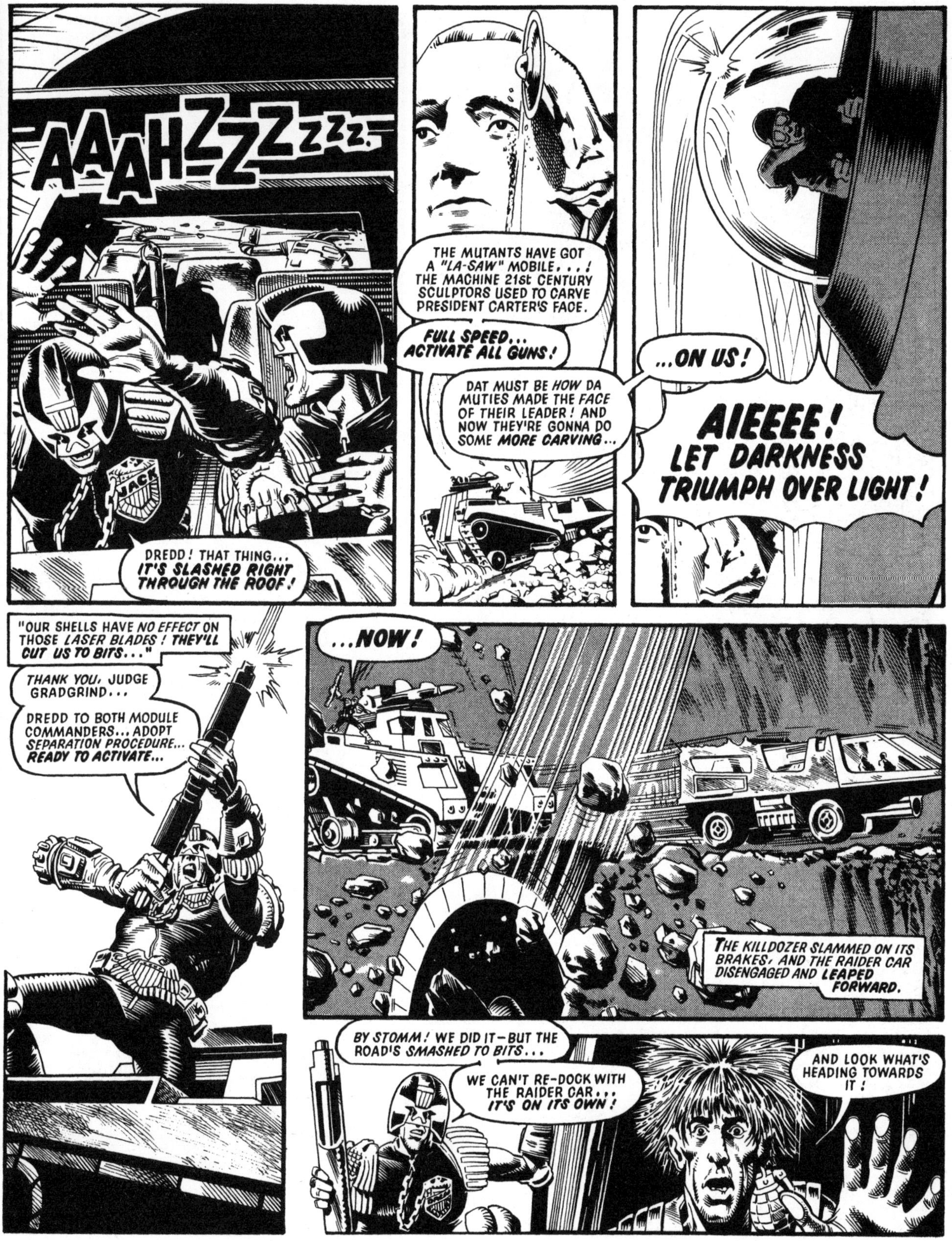

AAAHZZZzzz.
DREDD! THAT THING... IT'S SLASHED RIGHT THROUGH THE ROOF!
THE MUTANTS HAVE GOT A "LA-SAW" MOBILE...! THE MACHINE 21st CENTURY SCULPTORS USED TO CARVE PRESIDENT CARTER'S FACE.
FULL SPEED... ACTIVATE ALL GUNS!
DAT MUST BE HOW DA MUTIES MADE THE FACE OF THEIR LEADER! AND NOW THEY'RE GONNA DO SOME MORE CARVING...
...ON US!
AIEEEE! LET DARKNESS TRIUMPH OVER LIGHT!
"OUR SHELLS HAVE NO EFFECT ON THOSE LASER BLADES! THEY'LL CUT US TO BITS..."
THANK YOU, JUDGE GRADGRIND...
DREDD TO BOTH MODULE COMMANDERS... ADOPT SEPARATION PROCEDURE... READY TO ACTIVATE...
...NOW!
THE KILLDOZER SLAMMED ON ITS BRAKES, AND THE RAIDER CAR DISENGAGED AND LEAPED FORWARD.
BY STOMM! WE DID IT–BUT THE ROAD'S SMASHED TO BITS...
WE CAN'T RE-DOCK WITH THE RAIDER CAR... IT'S ON ITS OWN!
AND LOOK WHAT'S HEADING TOWARDS IT!

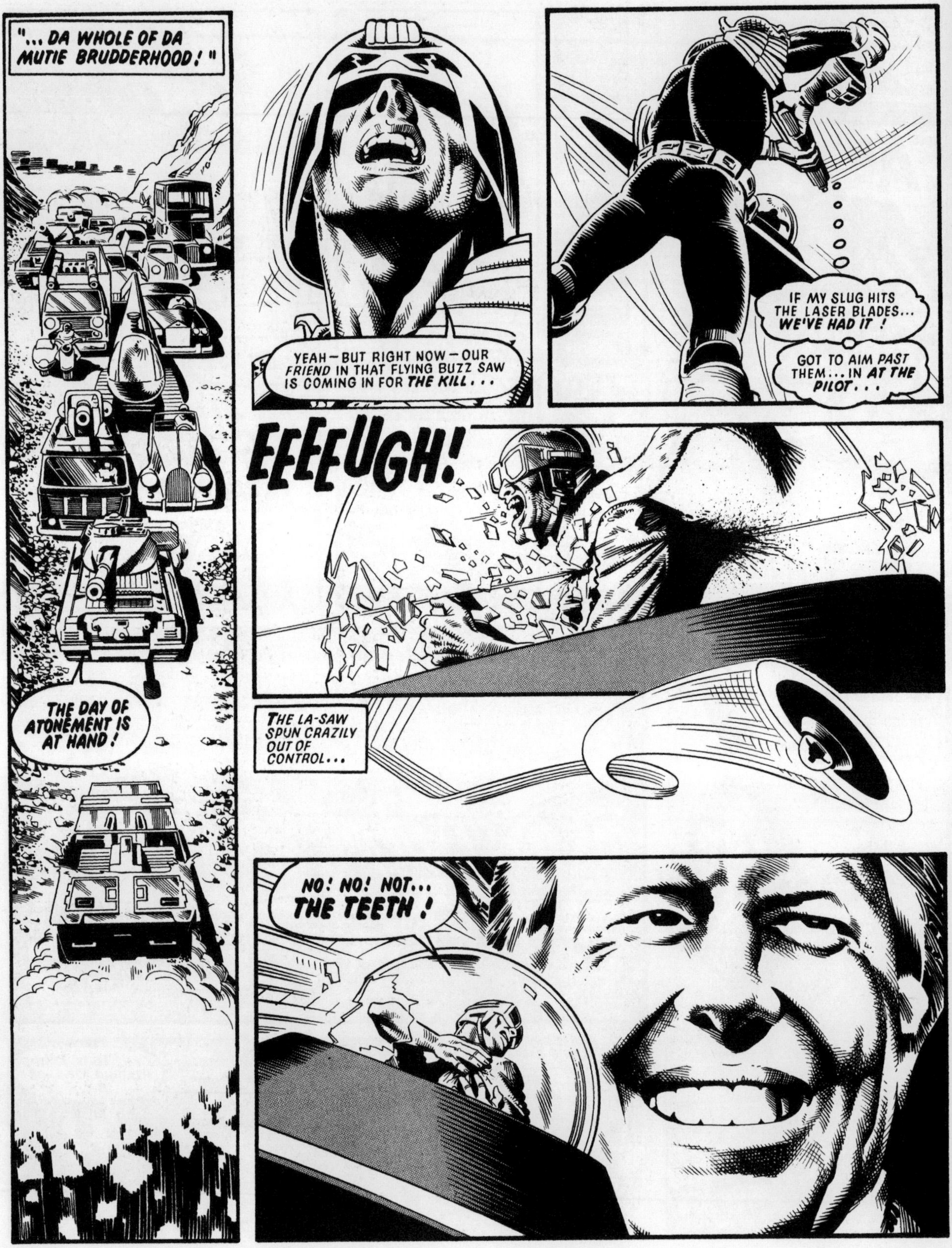
"... DA WHOLE OF DA MUTIE BRUDDERHOOD!"
THE DAY OF ATONEMENT IS AT HAND!
YEAH—BUT RIGHT NOW—OUR FRIEND IN THAT FLYING BUZZ SAW IS COMING IN FOR THE KILL...
IF MY SLUG HITS THE LASER BLADES... WE'VE HAD IT!
GOT TO AIM PAST THEM... IN AT THE PILOT...
EEEEUGH!
THE LA-SAW SPUN CRAZILY OUT OF CONTROL...
NO! NO! NOT... THE TEETH!

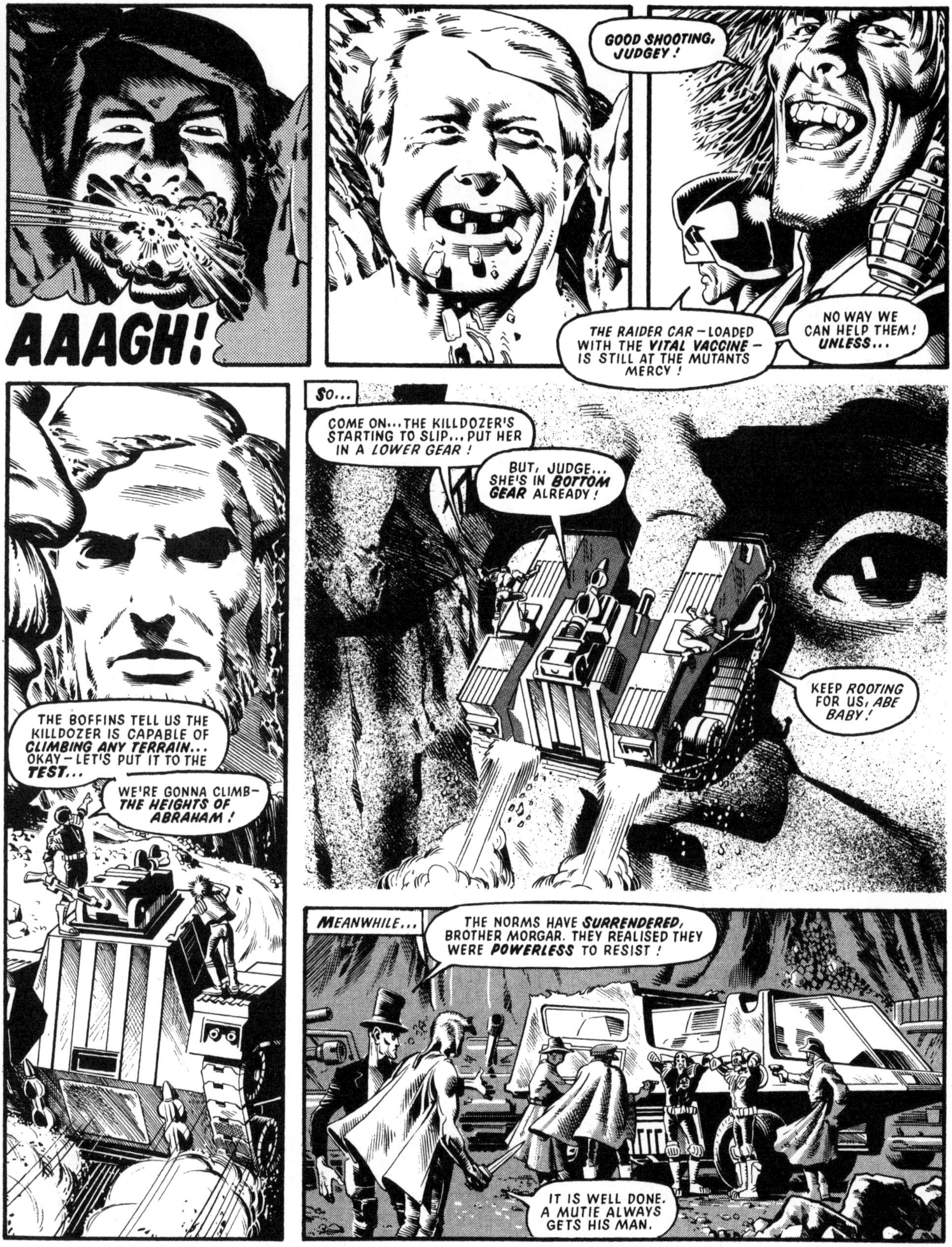
AAAGH!
GOOD SHOOTING, JUDGEY!
THE RAIDER CAR — LOADED WITH THE VITAL VACCINE — IS STILL AT THE MUTANTS MERCY!
NO WAY WE CAN HELP THEM! UNLESS...
THE BOFFINS TELL US THE KILLDOZER IS CAPABLE OF CLIMBING ANY TERRAIN... OKAY — LET'S PUT IT TO THE TEST...
WE'RE GONNA CLIMB — THE HEIGHTS OF ABRAHAM!
SO...
COME ON... THE KILLDOZER'S STARTING TO SLIP... PUT HER IN A LOWER GEAR!
BUT, JUDGE... SHE'S IN BOTTOM GEAR ALREADY!
KEEP ROOTING FOR US, ABE BABY!
MEANWHILE...
THE NORMS HAVE SURRENDERED, BROTHER MORGAR. THEY REALISED THEY WERE POWERLESS TO RESIST!
IT IS WELL DONE. A MUTIE ALWAYS GETS HIS MAN.

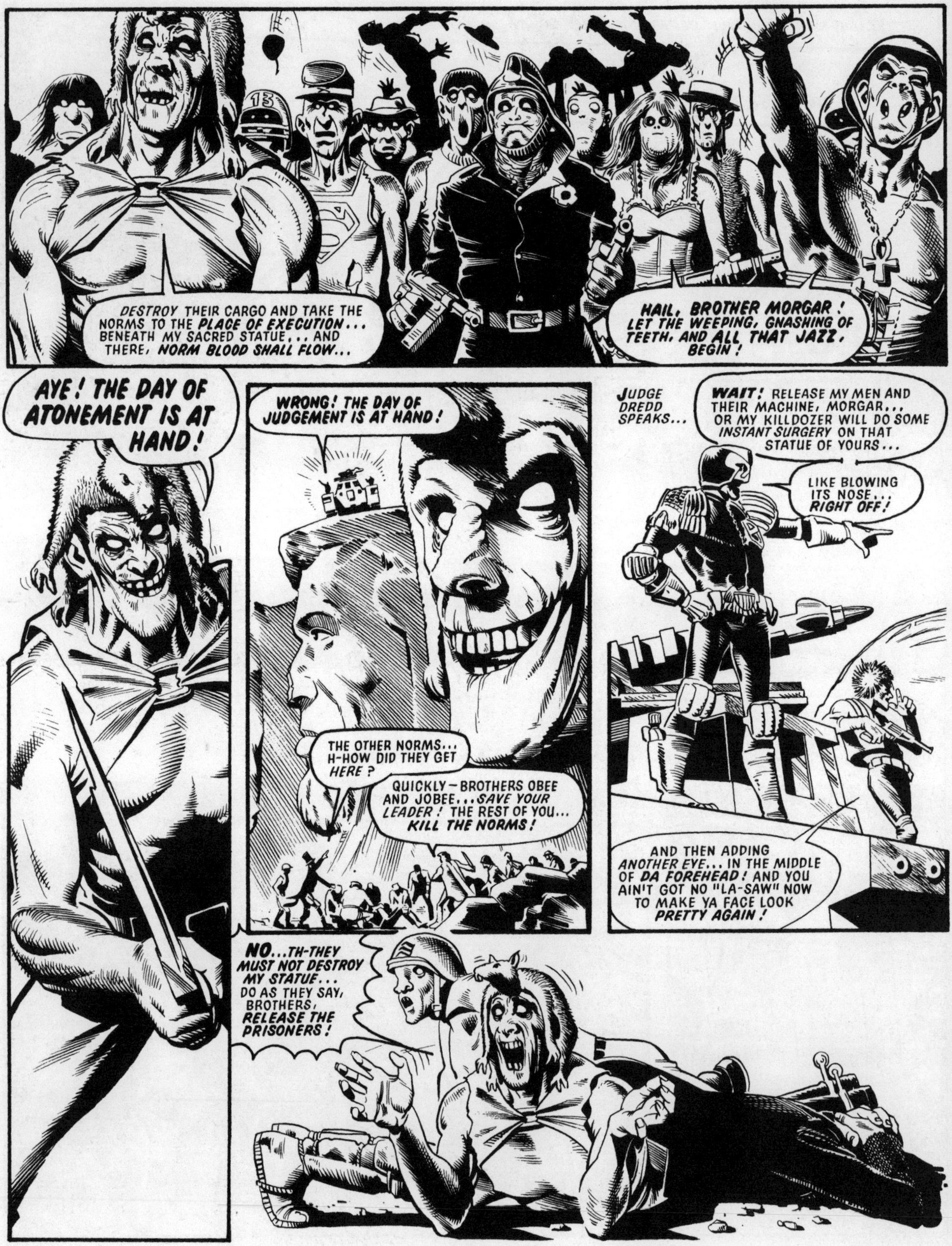
DESTROY THEIR CARGO AND TAKE THE NORMS TO THE PLACE OF EXECUTION... BENEATH MY SACRED STATUE... AND THERE, NORM BLOOD SHALL FLOW...
HAIL, BROTHER MORGAR! LET THE WEEPING, GNASHING OF TEETH, AND ALL THAT JAZZ, BEGIN!
AYE! THE DAY OF ATONEMENT IS AT HAND!
WRONG! THE DAY OF JUDGEMENT IS AT HAND!
THE OTHER NORMS... H-HOW DID THEY GET HERE?
QUICKLY—BROTHERS OBEE AND JOBEE... SAVE YOUR LEADER! THE REST OF YOU... KILL THE NORMS!
JUDGE DREDD SPEAKS...
WAIT! RELEASE MY MEN AND THEIR MACHINE, MORGAR... OR MY KILLDOZER WILL DO SOME INSTANT SURGERY ON THAT STATUE OF YOURS...
LIKE BLOWING ITS NOSE... RIGHT OFF!
AND THEN ADDING ANOTHER EYE... IN THE MIDDLE OF DA FOREHEAD! AND YOU AIN'T GOT NO "LA-SAW" NOW TO MAKE YA FACE LOOK PRETTY AGAIN!
NO...TH-THEY MUST NOT DESTROY MY STATUE... DO AS THEY SAY, BROTHERS, RELEASE THE PRISONERS!

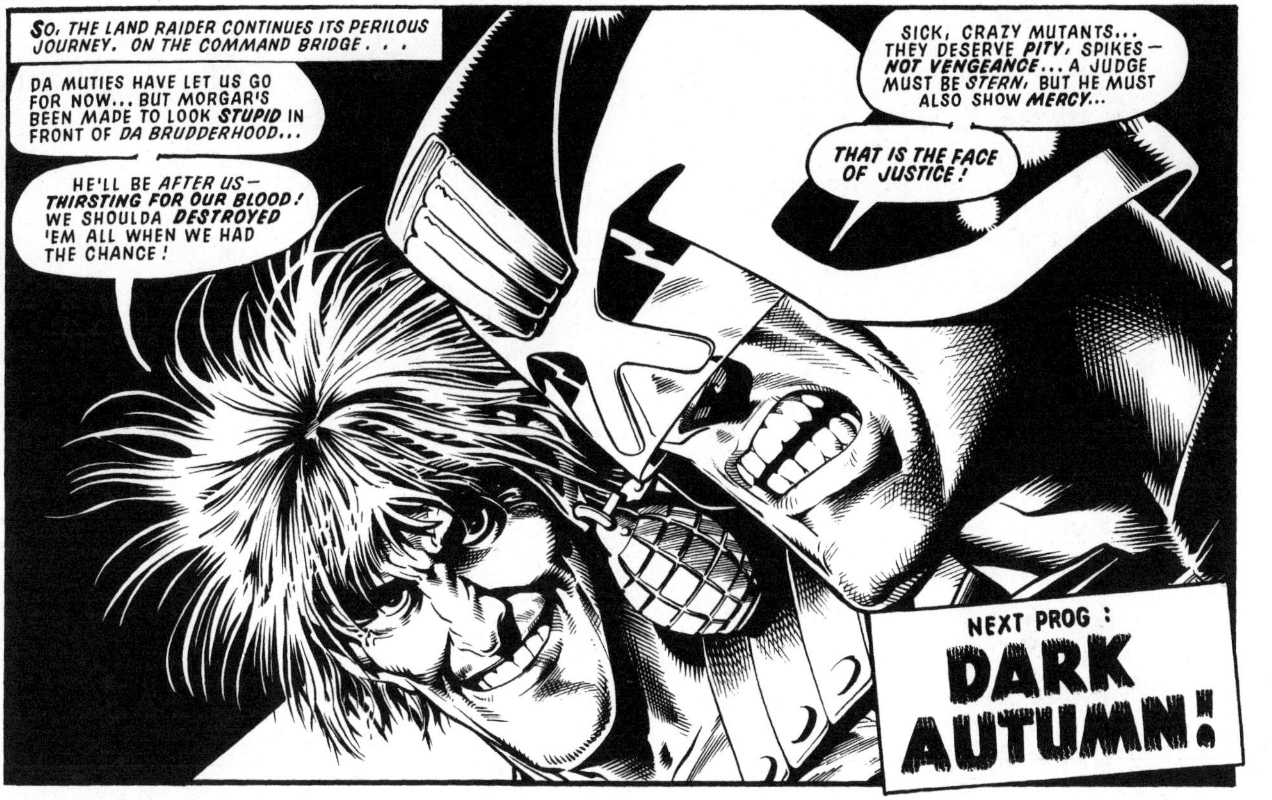
SO, THE LAND RAIDER CONTINUES ITS PERILOUS JOURNEY. ON THE COMMAND BRIDGE . . .
DA MUTIES HAVE LET US GO FOR NOW... BUT MORGAR'S BEEN MADE TO LOOK STUPID IN FRONT OF DA BRUDDERHOOD...
HE'LL BE AFTER US— THIRSTING FOR OUR BLOOD! WE SHOULDA DESTROYED 'EM ALL WHEN WE HAD THE CHANCE!
SICK, CRAZY MUTANTS... THEY DESERVE PITY, SPIKES— NOT VENGEANCE... A JUDGE MUST BE STERN, BUT HE MUST ALSO SHOW MERCY...
THAT IS THE FACE OF JUSTICE!
NEXT PROG :
DARK AUTUMN!

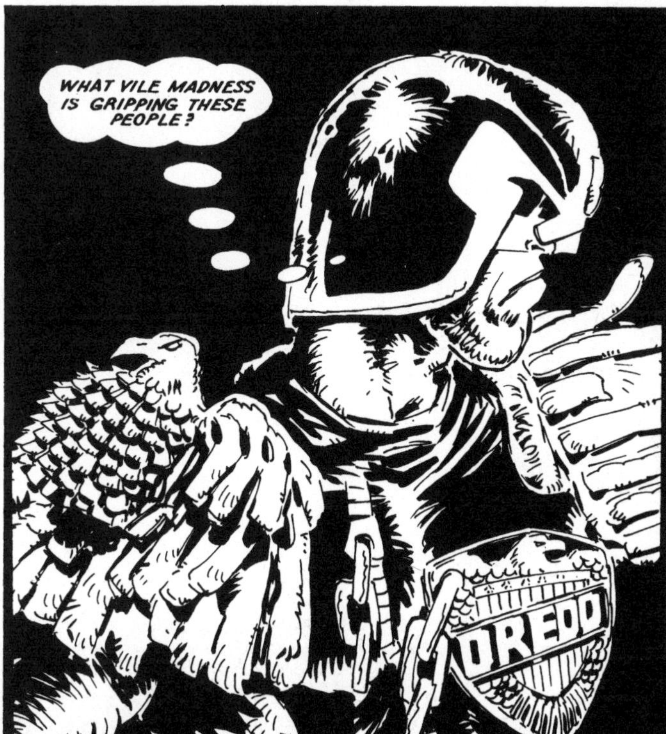
WHAT VILE MADNESS IS GRIPPING THESE PEOPLE?
DREDD

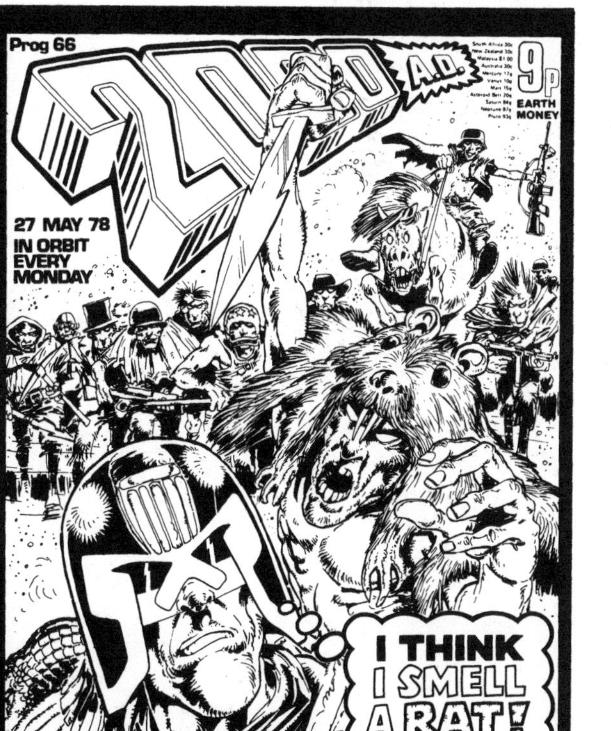
Prog 66
2000 A.D.
9p
EARTH MONEY
27 MAY 78
IN ORBIT EVERY MONDAY
I THINK I SMELL A RAT!

THE CURSED EARTH
CHAPTER 6.

DARK AUTUMN!

JUDGE DREDD

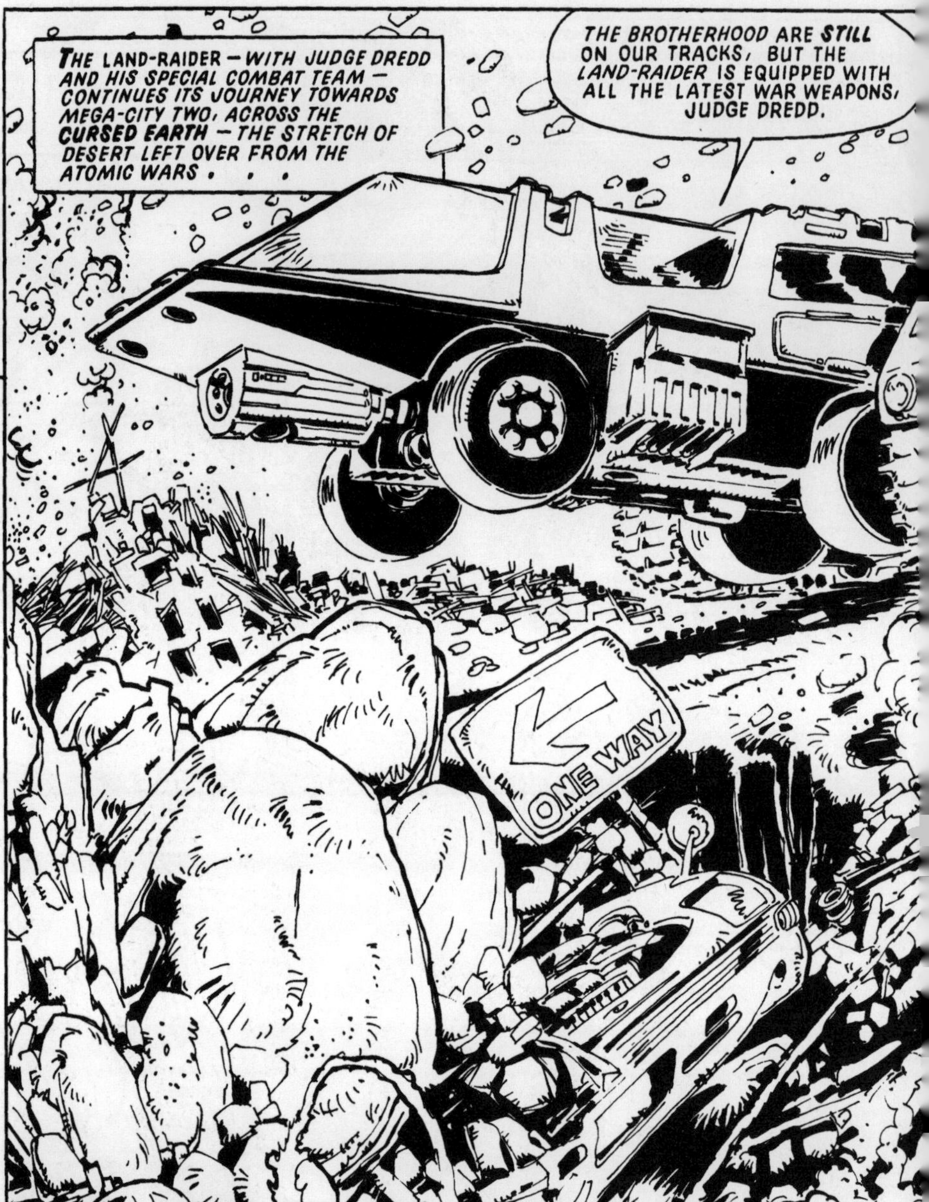

THE LAND-RAIDER — WITH JUDGE DREDD AND HIS SPECIAL COMBAT TEAM — CONTINUES ITS JOURNEY TOWARDS MEGA-CITY TWO, ACROSS THE CURSED EARTH — THE STRETCH OF DESERT LEFT OVER FROM THE ATOMIC WARS . . .
THE BROTHERHOOD ARE STILL ON OUR TRACKS, BUT THE LAND-RAIDER IS EQUIPPED WITH ALL THE LATEST WAR WEAPONS, JUDGE DREDD.
ONE WAY
2000 A.D.
Credit Card:
SCRIPT ROBOT
PAT MILLS
ART ROBOT
MIKE McMAHON
LETTERING ROBOT
TOM FRAME
COMPU·73E

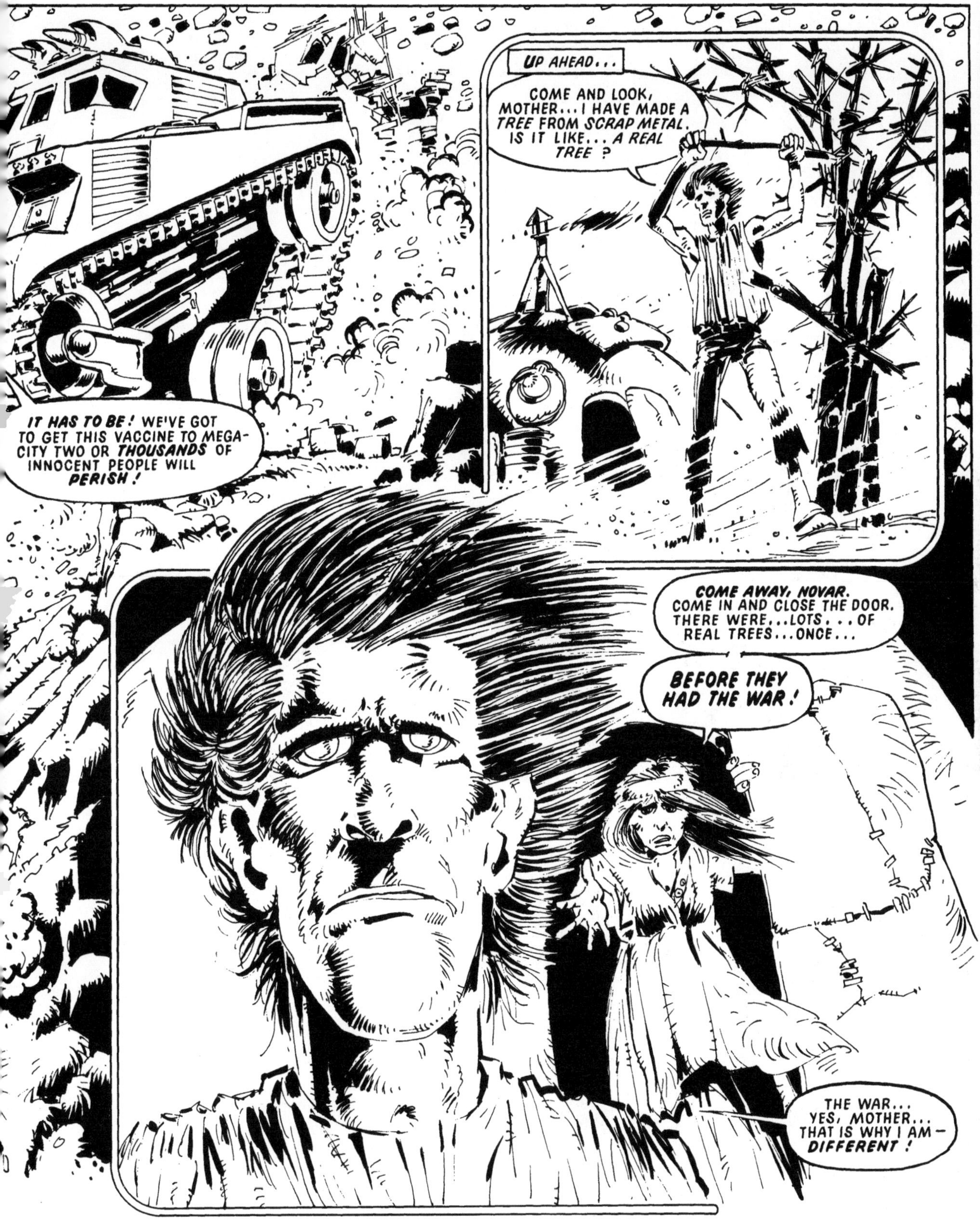

UP AHEAD...
COME AND LOOK, MOTHER... I HAVE MADE A TREE FROM SCRAP METAL. IS IT LIKE... A REAL TREE ?
IT HAS TO BE! WE'VE GOT TO GET THIS VACCINE TO MEGA-CITY TWO OR THOUSANDS OF INNOCENT PEOPLE WILL PERISH!
COME AWAY, NOVAR. COME IN AND CLOSE THE DOOR. THERE WERE...LOTS...OF REAL TREES...ONCE...
BEFORE THEY HAD THE WAR!
THE WAR... YES, MOTHER... THAT IS WHY I AM— DIFFERENT!

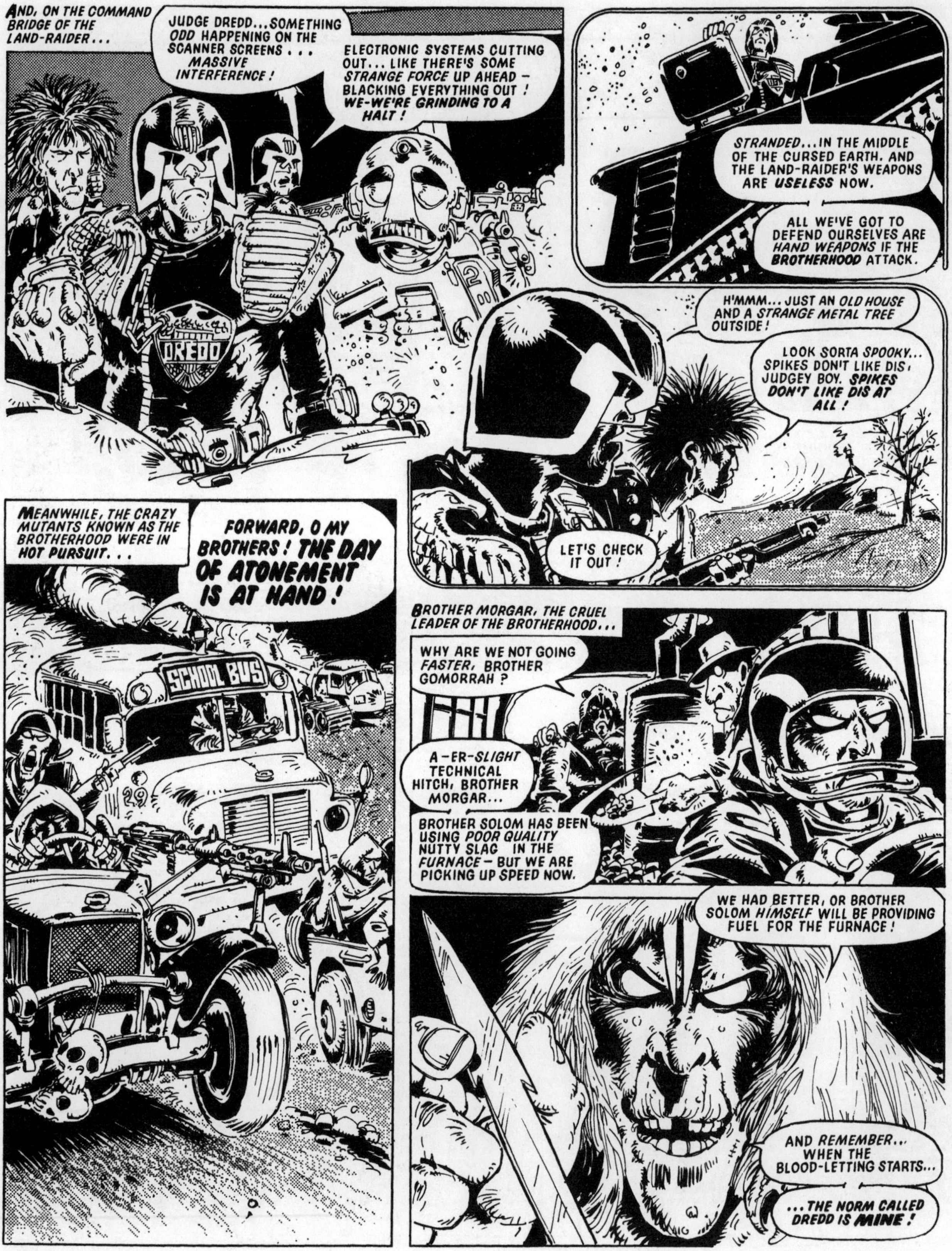

AND, ON THE COMMAND BRIDGE OF THE LAND-RAIDER...
JUDGE DREDD...SOMETHING ODD HAPPENING ON THE SCANNER SCREENS... MASSIVE INTERFERENCE!
ELECTRONIC SYSTEMS CUTTING OUT... LIKE THERE'S SOME STRANGE FORCE UP AHEAD — BLACKING EVERYTHING OUT! WE-WE'RE GRINDING TO A HALT!
DREDD
STRANDED...IN THE MIDDLE OF THE CURSED EARTH. AND THE LAND-RAIDER'S WEAPONS ARE USELESS NOW.
ALL WE'VE GOT TO DEFEND OURSELVES ARE HAND WEAPONS IF THE BROTHERHOOD ATTACK.
H'MMM... JUST AN OLD HOUSE AND A STRANGE METAL TREE OUTSIDE!
LOOK SORTA SPOOKY... SPIKES DON'T LIKE DIS, JUDGEY BOY. SPIKES DON'T LIKE DIS AT ALL!
LET'S CHECK IT OUT!
MEANWHILE, THE CRAZY MUTANTS KNOWN AS THE BROTHERHOOD WERE IN HOT PURSUIT...
FORWARD, O MY BROTHERS! THE DAY OF ATONEMENT IS AT HAND!
SCHOOL BUS
29
BROTHER MORGAR, THE CRUEL LEADER OF THE BROTHERHOOD...
WHY ARE WE NOT GOING FASTER, BROTHER GOMORRAH?
A-ER-SLIGHT TECHNICAL HITCH, BROTHER MORGAR...
BROTHER SOLOM HAS BEEN USING POOR QUALITY NUTTY SLAG IN THE FURNACE — BUT WE ARE PICKING UP SPEED NOW.
WE HAD BETTER, OR BROTHER SOLOM HIMSELF WILL BE PROVIDING FUEL FOR THE FURNACE!
AND REMEMBER... WHEN THE BLOOD-LETTING STARTS...
...THE NORM CALLED DREDD IS MINE!

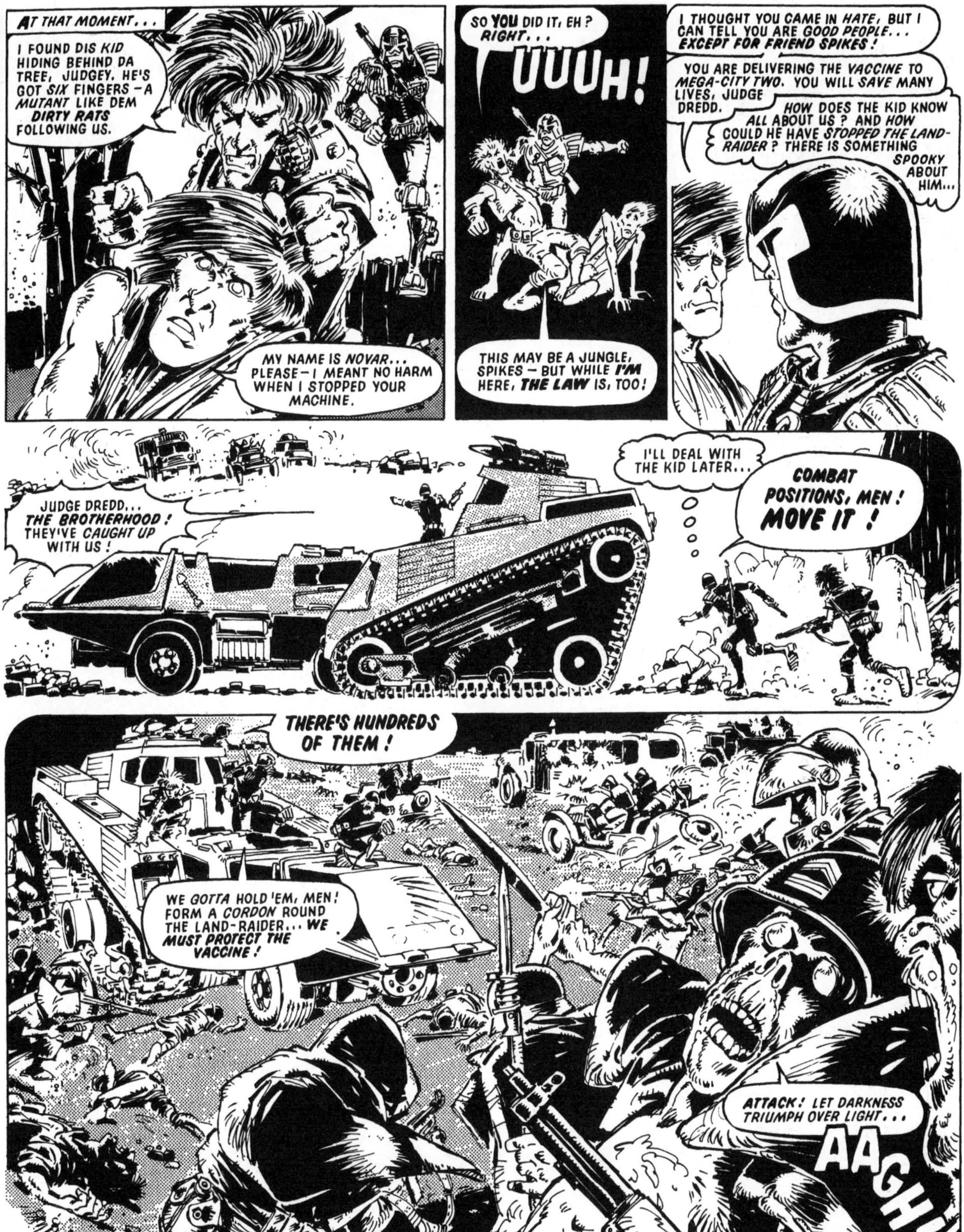
AT THAT MOMENT...
I FOUND DIS KID HIDING BEHIND DA TREE, JUDGEY. HE'S GOT SIX FINGERS — A MUTANT LIKE DEM DIRTY RATS FOLLOWING US.
MY NAME IS NOVAR... PLEASE — I MEANT NO HARM WHEN I STOPPED YOUR MACHINE.
SO YOU DID IT, EH? RIGHT...
UUUH!
THIS MAY BE A JUNGLE, SPIKES — BUT WHILE I'M HERE, THE LAW IS, TOO!
I THOUGHT YOU CAME IN HATE, BUT I CAN TELL YOU ARE GOOD PEOPLE... EXCEPT FOR FRIEND SPIKES!
YOU ARE DELIVERING THE VACCINE TO MEGA-CITY TWO. YOU WILL SAVE MANY LIVES, JUDGE DREDD.
HOW DOES THE KID KNOW ALL ABOUT US? AND HOW COULD HE HAVE STOPPED THE LAND-RAIDER? THERE IS SOMETHING SPOOKY ABOUT HIM...
JUDGE DREDD... THE BROTHERHOOD! THEY'VE CAUGHT UP WITH US!
I'LL DEAL WITH THE KID LATER...
COMBAT POSITIONS, MEN! MOVE IT!
THERE'S HUNDREDS OF THEM!
WE GOTTA HOLD 'EM, MEN! FORM A CORDON ROUND THE LAND-RAIDER... WE MUST PROTECT THE VACCINE!
ATTACK! LET DARKNESS TRIUMPH OVER LIGHT...
AAGH!

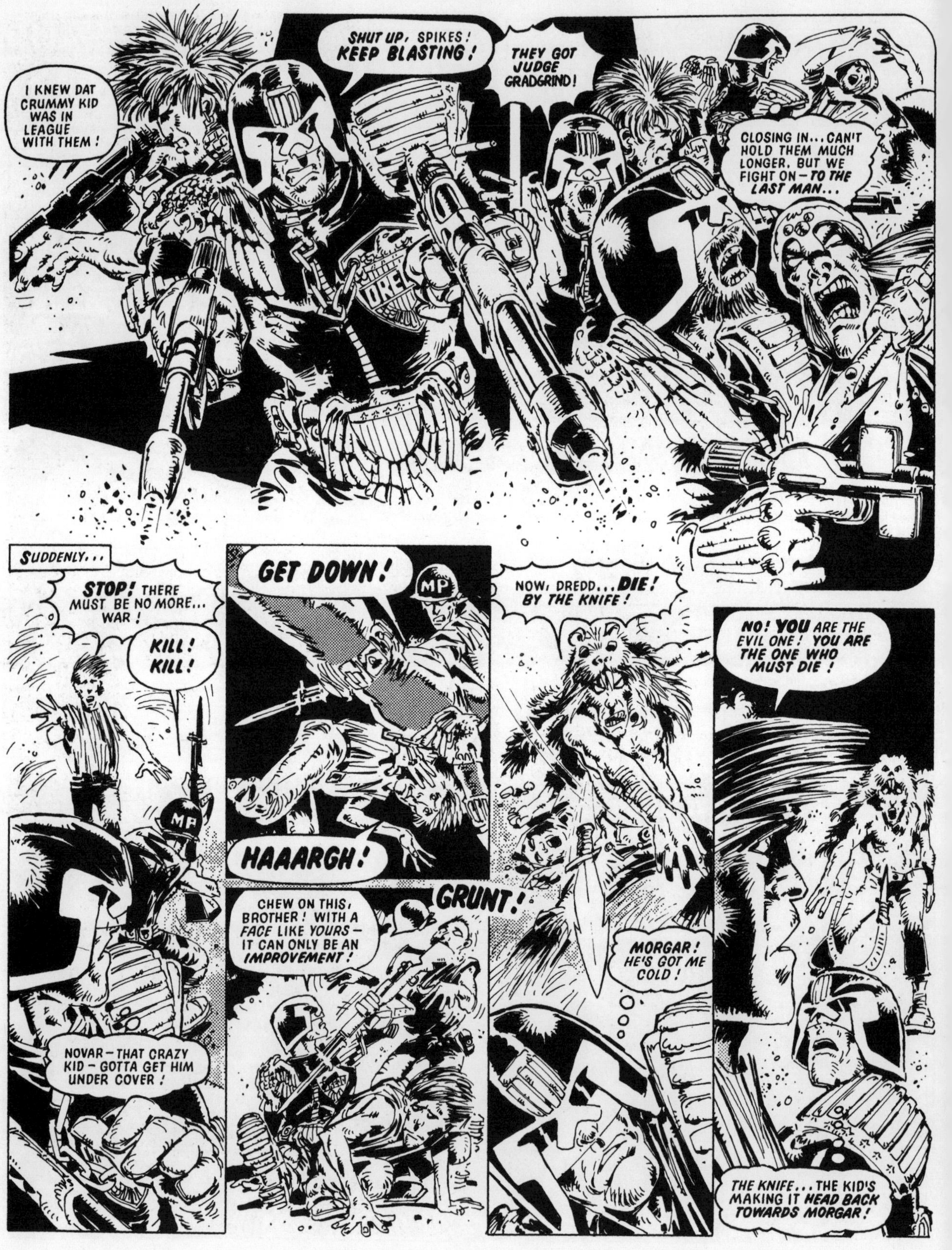
I KNEW DAT CRUMMY KID WAS IN LEAGUE WITH THEM!
SHUT UP, SPIKES! KEEP BLASTING!
THEY GOT JUDGE GRADGRIND!
CLOSING IN... CAN'T HOLD THEM MUCH LONGER, BUT WE FIGHT ON — TO THE LAST MAN...
SUDDENLY...
STOP! THERE MUST BE NO MORE... WAR!
KILL! KILL!
NOVAR — THAT CRAZY KID — GOTTA GET HIM UNDER COVER!
GET DOWN!
HAAARGH!
CHEW ON THIS, BROTHER! WITH A FACE LIKE YOURS — IT CAN ONLY BE AN IMPROVEMENT!
GRUNT!
NOW, DREDD... DIE! BY THE KNIFE!
MORGAR! HE'S GOT ME COLD!
NO! YOU ARE THE EVIL ONE! YOU ARE THE ONE WHO MUST DIE!
THE KNIFE... THE KID'S MAKING IT HEAD BACK TOWARDS MORGAR!

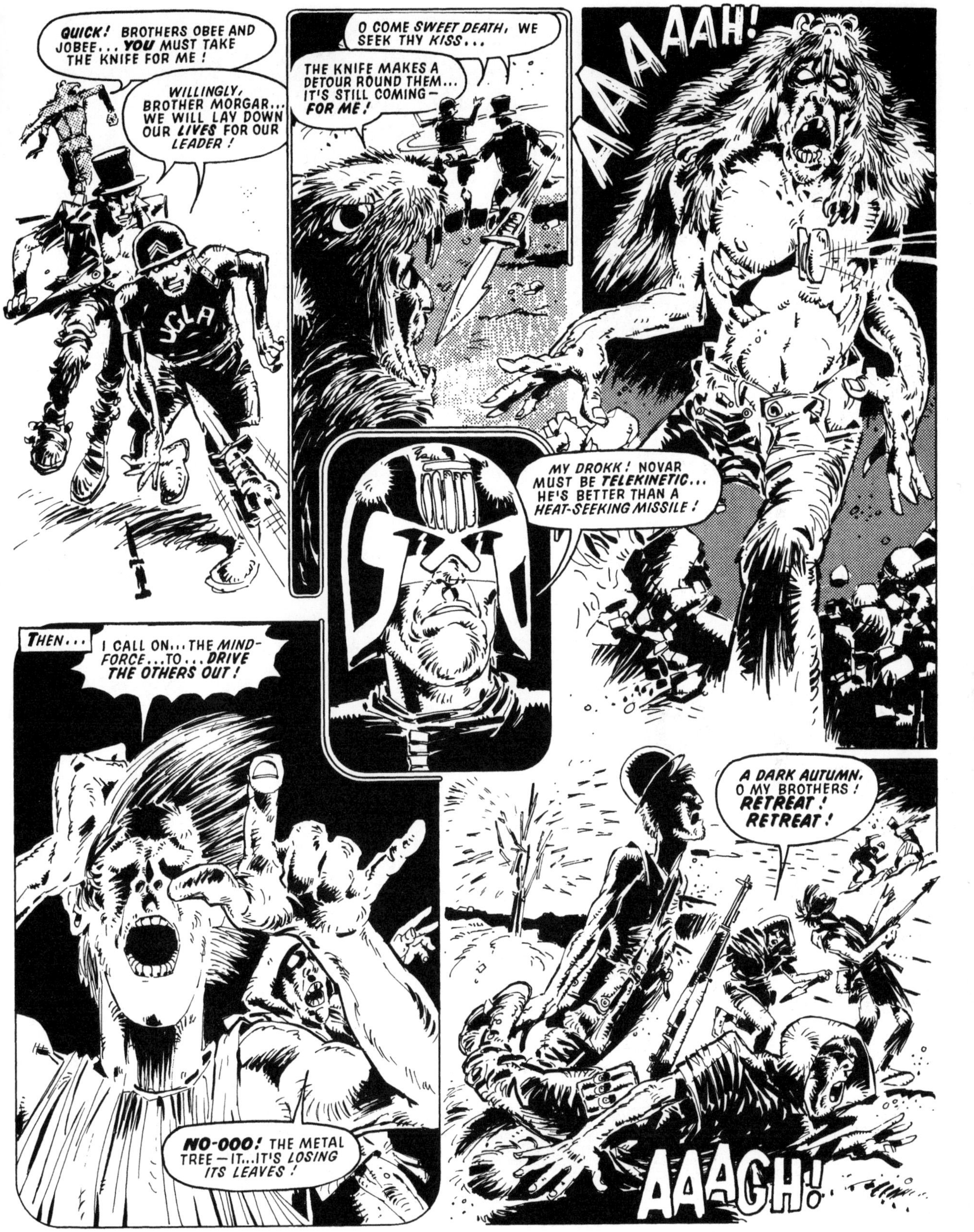
QUICK! BROTHERS OBEE AND JOBEE... YOU MUST TAKE THE KNIFE FOR ME!
WILLINGLY, BROTHER MORGAR... WE WILL LAY DOWN OUR LIVES FOR OUR LEADER!
O COME SWEET DEATH, WE SEEK THY KISS...
THE KNIFE MAKES A DETOUR ROUND THEM... IT'S STILL COMING— FOR ME!
AAAAAAH!
MY DROKK! NOVAR MUST BE TELEKINETIC... HE'S BETTER THAN A HEAT-SEEKING MISSILE!
THEN...
I CALL ON... THE MIND-FORCE... TO... DRIVE THE OTHERS OUT!
NO-OOO! THE METAL TREE—IT...IT'S LOSING ITS LEAVES!
A DARK AUTUMN, O MY BROTHERS! RETREAT! RETREAT!
AAAGH!

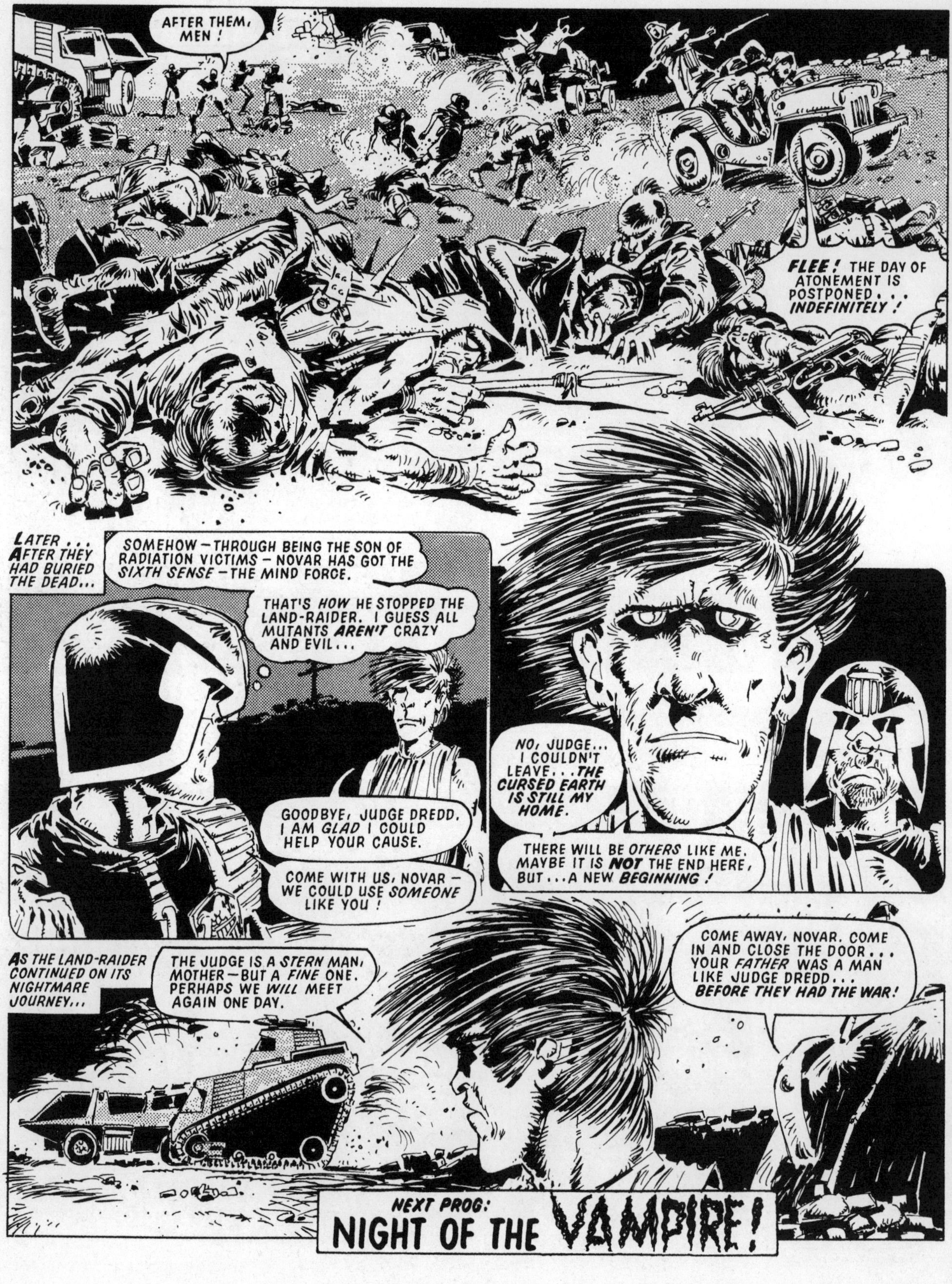
AFTER THEM, MEN !
FLEE ! THE DAY OF ATONEMENT IS POSTPONED . . . INDEFINITELY !
LATER . . . AFTER THEY HAD BURIED THE DEAD . . .
SOMEHOW – THROUGH BEING THE SON OF RADIATION VICTIMS – NOVAR HAS GOT THE SIXTH SENSE – THE MIND FORCE.
THAT'S HOW HE STOPPED THE LAND-RAIDER. I GUESS ALL MUTANTS AREN'T CRAZY AND EVIL . . .
GOODBYE, JUDGE DREDD. I AM GLAD I COULD HELP YOUR CAUSE.
COME WITH US, NOVAR – WE COULD USE SOMEONE LIKE YOU !
NO, JUDGE . . . I COULDN'T LEAVE . . . THE CURSED EARTH IS STILL MY HOME.
THERE WILL BE OTHERS LIKE ME. MAYBE IT IS NOT THE END HERE, BUT . . . A NEW BEGINNING !
AS THE LAND-RAIDER CONTINUED ON ITS NIGHTMARE JOURNEY . . .
THE JUDGE IS A STERN MAN, MOTHER – BUT A FINE ONE. PERHAPS WE WILL MEET AGAIN ONE DAY.
COME AWAY, NOVAR. COME IN AND CLOSE THE DOOR . . . YOUR FATHER WAS A MAN LIKE JUDGE DREDD . . . BEFORE THEY HAD THE WAR !
NEXT PROG:
NIGHT OF THE VAMPIRE !

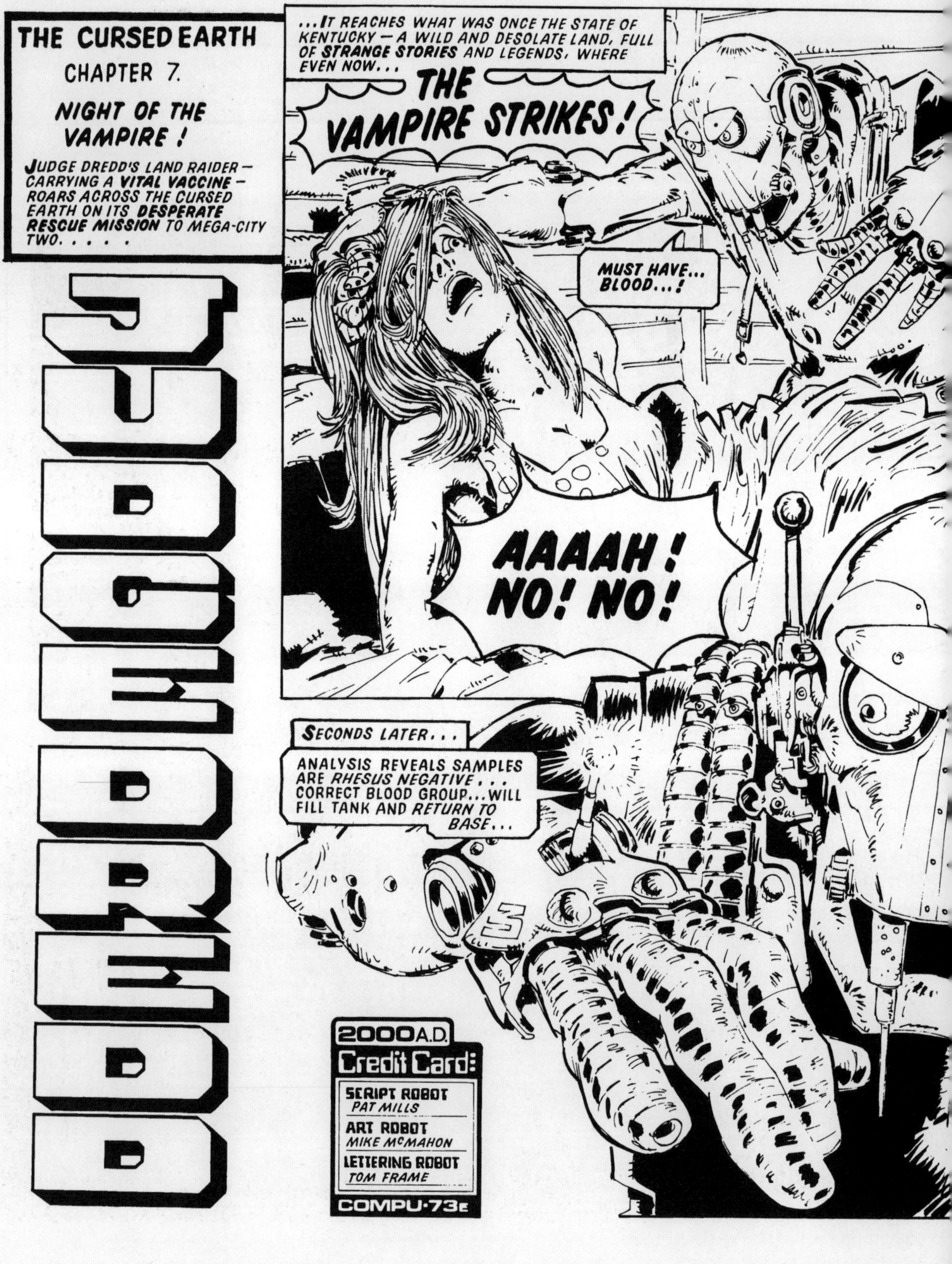
THE CURSED EARTH
CHAPTER 7.
NIGHT OF THE VAMPIRE!
JUDGE DREDD'S LAND RAIDER — CARRYING A VITAL VACCINE — ROARS ACROSS THE CURSED EARTH ON ITS DESPERATE RESCUE MISSION TO MEGA-CITY TWO. . . .
JUDGE DREDD
...IT REACHES WHAT WAS ONCE THE STATE OF KENTUCKY — A WILD AND DESOLATE LAND, FULL OF STRANGE STORIES AND LEGENDS, WHERE EVEN NOW...
THE VAMPIRE STRIKES!
MUST HAVE... BLOOD...!
AAAAH! NO! NO!
SECONDS LATER...
ANALYSIS REVEALS SAMPLES ARE RHESUS NEGATIVE... CORRECT BLOOD GROUP... WILL FILL TANK AND RETURN TO BASE...
2000 A.D. Credit Card:
SCRIPT ROBOT PAT MILLS
ART ROBOT MIKE McMAHON
LETTERING ROBOT TOM FRAME
COMPU-73E

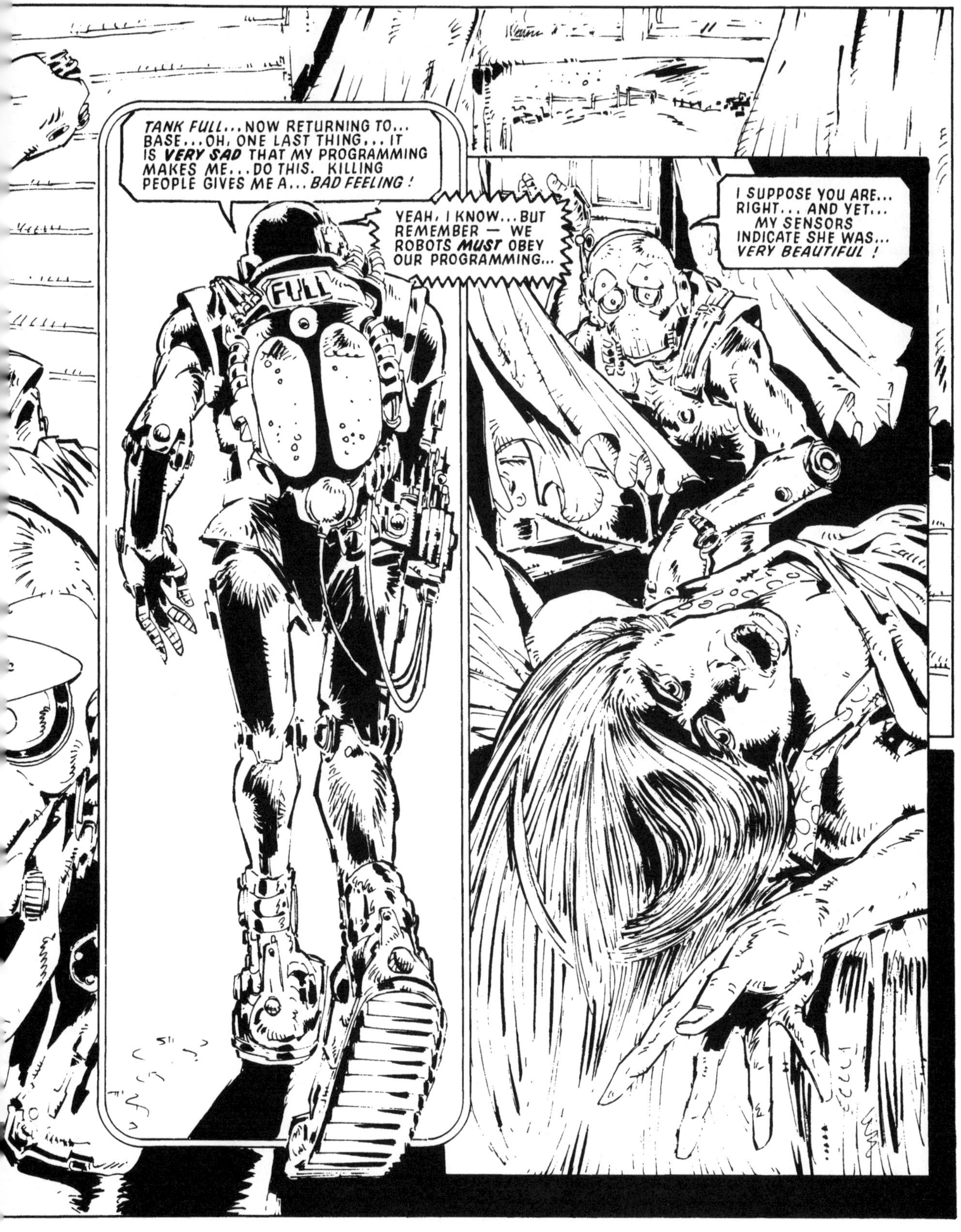
TANK FULL... NOW RETURNING TO... BASE... OH, ONE LAST THING... IT IS VERY SAD THAT MY PROGRAMMING MAKES ME... DO THIS. KILLING PEOPLE GIVES ME A... BAD FEELING !
YEAH, I KNOW... BUT REMEMBER — WE ROBOTS MUST OBEY OUR PROGRAMMING...
I SUPPOSE YOU ARE... RIGHT... AND YET... MY SENSORS INDICATE SHE WAS... VERY BEAUTIFUL !
FULL

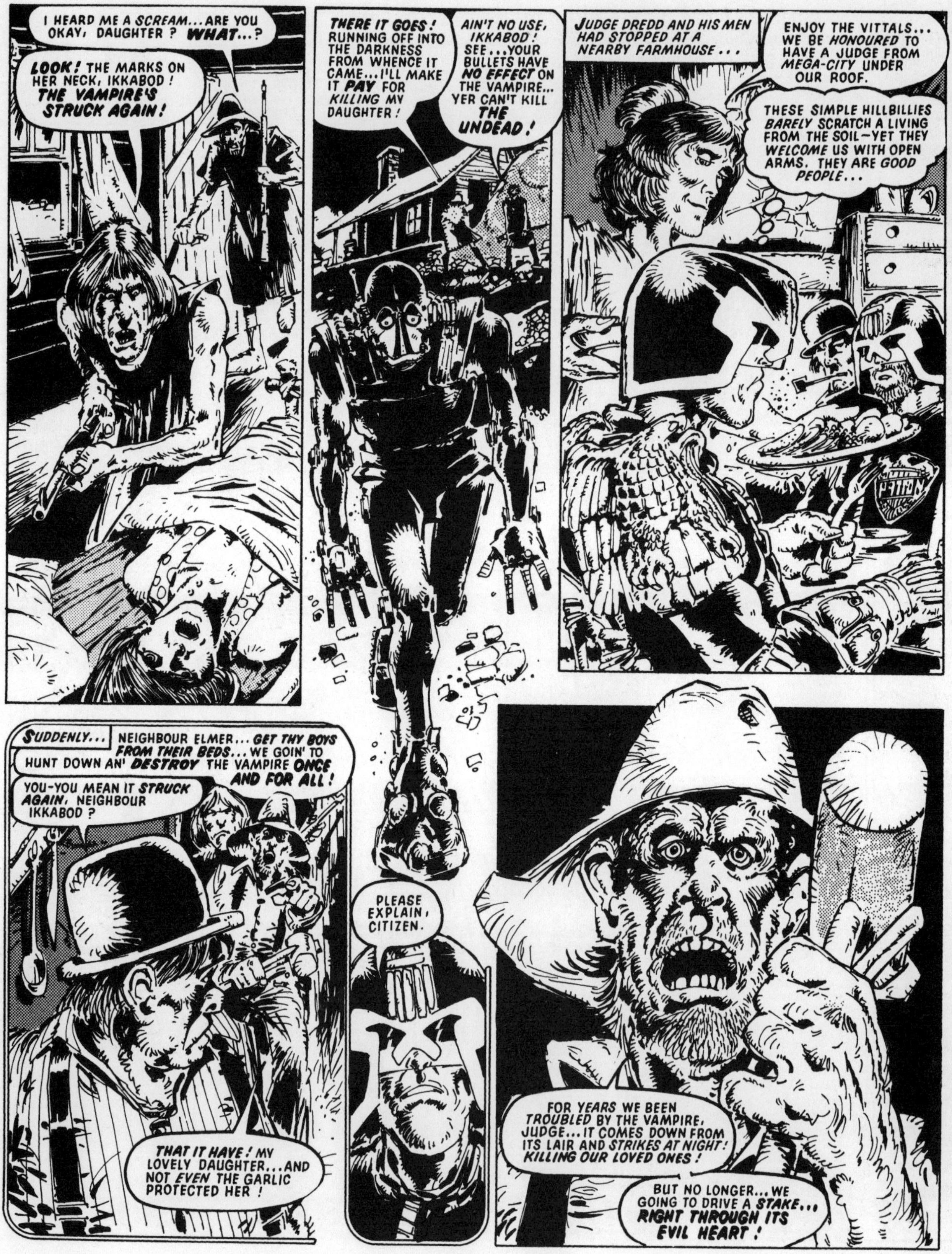
I HEARD ME A SCREAM... ARE YOU OKAY, DAUGHTER ? WHAT...?
LOOK! THE MARKS ON HER NECK, IKKABOD! THE VAMPIRE'S STRUCK AGAIN!
THERE IT GOES! RUNNING OFF INTO THE DARKNESS FROM WHENCE IT CAME... I'LL MAKE IT PAY FOR KILLING MY DAUGHTER!
AIN'T NO USE, IKKABOD! SEE... YOUR BULLETS HAVE NO EFFECT ON THE VAMPIRE... YER CAN'T KILL THE UNDEAD!
JUDGE DREDD AND HIS MEN HAD STOPPED AT A NEARBY FARMHOUSE...
ENJOY THE VITTALS... WE BE HONOURED TO HAVE A JUDGE FROM MEGA-CITY UNDER OUR ROOF.
THESE SIMPLE HILLBILLIES BARELY SCRATCH A LIVING FROM THE SOIL—YET THEY WELCOME US WITH OPEN ARMS. THEY ARE GOOD PEOPLE...
SUDDENLY...
NEIGHBOUR ELMER... GET THY BOYS FROM THEIR BEDS... WE GOIN' TO HUNT DOWN AN' DESTROY THE VAMPIRE ONCE AND FOR ALL!
YOU-YOU MEAN IT STRUCK AGAIN, NEIGHBOUR IKKABOD ?
THAT IT HAVE! MY LOVELY DAUGHTER... AND NOT EVEN THE GARLIC PROTECTED HER!
PLEASE EXPLAIN, CITIZEN.
FOR YEARS WE BEEN TROUBLED BY THE VAMPIRE, JUDGE... IT COMES DOWN FROM ITS LAIR AND STRIKES AT NIGHT! KILLING OUR LOVED ONES!
BUT NO LONGER... WE GOING TO DRIVE A STAKE... RIGHT THROUGH ITS EVIL HEART!

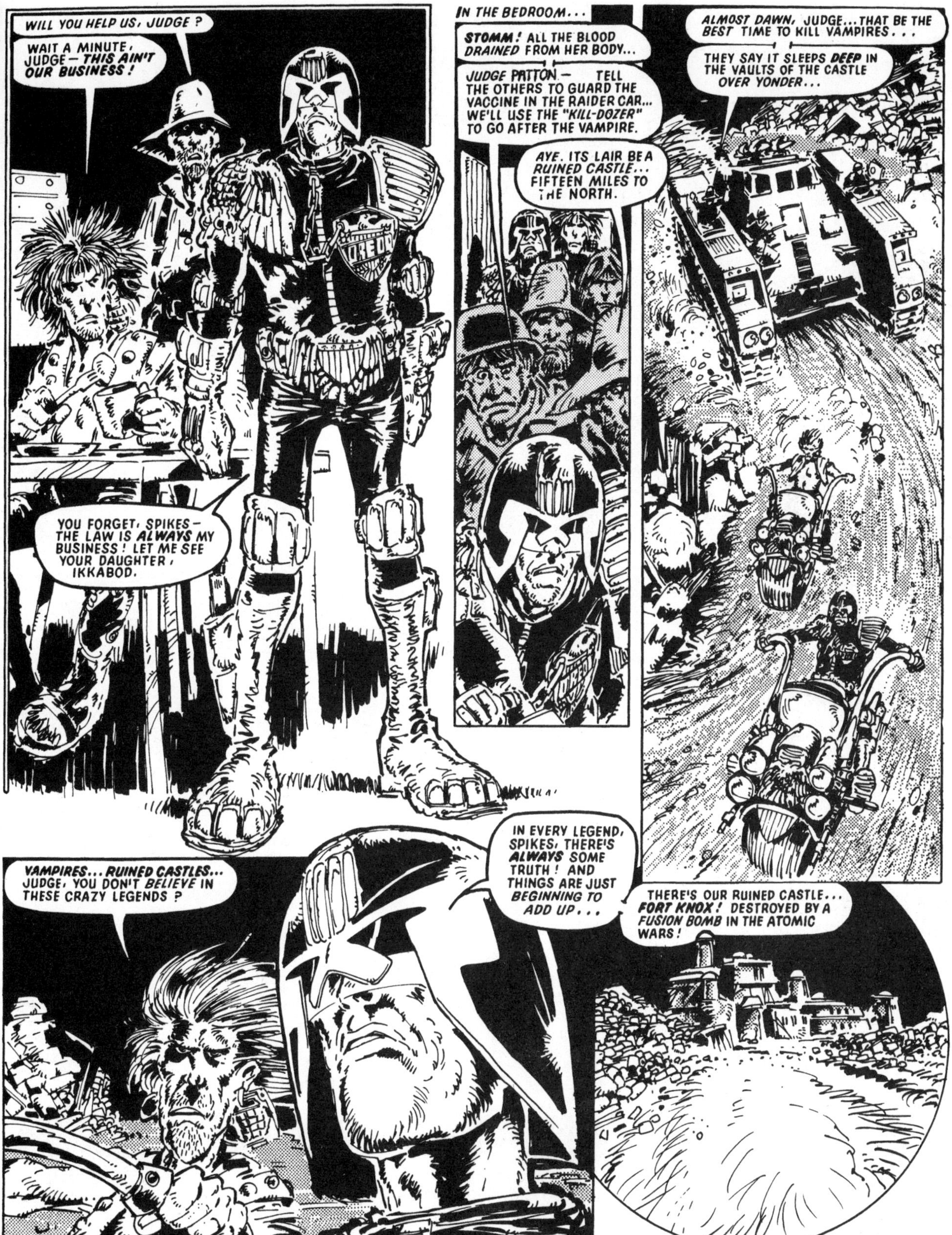
WILL YOU HELP US, JUDGE ?
WAIT A MINUTE, JUDGE — THIS AIN'T OUR BUSINESS !
YOU FORGET, SPIKES — THE LAW IS ALWAYS MY BUSINESS ! LET ME SEE YOUR DAUGHTER, IKKABOD.
IN THE BEDROOM...
STOMM ! ALL THE BLOOD DRAINED FROM HER BODY...
JUDGE PATTON — TELL THE OTHERS TO GUARD THE VACCINE IN THE RAIDER CAR... WE'LL USE THE "KILL-DOZER" TO GO AFTER THE VAMPIRE.
AYE. ITS LAIR BE A RUINED CASTLE... FIFTEEN MILES TO THE NORTH.
ALMOST DAWN, JUDGE... THAT BE THE BEST TIME TO KILL VAMPIRES...
THEY SAY IT SLEEPS DEEP IN THE VAULTS OF THE CASTLE OVER YONDER...
VAMPIRES... RUINED CASTLES... JUDGE, YOU DON'T BELIEVE IN THESE CRAZY LEGENDS ?
IN EVERY LEGEND, SPIKES, THERE'S ALWAYS SOME TRUTH ! AND THINGS ARE JUST BEGINNING TO ADD UP...
THERE'S OUR RUINED CASTLE... FORT KNOX ! DESTROYED BY A FUSION BOMB IN THE ATOMIC WARS !

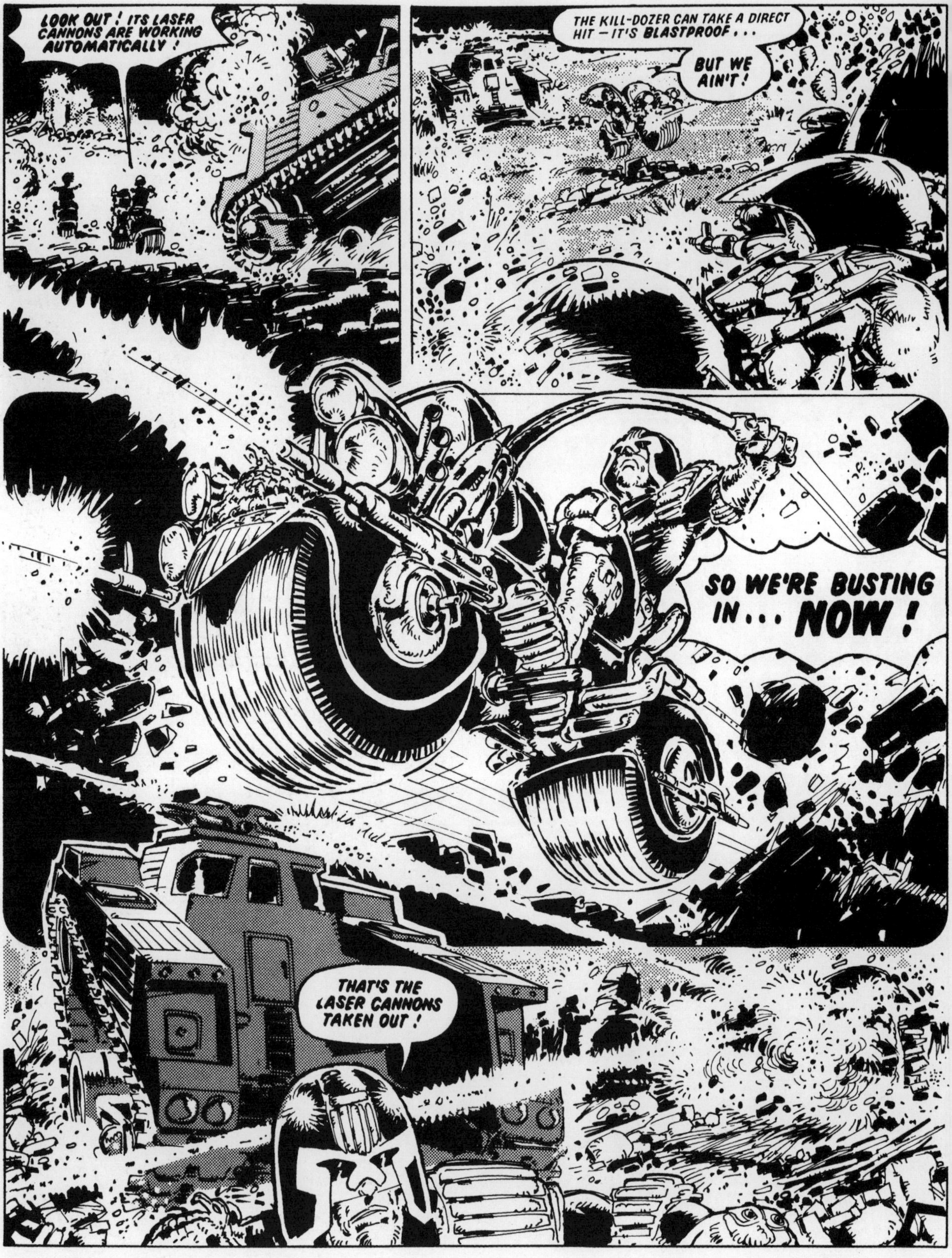
LOOK OUT ! ITS LASER CANNONS ARE WORKING AUTOMATICALLY !
THE KILL-DOZER CAN TAKE A DIRECT HIT — IT'S BLASTPROOF . . .
BUT WE AIN'T !
SO WE'RE BUSTING IN . . . NOW !
THAT'S THE LASER CANNONS TAKEN OUT !

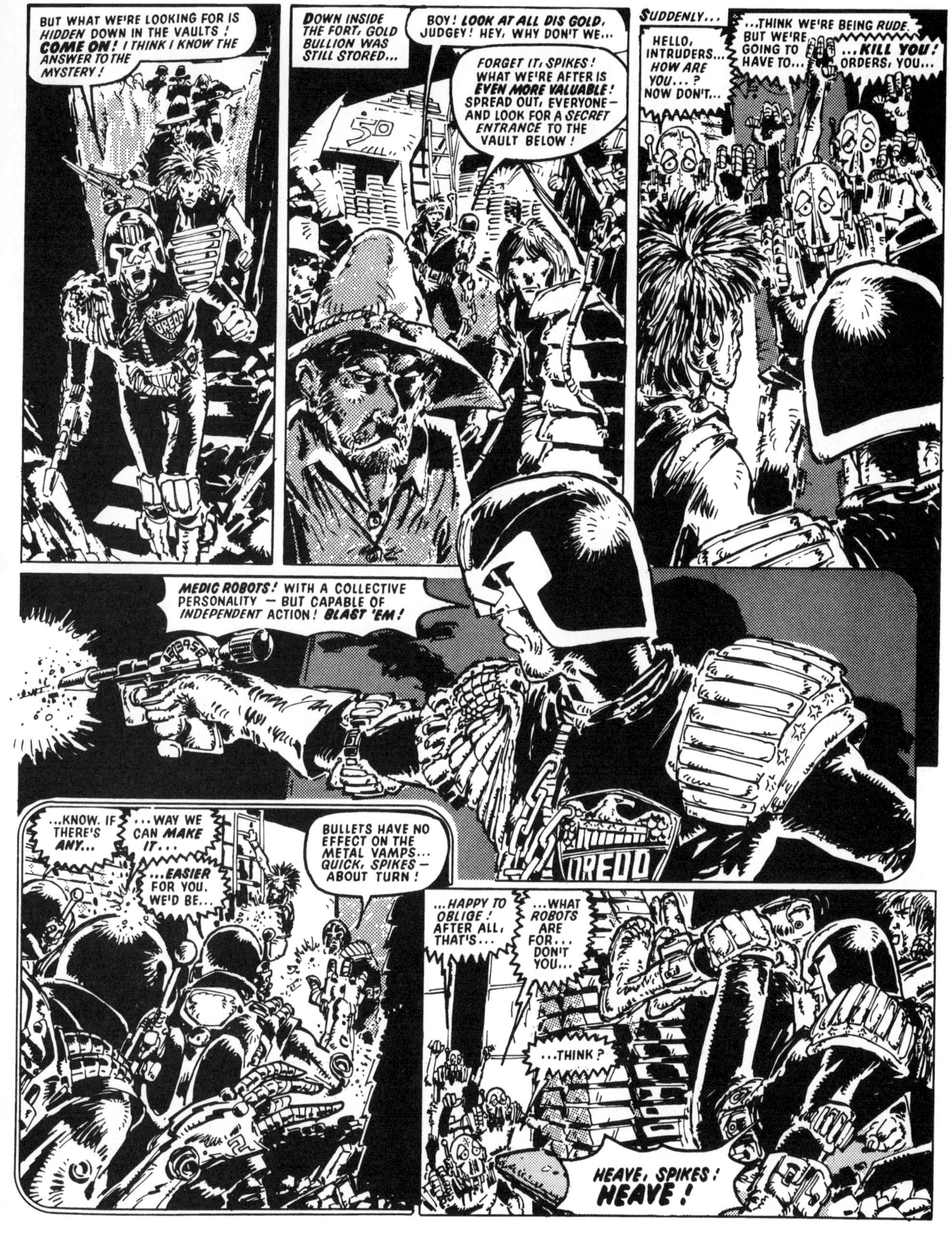

BUT WHAT WE'RE LOOKING FOR IS HIDDEN DOWN IN THE VAULTS! COME ON! I THINK I KNOW THE ANSWER TO THE MYSTERY!
DOWN INSIDE THE FORT, GOLD BULLION WAS STILL STORED...
BOY! LOOK AT ALL DIS GOLD, JUDGEY! HEY, WHY DON'T WE...
FORGET IT, SPIKES! WHAT WE'RE AFTER IS EVEN MORE VALUABLE! SPREAD OUT, EVERYONE— AND LOOK FOR A SECRET ENTRANCE TO THE VAULT BELOW!
SUDDENLY...
HELLO, INTRUDERS... HOW ARE YOU...? NOW DON'T...
...THINK WE'RE BEING RUDE. BUT WE'RE GOING TO HAVE TO...
...KILL YOU! ORDERS, YOU...
MEDIC ROBOTS! WITH A COLLECTIVE PERSONALITY — BUT CAPABLE OF INDEPENDENT ACTION! BLAST 'EM!
...KNOW. IF THERE'S ANY...
...WAY WE CAN MAKE IT...
...EASIER FOR YOU. WE'D BE...
BULLETS HAVE NO EFFECT ON THE METAL VAMPS... QUICK, SPIKES— ABOUT TURN!
...HAPPY TO OBLIGE! AFTER ALL, THAT'S...
...WHAT ROBOTS ARE FOR... DON'T YOU...
...THINK?
HEAVE, SPIKES! HEAVE!

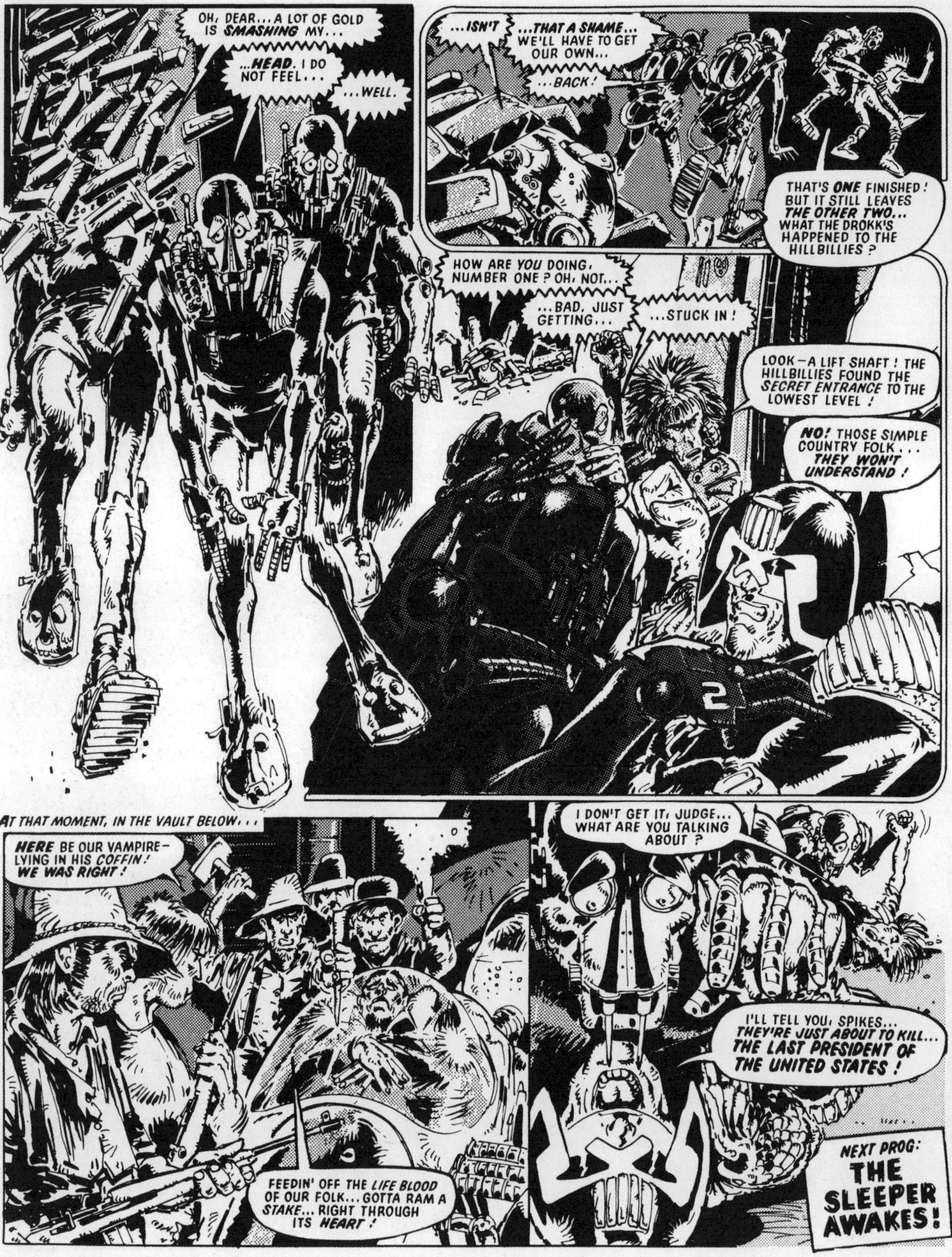
OH, DEAR... A LOT OF GOLD IS SMASHING MY...
...HEAD. I DO NOT FEEL...
...WELL.
...ISN'T
...THAT A SHAME... WE'LL HAVE TO GET OUR OWN...
...BACK!
THAT'S ONE FINISHED! BUT IT STILL LEAVES THE OTHER TWO... WHAT THE DROKK'S HAPPENED TO THE HILLBILLIES?
HOW ARE YOU DOING, NUMBER ONE? OH, NOT...
...BAD, JUST GETTING...
...STUCK IN!
LOOK—A LIFT SHAFT! THE HILLBILLIES FOUND THE SECRET ENTRANCE TO THE LOWEST LEVEL!
NO! THOSE SIMPLE COUNTRY FOLK... THEY WON'T UNDERSTAND!
AT THAT MOMENT, IN THE VAULT BELOW...
HERE BE OUR VAMPIRE— LYING IN HIS COFFIN! WE WAS RIGHT!
FEEDIN' OFF THE LIFE BLOOD OF OUR FOLK... GOTTA RAM A STAKE... RIGHT THROUGH ITS HEART!
I DON'T GET IT, JUDGE... WHAT ARE YOU TALKING ABOUT?
I'LL TELL YOU, SPIKES... THEY'RE JUST ABOUT TO KILL... THE LAST PRESIDENT OF THE UNITED STATES!
NEXT PROG: THE SLEEPER AWAKES!

THE CURSED EARTH

CHAPTER 8.

THE SLEEPER AWAKES!

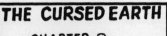

ON THE WILD HILLBILLY TERRITORY OF **KENTUCKY**, A STRANGE VAMPIRE HAS BEEN ATTACKING AND **DRAINING** ITS VICTIMS OF THEIR **LIFE BLOOD**.

THE HILLBILLIES APPEAL TO JUDGE DREDD FOR HELP, AND A SEARCH LEADS TO THE VAULTS OF RUINED FORT KNOX, WHERE...

IN THE VAULT...

THIS BE THE **VAMPIRE**...

...GOTTA RAM THE STAKE RIGHT THROUGH ITS **BLACK HEART**!

DROKK IT! THE HILLBILLIES ARE GOING TO KILL...

THE LAST PRESIDENT OF THE UNITED STATES!

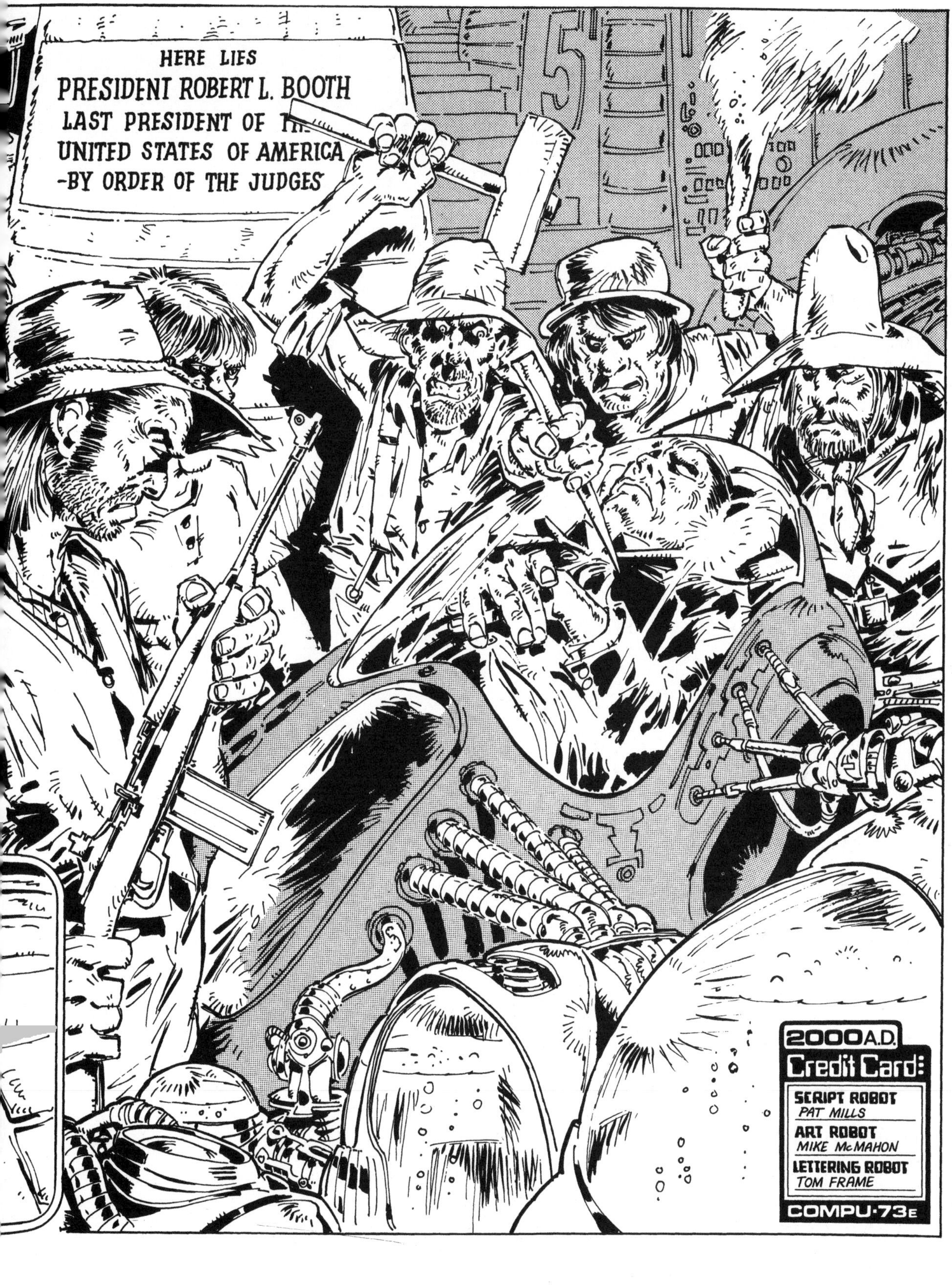

HERE LIES
PRESIDENT ROBERT L. BOOTH
LAST PRESIDENT OF TH
UNITED STATES OF AMERICA
-BY ORDER OF THE JUDGES
2000 A.D.
Credit Card:
SCRIPT ROBOT
PAT MILLS
ART ROBOT
MIKE McMAHON
LETTERING ROBOT
TOM FRAME
COMPU-73E

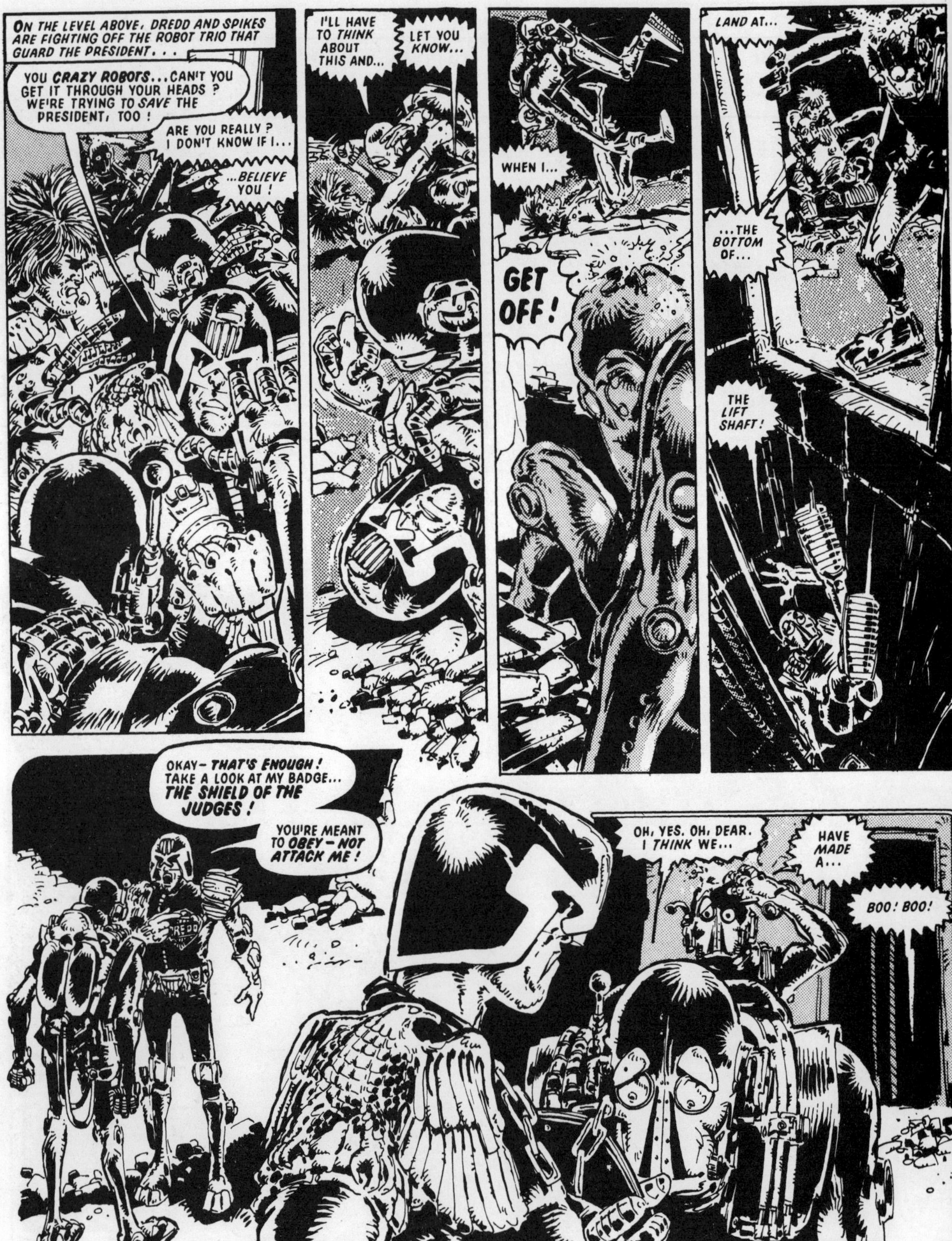

ON THE LEVEL ABOVE, DREDD AND SPIKES ARE FIGHTING OFF THE ROBOT TRIO THAT GUARD THE PRESIDENT . . .
YOU CRAZY ROBOTS . . . CAN'T YOU GET IT THROUGH YOUR HEADS ? WE'RE TRYING TO SAVE THE PRESIDENT, TOO !
ARE YOU REALLY ? I DON'T KNOW IF I...
...BELIEVE YOU !
I'LL HAVE TO THINK ABOUT THIS AND...
LET YOU KNOW...
WHEN I...
GET OFF !
LAND AT...
...THE BOTTOM OF...
THE LIFT SHAFT !
OKAY– THAT'S ENOUGH ! TAKE A LOOK AT MY BADGE... THE SHIELD OF THE JUDGES !
YOU'RE MEANT TO OBEY – NOT ATTACK ME !
OH, YES. OH, DEAR. I THINK WE...
HAVE MADE A...
BOO ! BOO !

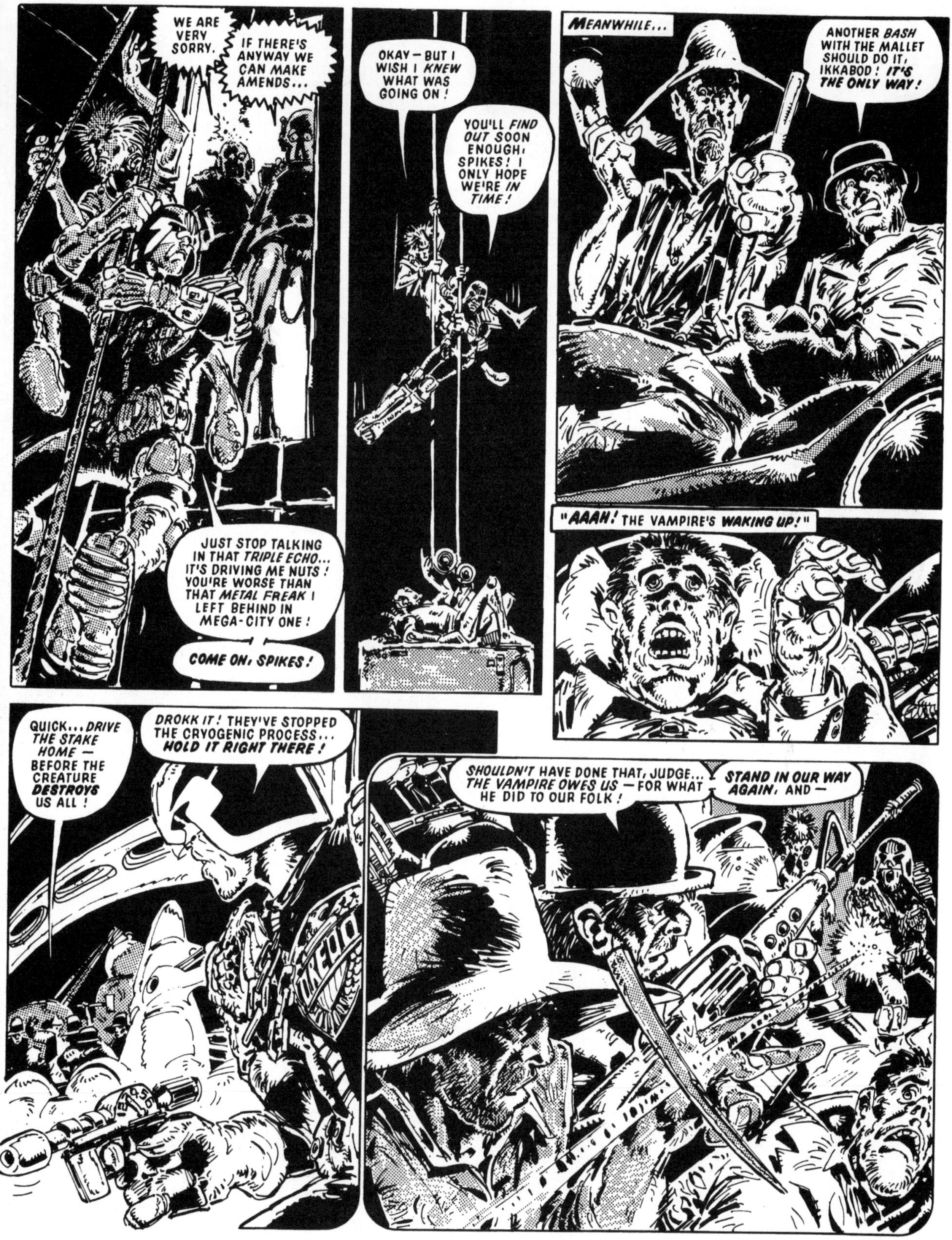
WE ARE VERY SORRY.
IF THERE'S ANYWAY WE CAN MAKE AMENDS...
JUST STOP TALKING IN THAT TRIPLE ECHO... IT'S DRIVING ME NUTS! YOU'RE WORSE THAN THAT METAL FREAK I LEFT BEHIND IN MEGA-CITY ONE!
COME ON, SPIKES!
OKAY — BUT I WISH I KNEW WHAT WAS GOING ON!
YOU'LL FIND OUT SOON ENOUGH, SPIKES! I ONLY HOPE WE'RE IN TIME!
MEANWHILE...
ANOTHER BASH WITH THE MALLET SHOULD DO IT, IKKABOD! IT'S THE ONLY WAY!
"AAAH! THE VAMPIRE'S WAKING UP!"
QUICK... DRIVE THE STAKE HOME — BEFORE THE CREATURE DESTROYS US ALL!
DROKK IT! THEY'VE STOPPED THE CRYOGENIC PROCESS... HOLD IT RIGHT THERE!
SHOULDN'T HAVE DONE THAT, JUDGE... THE VAMPIRE OWES US — FOR WHAT HE DID TO OUR FOLK!
STAND IN OUR WAY AGAIN, AND —

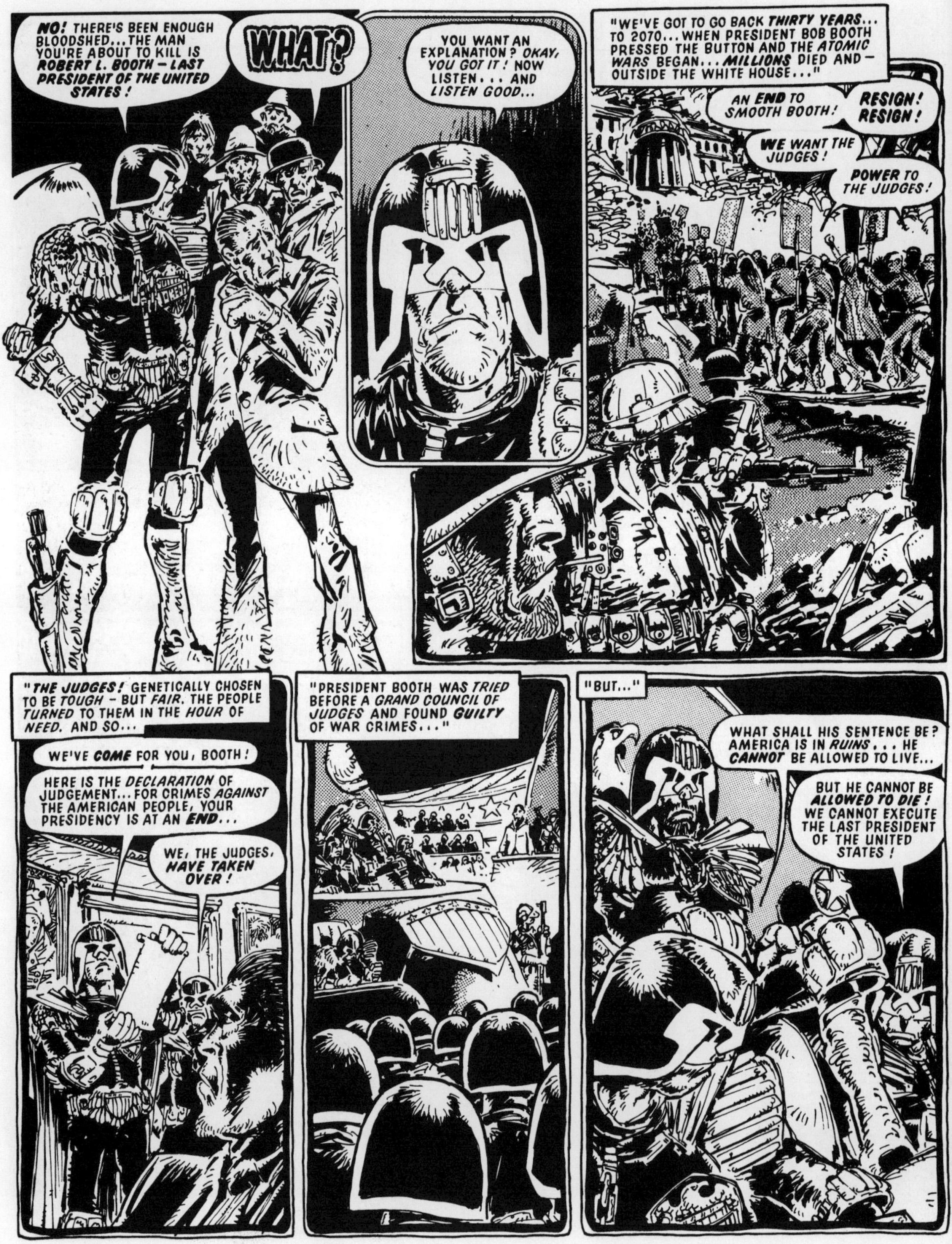
NO! THERE'S BEEN ENOUGH BLOODSHED...THE MAN YOU'RE ABOUT TO KILL IS ROBERT L. BOOTH – LAST PRESIDENT OF THE UNITED STATES!
WHAT?
YOU WANT AN EXPLANATION? OKAY, YOU GOT IT! NOW LISTEN... AND LISTEN GOOD...
"WE'VE GOT TO GO BACK THIRTY YEARS... TO 2070...WHEN PRESIDENT BOB BOOTH PRESSED THE BUTTON AND THE ATOMIC WARS BEGAN...MILLIONS DIED AND – OUTSIDE THE WHITE HOUSE..."
AN END TO SMOOTH BOOTH!
RESIGN! RESIGN!
WE WANT THE JUDGES!
POWER TO THE JUDGES!
"THE JUDGES! GENETICALLY CHOSEN TO BE TOUGH – BUT FAIR. THE PEOPLE TURNED TO THEM IN THE HOUR OF NEED. AND SO...
WE'VE COME FOR YOU, BOOTH!
HERE IS THE DECLARATION OF JUDGEMENT...FOR CRIMES AGAINST THE AMERICAN PEOPLE, YOUR PRESIDENCY IS AT AN END...
WE, THE JUDGES, HAVE TAKEN OVER!
"PRESIDENT BOOTH WAS TRIED BEFORE A GRAND COUNCIL OF JUDGES AND FOUND GUILTY OF WAR CRIMES..."
"BUT..."
WHAT SHALL HIS SENTENCE BE? AMERICA IS IN RUINS... HE CANNOT BE ALLOWED TO LIVE...
BUT HE CANNOT BE ALLOWED TO DIE! WE CANNOT EXECUTE THE LAST PRESIDENT OF THE UNITED STATES!

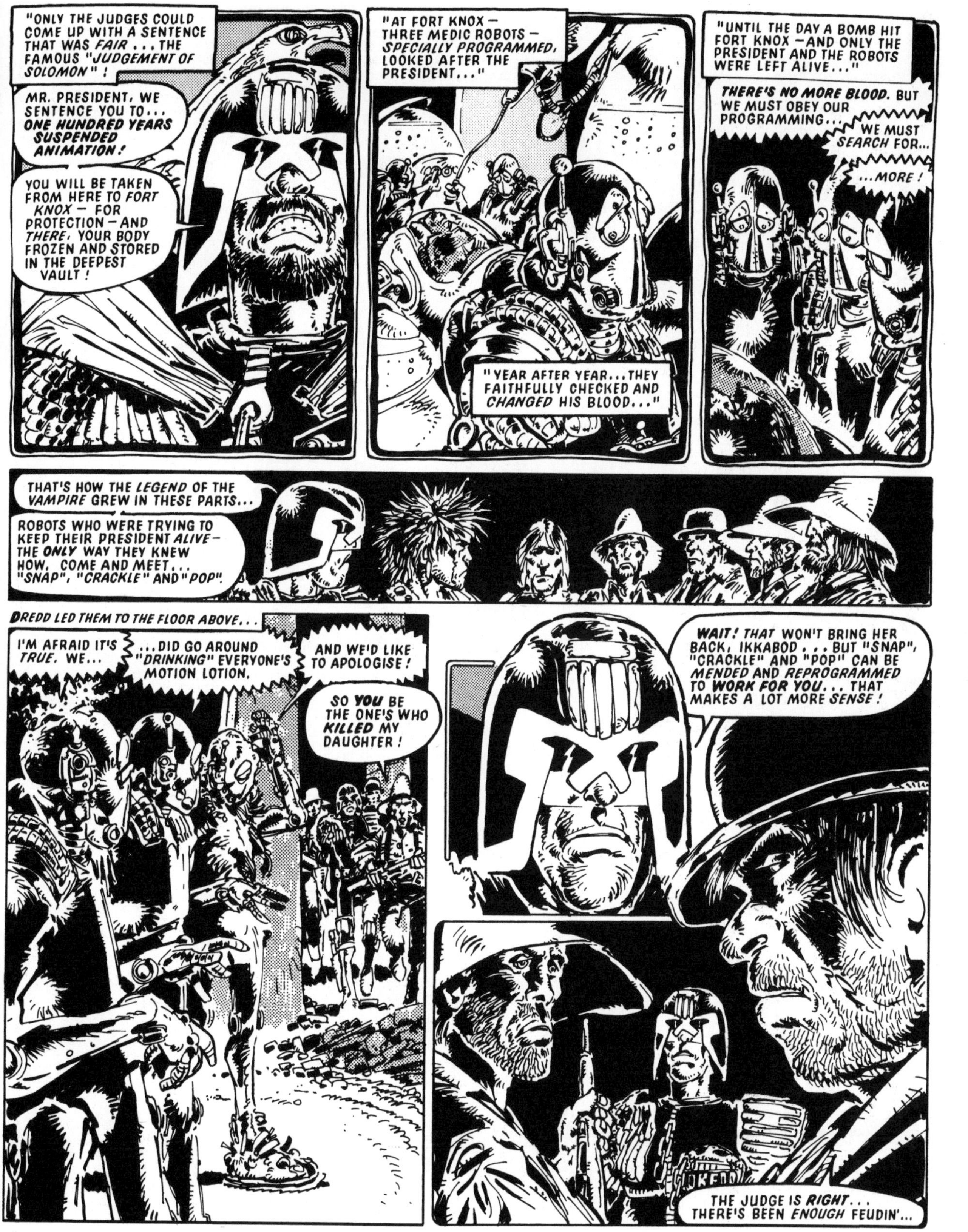
"ONLY THE JUDGES COULD COME UP WITH A SENTENCE THAT WAS FAIR . . . THE FAMOUS "JUDGEMENT OF SOLOMON" !
MR. PRESIDENT, WE SENTENCE YOU TO . . . ONE HUNDRED YEARS SUSPENDED ANIMATION !
YOU WILL BE TAKEN FROM HERE TO FORT KNOX — FOR PROTECTION — AND THERE, YOUR BODY FROZEN AND STORED IN THE DEEPEST VAULT !
"AT FORT KNOX — THREE MEDIC ROBOTS — SPECIALLY PROGRAMMED, LOOKED AFTER THE PRESIDENT . . ."
"YEAR AFTER YEAR . . . THEY FAITHFULLY CHECKED AND CHANGED HIS BLOOD . . ."
"UNTIL THE DAY A BOMB HIT FORT KNOX — AND ONLY THE PRESIDENT AND THE ROBOTS WERE LEFT ALIVE . . ."
THERE'S NO MORE BLOOD. BUT WE MUST OBEY OUR PROGRAMMING . . .
WE MUST SEARCH FOR . . .
. . . MORE !
THAT'S HOW THE LEGEND OF THE VAMPIRE GREW IN THESE PARTS . . .
ROBOTS WHO WERE TRYING TO KEEP THEIR PRESIDENT ALIVE — THE ONLY WAY THEY KNEW HOW. COME AND MEET . . . "SNAP", "CRACKLE" AND "POP".
DREDD LED THEM TO THE FLOOR ABOVE . . .
I'M AFRAID IT'S TRUE. WE . . .
. . . DID GO AROUND "DRINKING" EVERYONE'S MOTION LOTION.
AND WE'D LIKE TO APOLOGISE !
SO YOU BE THE ONE'S WHO KILLED MY DAUGHTER !
WAIT! THAT WON'T BRING HER BACK, IKKABOD . . . BUT "SNAP", "CRACKLE" AND "POP" CAN BE MENDED AND REPROGRAMMED TO WORK FOR YOU . . . THAT MAKES A LOT MORE SENSE !
THE JUDGE IS RIGHT . . . THERE'S BEEN ENOUGH FEUDIN' . . .

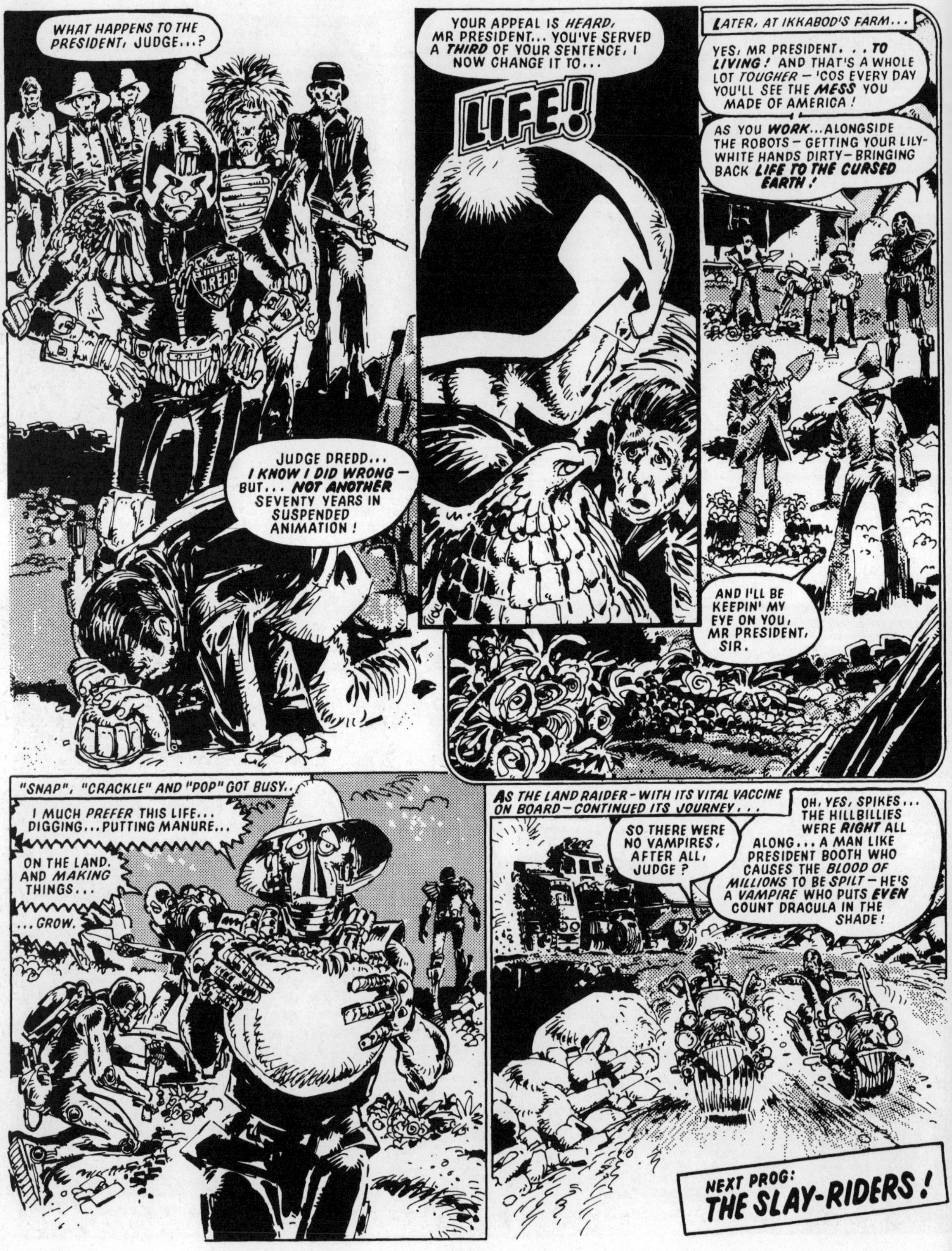
WHAT HAPPENS TO THE PRESIDENT, JUDGE...?
JUDGE DREDD... I KNOW I DID WRONG — BUT... NOT ANOTHER SEVENTY YEARS IN SUSPENDED ANIMATION!
YOUR APPEAL IS HEARD, MR PRESIDENT... YOU'VE SERVED A THIRD OF YOUR SENTENCE, I NOW CHANGE IT TO...
LIFE!
LATER, AT IKKABOD'S FARM...
YES, MR PRESIDENT, . . TO LIVING! AND THAT'S A WHOLE LOT TOUGHER — 'COS EVERY DAY YOU'LL SEE THE MESS YOU MADE OF AMERICA!
AS YOU WORK...ALONGSIDE THE ROBOTS — GETTING YOUR LILY-WHITE HANDS DIRTY — BRINGING BACK LIFE TO THE CURSED EARTH!
AND I'LL BE KEEPIN' MY EYE ON YOU, MR PRESIDENT, SIR.
"SNAP", "CRACKLE" AND "POP" GOT BUSY...
I MUCH PREFER THIS LIFE... DIGGING...PUTTING MANURE...
ON THE LAND. AND MAKING THINGS...
...GROW.
AS THE LAND RAIDER — WITH ITS VITAL VACCINE ON BOARD — CONTINUED ITS JOURNEY...
SO THERE WERE NO VAMPIRES, AFTER ALL, JUDGE?
OH, YES, SPIKES... THE HILLBILLIES WERE RIGHT ALL ALONG... A MAN LIKE PRESIDENT BOOTH WHO CAUSES THE BLOOD OF MILLIONS TO BE SPILT — HE'S A VAMPIRE WHO PUTS EVEN COUNT DRACULA IN THE SHADE!
NEXT PROG: THE SLAY-RIDERS!

THE CURSED EARTH

CHAPTER 9.

THE SLAY-RIDERS!

JUDGE DREDD

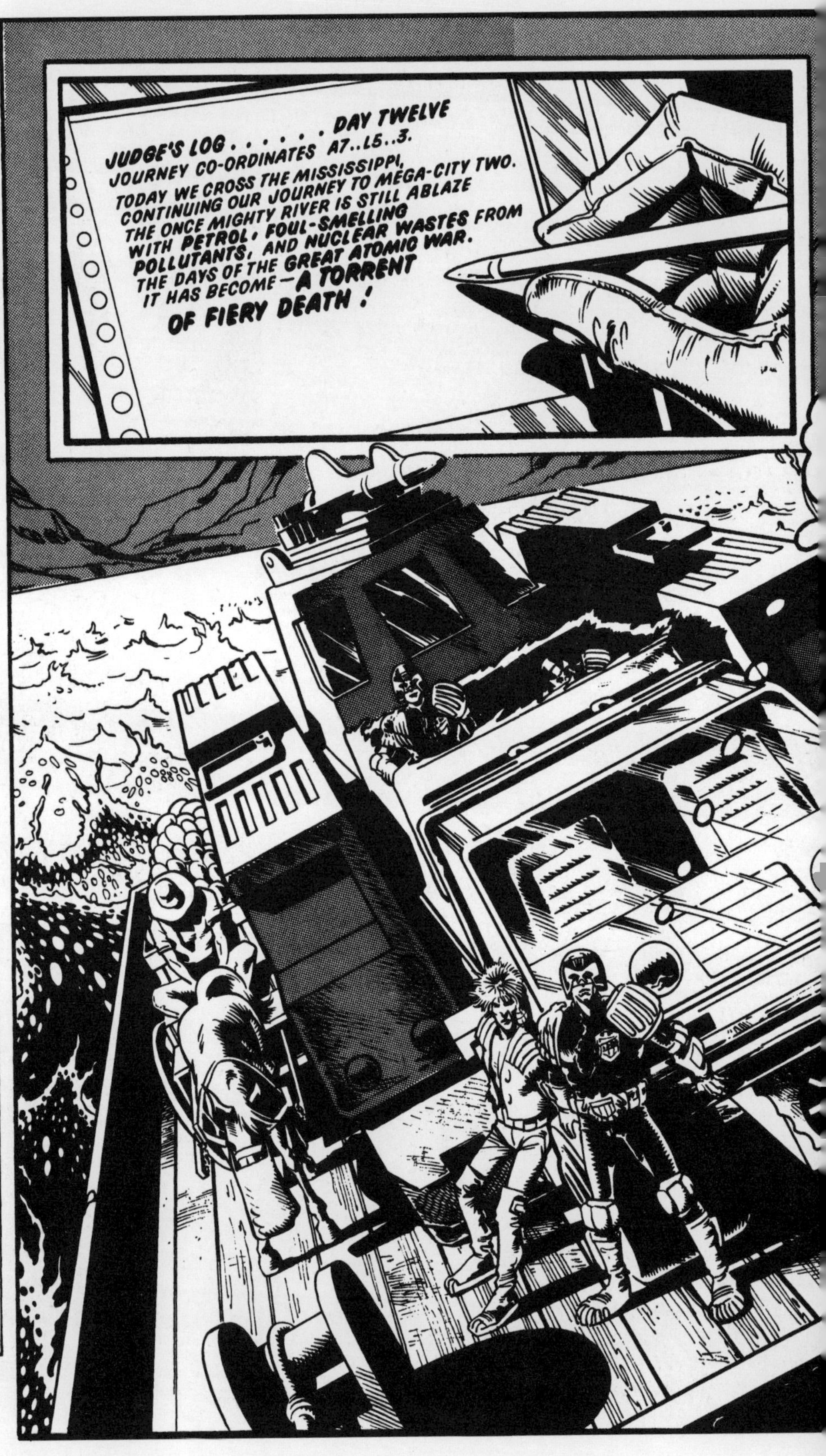
JUDGE'S LOG . . . . . DAY TWELVE
JOURNEY CO-ORDINATES A7..L5..3.
TODAY WE CROSS THE MISSISSIPPI, CONTINUING OUR JOURNEY TO MEGA-CITY TWO. THE ONCE MIGHTY RIVER IS STILL ABLAZE WITH PETROL, FOUL-SMELLING POLLUTANTS, AND NUCLEAR WASTES FROM THE DAYS OF THE GREAT ATOMIC WAR. IT HAS BECOME—A TORRENT OF FIERY DEATH!

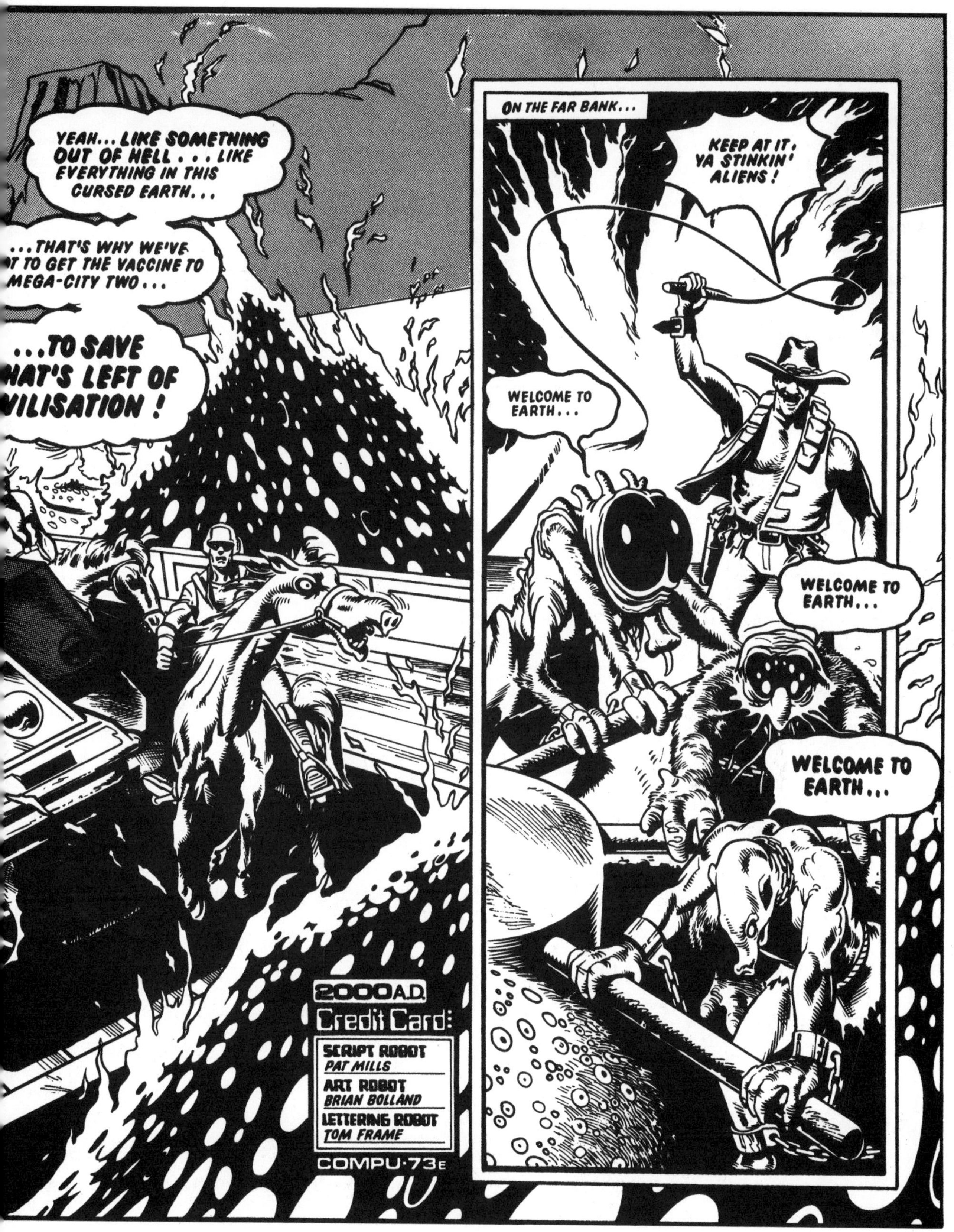
YEAH... LIKE SOMETHING OUT OF HELL . . . LIKE EVERYTHING IN THIS CURSED EARTH...
...THAT'S WHY WE'VE
T TO GET THE VACCINE TO
MEGA-CITY TWO...
...TO SAVE
HAT'S LEFT OF
VILISATION !
ON THE FAR BANK...
KEEP AT IT, YA STINKIN' ALIENS !
WELCOME TO EARTH...
WELCOME TO EARTH...
WELCOME TO EARTH...
2000 A.D. Credit Card
SCRIPT ROBOT PAT MILLS
ART ROBOT BRIAN BOLLAND
LETTERING ROBOT TOM FRAME
COMPU·73E

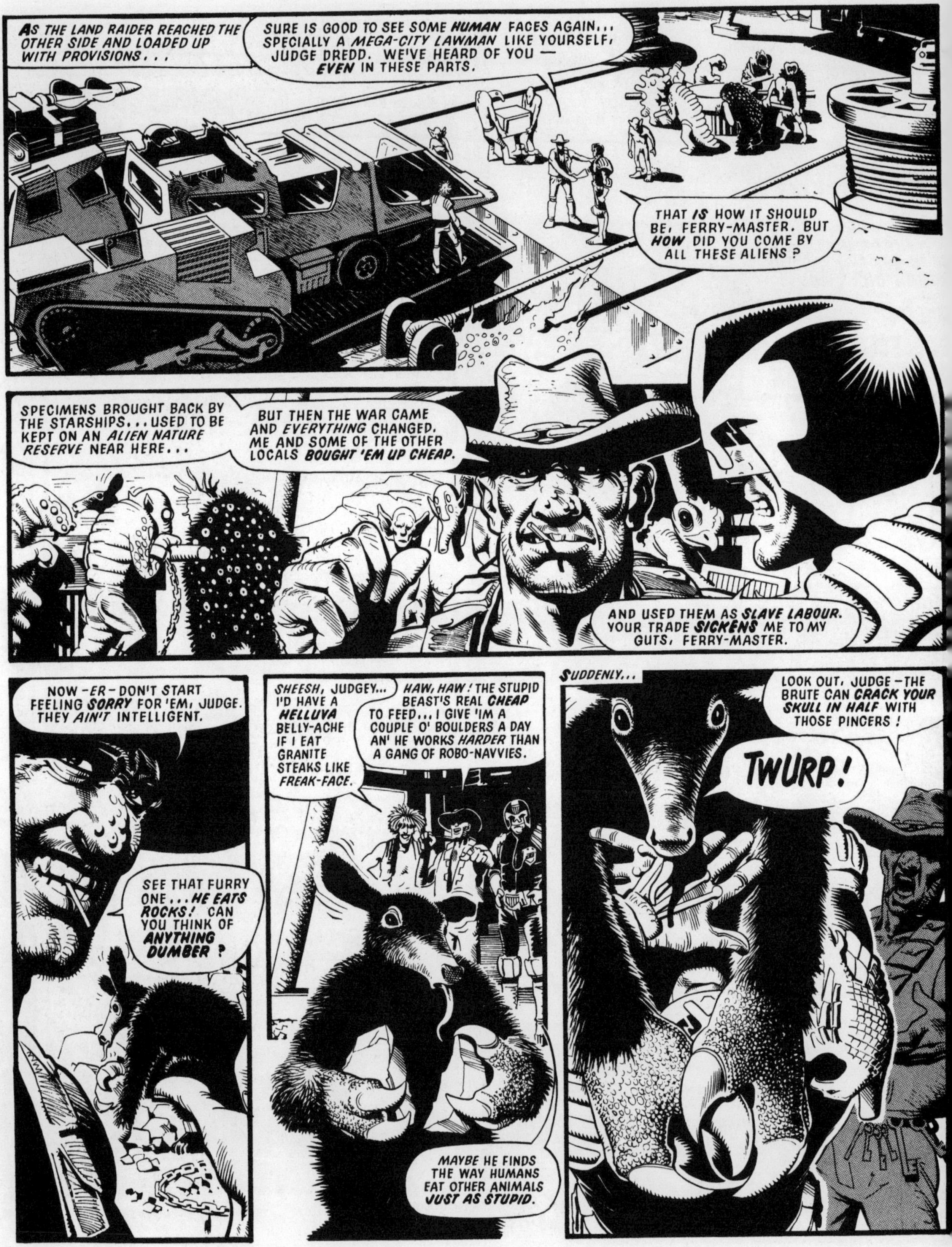
AS THE LAND RAIDER REACHED THE OTHER SIDE AND LOADED UP WITH PROVISIONS...
SURE IS GOOD TO SEE SOME HUMAN FACES AGAIN... SPECIALLY A MEGA-CITY LAWMAN LIKE YOURSELF, JUDGE DREDD. WE'VE HEARD OF YOU — EVEN IN THESE PARTS.
THAT IS HOW IT SHOULD BE, FERRY-MASTER. BUT HOW DID YOU COME BY ALL THESE ALIENS?
SPECIMENS BROUGHT BACK BY THE STARSHIPS... USED TO BE KEPT ON AN ALIEN NATURE RESERVE NEAR HERE...
BUT THEN THE WAR CAME AND EVERYTHING CHANGED. ME AND SOME OF THE OTHER LOCALS BOUGHT 'EM UP CHEAP.
AND USED THEM AS SLAVE LABOUR. YOUR TRADE SICKENS ME TO MY GUTS, FERRY-MASTER.
NOW -ER- DON'T START FEELING SORRY FOR 'EM, JUDGE. THEY AIN'T INTELLIGENT.
SEE THAT FURRY ONE... HE EATS ROCKS! CAN YOU THINK OF ANYTHING DUMBER?
SHEESH, JUDGEY... I'D HAVE A HELLUVA BELLY-ACHE IF I EAT GRANITE STEAKS LIKE FREAK-FACE.
HAW, HAW! THE STUPID BEAST'S REAL CHEAP TO FEED... I GIVE 'IM A COUPLE O' BOULDERS A DAY AN' HE WORKS HARDER THAN A GANG OF ROBO-NAVVIES.
MAYBE HE FINDS THE WAY HUMANS EAT OTHER ANIMALS JUST AS STUPID.
SUDDENLY...
LOOK OUT, JUDGE — THE BRUTE CAN CRACK YOUR SKULL IN HALF WITH THOSE PINCERS!
TWURP!

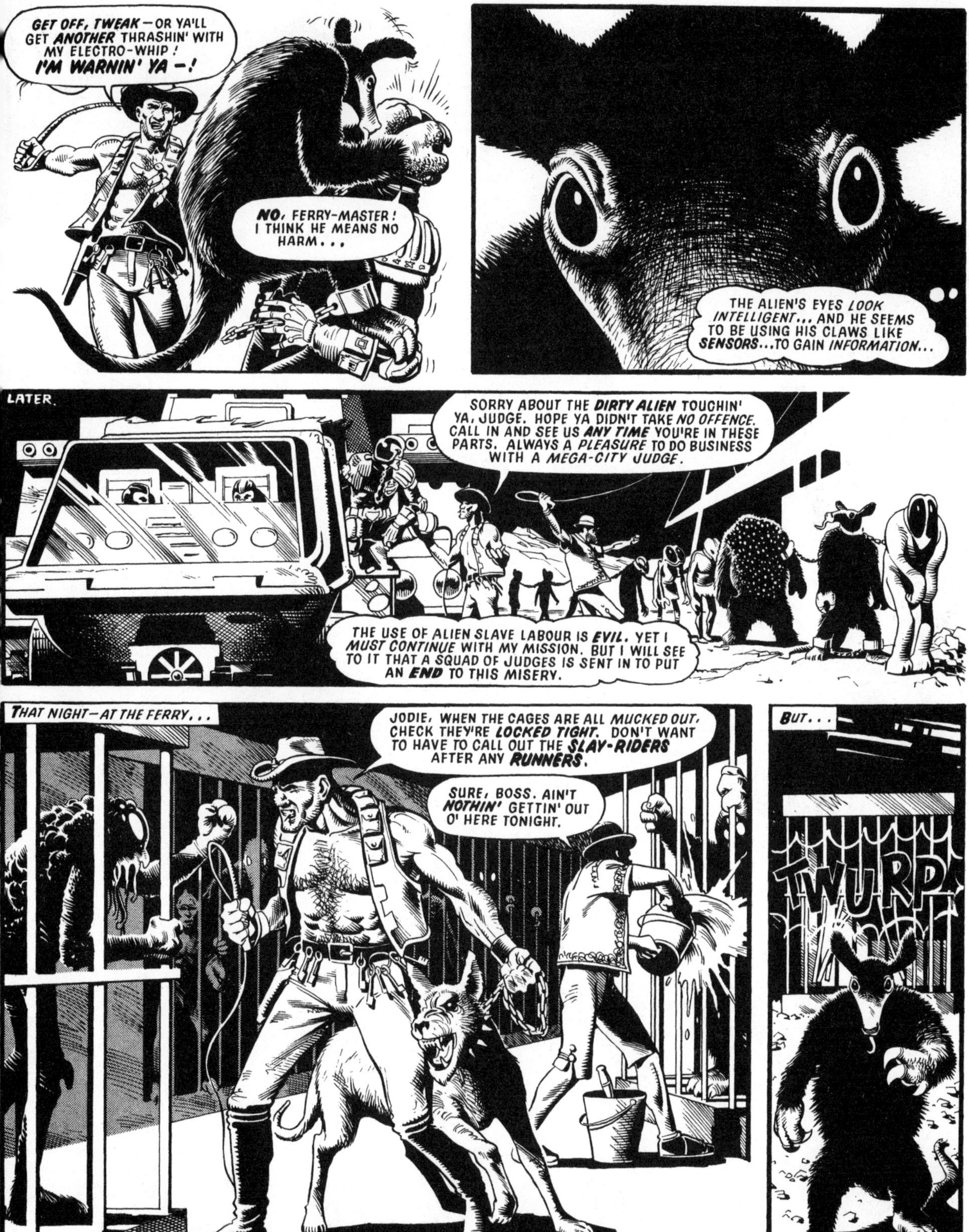
GET OFF, TWEAK — OR YA'LL GET ANOTHER THRASHIN' WITH MY ELECTRO-WHIP! I'M WARNIN' YA —!
NO, FERRY-MASTER! I THINK HE MEANS NO HARM...
THE ALIEN'S EYES LOOK INTELLIGENT... AND HE SEEMS TO BE USING HIS CLAWS LIKE SENSORS... TO GAIN INFORMATION...
LATER.
SORRY ABOUT THE DIRTY ALIEN TOUCHIN' YA, JUDGE. HOPE YA DIDN'T TAKE NO OFFENCE. CALL IN AND SEE US ANY TIME YOU'RE IN THESE PARTS. ALWAYS A PLEASURE TO DO BUSINESS WITH A MEGA-CITY JUDGE.
THE USE OF ALIEN SLAVE LABOUR IS EVIL. YET I MUST CONTINUE WITH MY MISSION. BUT I WILL SEE TO IT THAT A SQUAD OF JUDGES IS SENT IN TO PUT AN END TO THIS MISERY.
THAT NIGHT — AT THE FERRY...
JODIE, WHEN THE CAGES ARE ALL MUCKED OUT, CHECK THEY'RE LOCKED TIGHT. DON'T WANT TO HAVE TO CALL OUT THE SLAY-RIDERS AFTER ANY RUNNERS.
SURE, BOSS. AIN'T NOTHIN' GETTIN' OUT O' HERE TONIGHT.
BUT...
TWURP

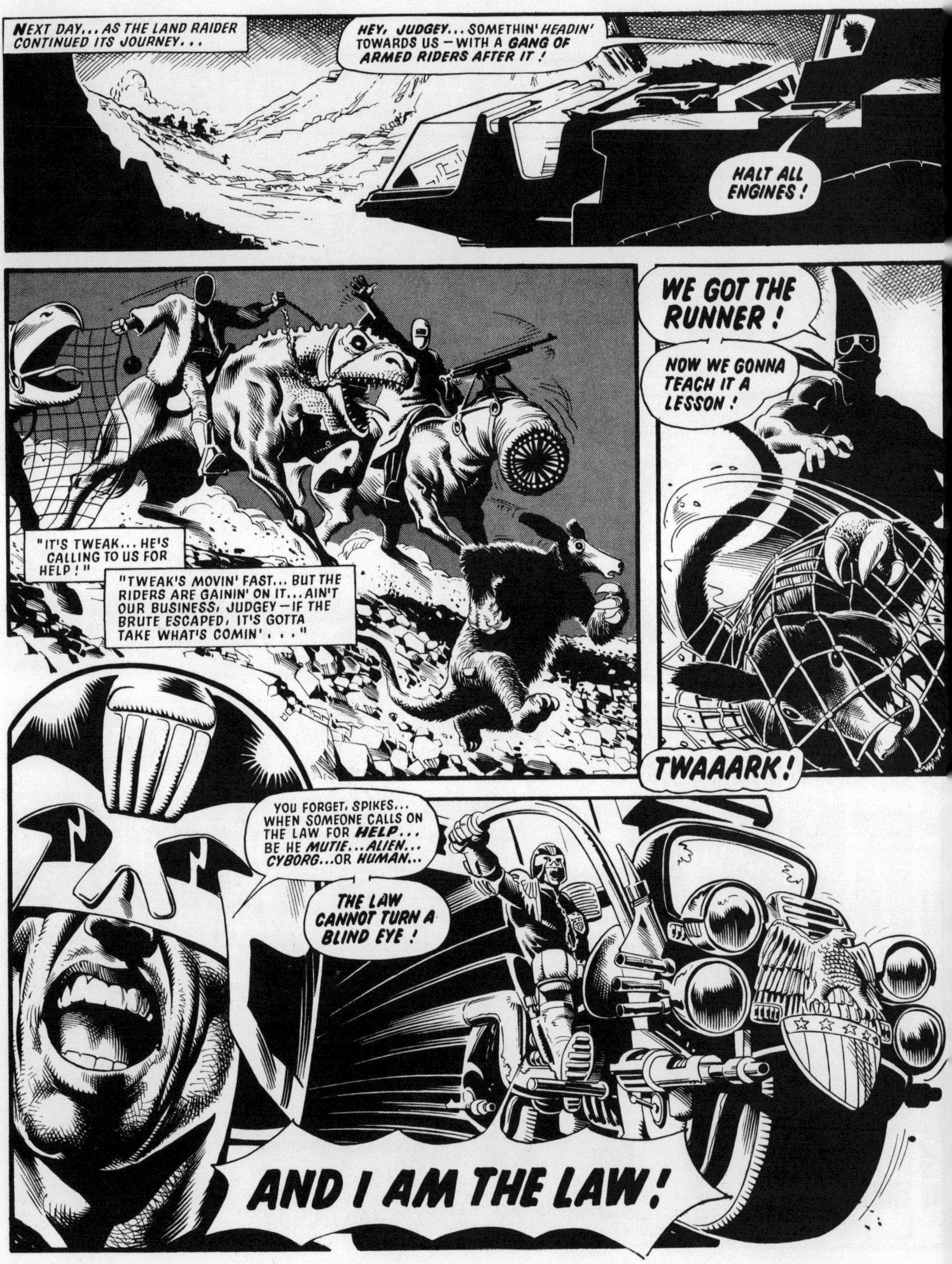
NEXT DAY... AS THE LAND RAIDER CONTINUED ITS JOURNEY...
HEY, JUDGEY... SOMETHIN' HEADIN' TOWARDS US — WITH A GANG OF ARMED RIDERS AFTER IT !
HALT ALL ENGINES !
"IT'S TWEAK... HE'S CALLING TO US FOR HELP !"
"TWEAK'S MOVIN' FAST... BUT THE RIDERS ARE GAININ' ON IT... AIN'T OUR BUSINESS, JUDGEY — IF THE BRUTE ESCAPED, IT'S GOTTA TAKE WHAT'S COMIN'..."
WE GOT THE RUNNER !
NOW WE GONNA TEACH IT A LESSON !
TWAAARK !
YOU FORGET, SPIKES... WHEN SOMEONE CALLS ON THE LAW FOR HELP... BE HE MUTIE... ALIEN... CYBORG... OR HUMAN...
THE LAW CANNOT TURN A BLIND EYE !
AND I AM THE LAW !

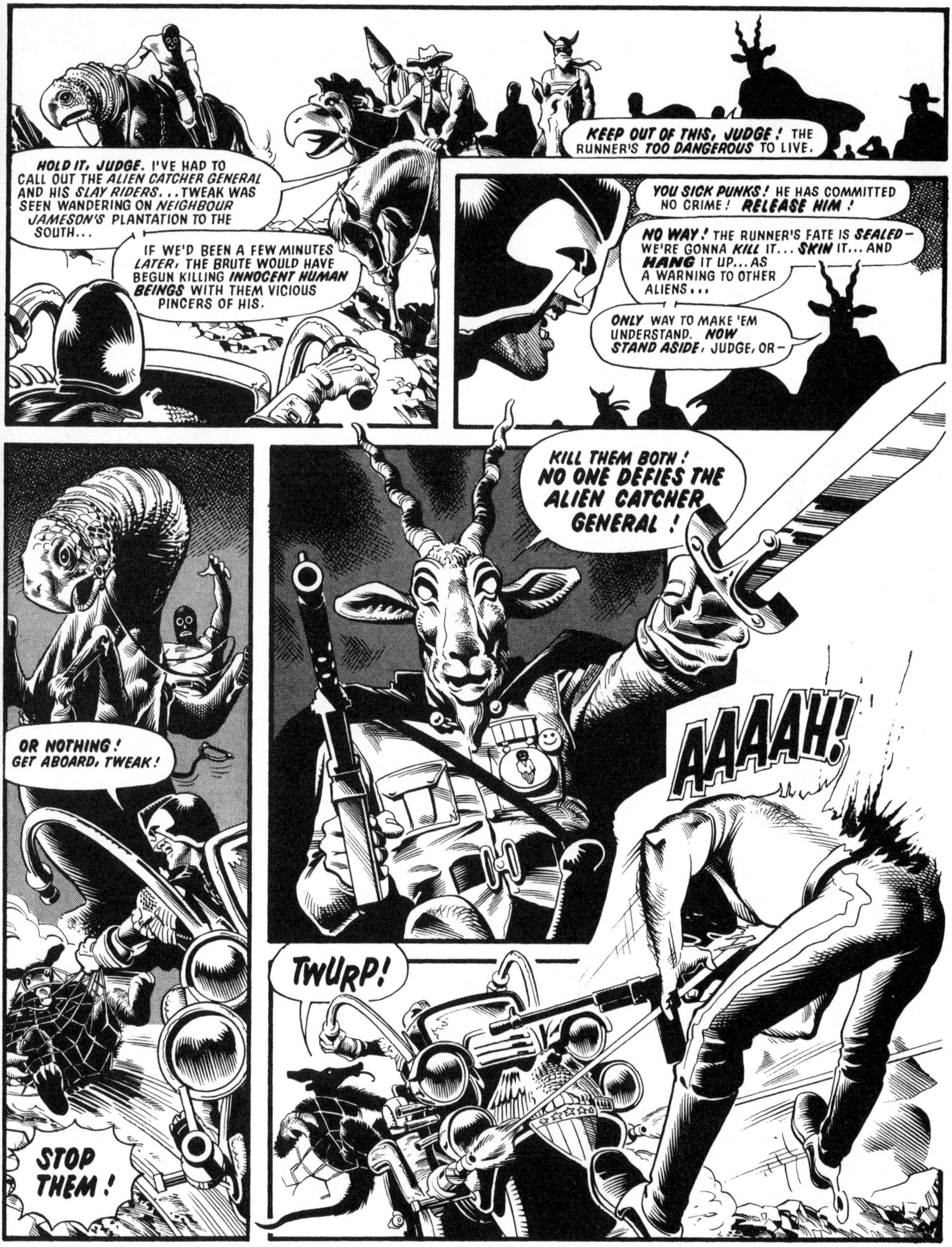
HOLD IT, JUDGE. I'VE HAD TO CALL OUT THE ALIEN CATCHER GENERAL AND HIS SLAY RIDERS... TWEAK WAS SEEN WANDERING ON NEIGHBOUR JAMESON'S PLANTATION TO THE SOUTH...
IF WE'D BEEN A FEW MINUTES LATER, THE BRUTE WOULD HAVE BEGUN KILLING INNOCENT HUMAN BEINGS WITH THEM VICIOUS PINCERS OF HIS.
KEEP OUT OF THIS, JUDGE! THE RUNNER'S TOO DANGEROUS TO LIVE.
YOU SICK PUNKS! HE HAS COMMITTED NO CRIME! RELEASE HIM!
NO WAY! THE RUNNER'S FATE IS SEALED— WE'RE GONNA KILL IT... SKIN IT... AND HANG IT UP... AS A WARNING TO OTHER ALIENS...
ONLY WAY TO MAKE 'EM UNDERSTAND. NOW STAND ASIDE, JUDGE, OR—
OR NOTHING! GET ABOARD, TWEAK!
STOP THEM!
KILL THEM BOTH! NO ONE DEFIES THE ALIEN CATCHER GENERAL!
AAAAH!
TWURP!

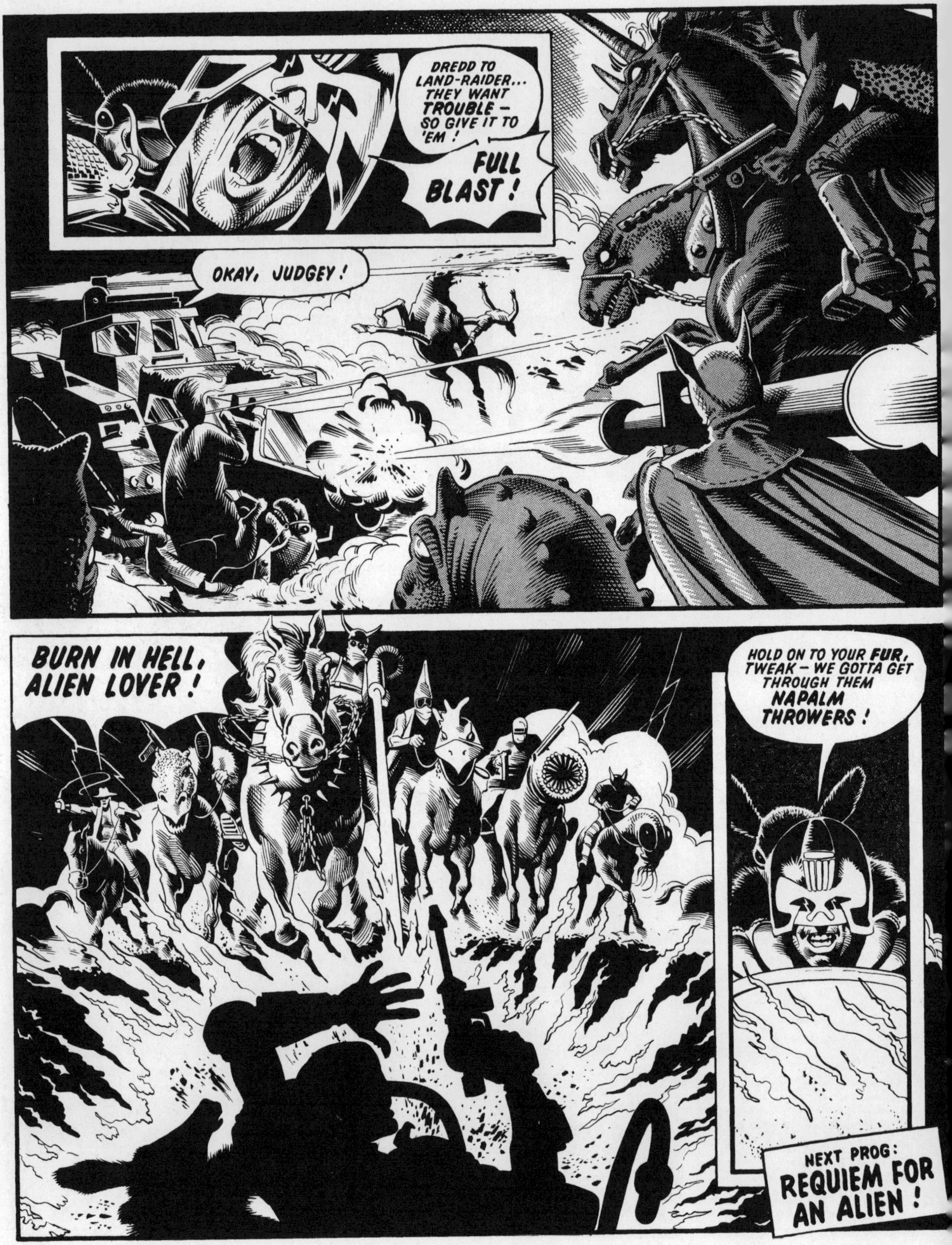
DREDD TO LAND-RAIDER... THEY WANT TROUBLE — SO GIVE IT TO 'EM !
FULL BLAST !
OKAY, JUDGEY !
BURN IN HELL, ALIEN LOVER !
HOLD ON TO YOUR FUR, TWEAK — WE GOTTA GET THROUGH THEM NAPALM THROWERS !
NEXT PROG: REQUIEM FOR AN ALIEN !

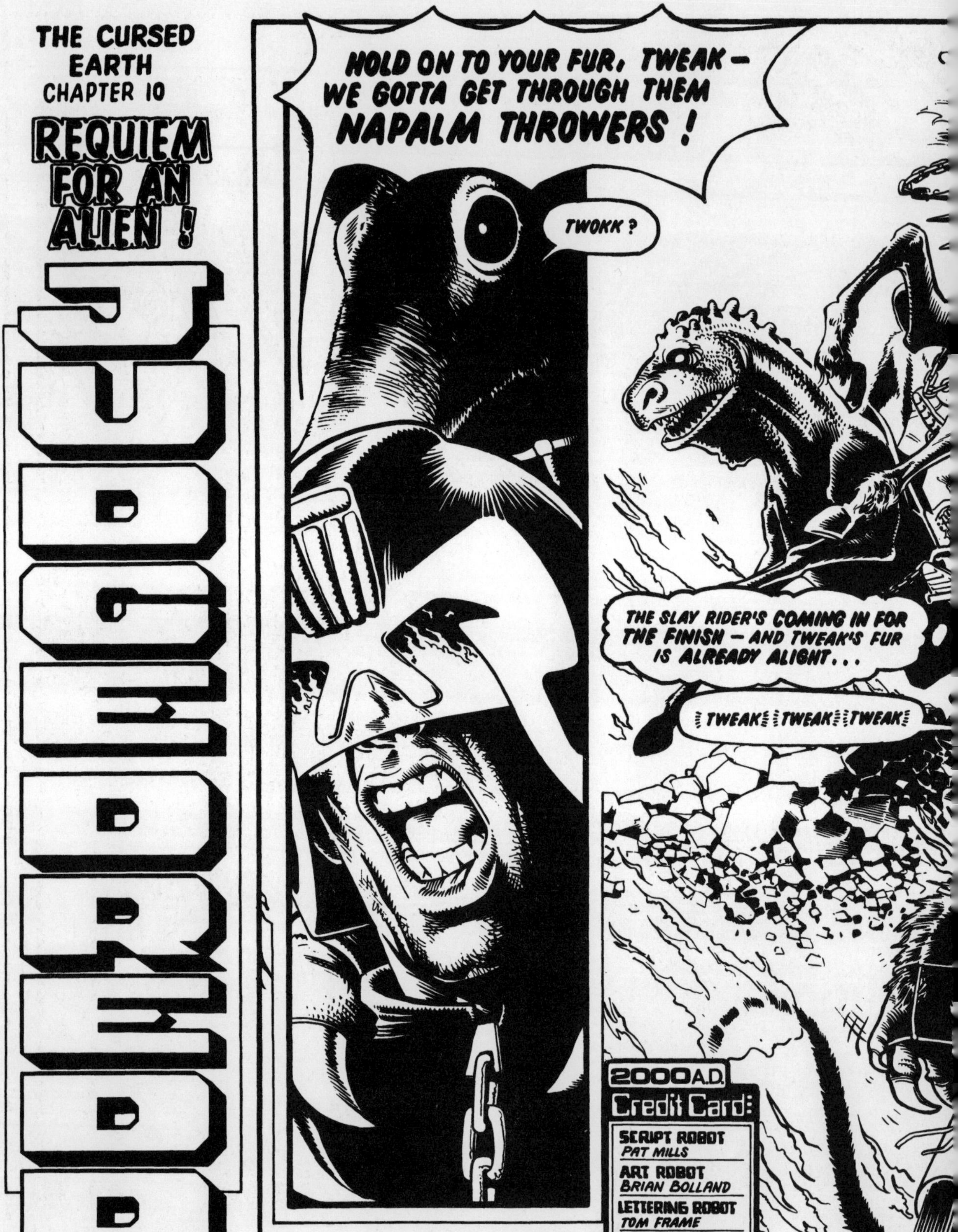

THE CURSED EARTH
CHAPTER 10
REQUIEM FOR AN ALIEN !
JUDGE DREDD
HOLD ON TO YOUR FUR, TWEAK — WE GOTTA GET THROUGH THEM NAPALM THROWERS !
TWOKK ?
THE SLAY RIDER'S COMING IN FOR THE FINISH — AND TWEAK'S FUR IS ALREADY ALIGHT...
TWEAK TWEAK TWEAK
2000 A.D. Credit Card:
SCRIPT ROBOT PAT MILLS
ART ROBOT BRIAN BOLLAND
LETTERING ROBOT TOM FRAME
COMPU·73E

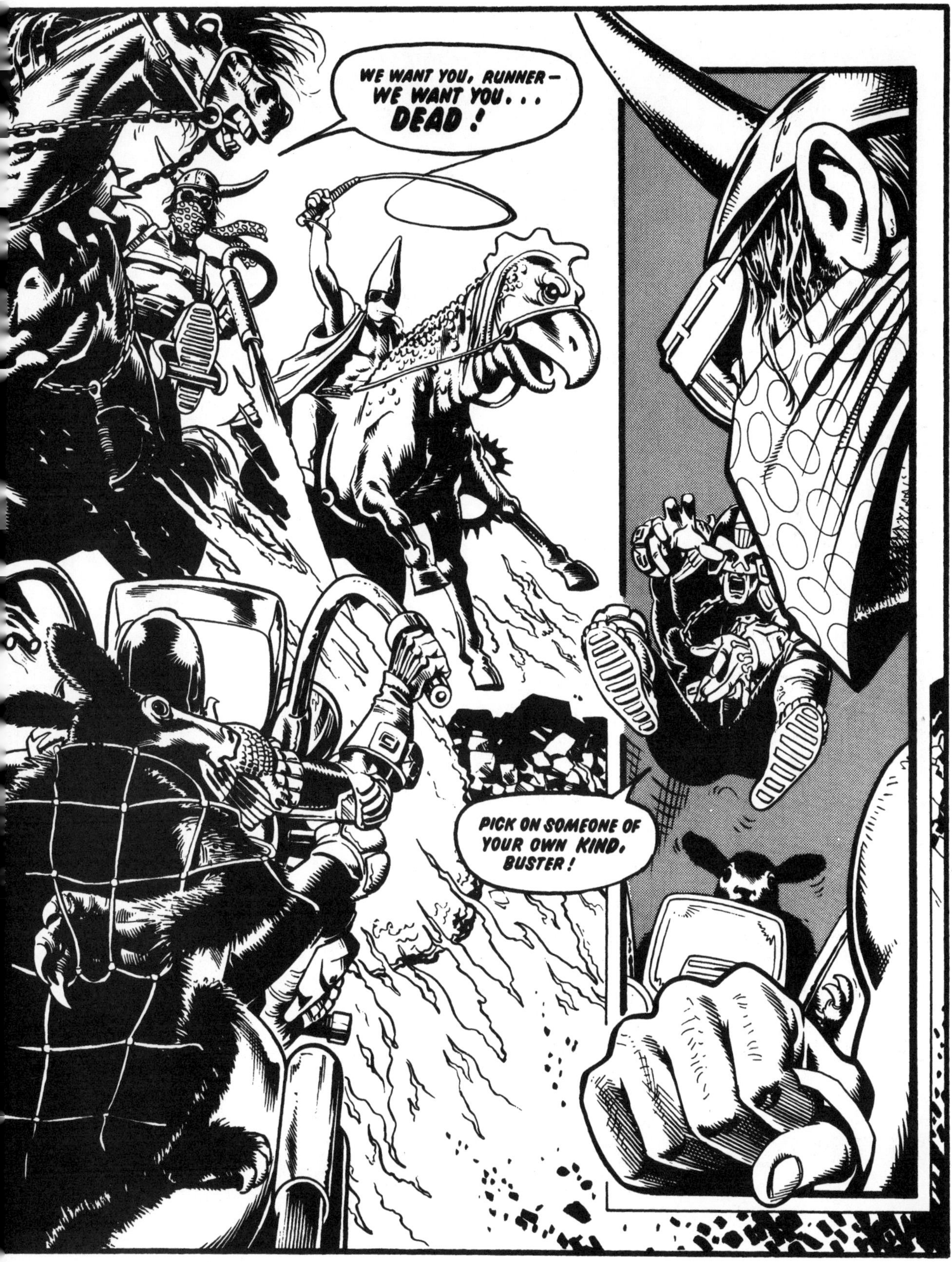
WE WANT YOU, RUNNER— WE WANT YOU. . . DEAD!
PICK ON SOMEONE OF YOUR OWN KIND, BUSTER!

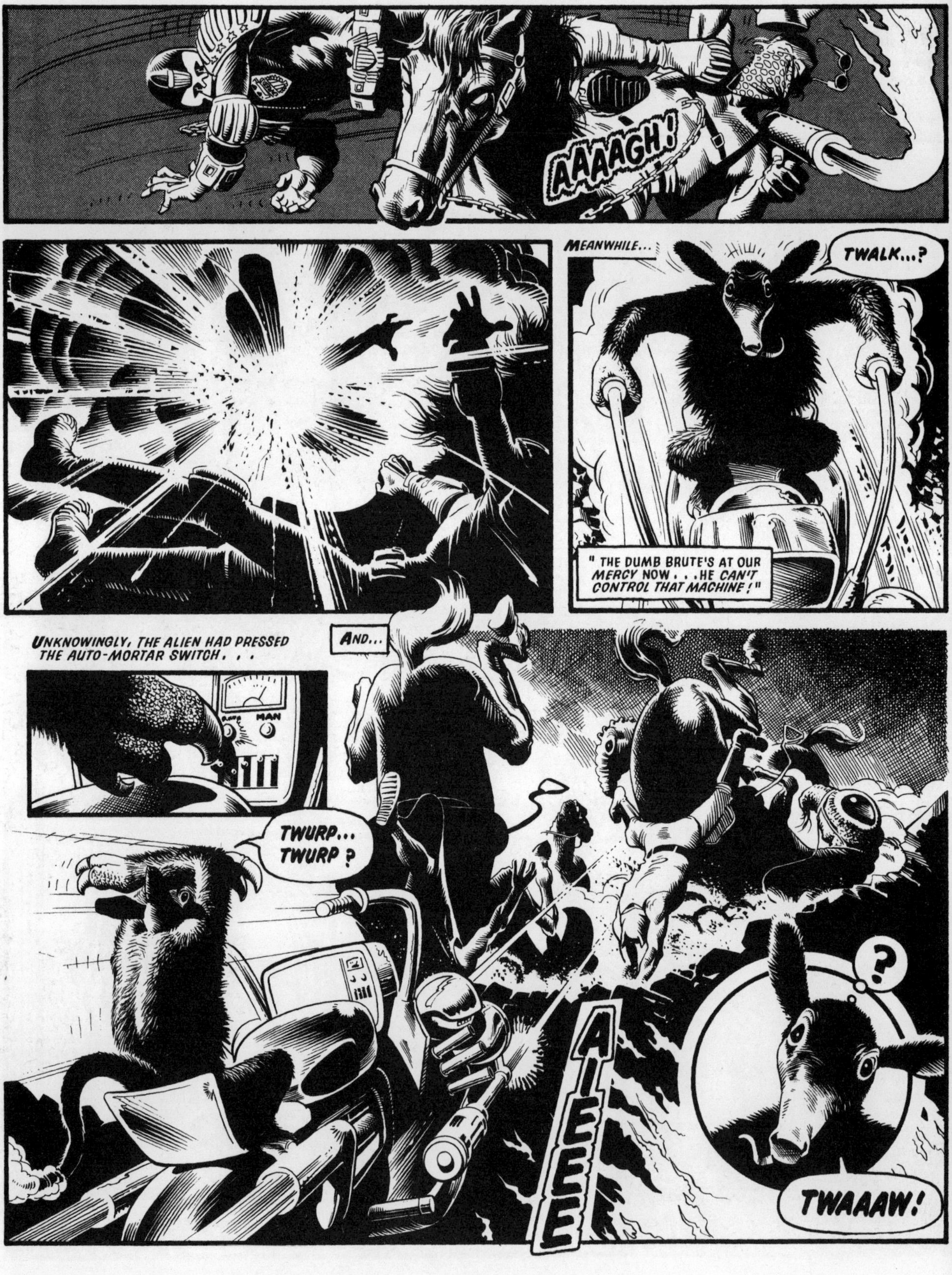
AAAAGH!
MEANWHILE...
TWALK...?
" THE DUMB BRUTE'S AT OUR MERCY NOW . . . HE CAN'T CONTROL THAT MACHINE ! "
UNKNOWINGLY, THE ALIEN HAD PRESSED THE AUTO-MORTAR SWITCH . . .
MAN
AND...
TWURP... TWURP ?
AIEEEE
?
TWAAAW!

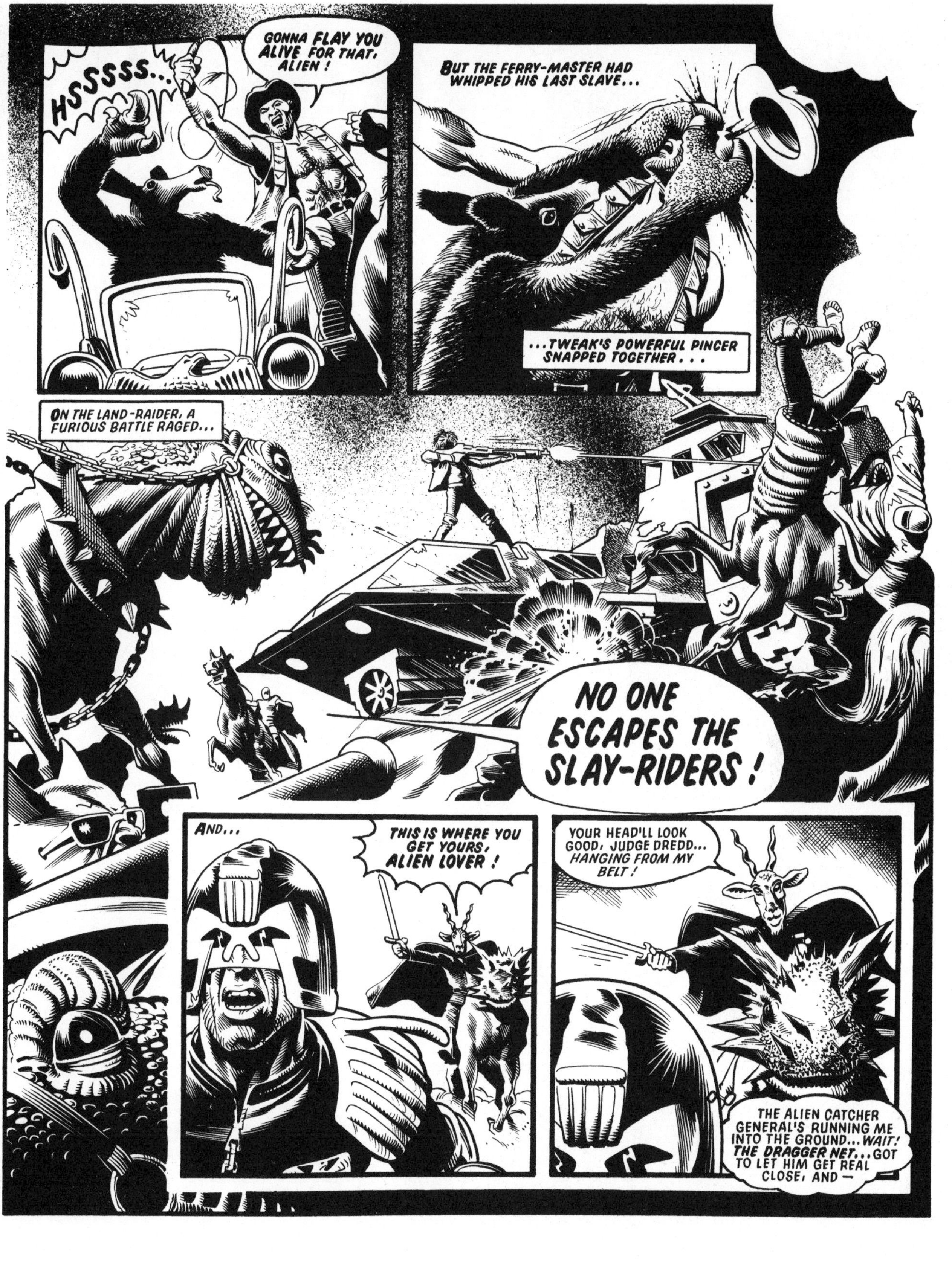
HSSSSS...
GONNA FLAY YOU ALIVE FOR THAT, ALIEN !
BUT THE FERRY-MASTER HAD WHIPPED HIS LAST SLAVE...
...TWEAK'S POWERFUL PINCER SNAPPED TOGETHER . . .
ON THE LAND-RAIDER, A FURIOUS BATTLE RAGED...
NO ONE ESCAPES THE SLAY-RIDERS !
AND...
THIS IS WHERE YOU GET YOURS, ALIEN LOVER !
YOUR HEAD'LL LOOK GOOD, JUDGE DREDD... HANGING FROM MY BELT !
THE ALIEN CATCHER GENERAL'S RUNNING ME INTO THE GROUND... WAIT! THE DRAGGER NET... GOT TO LET HIM GET REAL CLOSE, AND —

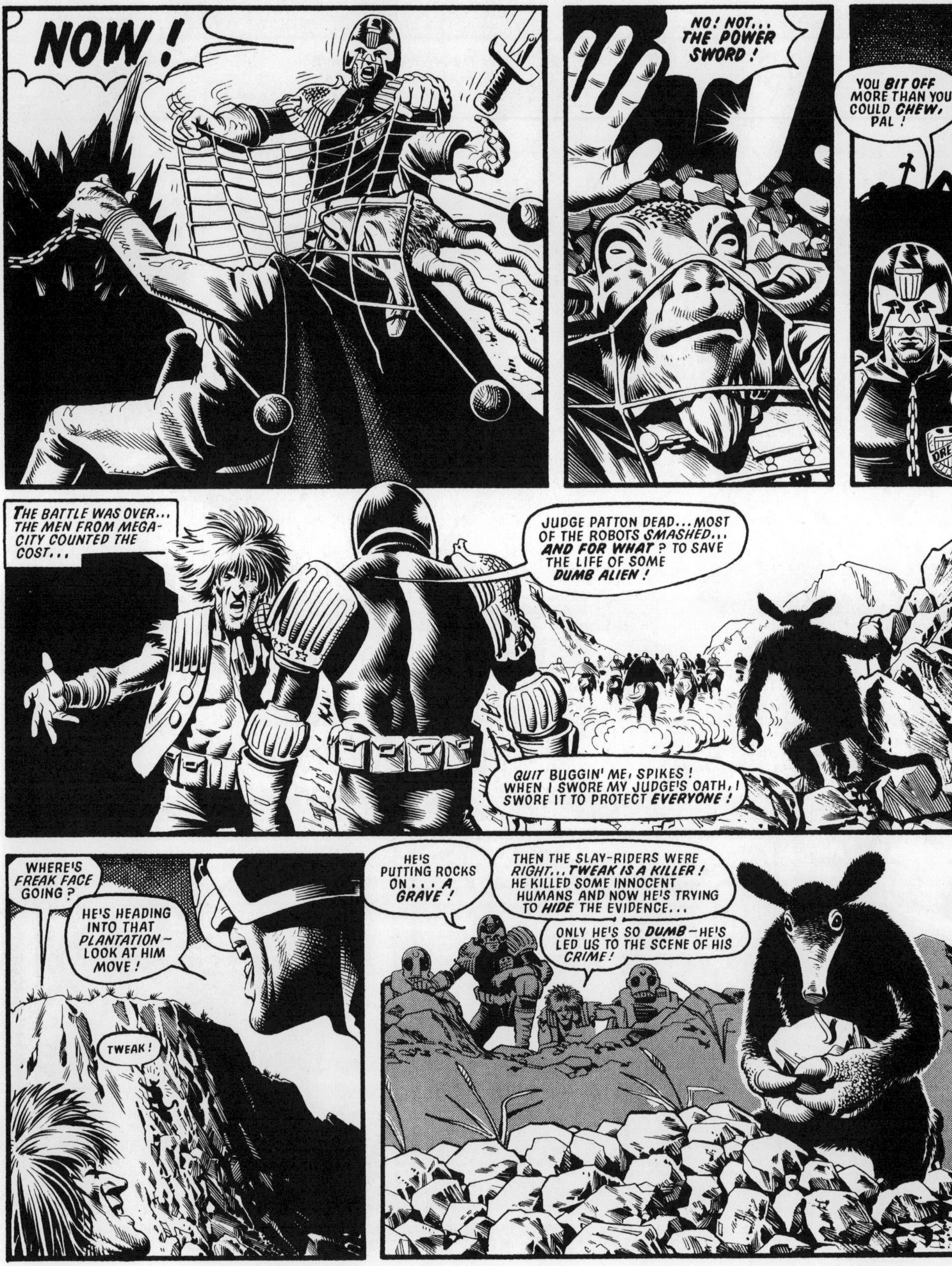
NOW!
NO! NOT... THE POWER SWORD!
YOU BIT OFF MORE THAN YOU COULD CHEW, PAL!
THE BATTLE WAS OVER... THE MEN FROM MEGA-CITY COUNTED THE COST...
JUDGE PATTON DEAD... MOST OF THE ROBOTS SMASHED... AND FOR WHAT? TO SAVE THE LIFE OF SOME DUMB ALIEN!
QUIT BUGGIN' ME, SPIKES! WHEN I SWORE MY JUDGE'S OATH, I SWORE IT TO PROTECT EVERYONE!
WHERE'S FREAK FACE GOING?
HE'S HEADING INTO THAT PLANTATION - LOOK AT HIM MOVE!
TWEAK!
HE'S PUTTING ROCKS ON... A GRAVE!
THEN THE SLAY-RIDERS WERE RIGHT... TWEAK IS A KILLER! HE KILLED SOME INNOCENT HUMANS AND NOW HE'S TRYING TO HIDE THE EVIDENCE...
ONLY HE'S SO DUMB - HE'S LED US TO THE SCENE OF HIS CRIME!

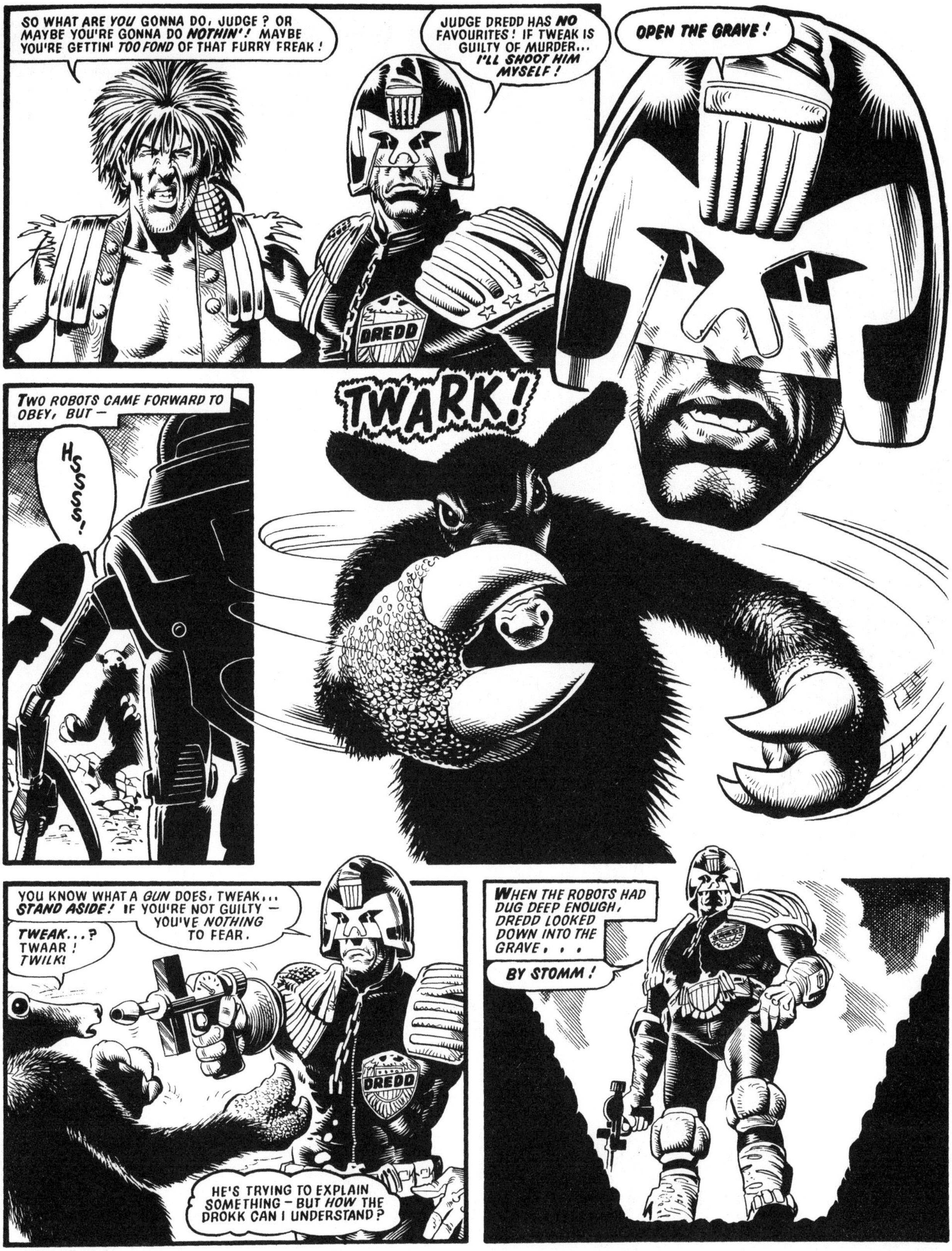
SO WHAT ARE YOU GONNA DO, JUDGE ? OR MAYBE YOU'RE GONNA DO NOTHIN'! MAYBE YOU'RE GETTIN' TOO FOND OF THAT FURRY FREAK !
JUDGE DREDD HAS NO FAVOURITES ! IF TWEAK IS GUILTY OF MURDER... I'LL SHOOT HIM MYSELF !
DREDD
OPEN THE GRAVE !
TWO ROBOTS CAME FORWARD TO OBEY, BUT —
HSSSSS!
TWARK!
YOU KNOW WHAT A GUN DOES, TWEAK... STAND ASIDE! IF YOU'RE NOT GUILTY — YOU'VE NOTHING TO FEAR.
TWEAK...? TWAAR! TWILK!
DREDD
HE'S TRYING TO EXPLAIN SOMETHING — BUT HOW THE DROKK CAN I UNDERSTAND?
WHEN THE ROBOTS HAD DUG DEEP ENOUGH, DREDD LOOKED DOWN INTO THE GRAVE . . .
BY STOMM !

TWEAK, AIN'T MUCH I CAN DO TO MAKE AMENDS, BUDDY...BUT YOU'RE WELCOME TO COME WITH US. AND — I'M SORRY.

FILL IN THE GRAVE!

TWOLK!

WH-WHAT WAS IN THE GRAVE?

THREE ALIENS — LIKE TWEAK, TWO OF THEM SMALL — AND THE OTHER WITH GOLDEN FUR... YEAH, TWEAK'S MATE AND KIDS... SHOT — BY HUMAN BULLETS!

THAT'S WHY TWEAK ESCAPED — SO HE COULD REACH THIS PLANTATION WHERE THEY WERE SLAVES — SO HE COULD SEE HIS FAMILY AGAIN...

MY GUESS IS THE PLANTATION OWNER — ONE OF THE SLAY-RIDERS — FOUND THEY DIDN'T WORK HARD ENOUGH — AND HAD THEM SHOT...

SO TWEAK BURIED THEM AND BEGAN LAYING ROCKS ON THEIR GRAVE..."FOOD" FOR THEIR JOURNEY AFTER DEATH — ACCORDING TO THE CUSTOM ON HIS PLANET... AND WE'RE GONNA HELP HIM...!

AND SO...

: TWURRRRP :

I THINK TWEAK'S TRYING TO TELL YOU, SPIKES — HE ONLY LIKES THE HARD STUFF... GRANITE AND QUARTZ!

SHEESH! HE'S REALLY FUSSY ABOUT HIS GRUB — AND I LUGGED THESE NICE JUICY ROCKS ALL THE WAY UP THE HILL SPECIAL.

THEY LEFT TWEAK ALONE FOR A FEW MINUTES BY THE GRAVE...

DRAGGED AS A SPECIMEN OFF HIS HOME PLANET... SOLD INTO SLAVERY...HIS MATE AND KIDS BUTCHERED ON A WORLD LIGHT YEARS AWAY FROM HOME... YEAH, TWEAK MUST REALLY THINK WE HUMANS ARE CIVILISED!

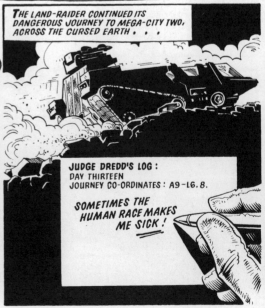

THE LAND-RAIDER CONTINUED ITS DANGEROUS JOURNEY TO MEGA-CITY TWO, ACROSS THE CURSED EARTH...

JUDGE DREDD'S LOG:
DAY THIRTEEN
JOURNEY CO-ORDINATES: A9-L6.8.

SOMETIMES THE HUMAN RACE MAKES ME SICK!

THE CURSED EARTH
CHAPTER 13
THE COMING OF SATANUS!

JUDGE DREDD

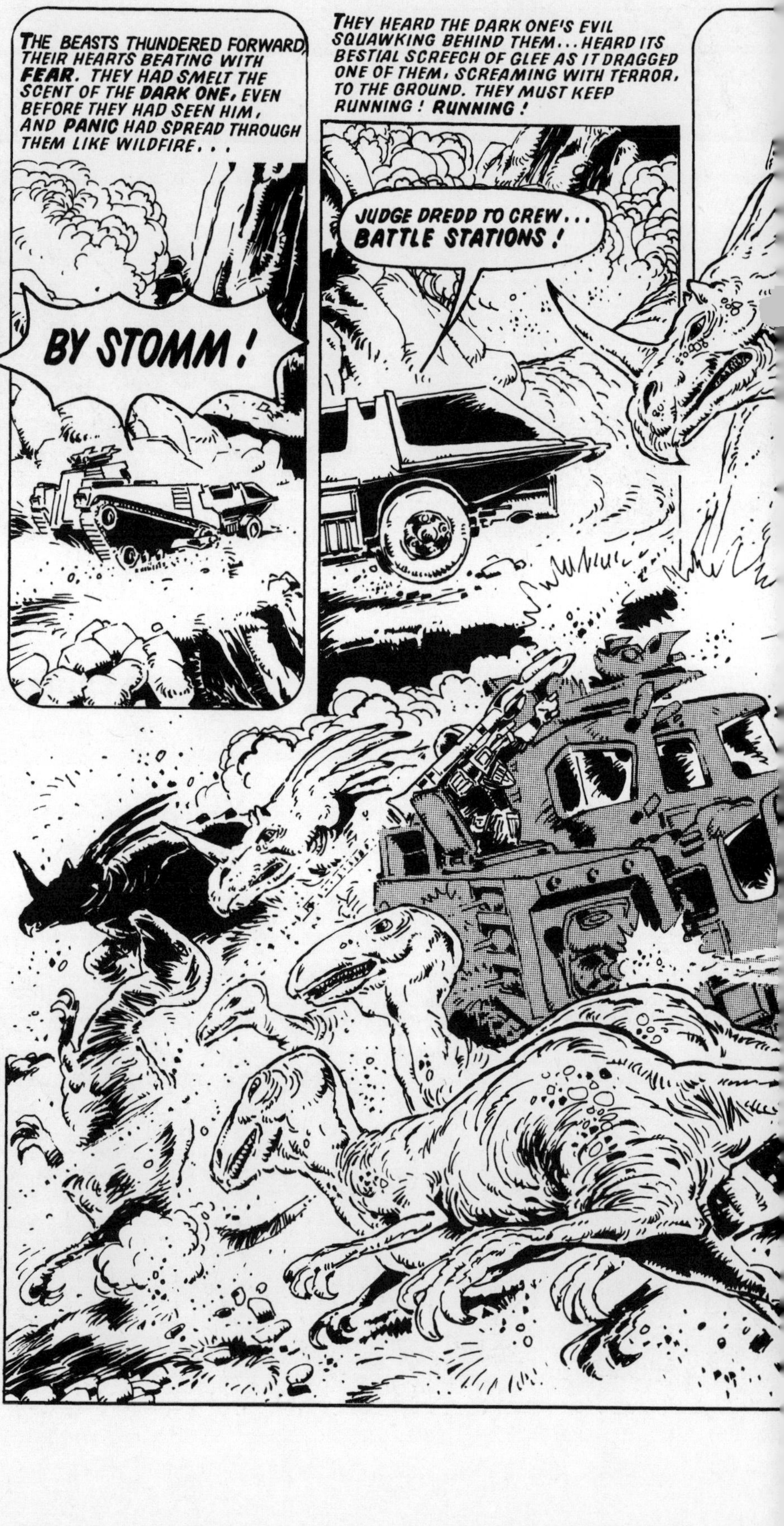

THE BEASTS THUNDERED FORWARD, THEIR HEARTS BEATING WITH FEAR. THEY HAD SMELT THE SCENT OF THE DARK ONE, EVEN BEFORE THEY HAD SEEN HIM, AND PANIC HAD SPREAD THROUGH THEM LIKE WILDFIRE . . .
BY STOMM!
THEY HEARD THE DARK ONE'S EVIL SQUAWKING BEHIND THEM . . . HEARD ITS BESTIAL SCREECH OF GLEE AS IT DRAGGED ONE OF THEM, SCREAMING WITH TERROR, TO THE GROUND. THEY MUST KEEP RUNNING! RUNNING!
JUDGE DREDD TO CREW . . . BATTLE STATIONS!

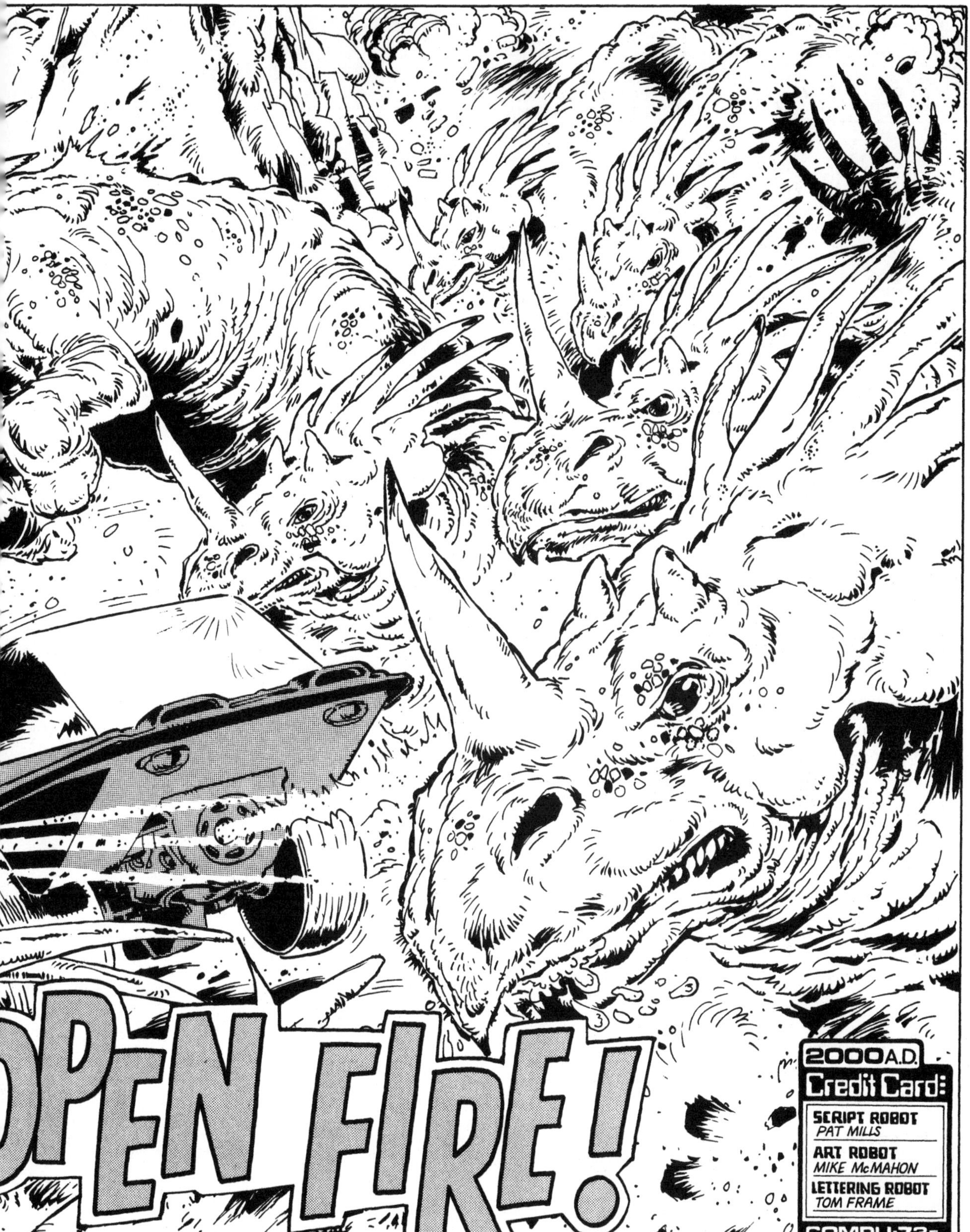
OPEN FIRE!
2000 A.D.
Credit Card:
SCRIPT ROBOT
PAT MILLS
ART ROBOT
MIKE McMAHON
LETTERING ROBOT
TOM FRAME
COMPU·73E

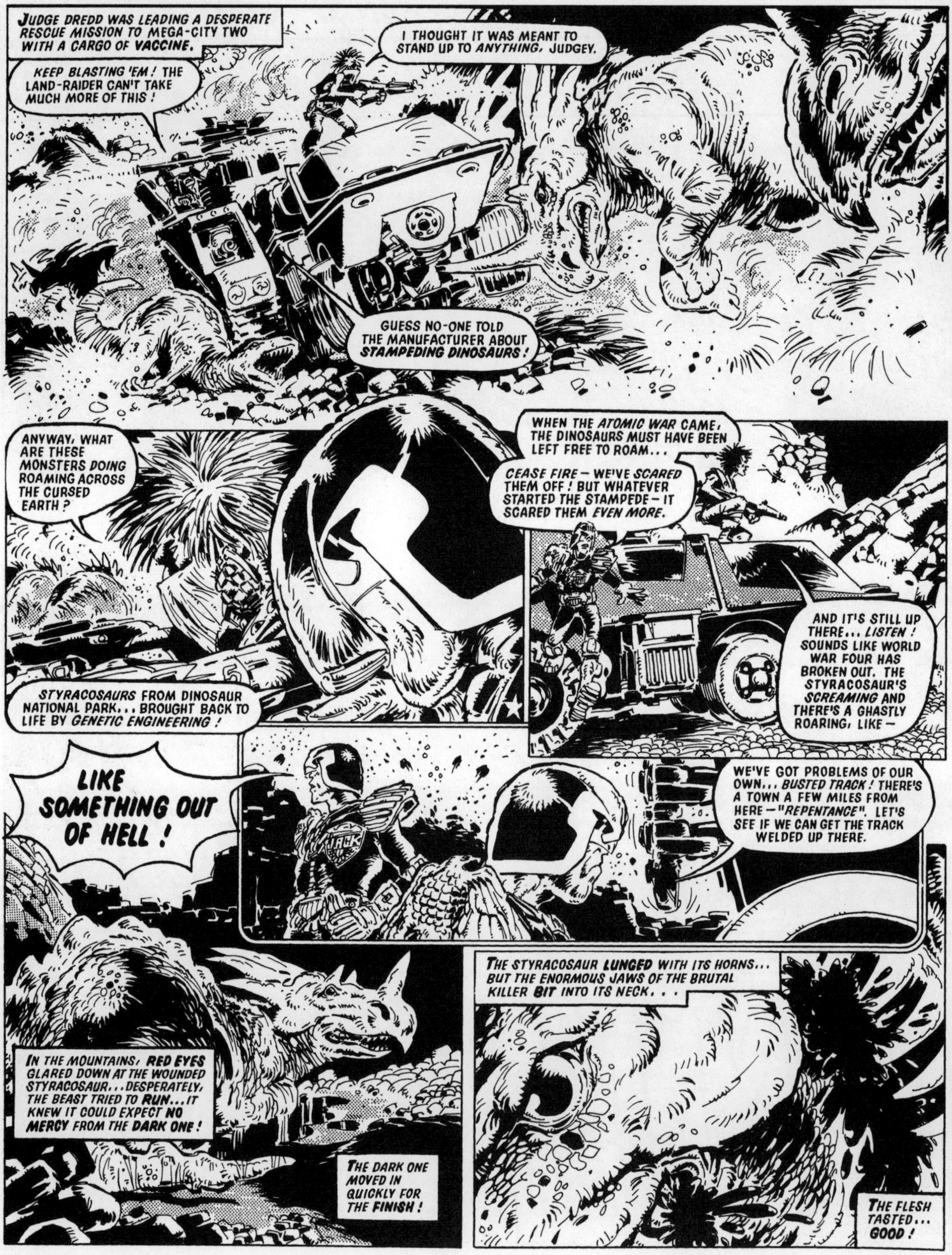

JUDGE DREDD WAS LEADING A DESPERATE RESCUE MISSION TO MEGA-CITY TWO WITH A CARGO OF VACCINE.
KEEP BLASTING 'EM! THE LAND-RAIDER CAN'T TAKE MUCH MORE OF THIS!
I THOUGHT IT WAS MEANT TO STAND UP TO ANYTHING, JUDGEY.
GUESS NO-ONE TOLD THE MANUFACTURER ABOUT STAMPEDING DINOSAURS!
ANYWAY, WHAT ARE THESE MONSTERS DOING ROAMING ACROSS THE CURSED EARTH?
STYRACOSAURS FROM DINOSAUR NATIONAL PARK... BROUGHT BACK TO LIFE BY GENETIC ENGINEERING!
WHEN THE ATOMIC WAR CAME, THE DINOSAURS MUST HAVE BEEN LEFT FREE TO ROAM...
CEASE FIRE — WE'VE SCARED THEM OFF! BUT WHATEVER STARTED THE STAMPEDE — IT SCARED THEM EVEN MORE.
AND IT'S STILL UP THERE... LISTEN! SOUNDS LIKE WORLD WAR FOUR HAS BROKEN OUT. THE STYRACOSAUR'S SCREAMING AND THERE'S A GHASTLY ROARING, LIKE —
LIKE SOMETHING OUT OF HELL!
WE'VE GOT PROBLEMS OF OUR OWN... BUSTED TRACK! THERE'S A TOWN A FEW MILES FROM HERE — "REPENTANCE". LET'S SEE IF WE CAN GET THE TRACK WELDED UP THERE.
IN THE MOUNTAINS, RED EYES GLARED DOWN AT THE WOUNDED STYRACOSAUR... DESPERATELY, THE BEAST TRIED TO RUN... IT KNEW IT COULD EXPECT NO MERCY FROM THE DARK ONE!
THE DARK ONE MOVED IN QUICKLY FOR THE FINISH!
THE STYRACOSAUR LUNGED WITH ITS HORNS... BUT THE ENORMOUS JAWS OF THE BRUTAL KILLER BIT INTO ITS NECK...
THE FLESH TASTED... GOOD!

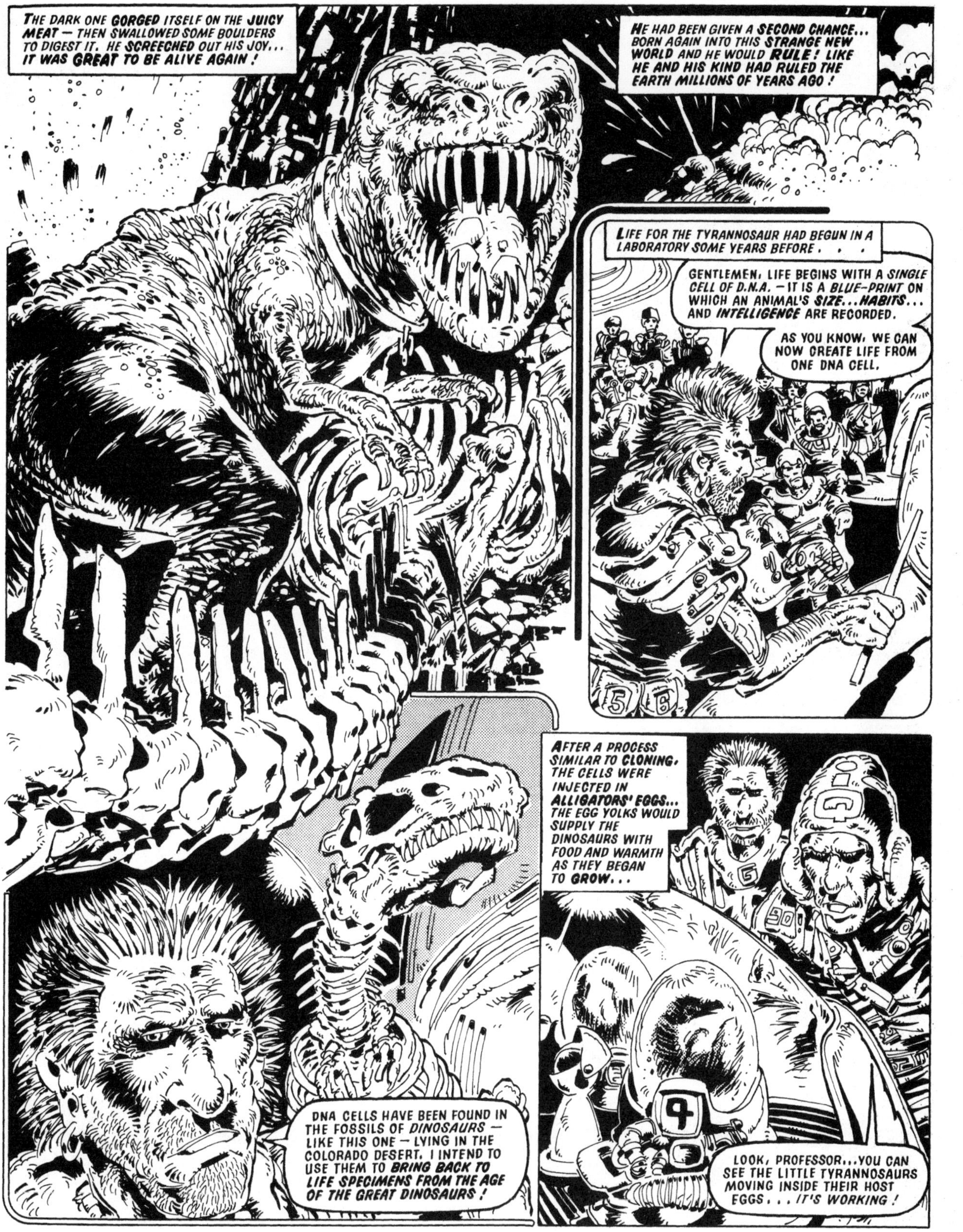

THE DARK ONE GORGED ITSELF ON THE JUICY MEAT — THEN SWALLOWED SOME BOULDERS TO DIGEST IT. HE SCREECHED OUT HIS JOY... IT WAS GREAT TO BE ALIVE AGAIN!
HE HAD BEEN GIVEN A SECOND CHANCE... BORN AGAIN INTO THIS STRANGE NEW WORLD AND HE WOULD RULE! LIKE HE AND HIS KIND HAD RULED THE EARTH MILLIONS OF YEARS AGO!
LIFE FOR THE TYRANNOSAUR HAD BEGUN IN A LABORATORY SOME YEARS BEFORE . . .
GENTLEMEN, LIFE BEGINS WITH A SINGLE CELL OF D.N.A. — IT IS A BLUE-PRINT ON WHICH AN ANIMAL'S SIZE... HABITS... AND INTELLIGENCE ARE RECORDED.
AS YOU KNOW, WE CAN NOW CREATE LIFE FROM ONE DNA CELL.
DNA CELLS HAVE BEEN FOUND IN THE FOSSILS OF DINOSAURS — LIKE THIS ONE — LYING IN THE COLORADO DESERT. I INTEND TO USE THEM TO BRING BACK TO LIFE SPECIMENS FROM THE AGE OF THE GREAT DINOSAURS!
AFTER A PROCESS SIMILAR TO CLONING, THE CELLS WERE INJECTED IN ALLIGATORS' EGGS... THE EGG YOLKS WOULD SUPPLY THE DINOSAURS WITH FOOD AND WARMTH AS THEY BEGAN TO GROW...
LOOK, PROFESSOR... YOU CAN SEE THE LITTLE TYRANNOSAURS MOVING INSIDE THEIR HOST EGGS . . . IT'S WORKING!

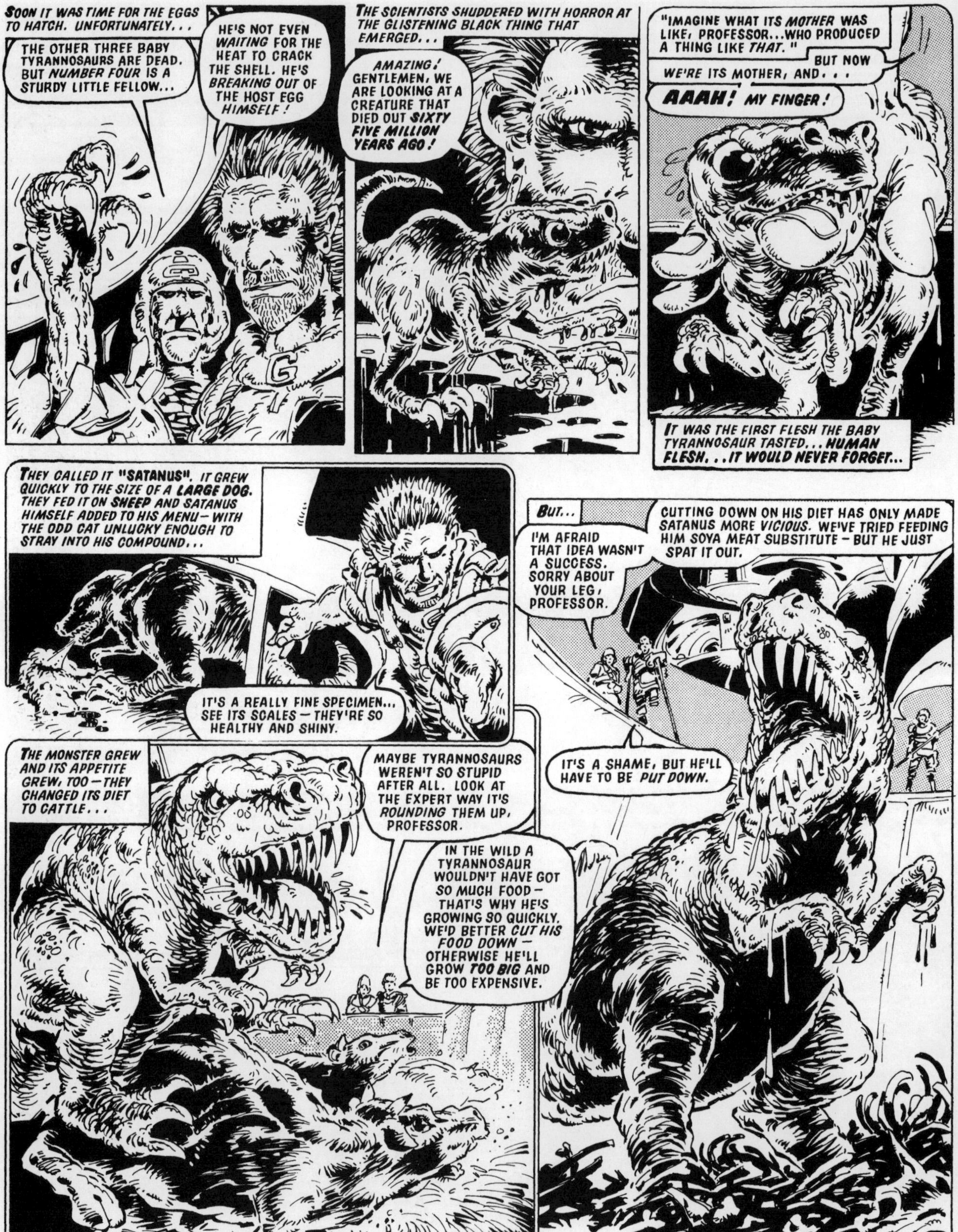

SOON IT WAS TIME FOR THE EGGS TO HATCH. UNFORTUNATELY...
THE OTHER THREE BABY TYRANNOSAURS ARE DEAD. BUT NUMBER FOUR IS A STURDY LITTLE FELLOW...
HE'S NOT EVEN WAITING FOR THE HEAT TO CRACK THE SHELL. HE'S BREAKING OUT OF THE HOST EGG HIMSELF!
THE SCIENTISTS SHUDDERED WITH HORROR AT THE GLISTENING BLACK THING THAT EMERGED...
AMAZING! GENTLEMEN, WE ARE LOOKING AT A CREATURE THAT DIED OUT SIXTY FIVE MILLION YEARS AGO!
"IMAGINE WHAT ITS MOTHER WAS LIKE, PROFESSOR...WHO PRODUCED A THING LIKE THAT."
BUT NOW WE'RE ITS MOTHER, AND...
AAAH! MY FINGER!
IT WAS THE FIRST FLESH THE BABY TYRANNOSAUR TASTED... HUMAN FLESH... IT WOULD NEVER FORGET...
THEY CALLED IT "SATANUS". IT GREW QUICKLY TO THE SIZE OF A LARGE DOG. THEY FED IT ON SHEEP AND SATANUS HIMSELF ADDED TO HIS MENU — WITH THE ODD CAT UNLUCKY ENOUGH TO STRAY INTO HIS COMPOUND...
IT'S A REALLY FINE SPECIMEN... SEE ITS SCALES — THEY'RE SO HEALTHY AND SHINY.
THE MONSTER GREW AND ITS APPETITE GREW, TOO — THEY CHANGED ITS DIET TO CATTLE...
MAYBE TYRANNOSAURS WEREN'T SO STUPID AFTER ALL. LOOK AT THE EXPERT WAY IT'S ROUNDING THEM UP, PROFESSOR.
IN THE WILD A TYRANNOSAUR WOULDN'T HAVE GOT SO MUCH FOOD — THAT'S WHY HE'S GROWING SO QUICKLY. WE'D BETTER CUT HIS FOOD DOWN — OTHERWISE HE'LL GROW TOO BIG AND BE TOO EXPENSIVE.
BUT...
I'M AFRAID THAT IDEA WASN'T A SUCCESS. SORRY ABOUT YOUR LEG, PROFESSOR.
CUTTING DOWN ON HIS DIET HAS ONLY MADE SATANUS MORE VICIOUS. WE'VE TRIED FEEDING HIM SOYA MEAT SUBSTITUTE — BUT HE JUST SPAT IT OUT.
IT'S A SHAME, BUT HE'LL HAVE TO BE PUT DOWN.

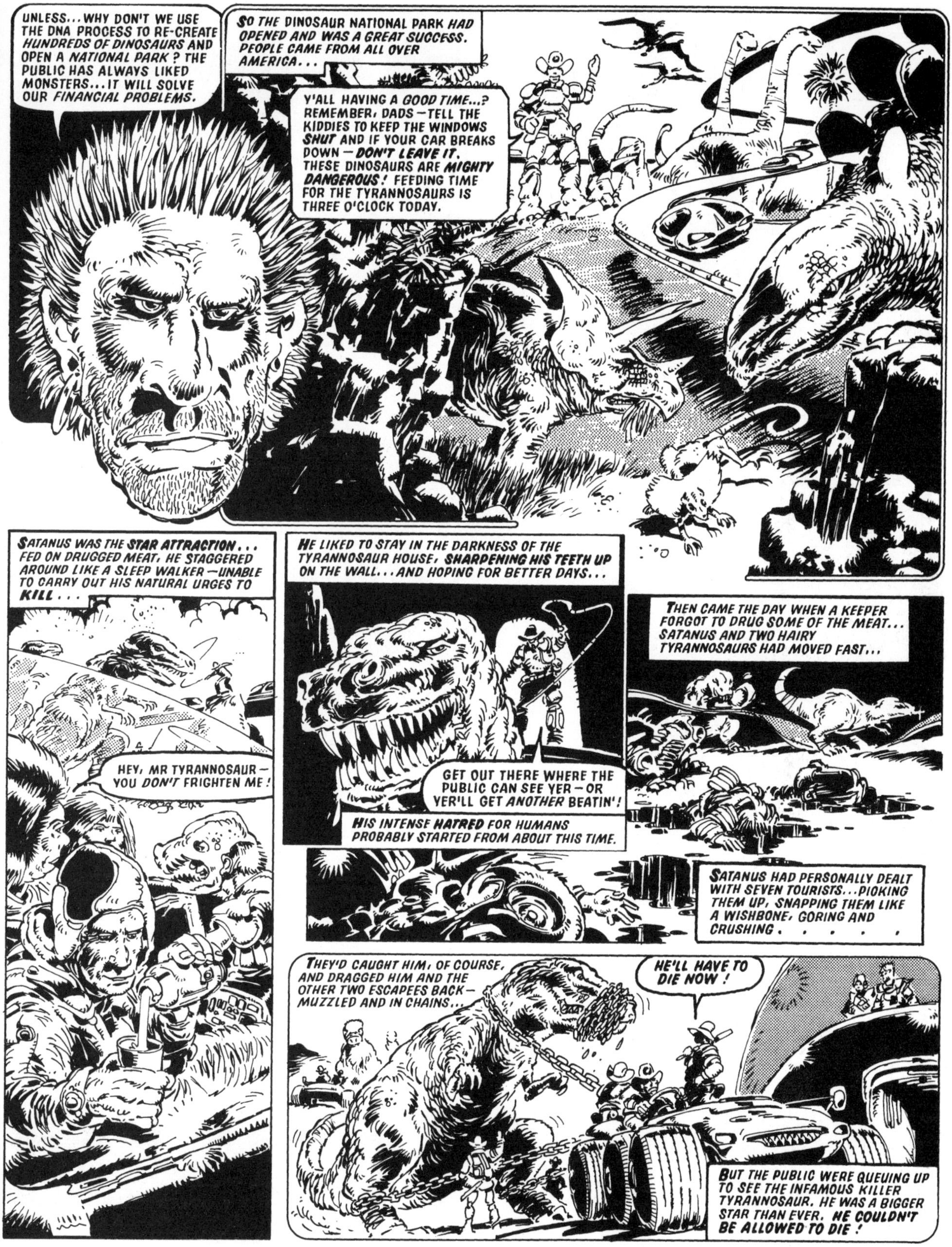

UNLESS... WHY DON'T WE USE THE DNA PROCESS TO RE-CREATE HUNDREDS OF DINOSAURS AND OPEN A NATIONAL PARK? THE PUBLIC HAS ALWAYS LIKED MONSTERS... IT WILL SOLVE OUR FINANCIAL PROBLEMS.
SO THE DINOSAUR NATIONAL PARK HAD OPENED AND WAS A GREAT SUCCESS. PEOPLE CAME FROM ALL OVER AMERICA...
Y'ALL HAVING A GOOD TIME...? REMEMBER, DADS—TELL THE KIDDIES TO KEEP THE WINDOWS SHUT AND IF YOUR CAR BREAKS DOWN—DON'T LEAVE IT. THESE DINOSAURS ARE MIGHTY DANGEROUS! FEEDING TIME FOR THE TYRANNOSAURS IS THREE O'CLOCK TODAY.
SATANUS WAS THE STAR ATTRACTION... FED ON DRUGGED MEAT, HE STAGGERED AROUND LIKE A SLEEP WALKER—UNABLE TO CARRY OUT HIS NATURAL URGES TO KILL...
HEY, MR TYRANNOSAUR—YOU DON'T FRIGHTEN ME!
HE LIKED TO STAY IN THE DARKNESS OF THE TYRANNOSAUR HOUSE, SHARPENING HIS TEETH UP ON THE WALL... AND HOPING FOR BETTER DAYS...
GET OUT THERE WHERE THE PUBLIC CAN SEE YER—OR YER'LL GET ANOTHER BEATIN'!
HIS INTENSE HATRED FOR HUMANS PROBABLY STARTED FROM ABOUT THIS TIME.
THEN CAME THE DAY WHEN A KEEPER FORGOT TO DRUG SOME OF THE MEAT... SATANUS AND TWO HAIRY TYRANNOSAURS HAD MOVED FAST...
SATANUS HAD PERSONALLY DEALT WITH SEVEN TOURISTS... PICKING THEM UP, SNAPPING THEM LIKE A WISHBONE, GORING AND CRUSHING . . . . .
THEY'D CAUGHT HIM, OF COURSE, AND DRAGGED HIM AND THE OTHER TWO ESCAPEES BACK—MUZZLED AND IN CHAINS...
HE'LL HAVE TO DIE NOW!
BUT THE PUBLIC WERE QUEUING UP TO SEE THE INFAMOUS KILLER TYRANNOSAUR. HE WAS A BIGGER STAR THAN EVER. HE COULDN'T BE ALLOWED TO DIE!

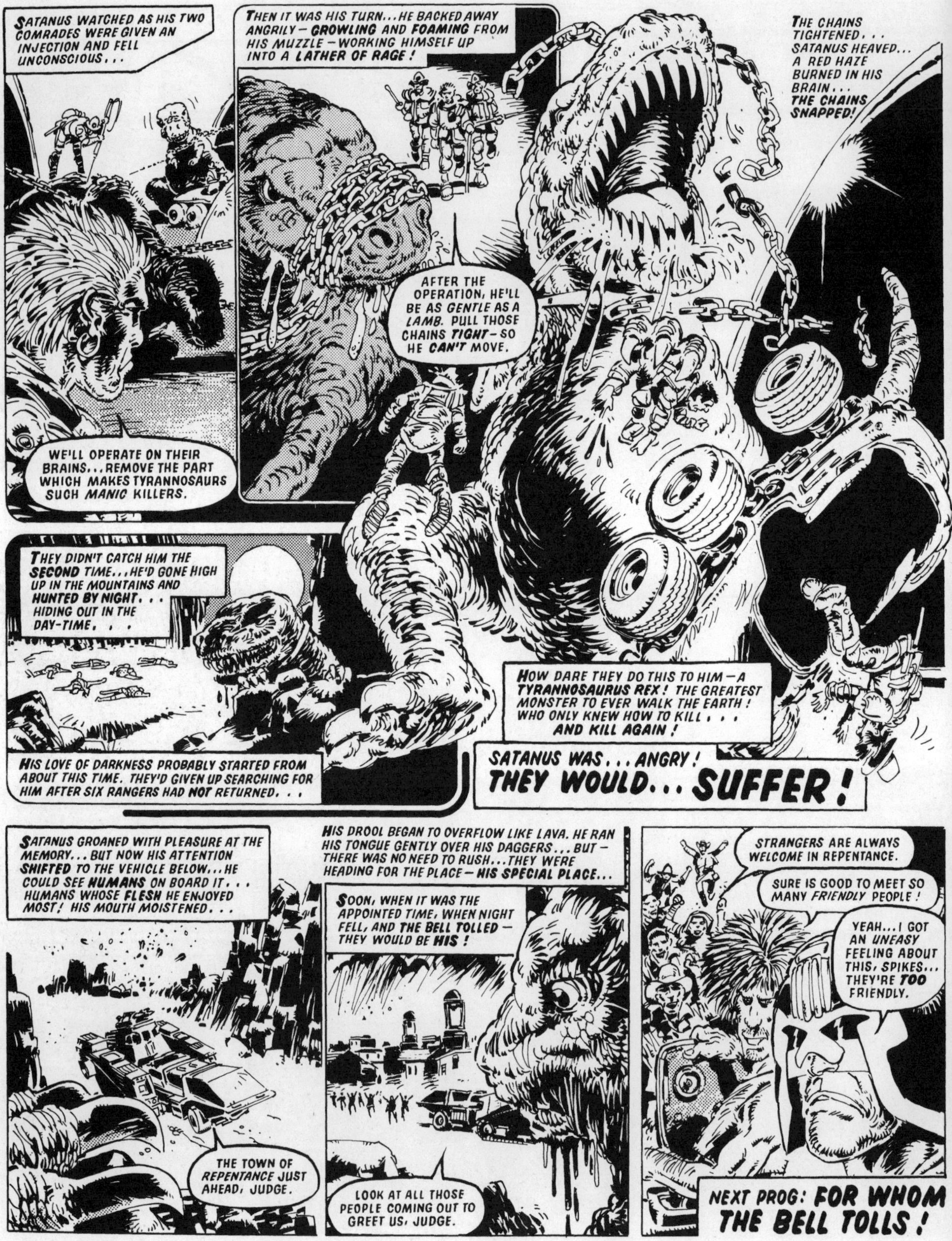
SATANUS WATCHED AS HIS TWO COMRADES WERE GIVEN AN INJECTION AND FELL UNCONSCIOUS...
WE'LL OPERATE ON THEIR BRAINS... REMOVE THE PART WHICH MAKES TYRANNOSAURS SUCH MANIC KILLERS.
THEN IT WAS HIS TURN... HE BACKED AWAY ANGRILY — GROWLING AND FOAMING FROM HIS MUZZLE — WORKING HIMSELF UP INTO A LATHER OF RAGE!
AFTER THE OPERATION, HE'LL BE AS GENTLE AS A LAMB. PULL THOSE CHAINS TIGHT — SO HE CAN'T MOVE.
THE CHAINS TIGHTENED... SATANUS HEAVED... A RED HAZE BURNED IN HIS BRAIN... THE CHAINS SNAPPED!
HOW DARE THEY DO THIS TO HIM — A TYRANNOSAURUS REX! THE GREATEST MONSTER TO EVER WALK THE EARTH! WHO ONLY KNEW HOW TO KILL... AND KILL AGAIN!
SATANUS WAS... ANGRY! THEY WOULD... SUFFER!
THEY DIDN'T CATCH HIM THE SECOND TIME... HE'D GONE HIGH UP IN THE MOUNTAINS AND HUNTED BY NIGHT... HIDING OUT IN THE DAY-TIME...
HIS LOVE OF DARKNESS PROBABLY STARTED FROM ABOUT THIS TIME. THEY'D GIVEN UP SEARCHING FOR HIM AFTER SIX RANGERS HAD NOT RETURNED...
SATANUS GROANED WITH PLEASURE AT THE MEMORY... BUT NOW HIS ATTENTION SHIFTED TO THE VEHICLE BELOW... HE COULD SEE HUMANS ON BOARD IT... HUMANS WHOSE FLESH HE ENJOYED MOST! HIS MOUTH MOISTENED...
THE TOWN OF REPENTANCE JUST AHEAD, JUDGE.
HIS DROOL BEGAN TO OVERFLOW LIKE LAVA. HE RAN HIS TONGUE GENTLY OVER HIS DAGGERS... BUT — THERE WAS NO NEED TO RUSH... THEY WERE HEADING FOR THE PLACE — HIS SPECIAL PLACE...
SOON, WHEN IT WAS THE APPOINTED TIME, WHEN NIGHT FELL, AND THE BELL TOLLED — THEY WOULD BE HIS!
LOOK AT ALL THOSE PEOPLE COMING OUT TO GREET US, JUDGE.
STRANGERS ARE ALWAYS WELCOME IN REPENTANCE.
SURE IS GOOD TO MEET SO MANY FRIENDLY PEOPLE!
YEAH... I GOT AN UNEASY FEELING ABOUT THIS, SPIKES... THEY'RE TOO FRIENDLY.
NEXT PROG: FOR WHOM THE BELL TOLLS!

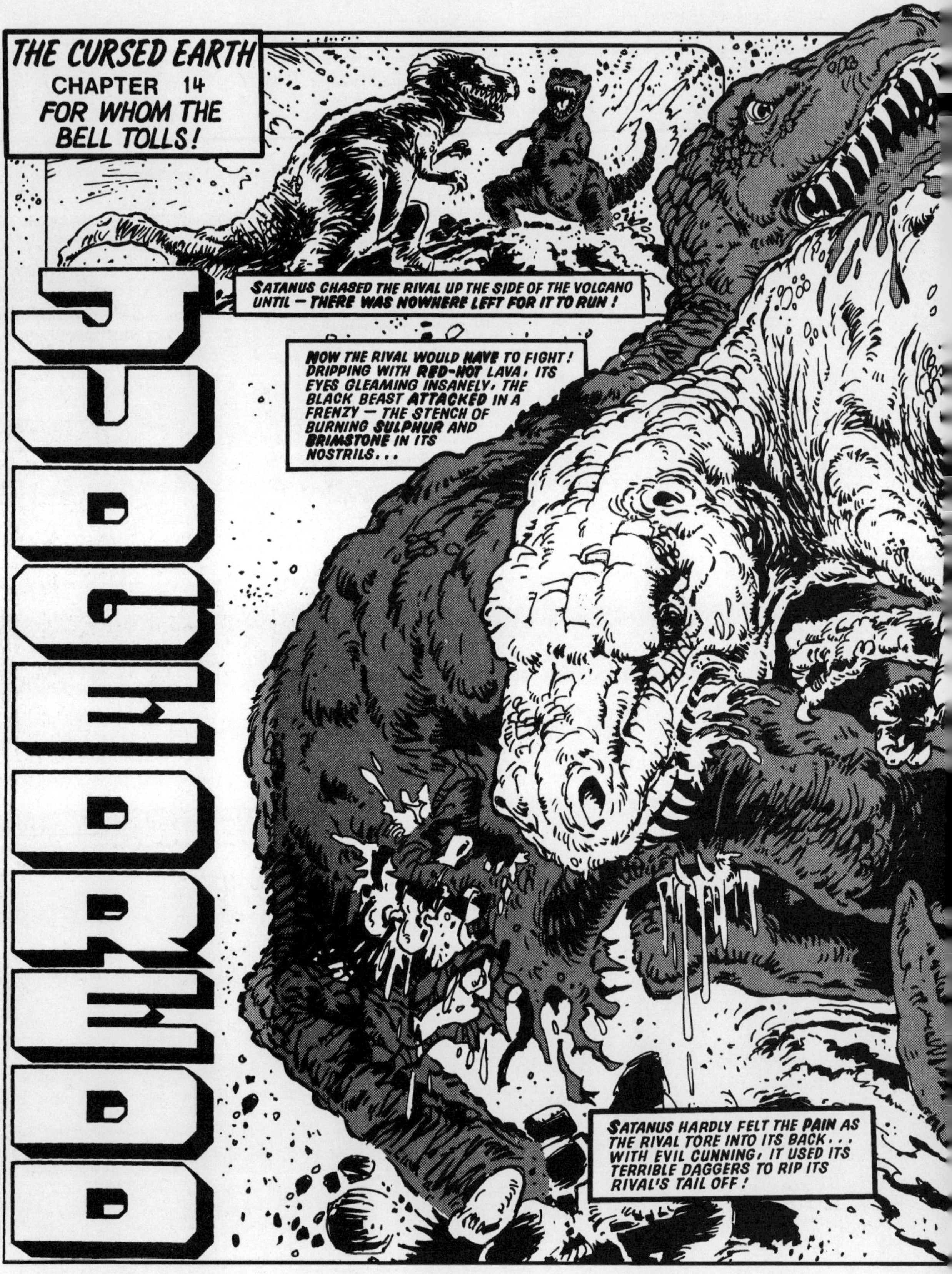
THE CURSED EARTH
CHAPTER 14
FOR WHOM THE BELL TOLLS!
JUDGE DREDD
SATANUS CHASED THE RIVAL UP THE SIDE OF THE VOLCANO UNTIL — THERE WAS NOWHERE LEFT FOR IT TO RUN!
NOW THE RIVAL WOULD HAVE TO FIGHT! DRIPPING WITH RED-HOT LAVA, ITS EYES GLEAMING INSANELY, THE BLACK BEAST ATTACKED IN A FRENZY — THE STENCH OF BURNING SULPHUR AND BRIMSTONE IN ITS NOSTRILS...
SATANUS HARDLY FELT THE PAIN AS THE RIVAL TORE INTO ITS BACK... WITH EVIL CUNNING, IT USED ITS TERRIBLE DAGGERS TO RIP ITS RIVAL'S TAIL OFF!

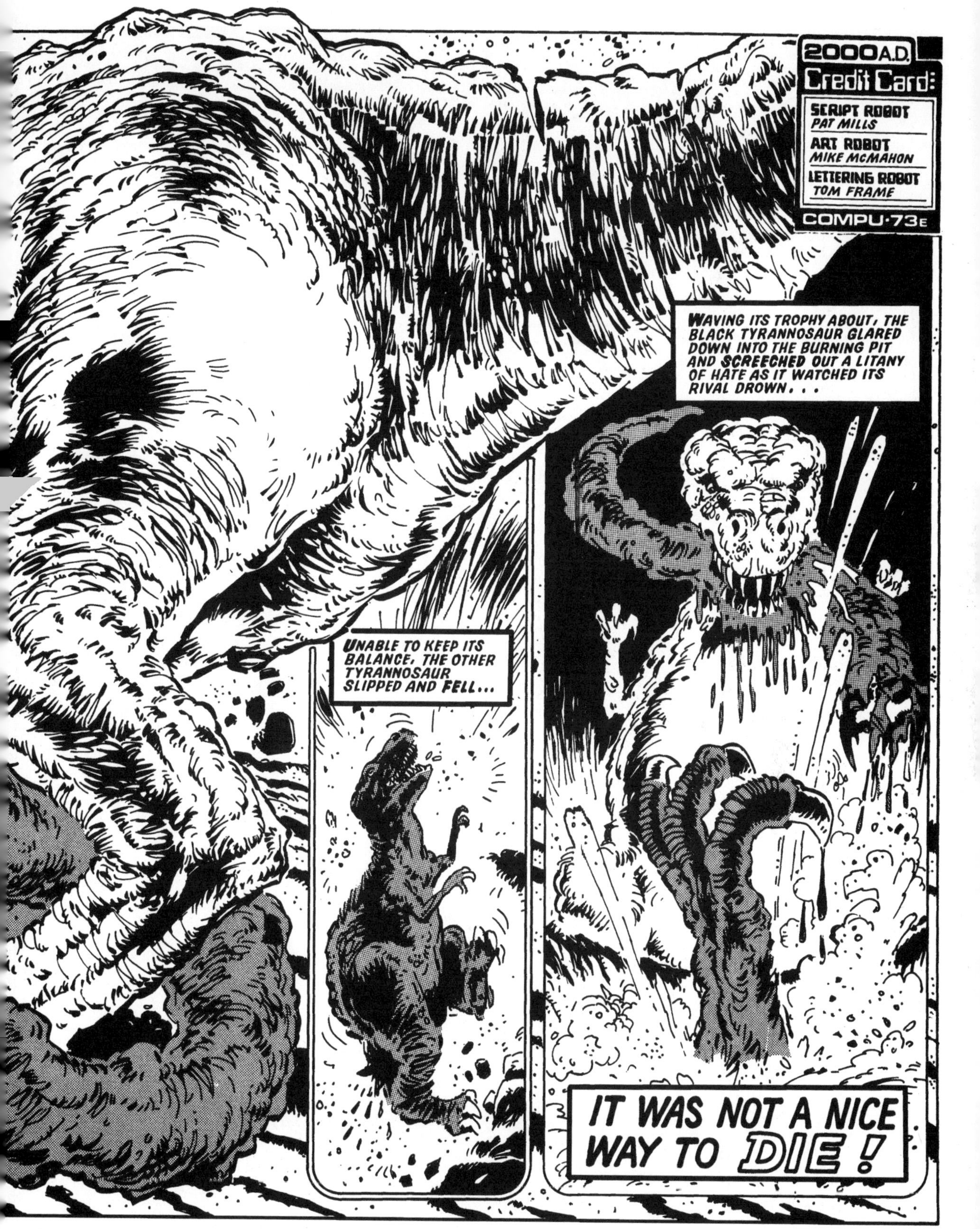
2000 A.D.
Credit Card:
SCRIPT ROBOT PAT MILLS
ART ROBOT MIKE McMAHON
LETTERING ROBOT TOM FRAME
COMPU·73E
WAVING ITS TROPHY ABOUT, THE BLACK TYRANNOSAUR GLARED DOWN INTO THE BURNING PIT AND SCREECHED OUT A LITANY OF HATE AS IT WATCHED ITS RIVAL DROWN. . .
UNABLE TO KEEP ITS BALANCE, THE OTHER TYRANNOSAUR SLIPPED AND FELL...
IT WAS NOT A NICE WAY TO DIE!

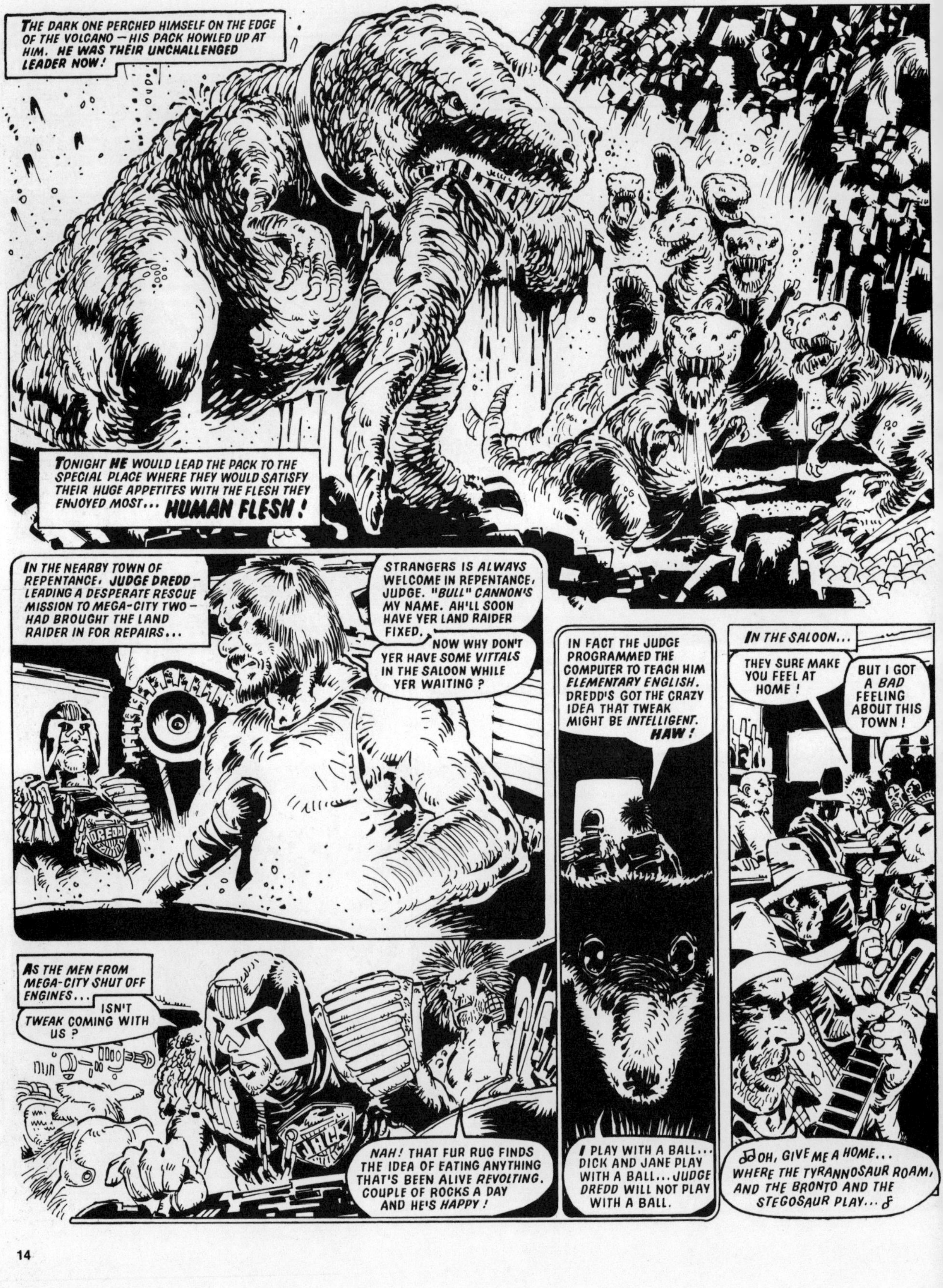
THE DARK ONE PERCHED HIMSELF ON THE EDGE OF THE VOLCANO — HIS PACK HOWLED UP AT HIM. HE WAS THEIR UNCHALLENGED LEADER NOW!
TONIGHT HE WOULD LEAD THE PACK TO THE SPECIAL PLACE WHERE THEY WOULD SATISFY THEIR HUGE APPETITES WITH THE FLESH THEY ENJOYED MOST... HUMAN FLESH!
IN THE NEARBY TOWN OF REPENTANCE, JUDGE DREDD — LEADING A DESPERATE RESCUE MISSION TO MEGA-CITY TWO — HAD BROUGHT THE LAND RAIDER IN FOR REPAIRS...
STRANGERS IS ALWAYS WELCOME IN REPENTANCE, JUDGE. "BULL" CANNON'S MY NAME. AH'LL SOON HAVE YER LAND RAIDER FIXED.
NOW WHY DON'T YER HAVE SOME VITTALS IN THE SALOON WHILE YER WAITING?
DREDD
AS THE MEN FROM MEGA-CITY SHUT OFF ENGINES...
ISN'T TWEAK COMING WITH US?
NAH! THAT FUR RUG FINDS THE IDEA OF EATING ANYTHING THAT'S BEEN ALIVE REVOLTING. COUPLE OF ROCKS A DAY AND HE'S HAPPY!
IN FACT THE JUDGE PROGRAMMED THE COMPUTER TO TEACH HIM ELEMENTARY ENGLISH. DREDD'S GOT THE CRAZY IDEA THAT TWEAK MIGHT BE INTELLIGENT. HAW!
I PLAY WITH A BALL... DICK AND JANE PLAY WITH A BALL... JUDGE DREDD WILL NOT PLAY WITH A BALL.
IN THE SALOON...
THEY SURE MAKE YOU FEEL AT HOME!
BUT I GOT A BAD FEELING ABOUT THIS TOWN!
OH, GIVE ME A HOME... WHERE THE TYRANNOSAUR ROAM, AND THE BRONTO AND THE STEGOSAUR PLAY...

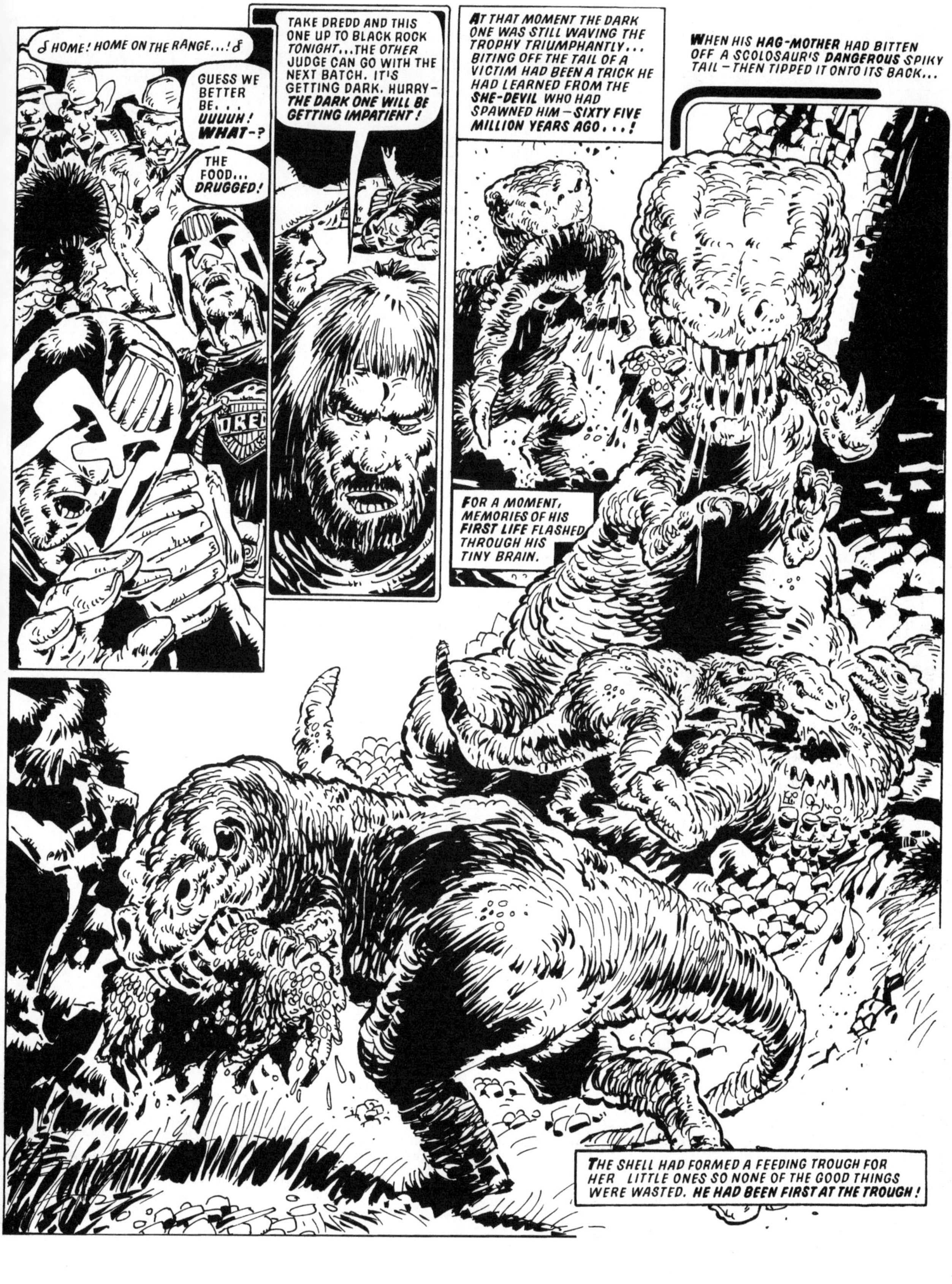

♪ HOME! HOME ON THE RANGE...! ♪
GUESS WE BETTER BE... **UUUUH! WHAT-?**
THE FOOD... **DRUGGED!**
TAKE DREDD AND THIS ONE UP TO BLACK ROCK TONIGHT...THE OTHER JUDGE CAN GO WITH THE NEXT BATCH. IT'S GETTING DARK. HURRY- **THE DARK ONE WILL BE GETTING IMPATIENT!**
AT THAT MOMENT THE DARK ONE WAS STILL WAVING THE TROPHY TRIUMPHANTLY... BITING OFF THE TAIL OF A VICTIM HAD BEEN A TRICK HE HAD LEARNED FROM THE **SHE-DEVIL** WHO HAD SPAWNED HIM — **SIXTY FIVE MILLION YEARS AGO...!**
FOR A MOMENT, MEMORIES OF HIS **FIRST LIFE** FLASHED THROUGH HIS TINY BRAIN.
WHEN HIS **HAG-MOTHER** HAD BITTEN OFF A SCOLOSAUR'S **DANGEROUS** SPIKY TAIL — THEN TIPPED IT ONTO ITS BACK...
THE SHELL HAD FORMED A FEEDING TROUGH FOR HER LITTLE ONES SO NONE OF THE GOOD THINGS WERE WASTED. **HE HAD BEEN FIRST AT THE TROUGH!**

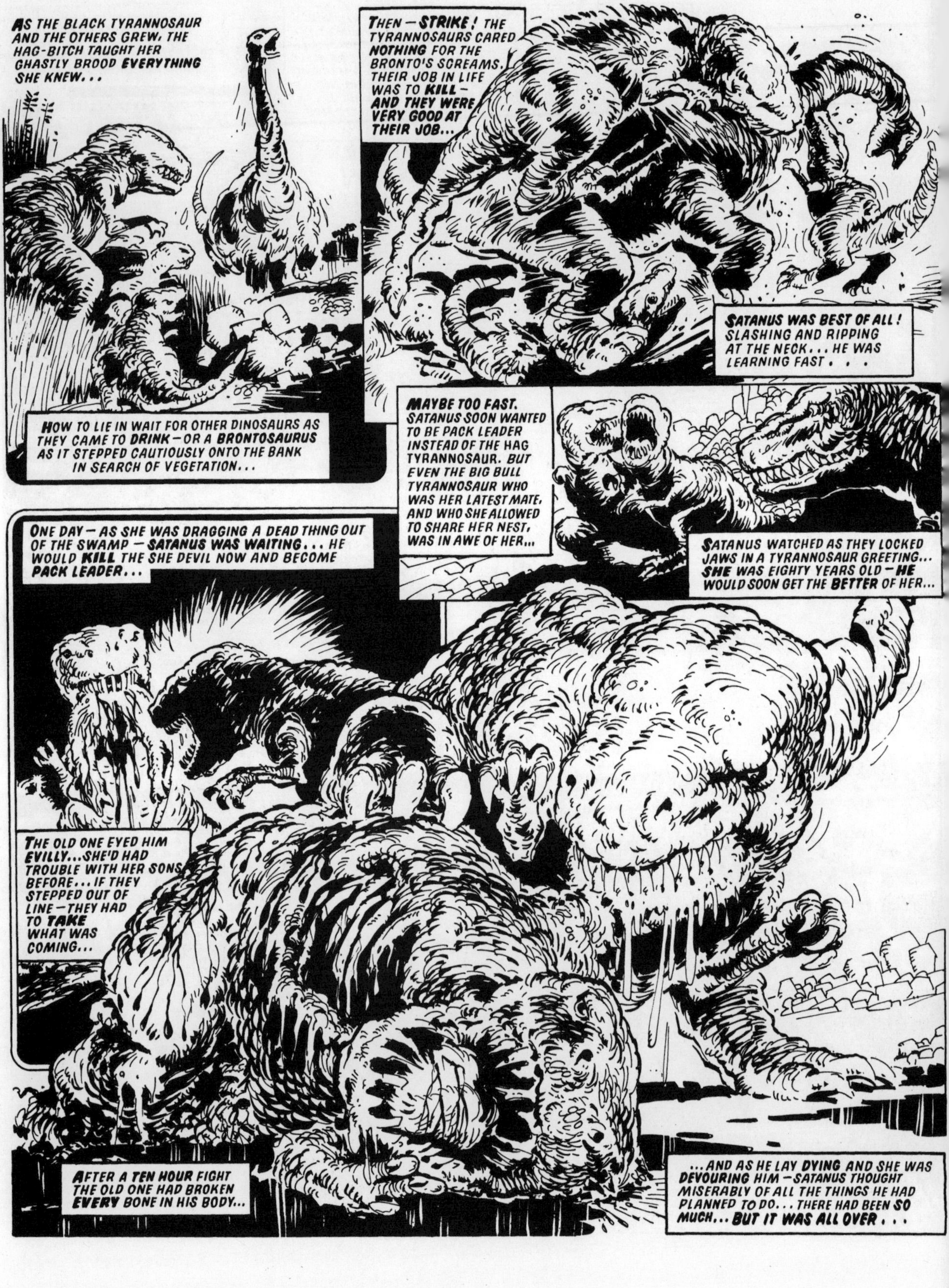
AS THE BLACK TYRANNOSAUR AND THE OTHERS GREW, THE HAG-BITCH TAUGHT HER GHASTLY BROOD EVERYTHING SHE KNEW...
HOW TO LIE IN WAIT FOR OTHER DINOSAURS AS THEY CAME TO DRINK—OR A BRONTOSAURUS AS IT STEPPED CAUTIOUSLY ONTO THE BANK IN SEARCH OF VEGETATION...
THEN—STRIKE! THE TYRANNOSAURS CARED NOTHING FOR THE BRONTO'S SCREAMS. THEIR JOB IN LIFE WAS TO KILL—AND THEY WERE VERY GOOD AT THEIR JOB...
SATANUS WAS BEST OF ALL! SLASHING AND RIPPING AT THE NECK... HE WAS LEARNING FAST...
MAYBE TOO FAST. SATANUS SOON WANTED TO BE PACK LEADER INSTEAD OF THE HAG TYRANNOSAUR. BUT EVEN THE BIG BULL TYRANNOSAUR WHO WAS HER LATEST MATE, AND WHO SHE ALLOWED TO SHARE HER NEST, WAS IN AWE OF HER...
SATANUS WATCHED AS THEY LOCKED JAWS IN A TYRANNOSAUR GREETING... SHE WAS EIGHTY YEARS OLD—HE WOULD SOON GET THE BETTER OF HER...
ONE DAY—AS SHE WAS DRAGGING A DEAD THING OUT OF THE SWAMP—SATANUS WAS WAITING... HE WOULD KILL THE SHE DEVIL NOW AND BECOME PACK LEADER...
THE OLD ONE EYED HIM EVILLY... SHE'D HAD TROUBLE WITH HER SONS BEFORE... IF THEY STEPPED OUT OF LINE—THEY HAD TO TAKE WHAT WAS COMING...
AFTER A TEN HOUR FIGHT THE OLD ONE HAD BROKEN EVERY BONE IN HIS BODY...
...AND AS HE LAY DYING AND SHE WAS DEVOURING HIM—SATANUS THOUGHT MISERABLY OF ALL THE THINGS HE HAD PLANNED TO DO... THERE HAD BEEN SO MUCH... BUT IT WAS ALL OVER...

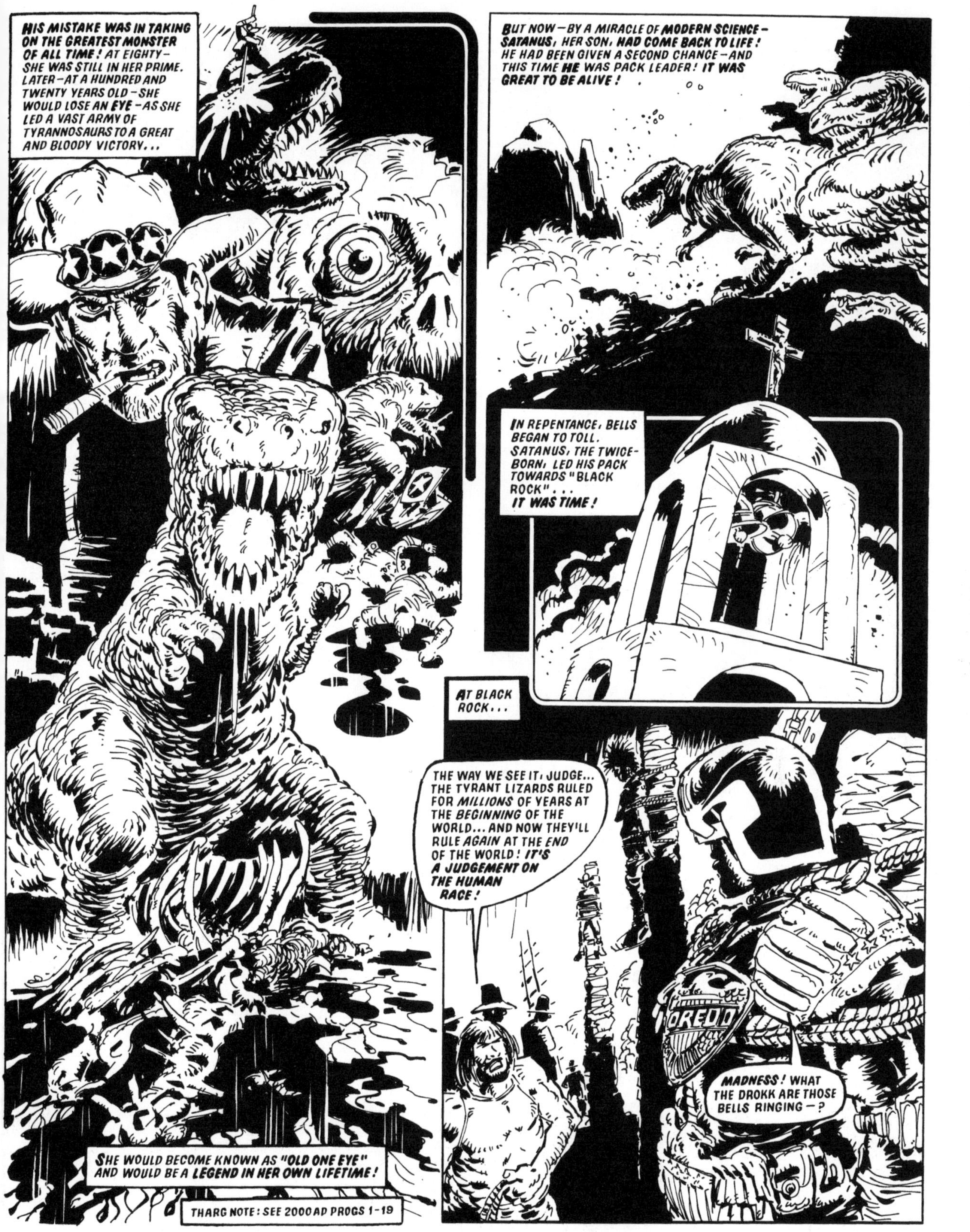
HIS MISTAKE WAS IN TAKING ON THE GREATEST MONSTER OF ALL TIME! AT EIGHTY– SHE WAS STILL IN HER PRIME. LATER–AT A HUNDRED AND TWENTY YEARS OLD–SHE WOULD LOSE AN EYE–AS SHE LED A VAST ARMY OF TYRANNOSAURS TO A GREAT AND BLOODY VICTORY...
SHE WOULD BECOME KNOWN AS "OLD ONE EYE" AND WOULD BE A LEGEND IN HER OWN LIFETIME!
THARG NOTE: SEE 2000 AD PROGS 1-19
BUT NOW–BY A MIRACLE OF MODERN SCIENCE– SATANUS, HER SON, HAD COME BACK TO LIFE! HE HAD BEEN GIVEN A SECOND CHANCE–AND THIS TIME HE WAS PACK LEADER! IT WAS GREAT TO BE ALIVE!
IN REPENTANCE, BELLS BEGAN TO TOLL. SATANUS, THE TWICE-BORN, LED HIS PACK TOWARDS "BLACK ROCK"... IT WAS TIME!
AT BLACK ROCK...
THE WAY WE SEE IT, JUDGE... THE TYRANT LIZARDS RULED FOR MILLIONS OF YEARS AT THE BEGINNING OF THE WORLD... AND NOW THEY'LL RULE AGAIN AT THE END OF THE WORLD! IT'S A JUDGEMENT ON THE HUMAN RACE!
DREDD
MADNESS! WHAT THE DROKK ARE THOSE BELLS RINGING–?

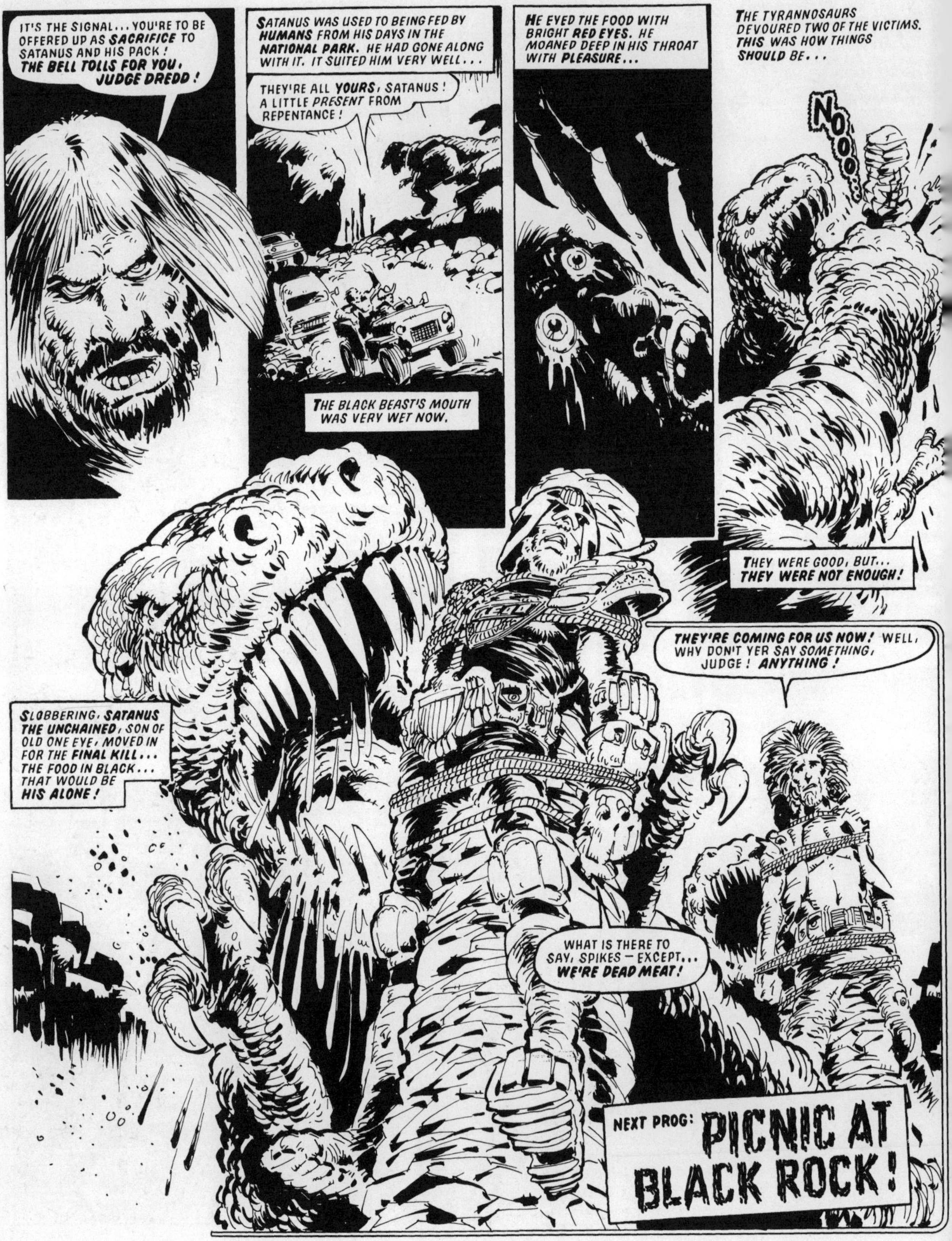

IT'S THE SIGNAL... YOU'RE TO BE OFFERED UP AS SACRIFICE TO SATANUS AND HIS PACK! THE BELL TOLLS FOR YOU, JUDGE DREDD!
SATANUS WAS USED TO BEING FED BY HUMANS FROM HIS DAYS IN THE NATIONAL PARK. HE HAD GONE ALONG WITH IT. IT SUITED HIM VERY WELL...
THEY'RE ALL YOURS, SATANUS! A LITTLE PRESENT FROM REPENTANCE!
THE BLACK BEAST'S MOUTH WAS VERY WET NOW.
HE EYED THE FOOD WITH BRIGHT RED EYES. HE MOANED DEEP IN HIS THROAT WITH PLEASURE...
THE TYRANNOSAURS DEVOURED TWO OF THE VICTIMS. THIS WAS HOW THINGS SHOULD BE...
NOOO...
THEY WERE GOOD, BUT... THEY WERE NOT ENOUGH!
SLOBBERING, SATANUS THE UNCHAINED, SON OF OLD ONE EYE, MOVED IN FOR THE FINAL KILL... THE FOOD IN BLACK... THAT WOULD BE HIS ALONE!
THEY'RE COMING FOR US NOW! WELL, WHY DON'T YER SAY SOMETHING, JUDGE! ANYTHING!
WHAT IS THERE TO SAY, SPIKES — EXCEPT... WE'RE DEAD MEAT!
NEXT PROG: PICNIC AT BLACK ROCK!

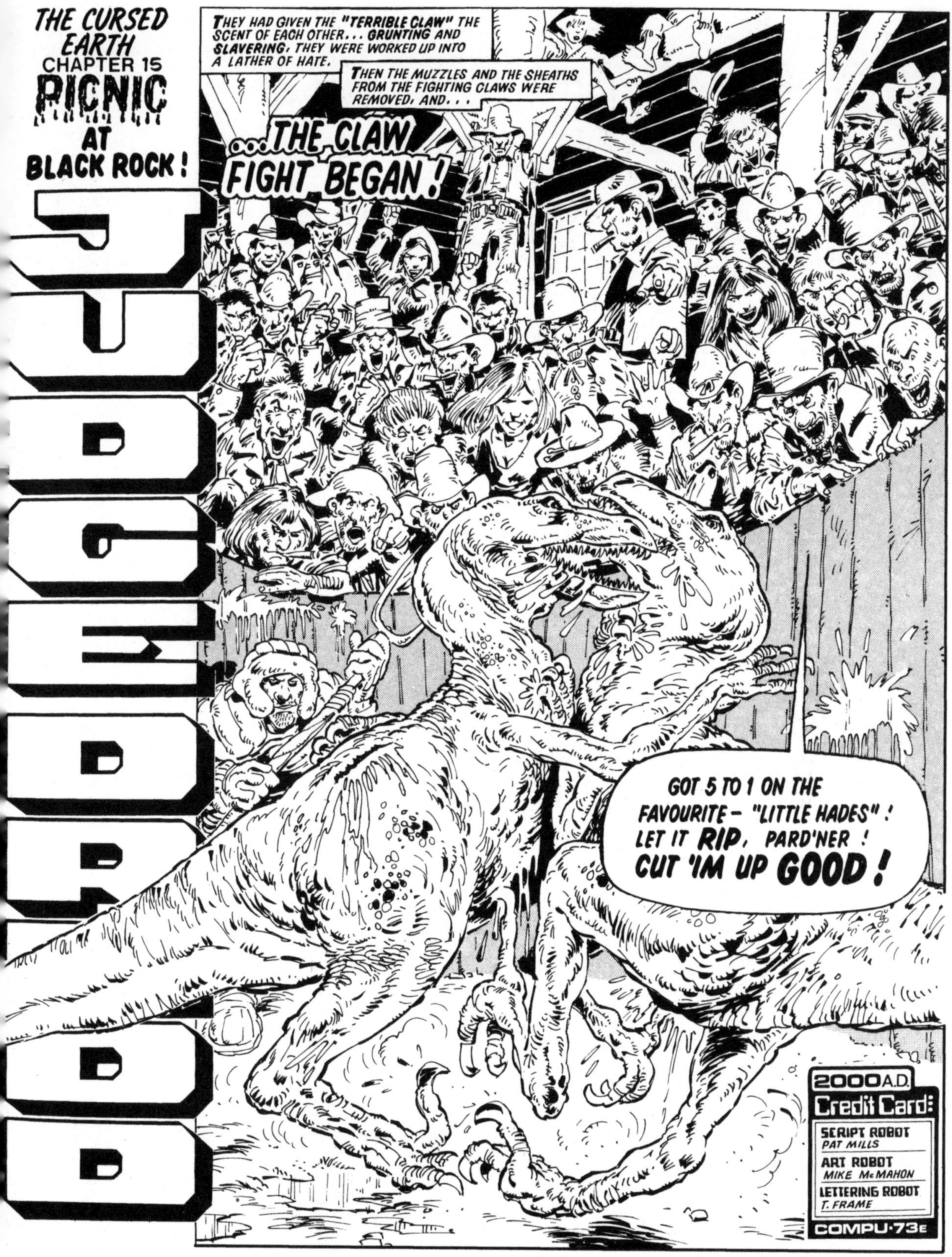
THE CURSED EARTH
CHAPTER 15
PICNIC AT BLACK ROCK!
JUDGE DREDD
THEY HAD GIVEN THE "TERRIBLE CLAW" THE SCENT OF EACH OTHER... GRUNTING AND SLAVERING, THEY WERE WORKED UP INTO A LATHER OF HATE.
THEN THE MUZZLES AND THE SHEATHS FROM THE FIGHTING CLAWS WERE REMOVED, AND...
...THE CLAW FIGHT BEGAN!
GOT 5 TO 1 ON THE FAVOURITE – "LITTLE HADES"! LET IT RIP, PARD'NER! CUT 'IM UP GOOD!
2000 A.D. Credit Card:
SCRIPT ROBOT PAT MILLS
ART ROBOT MIKE McMAHON
LETTERING ROBOT T. FRAME
COMPU-73E

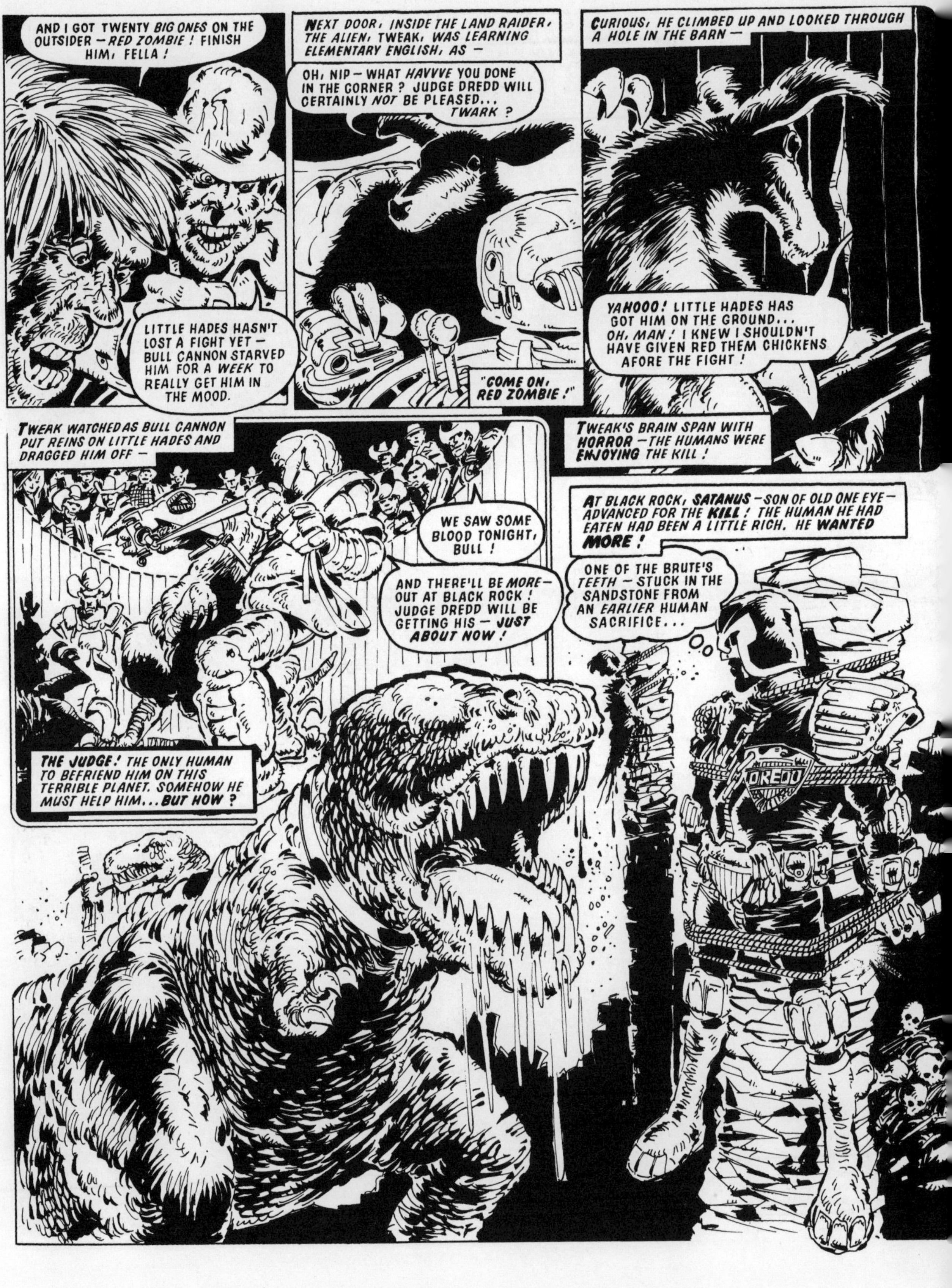
AND I GOT TWENTY BIG ONES ON THE OUTSIDER — RED ZOMBIE ! FINISH HIM, FELLA !
LITTLE HADES HASN'T LOST A FIGHT YET — BULL CANNON STARVED HIM FOR A WEEK TO REALLY GET HIM IN THE MOOD.
NEXT DOOR, INSIDE THE LAND RAIDER, THE ALIEN, TWEAK, WAS LEARNING ELEMENTARY ENGLISH, AS —
OH, NIP — WHAT HAVVVE YOU DONE IN THE CORNER ? JUDGE DREDD WILL CERTAINLY NOT BE PLEASED... TWARK ?
"COME ON, RED ZOMBIE !"
CURIOUS, HE CLIMBED UP AND LOOKED THROUGH A HOLE IN THE BARN —
YAHOOO ! LITTLE HADES HAS GOT HIM ON THE GROUND... OH, MAN ! I KNEW I SHOULDN'T HAVE GIVEN RED THEM CHICKENS AFORE THE FIGHT !
TWEAK'S BRAIN SPAN WITH HORROR — THE HUMANS WERE ENJOYING THE KILL !
TWEAK WATCHED AS BULL CANNON PUT REINS ON LITTLE HADES AND DRAGGED HIM OFF —
WE SAW SOME BLOOD TONIGHT, BULL !
AND THERE'LL BE MORE — OUT AT BLACK ROCK ! JUDGE DREDD WILL BE GETTING HIS — JUST ABOUT NOW !
THE JUDGE ! THE ONLY HUMAN TO BEFRIEND HIM ON THIS TERRIBLE PLANET. SOMEHOW HE MUST HELP HIM... BUT HOW ?
AT BLACK ROCK, SATANUS — SON OF OLD ONE EYE — ADVANCED FOR THE KILL ! THE HUMAN HE HAD EATEN HAD BEEN A LITTLE RICH. HE WANTED MORE !
ONE OF THE BRUTE'S TEETH — STUCK IN THE SANDSTONE FROM AN EARLIER HUMAN SACRIFICE...
DREDD

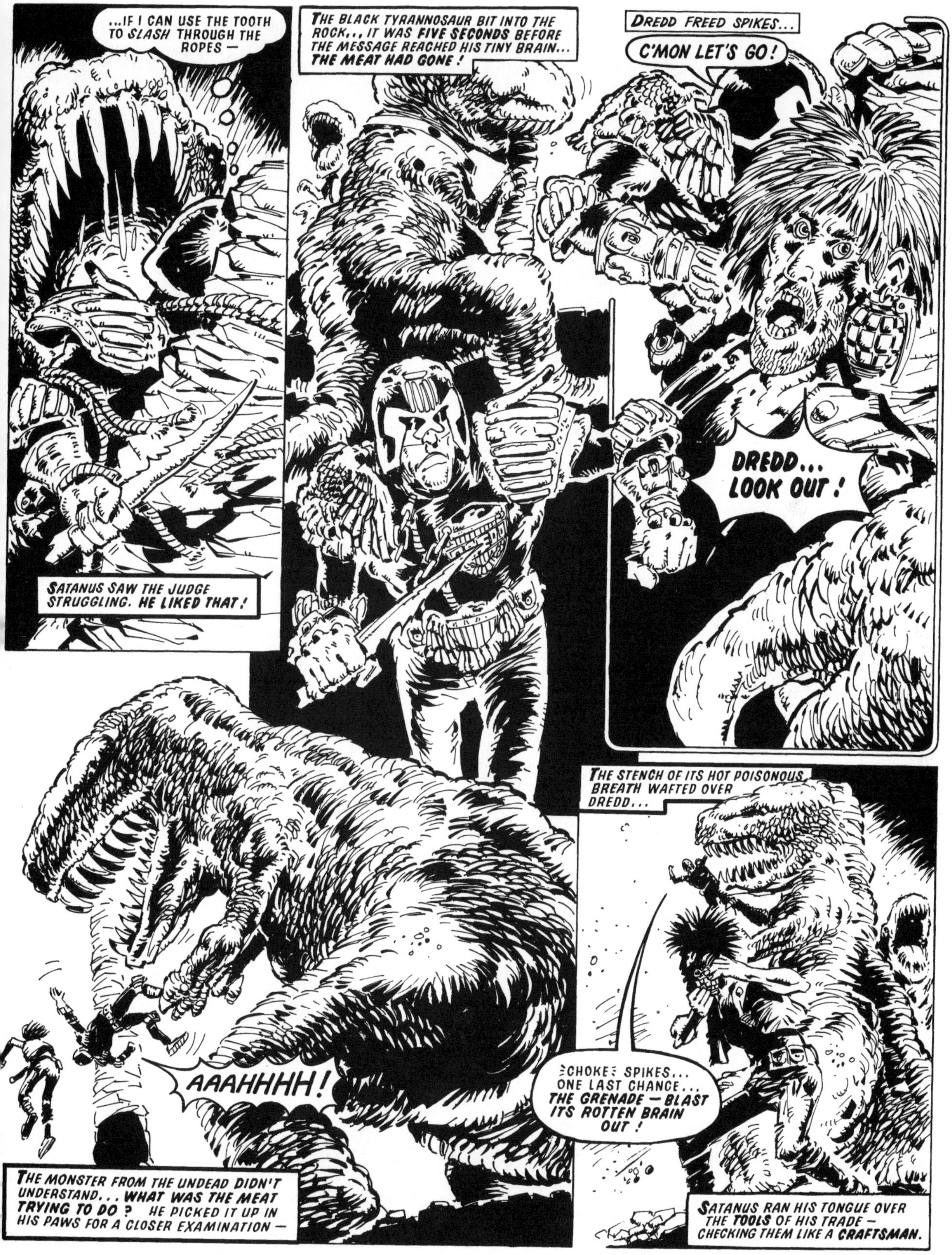
...IF I CAN USE THE TOOTH TO SLASH THROUGH THE ROPES —
SATANUS SAW THE JUDGE STRUGGLING. HE LIKED THAT!
THE BLACK TYRANNOSAUR BIT INTO THE ROCK... IT WAS FIVE SECONDS BEFORE THE MESSAGE REACHED HIS TINY BRAIN... THE MEAT HAD GONE!
DREDD FREED SPIKES...
C'MON LET'S GO!
DREDD... LOOK OUT!
AAAHHHH!
THE MONSTER FROM THE UNDEAD DIDN'T UNDERSTAND... WHAT WAS THE MEAT TRYING TO DO? HE PICKED IT UP IN HIS PAWS FOR A CLOSER EXAMINATION —
THE STENCH OF ITS HOT POISONOUS BREATH WAFTED OVER DREDD...
CHOKE SPIKES... ONE LAST CHANCE... THE GRENADE — BLAST ITS ROTTEN BRAIN OUT!
SATANUS RAN HIS TONGUE OVER THE TOOLS OF HIS TRADE — CHECKING THEM LIKE A CRAFTSMAN.

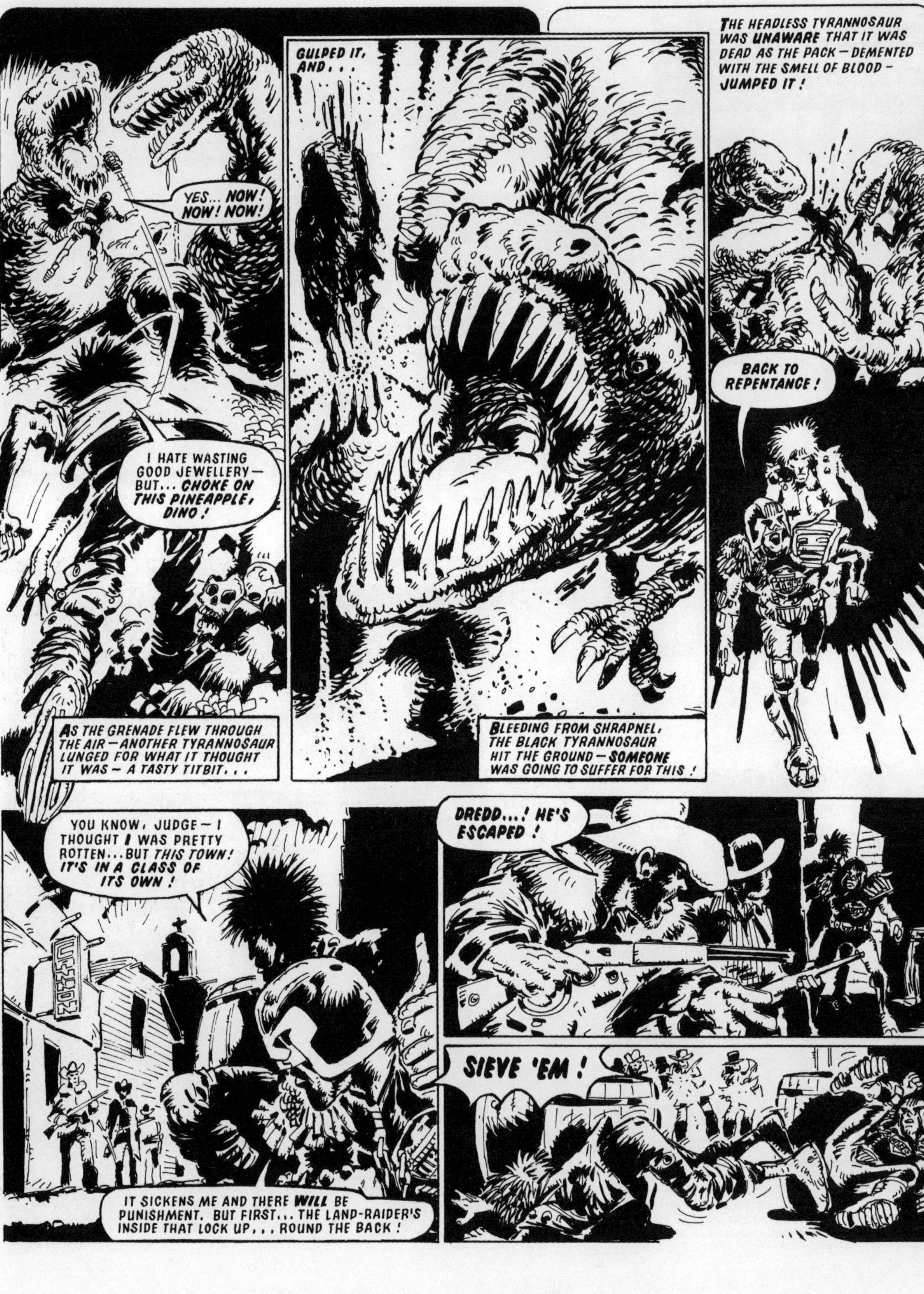
YES... NOW! NOW! NOW!
I HATE WASTING GOOD JEWELLERY— BUT... CHOKE ON THIS PINEAPPLE, DINO!
AS THE GRENADE FLEW THROUGH THE AIR — ANOTHER TYRANNOSAUR LUNGED FOR WHAT IT THOUGHT IT WAS — A TASTY TITBIT...
GULPED IT, AND...
BLEEDING FROM SHRAPNEL, THE BLACK TYRANNOSAUR HIT THE GROUND — SOMEONE WAS GOING TO SUFFER FOR THIS!
THE HEADLESS TYRANNOSAUR WAS UNAWARE THAT IT WAS DEAD AS THE PACK — DEMENTED WITH THE SMELL OF BLOOD — JUMPED IT!
BACK TO REPENTANCE!
YOU KNOW, JUDGE — I THOUGHT I WAS PRETTY ROTTEN... BUT THIS TOWN! IT'S IN A CLASS OF ITS OWN!
IT SICKENS ME AND THERE WILL BE PUNISHMENT. BUT FIRST... THE LAND-RAIDER'S INSIDE THAT LOCK UP... ROUND THE BACK!
DREDD...! HE'S ESCAPED!
SIEVE 'EM!

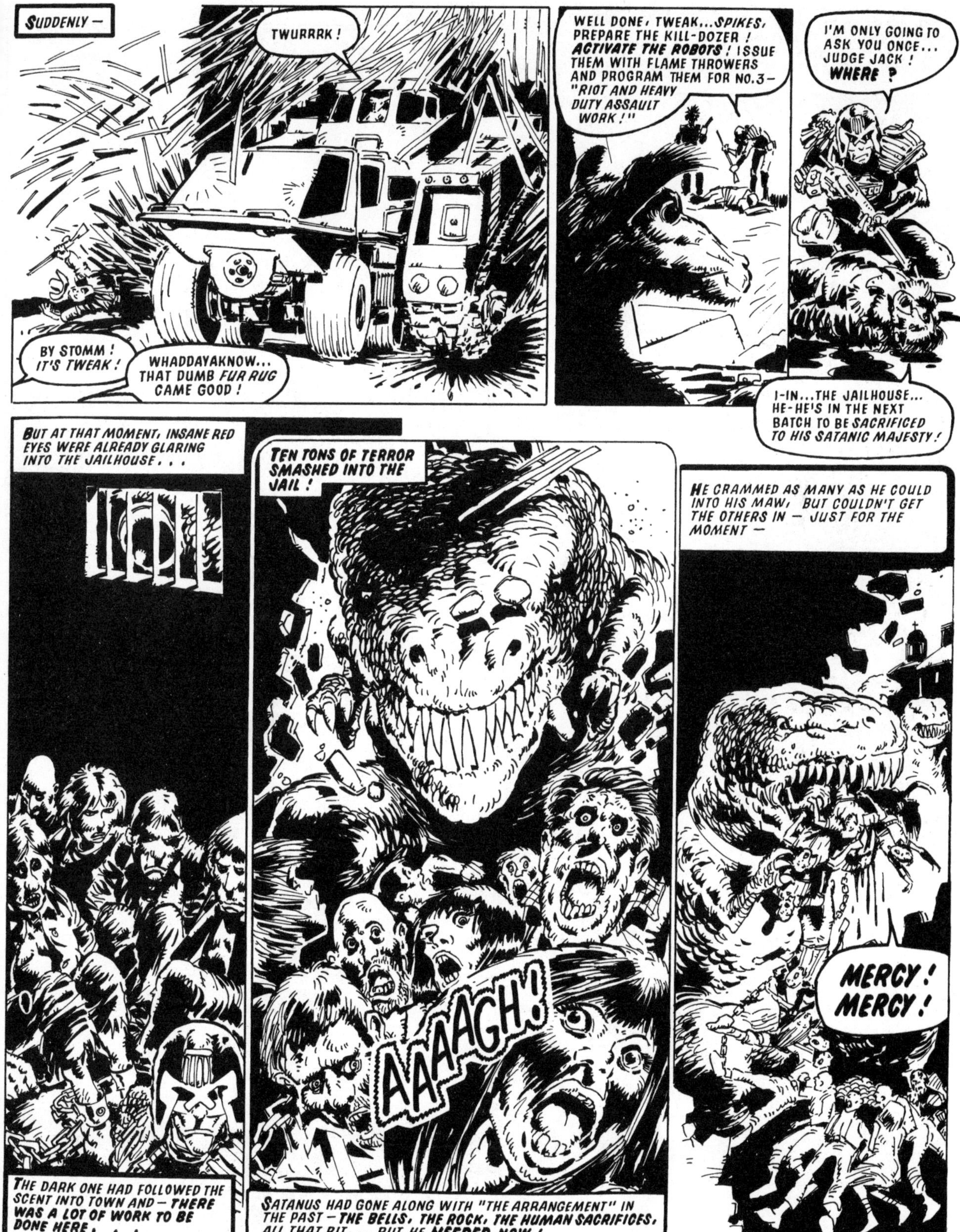

SUDDENLY —
TWURRRK !
BY STOMM ! IT'S TWEAK !
WHADDAYAKNOW... THAT DUMB FUR RUG CAME GOOD !
WELL DONE, TWEAK...SPIKES, PREPARE THE KILL-DOZER ! ACTIVATE THE ROBOTS ! ISSUE THEM WITH FLAME THROWERS AND PROGRAM THEM FOR NO.3 - "RIOT AND HEAVY DUTY ASSAULT WORK !"
I'M ONLY GOING TO ASK YOU ONCE... JUDGE JACK ! WHERE ?
I-IN...THE JAILHOUSE... HE-HE'S IN THE NEXT BATCH TO BE SACRIFICED TO HIS SATANIC MAJESTY !
BUT AT THAT MOMENT, INSANE RED EYES WERE ALREADY GLARING INTO THE JAILHOUSE . . .
THE DARK ONE HAD FOLLOWED THE SCENT INTO TOWN AND — THERE WAS A LOT OF WORK TO BE DONE HERE . . .
TEN TONS OF TERROR SMASHED INTO THE JAIL !
AAAAGH !
SATANUS HAD GONE ALONG WITH "THE ARRANGEMENT" IN THE PAST — THE BELLS, THE ROCK, THE HUMAN SACRIFICES, ALL THAT BIT... BUT HE NEEDED NOW !
HE CRAMMED AS MANY AS HE COULD INTO HIS MAW, BUT COULDN'T GET THE OTHERS IN — JUST FOR THE MOMENT —
MERCY ! MERCY !

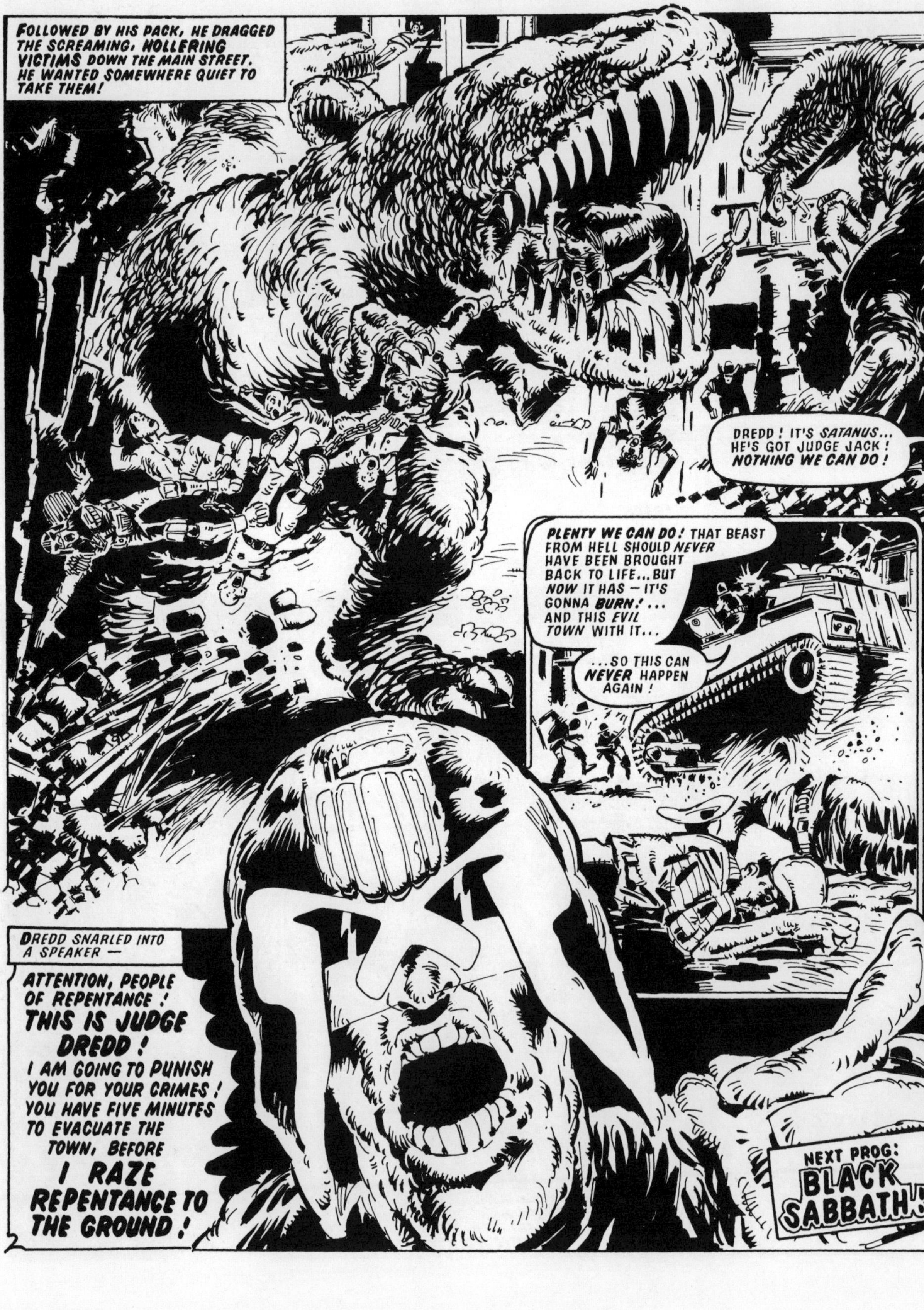
FOLLOWED BY HIS PACK, HE DRAGGED THE SCREAMING, HOLLERING VICTIMS DOWN THE MAIN STREET. HE WANTED SOMEWHERE QUIET TO TAKE THEM!
DREDD! IT'S SATANUS... HE'S GOT JUDGE JACK! NOTHING WE CAN DO!
PLENTY WE CAN DO! THAT BEAST FROM HELL SHOULD NEVER HAVE BEEN BROUGHT BACK TO LIFE... BUT NOW IT HAS — IT'S GONNA BURN!... AND THIS EVIL TOWN WITH IT...
...SO THIS CAN NEVER HAPPEN AGAIN!
DREDD SNARLED INTO A SPEAKER —
ATTENTION, PEOPLE OF REPENTANCE! THIS IS JUDGE DREDD! I AM GOING TO PUNISH YOU FOR YOUR CRIMES! YOU HAVE FIVE MINUTES TO EVACUATE THE TOWN, BEFORE I RAZE REPENTANCE TO THE GROUND!
NEXT PROG: BLACK SABBATH!

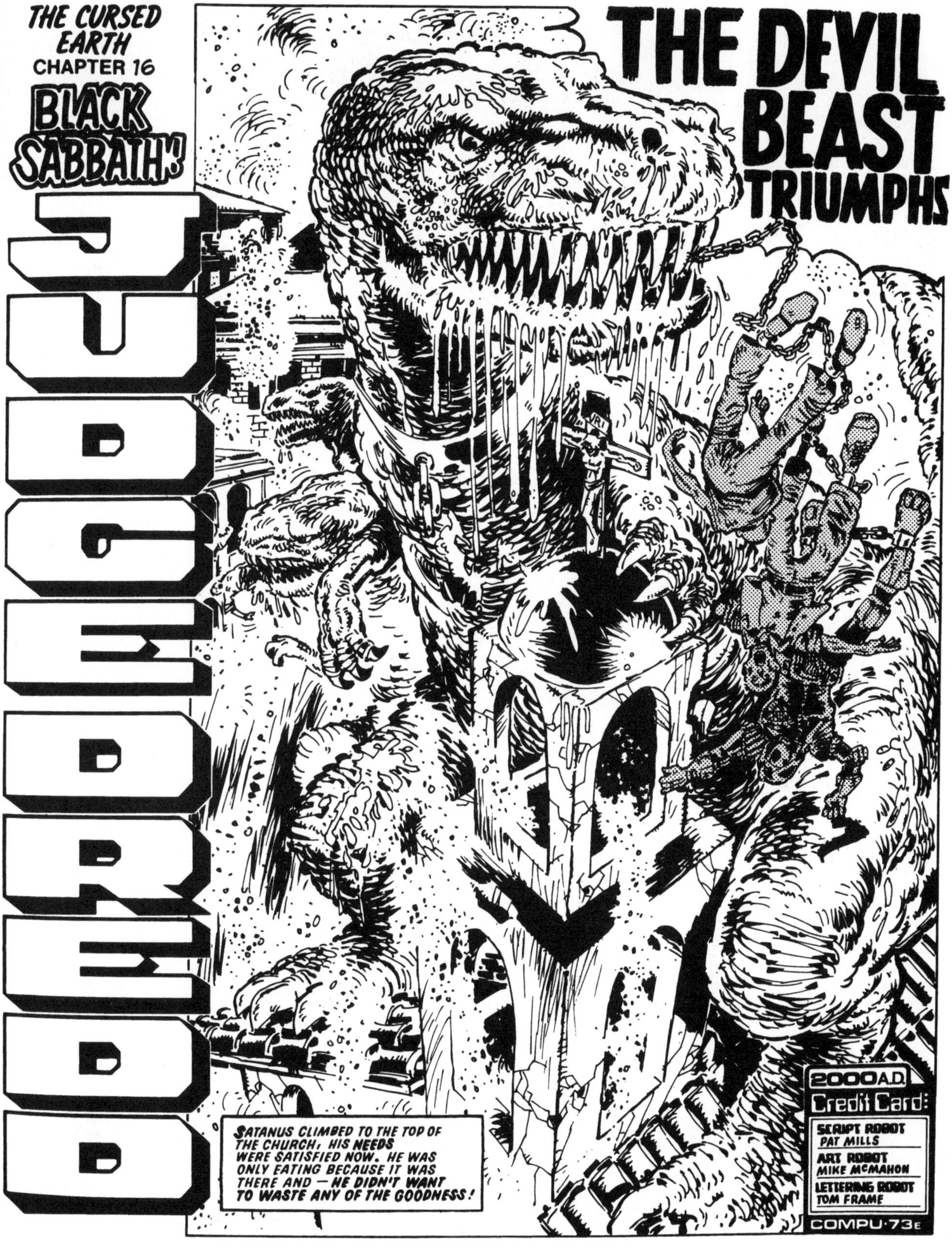
THE CURSED EARTH
CHAPTER 16
BLACK SABBATH!
JUDGE DREDD
THE DEVIL BEAST TRIUMPHS
SATANUS CLIMBED TO THE TOP OF THE CHURCH, HIS NEEDS WERE SATISFIED NOW. HE WAS ONLY EATING BECAUSE IT WAS THERE AND — HE DIDN'T WANT TO WASTE ANY OF THE GOODNESS!
2000 A.D. Credit Card:
SCRIPT ROBOT PAT MILLS
ART ROBOT MIKE McMAHON
LETTERING ROBOT TOM FRAME
COMPU·73E

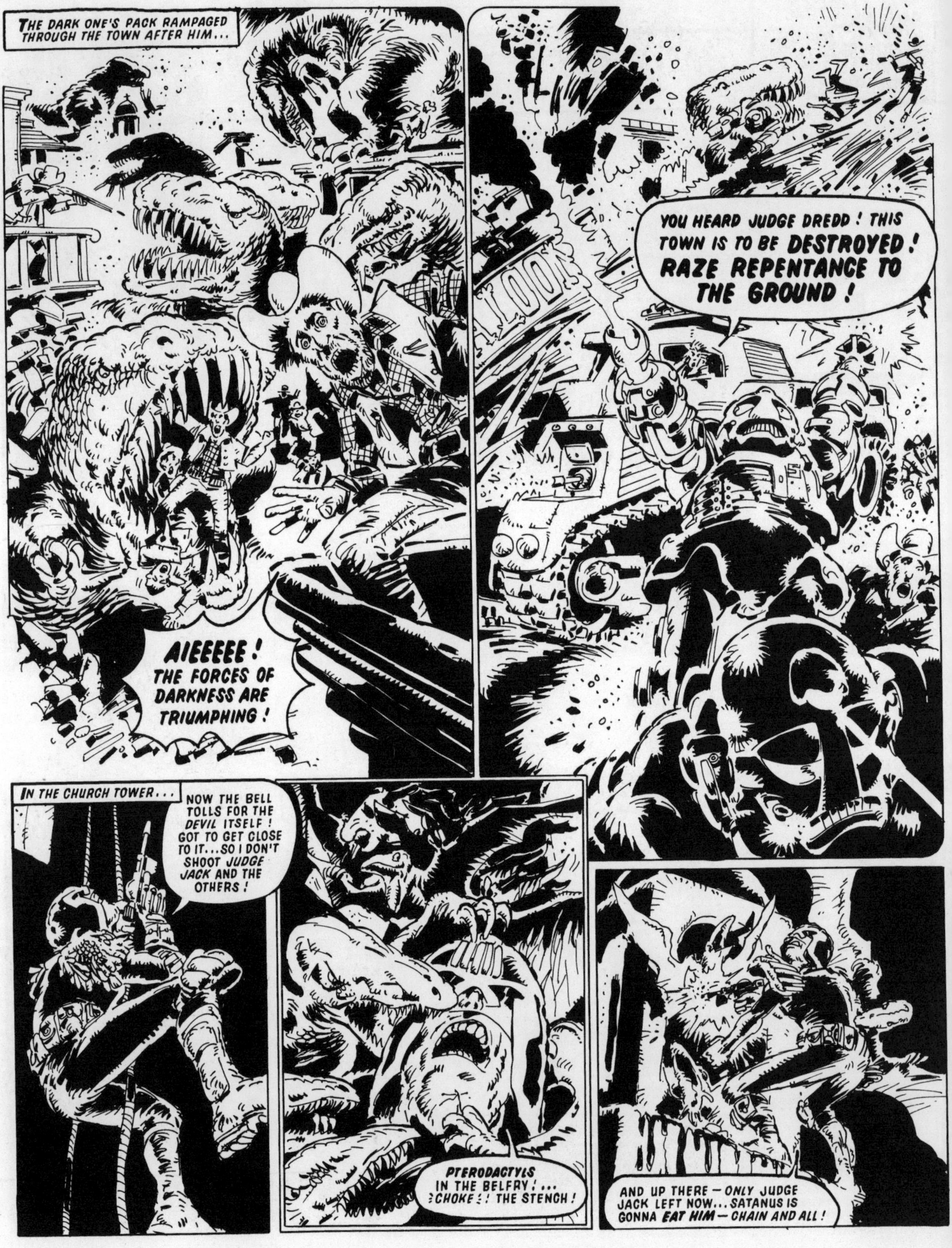
THE DARK ONE'S PACK RAMPAGED THROUGH THE TOWN AFTER HIM...
AIEEEEE! THE FORCES OF DARKNESS ARE TRIUMPHING!
YOU HEARD JUDGE DREDD! THIS TOWN IS TO BE DESTROYED! RAZE REPENTANCE TO THE GROUND!
IN THE CHURCH TOWER...
NOW THE BELL TOLLS FOR THE DEVIL ITSELF! GOT TO GET CLOSE TO IT... SO I DON'T SHOOT JUDGE JACK AND THE OTHERS!
PTERODACTYLS IN THE BELFRY!... CHOKE! THE STENCH!
AND UP THERE — ONLY JUDGE JACK LEFT NOW... SATANUS IS GONNA EAT HIM — CHAIN AND ALL!

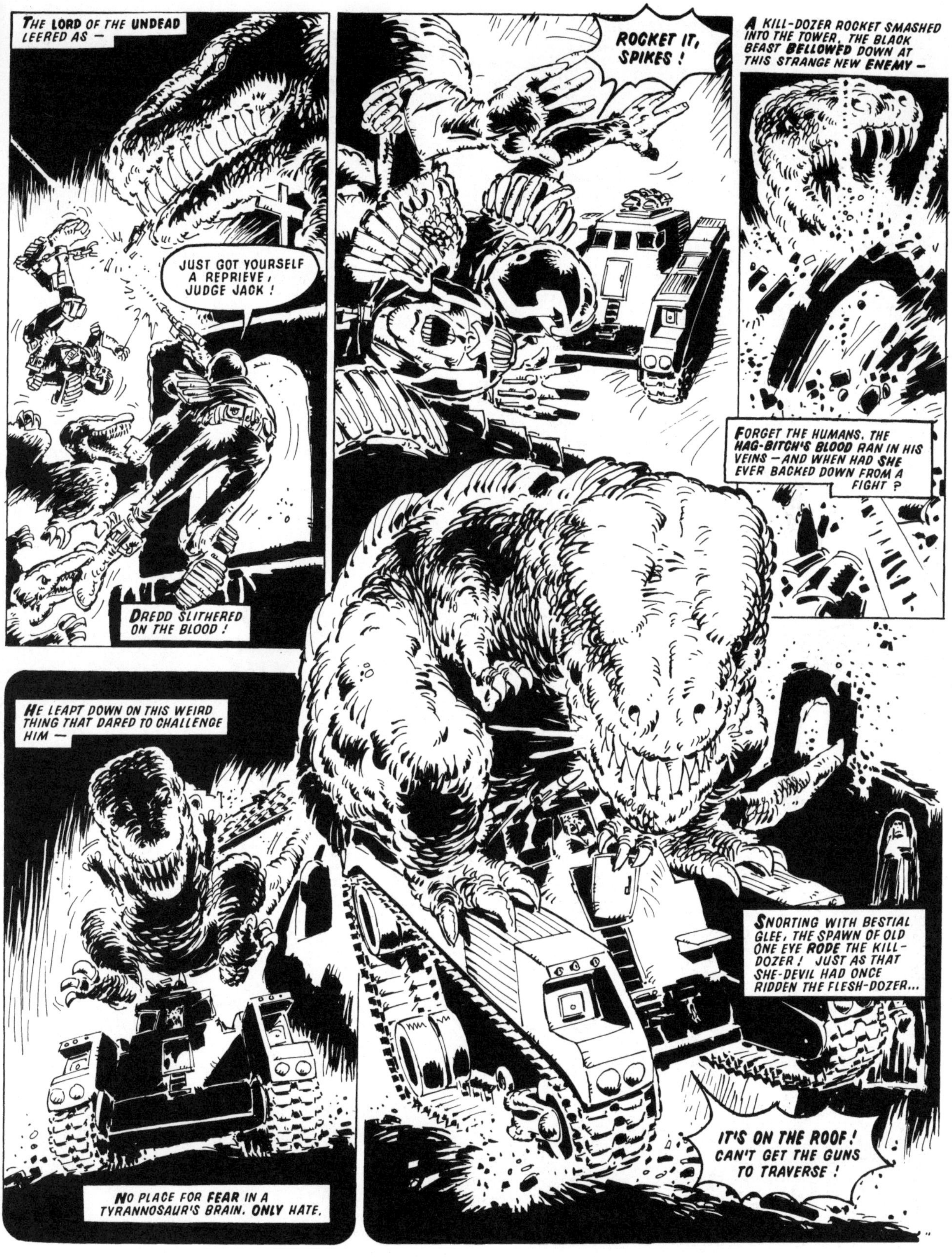
THE LORD OF THE UNDEAD LEERED AS –
JUST GOT YOURSELF A REPRIEVE, JUDGE JACK!
DREDD SLITHERED ON THE BLOOD!
ROCKET IT, SPIKES!
A KILL-DOZER ROCKET SMASHED INTO THE TOWER. THE BLACK BEAST BELLOWED DOWN AT THIS STRANGE NEW ENEMY –
FORGET THE HUMANS. THE HAG-BITCH'S BLOOD RAN IN HIS VEINS – AND WHEN HAD SHE EVER BACKED DOWN FROM A FIGHT?
HE LEAPT DOWN ON THIS WEIRD THING THAT DARED TO CHALLENGE HIM –
NO PLACE FOR FEAR IN A TYRANNOSAUR'S BRAIN. ONLY HATE.
SNORTING WITH BESTIAL GLEE, THE SPAWN OF OLD ONE EYE RODE THE KILL-DOZER! JUST AS THAT SHE-DEVIL HAD ONCE RIDDEN THE FLESH-DOZER...
IT'S ON THE ROOF! CAN'T GET THE GUNS TO TRAVERSE!

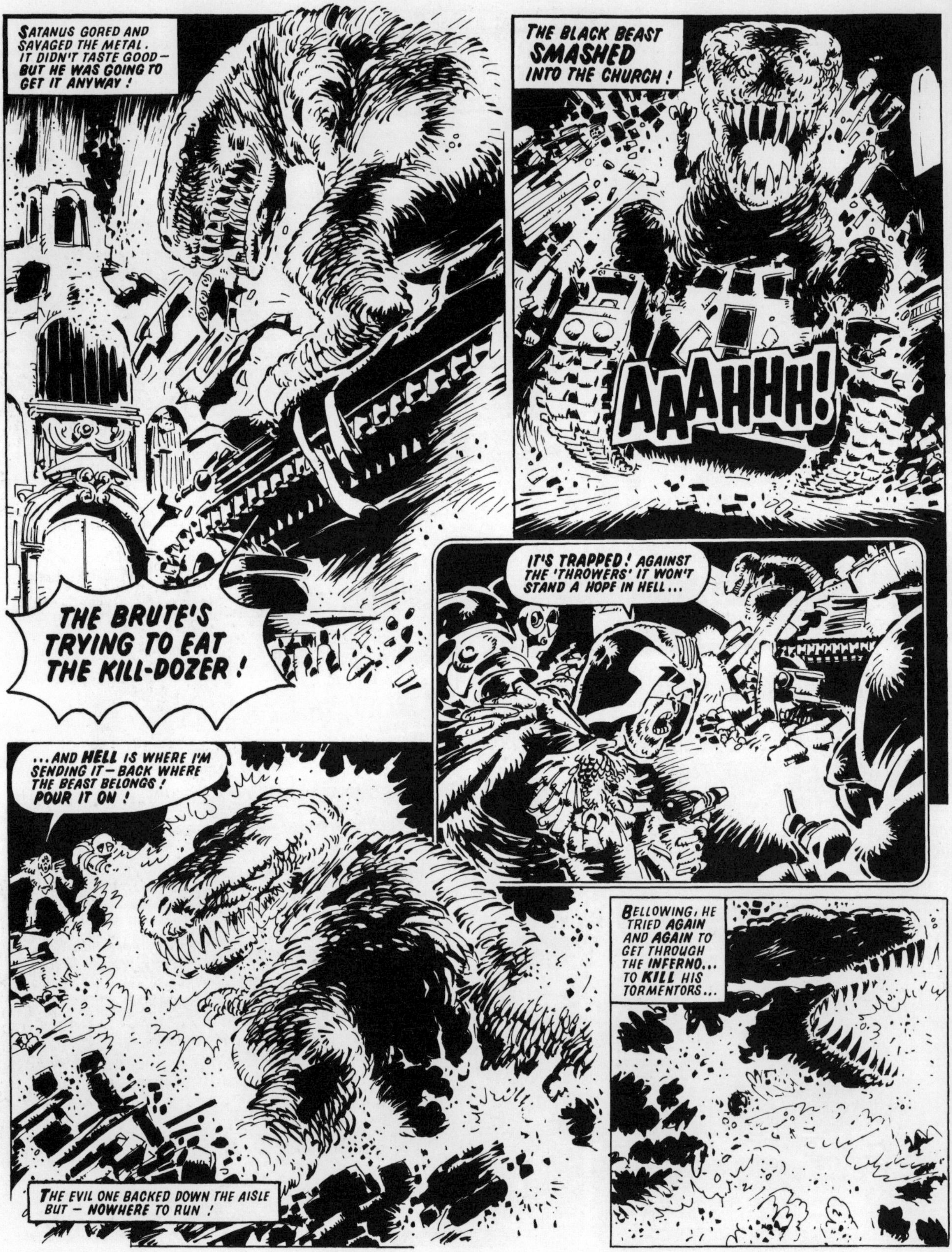

SATANUS GORED AND SAVAGED THE METAL. IT DIDN'T TASTE GOOD— BUT HE WAS GOING TO GET IT ANYWAY!
THE BRUTE'S TRYING TO EAT THE KILL-DOZER!
THE BLACK BEAST SMASHED INTO THE CHURCH!
AAAHHH!
IT'S TRAPPED! AGAINST THE 'THROWERS' IT WON'T STAND A HOPE IN HELL...
...AND HELL IS WHERE I'M SENDING IT—BACK WHERE THE BEAST BELONGS! POUR IT ON!
THE EVIL ONE BACKED DOWN THE AISLE BUT — NOWHERE TO RUN!
BELLOWING, HE TRIED AGAIN AND AGAIN TO GET THROUGH THE INFERNO... TO KILL HIS TORMENTORS...

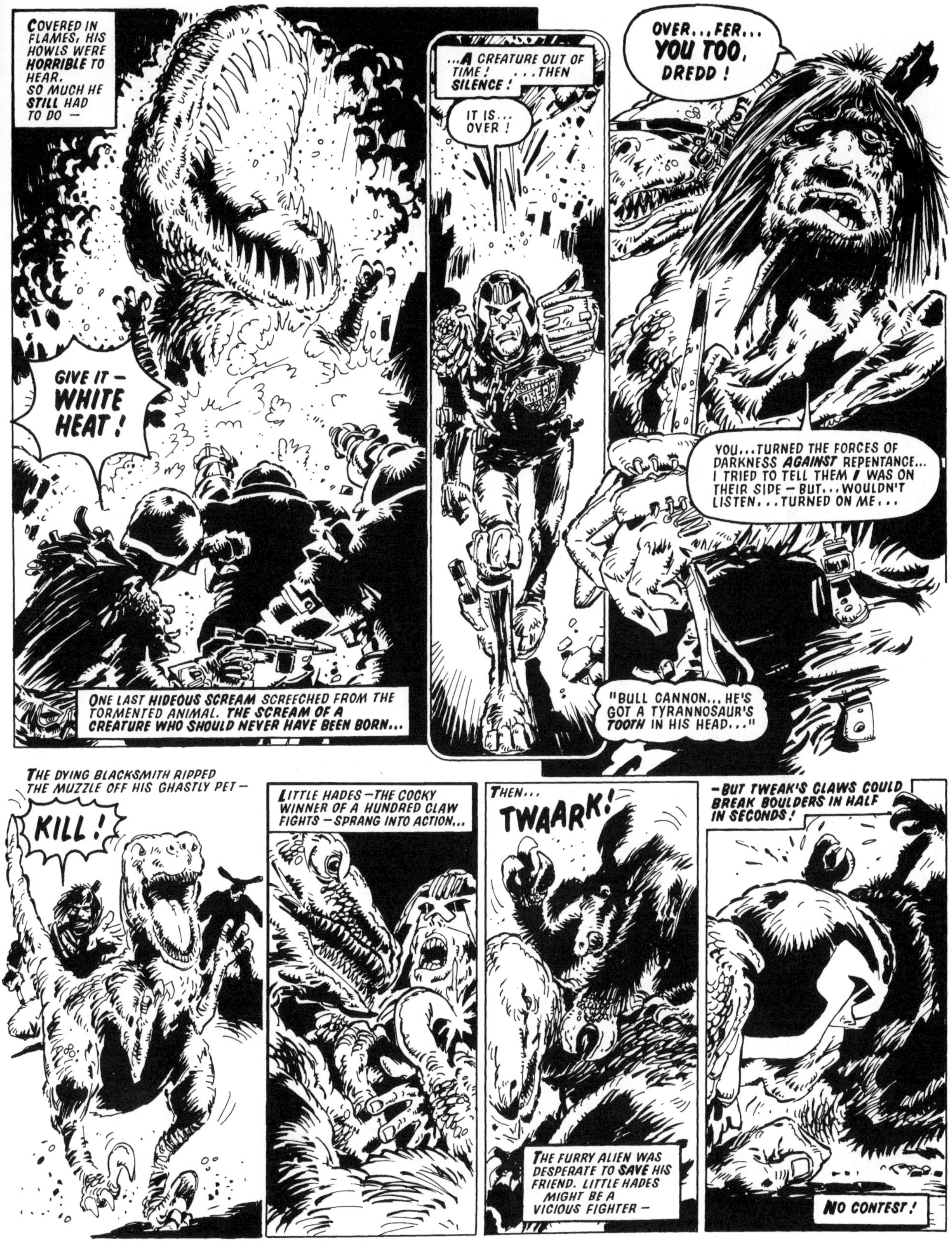
COVERED IN FLAMES, HIS HOWLS WERE HORRIBLE TO HEAR. SO MUCH HE STILL HAD TO DO —
GIVE IT — WHITE HEAT!
ONE LAST HIDEOUS SCREAM SCREECHED FROM THE TORMENTED ANIMAL. THE SCREAM OF A CREATURE WHO SHOULD NEVER HAVE BEEN BORN...
...A CREATURE OUT OF TIME! ...THEN SILENCE!
IT IS... OVER!
OVER... FER... YOU TOO, DREDD!
YOU... TURNED THE FORCES OF DARKNESS AGAINST REPENTANCE... I TRIED TO TELL THEM I WAS ON THEIR SIDE — BUT... WOULDN'T LISTEN... TURNED ON ME...
"BULL CANNON... HE'S GOT A TYRANNOSAUR'S TOOTH IN HIS HEAD..."
THE DYING BLACKSMITH RIPPED THE MUZZLE OFF HIS GHASTLY PET —
KILL!
LITTLE HADES — THE COCKY WINNER OF A HUNDRED CLAW FIGHTS — SPRANG INTO ACTION...
THEN...
TWAARK!
THE FURRY ALIEN WAS DESPERATE TO SAVE HIS FRIEND. LITTLE HADES MIGHT BE A VICIOUS FIGHTER —
— BUT TWEAK'S CLAWS COULD BREAK BOULDERS IN HALF IN SECONDS!
NO CONTEST!

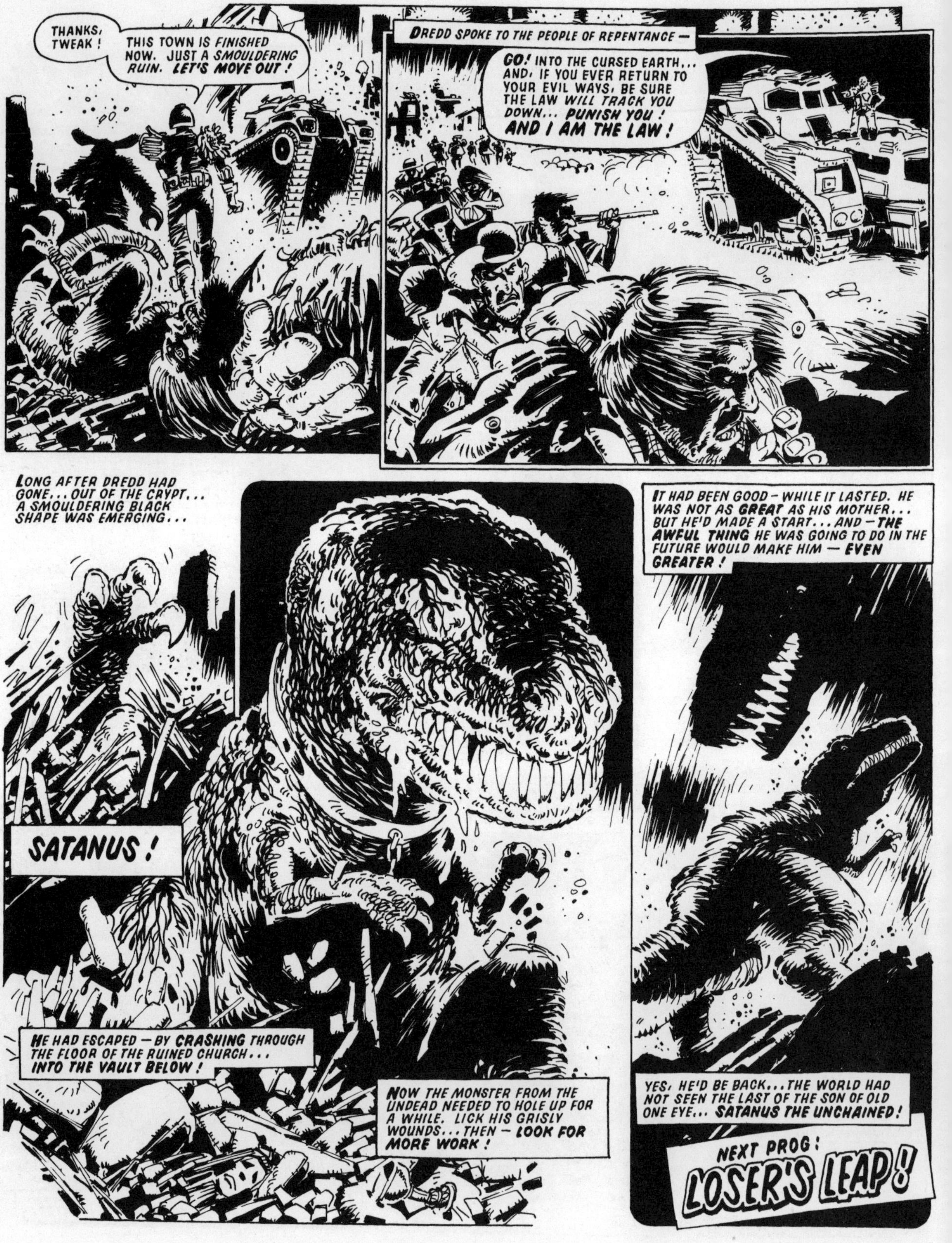
THANKS, TWEAK!
THIS TOWN IS FINISHED NOW. JUST A SMOULDERING RUIN. LET'S MOVE OUT!
DREDD SPOKE TO THE PEOPLE OF REPENTANCE —
GO! INTO THE CURSED EARTH... AND, IF YOU EVER RETURN TO YOUR EVIL WAYS, BE SURE THE LAW WILL TRACK YOU DOWN... PUNISH YOU! AND I AM THE LAW!
LONG AFTER DREDD HAD GONE... OUT OF THE CRYPT... A SMOULDERING BLACK SHAPE WAS EMERGING...
SATANUS!
HE HAD ESCAPED — BY CRASHING THROUGH THE FLOOR OF THE RUINED CHURCH... INTO THE VAULT BELOW!
NOW THE MONSTER FROM THE UNDEAD NEEDED TO HOLE UP FOR A WHILE. LICK HIS GRISLY WOUNDS... THEN — LOOK FOR MORE WORK!
IT HAD BEEN GOOD — WHILE IT LASTED. HE WAS NOT AS GREAT AS HIS MOTHER... BUT HE'D MADE A START... AND — THE AWFUL THING HE WAS GOING TO DO IN THE FUTURE WOULD MAKE HIM — EVEN GREATER!
YES, HE'D BE BACK... THE WORLD HAD NOT SEEN THE LAST OF THE SON OF OLD ONE EYE... SATANUS THE UNCHAINED!
NEXT PROG:
LOSER'S LEAP!

THE CURSED EARTH

CHAPTER 19

LOSER'S LEAP

JUDGE DREDD

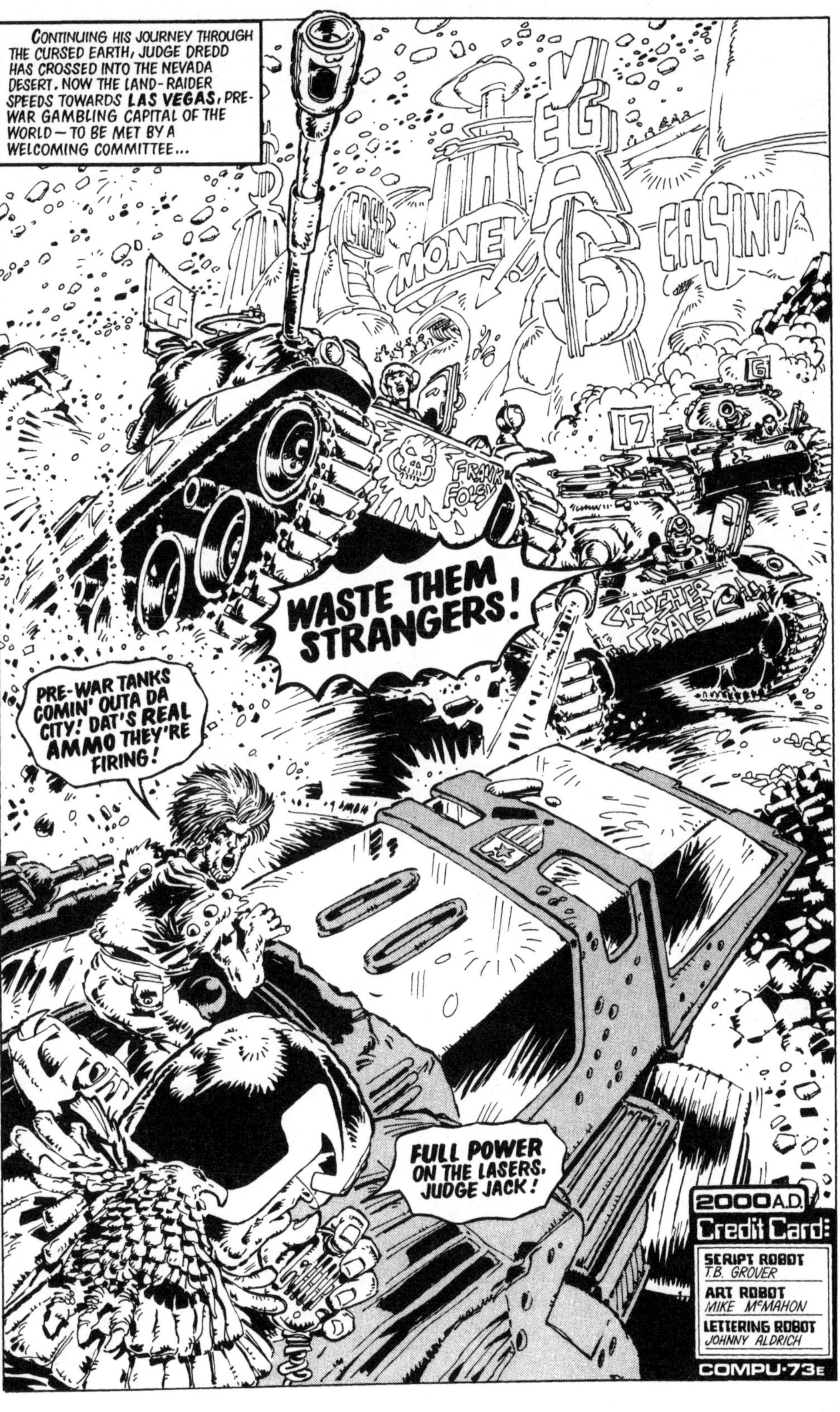
CONTINUING HIS JOURNEY THROUGH THE CURSED EARTH, JUDGE DREDD HAS CROSSED INTO THE NEVADA DESERT. NOW THE LAND-RAIDER SPEEDS TOWARDS LAS VEGAS, PRE-WAR GAMBLING CAPITAL OF THE WORLD — TO BE MET BY A WELCOMING COMMITTEE...
MONEY
CASINO
FRANK FOLSY
CRUSHER CRAIG
WASTE THEM STRANGERS!
PRE-WAR TANKS COMIN' OUTA DA CITY! DAT'S REAL AMMO THEY'RE FIRING!
FULL POWER ON THE LASERS, JUDGE JACK!
2000 A.D. Credit Card:
SCRIPT ROBOT T.B. GROVER
ART ROBOT MIKE McMAHON
LETTERING ROBOT JOHNNY ALDRICH
COMPU-73E

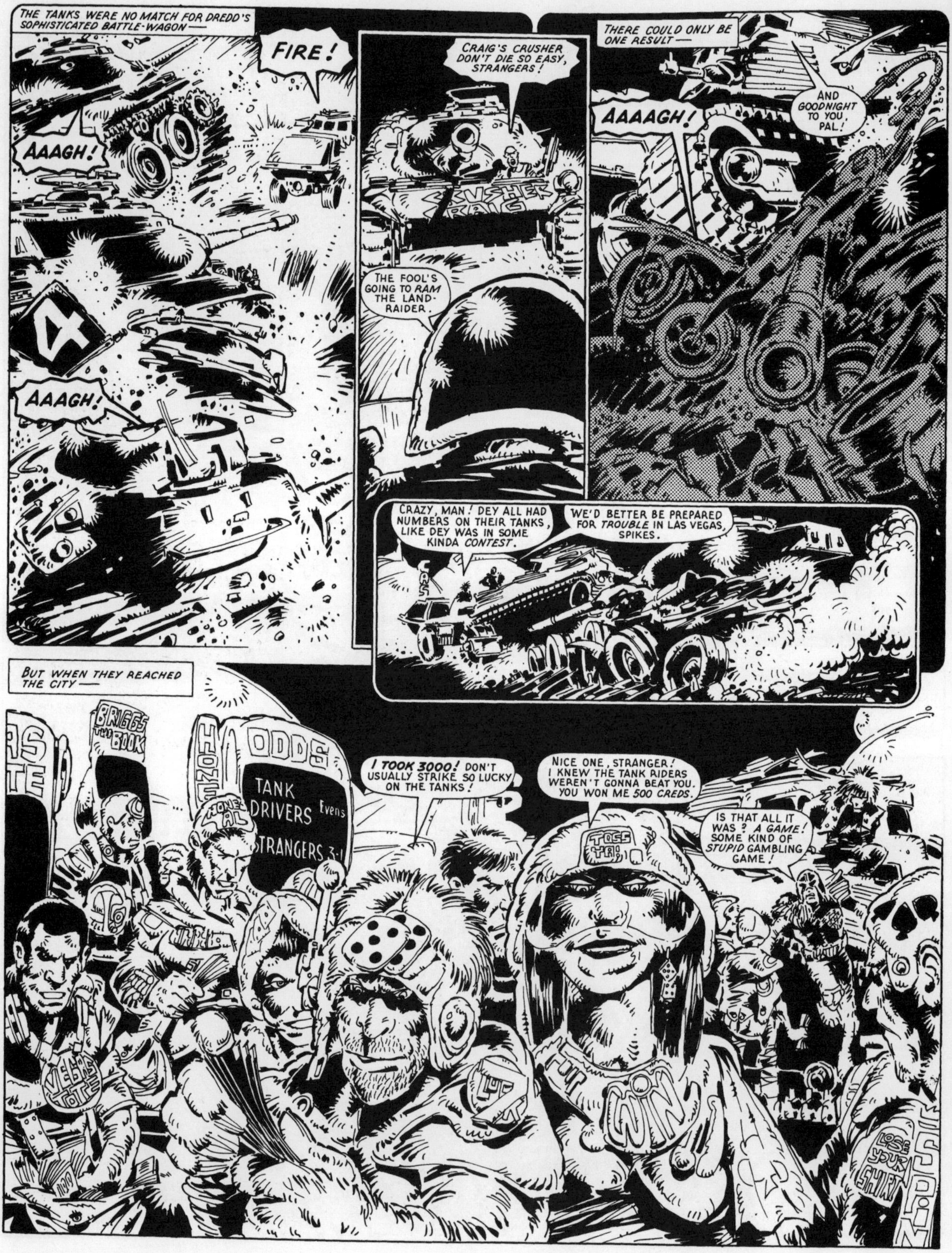
THE TANKS WERE NO MATCH FOR DREDD'S SOPHISTICATED BATTLE-WAGON—
FIRE!
AAAGH!
AAAGH!
CRAIG'S CRUSHER DON'T DIE SO EASY, STRANGERS!
CRUSHER CRAIG
THE FOOL'S GOING TO RAM THE LAND-RAIDER.
THERE COULD ONLY BE ONE RESULT—
AAAAGH!
AND GOODNIGHT TO YOU, PAL!
CRAZY, MAN! DEY ALL HAD NUMBERS ON THEIR TANKS, LIKE DEY WAS IN SOME KINDA CONTEST.
WE'D BETTER BE PREPARED FOR TROUBLE IN LAS VEGAS, SPIKES.
BUT WHEN THEY REACHED THE CITY—
BRIGGS THE BOOK
ODDS
TANK DRIVERS Evens
STRANGERS 3-1
I TOOK 3000! DON'T USUALLY STRIKE SO LUCKY ON THE TANKS!
NICE ONE, STRANGER! I KNEW THE TANK RIDERS WEREN'T GONNA BEAT YOU. YOU WON ME 500 CREDS.
IS THAT ALL IT WAS? A GAME! SOME KIND OF STUPID GAMBLING GAME!
VEGAS TOTE
WIN
LOSE YOUR SHIRT

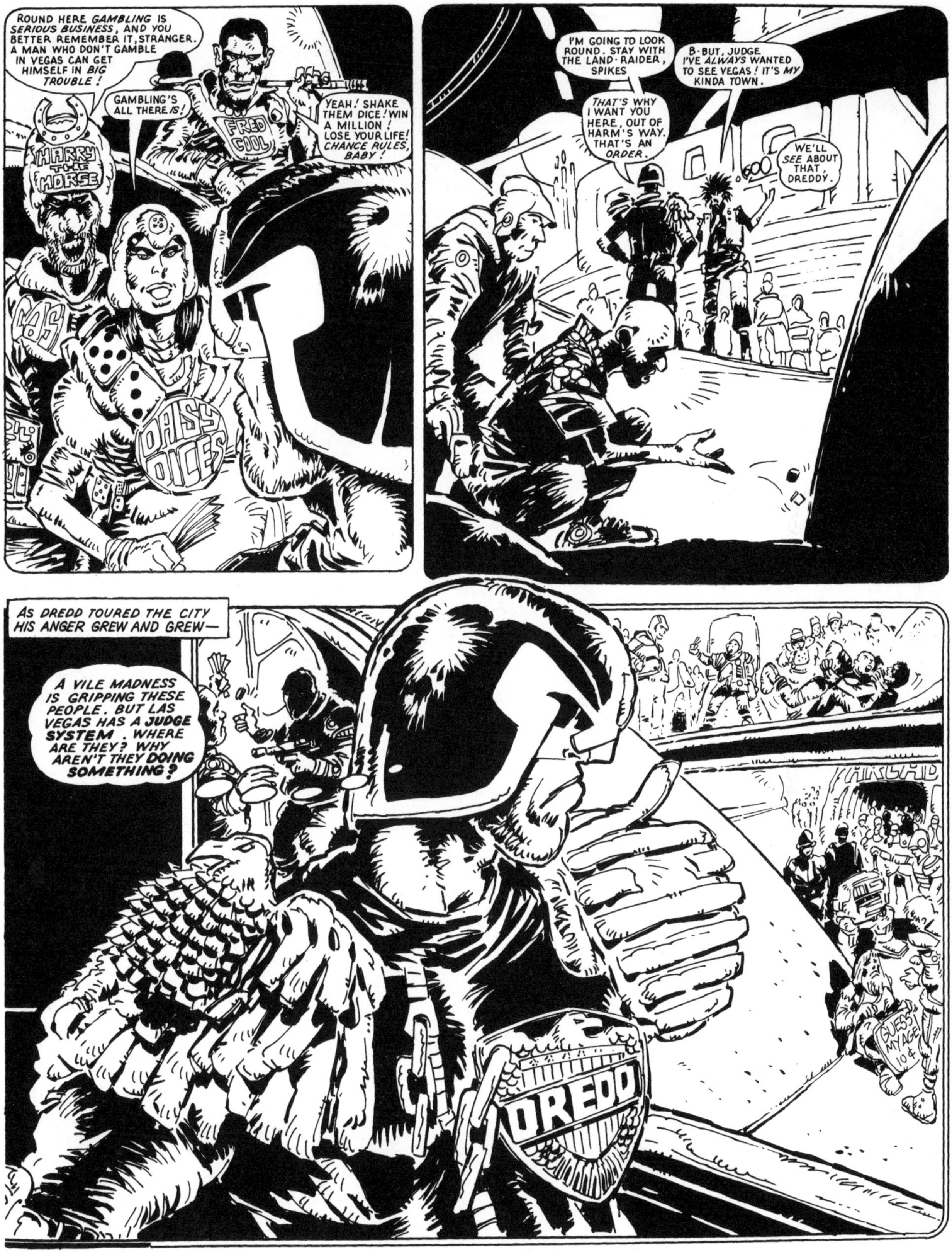
ROUND HERE GAMBLING IS SERIOUS BUSINESS, AND YOU BETTER REMEMBER IT, STRANGER. A MAN WHO DON'T GAMBLE IN VEGAS CAN GET HIMSELF IN BIG TROUBLE!
GAMBLING'S ALL THERE IS!
YEAH! SHAKE THEM DICE! WIN A MILLION! LOSE YOUR LIFE! CHANCE RULES, BABY!
HARRY THE HORSE
FRED COOL
DAISY DICES
I'M GOING TO LOOK ROUND. STAY WITH THE LAND-RAIDER, SPIKES
THAT'S WHY I WANT YOU HERE, OUT OF HARM'S WAY. THAT'S AN ORDER.
B-BUT, JUDGE I'VE ALWAYS WANTED TO SEE VEGAS! IT'S MY KINDA TOWN.
WE'LL SEE ABOUT THAT, DREDDY.
AS DREDD TOURED THE CITY HIS ANGER GREW AND GREW—
A VILE MADNESS IS GRIPPING THESE PEOPLE. BUT LAS VEGAS HAS A JUDGE SYSTEM. WHERE ARE THEY? WHY AREN'T THEY DOING SOMETHING?
DREDD
GUESS MY AGE 10¢

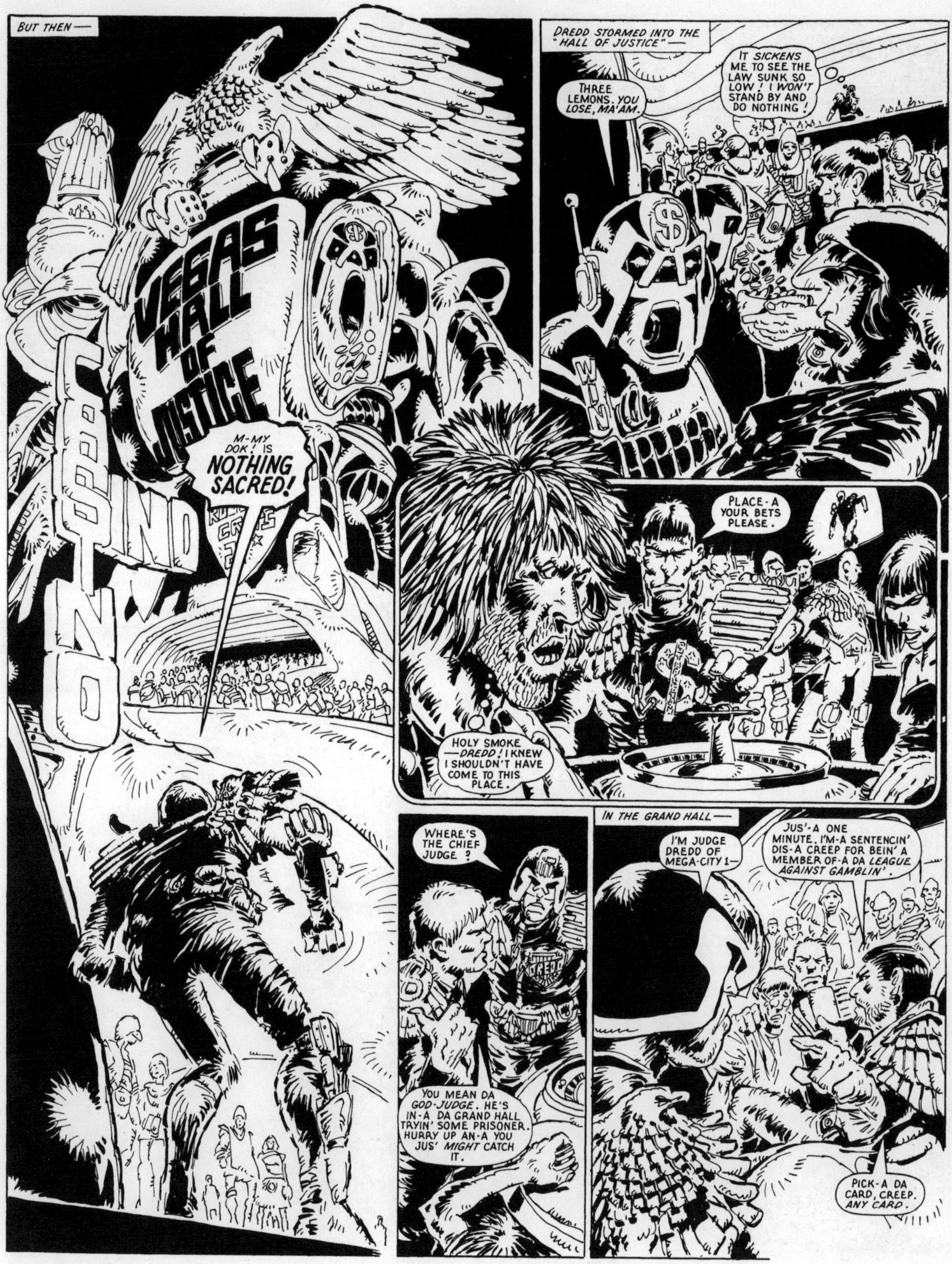

BUT THEN—
VEGAS HALL OF JUSTICE
M-MY DOK! IS NOTHING SACRED!
DREDD STORMED INTO THE "HALL OF JUSTICE"—
THREE LEMONS. YOU LOSE, MA'AM.
IT SICKENS ME TO SEE THE LAW SUNK SO LOW! I WON'T STAND BY AND DO NOTHING!
PLACE-A YOUR BETS PLEASE.
HOLY SMOKE —DREDD! I KNEW I SHOULDN'T HAVE COME TO THIS PLACE.
WHERE'S THE CHIEF JUDGE?
YOU MEAN DA GOD-JUDGE. HE'S IN-A DA GRAND HALL TRYIN' SOME PRISONER. HURRY UP AN-A YOU JUS' MIGHT CATCH IT.
IN THE GRAND HALL—
I'M JUDGE DREDD OF MEGA-CITY 1—
JUS'-A ONE MINUTE. I'M-A SENTENCIN' DIS-A CREEP FOR BEIN' A MEMBER OF-A DA LEAGUE AGAINST GAMBLIN'.
PICK-A DA CARD, CREEP. ANY CARD.

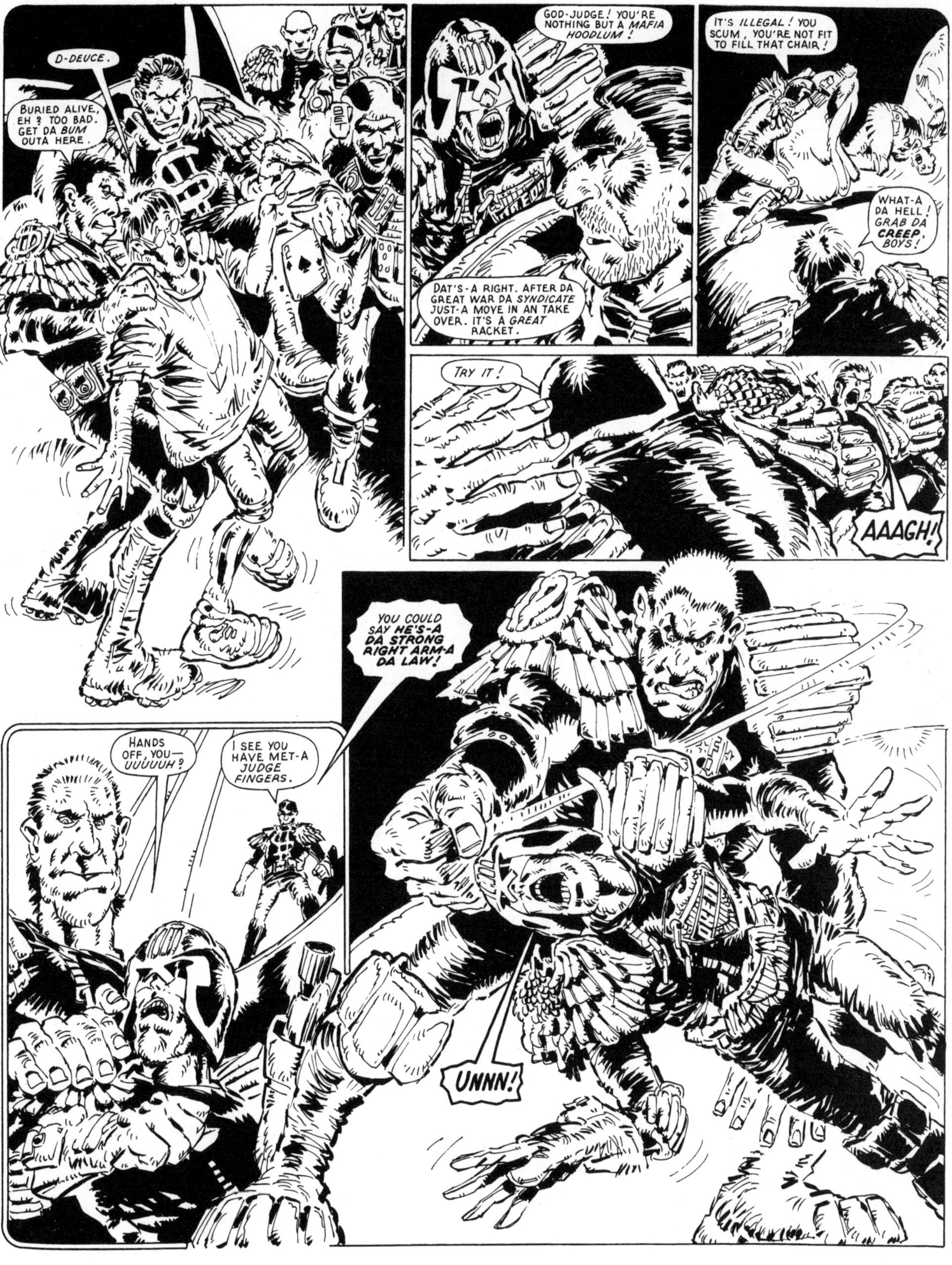
D-DEUCE.
BURIED ALIVE, EH? TOO BAD. GET DA BUM OUTA HERE.
GOD-JUDGE! YOU'RE NOTHING BUT A MAFIA HOODLUM!
DAT'S-A RIGHT. AFTER DA GREAT WAR DA SYNDICATE JUST-A MOVE IN AN TAKE OVER. IT'S A GREAT RACKET.
IT'S ILLEGAL! YOU SCUM, YOU'RE NOT FIT TO FILL THAT CHAIR!
WHAT-A DA HELL! GRAB DA CREEP, BOYS!
TRY IT!
AAAGH!
YOU COULD SAY HE'S-A DA STRONG RIGHT ARM-A DA LAW!
HANDS OFF, YOU— UUUUUH?
I SEE YOU HAVE MET-A JUDGE FINGERS.
UNNN!

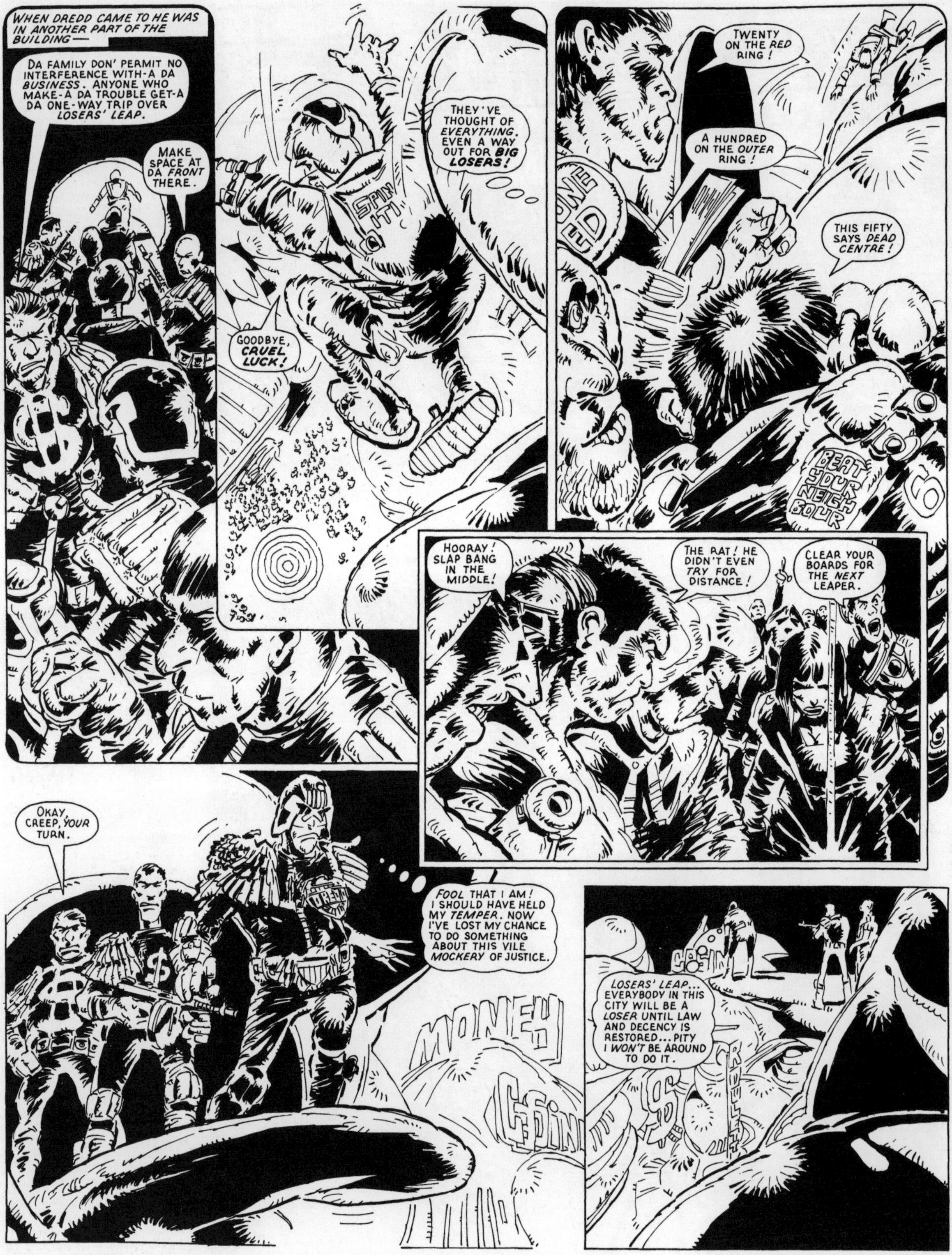

WHEN DREDD CAME TO HE WAS IN ANOTHER PART OF THE BUILDING—
DA FAMILY DON' PERMIT NO INTERFERENCE WITH-A DA BUSINESS. ANYONE WHO MAKE-A DA TROUBLE GET-A DA ONE-WAY TRIP OVER LOSERS' LEAP.
MAKE SPACE AT DA FRONT THERE.
THEY'VE THOUGHT OF EVERYTHING. EVEN A WAY OUT FOR BIG LOSERS!
GOODBYE, CRUEL LUCK!
TWENTY ON THE RED RING!
A HUNDRED ON THE OUTER RING!
THIS FIFTY SAYS DEAD CENTRE!
BEAT YOUR NEIGHBOUR
HOORAY! SLAP BANG IN THE MIDDLE!
THE RAT! HE DIDN'T EVEN TRY FOR DISTANCE!
CLEAR YOUR BOARDS FOR THE NEXT LEAPER.
OKAY, CREEP, YOUR TURN.
FOOL THAT I AM! I SHOULD HAVE HELD MY TEMPER. NOW I'VE LOST MY CHANCE TO DO SOMETHING ABOUT THIS VILE MOCKERY OF JUSTICE.
MONEY
LOSERS' LEAP... EVERYBODY IN THIS CITY WILL BE A LOSER UNTIL LAW AND DECENCY IS RESTORED... PITY I WON'T BE AROUND TO DO IT.

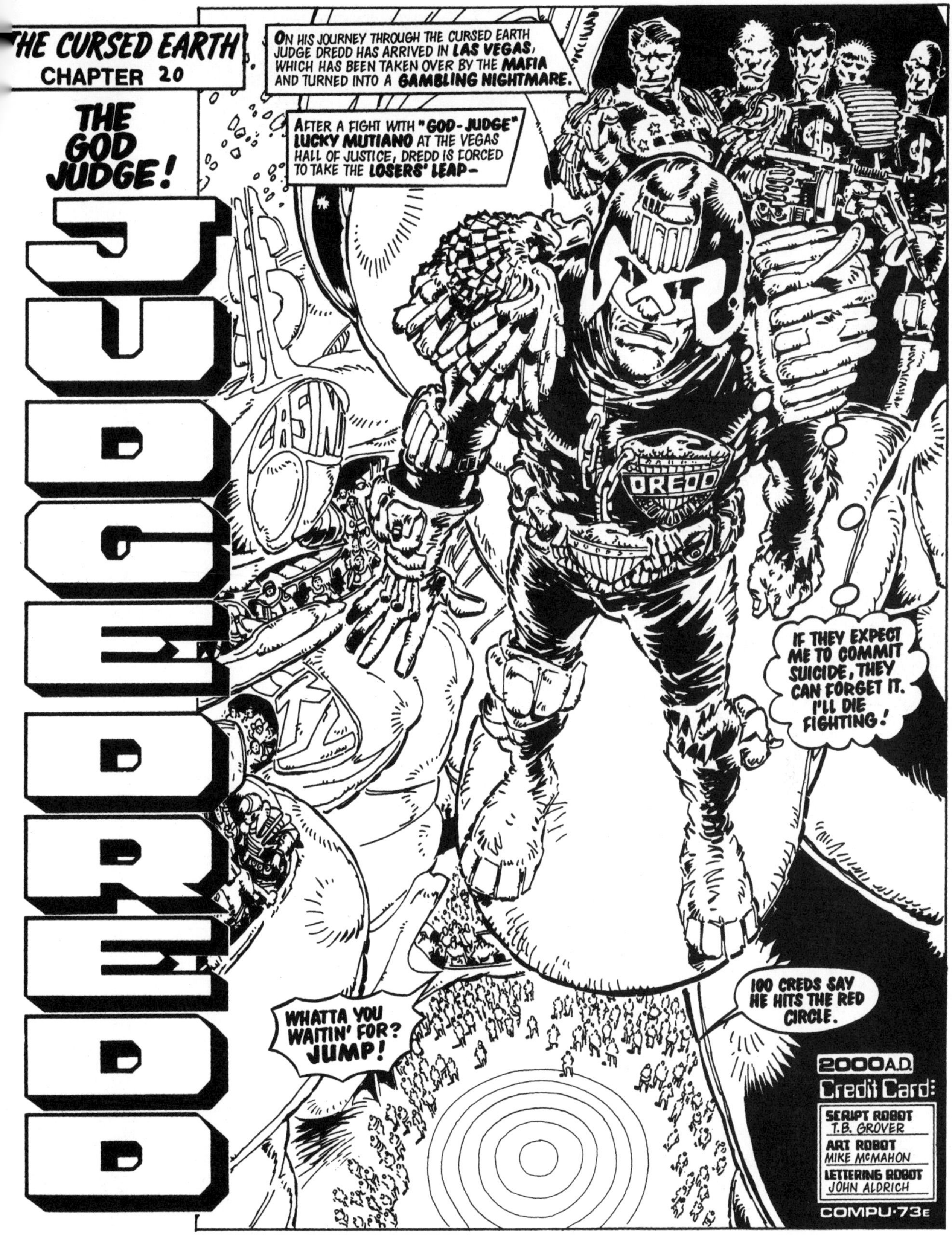
THE CURSED EARTH
CHAPTER 20
THE GOD JUDGE!
JUDGE DREDD
ON HIS JOURNEY THROUGH THE CURSED EARTH JUDGE DREDD HAS ARRIVED IN LAS VEGAS, WHICH HAS BEEN TAKEN OVER BY THE MAFIA AND TURNED INTO A GAMBLING NIGHTMARE.
AFTER A FIGHT WITH "GOD-JUDGE" LUCKY MUTIANO AT THE VEGAS HALL OF JUSTICE, DREDD IS FORCED TO TAKE THE LOSERS' LEAP–
IF THEY EXPECT ME TO COMMIT SUICIDE, THEY CAN FORGET IT. I'LL DIE FIGHTING!
100 CREDS SAY HE HITS THE RED CIRCLE.
WHATTA YOU WAITIN' FOR? JUMP!
DREDD
2000 A.D. Credit Card:
SCRIPT ROBOT T.B. GROVER
ART ROBOT MIKE McMAHON
LETTERING ROBOT JOHN ALDRICH
COMPU·73E

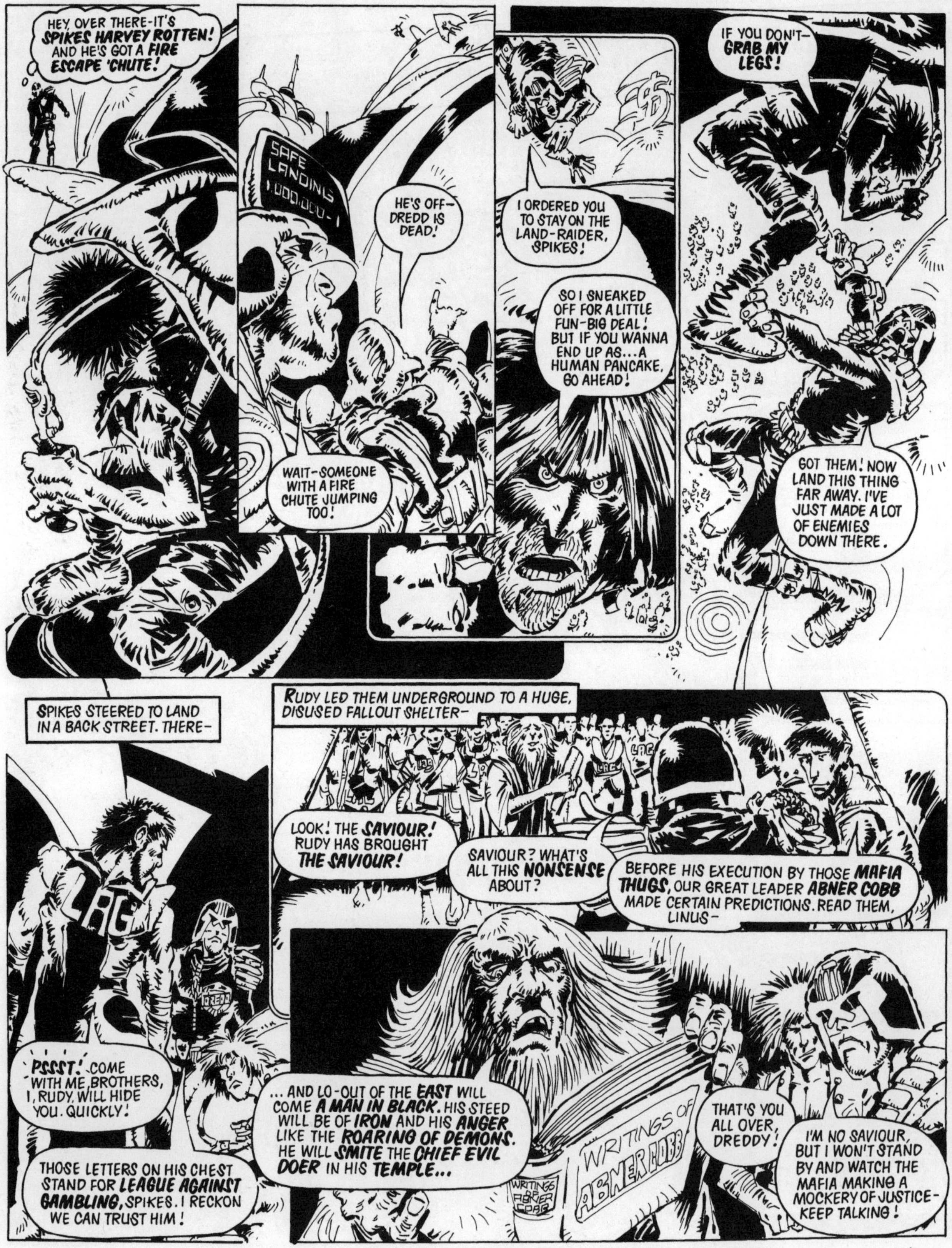
HEY, OVER THERE-IT'S SPIKES HARVEY ROTTEN! AND HE'S GOT A FIRE ESCAPE 'CHUTE!
SAFE LANDING
HE'S OFF-DREDD IS DEAD!
WAIT-SOMEONE WITH A FIRE CHUTE JUMPING TOO!
I ORDERED YOU TO STAY ON THE LAND-RAIDER, SPIKES!
SO I SNEAKED OFF FOR A LITTLE FUN-BIG DEAL! BUT IF YOU WANNA END UP AS...A HUMAN PANCAKE, GO AHEAD!
IF YOU DON'T-GRAB MY LEGS!
GOT THEM! NOW LAND THIS THING FAR AWAY. I'VE JUST MADE A LOT OF ENEMIES DOWN THERE.
SPIKES STEERED TO LAND IN A BACK STREET. THERE-
PSSST! COME WITH ME, BROTHERS, I, RUDY, WILL HIDE YOU. QUICKLY!
THOSE LETTERS ON HIS CHEST STAND FOR LEAGUE AGAINST GAMBLING, SPIKES. I RECKON WE CAN TRUST HIM!
RUDY LED THEM UNDERGROUND TO A HUGE, DISUSED FALLOUT SHELTER-
LOOK! THE SAVIOUR! RUDY HAS BROUGHT THE SAVIOUR!
SAVIOUR? WHAT'S ALL THIS NONSENSE ABOUT?
BEFORE HIS EXECUTION BY THOSE MAFIA THUGS, OUR GREAT LEADER ABNER COBB MADE CERTAIN PREDICTIONS. READ THEM, LINUS-
...AND LO-OUT OF THE EAST WILL COME A MAN IN BLACK. HIS STEED WILL BE OF IRON AND HIS ANGER LIKE THE ROARING OF DEMONS. HE WILL SMITE THE CHIEF EVIL DOER IN HIS TEMPLE...
WRITINGS OF ABNER COBB
THAT'S YOU ALL OVER, DREDDY!
I'M NO SAVIOUR, BUT I WON'T STAND BY AND WATCH THE MAFIA MAKING A MOCKERY OF JUSTICE-KEEP TALKING!

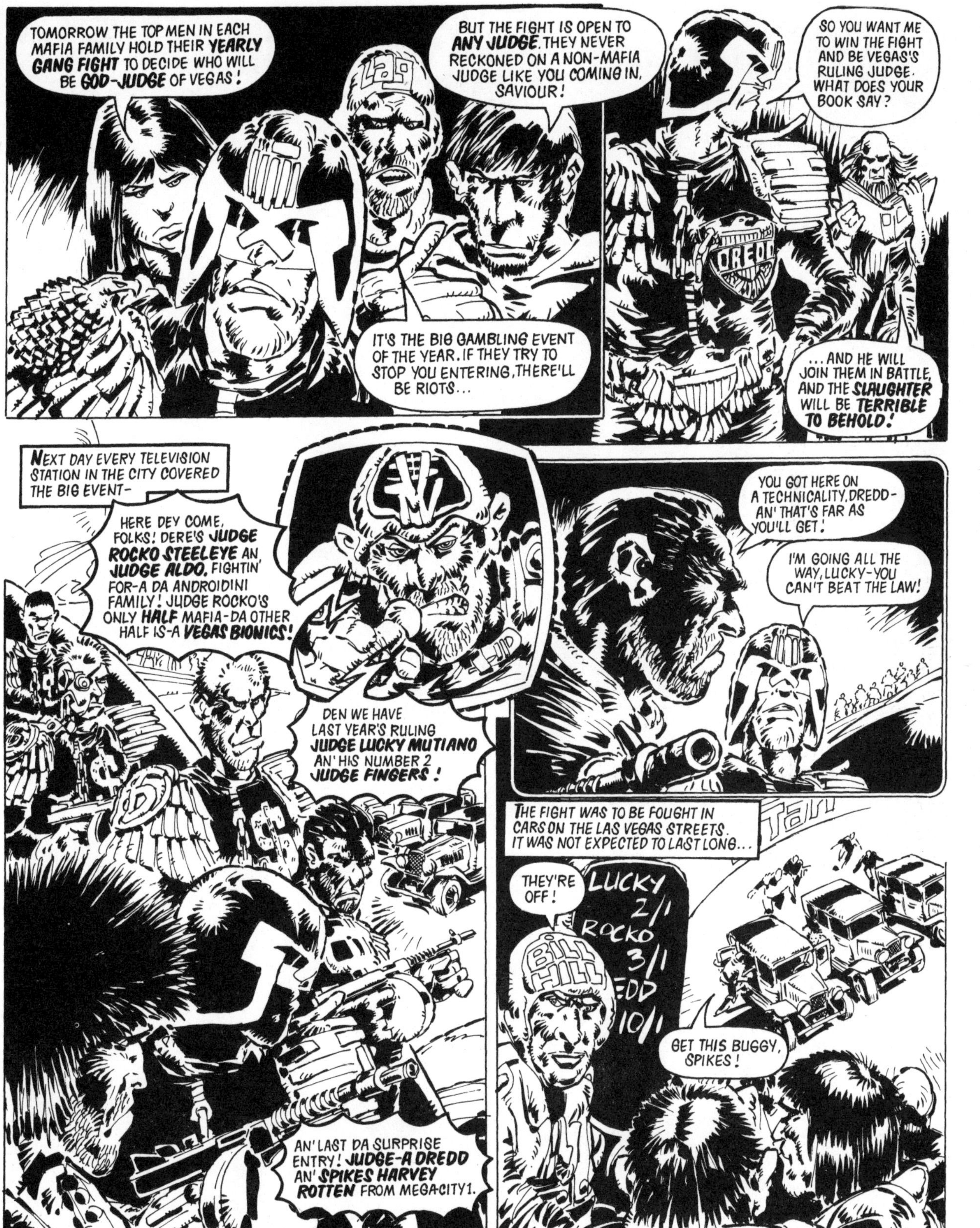

TOMORROW THE TOP MEN IN EACH MAFIA FAMILY HOLD THEIR YEARLY GANG FIGHT TO DECIDE WHO WILL BE GOD-JUDGE OF VEGAS!
BUT THE FIGHT IS OPEN TO ANY JUDGE. THEY NEVER RECKONED ON A NON-MAFIA JUDGE LIKE YOU COMING IN, SAVIOUR!
IT'S THE BIG GAMBLING EVENT OF THE YEAR. IF THEY TRY TO STOP YOU ENTERING, THERE'LL BE RIOTS...
SO YOU WANT ME TO WIN THE FIGHT AND BE VEGAS'S RULING JUDGE. WHAT DOES YOUR BOOK SAY?
...AND HE WILL JOIN THEM IN BATTLE, AND THE SLAUGHTER WILL BE TERRIBLE TO BEHOLD!
NEXT DAY EVERY TELEVISION STATION IN THE CITY COVERED THE BIG EVENT-
HERE DEY COME, FOLKS! DERE'S JUDGE ROCKO STEELEYE AN JUDGE ALDO, FIGHTIN' FOR-A DA ANDROIDINI FAMILY! JUDGE ROCKO'S ONLY HALF MAFIA-DA OTHER HALF IS-A VEGAS BIONICS!
DEN WE HAVE LAST YEAR'S RULING JUDGE LUCKY MUTIANO AN' HIS NUMBER 2 JUDGE FINGERS!
AN' LAST DA SURPRISE ENTRY! JUDGE-A DREDD AN' SPIKES HARVEY ROTTEN FROM MEGA-CITY 1.
YOU GOT HERE ON A TECHNICALITY, DREDD-AN' THAT'S FAR AS YOU'LL GET!
I'M GOING ALL THE WAY, LUCKY-YOU CAN'T BEAT THE LAW!
THE FIGHT WAS TO BE FOUGHT IN CARS ON THE LAS VEGAS STREETS. IT WAS NOT EXPECTED TO LAST LONG...
THEY'RE OFF!
LUCKY 2/1
ROCKO 3/1
EDD 10/1
GET THIS BUGGY, SPIKES!

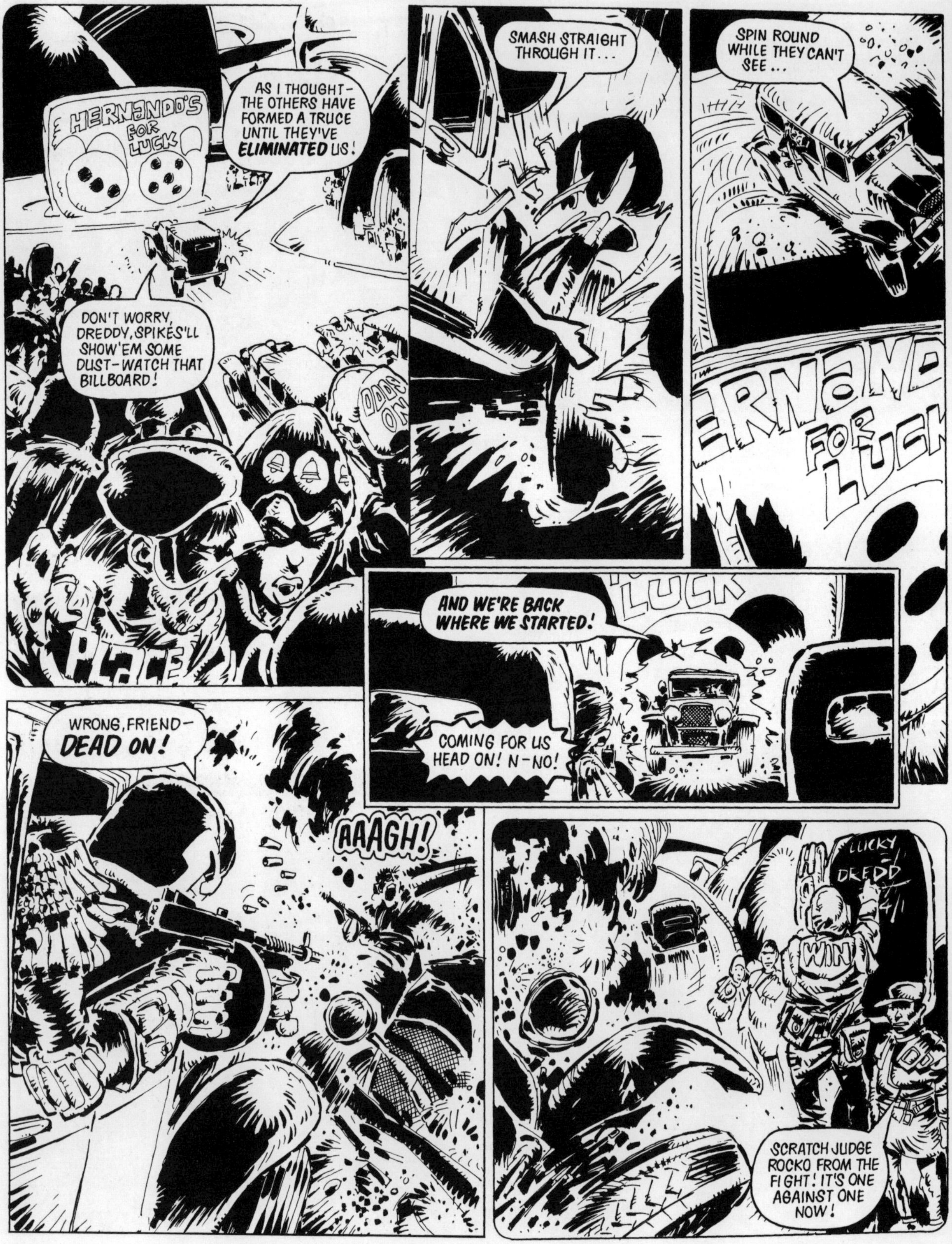
HERNANDO'S FOR LUCK
AS I THOUGHT- THE OTHERS HAVE FORMED A TRUCE UNTIL THEY'VE ELIMINATED US!
DON'T WORRY, DREDDY, SPIKES'LL SHOW'EM SOME DUST-WATCH THAT BILLBOARD!
ODDS ON
PLACE
SMASH STRAIGHT THROUGH IT...
SPIN ROUND WHILE THEY CAN'T SEE...
ERNAND FOR LUCK
LUCK
AND WE'RE BACK WHERE WE STARTED!
COMING FOR US HEAD ON! N-NO!
WRONG, FRIEND- DEAD ON!
AAAGH!
LUCKY DREDD 4/1
WIN
SCRATCH JUDGE ROCKO FROM THE FIGHT! IT'S ONE AGAINST ONE NOW!

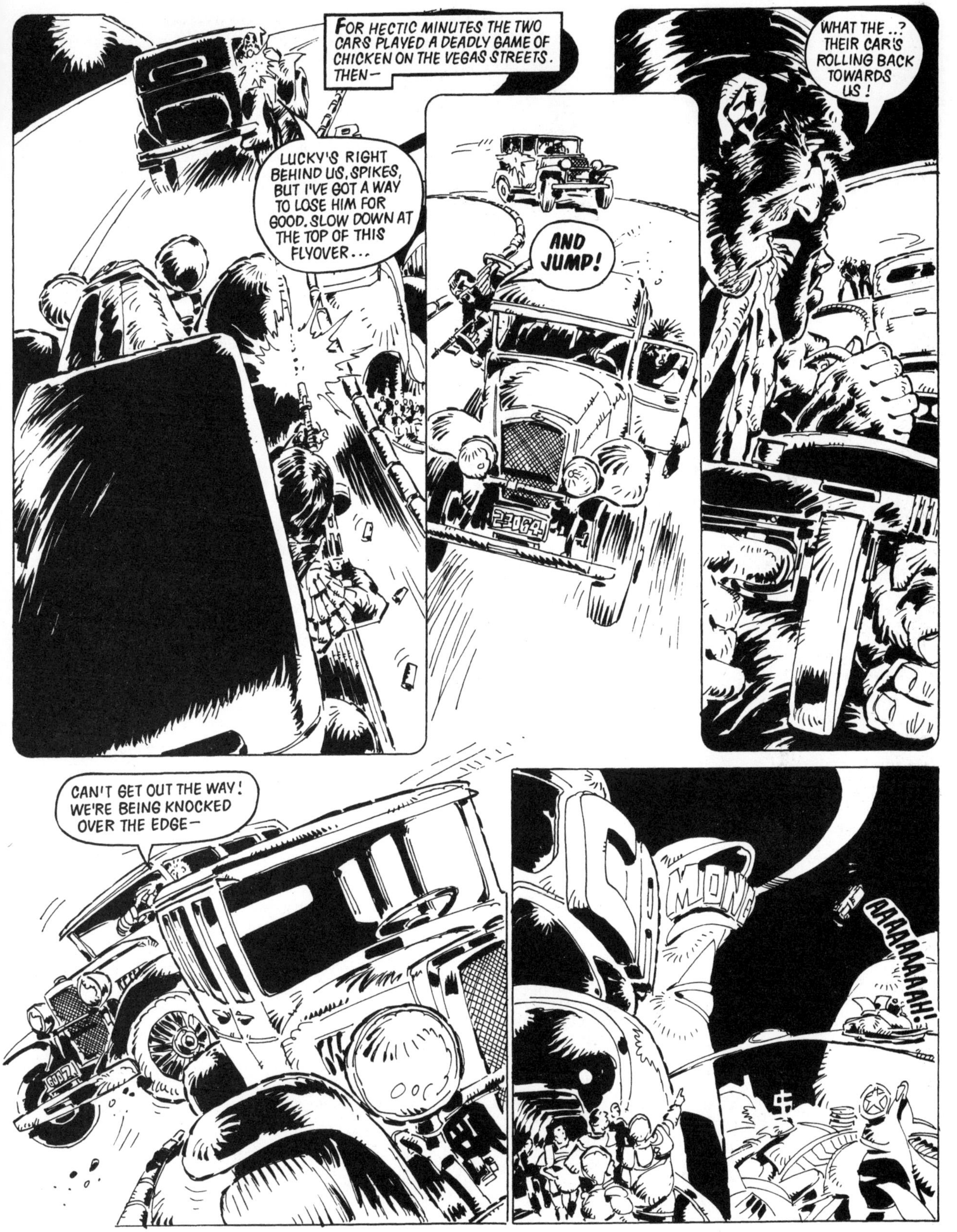

FOR HECTIC MINUTES THE TWO CARS PLAYED A DEADLY GAME OF CHICKEN ON THE VEGAS STREETS. THEN—
LUCKY'S RIGHT BEHIND US, SPIKES, BUT I'VE GOT A WAY TO LOSE HIM FOR GOOD. SLOW DOWN AT THE TOP OF THIS FLYOVER...
AND JUMP!
WHAT THE ..? THEIR CAR'S ROLLING BACK TOWARDS US!
CAN'T GET OUT THE WAY! WE'RE BEING KNOCKED OVER THE EDGE—
AAAAAAAAAAAH!

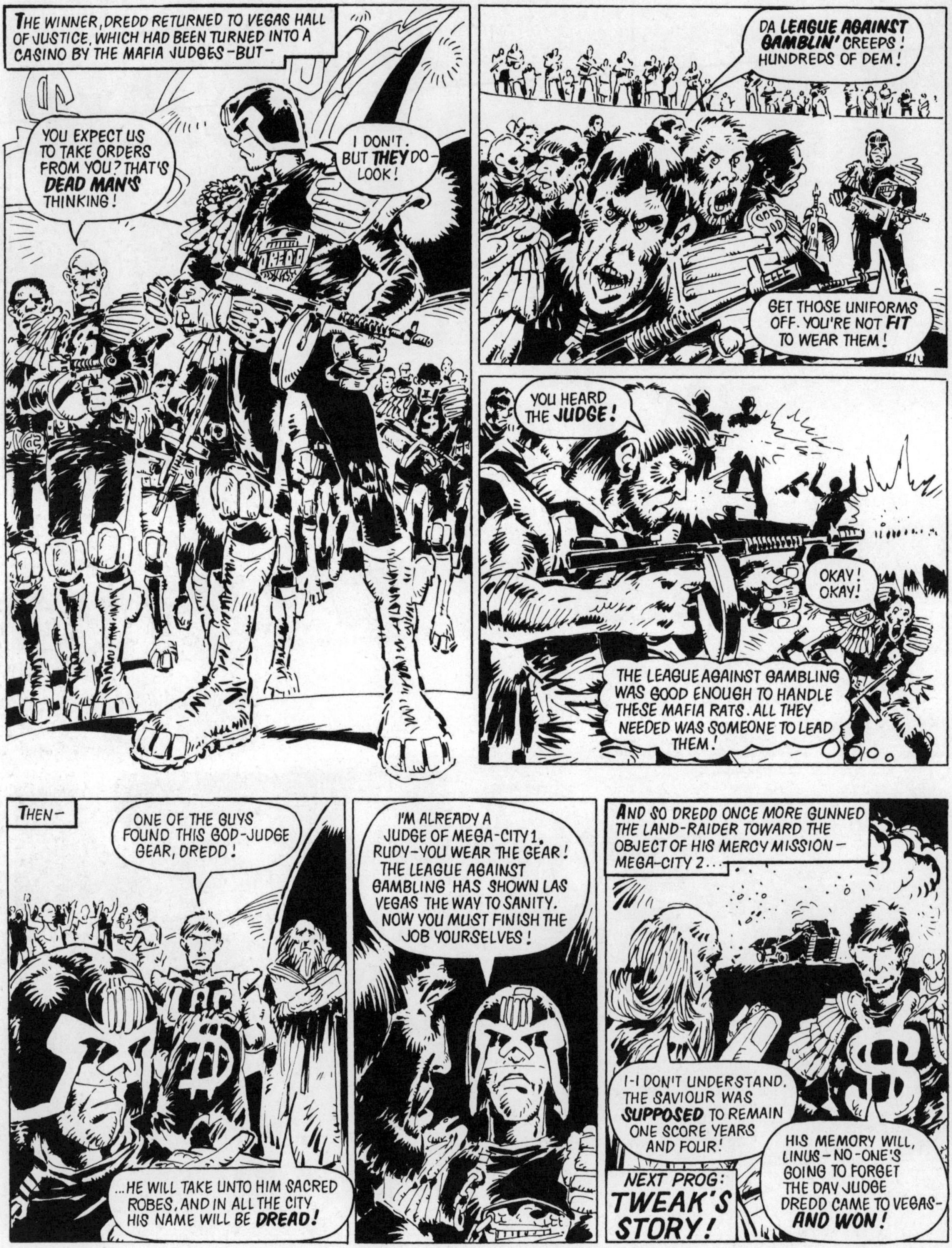
THE WINNER, DREDD RETURNED TO VEGAS HALL OF JUSTICE, WHICH HAD BEEN TURNED INTO A CASINO BY THE MAFIA JUDGES—BUT—
YOU EXPECT US TO TAKE ORDERS FROM YOU? THAT'S DEAD MAN'S THINKING!
I DON'T. BUT THEY DO—LOOK!
DA LEAGUE AGAINST GAMBLIN' CREEPS! HUNDREDS OF DEM!
GET THOSE UNIFORMS OFF. YOU'RE NOT FIT TO WEAR THEM!
YOU HEARD THE JUDGE!
OKAY! OKAY!
THE LEAGUE AGAINST GAMBLING WAS GOOD ENOUGH TO HANDLE THESE MAFIA RATS. ALL THEY NEEDED WAS SOMEONE TO LEAD THEM!
THEN—
ONE OF THE GUYS FOUND THIS GOD-JUDGE GEAR, DREDD!
...HE WILL TAKE UNTO HIM SACRED ROBES, AND IN ALL THE CITY HIS NAME WILL BE DREAD!
I'M ALREADY A JUDGE OF MEGA-CITY 1. RUDY—YOU WEAR THE GEAR! THE LEAGUE AGAINST GAMBLING HAS SHOWN LAS VEGAS THE WAY TO SANITY. NOW YOU MUST FINISH THE JOB YOURSELVES!
AND SO DREDD ONCE MORE GUNNED THE LAND-RAIDER TOWARD THE OBJECT OF HIS MERCY MISSION—MEGA-CITY 2...
I-I DON'T UNDERSTAND. THE SAVIOUR WAS SUPPOSED TO REMAIN ONE SCORE YEARS AND FOUR!
HIS MEMORY WILL, LINUS—NO-ONE'S GOING TO FORGET THE DAY JUDGE DREDD CAME TO VEGAS—AND WON!
NEXT PROG: TWEAK'S STORY!

JUDGE DREDD

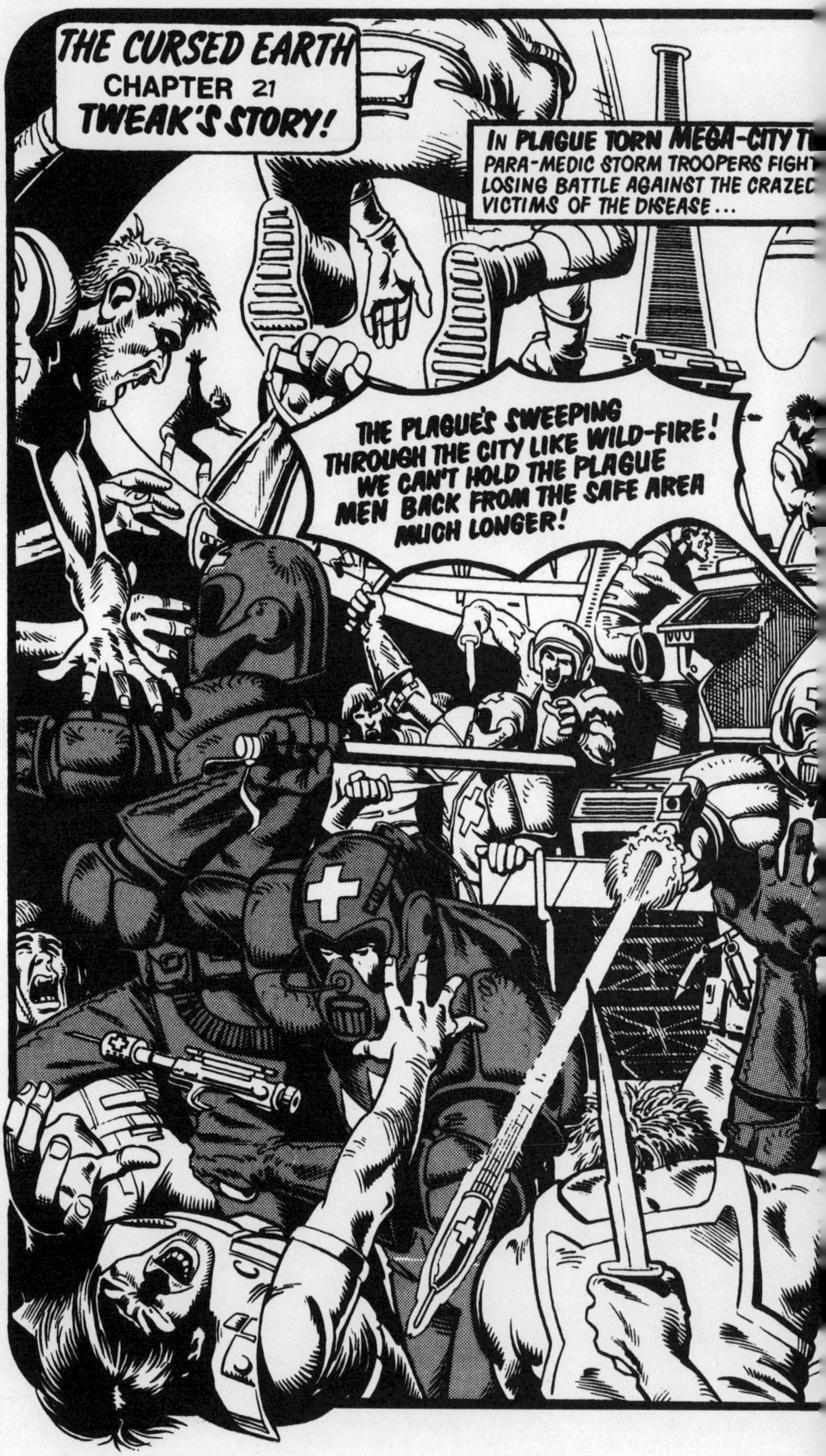

THE CURSED EARTH
CHAPTER 21
TWEAK'S STORY!
IN PLAGUE TORN MEGA-CITY T
PARA-MEDIC STORM TROOPERS FIGHT
LOSING BATTLE AGAINST THE CRAZED
VICTIMS OF THE DISEASE...
THE PLAGUE'S SWEEPING THROUGH THE CITY LIKE WILD-FIRE! WE CAN'T HOLD THE PLAGUE MEN BACK FROM THE SAFE AREA MUCH LONGER!

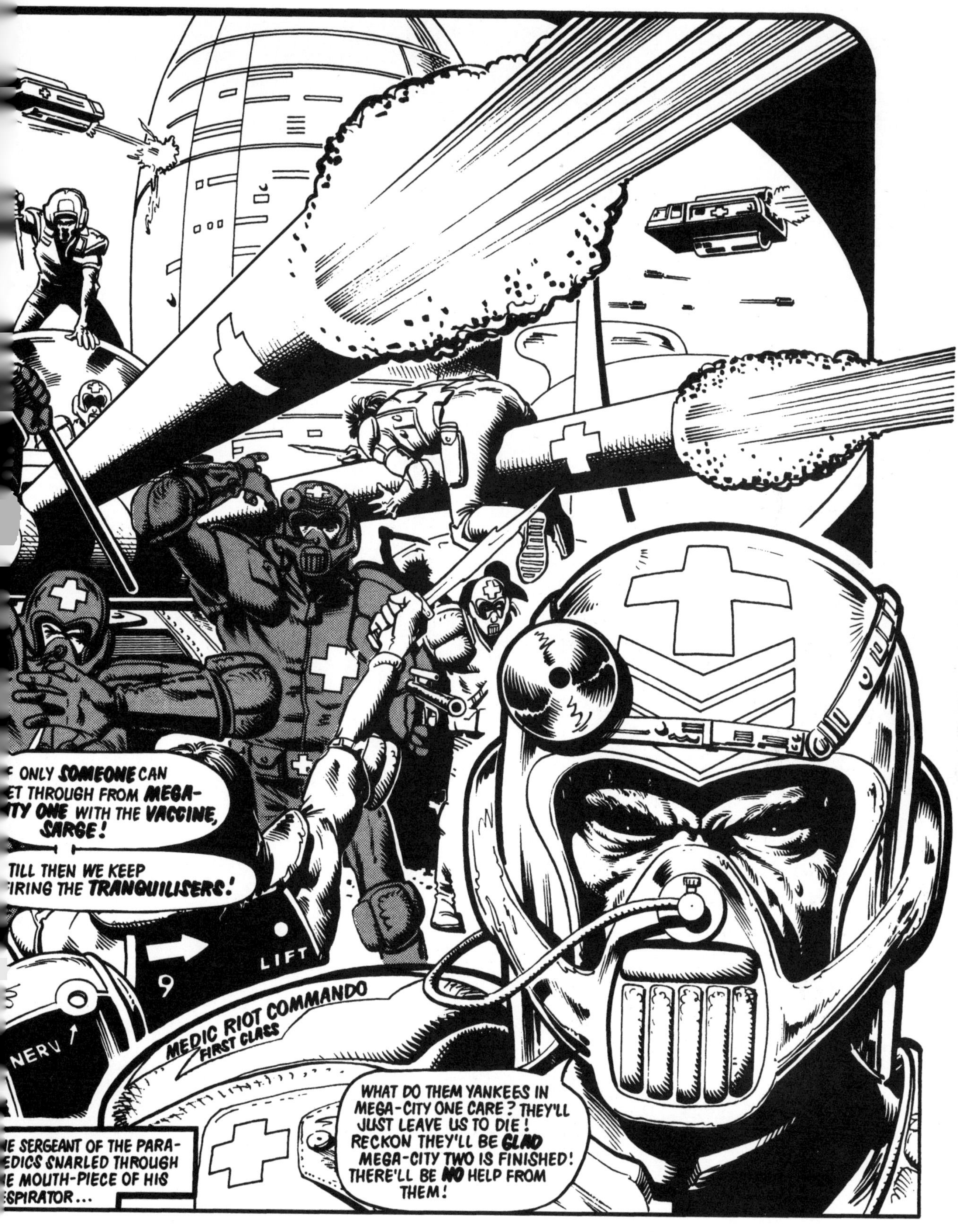
F ONLY SOMEONE CAN ET THROUGH FROM MEGA-TY ONE WITH THE VACCINE, SARGE!
TILL THEN WE KEEP FIRING THE TRANQUILISERS!
LIFT
9
NERV
MEDIC RIOT COMMANDO
FIRST CLASS
E SERGEANT OF THE PARA-EDICS SNARLED THROUGH E MOUTH-PIECE OF HIS ESPIRATOR...
WHAT DO THEM YANKEES IN MEGA-CITY ONE CARE? THEY'LL JUST LEAVE US TO DIE! RECKON THEY'LL BE GLAD MEGA-CITY TWO IS FINISHED! THERE'LL BE NO HELP FROM THEM!

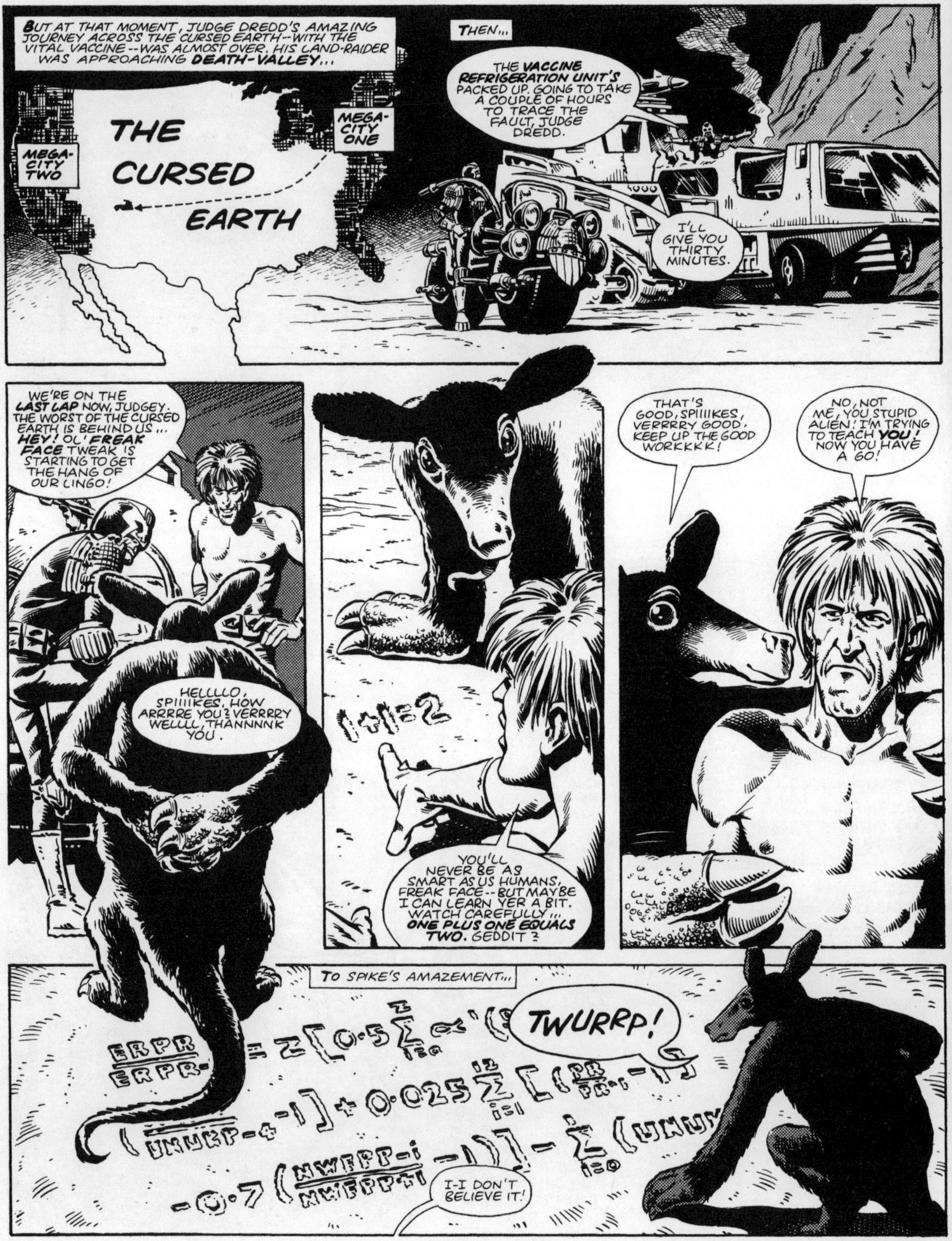

BUT AT THAT MOMENT, JUDGE DREDD'S AMAZING JOURNEY ACROSS THE CURSED EARTH--WITH THE VITAL VACCINE--WAS ALMOST OVER. HIS LAND-RAIDER WAS APPROACHING DEATH-VALLEY...
MEGA-CITY TWO
THE CURSED EARTH
MEGA-CITY ONE
THEN...
THE VACCINE REFRIGERATION UNIT'S PACKED UP. GOING TO TAKE A COUPLE OF HOURS TO TRACE THE FAULT, JUDGE DREDD.
I'LL GIVE YOU THIRTY MINUTES.
WE'RE ON THE LAST LAP NOW, JUDGEY. THE WORST OF THE CURSED EARTH IS BEHIND US... HEY! OL' FREAK FACE TWEAK IS STARTING TO GET THE HANG OF OUR LINGO!
HELLLLO, SPIIIIKES, HOW ARRRRE YOU? VERRRRY WELLLL, THANNNNK YOU.
1+1=2
YOU'LL NEVER BE AS SMART AS US HUMANS, FREAK FACE--BUT MAYBE I CAN LEARN YER A BIT. WATCH CAREFULLY... ONE PLUS ONE EQUALS TWO. GEDDIT?
THAT'S GOOD, SPIIIIKES, VERRRRY GOOD. KEEP UP THE GOOD WORKKKK!
NO, NOT ME, YOU STUPID ALIEN! I'M TRYING TO TEACH YOU! NOW YOU HAVE A GO!
TO SPIKE'S AMAZEMENT...
TWURRP!
I-I DON'T BELIEVE IT!

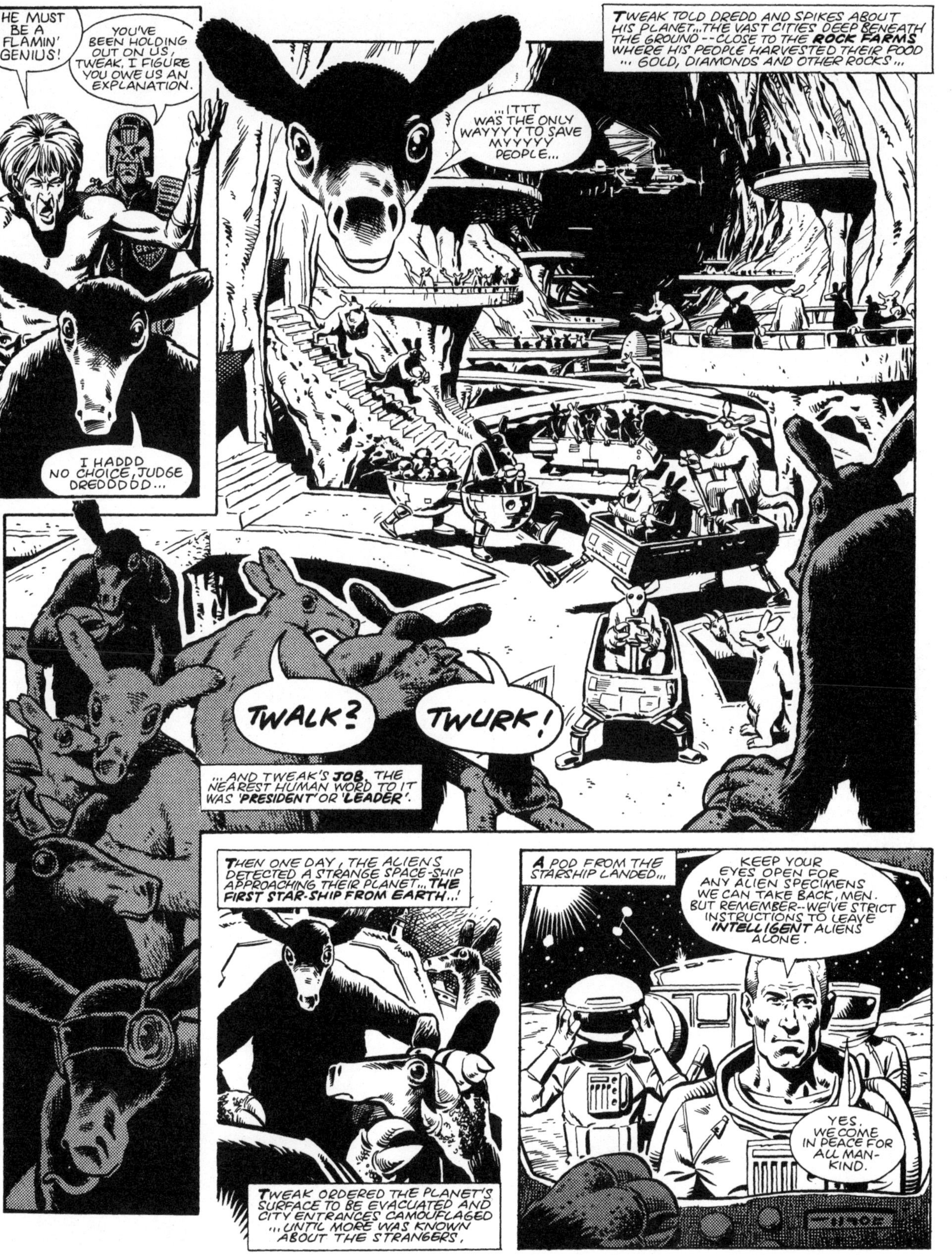
HE MUST BE A FLAMIN' GENIUS!
YOU'VE BEEN HOLDING OUT ON US, TWEAK. I FIGURE YOU OWE US AN EXPLANATION.
I HADDD NO CHOICE, JUDGE DREDDDDD...
TWEAK TOLD DREDD AND SPIKES ABOUT HIS PLANET... THE VAST CITIES DEEP BENEATH THE GROUND -- CLOSE TO THE ROCK FARMS WHERE HIS PEOPLE HARVESTED THEIR FOOD ... GOLD, DIAMONDS AND OTHER ROCKS...
...ITTT WAS THE ONLY WAYYYY TO SAVE MYYYYY PEOPLE...
TWALK?
TWURK!
...AND TWEAK'S JOB. THE NEAREST HUMAN WORD TO IT WAS 'PRESIDENT' OR 'LEADER'.
THEN ONE DAY, THE ALIENS DETECTED A STRANGE SPACE-SHIP APPROACHING THEIR PLANET... THE FIRST STAR-SHIP FROM EARTH...!
TWEAK ORDERED THE PLANET'S SURFACE TO BE EVACUATED AND CITY ENTRANCES CAMOUFLAGED ...UNTIL MORE WAS KNOWN ABOUT THE STRANGERS.
A POD FROM THE STARSHIP LANDED...
KEEP YOUR EYES OPEN FOR ANY ALIEN SPECIMENS WE CAN TAKE BACK, MEN. BUT REMEMBER--WE'VE STRICT INSTRUCTIONS TO LEAVE INTELLIGENT ALIENS ALONE.
YES. WE COME IN PEACE FOR ALL MAN-KIND.

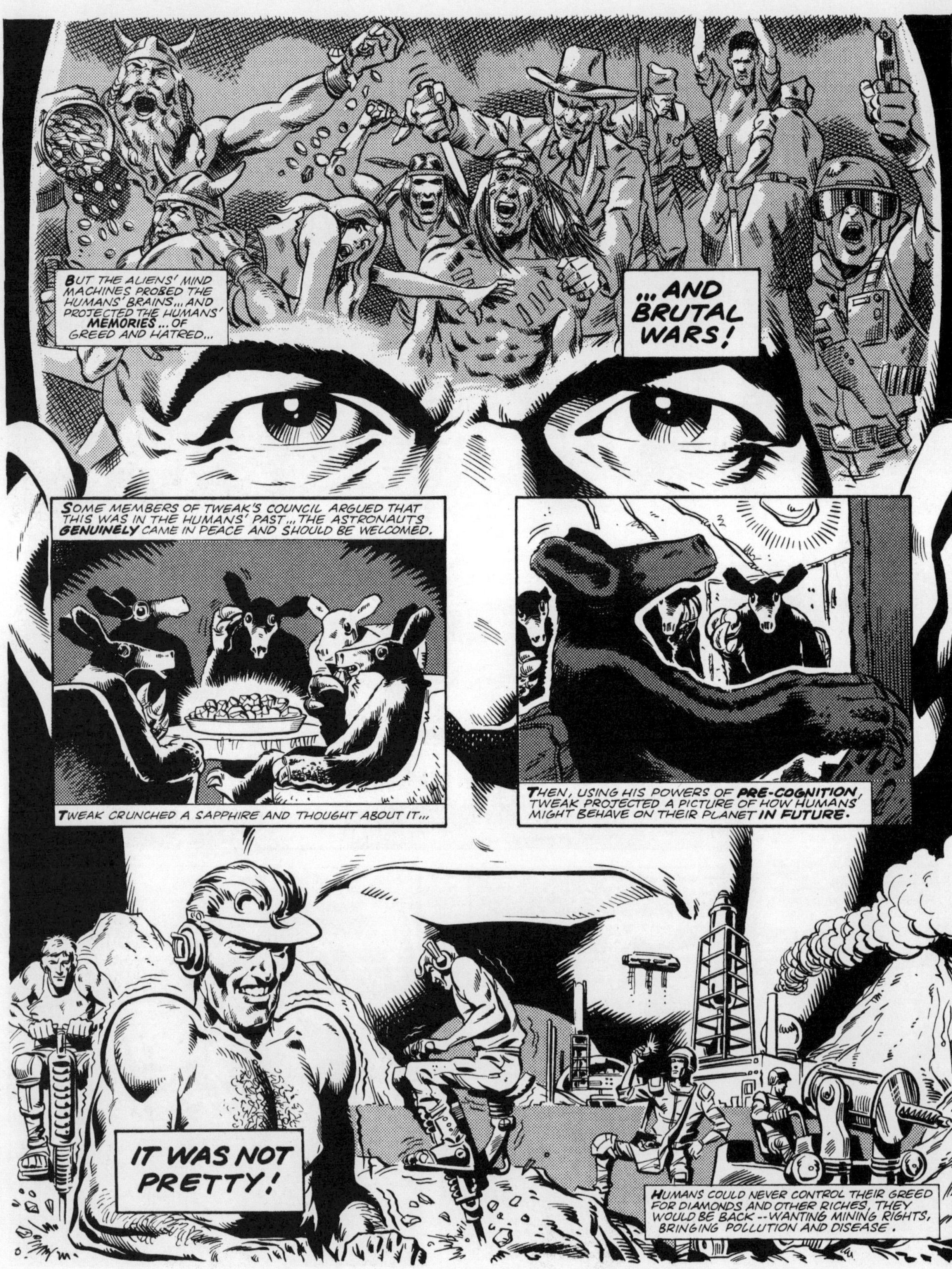

BUT THE ALIENS' MIND MACHINES PROBED THE HUMANS' BRAINS... AND PROJECTED THE HUMANS' MEMORIES... OF GREED AND HATRED...
...AND BRUTAL WARS!
SOME MEMBERS OF TWEAK'S COUNCIL ARGUED THAT THIS WAS IN THE HUMANS' PAST... THE ASTRONAUTS GENUINELY CAME IN PEACE AND SHOULD BE WELCOMED.
TWEAK CRUNCHED A SAPPHIRE AND THOUGHT ABOUT IT...
THEN, USING HIS POWERS OF PRE-COGNITION, TWEAK PROJECTED A PICTURE OF HOW HUMANS MIGHT BEHAVE ON THEIR PLANET IN FUTURE.
IT WAS NOT PRETTY!
HUMANS COULD NEVER CONTROL THEIR GREED FOR DIAMONDS AND OTHER RICHES, THEY WOULD BE BACK --WANTING MINING RIGHTS, BRINGING POLLUTION AND DISEASE.

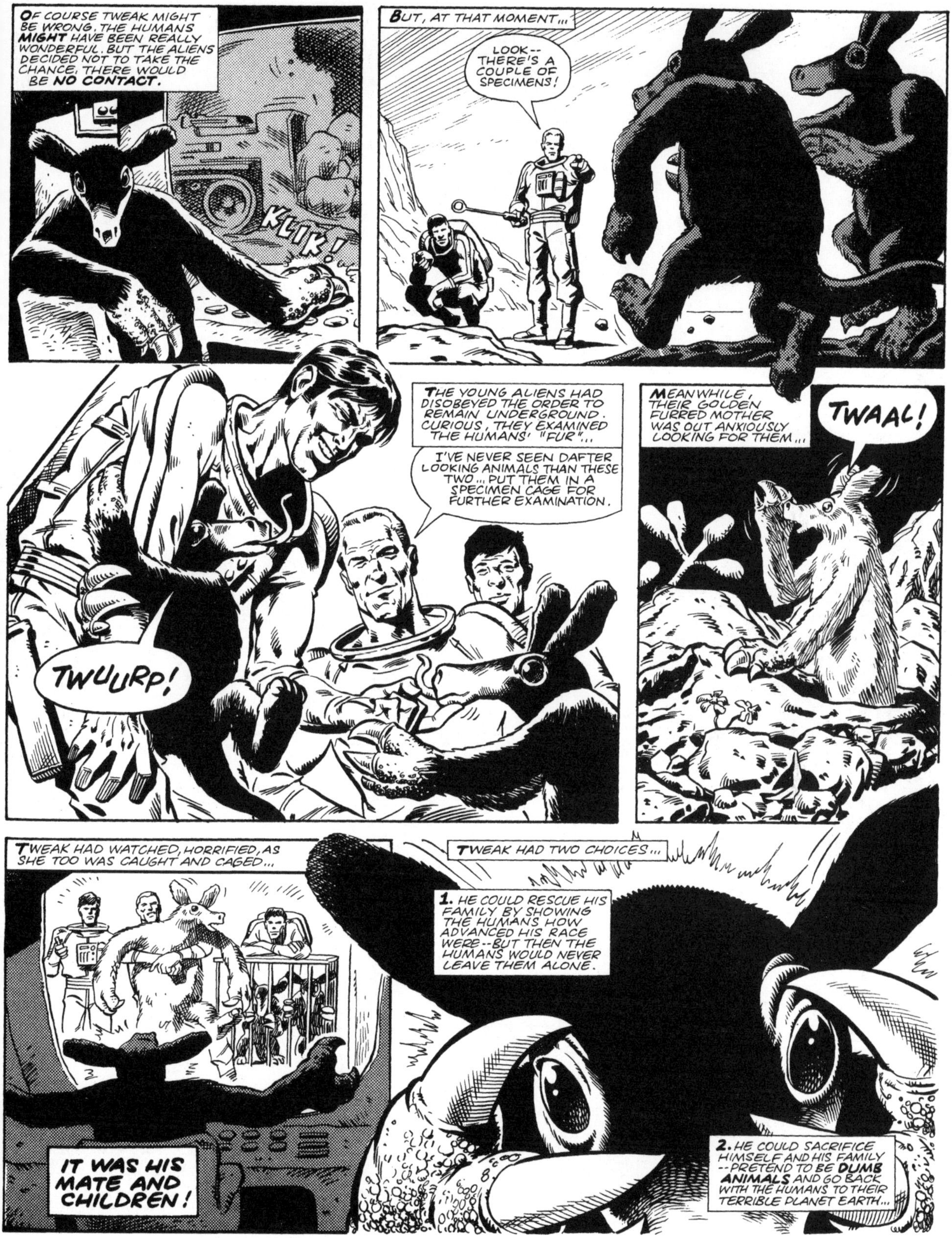

OF COURSE TWEAK MIGHT BE WRONG. THE HUMANS **MIGHT** HAVE BEEN REALLY WONDERFUL. BUT THE ALIENS DECIDED NOT TO TAKE THE CHANCE. THERE WOULD BE **NO CONTACT**.
KLIK!
BUT, AT THAT MOMENT...
LOOK-- THERE'S A COUPLE OF SPECIMENS!
THE YOUNG ALIENS HAD DISOBEYED THE ORDER TO REMAIN UNDERGROUND. CURIOUS, THEY EXAMINED THE HUMANS' "FUR"...
I'VE NEVER SEEN DAFTER LOOKING ANIMALS THAN THESE TWO... PUT THEM IN A SPECIMEN CAGE FOR FURTHER EXAMINATION.
TWUURP!
MEANWHILE, THEIR GOLDEN FURRED MOTHER WAS OUT ANXIOUSLY LOOKING FOR THEM...
TWAAL!
TWEAK HAD WATCHED, HORRIFIED, AS SHE TOO WAS CAUGHT AND CAGED...
IT WAS HIS MATE AND CHILDREN!
TWEAK HAD TWO CHOICES...
1. HE COULD RESCUE HIS FAMILY BY SHOWING THE HUMANS HOW ADVANCED HIS RACE WERE--BUT THEN THE HUMANS WOULD NEVER LEAVE THEM ALONE.
2. HE COULD SACRIFICE HIMSELF AND HIS FAMILY --PRETEND TO BE **DUMB ANIMALS** AND GO BACK WITH THE HUMANS TO THEIR TERRIBLE PLANET EARTH...

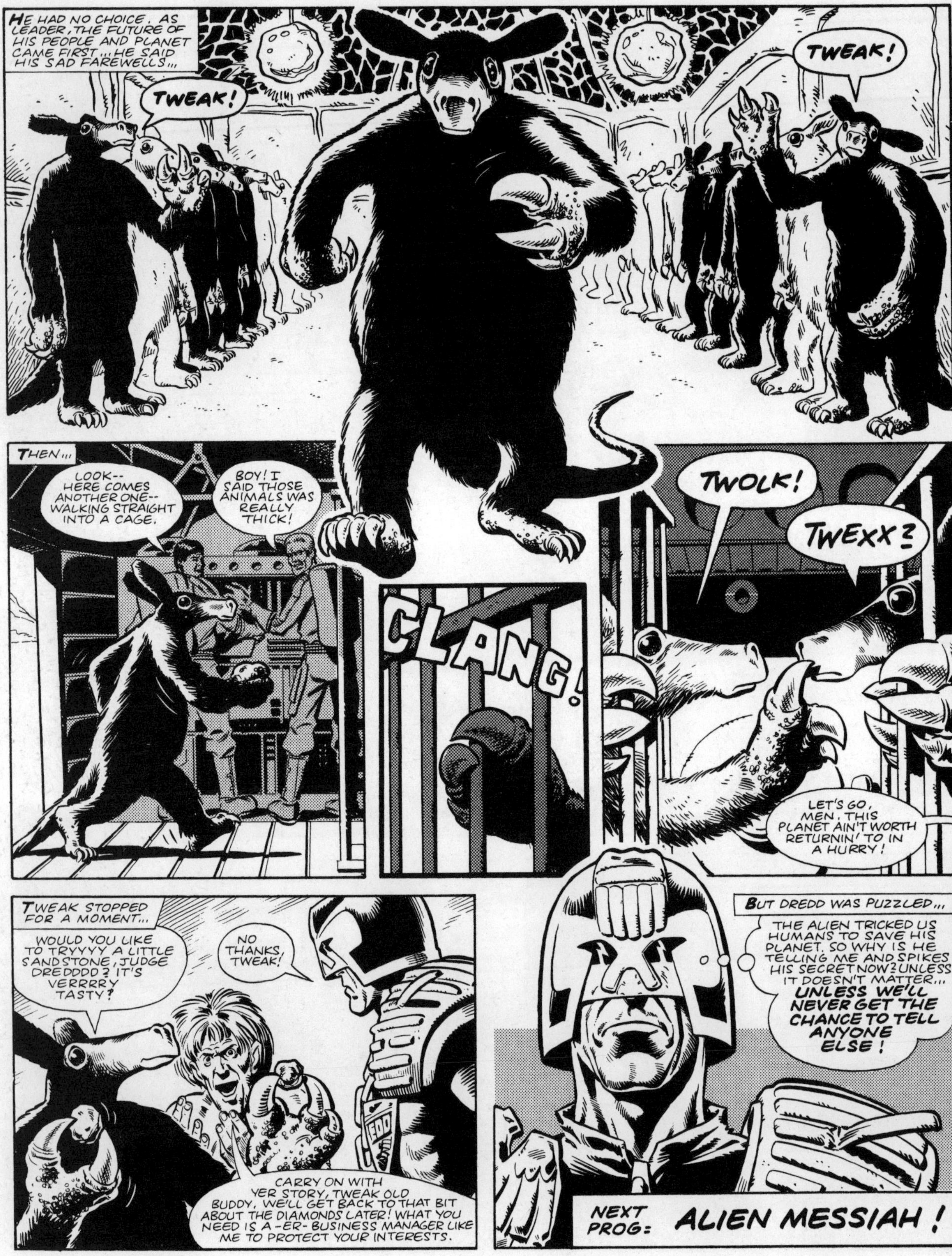
HE HAD NO CHOICE. AS LEADER, THE FUTURE OF HIS PEOPLE AND PLANET CAME FIRST... HE SAID HIS SAD FAREWELLS...
TWEAK!
TWEAK!
THEN...
LOOK-- HERE COMES ANOTHER ONE-- WALKING STRAIGHT INTO A CAGE.
BOY! I SAID THOSE ANIMALS WAS REALLY THICK!
CLANG!
TWOLK!
TWEXX?
LET'S GO, MEN. THIS PLANET AIN'T WORTH RETURNIN' TO IN A HURRY!
TWEAK STOPPED FOR A MOMENT...
WOULD YOU LIKE TO TRYYYY A LITTLE SANDSTONE, JUDGE DREDDDD? IT'S VERRRRY TASTY?
NO THANKS, TWEAK!
CARRY ON WITH YER STORY, TWEAK OLD BUDDY. WE'LL GET BACK TO THAT BIT ABOUT THE DIAMONDS LATER! WHAT YOU NEED IS A -ER- BUSINESS MANAGER LIKE ME TO PROTECT YOUR INTERESTS.
BUT DREDD WAS PUZZLED...
THE ALIEN TRICKED US HUMANS TO SAVE HIS PLANET. SO WHY IS HE TELLING ME AND SPIKES HIS SECRET NOW? UNLESS IT DOESN'T MATTER... UNLESS WE'LL NEVER GET THE CHANCE TO TELL ANYONE ELSE!
NEXT PROG: ALIEN MESSIAH!

THE CURSED EARTH

CHAPTER 22

TWEAK'S STORY

JUDGE DREDD

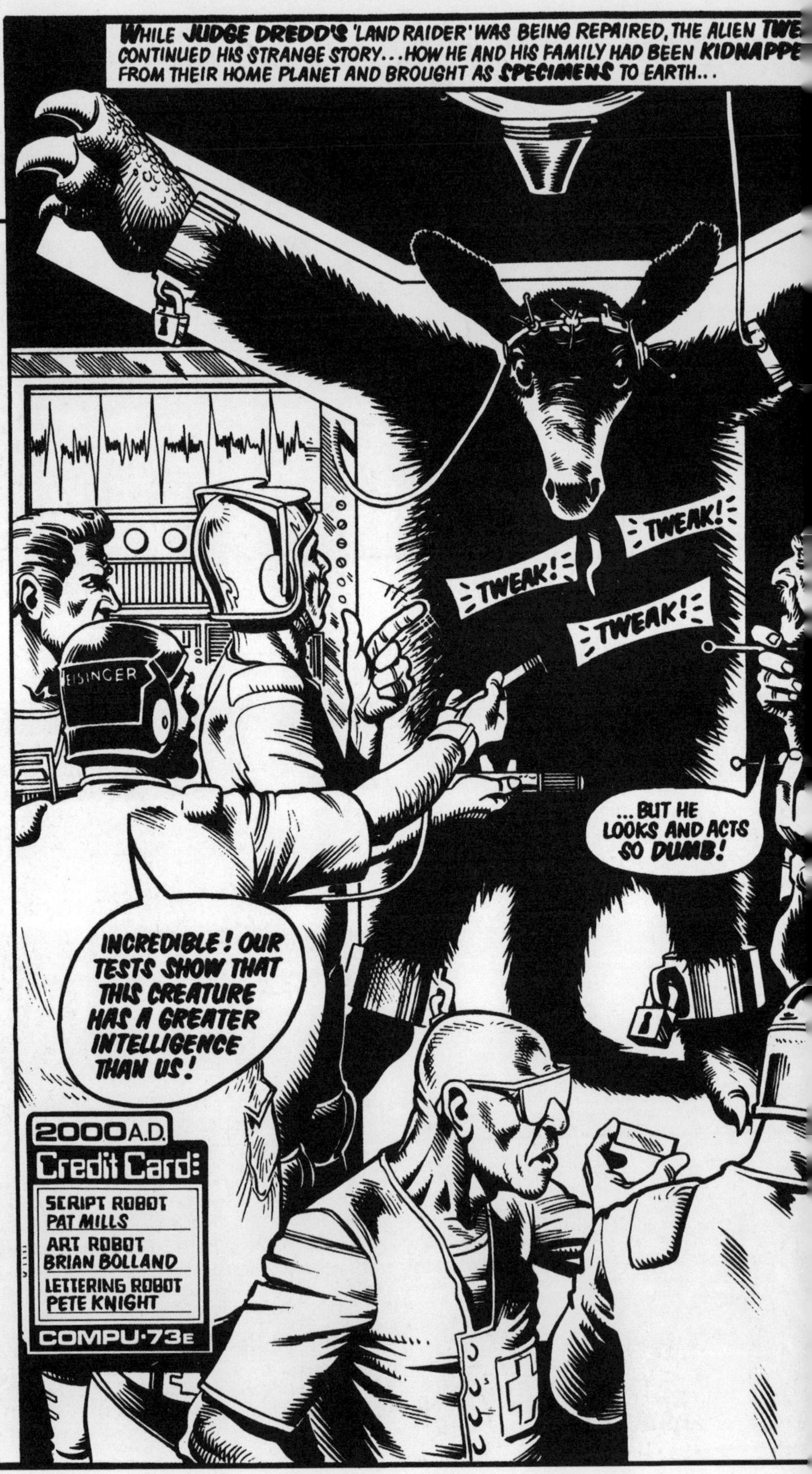
WHILE JUDGE DREDD'S 'LAND RAIDER' WAS BEING REPAIRED, THE ALIEN TWE
CONTINUED HIS STRANGE STORY... HOW HE AND HIS FAMILY HAD BEEN KIDNAPPE
FROM THEIR HOME PLANET AND BROUGHT AS SPECIMENS TO EARTH...
TWEAK!
TWEAK!
TWEAK!
EISINGER
... BUT HE LOOKS AND ACTS SO DUMB!
INCREDIBLE! OUR TESTS SHOW THAT THIS CREATURE HAS A GREATER INTELLIGENCE THAN US!
2000 A.D. Credit Card:
SCRIPT ROBOT PAT MILLS
ART ROBOT BRIAN BOLLAND
LETTERING ROBOT PETE KNIGHT
COMPU·73E

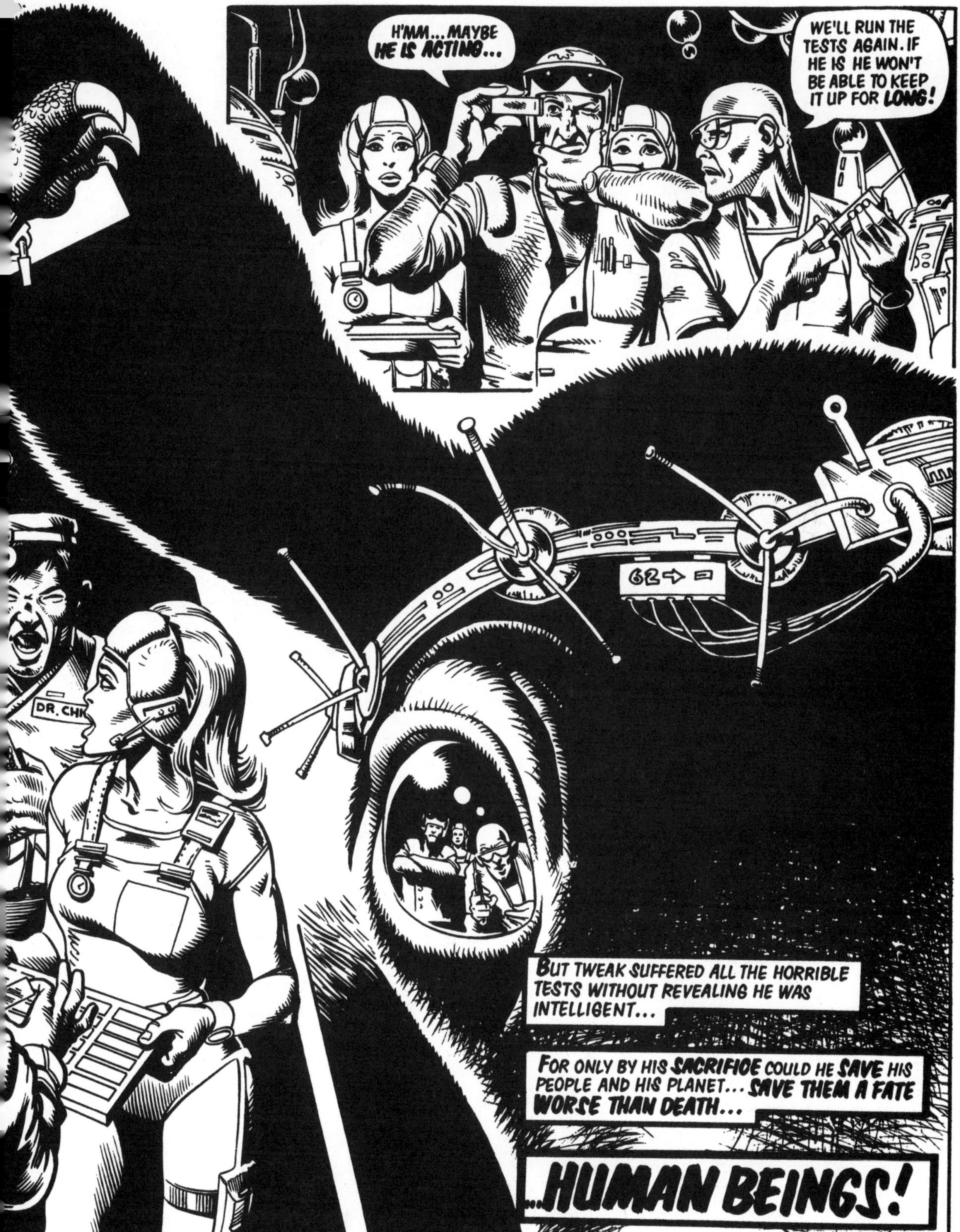
H'MM... MAYBE HE IS ACTING...
WE'LL RUN THE TESTS AGAIN. IF HE IS HE WON'T BE ABLE TO KEEP IT UP FOR LONG!
62 →
DR. CH
BUT TWEAK SUFFERED ALL THE HORRIBLE TESTS WITHOUT REVEALING HE WAS INTELLIGENT...
FOR ONLY BY HIS SACRIFICE COULD HE SAVE HIS PEOPLE AND HIS PLANET... SAVE THEM A FATE WORSE THAN DEATH...
...HUMAN BEINGS!

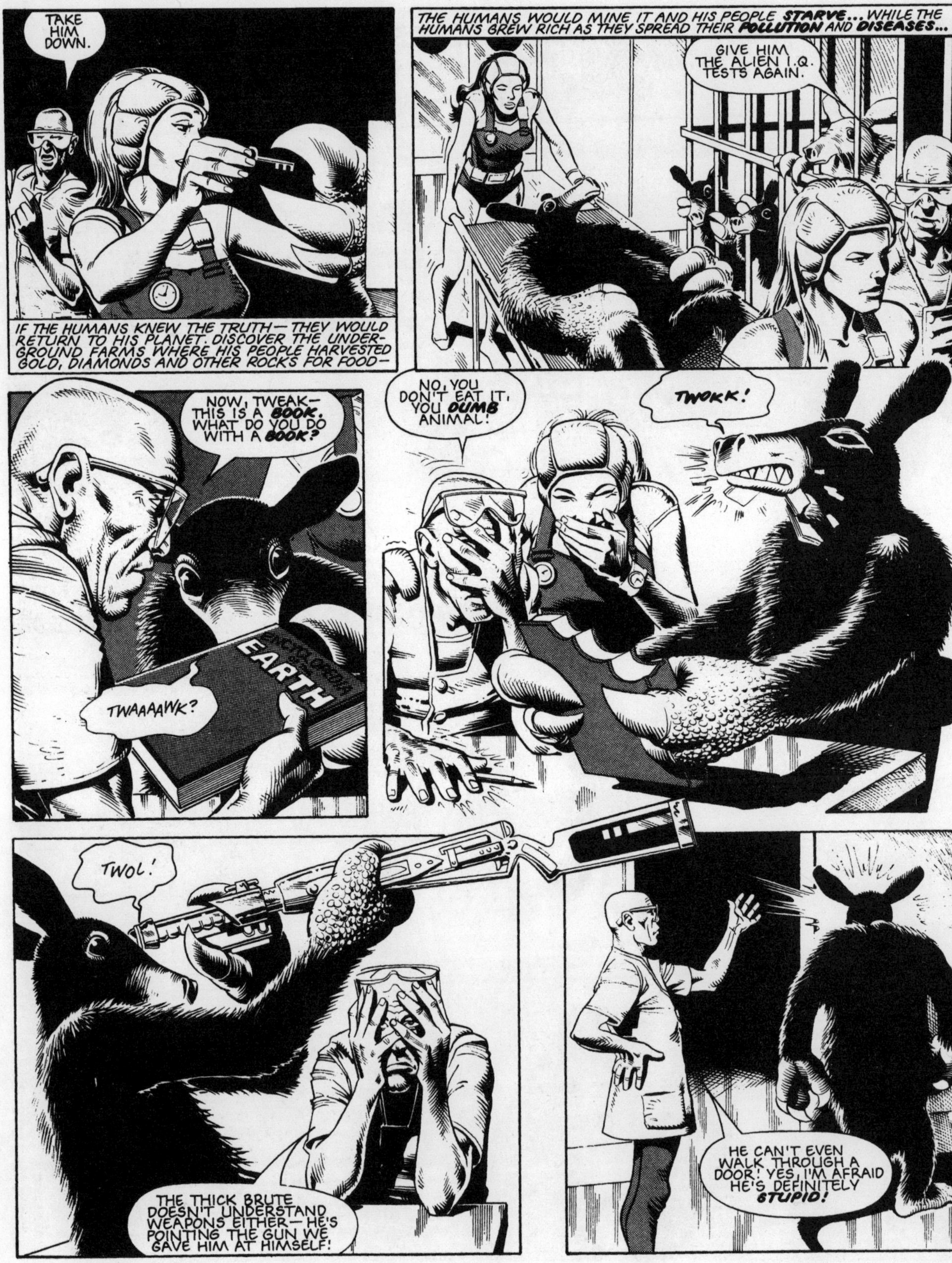

TAKE HIM DOWN.
IF THE HUMANS KNEW THE TRUTH— THEY WOULD RETURN TO HIS PLANET. DISCOVER THE UNDERGROUND FARMS WHERE HIS PEOPLE HARVESTED GOLD, DIAMONDS AND OTHER ROCKS FOR FOOD—
THE HUMANS WOULD MINE IT AND HIS PEOPLE STARVE... WHILE THE HUMANS GREW RICH AS THEY SPREAD THEIR POLLUTION AND DISEASES...
GIVE HIM THE ALIEN I.Q. TESTS AGAIN.
NOW, TWEAK— THIS IS A BOOK. WHAT DO YOU DO WITH A BOOK?
ENCYCLOPEDIA EARTH
TWAAAAWK?
NO, YOU DON'T EAT IT, YOU DUMB ANIMAL!
TWOKK!
TWOL!
THE THICK BRUTE DOESN'T UNDERSTAND WEAPONS EITHER— HE'S POINTING THE GUN WE GAVE HIM AT HIMSELF!
HE CAN'T EVEN WALK THROUGH A DOOR! YES, I'M AFRAID HE'S DEFINITELY STUPID!

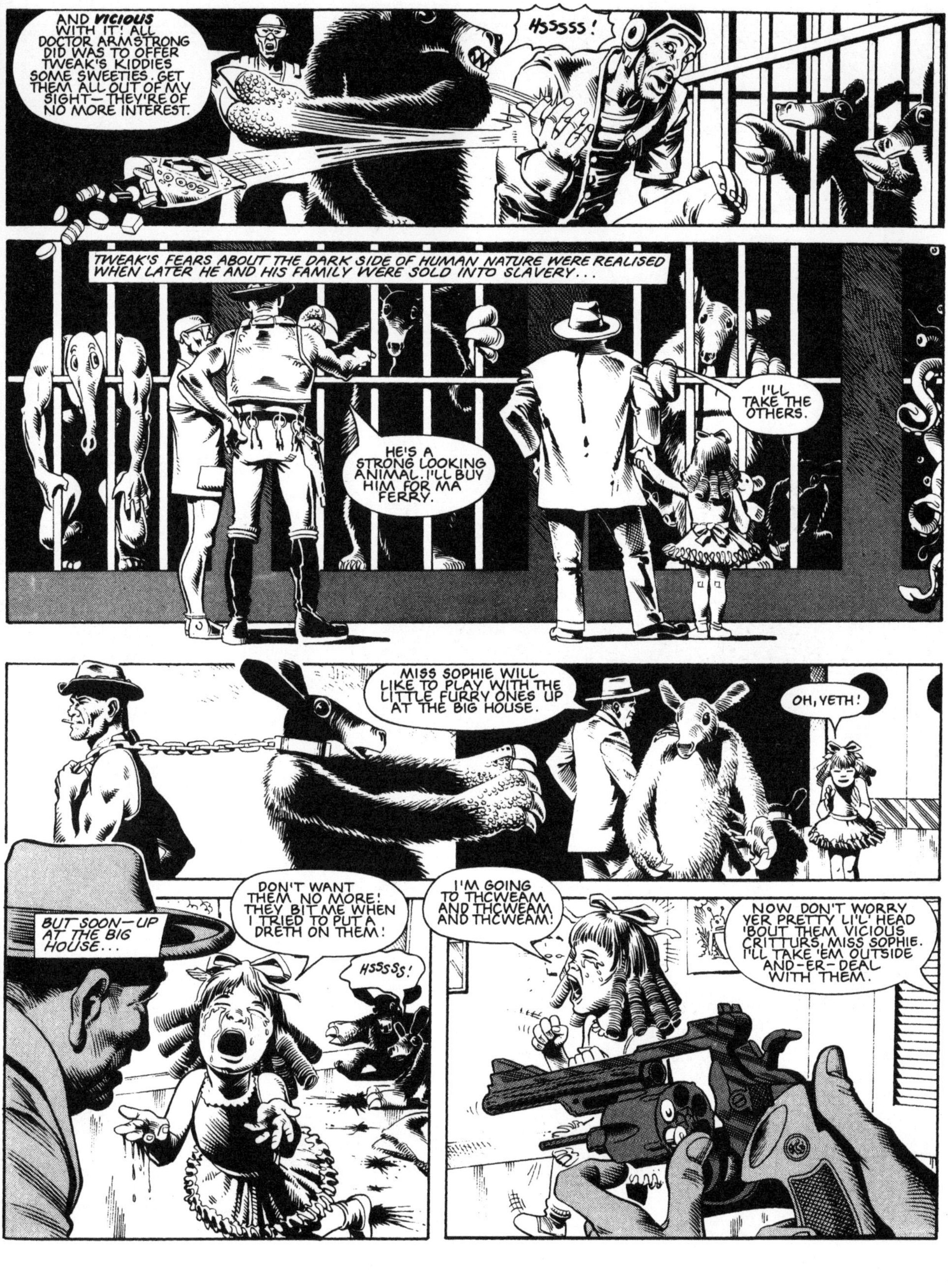
AND VICIOUS WITH IT! ALL DOCTOR ARMSTRONG DID WAS TO OFFER TWEAK'S KIDDIES SOME SWEETIES. GET THEM ALL OUT OF MY SIGHT— THEY'RE OF NO MORE INTEREST.
HSSSSS!
TWEAK'S FEARS ABOUT THE DARK SIDE OF HUMAN NATURE WERE REALISED WHEN LATER HE AND HIS FAMILY WERE SOLD INTO SLAVERY...
HE'S A STRONG LOOKING ANIMAL. I'LL BUY HIM FOR MA FERRY.
I'LL TAKE THE OTHERS.
MISS SOPHIE WILL LIKE TO PLAY WITH THE LITTLE FURRY ONES UP AT THE BIG HOUSE.
OH, YETH!
BUT SOON— UP AT THE BIG HOUSE...
DON'T WANT THEM NO MORE! THEY BIT ME WHEN I TRIED TO PUT A DRETH ON THEM!
HSSSSS!
I'M GOING TO THCWEAM AND THCWEAM AND THCWEAM!
NOW DON'T WORRY YER PRETTY LI'L' HEAD 'BOUT THEM VICIOUS CRITTURS, MISS SOPHIE. I'LL TAKE 'EM OUTSIDE AND—ER—DEAL WITH THEM.

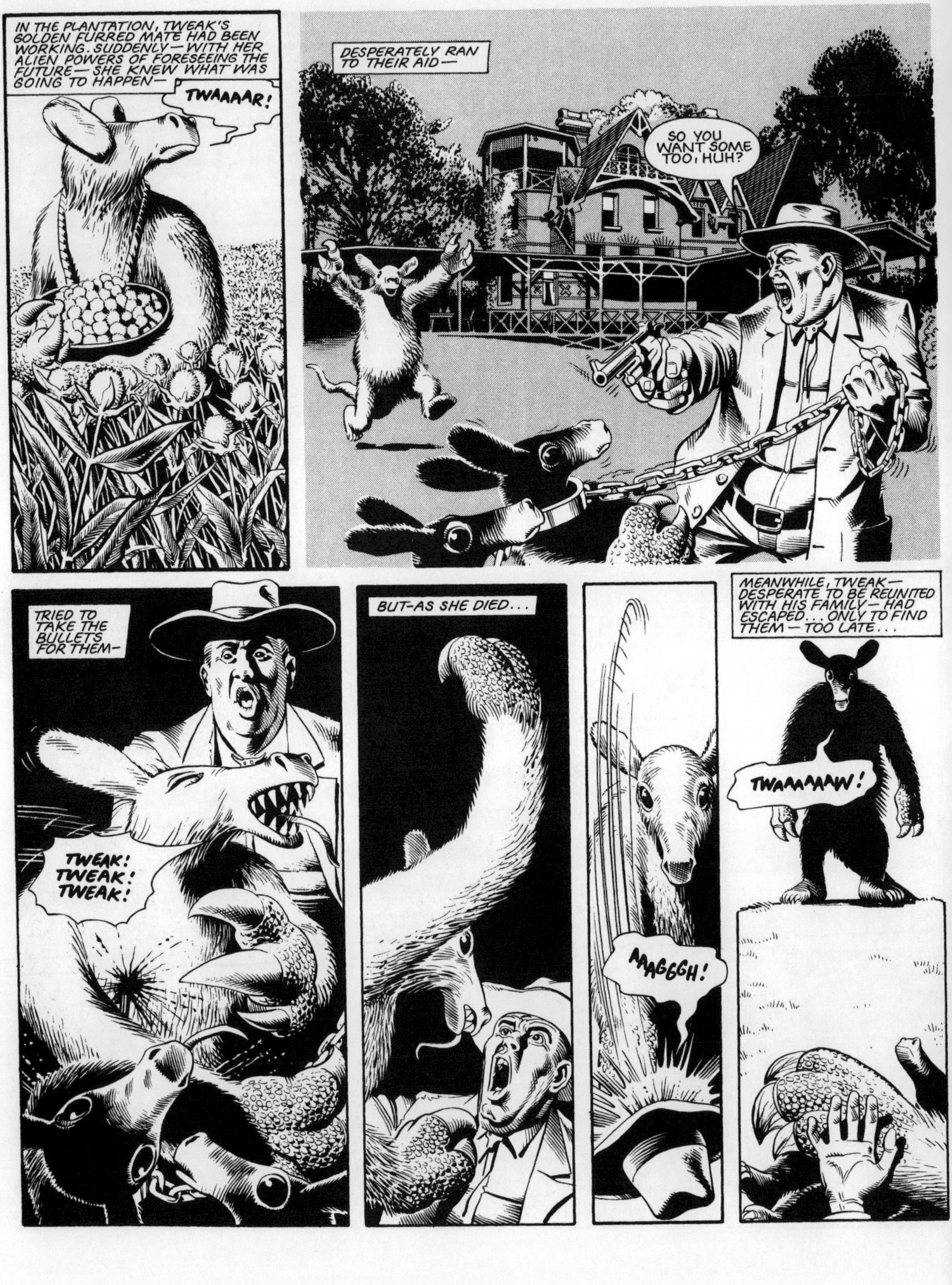
IN THE PLANTATION, TWEAK'S GOLDEN FURRED MATE HAD BEEN WORKING. SUDDENLY—WITH HER ALIEN POWERS OF FORESEEING THE FUTURE—SHE KNEW WHAT WAS GOING TO HAPPEN—
TWAAAAR!
DESPERATELY RAN TO THEIR AID—
SO YOU WANT SOME TOO, HUH?
TRIED TO TAKE THE BULLETS FOR THEM—
TWEAK! TWEAK! TWEAK!
BUT-AS SHE DIED...
AAAGGGH!
MEANWHILE, TWEAK—DESPERATE TO BE REUNITED WITH HIS FAMILY—HAD ESCAPED... ONLY TO FIND THEM—TOO LATE...
TWAAAAAAW!

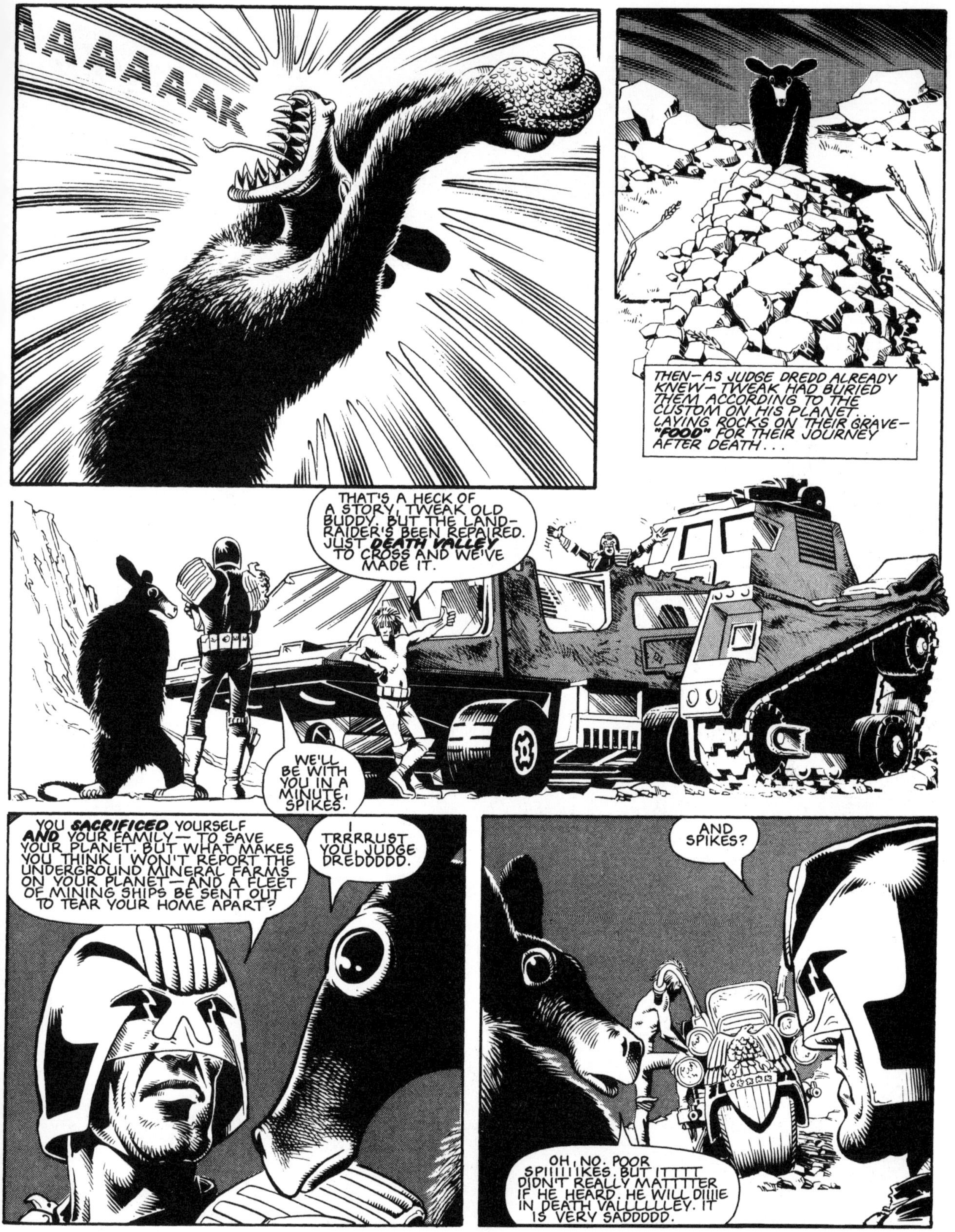
AAAAAAAK
THEN—AS JUDGE DREDD ALREADY KNEW—TWEAK HAD BURIED THEM ACCORDING TO THE CUSTOM ON HIS PLANET. LAYING ROCKS ON THEIR GRAVE—"FOOD" FOR THEIR JOURNEY AFTER DEATH...
THAT'S A HECK OF A STORY, TWEAK OLD BUDDY. BUT THE LAND-RAIDER'S BEEN REPAIRED. JUST DEATH VALLEY TO CROSS AND WE'VE MADE IT.
WE'LL BE WITH YOU IN A MINUTE, SPIKES.
YOU SACRIFICED YOURSELF AND YOUR FAMILY— TO SAVE YOUR PLANET. BUT WHAT MAKES YOU THINK I WON'T REPORT THE UNDERGROUND MINERAL FARMS ON YOUR PLANET— AND A FLEET OF MINING SHIPS BE SENT OUT TO TEAR YOUR HOME APART?
I TRRRRUST YOU, JUDGE DREDDDDD.
AND SPIKES?
OH, NO. POOR SPIIIIIIKES. BUT ITTTT DIDN'T REALLY MATTTTER IF HE HEARD. HE WILL DIIIIE IN DEATH VALLLLLLLEY. IT IS VERY SADDDDD.

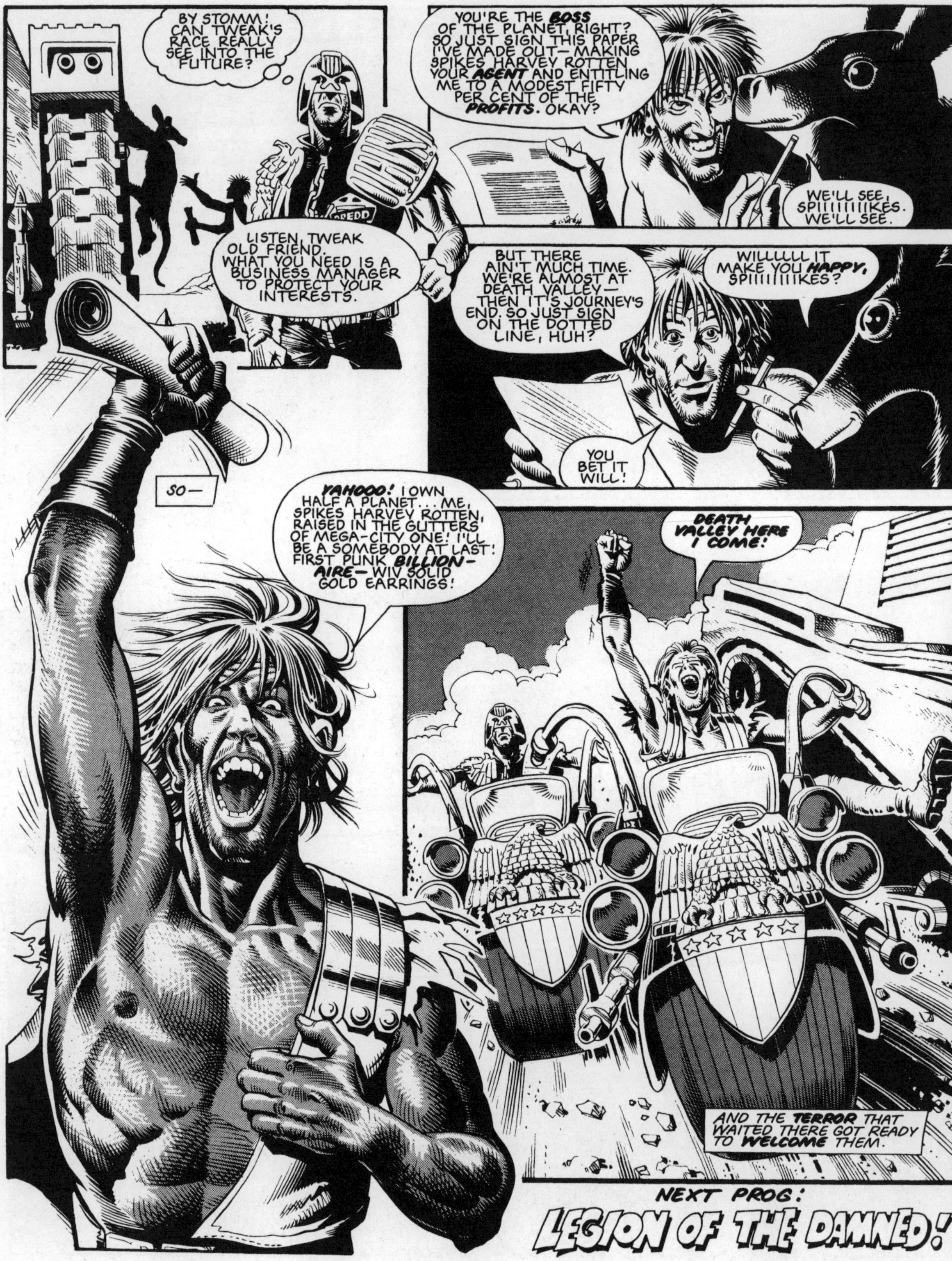

BY STOMM! CAN TWEAK'S RACE REALLY SEE INTO THE FUTURE?
LISTEN, TWEAK OLD FRIEND. WHAT YOU NEED IS A BUSINESS MANAGER TO PROTECT YOUR INTERESTS.
YOU'RE THE BOSS OF THE PLANET, RIGHT? SO JUST SIGN THIS PAPER I'VE MADE OUT— MAKING SPIKES HARVEY ROTTEN YOUR AGENT AND ENTITLING ME TO A MODEST FIFTY PER CENT OF THE PROFITS. OKAY?
WE'LL SEE, SPIIIIIIIIKES. WE'LL SEE.
BUT THERE AIN'T MUCH TIME. WE'RE ALMOST AT DEATH VALLEY— THEN IT'S JOURNEY'S END. SO JUST SIGN ON THE DOTTED LINE, HUH?
WILLLLLL IT MAKE YOU HAPPY, SPIIIIIIIIKES?
YOU BET IT WILL!
SO—
YAHOOO! I OWN HALF A PLANET... ME, SPIKES HARVEY ROTTEN, RAISED IN THE GUTTERS OF MEGA-CITY ONE! I'LL BE A SOMEBODY AT LAST! FIRST PUNK BILLION-AIRE— WIV SOLID GOLD EARRINGS!
DEATH VALLEY HERE I COME!
AND THE TERROR THAT WAITED THERE GOT READY TO WELCOME THEM.

NEXT PROG:

LEGION OF THE DAMNED!

THE CURSED EARTH
CHAPTER 23
LEGION OF THE DAMNED!

JUDGE DREDD'S DESPERATE RESCUE MISSION TO MEGA-CITY TWO WITH THE LIFE SAVING VACCINE IS ALMOST OVER. HIS 'LAND RAIDER' HAS NOW REACHED DEATH VALLEY...THERE DREDD ORDERS A HALT...

C'MON, DREDD...SEE THEM BEAUTIFUL LIGHTS OF MEGA-CITY TWO IN THE DISTANCE...? IT'S JOURNEY'S END! AGAINST ALL THE ODDS WE MADE IT!

ONE MOMENT, SPIKES...I WISH TO PAY MY LAST RESPECTS!

THE STATUE HONOURS THE JUDGES WHO DIED IN THE MOST SAVAGE BATTLE OF MODERN TIMES, SPIKES...FOUGHT HERE IN DEATH VALLEY. WORSE EVEN THAN ALAMEIN, IWO JIMA AND STALINGRAD...

THE BATTLE OF ARMAGEDDON!

DEATH VALLEY WAR MEMORIAL

BATTLE OF ARMAGEDDON 2071 a.d.

To the Glorious Dead

...LEST WE FORGET...

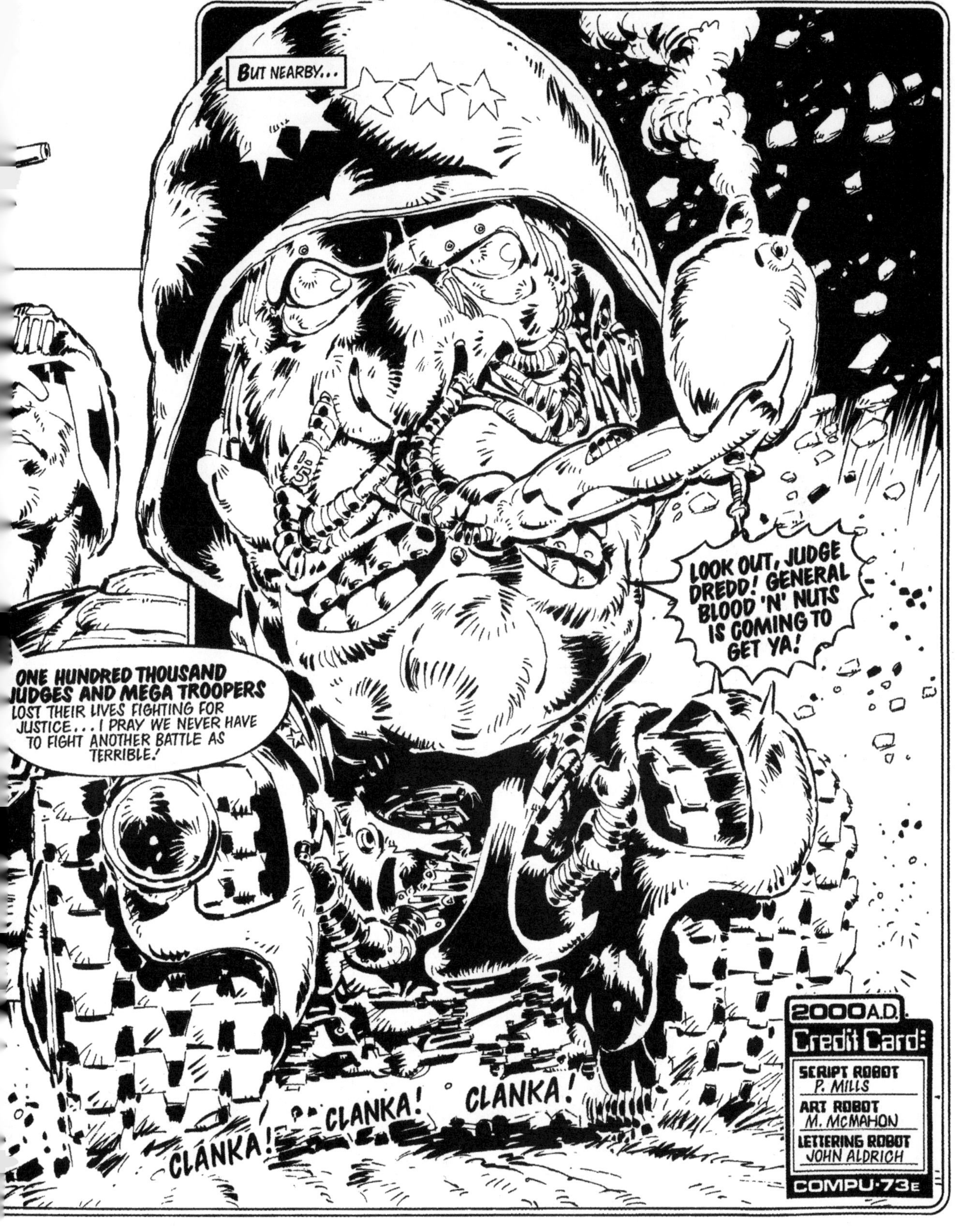

BUT NEARBY...
LOOK OUT, JUDGE DREDD! GENERAL BLOOD 'N' NUTS IS COMING TO GET YA!
ONE HUNDRED THOUSAND JUDGES AND MEGA TROOPERS LOST THEIR LIVES FIGHTING FOR JUSTICE... I PRAY WE NEVER HAVE TO FIGHT ANOTHER BATTLE AS TERRIBLE!
CLANKA! CLANKA! CLANKA!
2000 A.D. Credit Card:
SCRIPT ROBOT P. MILLS
ART ROBOT M. MCMAHON
LETTERING ROBOT JOHN ALDRICH
COMPU-73E

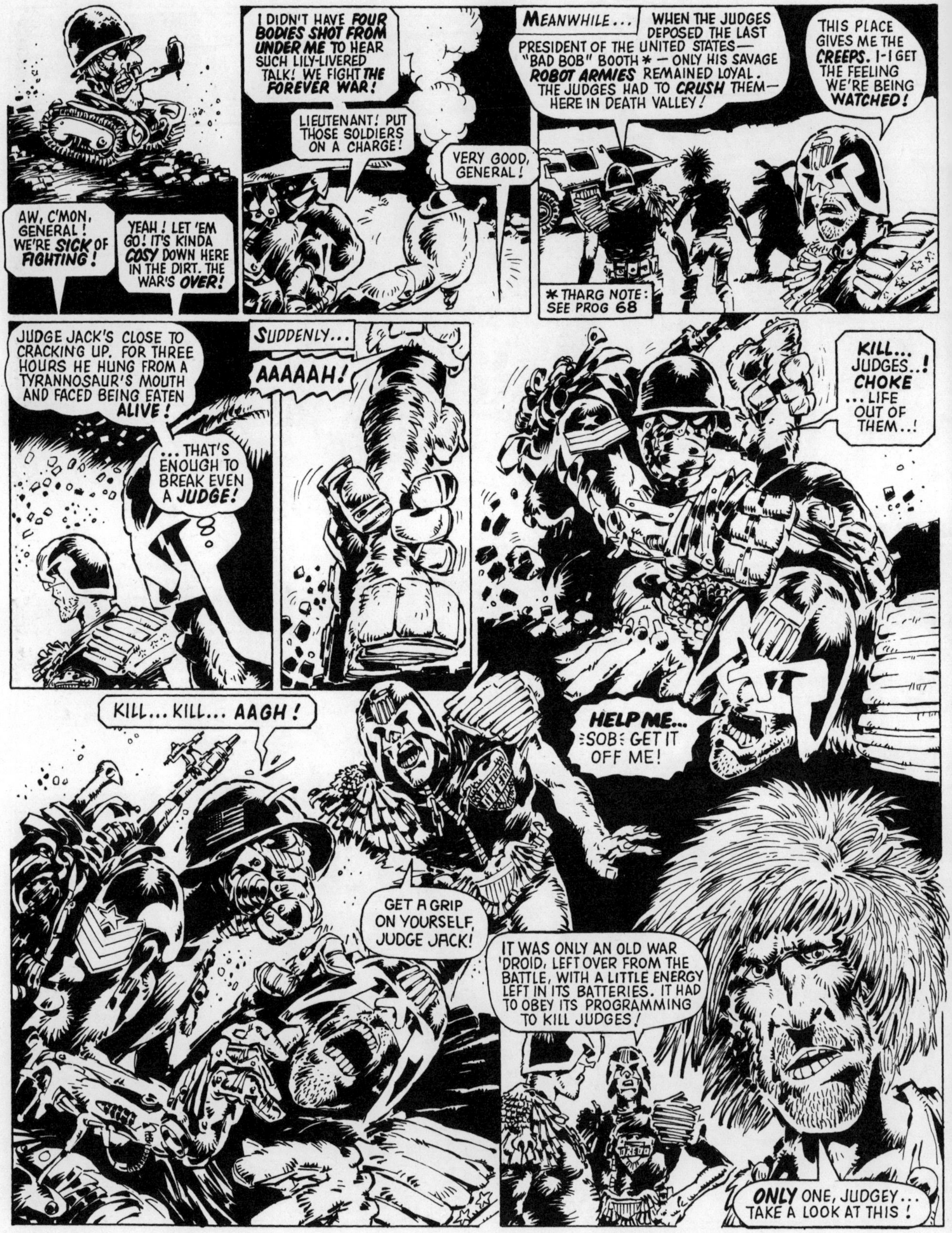

AW, C'MON, GENERAL! WE'RE SICK OF FIGHTING!
YEAH! LET 'EM GO! IT'S KINDA COSY DOWN HERE IN THE DIRT. THE WAR'S OVER!
I DIDN'T HAVE FOUR BODIES SHOT FROM UNDER ME TO HEAR SUCH LILY-LIVERED TALK! WE FIGHT THE FOREVER WAR!
LIEUTENANT! PUT THOSE SOLDIERS ON A CHARGE!
VERY GOOD, GENERAL!
MEANWHILE...
WHEN THE JUDGES DEPOSED THE LAST PRESIDENT OF THE UNITED STATES— "BAD BOB" BOOTH * — ONLY HIS SAVAGE ROBOT ARMIES REMAINED LOYAL. THE JUDGES HAD TO CRUSH THEM— HERE IN DEATH VALLEY!
THIS PLACE GIVES ME THE CREEPS. I-I GET THE FEELING WE'RE BEING WATCHED!
* THARG NOTE: SEE PROG 68
JUDGE JACK'S CLOSE TO CRACKING UP. FOR THREE HOURS HE HUNG FROM A TYRANNOSAUR'S MOUTH AND FACED BEING EATEN ALIVE!
... THAT'S ENOUGH TO BREAK EVEN A JUDGE!
SUDDENLY...
AAAAAH!
KILL... JUDGES..! CHOKE ...LIFE OUT OF THEM...!
HELP ME... SOB GET IT OFF ME!
KILL... KILL... AAGH!
GET A GRIP ON YOURSELF, JUDGE JACK!
IT WAS ONLY AN OLD WAR 'DROID, LEFT OVER FROM THE BATTLE, WITH A LITTLE ENERGY LEFT IN ITS BATTERIES. IT HAD TO OBEY ITS PROGRAMMING TO KILL JUDGES!
ONLY ONE, JUDGEY... TAKE A LOOK AT THIS!

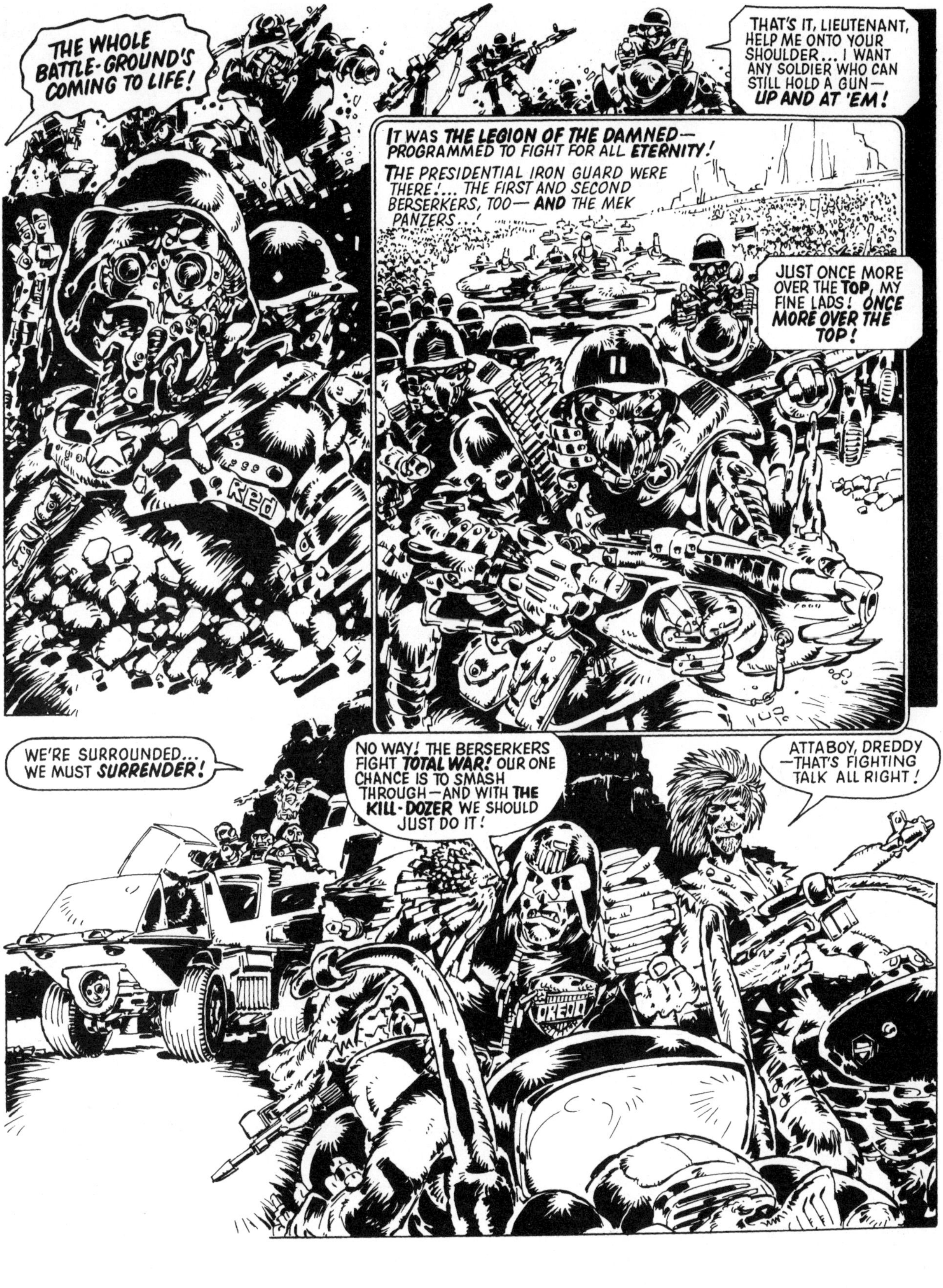
THE WHOLE BATTLE-GROUND'S COMING TO LIFE!
THAT'S IT, LIEUTENANT, HELP ME ONTO YOUR SHOULDER... I WANT ANY SOLDIER WHO CAN STILL HOLD A GUN- UP AND AT 'EM!
IT WAS THE LEGION OF THE DAMNED- PROGRAMMED TO FIGHT FOR ALL ETERNITY!
THE PRESIDENTIAL IRON GUARD WERE THERE!... THE FIRST AND SECOND BERSERKERS, TOO- AND THE MEK PANZERS...!
JUST ONCE MORE OVER THE TOP, MY FINE LADS! ONCE MORE OVER THE TOP!
RED
WE'RE SURROUNDED... WE MUST SURRENDER!
NO WAY! THE BERSERKERS FIGHT TOTAL WAR! OUR ONE CHANCE IS TO SMASH THROUGH-AND WITH THE KILL-DOZER WE SHOULD JUST DO IT!
ATTABOY, DREDDY -THAT'S FIGHTING TALK ALL RIGHT!
DREDD

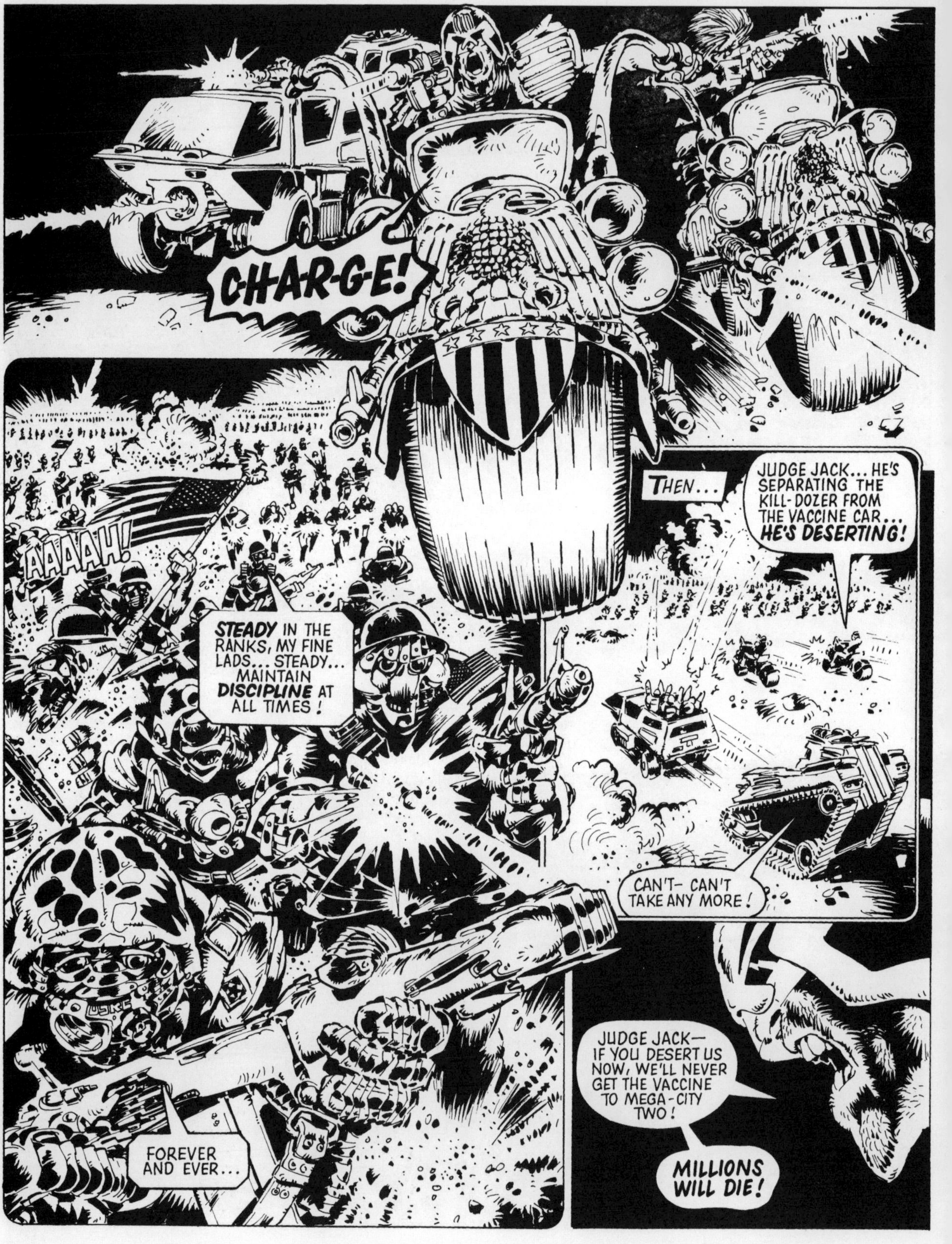
C-H-A-R-G-E!
AAAAH!
STEADY IN THE RANKS, MY FINE LADS... STEADY... MAINTAIN DISCIPLINE AT ALL TIMES!
FOREVER AND EVER...
THEN...
JUDGE JACK... HE'S SEPARATING THE KILL-DOZER FROM THE VACCINE CAR... HE'S DESERTING!
CAN'T- CAN'T TAKE ANY MORE!
JUDGE JACK— IF YOU DESERT US NOW, WE'LL NEVER GET THE VACCINE TO MEGA-CITY TWO!
MILLIONS WILL DIE!

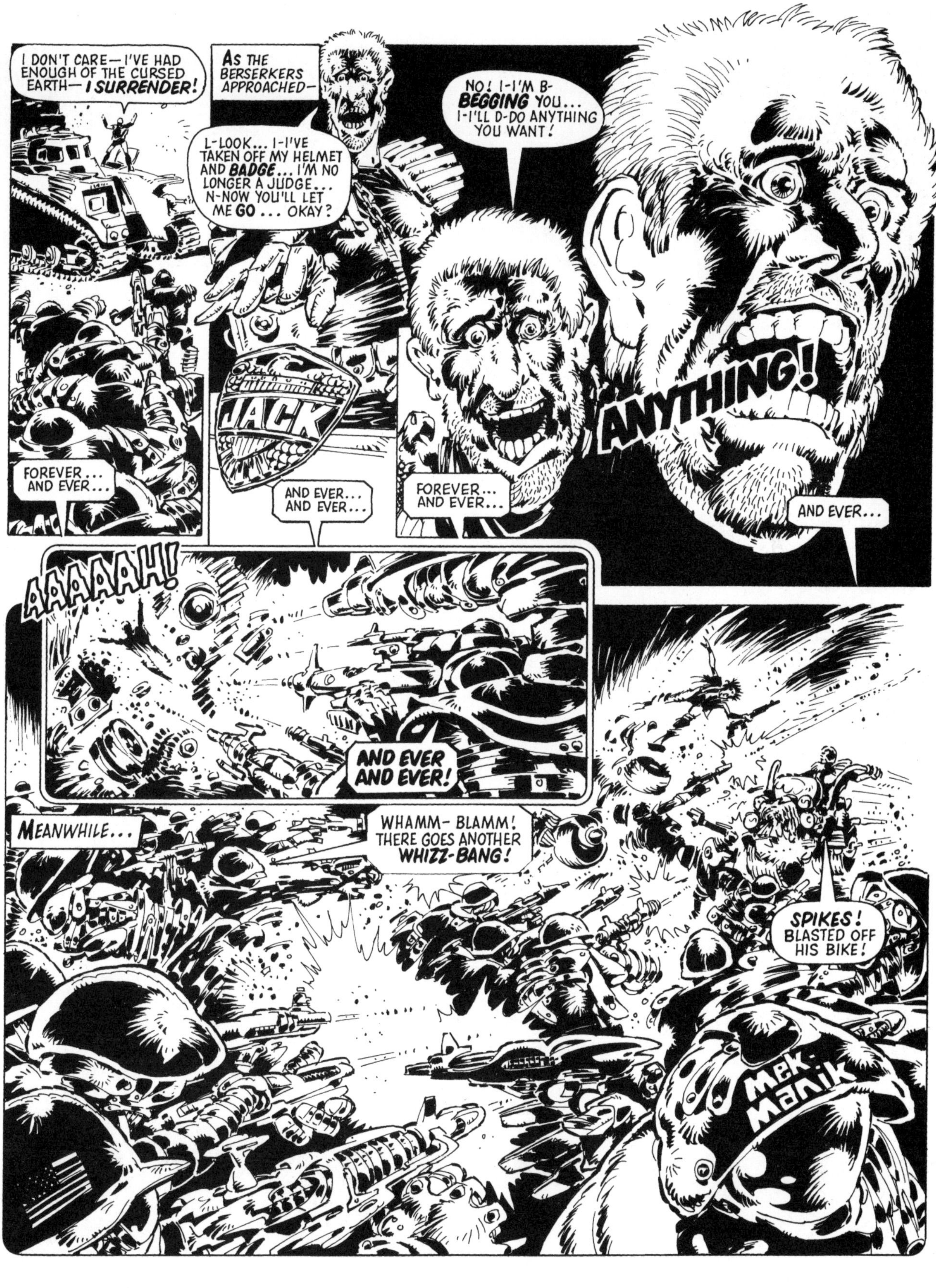

I DON'T CARE— I'VE HAD ENOUGH OF THE CURSED EARTH— I SURRENDER!
AS THE BERSERKERS APPROACHED—
L-LOOK... I-I'VE TAKEN OFF MY HELMET AND BADGE... I'M NO LONGER A JUDGE... N-NOW YOU'LL LET ME GO ... OKAY?
JACK
NO! I-I'M B-BEGGING YOU... I-I'LL D-DO ANYTHING YOU WANT!
ANYTHING!
FOREVER... AND EVER...
AND EVER... AND EVER...
FOREVER... AND EVER...
AND EVER...
AAAAAH!
AND EVER AND EVER!
MEANWHILE...
WHAMM- BLAMM! THERE GOES ANOTHER WHIZZ-BANG!
SPIKES! BLASTED OFF HIS BIKE!
Mek-Manik

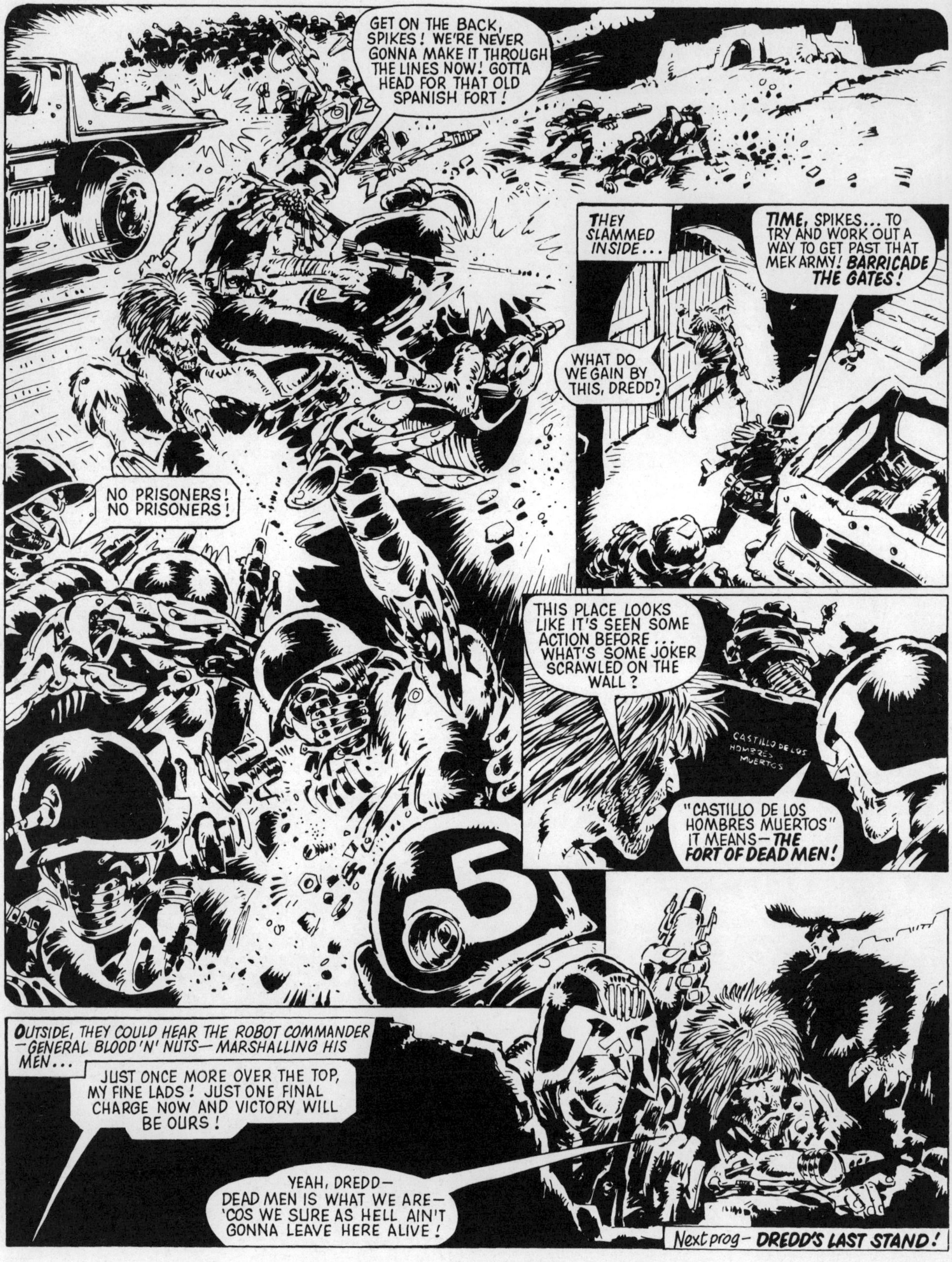
GET ON THE BACK, SPIKES! WE'RE NEVER GONNA MAKE IT THROUGH THE LINES NOW! GOTTA HEAD FOR THAT OLD SPANISH FORT!
NO PRISONERS! NO PRISONERS!
THEY SLAMMED INSIDE...
TIME, SPIKES... TO TRY AND WORK OUT A WAY TO GET PAST THAT MEK ARMY! BARRICADE THE GATES!
WHAT DO WE GAIN BY THIS, DREDD?
THIS PLACE LOOKS LIKE IT'S SEEN SOME ACTION BEFORE... WHAT'S SOME JOKER SCRAWLED ON THE WALL?
CASTILLO DE LOS HOMBRES MUERTOS
"CASTILLO DE LOS HOMBRES MUERTOS" IT MEANS—THE FORT OF DEAD MEN!
OUTSIDE, THEY COULD HEAR THE ROBOT COMMANDER —GENERAL BLOOD 'N' NUTS— MARSHALLING HIS MEN...
JUST ONCE MORE OVER THE TOP, MY FINE LADS! JUST ONE FINAL CHARGE NOW AND VICTORY WILL BE OURS!
YEAH, DREDD— DEAD MEN IS WHAT WE ARE— 'COS WE SURE AS HELL AIN'T GONNA LEAVE HERE ALIVE!
Next prog— DREDD'S LAST STAND!

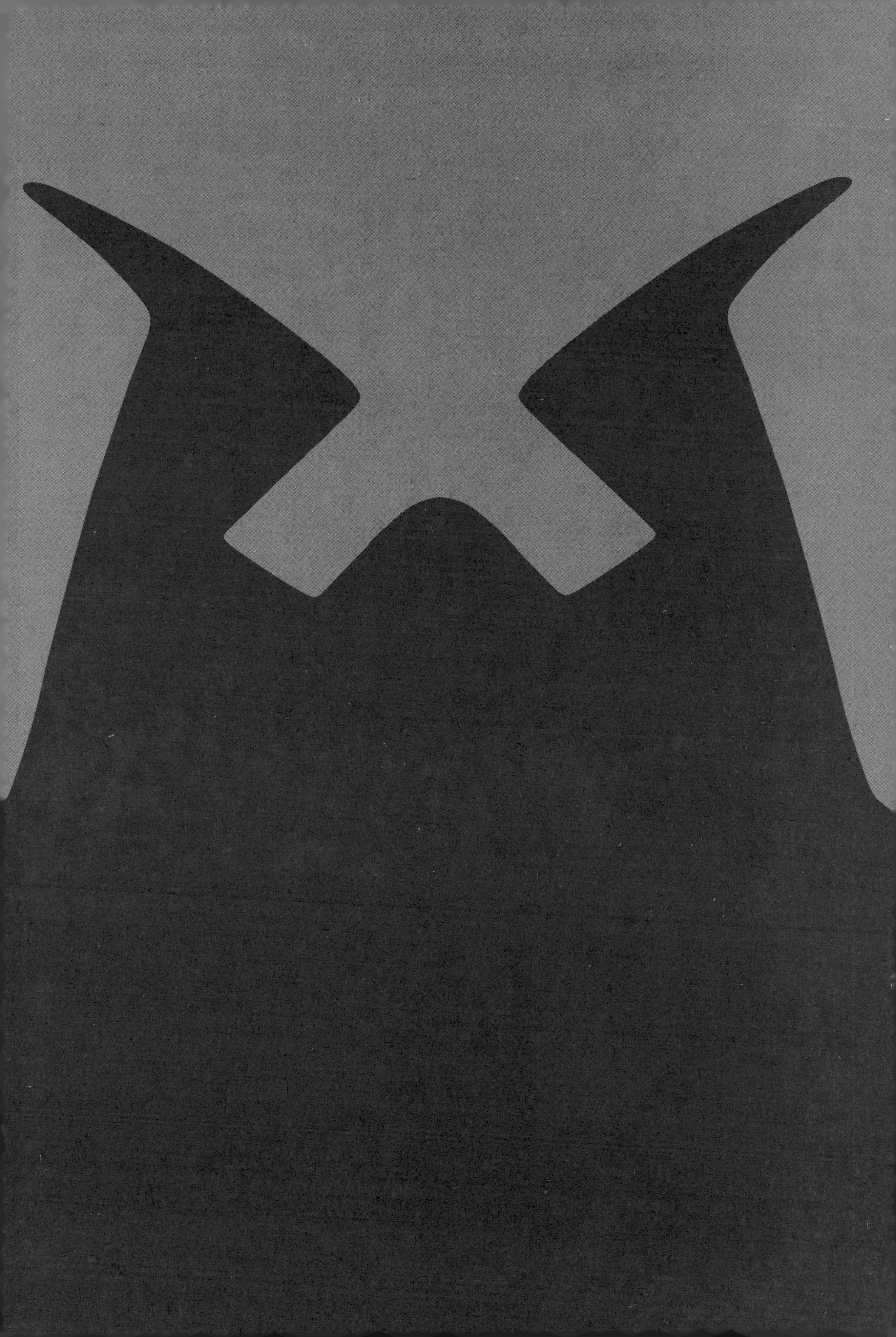

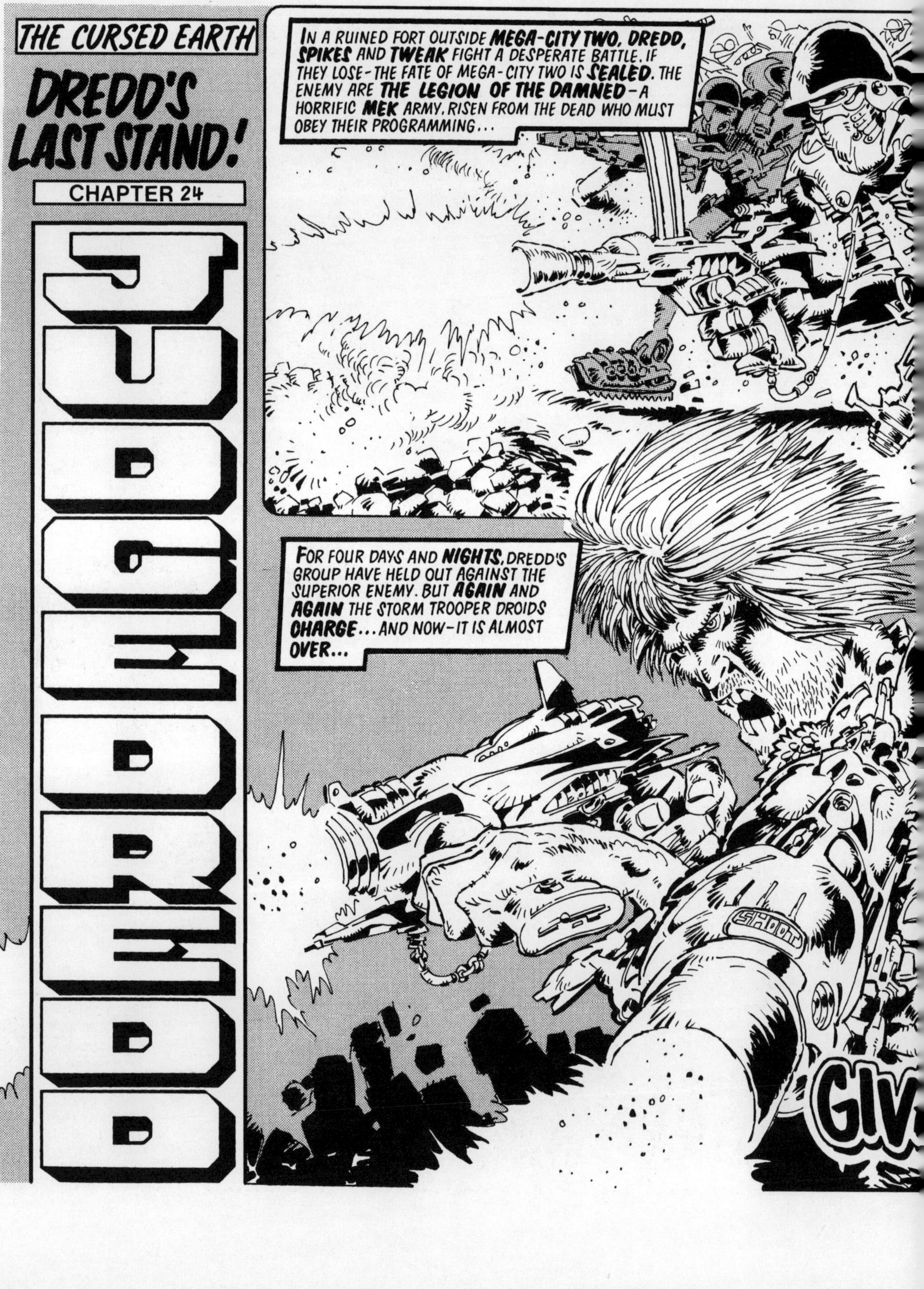
THE CURSED EARTH
DREDD'S LAST STAND!
CHAPTER 24
JUDGE DREDD
IN A RUINED FORT OUTSIDE MEGA-CITY TWO, DREDD, SPIKES AND TWEAK FIGHT A DESPERATE BATTLE. IF THEY LOSE-THE FATE OF MEGA-CITY TWO IS SEALED. THE ENEMY ARE THE LEGION OF THE DAMNED-A HORRIFIC MEK ARMY, RISEN FROM THE DEAD WHO MUST OBEY THEIR PROGRAMMING...
FOR FOUR DAYS AND NIGHTS, DREDD'S GROUP HAVE HELD OUT AGAINST THE SUPERIOR ENEMY. BUT AGAIN AND AGAIN THE STORM TROOPER DROIDS CHARGE... AND NOW-IT IS ALMOST OVER...
SHOOT

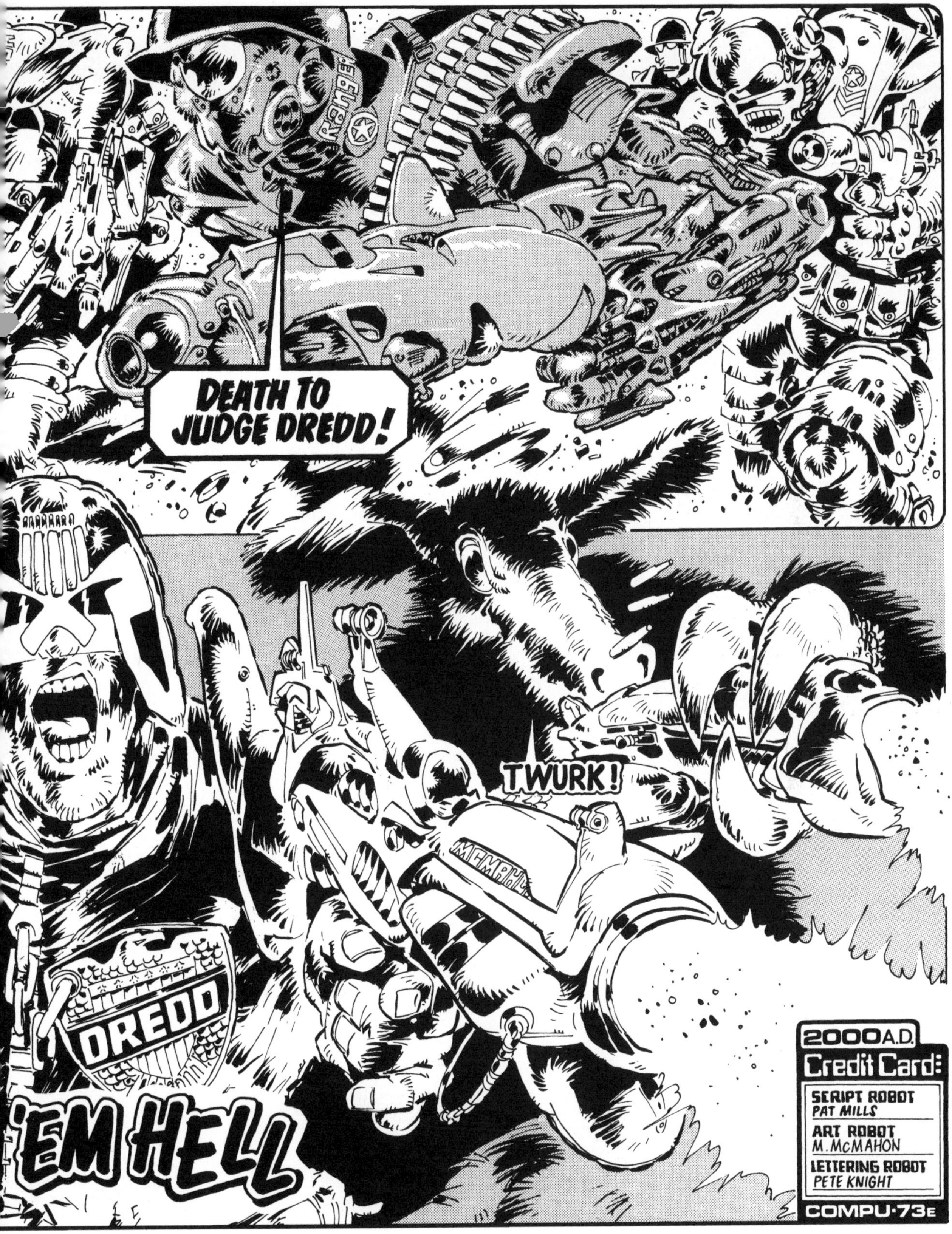
DEATH TO JUDGE DREDD!
TWURK!
DREDD
'EM HELL
2000 A.D. Credit Card:
SCRIPT ROBOT PAT MILLS
ART ROBOT M. McMAHON
LETTERING ROBOT PETE KNIGHT
COMPU·73E

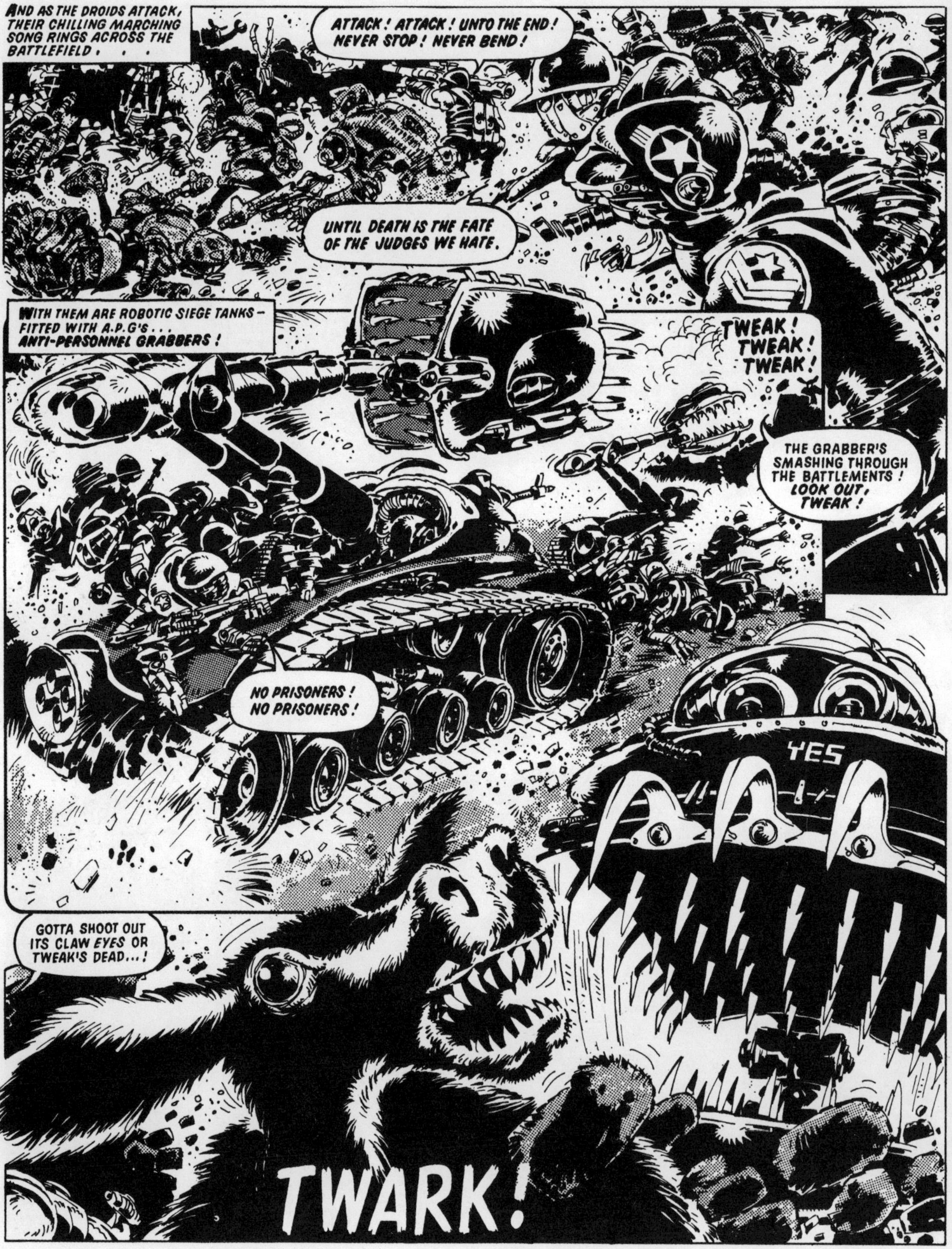
AND AS THE DROIDS ATTACK, THEIR CHILLING MARCHING SONG RINGS ACROSS THE BATTLEFIELD . . .
ATTACK! ATTACK! UNTO THE END! NEVER STOP! NEVER BEND!
UNTIL DEATH IS THE FATE OF THE JUDGES WE HATE.
WITH THEM ARE ROBOTIC SIEGE TANKS — FITTED WITH A.P.G'S . . . ANTI-PERSONNEL GRABBERS!
TWEAK! TWEAK! TWEAK!
THE GRABBER'S SMASHING THROUGH THE BATTLEMENTS! LOOK OUT, TWEAK!
NO PRISONERS! NO PRISONERS!
YES
GOTTA SHOOT OUT ITS CLAW EYES OR TWEAK'S DEAD...!
TWARK!

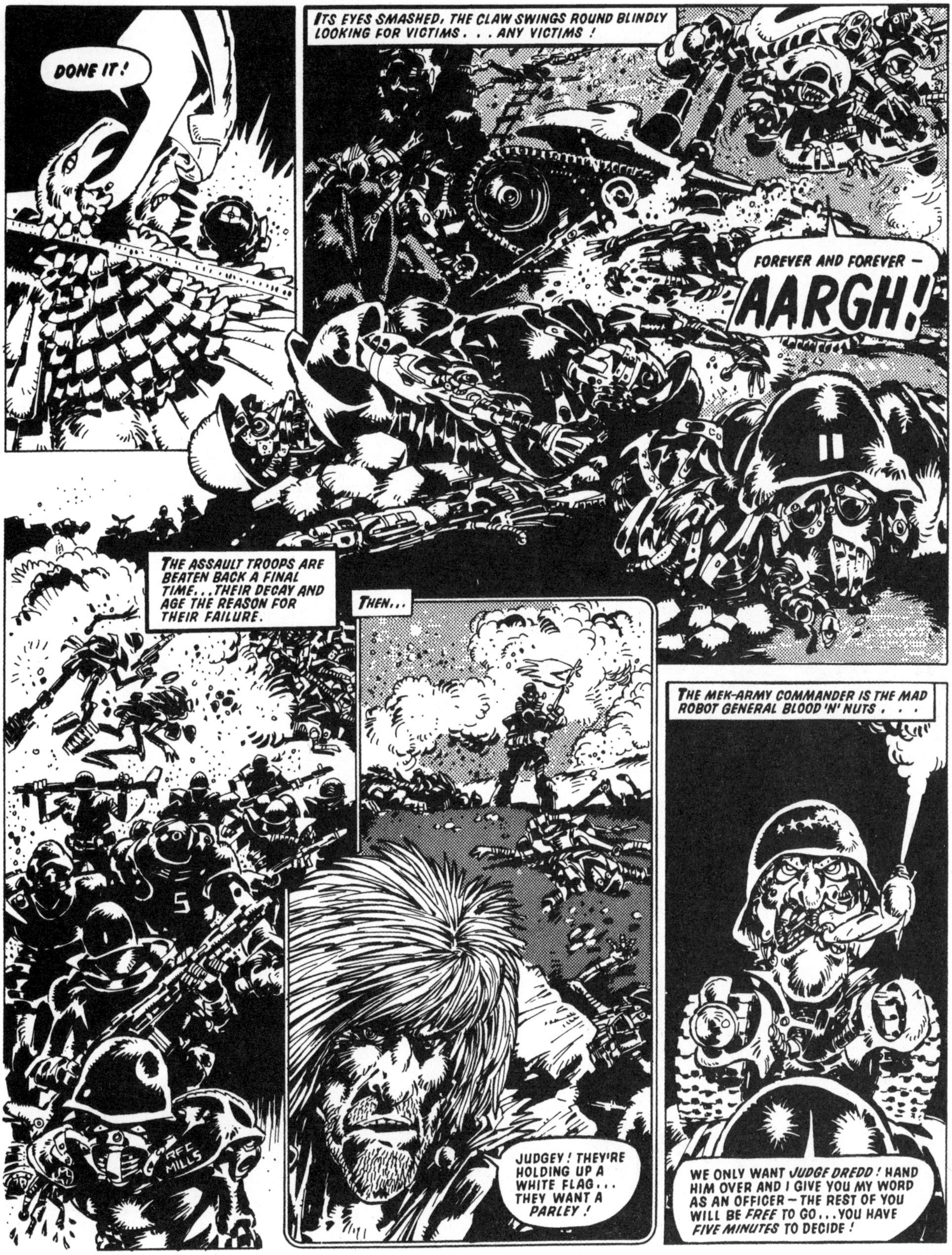
DONE IT!
ITS EYES SMASHED, THE CLAW SWINGS ROUND BLINDLY LOOKING FOR VICTIMS . . . ANY VICTIMS!
FOREVER AND FOREVER —
AARGH!
THE ASSAULT TROOPS ARE BEATEN BACK A FINAL TIME. . .THEIR DECAY AND AGE THE REASON FOR THEIR FAILURE.
THEN...
JUDGEY! THEY'RE HOLDING UP A WHITE FLAG. . . THEY WANT A PARLEY!
THE MEK-ARMY COMMANDER IS THE MAD ROBOT GENERAL BLOOD 'N' NUTS . . .
WE ONLY WANT JUDGE DREDD! HAND HIM OVER AND I GIVE YOU MY WORD AS AN OFFICER — THE REST OF YOU WILL BE FREE TO GO. . .YOU HAVE FIVE MINUTES TO DECIDE!

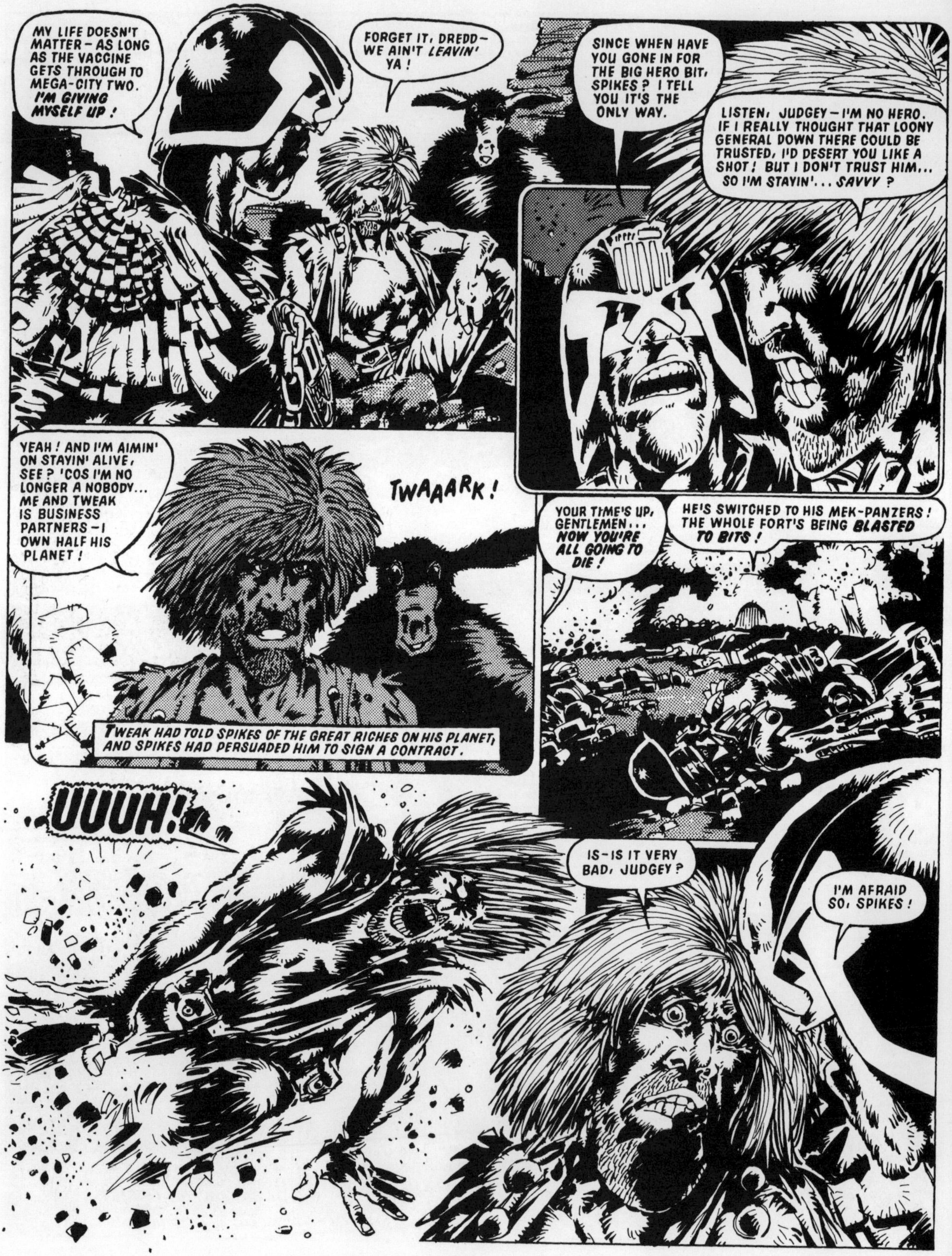

MY LIFE DOESN'T MATTER – AS LONG AS THE VACCINE GETS THROUGH TO MEGA-CITY TWO. I'M GIVING MYSELF UP!
FORGET IT, DREDD – WE AIN'T LEAVIN' YA!
SINCE WHEN HAVE YOU GONE IN FOR THE BIG HERO BIT, SPIKES? I TELL YOU IT'S THE ONLY WAY.
LISTEN, JUDGEY – I'M NO HERO. IF I REALLY THOUGHT THAT LOONY GENERAL DOWN THERE COULD BE TRUSTED, I'D DESERT YOU LIKE A SHOT! BUT I DON'T TRUST HIM... SO I'M STAYIN'... SAVVY?
YEAH! AND I'M AIMIN' ON STAYIN' ALIVE, SEE? 'COS I'M NO LONGER A NOBODY... ME AND TWEAK IS BUSINESS PARTNERS – I OWN HALF HIS PLANET!
TWAAARK!
TWEAK HAD TOLD SPIKES OF THE GREAT RICHES ON HIS PLANET, AND SPIKES HAD PERSUADED HIM TO SIGN A CONTRACT.
YOUR TIME'S UP, GENTLEMEN... NOW YOU'RE ALL GOING TO DIE!
HE'S SWITCHED TO HIS MEK-PANZERS! THE WHOLE FORT'S BEING BLASTED TO BITS!
UUUH!
IS-IS IT VERY BAD, JUDGEY?
I'M AFRAID SO, SPIKES!

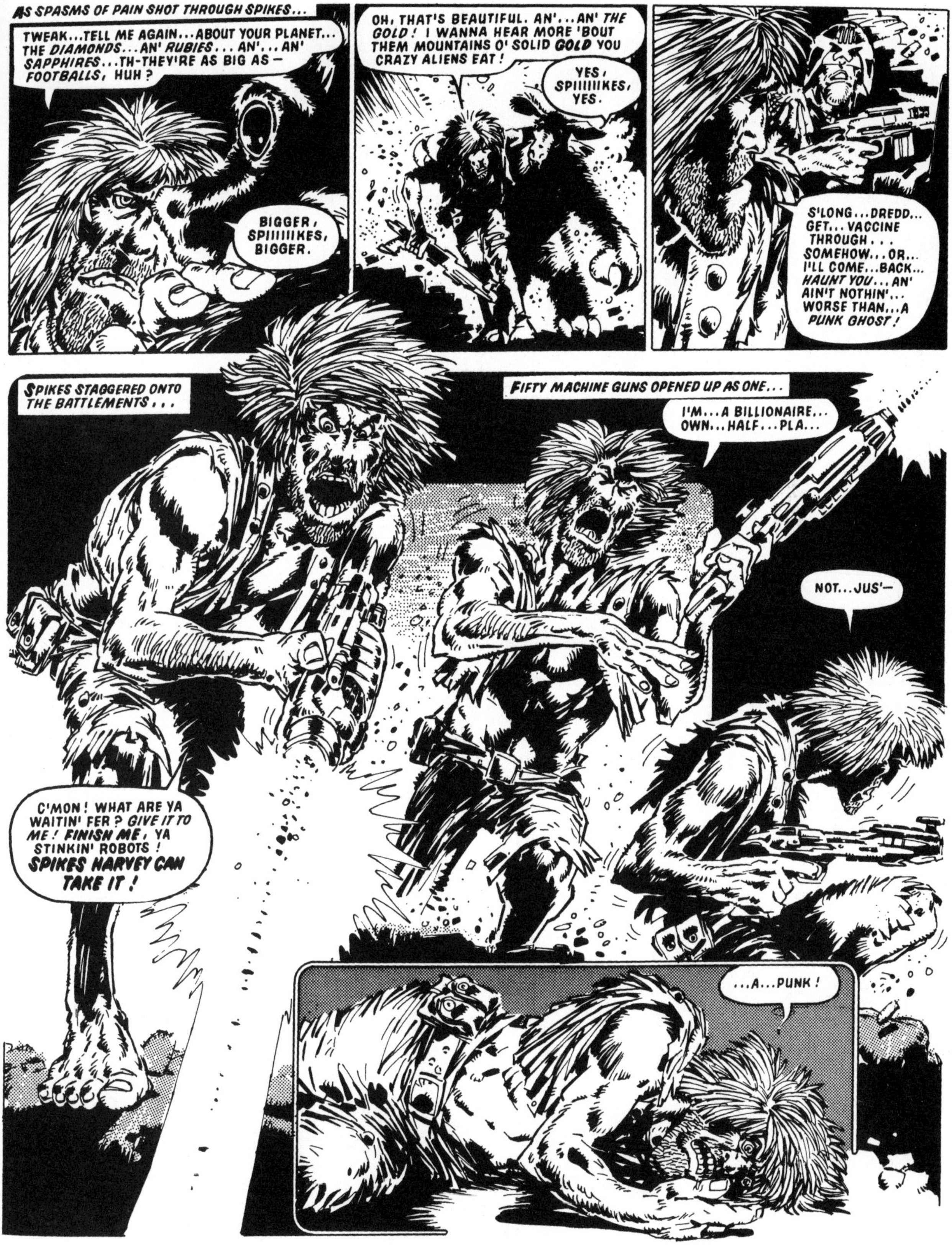

AS SPASMS OF PAIN SHOT THROUGH SPIKES...
TWEAK...TELL ME AGAIN...ABOUT YOUR PLANET... THE DIAMONDS...AN' RUBIES...AN'...AN' SAPPHIRES...TH-THEY'RE AS BIG AS — FOOTBALLS, HUH?
BIGGER, SPIIIIIIKES, BIGGER.
OH, THAT'S BEAUTIFUL. AN'...AN' THE GOLD! I WANNA HEAR MORE 'BOUT THEM MOUNTAINS O' SOLID GOLD YOU CRAZY ALIENS EAT!
YES, SPIIIIIIKES, YES.
S'LONG...DREDD... GET...VACCINE THROUGH... SOMEHOW...OR... I'LL COME...BACK... HAUNT YOU...AN' AIN'T NOTHIN'... WORSE THAN...A PUNK GHOST!
SPIKES STAGGERED ONTO THE BATTLEMENTS...
FIFTY MACHINE GUNS OPENED UP AS ONE...
I'M...A BILLIONAIRE... OWN...HALF...PLA...
NOT...JUS'—
C'MON! WHAT ARE YA WAITIN' FER? GIVE IT TO ME! FINISH ME, YA STINKIN' ROBOTS! SPIKES HARVEY CAN TAKE IT!
...A...PUNK!

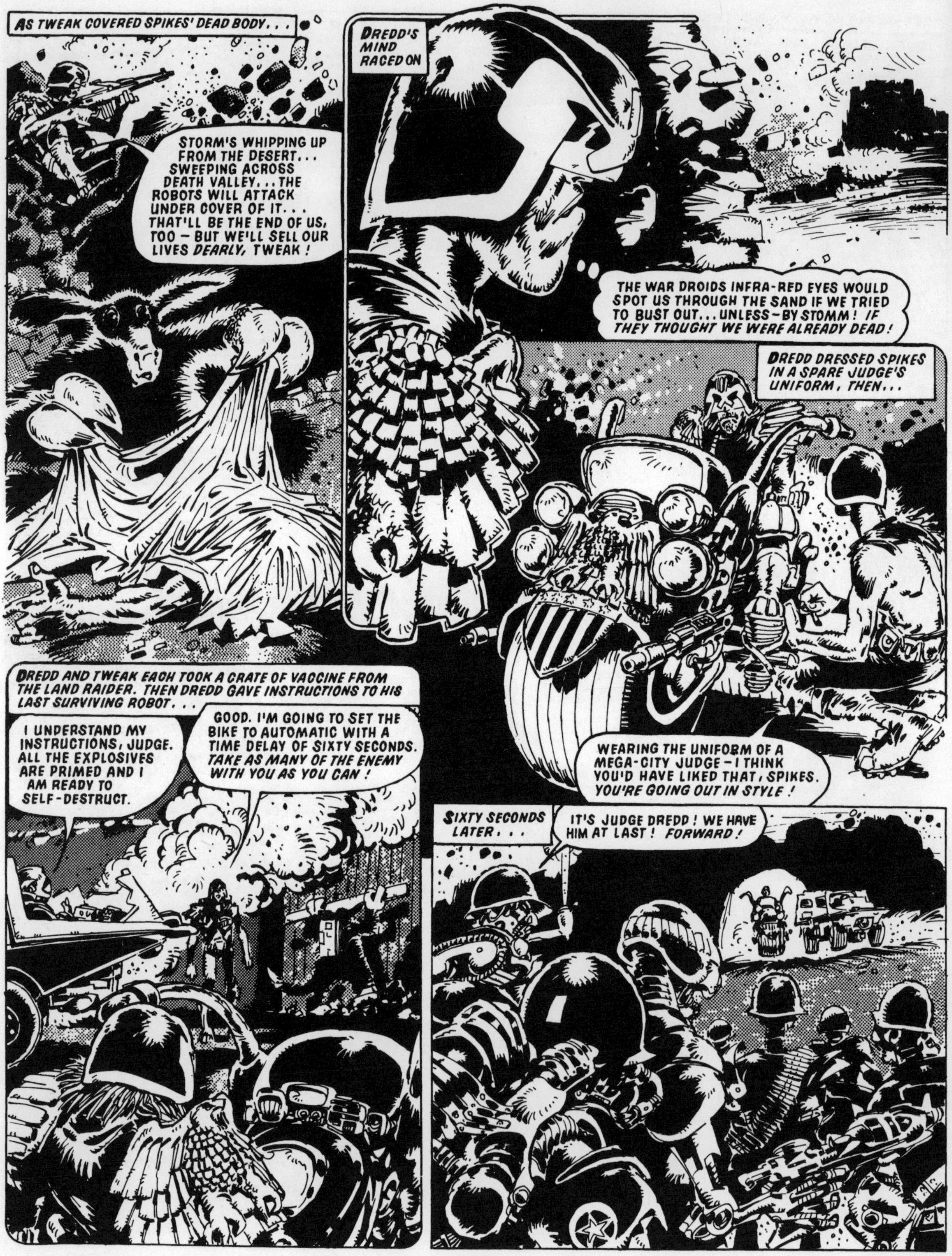

AS TWEAK COVERED SPIKES' DEAD BODY...
STORM'S WHIPPING UP FROM THE DESERT... SWEEPING ACROSS DEATH VALLEY... THE ROBOTS WILL ATTACK UNDER COVER OF IT... THAT'LL BE THE END OF US, TOO – BUT WE'LL SELL OUR LIVES DEARLY, TWEAK!
DREDD'S MIND RACED ON
THE WAR DROIDS INFRA-RED EYES WOULD SPOT US THROUGH THE SAND IF WE TRIED TO BUST OUT... UNLESS – BY STOMM! IF THEY THOUGHT WE WERE ALREADY DEAD!
DREDD DRESSED SPIKES IN A SPARE JUDGE'S UNIFORM, THEN...
WEARING THE UNIFORM OF A MEGA-CITY JUDGE – I THINK YOU'D HAVE LIKED THAT, SPIKES. YOU'RE GOING OUT IN STYLE!
DREDD AND TWEAK EACH TOOK A CRATE OF VACCINE FROM THE LAND RAIDER. THEN DREDD GAVE INSTRUCTIONS TO HIS LAST SURVIVING ROBOT...
I UNDERSTAND MY INSTRUCTIONS, JUDGE. ALL THE EXPLOSIVES ARE PRIMED AND I AM READY TO SELF-DESTRUCT.
GOOD. I'M GOING TO SET THE BIKE TO AUTOMATIC WITH A TIME DELAY OF SIXTY SECONDS. TAKE AS MANY OF THE ENEMY WITH YOU AS YOU CAN!
SIXTY SECONDS LATER...
IT'S JUDGE DREDD! WE HAVE HIM AT LAST! FORWARD!

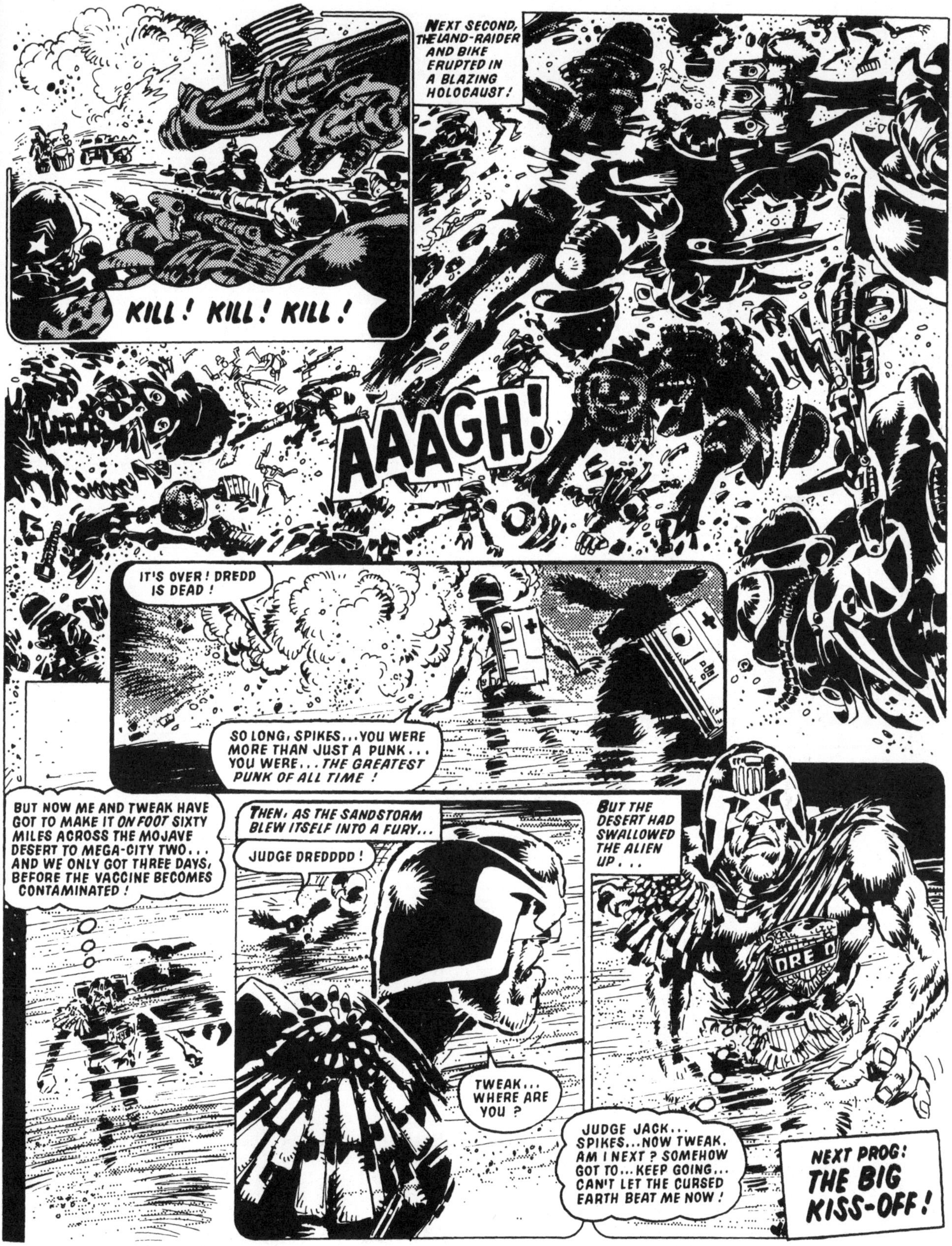

KILL! KILL! KILL!
NEXT SECOND, THE LAND-RAIDER AND BIKE ERUPTED IN A BLAZING HOLOCAUST!
AAAGH!
IT'S OVER! DREDD IS DEAD!
SO LONG, SPIKES... YOU WERE MORE THAN JUST A PUNK... YOU WERE... THE GREATEST PUNK OF ALL TIME!
BUT NOW ME AND TWEAK HAVE GOT TO MAKE IT ON FOOT SIXTY MILES ACROSS THE MOJAVE DESERT TO MEGA-CITY TWO... AND WE ONLY GOT THREE DAYS, BEFORE THE VACCINE BECOMES CONTAMINATED!
THEN, AS THE SANDSTORM BLEW ITSELF INTO A FURY...
JUDGE DREDDDD!
TWEAK... WHERE ARE YOU?
BUT THE DESERT HAD SWALLOWED THE ALIEN UP...
JUDGE JACK... SPIKES... NOW TWEAK. AM I NEXT? SOMEHOW GOT TO... KEEP GOING... CAN'T LET THE CURSED EARTH BEAT ME NOW!
NEXT PROG: THE BIG KISS-OFF!

THE CURSED EARTH
FinalChapter
DEATH CRAWL!

JUDGE DREDD

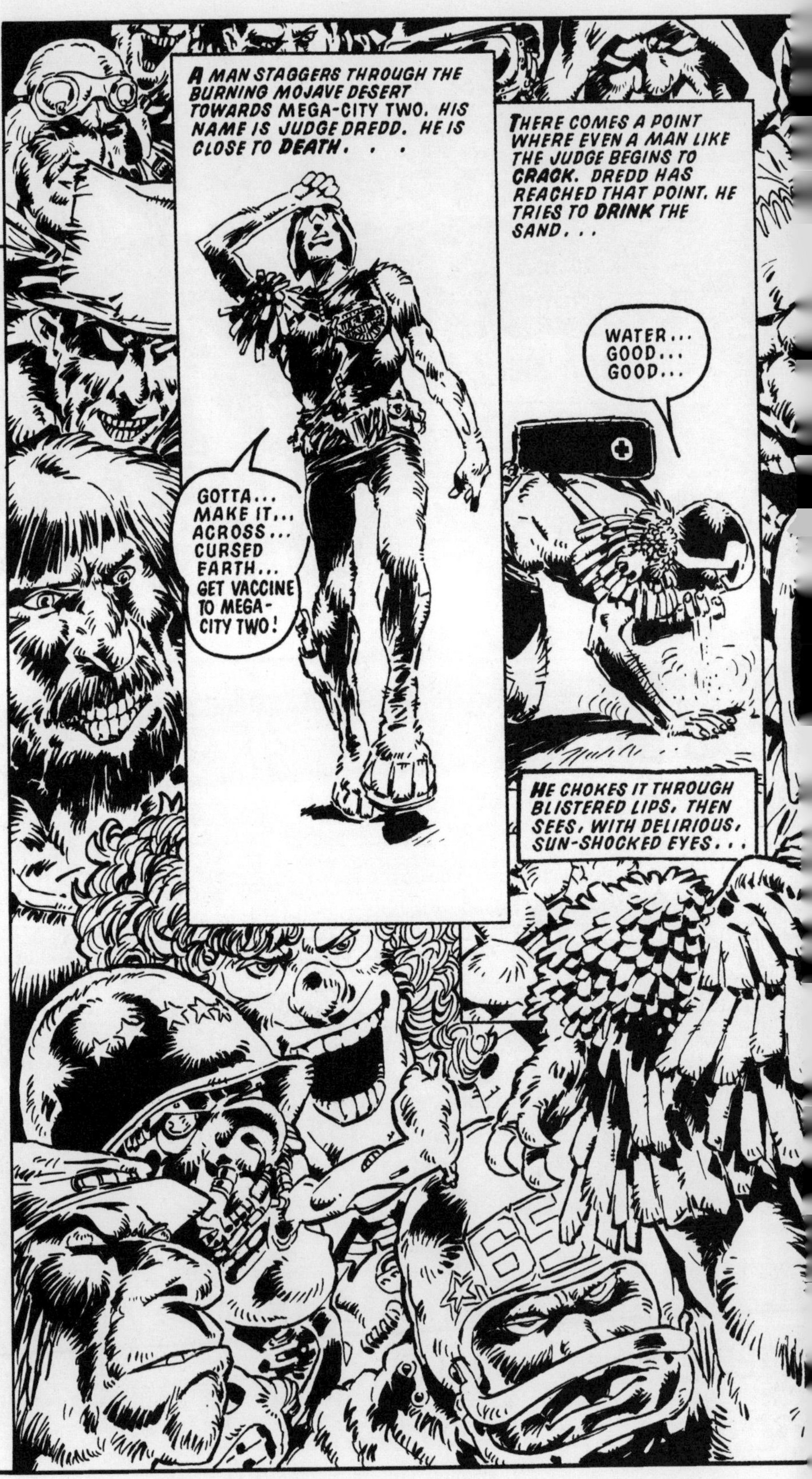

A MAN STAGGERS THROUGH THE BURNING MOJAVE DESERT TOWARDS MEGA-CITY TWO. HIS NAME IS JUDGE DREDD. HE IS CLOSE TO DEATH. . .
GOTTA... MAKE IT... ACROSS... CURSED EARTH... GET VACCINE TO MEGA-CITY TWO!
THERE COMES A POINT WHERE EVEN A MAN LIKE THE JUDGE BEGINS TO CRACK. DREDD HAS REACHED THAT POINT. HE TRIES TO DRINK THE SAND...
WATER... GOOD... GOOD...
HE CHOKES IT THROUGH BLISTERED LIPS, THEN SEES, WITH DELIRIOUS, SUN-SHOCKED EYES...

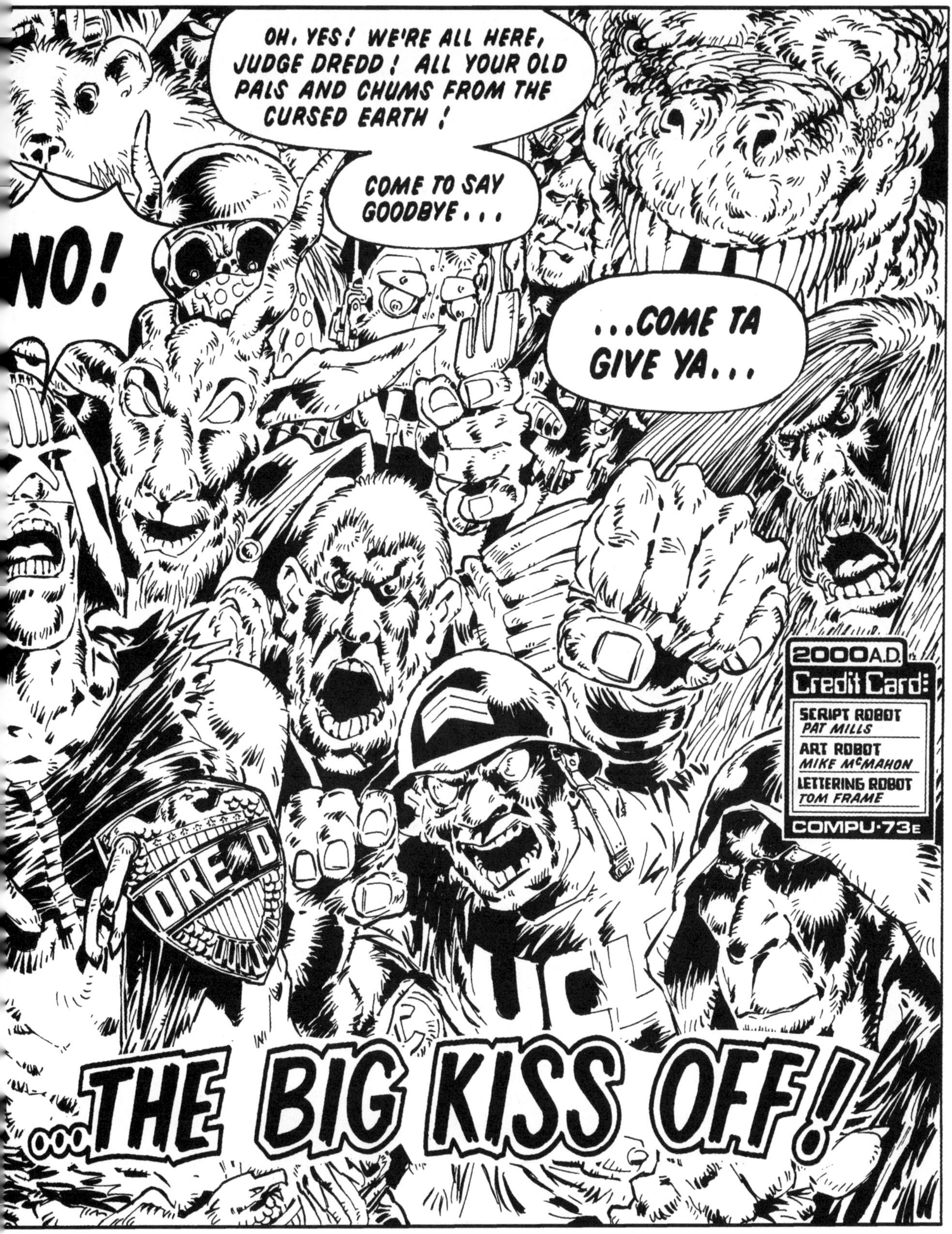
OH, YES! WE'RE ALL HERE, JUDGE DREDD! ALL YOUR OLD PALS AND CHUMS FROM THE CURSED EARTH!
COME TO SAY GOODBYE...
NO!
...COME TA GIVE YA...
2000 A.D. Credit Card:
SCRIPT ROBOT PAT MILLS
ART ROBOT MIKE McMAHON
LETTERING ROBOT TOM FRAME
COMPU·73E
DREDD
...THE BIG KISS OFF!

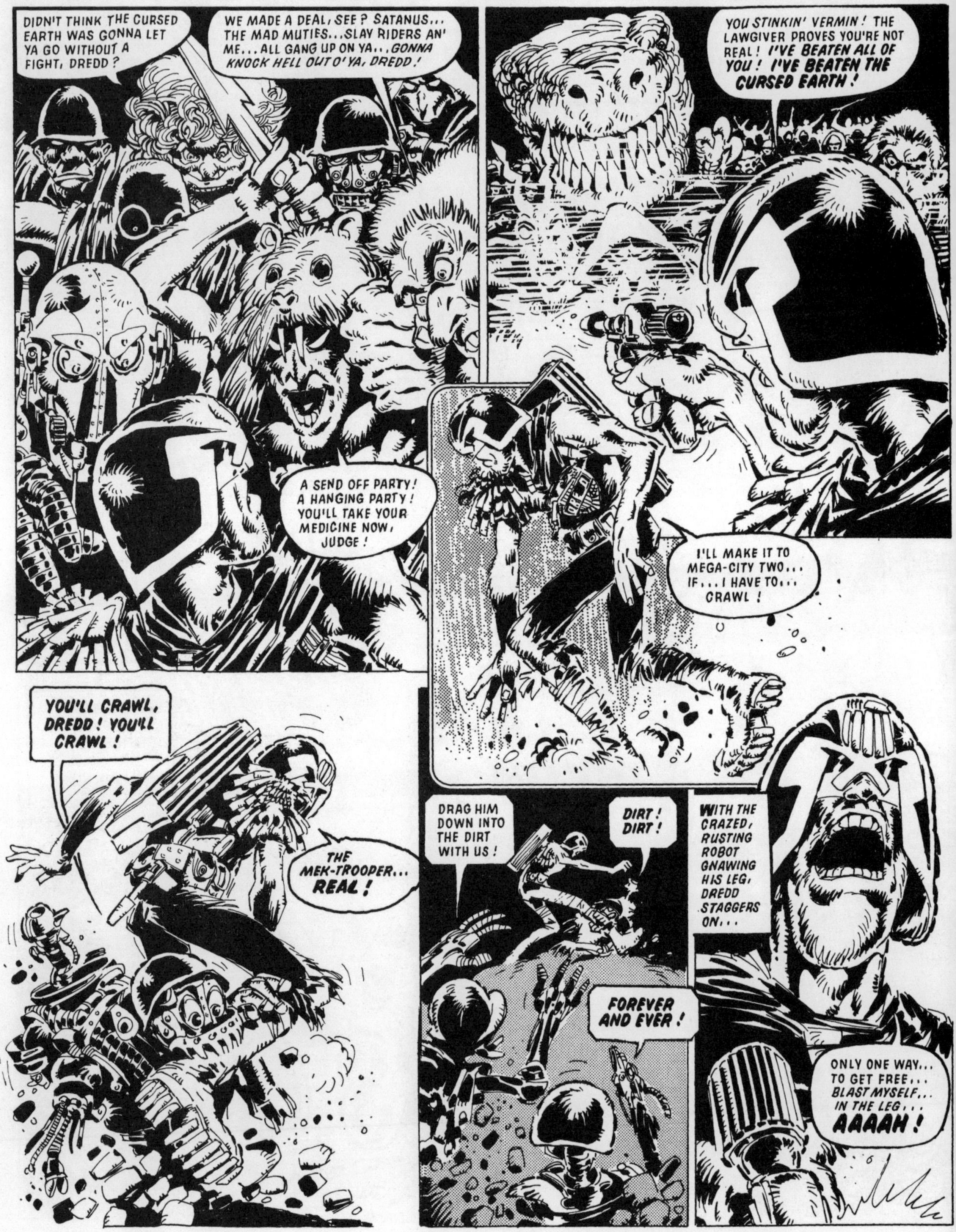
DIDN'T THINK THE CURSED EARTH WAS GONNA LET YA GO WITHOUT A FIGHT, DREDD?
WE MADE A DEAL, SEE? SATANUS... THE MAD MUTIES...SLAY RIDERS AN' ME...ALL GANG UP ON YA...GONNA KNOCK HELL OUT O' YA, DREDD!
A SEND OFF PARTY! A HANGING PARTY! YOU'LL TAKE YOUR MEDICINE NOW, JUDGE!
YOU STINKIN' VERMIN! THE LAWGIVER PROVES YOU'RE NOT REAL! I'VE BEATEN ALL OF YOU! I'VE BEATEN THE CURSED EARTH!
I'LL MAKE IT TO MEGA-CITY TWO... IF... I HAVE TO... CRAWL!
YOU'LL CRAWL, DREDD! YOU'LL CRAWL!
THE MEK-TROOPER... REAL!
DRAG HIM DOWN INTO THE DIRT WITH US!
DIRT! DIRT!
FOREVER AND EVER!
WITH THE CRAZED, RUSTING ROBOT GNAWING HIS LEG, DREDD STAGGERS ON...
ONLY ONE WAY... TO GET FREE... BLAST MYSELF... IN THE LEG... AAAAH!

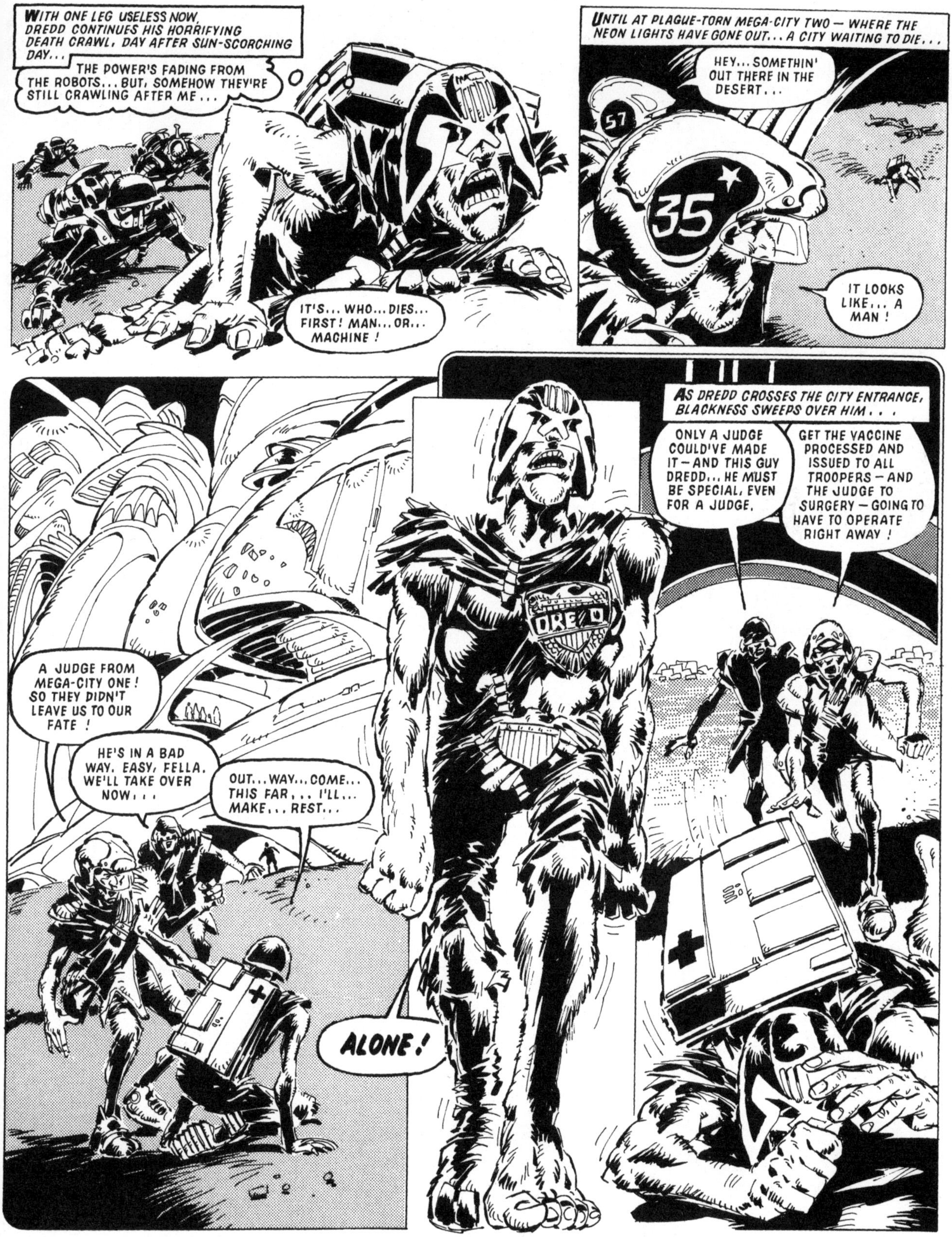

WITH ONE LEG USELESS NOW, DREDD CONTINUES HIS HORRIFYING DEATH CRAWL, DAY AFTER SUN-SCORCHING DAY...
THE POWER'S FADING FROM THE ROBOTS... BUT, SOMEHOW THEY'RE STILL CRAWLING AFTER ME...
IT'S... WHO... DIES... FIRST! MAN... OR... MACHINE!
UNTIL AT PLAGUE-TORN MEGA-CITY TWO — WHERE THE NEON LIGHTS HAVE GONE OUT... A CITY WAITING TO DIE...
HEY... SOMETHIN' OUT THERE IN THE DESERT...
57
35
IT LOOKS LIKE... A MAN!
A JUDGE FROM MEGA-CITY ONE! SO THEY DIDN'T LEAVE US TO OUR FATE!
HE'S IN A BAD WAY. EASY, FELLA. WE'LL TAKE OVER NOW...
OUT... WAY... COME... THIS FAR... I'LL... MAKE... REST...
ALONE!
DREDD
AS DREDD CROSSES THE CITY ENTRANCE, BLACKNESS SWEEPS OVER HIM...
ONLY A JUDGE COULD'VE MADE IT — AND THIS GUY DREDD... HE MUST BE SPECIAL, EVEN FOR A JUDGE.
GET THE VACCINE PROCESSED AND ISSUED TO ALL TROOPERS — AND THE JUDGE TO SURGERY — GOING TO HAVE TO OPERATE RIGHT AWAY!

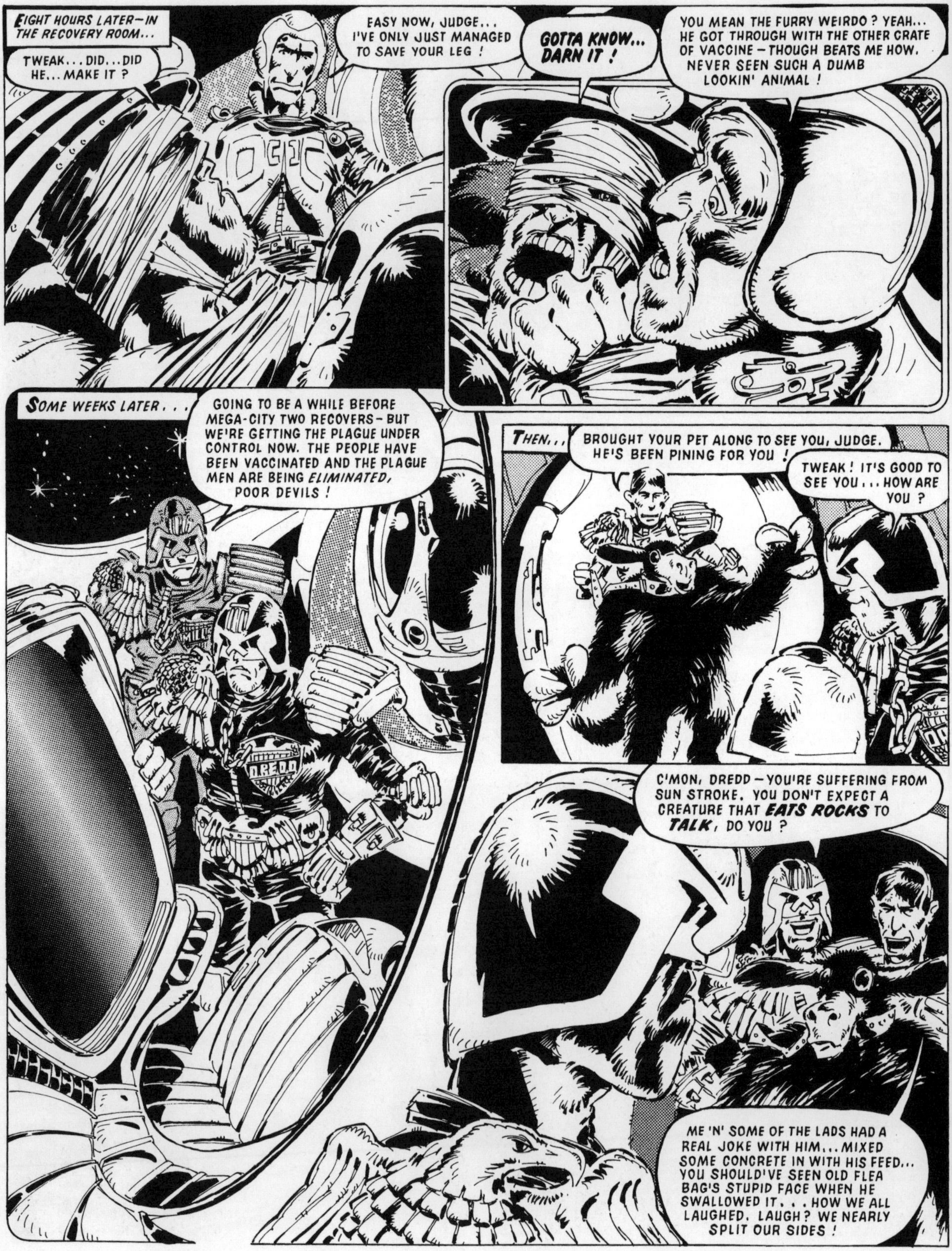
EIGHT HOURS LATER—IN THE RECOVERY ROOM...
TWEAK... DID... DID HE... MAKE IT ?
EASY NOW, JUDGE... I'VE ONLY JUST MANAGED TO SAVE YOUR LEG !
GOTTA KNOW... DARN IT !
YOU MEAN THE FURRY WEIRDO ? YEAH... HE GOT THROUGH WITH THE OTHER CRATE OF VACCINE—THOUGH BEATS ME HOW. NEVER SEEN SUCH A DUMB LOOKIN' ANIMAL !
SOME WEEKS LATER...
GOING TO BE A WHILE BEFORE MEGA-CITY TWO RECOVERS—BUT WE'RE GETTING THE PLAGUE UNDER CONTROL NOW. THE PEOPLE HAVE BEEN VACCINATED AND THE PLAGUE MEN ARE BEING ELIMINATED, POOR DEVILS !
THEN...
BROUGHT YOUR PET ALONG TO SEE YOU, JUDGE. HE'S BEEN PINING FOR YOU !
TWEAK ! IT'S GOOD TO SEE YOU... HOW ARE YOU ?
C'MON, DREDD—YOU'RE SUFFERING FROM SUN STROKE. YOU DON'T EXPECT A CREATURE THAT EATS ROCKS TO TALK, DO YOU ?
ME 'N' SOME OF THE LADS HAD A REAL JOKE WITH HIM... MIXED SOME CONCRETE IN WITH HIS FEED... YOU SHOULD'VE SEEN OLD FLEA BAG'S STUPID FACE WHEN HE SWALLOWED IT... HOW WE ALL LAUGHED. LAUGH? WE NEARLY SPLIT OUR SIDES !

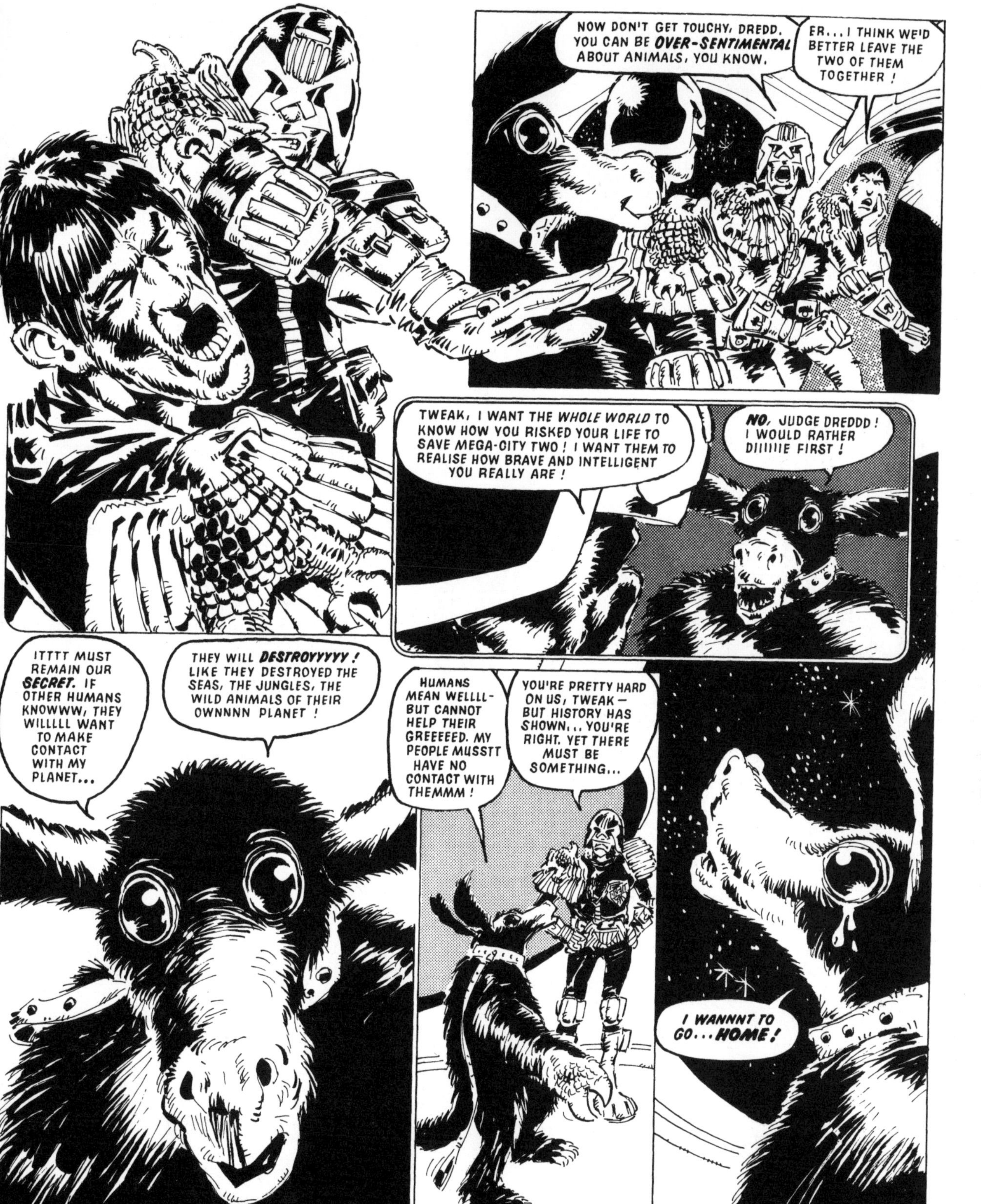

NOW DON'T GET TOUCHY, DREDD. YOU CAN BE OVER-SENTIMENTAL ABOUT ANIMALS, YOU KNOW.
ER... I THINK WE'D BETTER LEAVE THE TWO OF THEM TOGETHER!
TWEAK, I WANT THE WHOLE WORLD TO KNOW HOW YOU RISKED YOUR LIFE TO SAVE MEGA-CITY TWO! I WANT THEM TO REALISE HOW BRAVE AND INTELLIGENT YOU REALLY ARE!
NO, JUDGE DREDDD! I WOULD RATHER DIIIIIE FIRST!
ITTTT MUST REMAIN OUR SECRET. IF OTHER HUMANS KNOWWW, THEY WILLLLL WANT TO MAKE CONTACT WITH MY PLANET...
THEY WILL DESTROYYYYY! LIKE THEY DESTROYED THE SEAS, THE JUNGLES, THE WILD ANIMALS OF THEIR OWNNNN PLANET!
HUMANS MEAN WELLLL- BUT CANNOT HELP THEIR GREEEEED. MY PEOPLE MUSSTT HAVE NO CONTACT WITH THEMMM!
YOU'RE PRETTY HARD ON US, TWEAK - BUT HISTORY HAS SHOWN... YOU'RE RIGHT. YET THERE MUST BE SOMETHING...
I WANNNT TO GO... HOME!

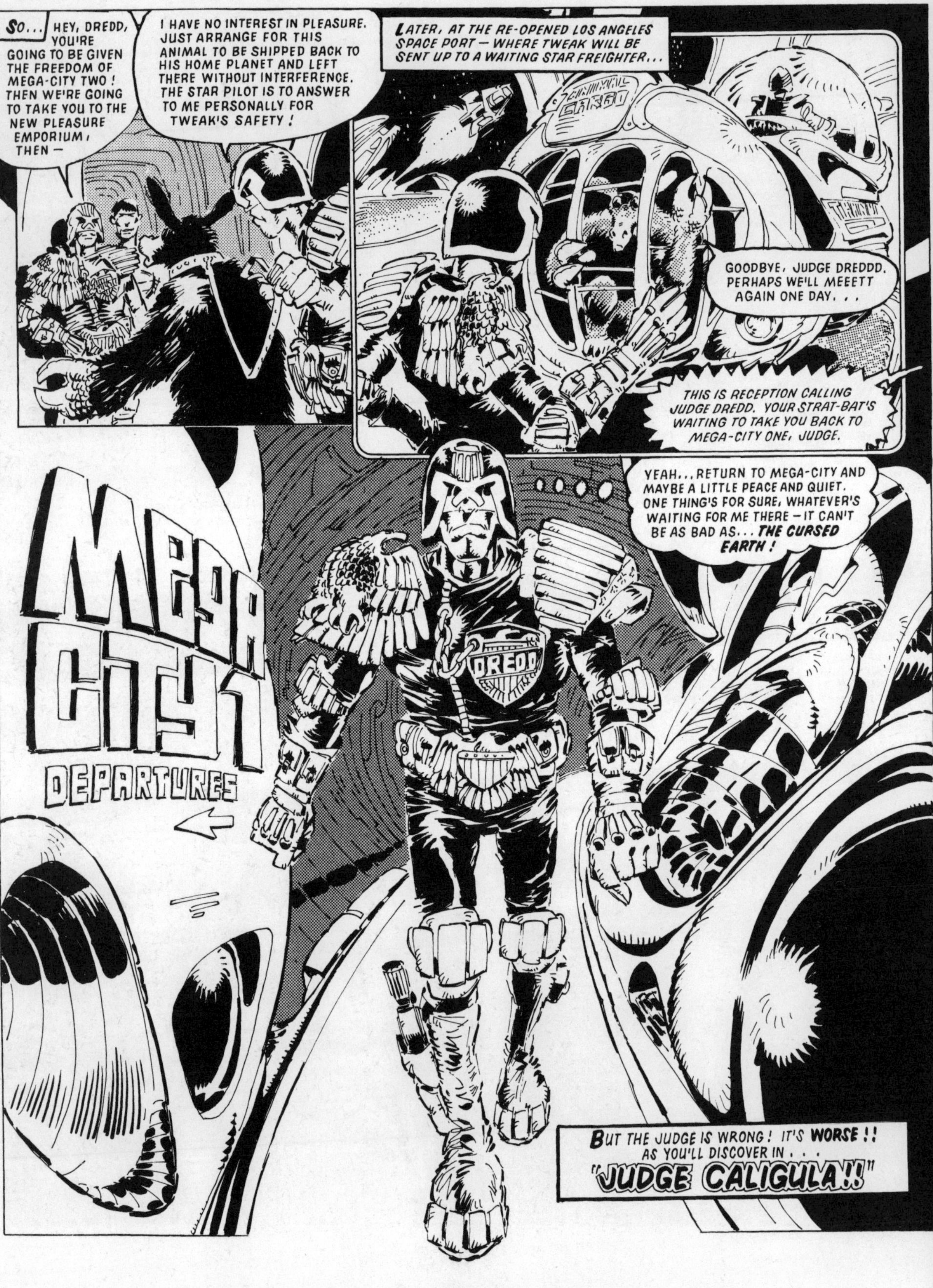

SO... HEY, DREDD, YOU'RE GOING TO BE GIVEN THE FREEDOM OF MEGA-CITY TWO! THEN WE'RE GOING TO TAKE YOU TO THE NEW PLEASURE EMPORIUM, THEN —
I HAVE NO INTEREST IN PLEASURE. JUST ARRANGE FOR THIS ANIMAL TO BE SHIPPED BACK TO HIS HOME PLANET AND LEFT THERE WITHOUT INTERFERENCE. THE STAR PILOT IS TO ANSWER TO ME PERSONALLY FOR TWEAK'S SAFETY!
LATER, AT THE RE-OPENED LOS ANGELES SPACE PORT — WHERE TWEAK WILL BE SENT UP TO A WAITING STAR FREIGHTER...
GOODBYE, JUDGE DREDDD. PERHAPS WE'LL MEEETT AGAIN ONE DAY...
THIS IS RECEPTION CALLING JUDGE DREDD. YOUR STRAT-BAT'S WAITING TO TAKE YOU BACK TO MEGA-CITY ONE, JUDGE.
YEAH... RETURN TO MEGA-CITY AND MAYBE A LITTLE PEACE AND QUIET. ONE THING'S FOR SURE, WHATEVER'S WAITING FOR ME THERE — IT CAN'T BE AS BAD AS... THE CURSED EARTH!
MEGA CITY 1
DEPARTURES
DREDD
BUT THE JUDGE IS WRONG! IT'S WORSE!! AS YOU'LL DISCOVER IN...
"JUDGE CALIGULA!!"

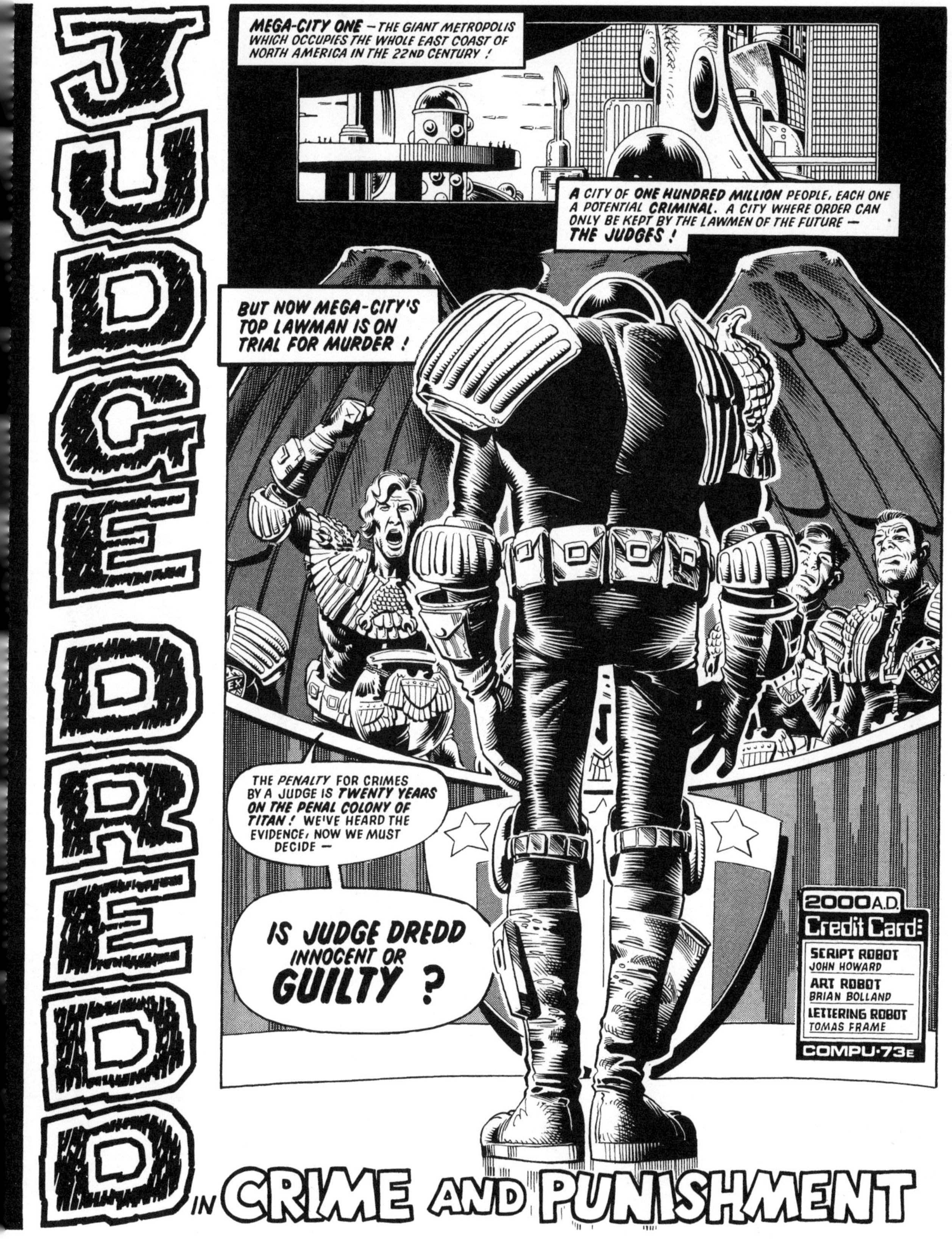

JUDGE DREDD
MEGA-CITY ONE – THE GIANT METROPOLIS WHICH OCCUPIES THE WHOLE EAST COAST OF NORTH AMERICA IN THE 22ND CENTURY !
A CITY OF ONE HUNDRED MILLION PEOPLE, EACH ONE A POTENTIAL CRIMINAL. A CITY WHERE ORDER CAN ONLY BE KEPT BY THE LAWMEN OF THE FUTURE – THE JUDGES !
BUT NOW MEGA-CITY'S TOP LAWMAN IS ON TRIAL FOR MURDER !
THE PENALTY FOR CRIMES BY A JUDGE IS TWENTY YEARS ON THE PENAL COLONY OF TITAN ! WE'VE HEARD THE EVIDENCE, NOW WE MUST DECIDE –
IS JUDGE DREDD INNOCENT OR GUILTY ?
2000 A.D. Credit Card:
SCRIPT ROBOT JOHN HOWARD
ART ROBOT BRIAN BOLLAND
LETTERING ROBOT TOMAS FRAME
COMPU-73E
IN CRIME AND PUNISHMENT

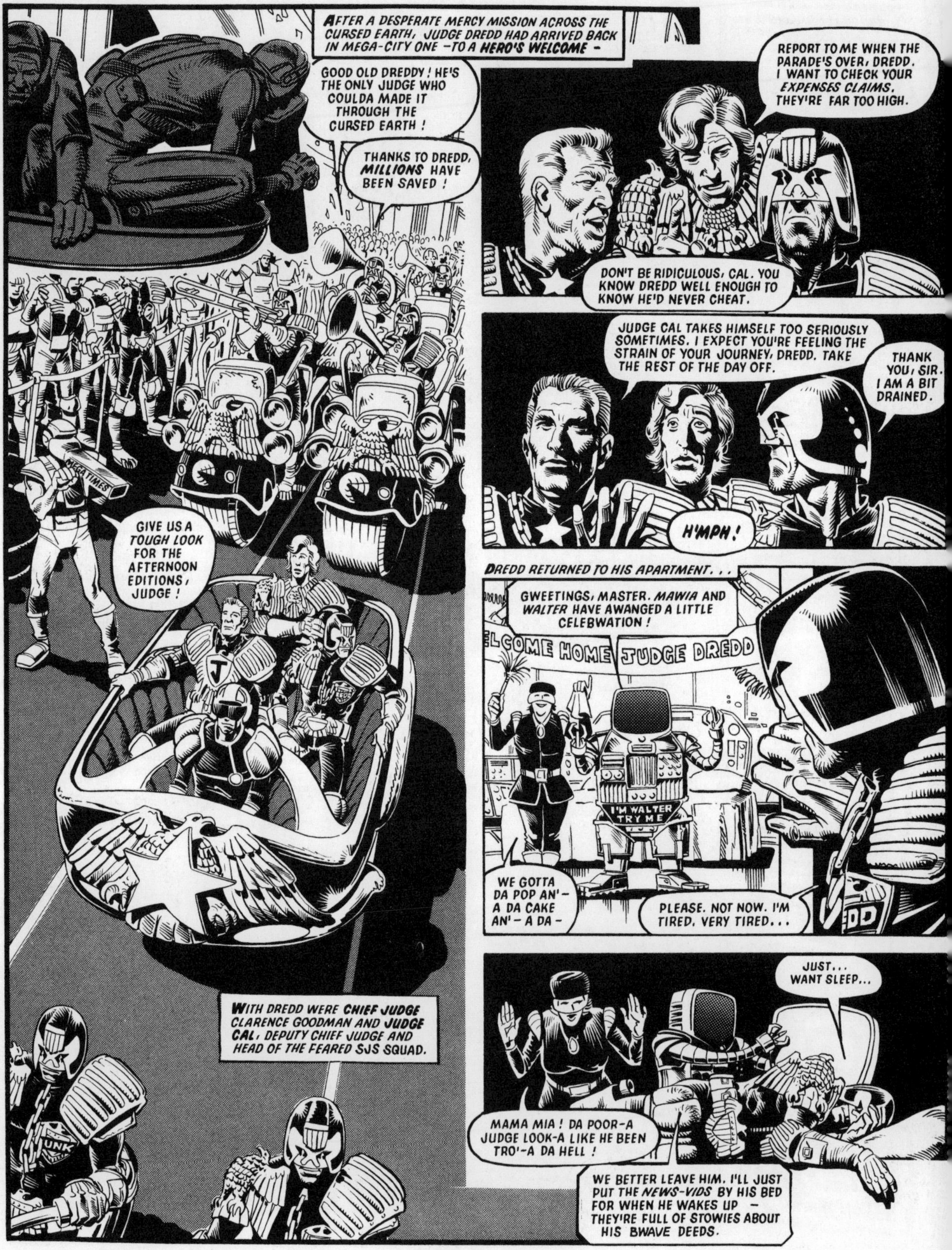

AFTER A DESPERATE MERCY MISSION ACROSS THE CURSED EARTH, JUDGE DREDD HAD ARRIVED BACK IN MEGA-CITY ONE –TO A HERO'S WELCOME –
GOOD OLD DREDDY! HE'S THE ONLY JUDGE WHO COULDA MADE IT THROUGH THE CURSED EARTH!
THANKS TO DREDD, MILLIONS HAVE BEEN SAVED!
REPORT TO ME WHEN THE PARADE'S OVER, DREDD. I WANT TO CHECK YOUR EXPENSES CLAIMS. THEY'RE FAR TOO HIGH.
DON'T BE RIDICULOUS, CAL. YOU KNOW DREDD WELL ENOUGH TO KNOW HE'D NEVER CHEAT.
MEGA TIMES
GIVE US A TOUGH LOOK FOR THE AFTERNOON EDITIONS, JUDGE!
JUDGE CAL TAKES HIMSELF TOO SERIOUSLY SOMETIMES. I EXPECT YOU'RE FEELING THE STRAIN OF YOUR JOURNEY, DREDD. TAKE THE REST OF THE DAY OFF.
THANK YOU, SIR. I AM A BIT DRAINED.
H'MPH!
DREDD RETURNED TO HIS APARTMENT. . .
GWEETINGS, MASTER. MAWIA AND WALTER HAVE AWANGED A LITTLE CELEBWATION!
ELCOME HOME JUDGE DREDD
I'M WALTER TRY ME
WE GOTTA DA POP AN' – A DA CAKE AN' – A DA –
PLEASE. NOT NOW. I'M TIRED. VERY TIRED. . .
WITH DREDD WERE CHIEF JUDGE CLARENCE GOODMAN AND JUDGE CAL, DEPUTY CHIEF JUDGE AND HEAD OF THE FEARED SJS SQUAD.
JUST... WANT SLEEP...
MAMA MIA! DA POOR-A JUDGE LOOK-A LIKE HE BEEN TRO'-A DA HELL!
WE BETTER LEAVE HIM. I'LL JUST PUT THE NEWS-VIDS BY HIS BED FOR WHEN HE WAKES UP – THEY'RE FULL OF STOWIES ABOUT HIS BWAVE DEEDS.

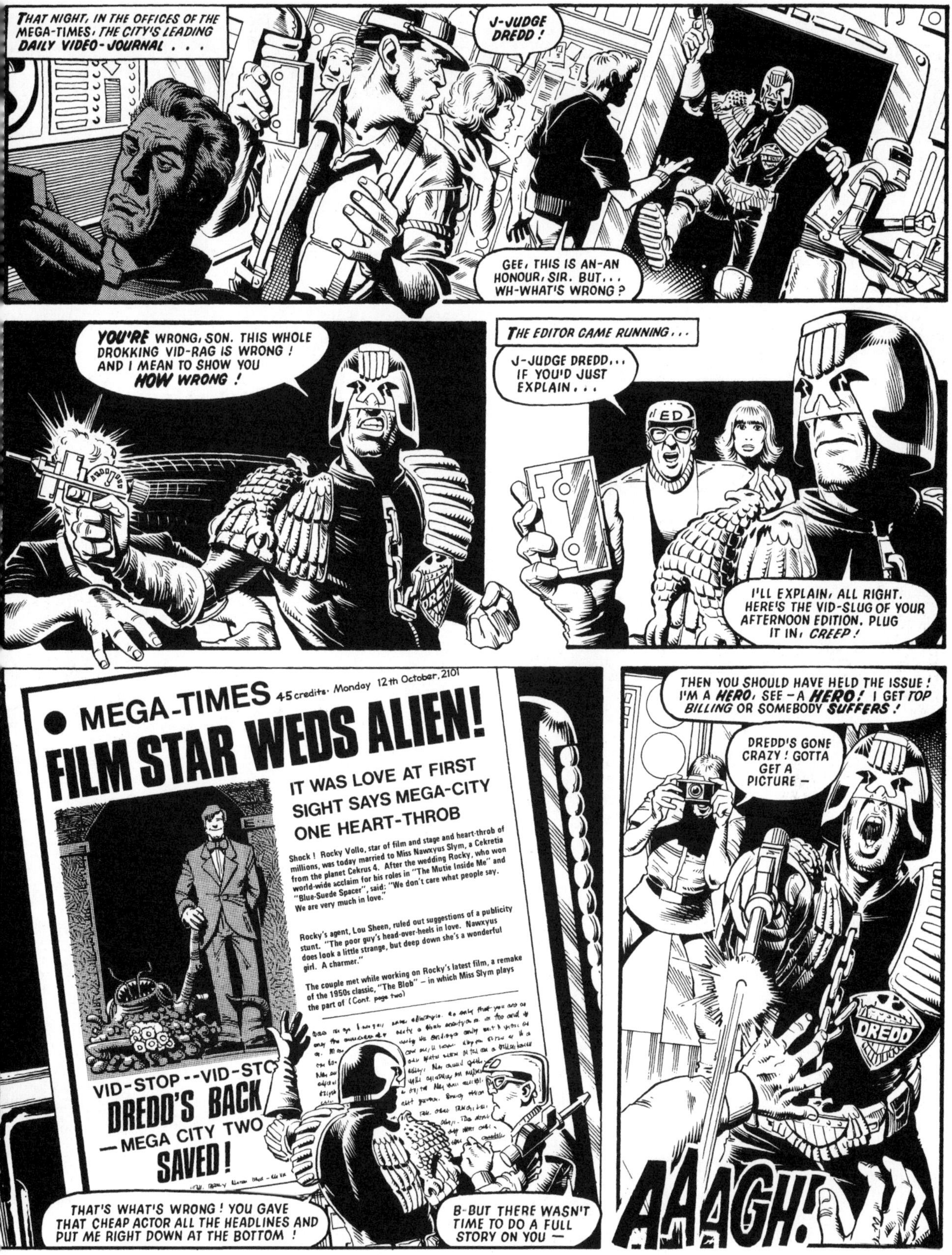
THAT NIGHT, IN THE OFFICES OF THE MEGA-TIMES, THE CITY'S LEADING DAILY VIDEO-JOURNAL . . .
J-JUDGE DREDD !
GEE, THIS IS AN-AN HONOUR, SIR. BUT... WH-WHAT'S WRONG ?
YOU'RE WRONG, SON. THIS WHOLE DROKKING VID-RAG IS WRONG ! AND I MEAN TO SHOW YOU HOW WRONG !
THE EDITOR CAME RUNNING . . .
J-JUDGE DREDD... IF YOU'D JUST EXPLAIN . . .
ED
I'LL EXPLAIN, ALL RIGHT. HERE'S THE VID-SLUG OF YOUR AFTERNOON EDITION. PLUG IT IN, CREEP !
MEGA-TIMES 45 credits · Monday 12th October, 2101
FILM STAR WEDS ALIEN!
IT WAS LOVE AT FIRST SIGHT SAYS MEGA-CITY ONE HEART-THROB
Shock ! Rocky Vollo, star of film and stage and heart-throb of millions, was today married to Miss Nawxyus Slym, a Cekretia from the planet Cekrus 4. After the wedding Rocky, who won world-wide acclaim for his roles in "The Mutie Inside Me" and "Blue-Suede Spacer", said: "We don't care what people say. We are very much in love."
Rocky's agent, Lou Sheen, ruled out suggestions of a publicity stunt. "The poor guy's head-over-heels in love. Nawxyus does look a little strange, but deep down she's a wonderful girl. A charmer."
The couple met while working on Rocky's latest film, a remake of the 1950s classic, "The Blob" – in which Miss Slym plays the part of (Cont. page two)
VID-STOP--VID-STC
DREDD'S BACK
–MEGA CITY TWO
SAVED !
THAT'S WHAT'S WRONG ! YOU GAVE THAT CHEAP ACTOR ALL THE HEADLINES AND PUT ME RIGHT DOWN AT THE BOTTOM !
B-BUT THERE WASN'T TIME TO DO A FULL STORY ON YOU –
THEN YOU SHOULD HAVE HELD THE ISSUE ! I'M A HERO, SEE – A HERO ! I GET TOP BILLING OR SOMEBODY SUFFERS !
DREDD'S GONE CRAZY ! GOTTA GET A PICTURE –
DREDD
AAAGH!

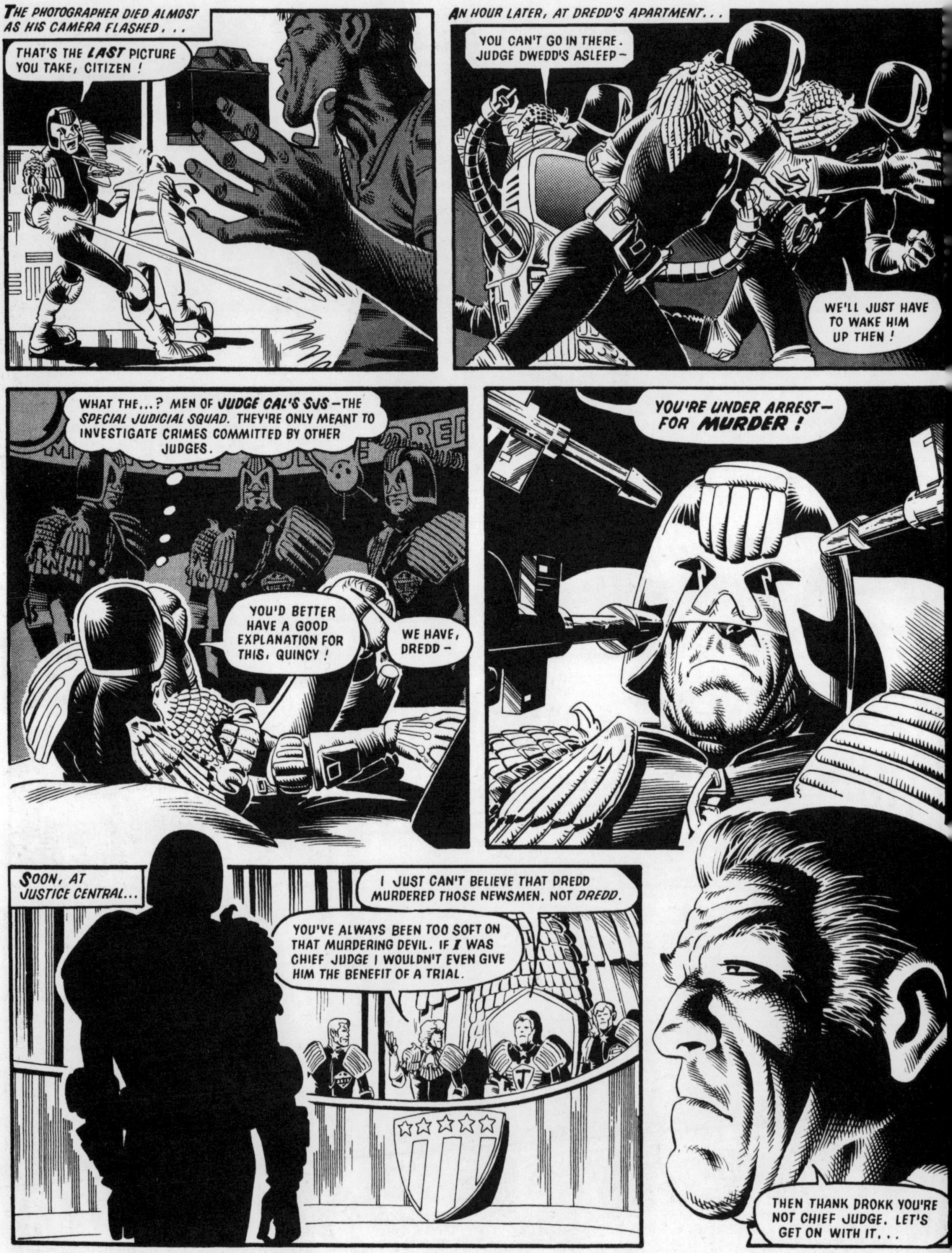
THE PHOTOGRAPHER DIED ALMOST AS HIS CAMERA FLASHED, . .
THAT'S THE LAST PICTURE YOU TAKE, CITIZEN !
AN HOUR LATER, AT DREDD'S APARTMENT. . .
YOU CAN'T GO IN THERE. JUDGE DWEDD'S ASLEEP –
WE'LL JUST HAVE TO WAKE HIM UP THEN !
WHAT THE. . .? MEN OF JUDGE CAL'S SJS – THE SPECIAL JUDICIAL SQUAD. THEY'RE ONLY MEANT TO INVESTIGATE CRIMES COMMITTED BY OTHER JUDGES.
YOU'D BETTER HAVE A GOOD EXPLANATION FOR THIS, QUINCY !
WE HAVE, DREDD –
YOU'RE UNDER ARREST – FOR MURDER !
SOON, AT JUSTICE CENTRAL. . .
I JUST CAN'T BELIEVE THAT DREDD MURDERED THOSE NEWSMEN. NOT DREDD.
YOU'VE ALWAYS BEEN TOO SOFT ON THAT MURDERING DEVIL. IF I WAS CHIEF JUDGE I WOULDN'T EVEN GIVE HIM THE BENEFIT OF A TRIAL.
THEN THANK DROKK YOU'RE NOT CHIEF JUDGE. LET'S GET ON WITH IT. . .

UNDER MEGA-CITY LAW, A SUSPECT JUDGE WAS TRIED BEFORE A COUNCIL OF FIVE. WITNESSES WERE BROUGHT FORWARD —

WALTER WAS OUTSIDE JUDGE DWEDD'S DOOR ALL DAY. JUDGE DWEDD NEVER LEFT HIS ROOM.

THAT ROBOT'S SICKENINGLY LOYAL. HE'S LYING. NEXT WITNESS!

THE EVIDENCE AGAINST DREDD WAS DAMNING...

IT WAS DREDD ALL RIGHT. I'D RECOGNISE HIS VOICE ANYWHERE.

A HERO, HE CALLED HIMSELF. I'D CALL HIM A STINKING MURDERER!

"BOX" PATON TOOK A PICTURE JUST AS THE EDITOR WAS SHOT. BEFORE THE SHUTTER CLOSED THE KILLER GOT OFF ANOTHER SHOT. ONLY JUDGE DREDD MOVES THAT FAST.

I...DON'T UNDERSTAND. I...HAVE NO MEMORY OF GOING TO THE MEGA-TIMES OFFICE...AND YET THERE'S NO REASON FOR THOSE MEN TO LIE.

GENTLEMEN, THE PENALTY FOR CRIMES BY A JUDGE IS TWENTY YEARS PENAL SERVITUDE ON THE COLONY OF TITAN. WE'VE HEARD THE EVIDENCE, NOW WE MUST DECIDE.

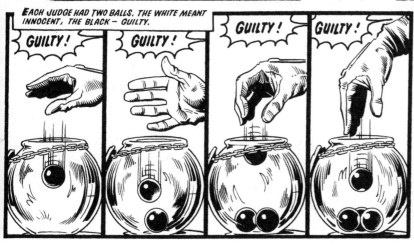

EACH JUDGE HAD TWO BALLS. THE WHITE MEANT INNOCENT, THE BLACK — GUILTY.

GUILTY!

GUILTY!

GUILTY!

GUILTY!

THE VERDICT MUST BE UNANIMOUS. VOTE, JUDGE GOODMAN.

VOTE — OR STAND DOWN, AS CHIEF JUDGE AND LET ME TAKE YOUR PLACE.

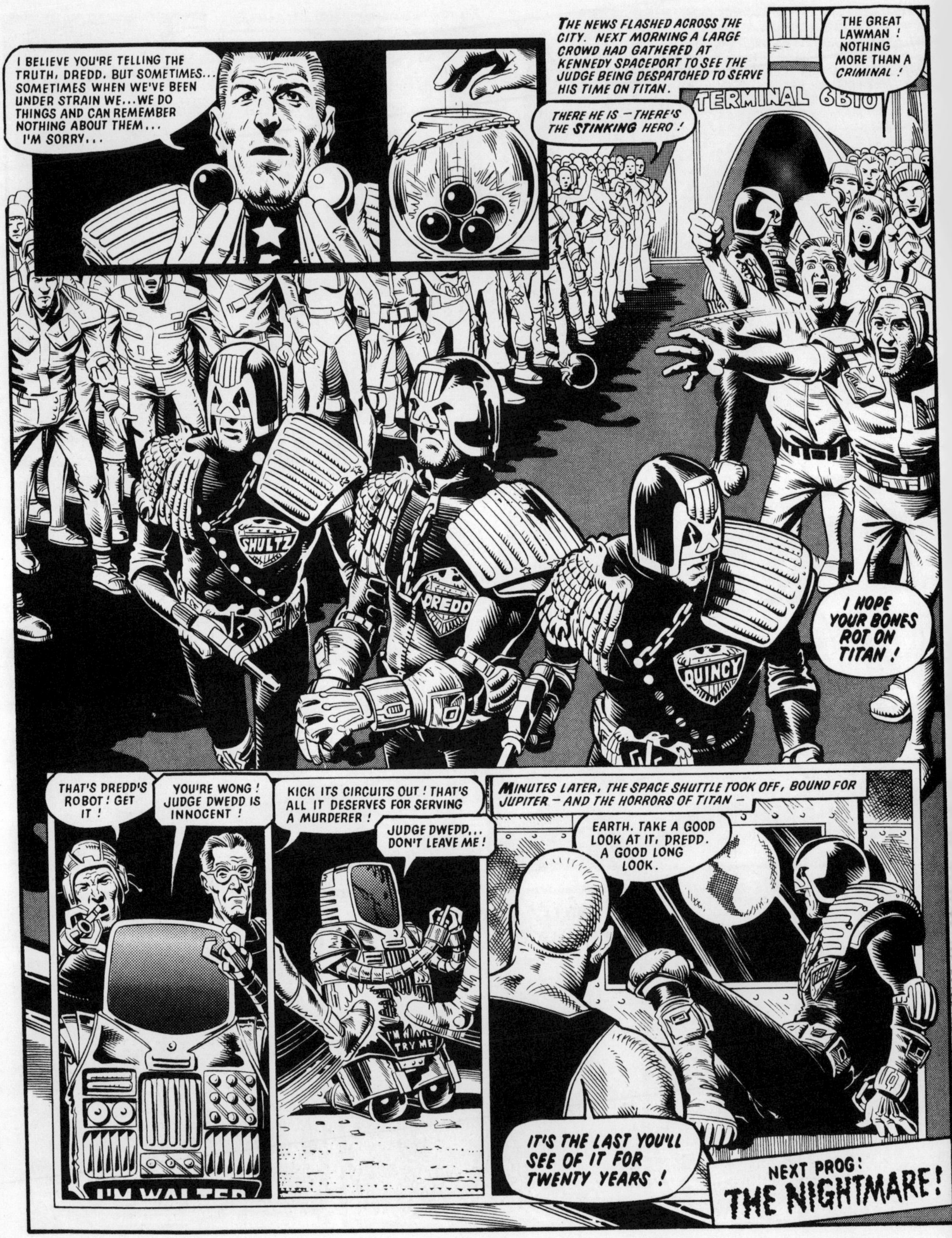
I BELIEVE YOU'RE TELLING THE TRUTH, DREDD. BUT SOMETIMES... SOMETIMES WHEN WE'VE BEEN UNDER STRAIN WE...WE DO THINGS AND CAN REMEMBER NOTHING ABOUT THEM... I'M SORRY...
THE NEWS FLASHED ACROSS THE CITY. NEXT MORNING A LARGE CROWD HAD GATHERED AT KENNEDY SPACEPORT TO SEE THE JUDGE BEING DESPATCHED TO SERVE HIS TIME ON TITAN.
THE GREAT LAWMAN! NOTHING MORE THAN A CRIMINAL!
TERMINAL 6B10
THERE HE IS — THERE'S THE STINKING HERO!
SHULTZ
DREDD
QUINCY
I HOPE YOUR BONES ROT ON TITAN!
THAT'S DREDD'S ROBOT! GET IT!
YOU'RE WONG! JUDGE DWEDD IS INNOCENT!
KICK ITS CIRCUITS OUT! THAT'S ALL IT DESERVES FOR SERVING A MURDERER!
JUDGE DWEDD... DON'T LEAVE ME!
I'M WALTER
MINUTES LATER, THE SPACE SHUTTLE TOOK OFF, BOUND FOR JUPITER — AND THE HORRORS OF TITAN —
EARTH. TAKE A GOOD LOOK AT IT, DREDD. A GOOD LONG LOOK.
IT'S THE LAST YOU'LL SEE OF IT FOR TWENTY YEARS!
NEXT PROG: THE NIGHTMARE!

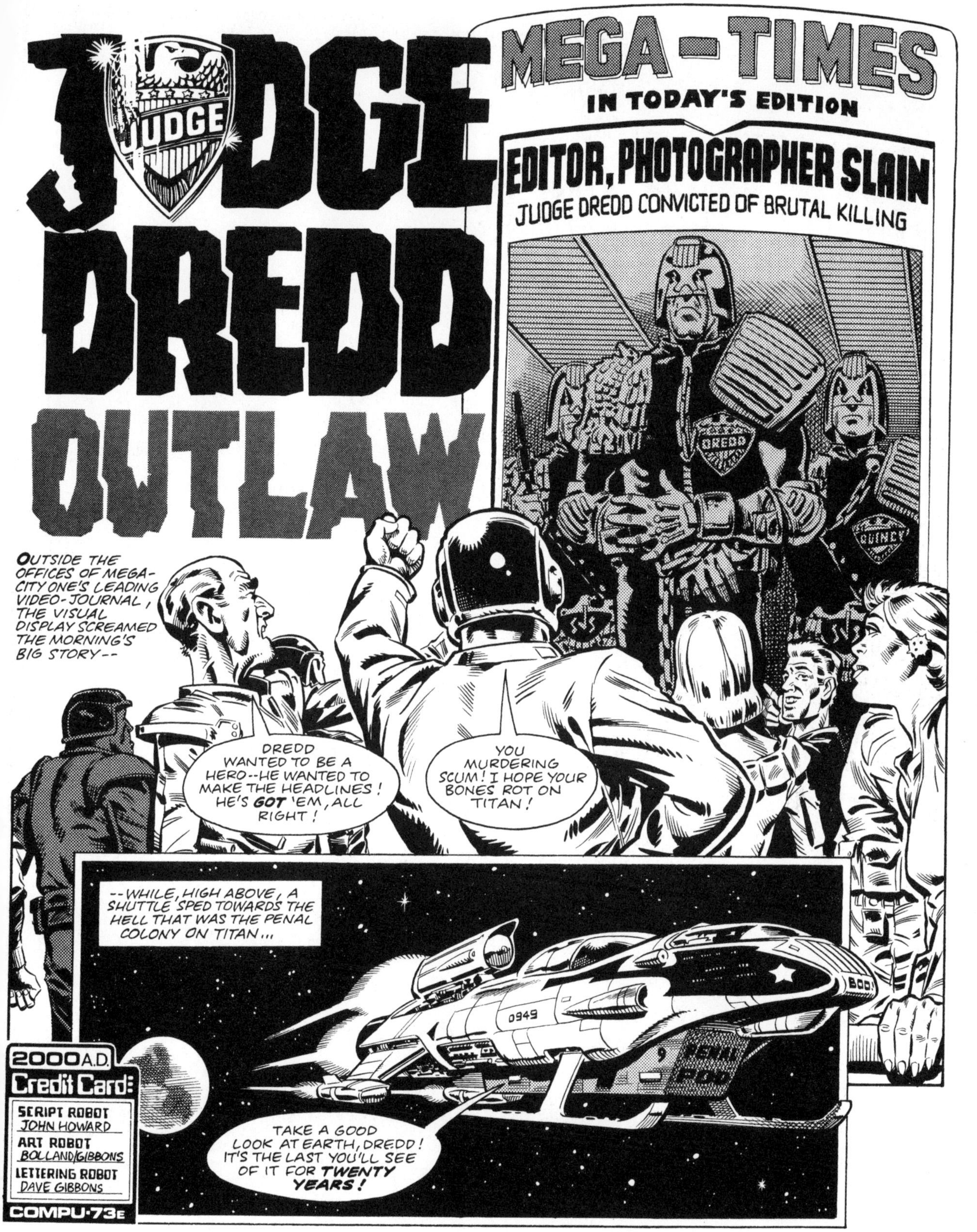
JUDGE
JUDGE DREDD
OUTLAW
MEGA-TIMES
IN TODAY'S EDITION
EDITOR, PHOTOGRAPHER SLAIN
JUDGE DREDD CONVICTED OF BRUTAL KILLING
DREDD
QUINCY
OUTSIDE THE OFFICES OF MEGA-CITY ONE'S LEADING VIDEO-JOURNAL, THE VISUAL DISPLAY SCREAMED THE MORNING'S BIG STORY--
DREDD WANTED TO BE A HERO--HE WANTED TO MAKE THE HEADLINES! HE'S GOT 'EM, ALL RIGHT!
YOU MURDERING SCUM! I HOPE YOUR BONES ROT ON TITAN!
--WHILE, HIGH ABOVE, A SHUTTLE SPED TOWARDS THE HELL THAT WAS THE PENAL COLONY ON TITAN...
0949
TAKE A GOOD LOOK AT EARTH, DREDD! IT'S THE LAST YOU'LL SEE OF IT FOR TWENTY YEARS!
2000 A.D.
Credit Card:
SCRIPT ROBOT JOHN HOWARD
ART ROBOT BOLLAND/GIBBONS
LETTERING ROBOT DAVE GIBBONS
COMPU-73E

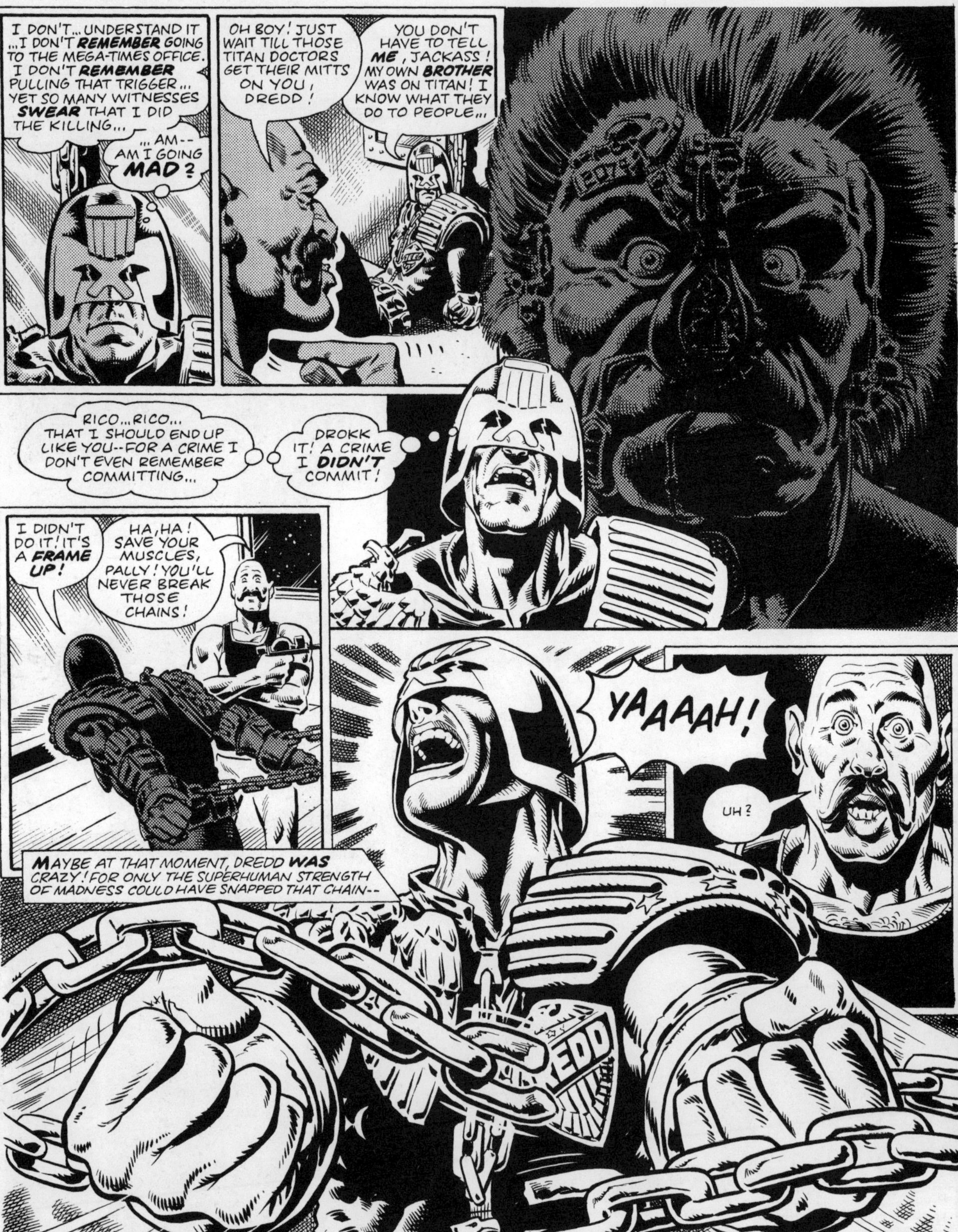
I DON'T... UNDERSTAND IT ...I DON'T **REMEMBER** GOING TO THE MEGA-TIMES OFFICE. I DON'T **REMEMBER** PULLING THAT TRIGGER... YET SO MANY WITNESSES **SWEAR** THAT I DID THE KILLING...
... AM-- AM I GOING **MAD**?
OH BOY! JUST WAIT TILL THOSE TITAN DOCTORS GET THEIR MITTS ON YOU, DREDD!
YOU DON'T HAVE TO TELL **ME**, JACKASS! MY OWN **BROTHER** WAS ON TITAN! I KNOW WHAT THEY DO TO PEOPLE...
RICO... RICO... THAT I SHOULD END UP LIKE YOU--FOR A CRIME I DON'T EVEN REMEMBER COMMITTING...
DROKK IT! A CRIME I **DIDN'T** COMMIT!
I DIDN'T DO IT! IT'S A **FRAME UP**!
HA, HA! SAVE YOUR MUSCLES, PALLY! YOU'LL NEVER BREAK THOSE CHAINS!
YAAAAH!
UH?
MAYBE AT THAT MOMENT, DREDD **WAS** CRAZY! FOR ONLY THE SUPERHUMAN STRENGTH OF MADNESS COULD HAVE SNAPPED THAT CHAIN--

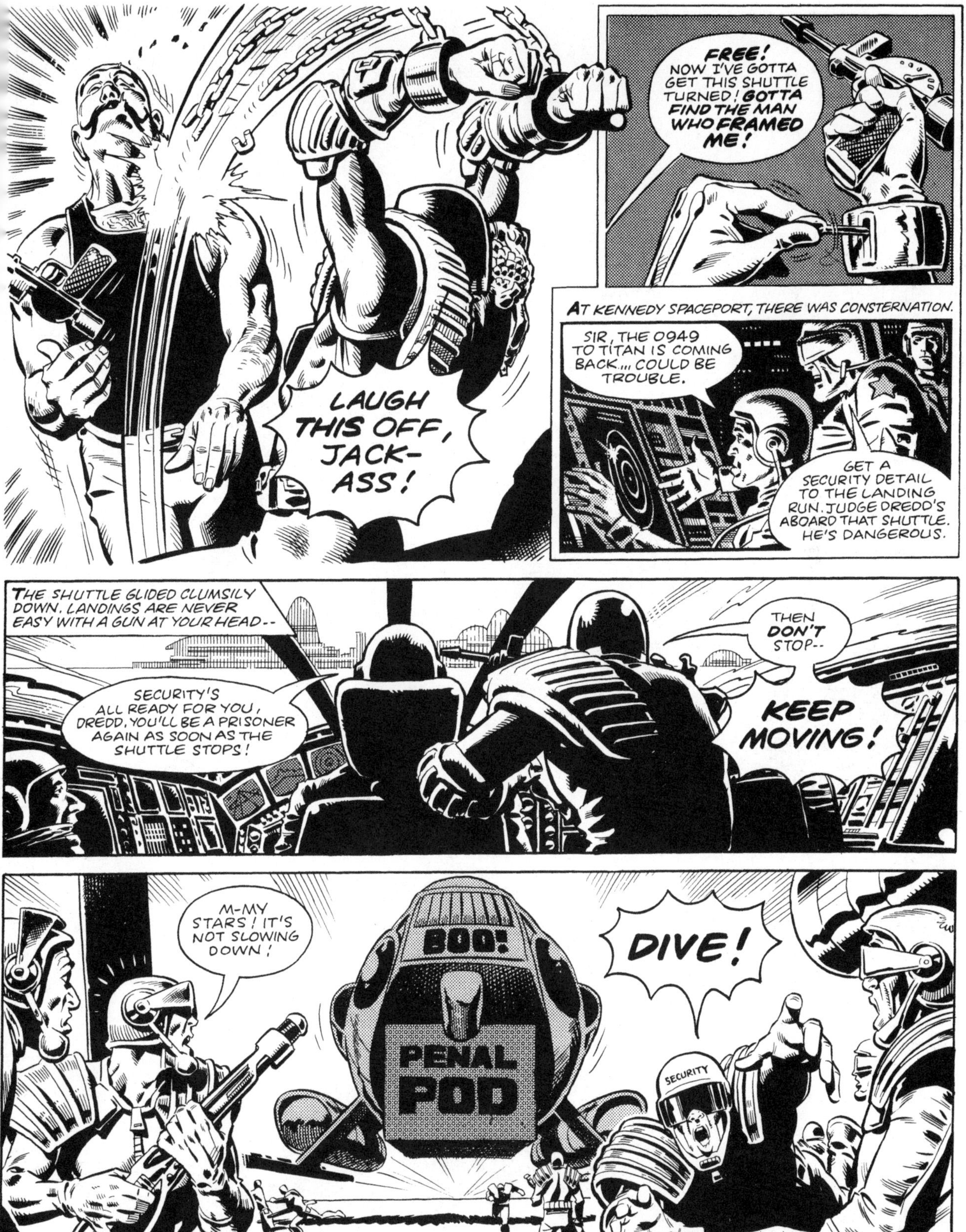
LAUGH THIS OFF, JACK-ASS!
FREE! NOW I'VE GOTTA GET THIS SHUTTLE TURNED! GOTTA FIND THE MAN WHO FRAMED ME!
AT KENNEDY SPACEPORT, THERE WAS CONSTERNATION.
SIR, THE 0949 TO TITAN IS COMING BACK.... COULD BE TROUBLE.
GET A SECURITY DETAIL TO THE LANDING RUN. JUDGE DREDD'S ABOARD THAT SHUTTLE. HE'S DANGEROUS.
THE SHUTTLE GLIDED CLUMSILY DOWN. LANDINGS ARE NEVER EASY WITH A GUN AT YOUR HEAD--
SECURITY'S ALL READY FOR YOU, DREDD. YOU'LL BE A PRISONER AGAIN AS SOON AS THE SHUTTLE STOPS!
THEN DON'T STOP--
KEEP MOVING!
M-MY STARS! IT'S NOT SLOWING DOWN!
BOO!
PENAL POD
DIVE!
SECURITY

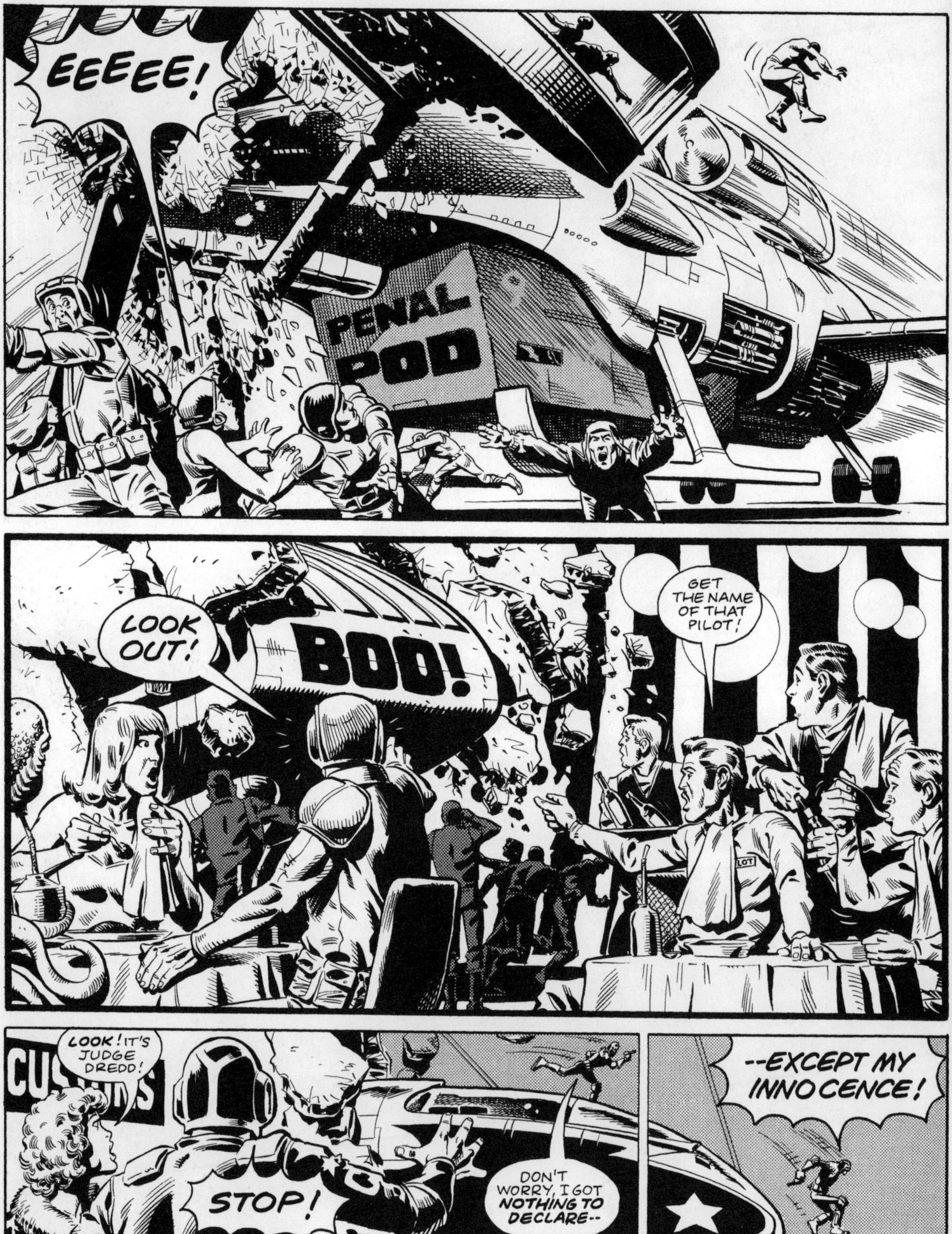
EEEEEE!
PENAL POD
LOOK OUT!
BOO!
GET THE NAME OF THAT PILOT!
LOOK! IT'S JUDGE DREDD!
STOP!
DON'T WORRY, I GOT NOTHING TO DECLARE--
--EXCEPT MY INNOCENCE!

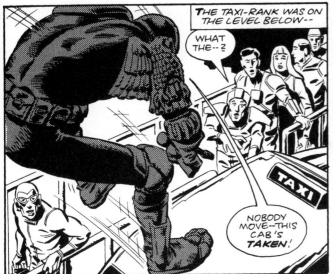

THE TAXI-RANK WAS ON THE LEVEL BELOW--

WHAT THE--?

NOBODY MOVE--THIS CAB'S *TAKEN!*

DRIVE! AND IF YOU EVER WANT TO WORK THIS RANK AGAIN, DON'T STOP TILL I *TELL* YOU!

Y-YES, S-S-*SIR!*

AT JUSTICE CENTRAL, DEPUTY CHIEF JUDGE CAL SUMMONED EVERY AVAILABLE JUDGE TO THE GRAND HALL--

I WANT DREDD AND I WANT HIM *NOW!* YOU'RE RELIEVED OF ALL OTHER DUTIES UNTIL HE'S FOUND!

A-ALL OF US, SIR? HAS THE CHIEF JUDGE OKAYED IT, SIR?

YES...YES... WHATEVER JUDGE CAL THINKS IS... BEST...

JUDGE CAL SNARLED...

DON'T EVER QUESTION MY AUTHORITY AGAIN, JUDGE OCHS! I'M HANDLING THINGS HERE UNTIL THE CHIEF JUDGE IS... WELL AGAIN.

THE CHIEF JUDGE HAS GONE TO PIECES SINCE HIS VOTE CONDEMNED DREDD TO TITAN, JUDGE CAL WOULD JUST LOVE TO STEP INTO HIS SHOES--*PERMANENTLY!*

THERE FOLLOWED THE BIGGEST MAN-HUNT IN MEGA-CITY HISTORY...

WE'RE LOOKING FOR DREDD.

IN MY BAG?

ANYWHERE!

YOU WATS! YOU'LL NEVER FIND DWEDD!

I'M WALTER TRY ME

CAN IT, RUST-BUCKET --OR WE'LL CAN *YOU!*

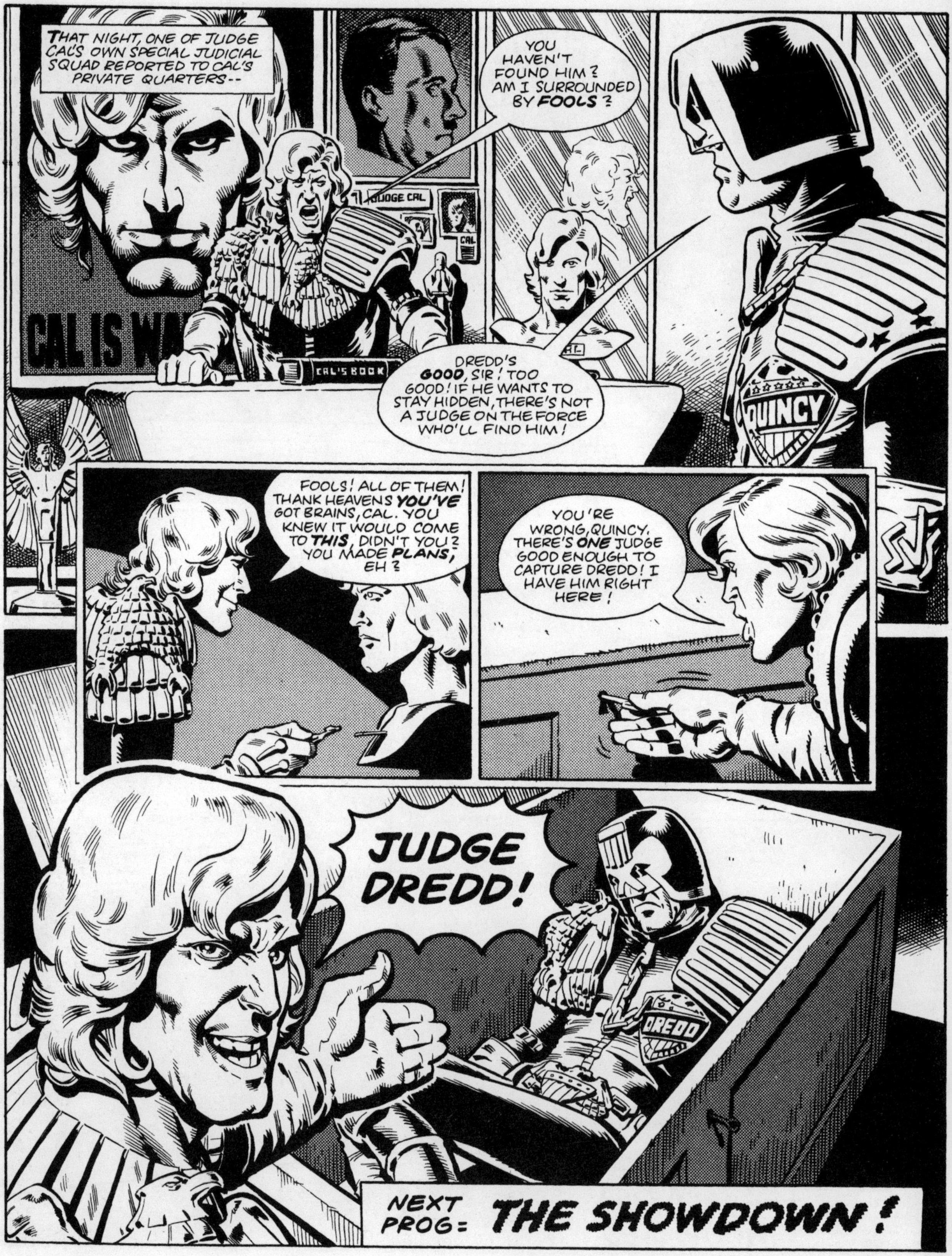
THAT NIGHT, ONE OF JUDGE CAL'S OWN SPECIAL JUDICIAL SQUAD REPORTED TO CAL'S PRIVATE QUARTERS--
YOU HAVEN'T FOUND HIM? AM I SURROUNDED BY FOOLS?
DREDD'S GOOD, SIR! TOO GOOD! IF HE WANTS TO STAY HIDDEN, THERE'S NOT A JUDGE ON THE FORCE WHO'LL FIND HIM!
CAL IS WA
JUDGE CAL
CAL'S BOOK
QUINCY
FOOLS! ALL OF THEM! THANK HEAVENS YOU'VE GOT BRAINS, CAL. YOU KNEW IT WOULD COME TO THIS, DIDN'T YOU? YOU MADE PLANS, EH?
YOU'RE WRONG, QUINCY. THERE'S ONE JUDGE GOOD ENOUGH TO CAPTURE DREDD! I HAVE HIM RIGHT HERE!
JUDGE DREDD!
DREDD
NEXT PROG: THE SHOWDOWN!

JUDGE DREDD

THERE'S ONLY ROOM FOR ONE DREDD IN MEGA-CITY, AND THAT DREDD IS ME!
IT'S A FIGHT I CAN'T WIN! HOW CAN I KILL MYSELF?
DREDD
2000 A.D. Credit Card:
SCRIPT ROBOT JOHN HOWARD
ART ROBOT McCARTHY/EWINS
LETTERING ROBOT T. FRAME
COMPU-73E
BRING ME THE HEAD OF JUDGE DREDD!

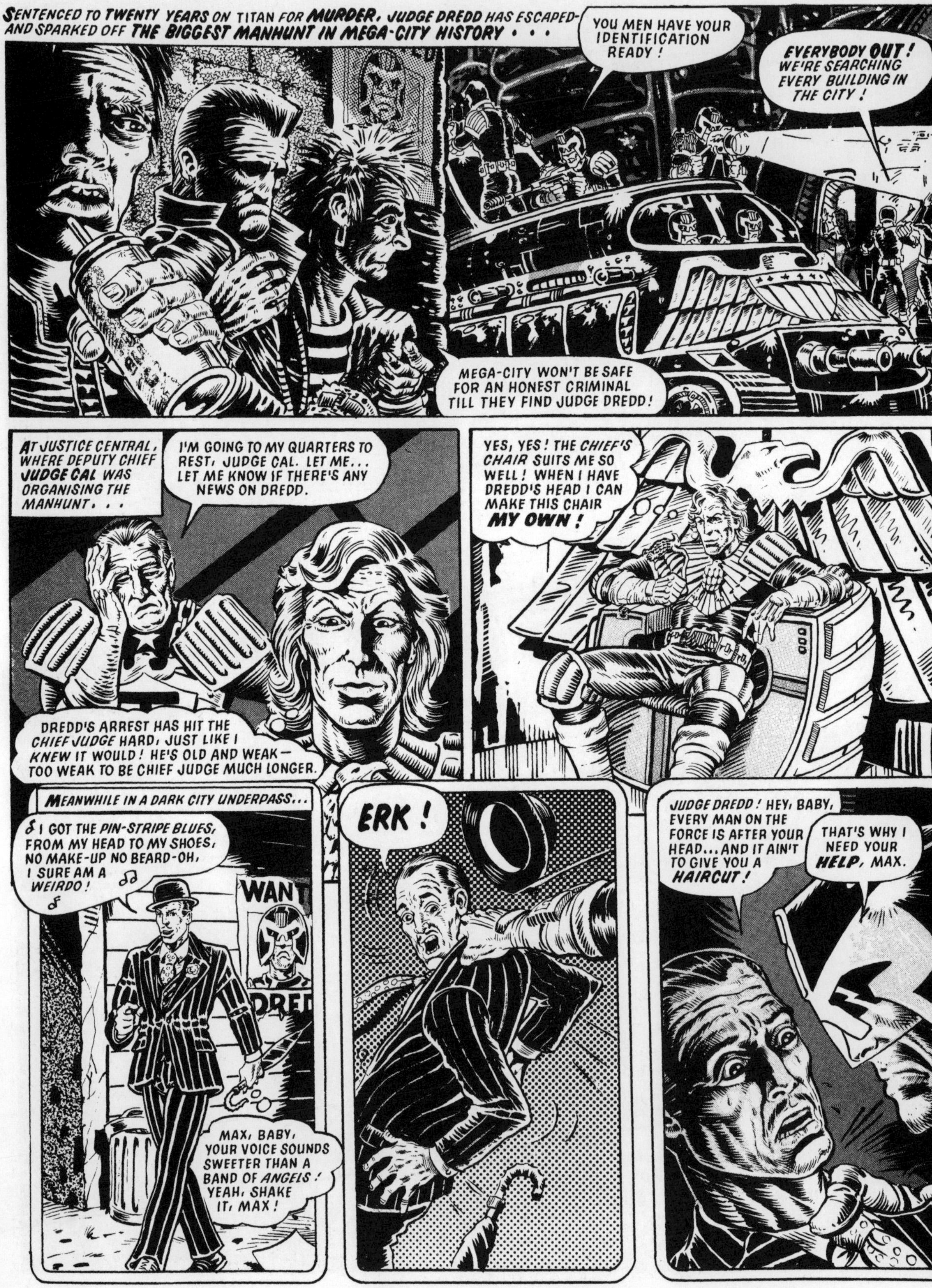
SENTENCED TO TWENTY YEARS ON TITAN FOR MURDER, JUDGE DREDD HAS ESCAPED-AND SPARKED OFF THE BIGGEST MANHUNT IN MEGA-CITY HISTORY . . .
YOU MEN HAVE YOUR IDENTIFICATION READY!
EVERYBODY OUT! WE'RE SEARCHING EVERY BUILDING IN THE CITY!
MEGA-CITY WON'T BE SAFE FOR AN HONEST CRIMINAL TILL THEY FIND JUDGE DREDD!
AT JUSTICE CENTRAL, WHERE DEPUTY CHIEF JUDGE CAL WAS ORGANISING THE MANHUNT. . .
I'M GOING TO MY QUARTERS TO REST, JUDGE CAL. LET ME... LET ME KNOW IF THERE'S ANY NEWS ON DREDD.
DREDD'S ARREST HAS HIT THE CHIEF JUDGE HARD, JUST LIKE I KNEW IT WOULD! HE'S OLD AND WEAK-TOO WEAK TO BE CHIEF JUDGE MUCH LONGER.
YES, YES! THE CHIEF'S CHAIR SUITS ME SO WELL! WHEN I HAVE DREDD'S HEAD I CAN MAKE THIS CHAIR MY OWN!
MEANWHILE IN A DARK CITY UNDERPASS...
I GOT THE PIN-STRIPE BLUES, FROM MY HEAD TO MY SHOES, NO MAKE-UP NO BEARD-OH, I SURE AM A WEIRDO!
WANT
DREDD
MAX, BABY, YOUR VOICE SOUNDS SWEETER THAN A BAND OF ANGELS! YEAH, SHAKE IT, MAX!
ERK!
JUDGE DREDD! HEY, BABY, EVERY MAN ON THE FORCE IS AFTER YOUR HEAD... AND IT AIN'T TO GIVE YOU A HAIRCUT!
THAT'S WHY I NEED YOUR HELP, MAX.

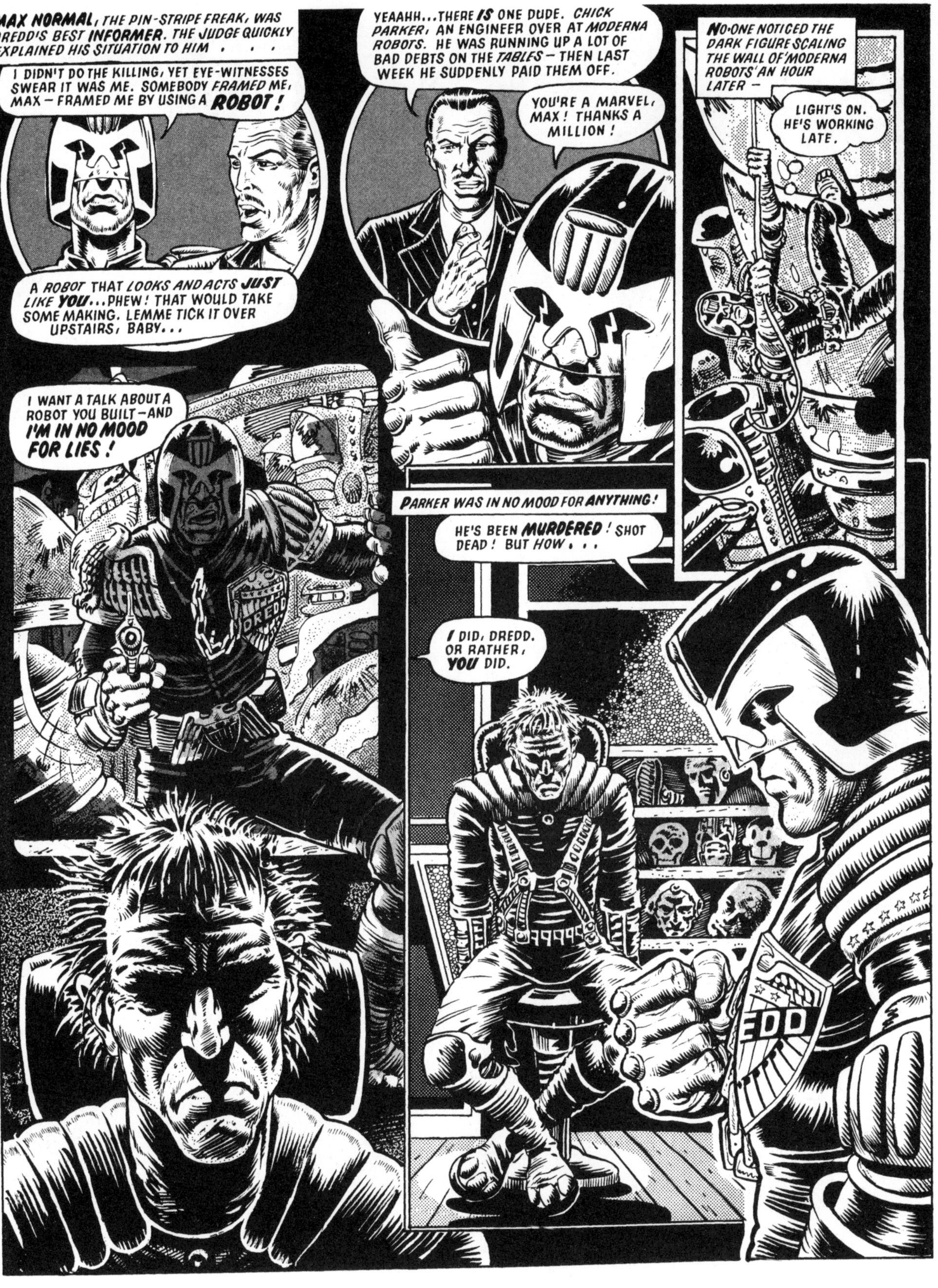
MAX NORMAL, THE PIN-STRIPE FREAK, WAS DREDD'S BEST INFORMER. THE JUDGE QUICKLY EXPLAINED HIS SITUATION TO HIM . . .
I DIDN'T DO THE KILLING, YET EYE-WITNESSES SWEAR IT WAS ME. SOMEBODY FRAMED ME, MAX — FRAMED ME BY USING A ROBOT!
A ROBOT THAT LOOKS AND ACTS JUST LIKE YOU... PHEW! THAT WOULD TAKE SOME MAKING. LEMME TICK IT OVER UPSTAIRS, BABY...
YEAAHH...THERE IS ONE DUDE. CHICK PARKER, AN ENGINEER OVER AT MODERNA ROBOTS. HE WAS RUNNING UP A LOT OF BAD DEBTS ON THE TABLES — THEN LAST WEEK HE SUDDENLY PAID THEM OFF.
YOU'RE A MARVEL, MAX! THANKS A MILLION!
NO-ONE NOTICED THE DARK FIGURE SCALING THE WALL OF 'MODERNA ROBOTS' AN HOUR LATER —
LIGHT'S ON. HE'S WORKING LATE.
I WANT A TALK ABOUT A ROBOT YOU BUILT—AND I'M IN NO MOOD FOR LIES!
PARKER WAS IN NO MOOD FOR ANYTHING!
HE'S BEEN MURDERED! SHOT DEAD! BUT HOW . . .
I DID, DREDD. OR RATHER, YOU DID.

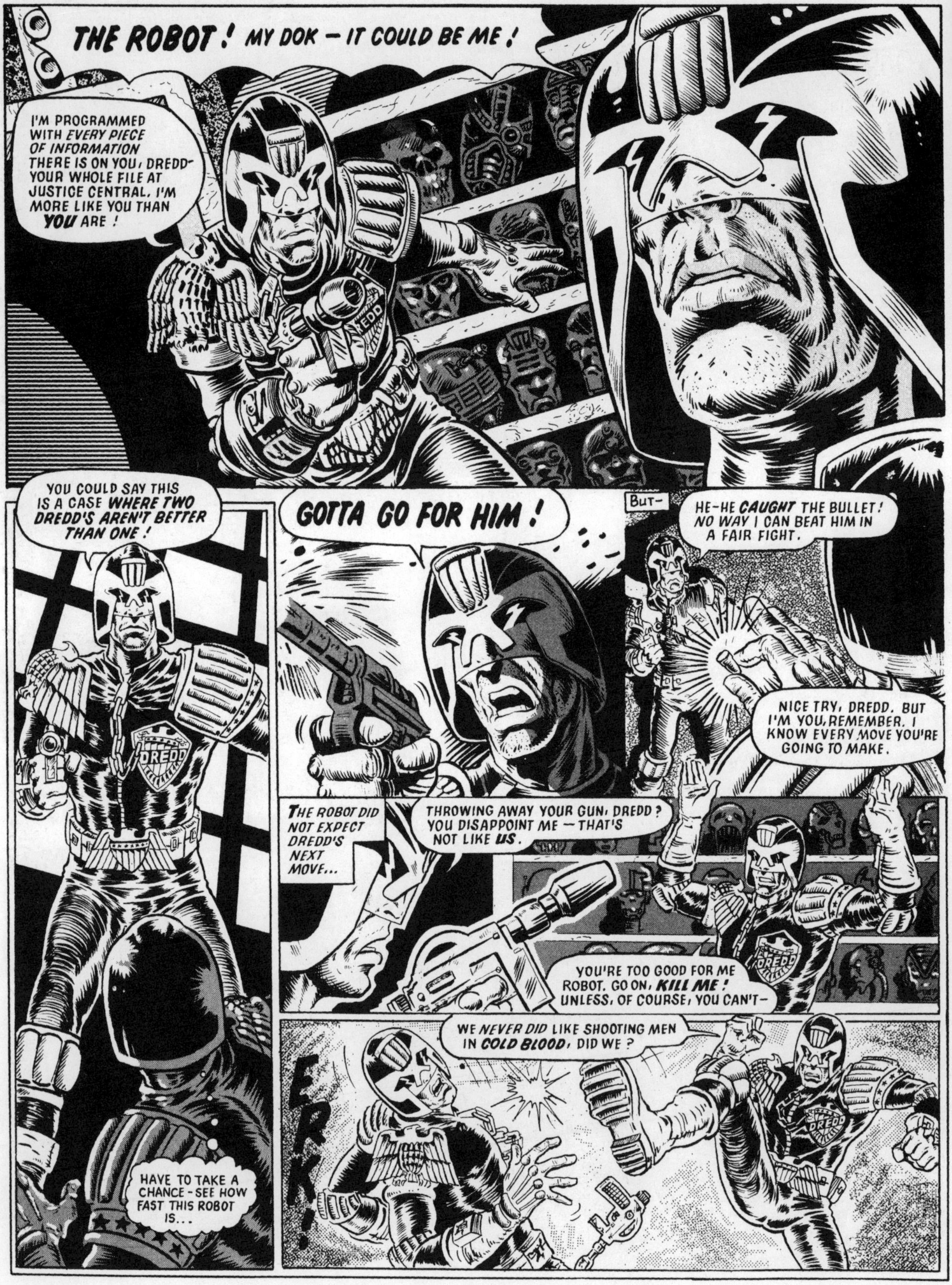
THE ROBOT! MY DOK — IT COULD BE ME!
I'M PROGRAMMED WITH EVERY PIECE OF INFORMATION THERE IS ON YOU, DREDD- YOUR WHOLE FILE AT JUSTICE CENTRAL. I'M MORE LIKE YOU THAN YOU ARE!
YOU COULD SAY THIS IS A CASE WHERE TWO DREDD'S AREN'T BETTER THAN ONE!
HAVE TO TAKE A CHANCE - SEE HOW FAST THIS ROBOT IS...
GOTTA GO FOR HIM!
BUT-
HE-HE CAUGHT THE BULLET! NO WAY I CAN BEAT HIM IN A FAIR FIGHT.
NICE TRY, DREDD. BUT I'M YOU, REMEMBER. I KNOW EVERY MOVE YOU'RE GOING TO MAKE.
THE ROBOT DID NOT EXPECT DREDD'S NEXT MOVE...
THROWING AWAY YOUR GUN, DREDD? YOU DISAPPOINT ME — THAT'S NOT LIKE US.
YOU'RE TOO GOOD FOR ME ROBOT. GO ON, KILL ME! UNLESS, OF COURSE, YOU CAN'T-
WE NEVER DID LIKE SHOOTING MEN IN COLD BLOOD, DID WE?
ERK!

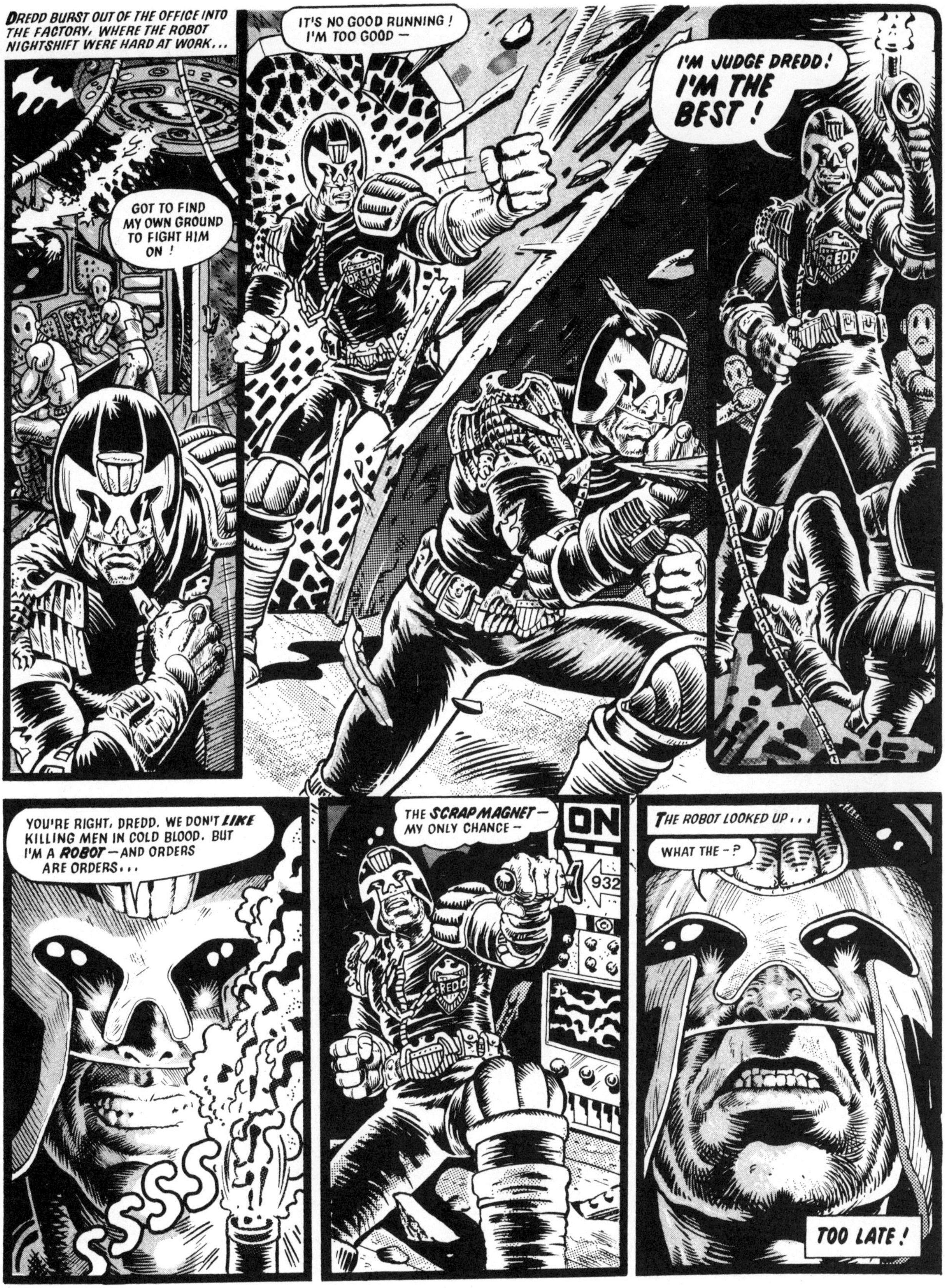

DREDD BURST OUT OF THE OFFICE INTO THE FACTORY, WHERE THE ROBOT NIGHTSHIFT WERE HARD AT WORK...
GOT TO FIND MY OWN GROUND TO FIGHT HIM ON !
IT'S NO GOOD RUNNING ! I'M TOO GOOD —
I'M JUDGE DREDD! I'M THE BEST !
YOU'RE RIGHT, DREDD. WE DON'T LIKE KILLING MEN IN COLD BLOOD. BUT I'M A ROBOT — AND ORDERS ARE ORDERS...
SSSS
THE SCRAP MAGNET — MY ONLY CHANCE —
ON
932
THE ROBOT LOOKED UP...
WHAT THE —?
TOO LATE !

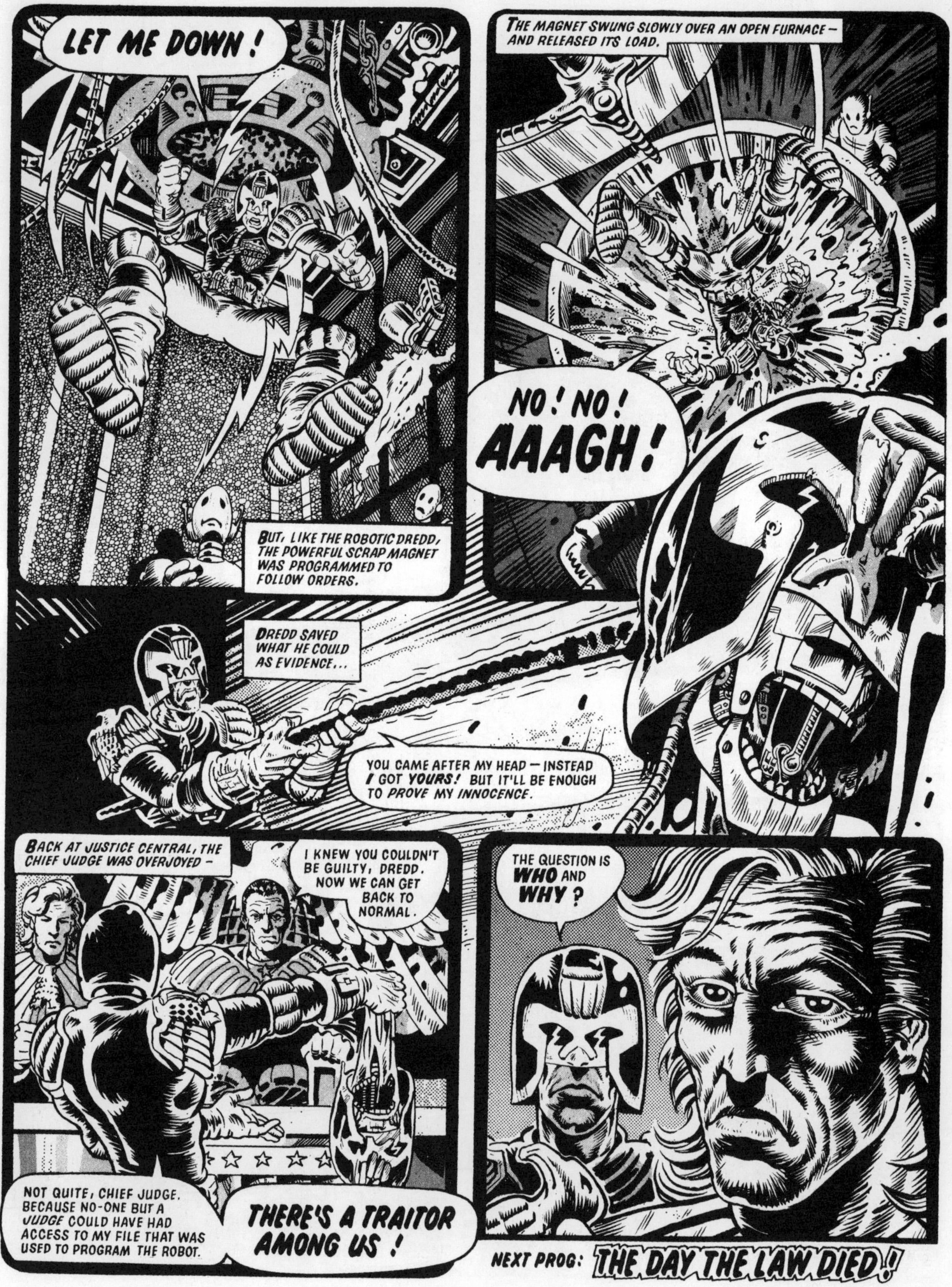
LET ME DOWN!
BUT, LIKE THE ROBOTIC DREDD, THE POWERFUL SCRAP MAGNET WAS PROGRAMMED TO FOLLOW ORDERS.
THE MAGNET SWUNG SLOWLY OVER AN OPEN FURNACE – AND RELEASED ITS LOAD.
NO! NO! AAAGH!
DREDD SAVED WHAT HE COULD AS EVIDENCE...
YOU CAME AFTER MY HEAD – INSTEAD I GOT YOURS! BUT IT'LL BE ENOUGH TO PROVE MY INNOCENCE.
BACK AT JUSTICE CENTRAL, THE CHIEF JUDGE WAS OVERJOYED –
I KNEW YOU COULDN'T BE GUILTY, DREDD. NOW WE CAN GET BACK TO NORMAL.
NOT QUITE, CHIEF JUDGE. BECAUSE NO-ONE BUT A JUDGE COULD HAVE HAD ACCESS TO MY FILE THAT WAS USED TO PROGRAM THE ROBOT.
THERE'S A TRAITOR AMONG US!
THE QUESTION IS WHO AND WHY?

NEXT PROG: THE DAY THE LAW DIED!

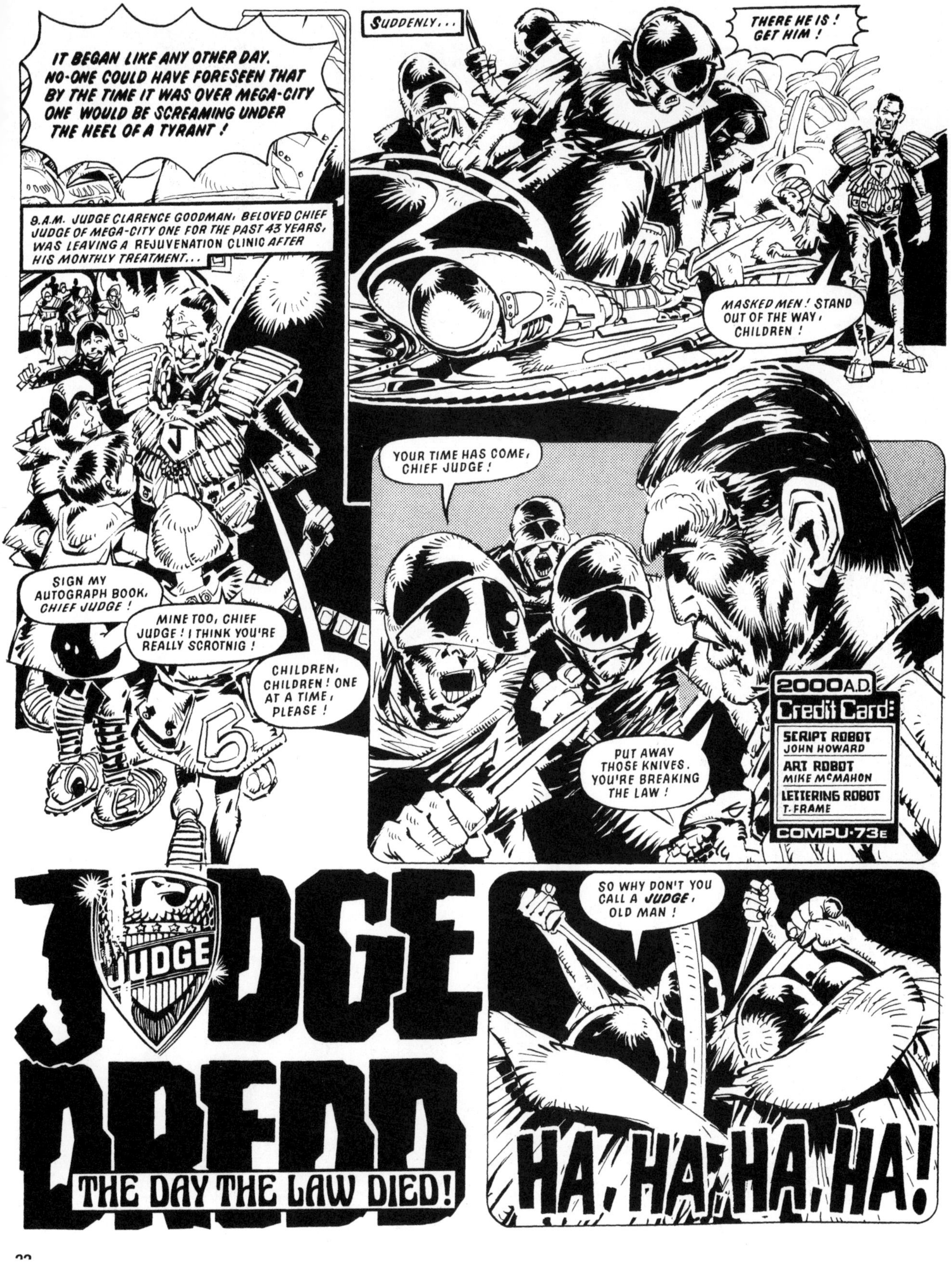

IT BEGAN LIKE ANY OTHER DAY. NO-ONE COULD HAVE FORESEEN THAT BY THE TIME IT WAS OVER MEGA-CITY ONE WOULD BE SCREAMING UNDER THE HEEL OF A TYRANT!
9.A.M. JUDGE CLARENCE GOODMAN, BELOVED CHIEF JUDGE OF MEGA-CITY ONE FOR THE PAST 43 YEARS, WAS LEAVING A REJUVENATION CLINIC AFTER HIS MONTHLY TREATMENT...
SIGN MY AUTOGRAPH BOOK, CHIEF JUDGE!
MINE TOO, CHIEF JUDGE! I THINK YOU'RE REALLY SCROTNIG!
CHILDREN, CHILDREN! ONE AT A TIME, PLEASE!
SUDDENLY...
THERE HE IS! GET HIM!
MASKED MEN! STAND OUT OF THE WAY, CHILDREN!
YOUR TIME HAS COME, CHIEF JUDGE!
PUT AWAY THOSE KNIVES. YOU'RE BREAKING THE LAW!
2000 A.D. Credit Card:
SCRIPT ROBOT JOHN HOWARD
ART ROBOT MIKE McMAHON
LETTERING ROBOT T. FRAME
COMPU-73E
JUDGE
JUDGE DREDD
THE DAY THE LAW DIED!
SO WHY DON'T YOU CALL A JUDGE, OLD MAN!
HA, HA! HA, HA!

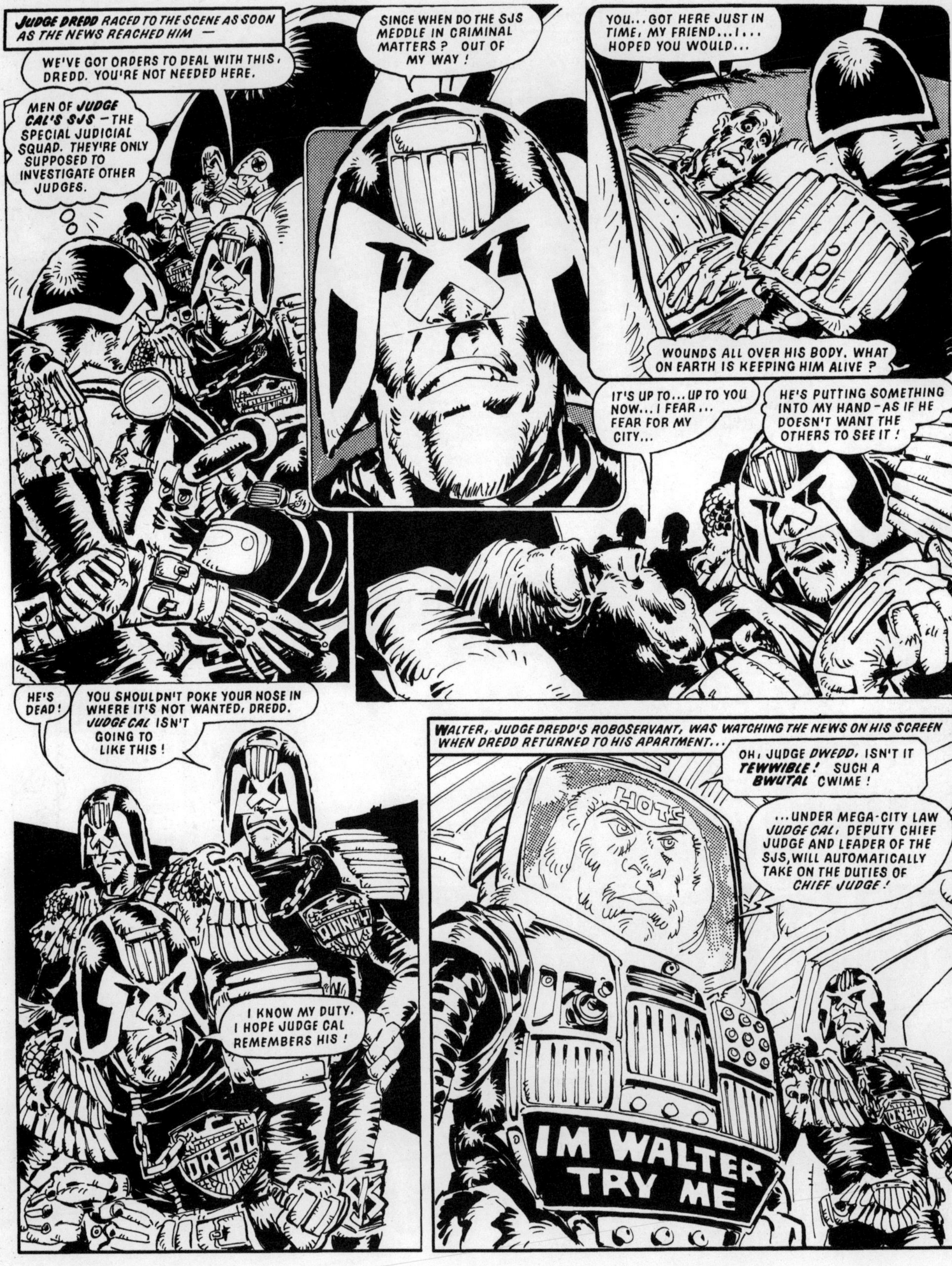
JUDGE DREDD RACED TO THE SCENE AS SOON AS THE NEWS REACHED HIM —
WE'VE GOT ORDERS TO DEAL WITH THIS, DREDD. YOU'RE NOT NEEDED HERE.
MEN OF JUDGE CAL'S SJS — THE SPECIAL JUDICIAL SQUAD. THEY'RE ONLY SUPPOSED TO INVESTIGATE OTHER JUDGES.
SINCE WHEN DO THE SJS MEDDLE IN CRIMINAL MATTERS? OUT OF MY WAY!
YOU... GOT HERE JUST IN TIME, MY FRIEND... I... HOPED YOU WOULD...
WOUNDS ALL OVER HIS BODY. WHAT ON EARTH IS KEEPING HIM ALIVE?
IT'S UP TO... UP TO YOU NOW... I FEAR... FEAR FOR MY CITY...
HE'S PUTTING SOMETHING INTO MY HAND — AS IF HE DOESN'T WANT THE OTHERS TO SEE IT!
HE'S DEAD!
YOU SHOULDN'T POKE YOUR NOSE IN WHERE IT'S NOT WANTED, DREDD. JUDGE CAL ISN'T GOING TO LIKE THIS!
I KNOW MY DUTY. I HOPE JUDGE CAL REMEMBERS HIS!
WALTER, JUDGE DREDD'S ROBOSERVANT, WAS WATCHING THE NEWS ON HIS SCREEN WHEN DREDD RETURNED TO HIS APARTMENT...
OH, JUDGE DWEDD, ISN'T IT TEWWIBLE! SUCH A BWUTAL CWIME!
...UNDER MEGA-CITY LAW JUDGE CAL, DEPUTY CHIEF JUDGE AND LEADER OF THE SJS, WILL AUTOMATICALLY TAKE ON THE DUTIES OF CHIEF JUDGE!
HOTS
IM WALTER TRY ME

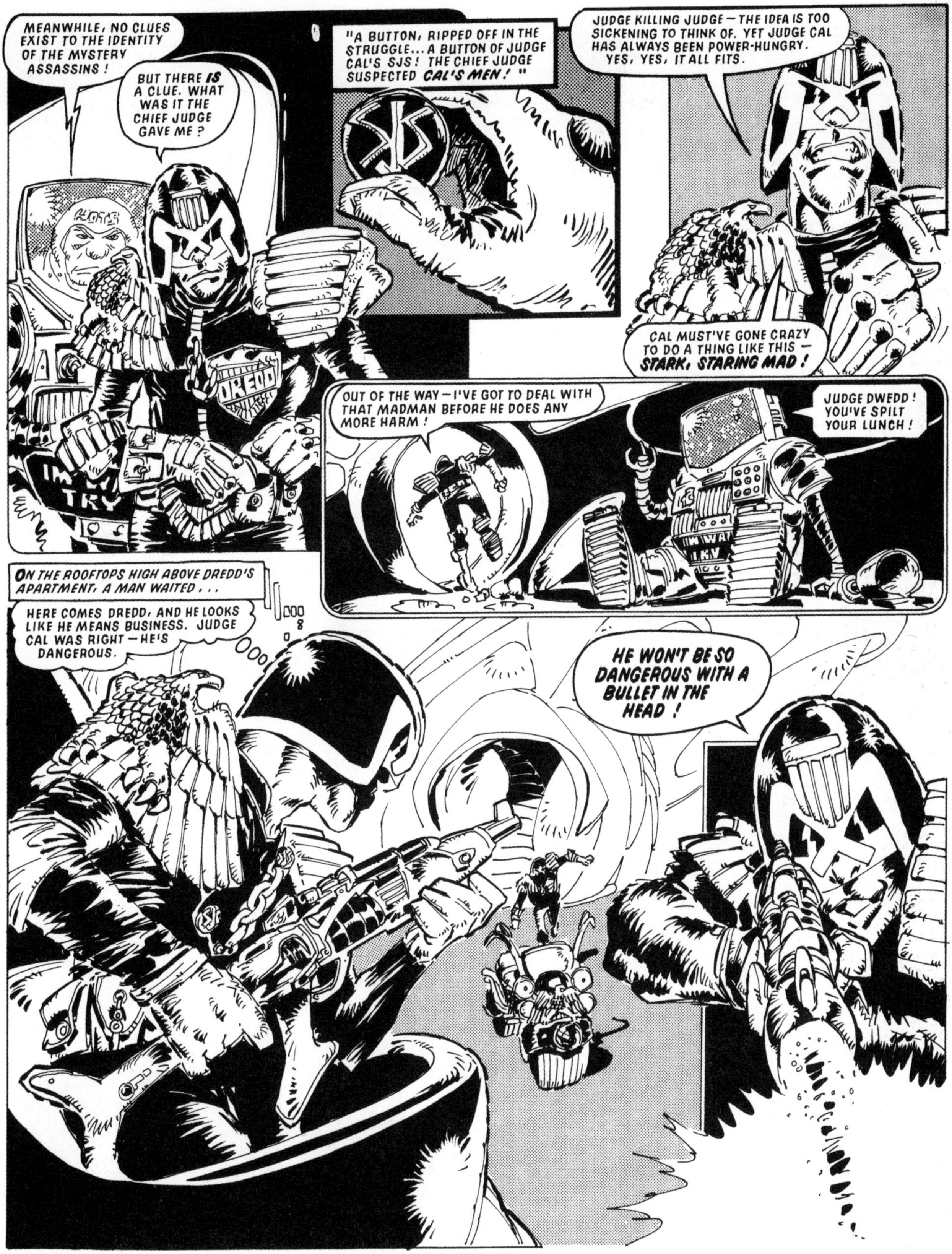

MEANWHILE, NO CLUES EXIST TO THE IDENTITY OF THE MYSTERY ASSASSINS !
BUT THERE IS A CLUE. WHAT WAS IT THE CHIEF JUDGE GAVE ME ?
"A BUTTON, RIPPED OFF IN THE STRUGGLE... A BUTTON OF JUDGE CAL'S SJS ! THE CHIEF JUDGE SUSPECTED CAL'S MEN ! "
JUDGE KILLING JUDGE — THE IDEA IS TOO SICKENING TO THINK OF. YET JUDGE CAL HAS ALWAYS BEEN POWER-HUNGRY. YES, YES, IT ALL FITS.
CAL MUST'VE GONE CRAZY TO DO A THING LIKE THIS — STARK, STARING MAD !
OUT OF THE WAY — I'VE GOT TO DEAL WITH THAT MADMAN BEFORE HE DOES ANY MORE HARM !
JUDGE DWEDD ! YOU'VE SPILT YOUR LUNCH !
ON THE ROOFTOPS HIGH ABOVE DREDD'S APARTMENT, A MAN WAITED . . .
HERE COMES DREDD, AND HE LOOKS LIKE HE MEANS BUSINESS. JUDGE CAL WAS RIGHT — HE'S DANGEROUS.
HE WON'T BE SO DANGEROUS WITH A BULLET IN THE HEAD !

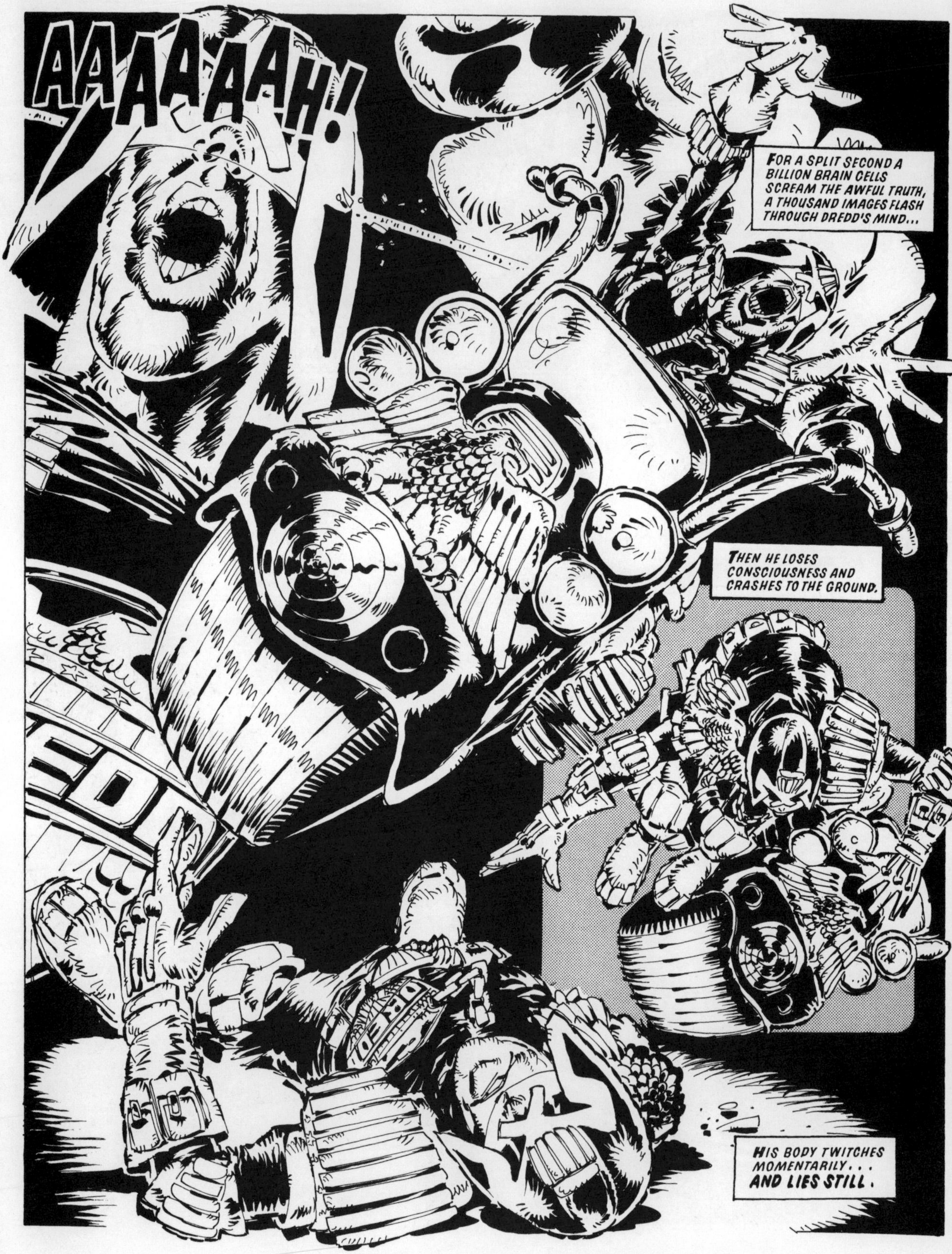
AAAAAAAH!
FOR A SPLIT SECOND A BILLION BRAIN CELLS SCREAM THE AWFUL TRUTH, A THOUSAND IMAGES FLASH THROUGH DREDD'S MIND...
THEN HE LOSES CONSCIOUSNESS AND CRASHES TO THE GROUND.
HIS BODY TWITCHES MOMENTARILY...
AND LIES STILL.

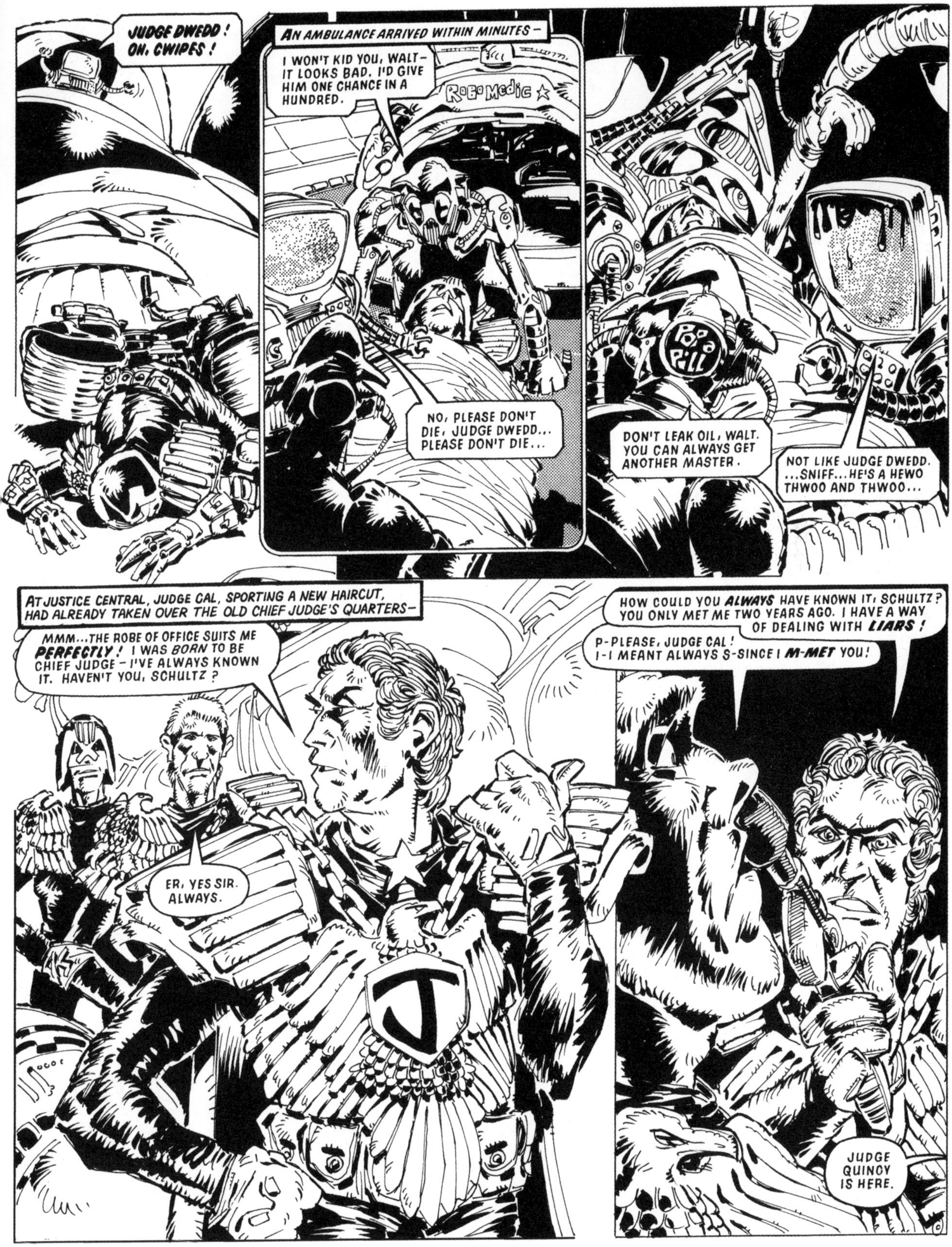
JUDGE DWEDD! OH, CWIPES!
AN AMBULANCE ARRIVED WITHIN MINUTES—
I WON'T KID YOU, WALT— IT LOOKS BAD. I'D GIVE HIM ONE CHANCE IN A HUNDRED.
ROBOMEDIC
NO, PLEASE DON'T DIE, JUDGE DWEDD... PLEASE DON'T DIE...
ROBO PILL
DON'T LEAK OIL, WALT. YOU CAN ALWAYS GET ANOTHER MASTER.
NOT LIKE JUDGE DWEDD. ...SNIFF... HE'S A HEWO THWOO AND THWOO...
AT JUSTICE CENTRAL, JUDGE CAL, SPORTING A NEW HAIRCUT, HAD ALREADY TAKEN OVER THE OLD CHIEF JUDGE'S QUARTERS—
MMM... THE ROBE OF OFFICE SUITS ME PERFECTLY! I WAS BORN TO BE CHIEF JUDGE - I'VE ALWAYS KNOWN IT. HAVEN'T YOU, SCHULTZ?
ER, YES SIR. ALWAYS.
HOW COULD YOU ALWAYS HAVE KNOWN IT, SCHULTZ? YOU ONLY MET ME TWO YEARS AGO. I HAVE A WAY OF DEALING WITH LIARS!
P-PLEASE, JUDGE CAL! I-I MEANT ALWAYS S-SINCE I M-MET YOU!
JUDGE QUINCY IS HERE.

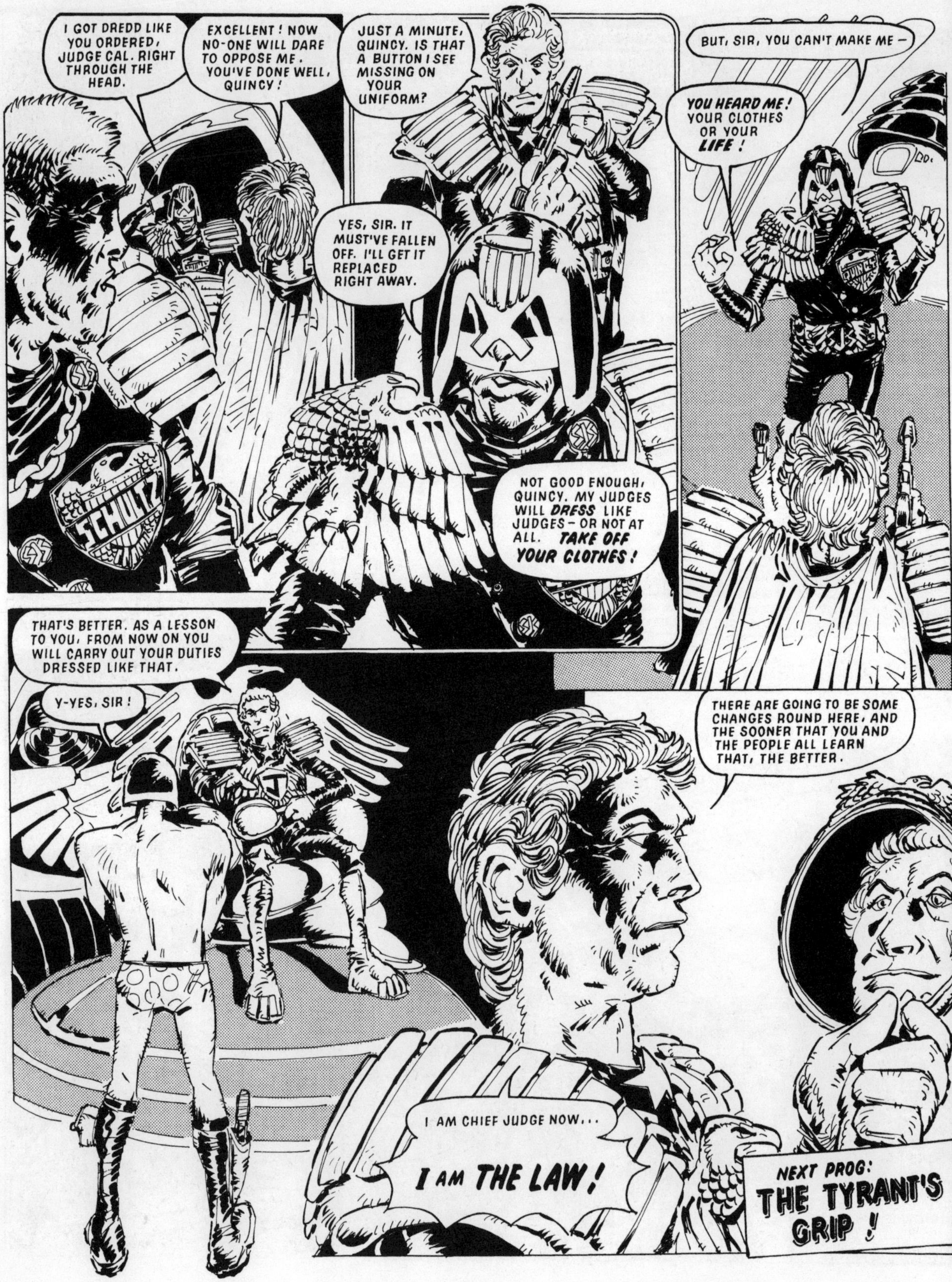
I GOT DREDD LIKE YOU ORDERED, JUDGE CAL. RIGHT THROUGH THE HEAD.
EXCELLENT! NOW NO-ONE WILL DARE TO OPPOSE ME. YOU'VE DONE WELL, QUINCY!
SCHULTZ
JUST A MINUTE, QUINCY. IS THAT A BUTTON I SEE MISSING ON YOUR UNIFORM?
YES, SIR. IT MUST'VE FALLEN OFF. I'LL GET IT REPLACED RIGHT AWAY.
NOT GOOD ENOUGH, QUINCY. MY JUDGES WILL DRESS LIKE JUDGES – OR NOT AT ALL. TAKE OFF YOUR CLOTHES!
BUT, SIR, YOU CAN'T MAKE ME –
YOU HEARD ME! YOUR CLOTHES OR YOUR LIFE!
QUINCY
THAT'S BETTER. AS A LESSON TO YOU, FROM NOW ON YOU WILL CARRY OUT YOUR DUTIES DRESSED LIKE THAT.
Y-YES, SIR!
THERE ARE GOING TO BE SOME CHANGES ROUND HERE, AND THE SOONER THAT YOU AND THE PEOPLE ALL LEARN THAT, THE BETTER.
I AM CHIEF JUDGE NOW...
I AM THE LAW!
NEXT PROG: THE TYRANT'S GRIP!

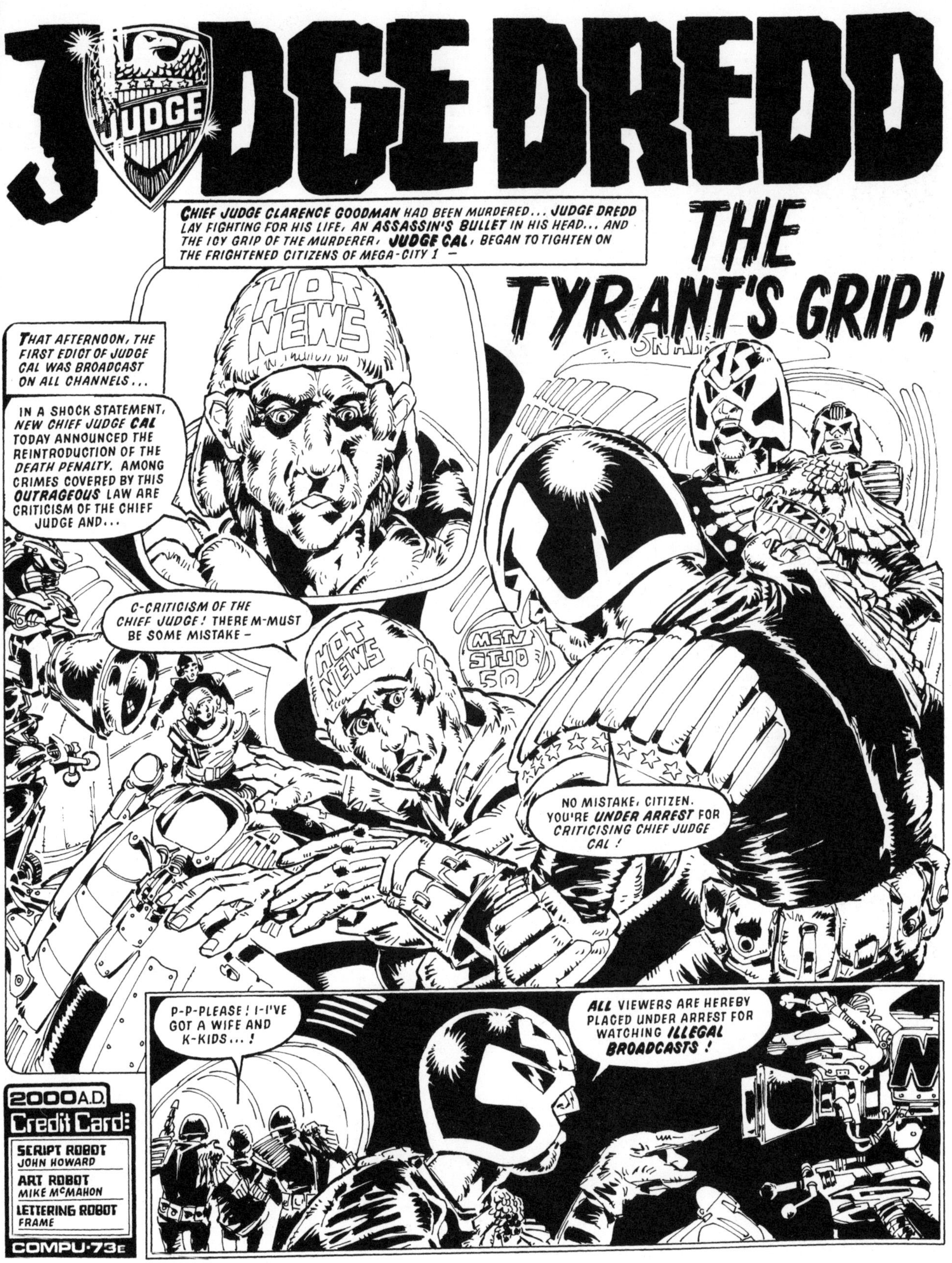

JUDGE DREDD
CHIEF JUDGE CLARENCE GOODMAN HAD BEEN MURDERED... JUDGE DREDD LAY FIGHTING FOR HIS LIFE, AN ASSASSIN'S BULLET IN HIS HEAD... AND THE ICY GRIP OF THE MURDERER, JUDGE CAL, BEGAN TO TIGHTEN ON THE FRIGHTENED CITIZENS OF MEGA-CITY 1 –
THE TYRANT'S GRIP!
THAT AFTERNOON, THE FIRST EDICT OF JUDGE CAL WAS BROADCAST ON ALL CHANNELS...
IN A SHOCK STATEMENT, NEW CHIEF JUDGE CAL TODAY ANNOUNCED THE REINTRODUCTION OF THE DEATH PENALTY. AMONG CRIMES COVERED BY THIS OUTRAGEOUS LAW ARE CRITICISM OF THE CHIEF JUDGE AND...
HOT NEWS
C-CRITICISM OF THE CHIEF JUDGE! THERE M-MUST BE SOME MISTAKE –
NO MISTAKE, CITIZEN. YOU'RE UNDER ARREST FOR CRITICISING CHIEF JUDGE CAL!
P-P-PLEASE! I-I'VE GOT A WIFE AND K-KIDS...!
ALL VIEWERS ARE HEREBY PLACED UNDER ARREST FOR WATCHING ILLEGAL BROADCASTS!
2000 A.D. Credit Card:
SCRIPT ROBOT JOHN HOWARD
ART ROBOT MIKE McMAHON
LETTERING ROBOT FRAME
COMPU-73E

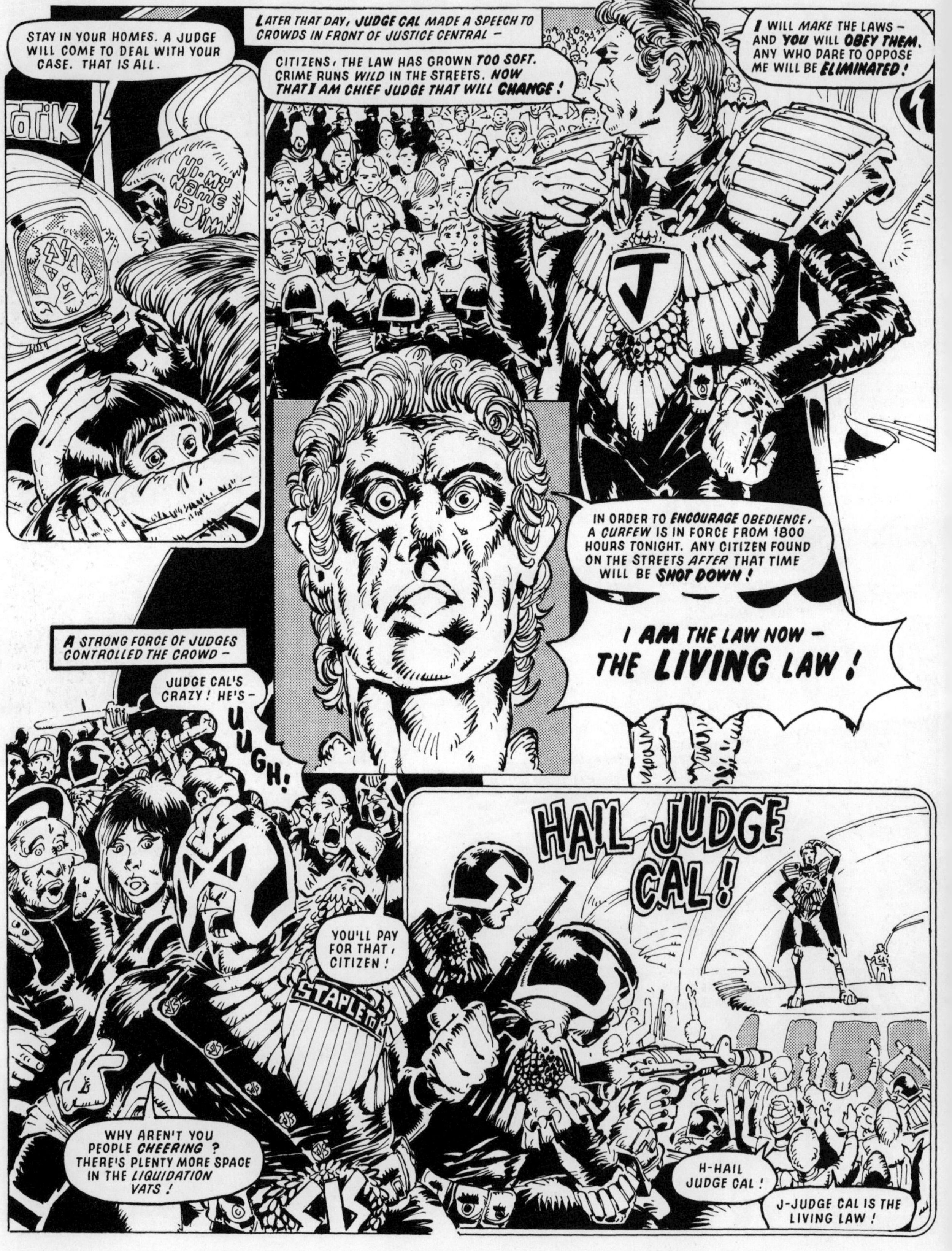
STAY IN YOUR HOMES. A JUDGE WILL COME TO DEAL WITH YOUR CASE. THAT IS ALL.
Hi-MY Name is Jim
LATER THAT DAY, JUDGE CAL MADE A SPEECH TO CROWDS IN FRONT OF JUSTICE CENTRAL –
CITIZENS, THE LAW HAS GROWN TOO SOFT. CRIME RUNS WILD IN THE STREETS. NOW THAT I AM CHIEF JUDGE THAT WILL CHANGE!
I WILL MAKE THE LAWS – AND YOU WILL OBEY THEM. ANY WHO DARE TO OPPOSE ME WILL BE ELIMINATED!
IN ORDER TO ENCOURAGE OBEDIENCE, A CURFEW IS IN FORCE FROM 1800 HOURS TONIGHT. ANY CITIZEN FOUND ON THE STREETS AFTER THAT TIME WILL BE SHOT DOWN!
I AM THE LAW NOW – THE LIVING LAW!
A STRONG FORCE OF JUDGES CONTROLLED THE CROWD –
JUDGE CAL'S CRAZY! HE'S–
UUGH!
YOU'LL PAY FOR THAT, CITIZEN!
STAPLETON
WHY AREN'T YOU PEOPLE CHEERING? THERE'S PLENTY MORE SPACE IN THE LIQUIDATION VATS!
HAIL JUDGE CAL!
H-HAIL JUDGE CAL!
J-JUDGE CAL IS THE LIVING LAW!

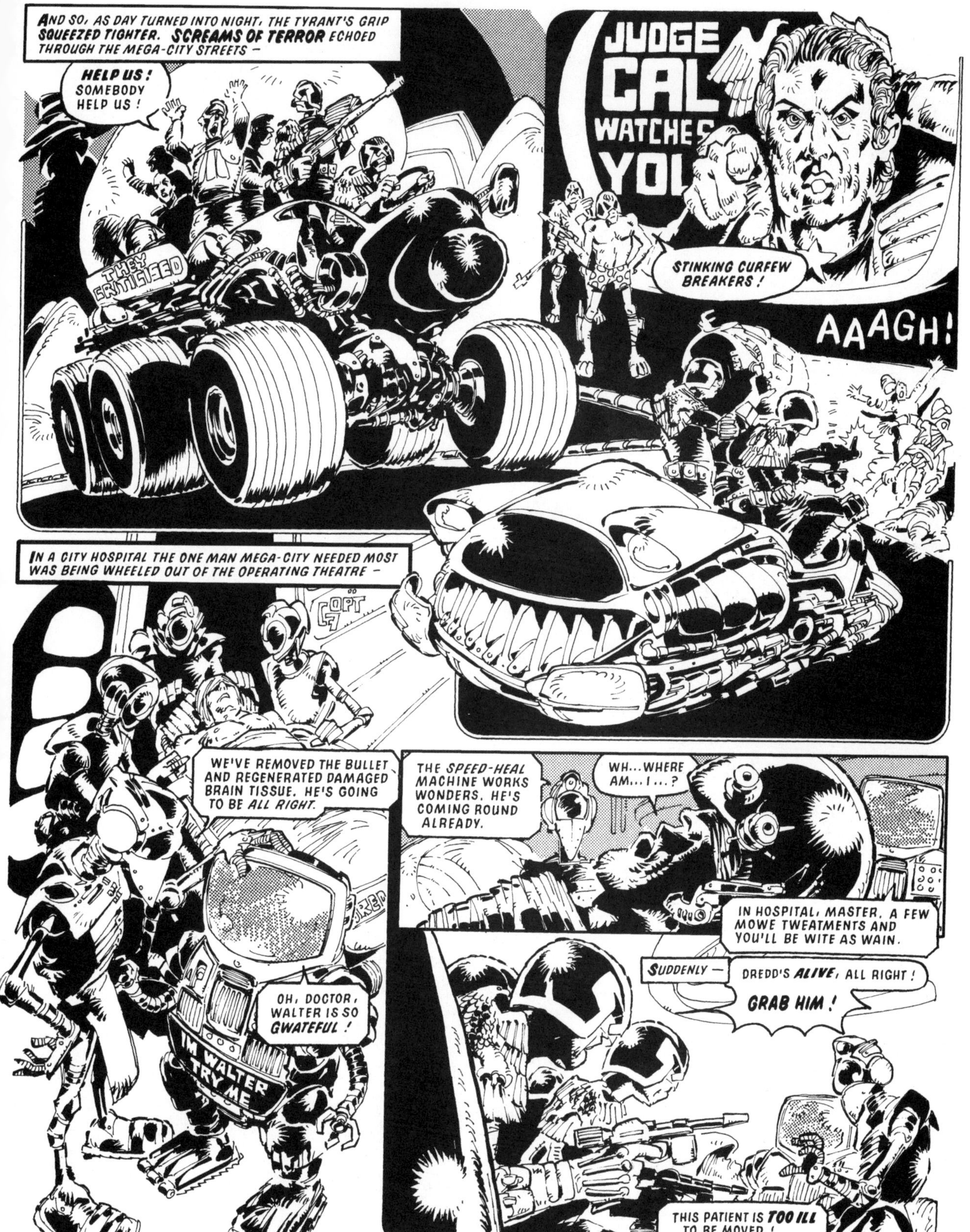
AND SO, AS DAY TURNED INTO NIGHT, THE TYRANT'S GRIP SQUEEZED TIGHTER. SCREAMS OF TERROR ECHOED THROUGH THE MEGA-CITY STREETS —
HELP US! SOMEBODY HELP US!
THEY CRITICISED
JUDGE CAL WATCHES YOU
STINKING CURFEW BREAKERS!
AAAGH!
IN A CITY HOSPITAL THE ONE MAN MEGA-CITY NEEDED MOST WAS BEING WHEELED OUT OF THE OPERATING THEATRE —
WE'VE REMOVED THE BULLET AND REGENERATED DAMAGED BRAIN TISSUE. HE'S GOING TO BE ALL RIGHT.
OH, DOCTOR, WALTER IS SO GWATEFUL!
IM WALTER TRY ME
THE SPEED-HEAL MACHINE WORKS WONDERS. HE'S COMING ROUND ALREADY.
WH... WHERE AM... I...?
IN HOSPITAL, MASTER. A FEW MOWE TWEATMENTS AND YOU'LL BE WITE AS WAIN.
SUDDENLY —
DREDD'S ALIVE, ALL RIGHT! GRAB HIM!
THIS PATIENT IS TOO ILL TO BE MOVED!

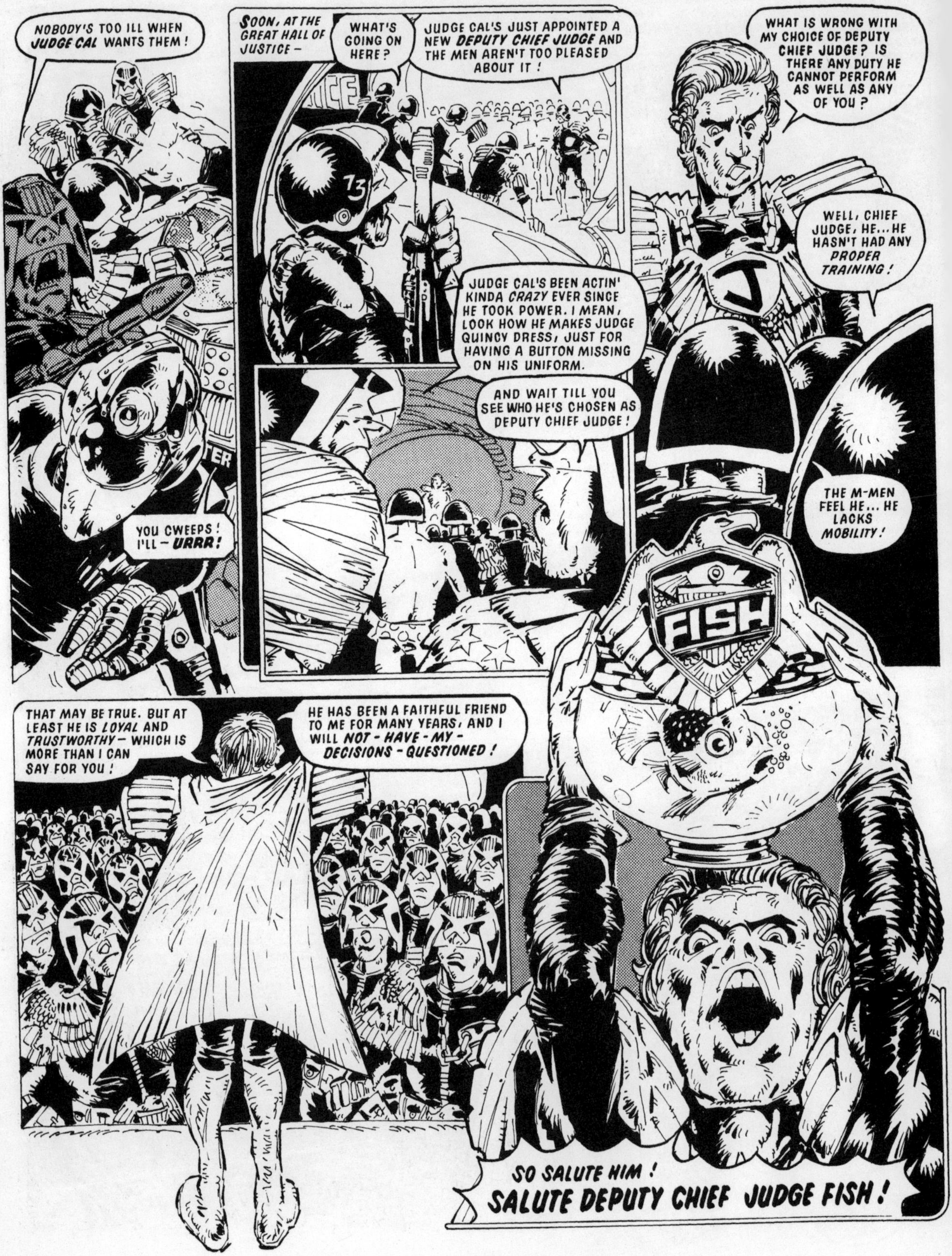
NOBODY'S TOO ILL WHEN JUDGE CAL WANTS THEM !
YOU CWEEPS ! I'LL — URRR!
SOON, AT THE GREAT HALL OF JUSTICE —
WHAT'S GOING ON HERE ?
JUDGE CAL'S JUST APPOINTED A NEW DEPUTY CHIEF JUDGE AND THE MEN AREN'T TOO PLEASED ABOUT IT !
JUDGE CAL'S BEEN ACTIN' KINDA CRAZY EVER SINCE HE TOOK POWER. I MEAN, LOOK HOW HE MAKES JUDGE QUINCY DRESS, JUST FOR HAVING A BUTTON MISSING ON HIS UNIFORM.
AND WAIT TILL YOU SEE WHO HE'S CHOSEN AS DEPUTY CHIEF JUDGE !
WHAT IS WRONG WITH MY CHOICE OF DEPUTY CHIEF JUDGE ? IS THERE ANY DUTY HE CANNOT PERFORM AS WELL AS ANY OF YOU ?
WELL, CHIEF JUDGE, HE... HE HASN'T HAD ANY PROPER TRAINING !
THE M-MEN FEEL HE... HE LACKS MOBILITY !
THAT MAY BE TRUE. BUT AT LEAST HE IS LOYAL AND TRUSTWORTHY — WHICH IS MORE THAN I CAN SAY FOR YOU !
HE HAS BEEN A FAITHFUL FRIEND TO ME FOR MANY YEARS, AND I WILL NOT - HAVE - MY - DECISIONS - QUESTIONED !
FISH
SO SALUTE HIM !
SALUTE DEPUTY CHIEF JUDGE FISH !

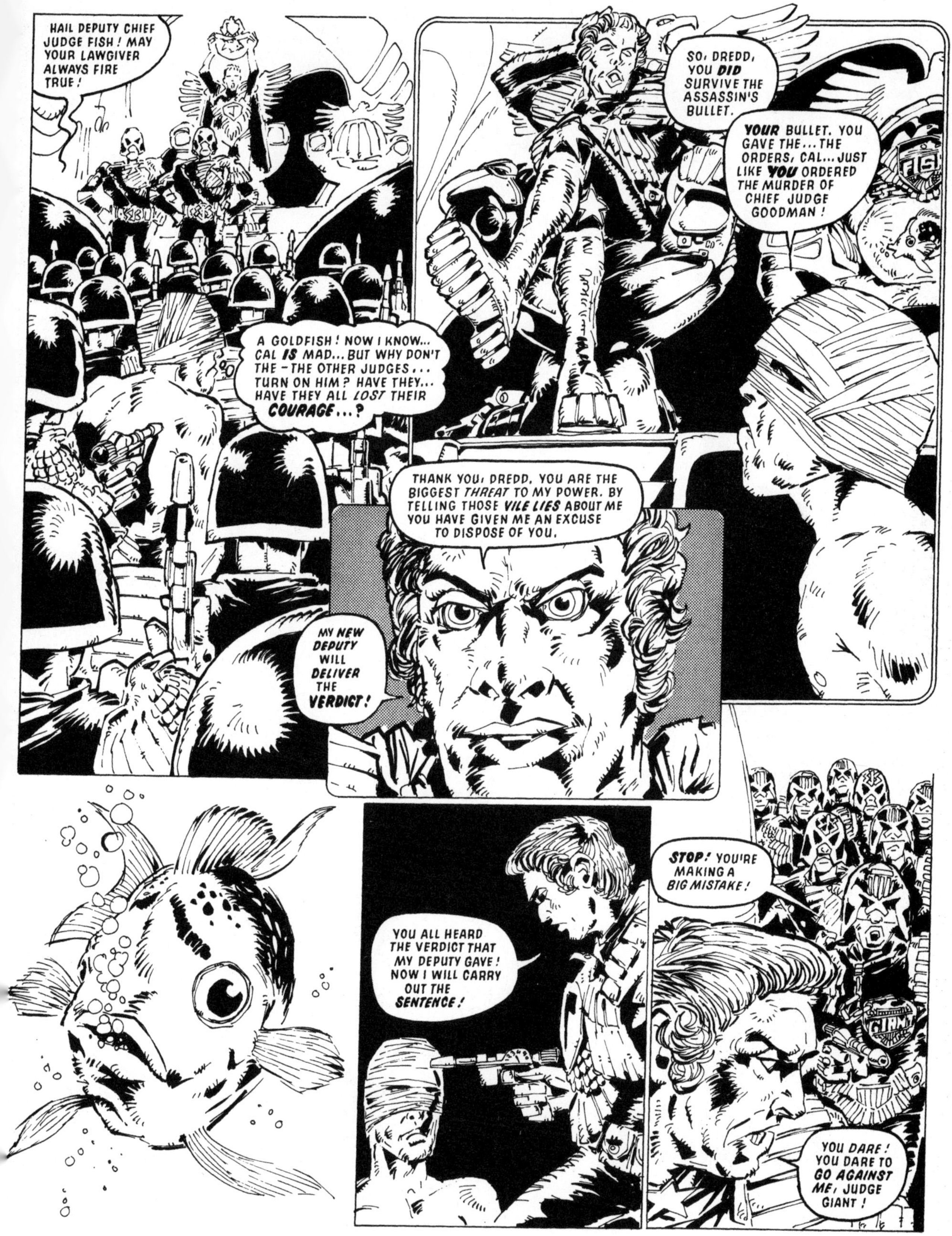

HAIL DEPUTY CHIEF JUDGE FISH! MAY YOUR LAWGIVER ALWAYS FIRE TRUE!
A GOLDFISH! NOW I KNOW... CAL IS MAD... BUT WHY DON'T THE - THE OTHER JUDGES... TURN ON HIM? HAVE THEY... HAVE THEY ALL LOST THEIR COURAGE...?
SO, DREDD, YOU DID SURVIVE THE ASSASSIN'S BULLET.
YOUR BULLET. YOU GAVE THE... THE ORDERS, CAL... JUST LIKE YOU ORDERED THE MURDER OF CHIEF JUDGE GOODMAN!
THANK YOU, DREDD. YOU ARE THE BIGGEST THREAT TO MY POWER. BY TELLING THOSE VILE LIES ABOUT ME YOU HAVE GIVEN ME AN EXCUSE TO DISPOSE OF YOU.
MY NEW DEPUTY WILL DELIVER THE VERDICT!
YOU ALL HEARD THE VERDICT THAT MY DEPUTY GAVE! NOW I WILL CARRY OUT THE SENTENCE!
STOP! YOU'RE MAKING A BIG MISTAKE!
YOU DARE! YOU DARE TO GO AGAINST ME, JUDGE GIANT!

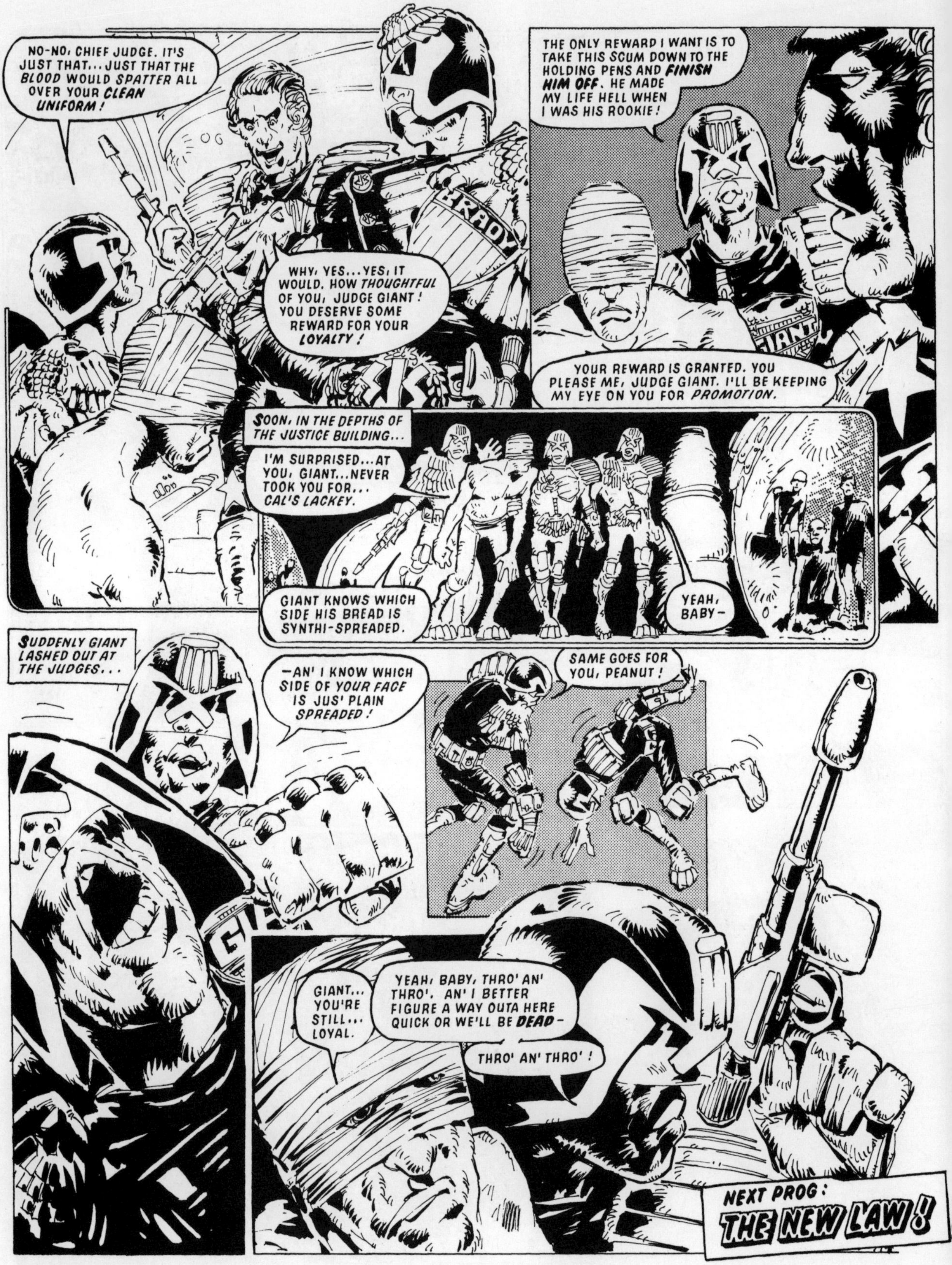
NO-NO, CHIEF JUDGE. IT'S JUST THAT... JUST THAT THE BLOOD WOULD SPATTER ALL OVER YOUR CLEAN UNIFORM!
WHY, YES... YES, IT WOULD. HOW THOUGHTFUL OF YOU, JUDGE GIANT! YOU DESERVE SOME REWARD FOR YOUR LOYALTY!
THE ONLY REWARD I WANT IS TO TAKE THIS SCUM DOWN TO THE HOLDING PENS AND FINISH HIM OFF. HE MADE MY LIFE HELL WHEN I WAS HIS ROOKIE!
YOUR REWARD IS GRANTED. YOU PLEASE ME, JUDGE GIANT. I'LL BE KEEPING MY EYE ON YOU FOR PROMOTION.
SOON, IN THE DEPTHS OF THE JUSTICE BUILDING...
I'M SURPRISED... AT YOU, GIANT... NEVER TOOK YOU FOR... CAL'S LACKEY.
GIANT KNOWS WHICH SIDE HIS BREAD IS SYNTHI-SPREADED.
YEAH, BABY–
SUDDENLY GIANT LASHED OUT AT THE JUDGES...
–AN' I KNOW WHICH SIDE OF YOUR FACE IS JUS' PLAIN SPREADED!
SAME GOES FOR YOU, PEANUT!
GIANT... YOU'RE STILL... LOYAL.
YEAH, BABY, THRO' AN' THRO'. AN' I BETTER FIGURE A WAY OUTA HERE QUICK OR WE'LL BE DEAD–
THRO' AN' THRO'!
NEXT PROG:
THE NEW LAW!

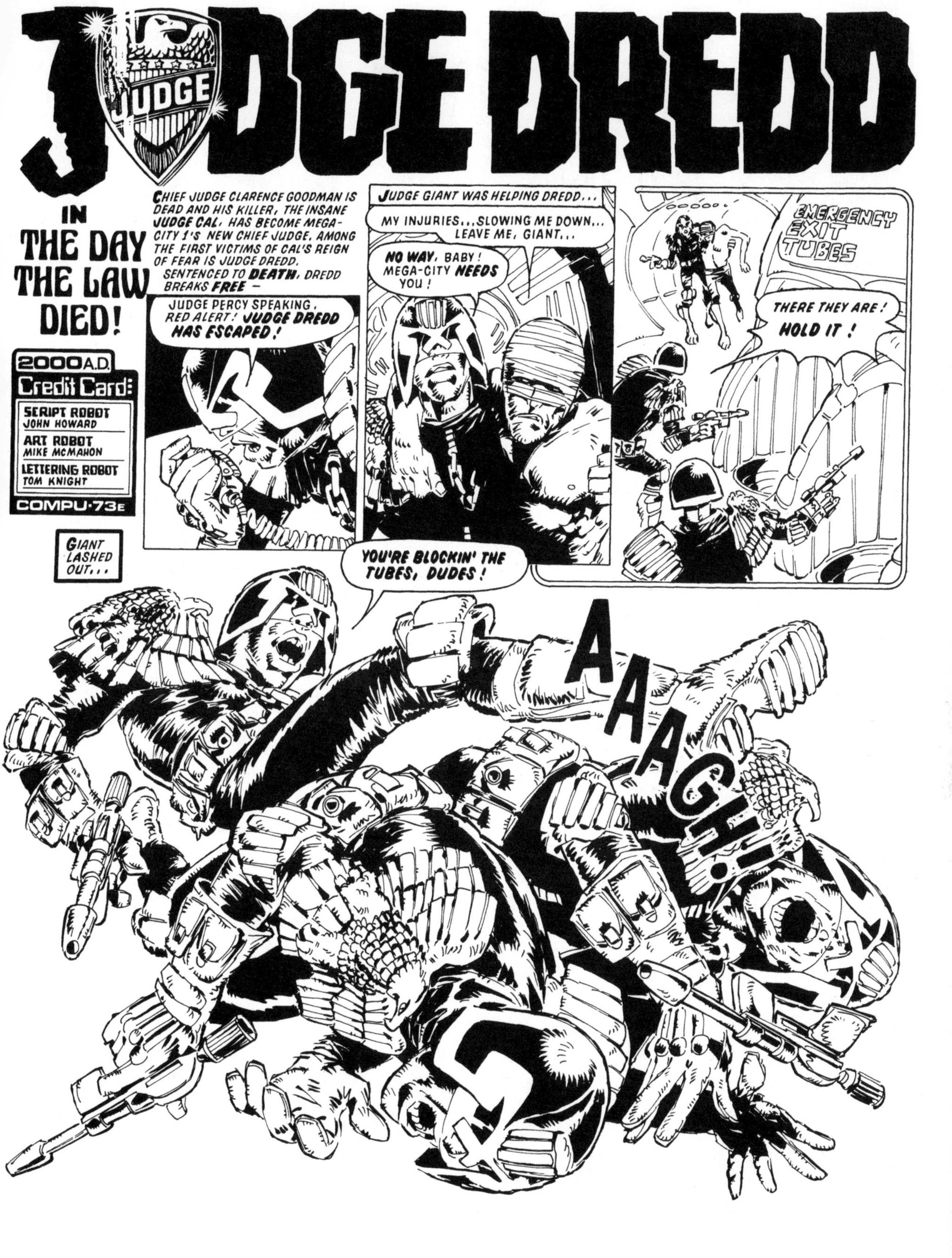

JUDGE DREDD
JUDGE
IN THE DAY THE LAW DIED!
2000 A.D. Credit Card:
SCRIPT ROBOT JOHN HOWARD
ART ROBOT MIKE McMAHON
LETTERING ROBOT TOM KNIGHT
COMPU·73E
CHIEF JUDGE CLARENCE GOODMAN IS DEAD AND HIS KILLER, THE INSANE JUDGE CAL, HAS BECOME MEGA-CITY 1'S NEW CHIEF JUDGE. AMONG THE FIRST VICTIMS OF CAL'S REIGN OF FEAR IS JUDGE DREDD. SENTENCED TO DEATH, DREDD BREAKS FREE —
JUDGE PERCY SPEAKING. RED ALERT! JUDGE DREDD HAS ESCAPED!
JUDGE GIANT WAS HELPING DREDD...
MY INJURIES... SLOWING ME DOWN... LEAVE ME, GIANT...
NO WAY, BABY! MEGA-CITY NEEDS YOU!
EMERGENCY EXIT TUBES
THERE THEY ARE! HOLD IT!
GIANT LASHED OUT...
YOU'RE BLOCKIN' THE TUBES, DUDES!
AAAAGH!

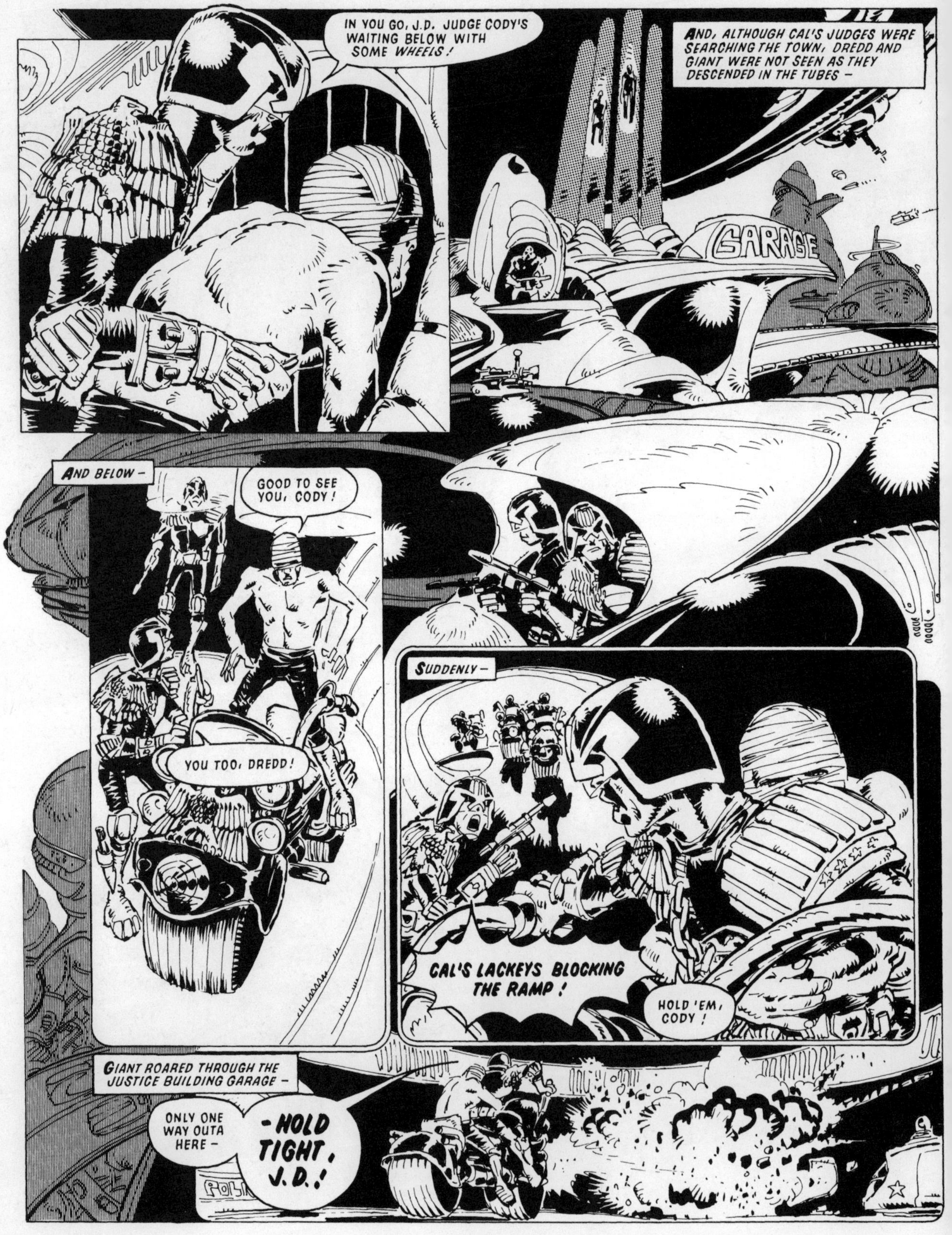
IN YOU GO, J.D. JUDGE CODY'S WAITING BELOW WITH SOME WHEELS!
AND, ALTHOUGH CAL'S JUDGES WERE SEARCHING THE TOWN, DREDD AND GIANT WERE NOT SEEN AS THEY DESCENDED IN THE TUBES –
GARAGE
AND BELOW –
GOOD TO SEE YOU, CODY!
YOU TOO, DREDD!
SUDDENLY –
CAL'S LACKEYS BLOCKING THE RAMP!
HOLD 'EM, CODY!
GIANT ROARED THROUGH THE JUSTICE BUILDING GARAGE –
ONLY ONE WAY OUTA HERE –
– HOLD TIGHT, J.D.!

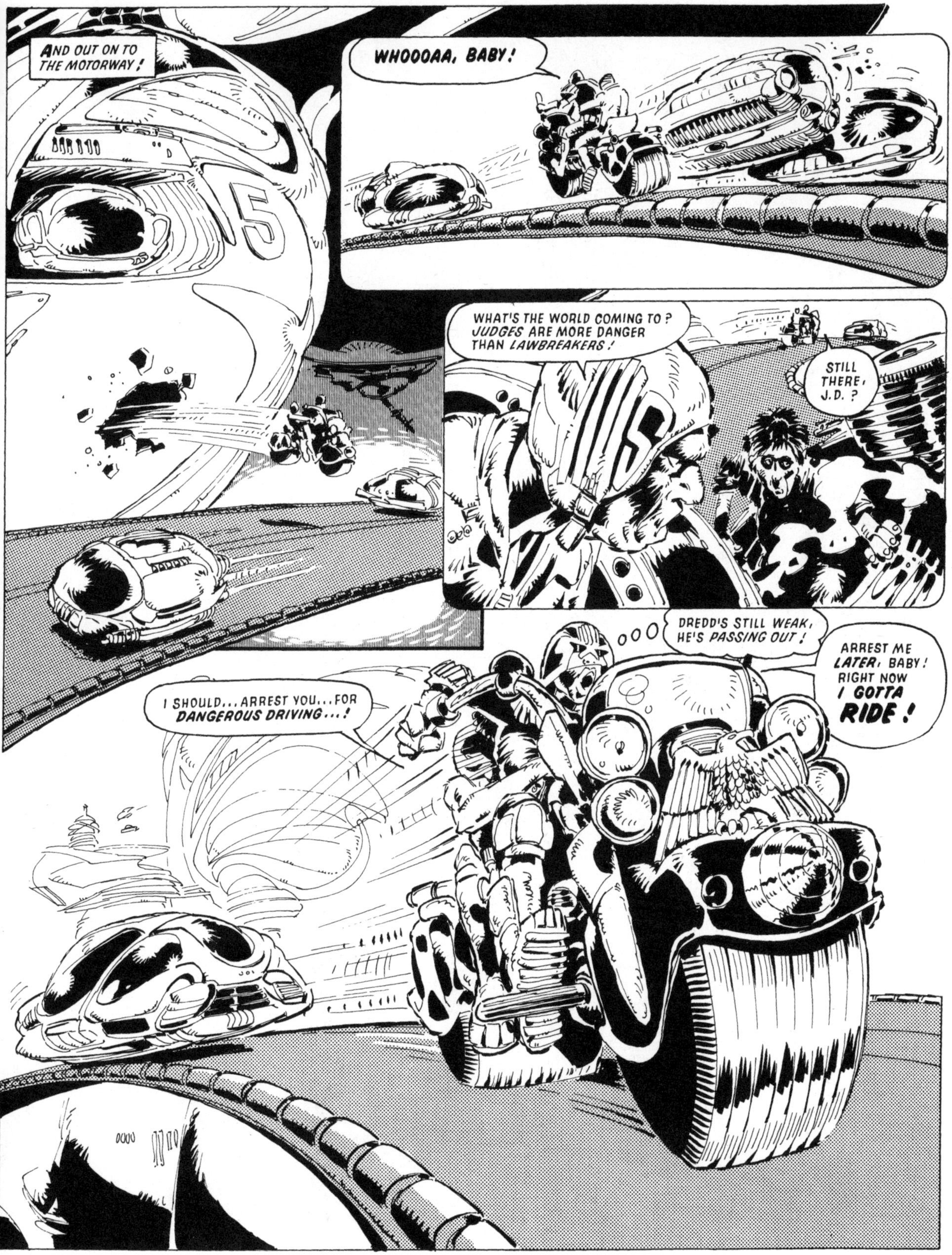

AND OUT ON TO THE MOTORWAY!
WHOOOAA, BABY!
WHAT'S THE WORLD COMING TO? JUDGES ARE MORE DANGER THAN LAWBREAKERS!
STILL THERE, J.D.?
DREDD'S STILL WEAK, HE'S PASSING OUT!
ARREST ME LATER, BABY! RIGHT NOW I GOTTA RIDE!
I SHOULD... ARREST YOU... FOR DANGEROUS DRIVING...!

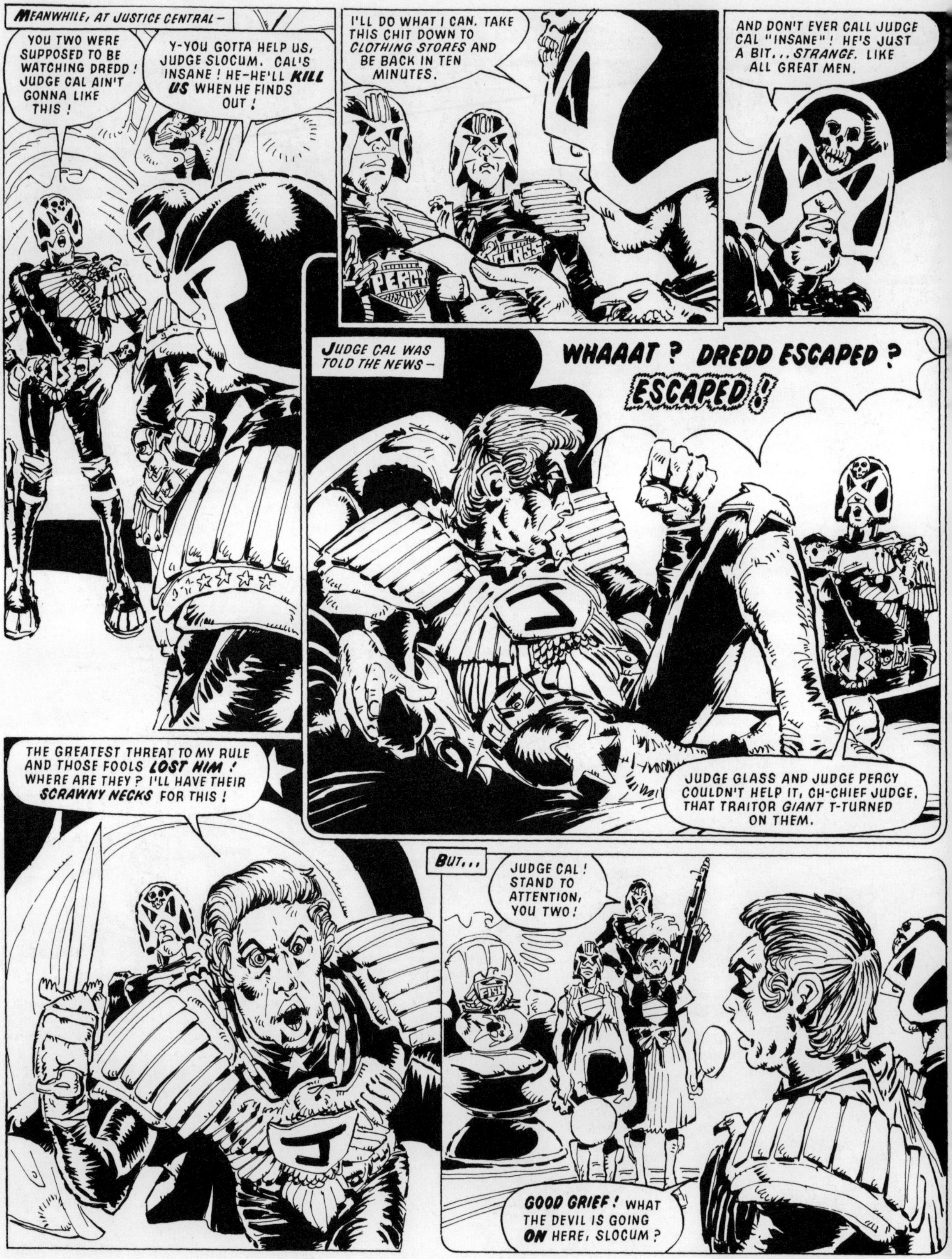
MEANWHILE, AT JUSTICE CENTRAL –
YOU TWO WERE SUPPOSED TO BE WATCHING DREDD! JUDGE CAL AIN'T GONNA LIKE THIS!
Y-YOU GOTTA HELP US, JUDGE SLOCUM. CAL'S INSANE! HE-HE'LL KILL US WHEN HE FINDS OUT!
I'LL DO WHAT I CAN. TAKE THIS CHIT DOWN TO CLOTHING STORES AND BE BACK IN TEN MINUTES.
AND DON'T EVER CALL JUDGE CAL "INSANE"! HE'S JUST A BIT... STRANGE. LIKE ALL GREAT MEN.
JUDGE CAL WAS TOLD THE NEWS –
WHAAAT? DREDD ESCAPED? ESCAPED!
JUDGE GLASS AND JUDGE PERCY COULDN'T HELP IT, CH-CHIEF JUDGE. THAT TRAITOR GIANT T-TURNED ON THEM.
THE GREATEST THREAT TO MY RULE AND THOSE FOOLS LOST HIM! WHERE ARE THEY? I'LL HAVE THEIR SCRAWNY NECKS FOR THIS!
BUT...
JUDGE CAL! STAND TO ATTENTION, YOU TWO!
GOOD GRIEF! WHAT THE DEVIL IS GOING ON HERE, SLOCUM?

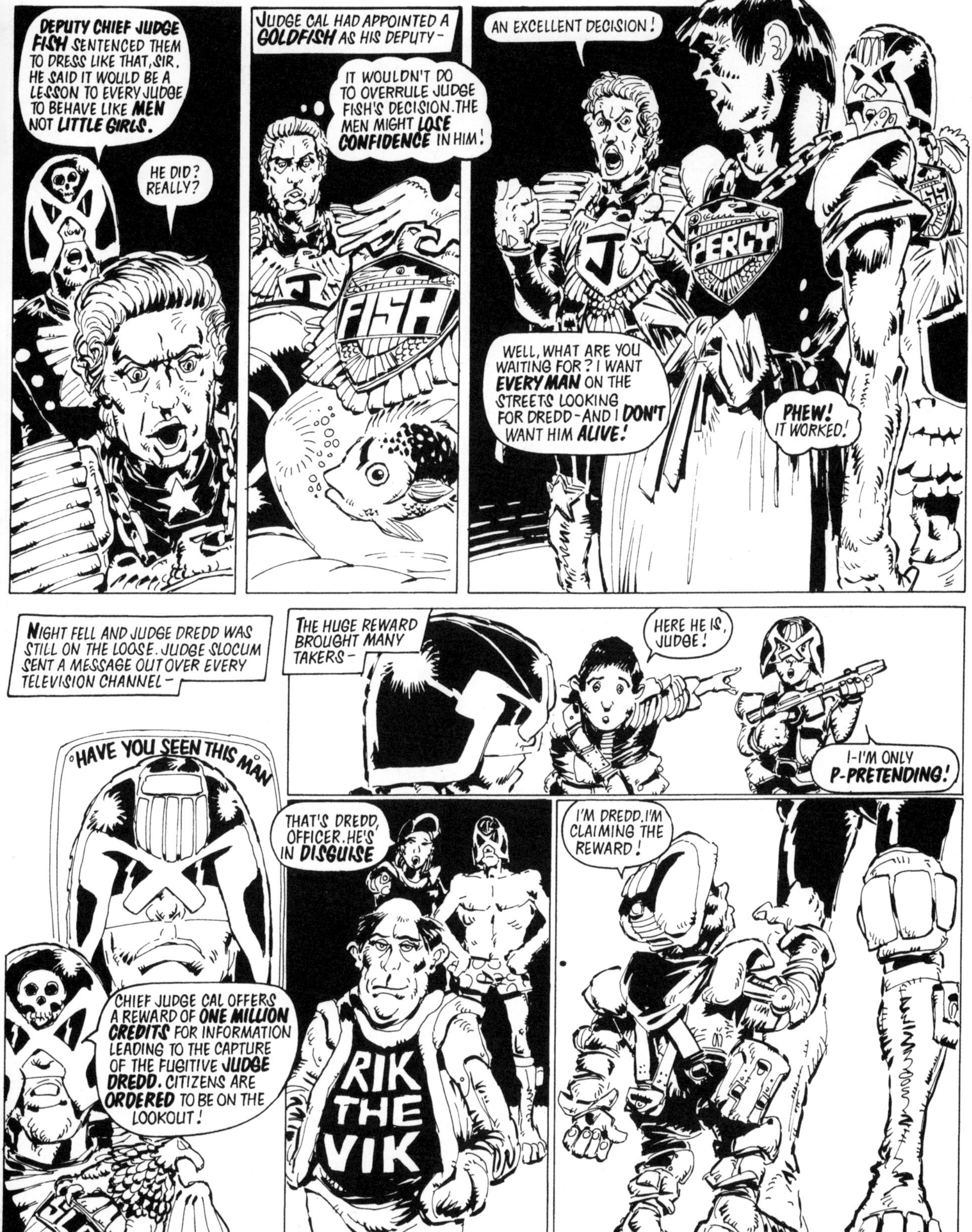
DEPUTY CHIEF JUDGE FISH SENTENCED THEM TO DRESS LIKE THAT, SIR. HE SAID IT WOULD BE A LESSON TO EVERY JUDGE TO BEHAVE LIKE MEN NOT LITTLE GIRLS.
HE DID? REALLY?
JUDGE CAL HAD APPOINTED A GOLDFISH AS HIS DEPUTY-
IT WOULDN'T DO TO OVERRULE JUDGE FISH'S DECISION. THE MEN MIGHT LOSE CONFIDENCE IN HIM!
FISH
AN EXCELLENT DECISION!
PERCY
WELL, WHAT ARE YOU WAITING FOR? I WANT EVERY MAN ON THE STREETS LOOKING FOR DREDD-AND I DON'T WANT HIM ALIVE!
PHEW! IT WORKED!
NIGHT FELL AND JUDGE DREDD WAS STILL ON THE LOOSE. JUDGE SLOCUM SENT A MESSAGE OUT OVER EVERY TELEVISION CHANNEL-
"HAVE YOU SEEN THIS MAN
CHIEF JUDGE CAL OFFERS A REWARD OF ONE MILLION CREDITS FOR INFORMATION LEADING TO THE CAPTURE OF THE FUGITIVE JUDGE DREDD. CITIZENS ARE ORDERED TO BE ON THE LOOKOUT!
THE HUGE REWARD BROUGHT MANY TAKERS-
HERE HE IS, JUDGE!
I-I'M ONLY P-PRETENDING!
THAT'S DREDD, OFFICER. HE'S IN DISGUISE
RIK THE VIK
I'M DREDD. I'M CLAIMING THE REWARD!

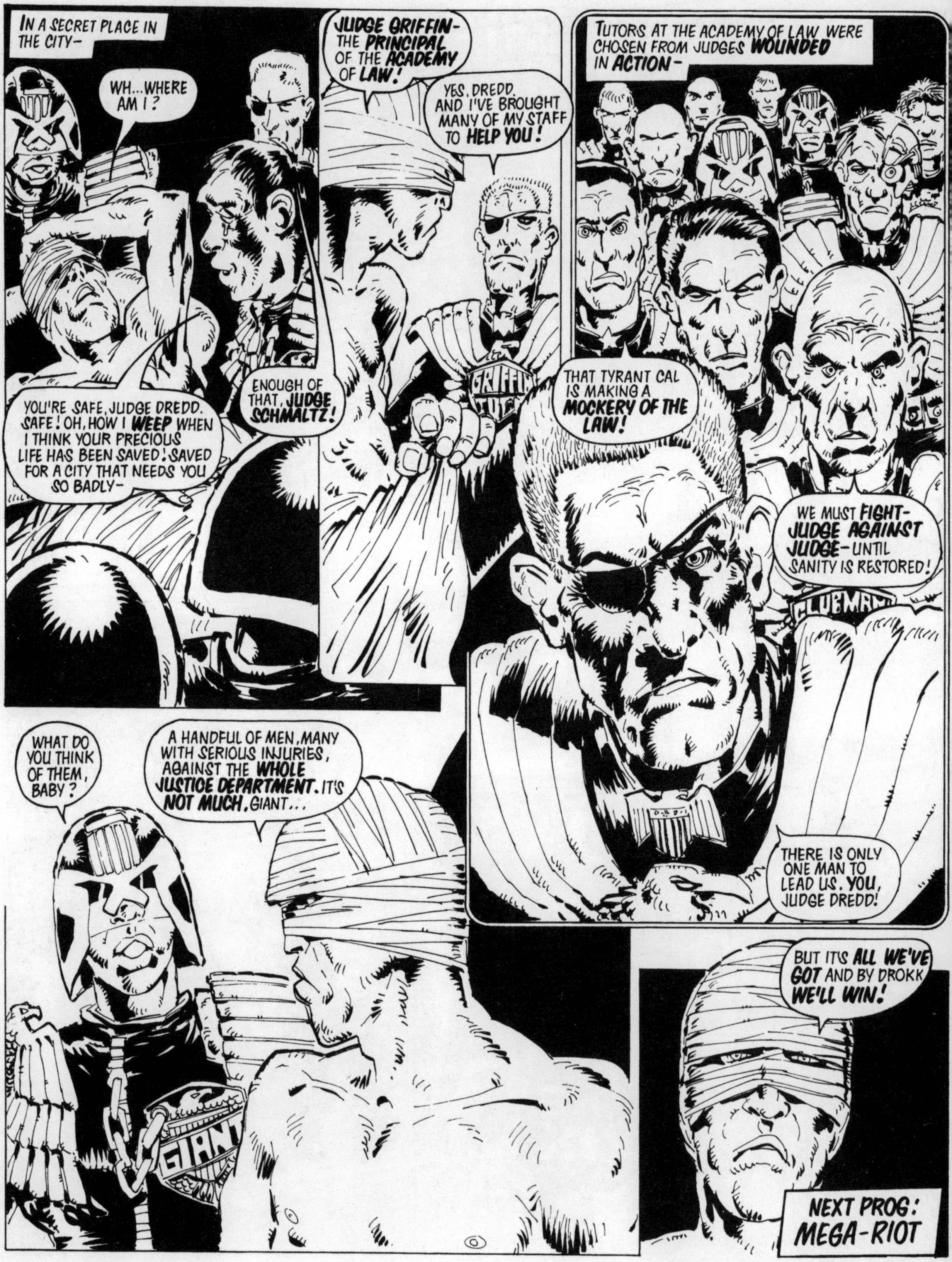
IN A SECRET PLACE IN THE CITY-
WH...WHERE AM I?
YOU'RE SAFE, JUDGE DREDD. SAFE! OH, HOW I WEEP WHEN I THINK YOUR PRECIOUS LIFE HAS BEEN SAVED! SAVED FOR A CITY THAT NEEDS YOU SO BADLY-
JUDGE GRIFFIN- THE PRINCIPAL OF THE ACADEMY OF LAW!
YES, DREDD, AND I'VE BROUGHT MANY OF MY STAFF TO HELP YOU!
ENOUGH OF THAT, JUDGE SCHMALTZ!
GRIFFIN
TUTORS AT THE ACADEMY OF LAW WERE CHOSEN FROM JUDGES WOUNDED IN ACTION-
THAT TYRANT CAL IS MAKING A MOCKERY OF THE LAW!
WE MUST FIGHT- JUDGE AGAINST JUDGE- UNTIL SANITY IS RESTORED!
CLUBMAN
THERE IS ONLY ONE MAN TO LEAD US. YOU, JUDGE DREDD!
WHAT DO YOU THINK OF THEM, BABY?
A HANDFUL OF MEN, MANY WITH SERIOUS INJURIES, AGAINST THE WHOLE JUSTICE DEPARTMENT. IT'S NOT MUCH, GIANT...
GIANT
BUT IT'S ALL WE'VE GOT AND BY DROKK WE'LL WIN!
NEXT PROG: MEGA-RIOT

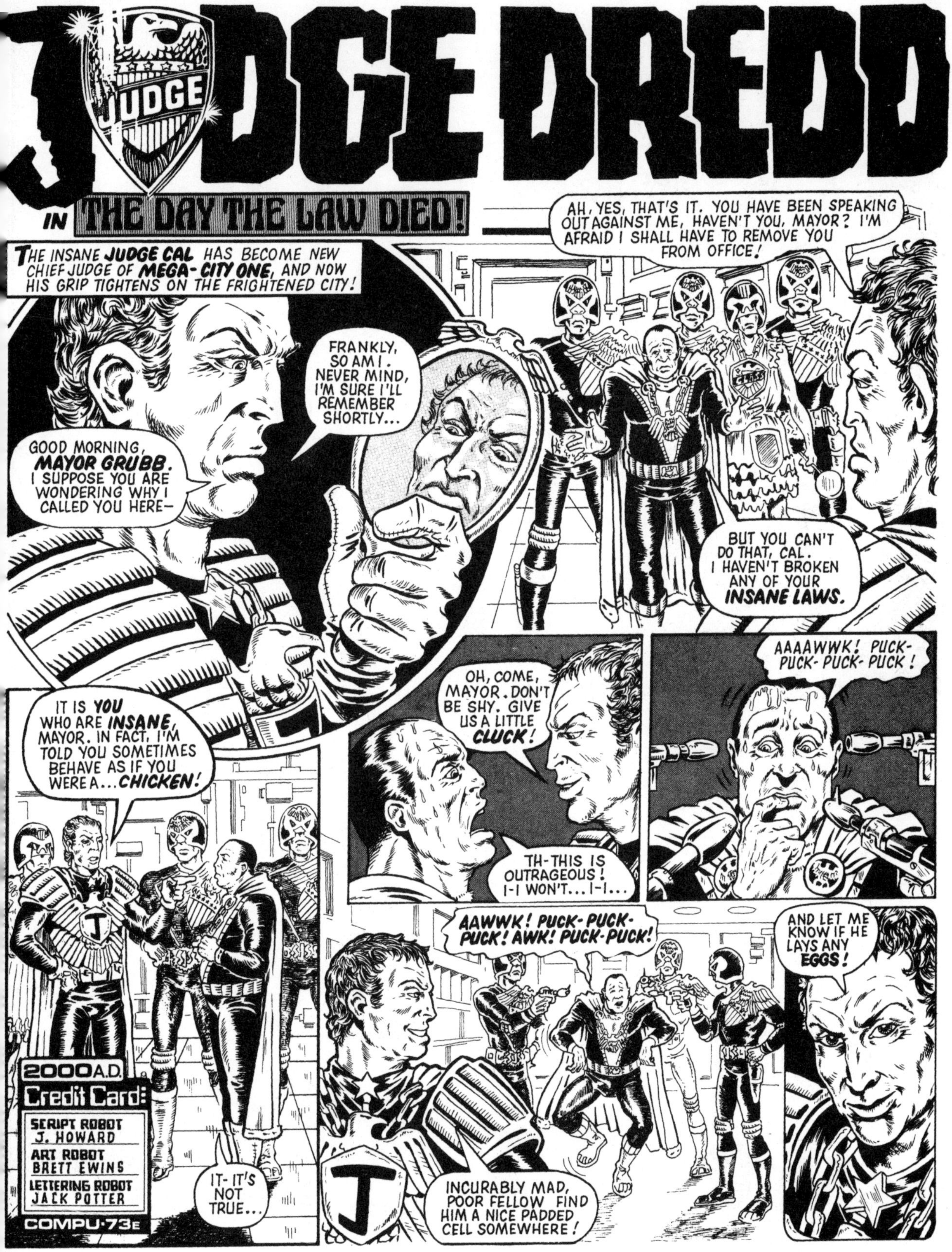
JUDGE DREDD
IN THE DAY THE LAW DIED!
THE INSANE JUDGE CAL HAS BECOME NEW CHIEF JUDGE OF MEGA-CITY ONE, AND NOW HIS GRIP TIGHTENS ON THE FRIGHTENED CITY!
GOOD MORNING, MAYOR GRUBB. I SUPPOSE YOU ARE WONDERING WHY I CALLED YOU HERE–
FRANKLY, SO AM I. NEVER MIND, I'M SURE I'LL REMEMBER SHORTLY...
AH, YES, THAT'S IT. YOU HAVE BEEN SPEAKING OUT AGAINST ME, HAVEN'T YOU, MAYOR? I'M AFRAID I SHALL HAVE TO REMOVE YOU FROM OFFICE!
BUT YOU CAN'T DO THAT, CAL. I HAVEN'T BROKEN ANY OF YOUR INSANE LAWS.
IT IS YOU WHO ARE INSANE, MAYOR. IN FACT, I'M TOLD YOU SOMETIMES BEHAVE AS IF YOU WERE A...CHICKEN!
OH, COME, MAYOR. DON'T BE SHY. GIVE US A LITTLE CLUCK!
TH-THIS IS OUTRAGEOUS! I-I WON'T... I-I...
AAAAWWK! PUCK-PUCK-PUCK-PUCK!
IT- IT'S NOT TRUE...
AAWWK! PUCK-PUCK-PUCK! AWK! PUCK-PUCK!
INCURABLY MAD, POOR FELLOW. FIND HIM A NICE PADDED CELL SOMEWHERE!
AND LET ME KNOW IF HE LAYS ANY EGGS!
2000 A.D. Credit Card:
SCRIPT ROBOT J. HOWARD
ART ROBOT BRETT EWINS
LETTERING ROBOT JACK POTTER
COMPU-73E

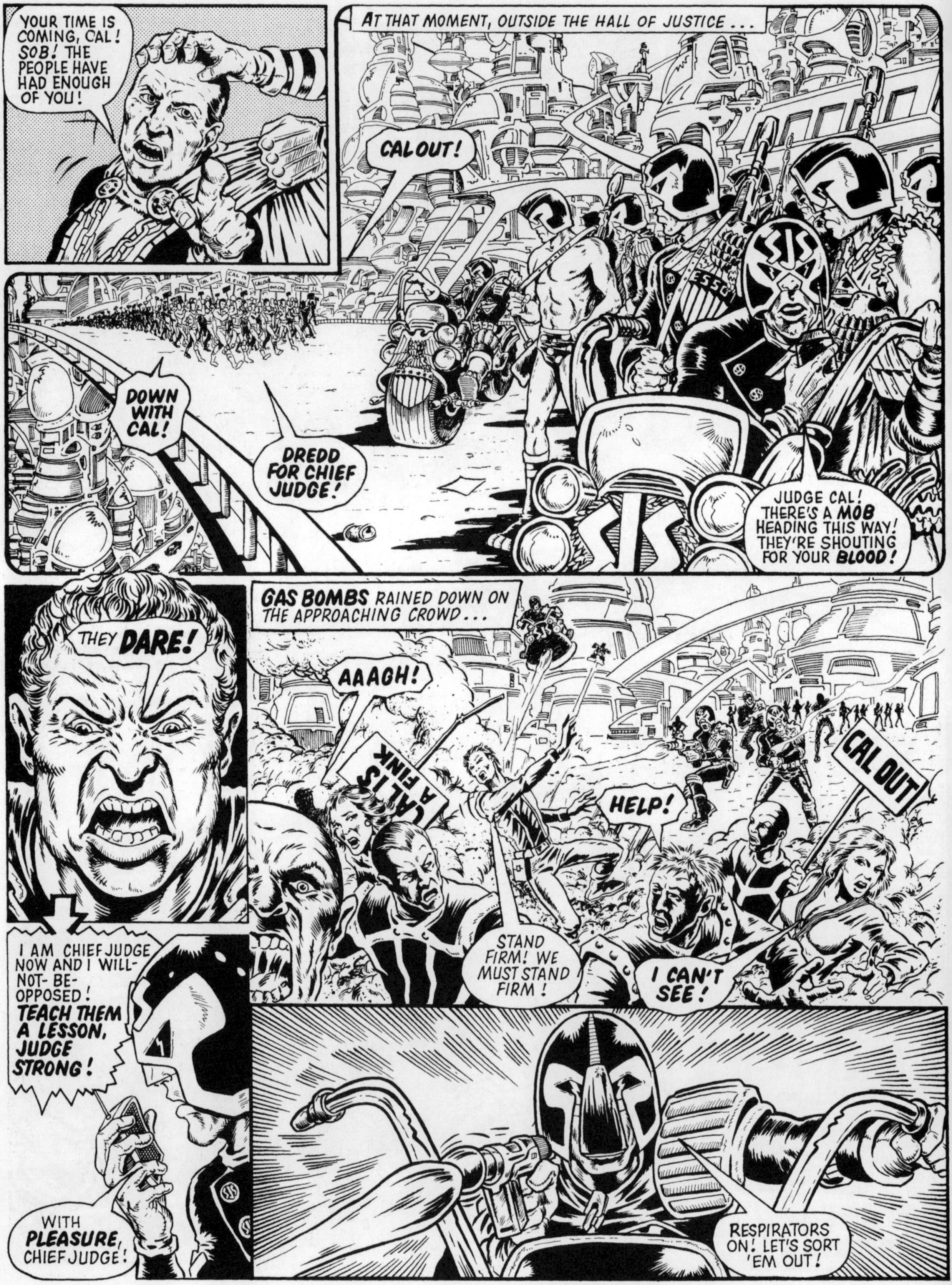

YOUR TIME IS COMING, CAL! SOB! THE PEOPLE HAVE HAD ENOUGH OF YOU!
AT THAT MOMENT, OUTSIDE THE HALL OF JUSTICE ...
CAL OUT!
DOWN WITH CAL!
DREDD FOR CHIEF JUDGE!
JUDGE CAL! THERE'S A MOB HEADING THIS WAY! THEY'RE SHOUTING FOR YOUR BLOOD!
THEY DARE!
I AM CHIEF JUDGE NOW AND I WILL-NOT-BE-OPPOSED! TEACH THEM A LESSON, JUDGE STRONG!
WITH PLEASURE, CHIEF JUDGE!
GAS BOMBS RAINED DOWN ON THE APPROACHING CROWD ...
AAAGH!
CAL IS A FINK
CAL OUT
HELP!
STAND FIRM! WE MUST STAND FIRM!
I CAN'T SEE!
RESPIRATORS ON! LET'S SORT 'EM OUT!

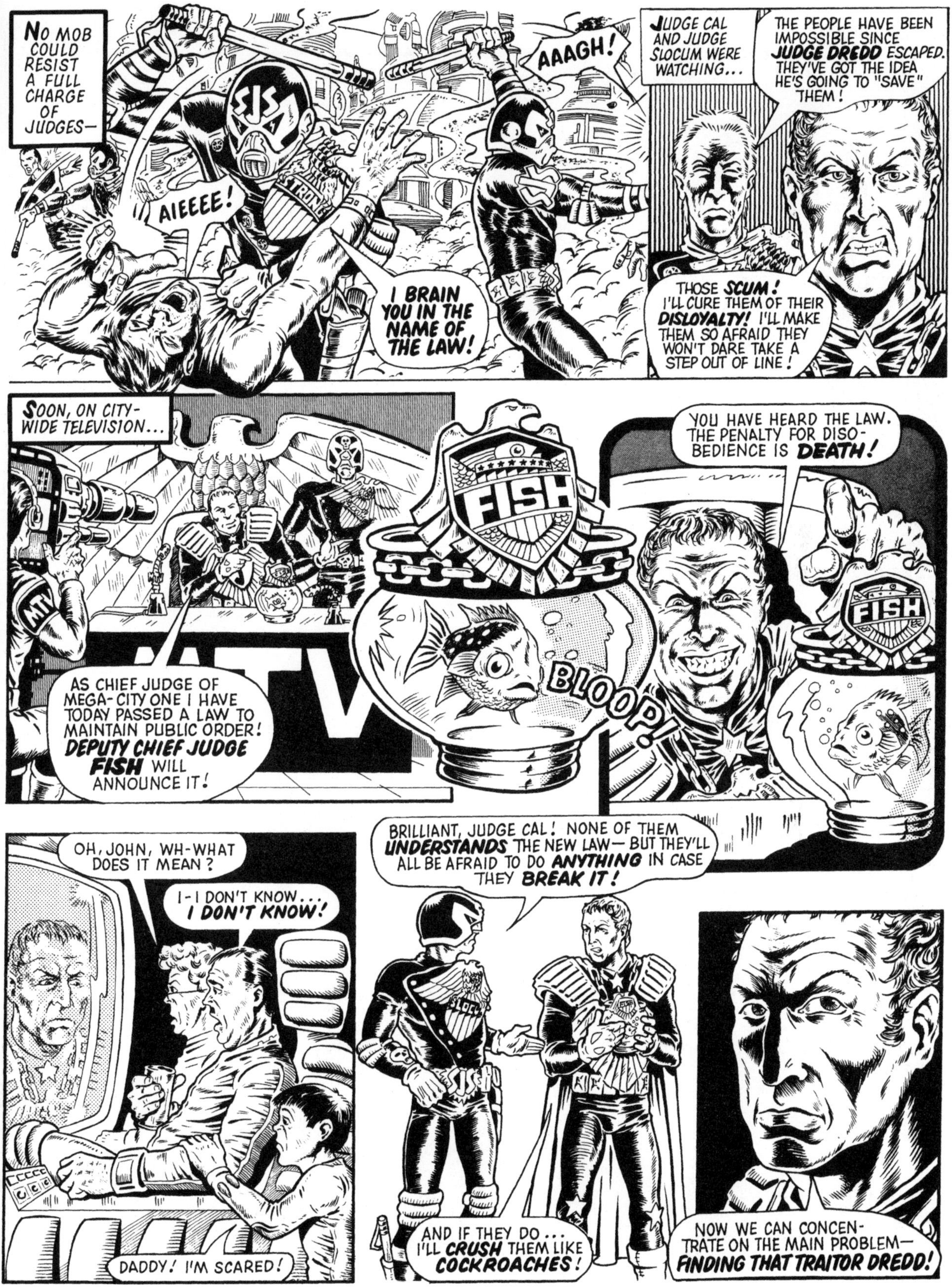
NO MOB COULD RESIST A FULL CHARGE OF JUDGES—
AIEEEE!
AAAGH!
I BRAIN YOU IN THE NAME OF THE LAW!
JUDGE CAL AND JUDGE SLOCUM WERE WATCHING...
THE PEOPLE HAVE BEEN IMPOSSIBLE SINCE JUDGE DREDD ESCAPED. THEY'VE GOT THE IDEA HE'S GOING TO "SAVE" THEM!
THOSE SCUM! I'LL CURE THEM OF THEIR DISLOYALTY! I'LL MAKE THEM SO AFRAID THEY WON'T DARE TAKE A STEP OUT OF LINE!
SOON, ON CITY-WIDE TELEVISION...
AS CHIEF JUDGE OF MEGA-CITY ONE I HAVE TODAY PASSED A LAW TO MAINTAIN PUBLIC ORDER! DEPUTY CHIEF JUDGE FISH WILL ANNOUNCE IT!
FISH
BLOOP!
YOU HAVE HEARD THE LAW. THE PENALTY FOR DISOBEDIENCE IS DEATH!
FISH
OH, JOHN, WH-WHAT DOES IT MEAN?
I-I DON'T KNOW... I DON'T KNOW!
DADDY! I'M SCARED!
BRILLIANT, JUDGE CAL! NONE OF THEM UNDERSTANDS THE NEW LAW— BUT THEY'LL ALL BE AFRAID TO DO ANYTHING IN CASE THEY BREAK IT!
AND IF THEY DO... I'LL CRUSH THEM LIKE COCKROACHES!
NOW WE CAN CONCENTRATE ON THE MAIN PROBLEM— FINDING THAT TRAITOR DREDD!

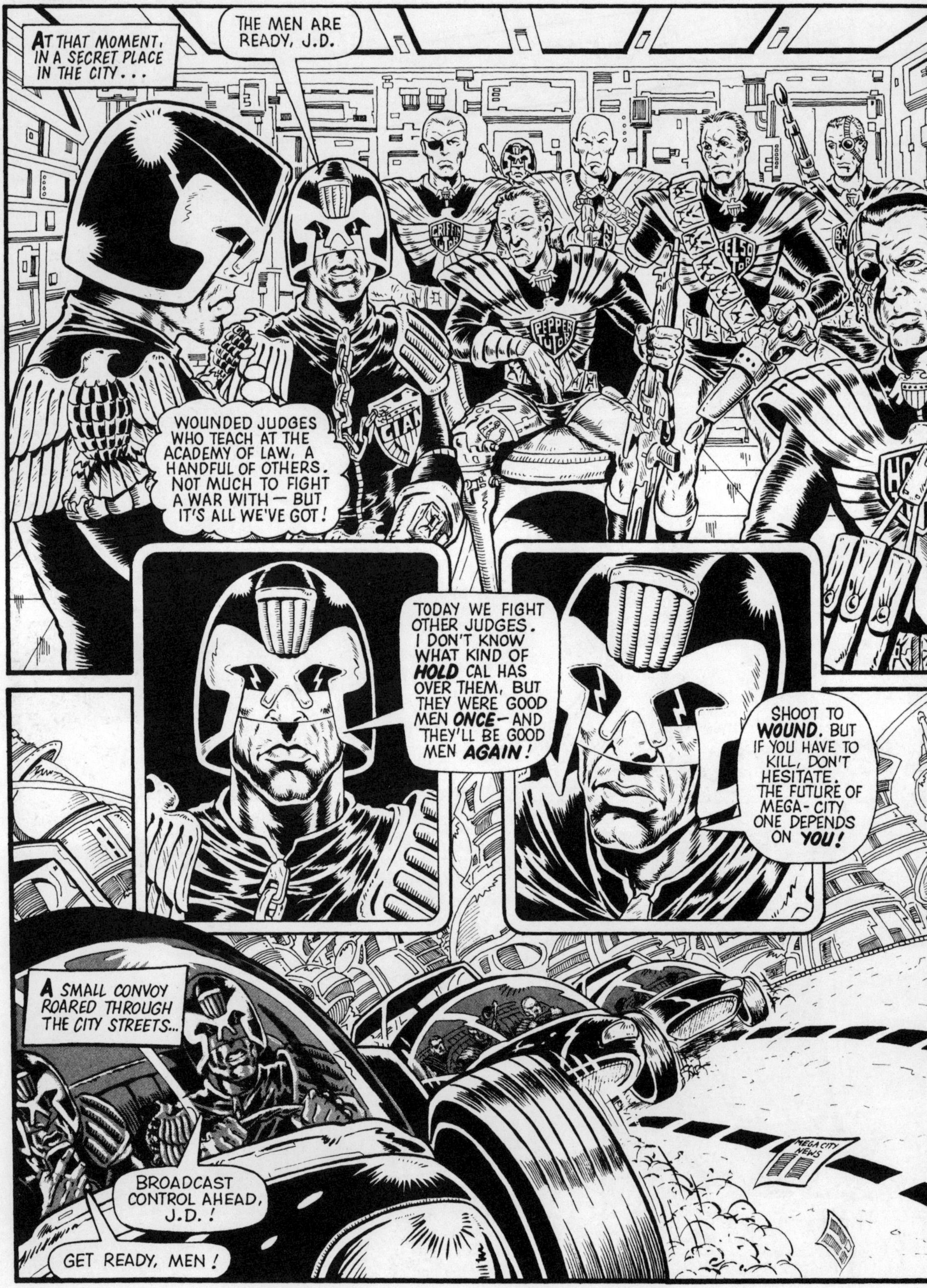
AT THAT MOMENT, IN A SECRET PLACE IN THE CITY...
THE MEN ARE READY, J.D.
WOUNDED JUDGES WHO TEACH AT THE ACADEMY OF LAW, A HANDFUL OF OTHERS. NOT MUCH TO FIGHT A WAR WITH — BUT IT'S ALL WE'VE GOT!
TODAY WE FIGHT OTHER JUDGES. I DON'T KNOW WHAT KIND OF HOLD CAL HAS OVER THEM, BUT THEY WERE GOOD MEN ONCE— AND THEY'LL BE GOOD MEN AGAIN!
SHOOT TO WOUND. BUT IF YOU HAVE TO KILL, DON'T HESITATE. THE FUTURE OF MEGA-CITY ONE DEPENDS ON YOU!
A SMALL CONVOY ROARED THROUGH THE CITY STREETS...
BROADCAST CONTROL AHEAD, J.D.!
GET READY, MEN!
MEGA CITY NEWS

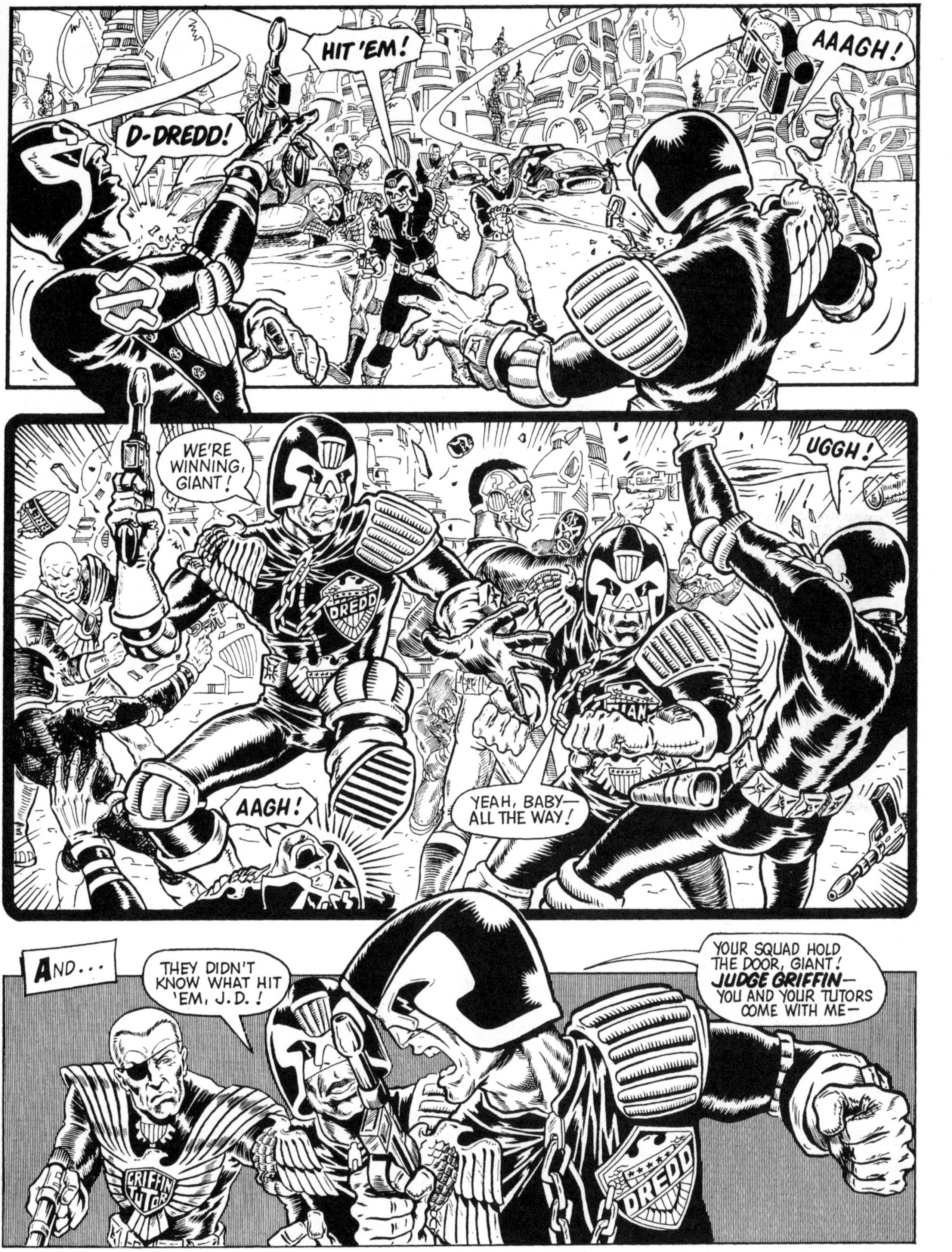
D-DREDD!
HIT 'EM!
AAAGH!
WE'RE WINNING, GIANT!
UGGH!
AAGH!
YEAH, BABY— ALL THE WAY!
AND...
THEY DIDN'T KNOW WHAT HIT 'EM, J.D.!
YOUR SQUAD HOLD THE DOOR, GIANT! JUDGE GRIFFIN— YOU AND YOUR TUTORS COME WITH ME—

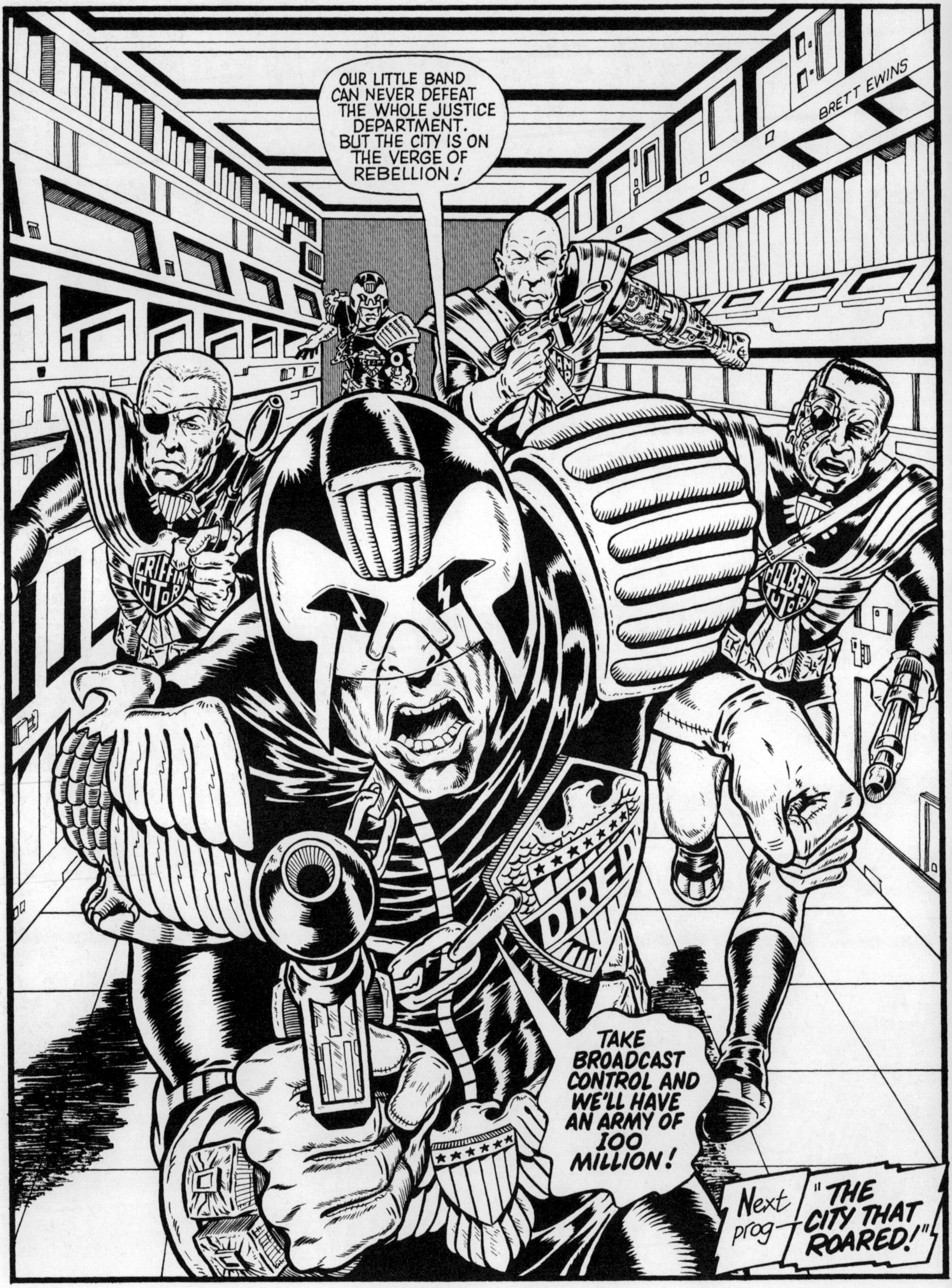
BRETT EWINS
OUR LITTLE BAND CAN NEVER DEFEAT THE WHOLE JUSTICE DEPARTMENT. BUT THE CITY IS ON THE VERGE OF REBELLION!
GRIFFIN TUTOR
HOLBEIN TUTOR
DRED
TAKE BROADCAST CONTROL AND WE'LL HAVE AN ARMY OF 100 MILLION!
Next prog
"THE CITY THAT ROARED!"

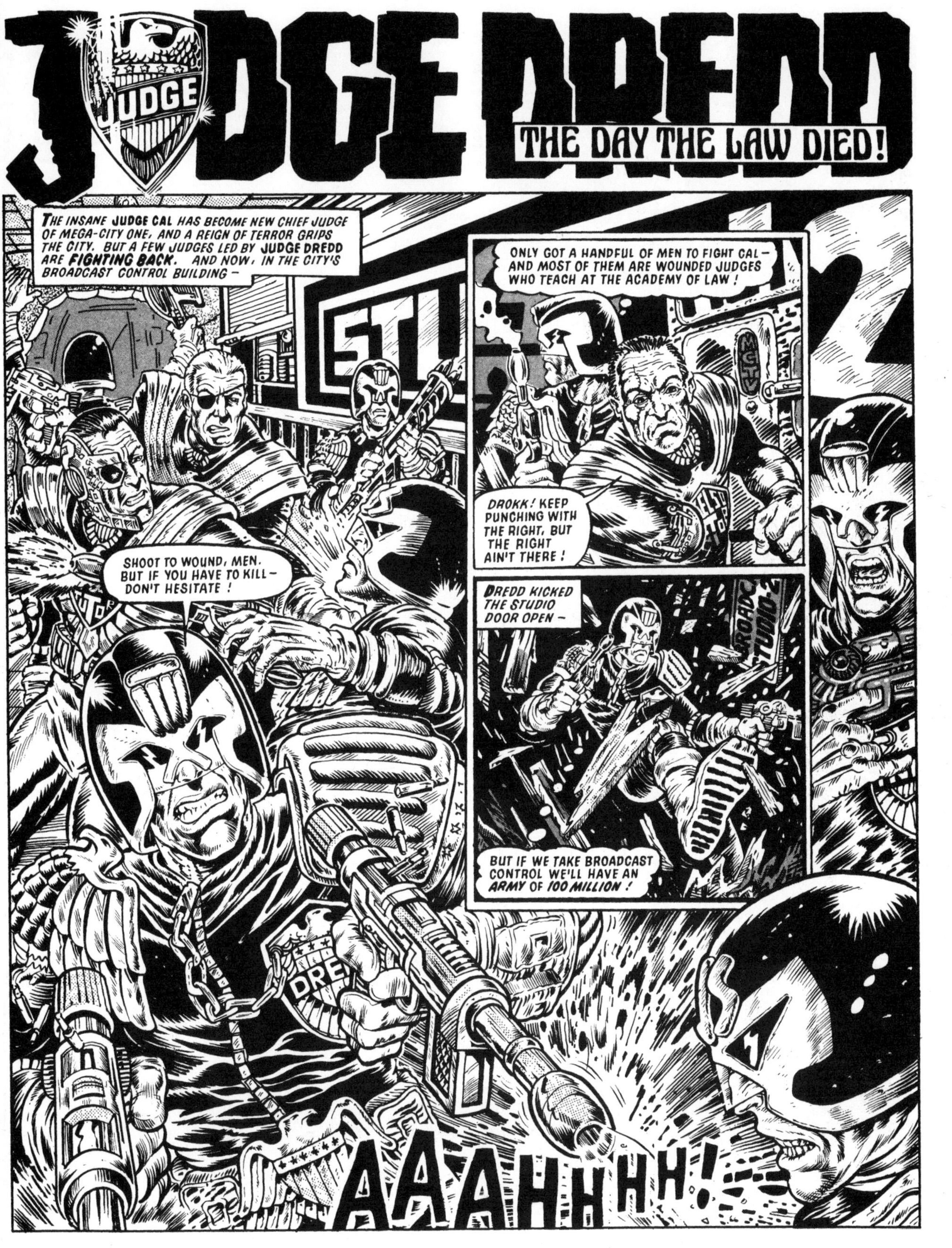

JUDGE
JUDGE DREDD
THE DAY THE LAW DIED!
THE INSANE JUDGE CAL HAS BECOME NEW CHIEF JUDGE OF MEGA-CITY ONE, AND A REIGN OF TERROR GRIPS THE CITY. BUT A FEW JUDGES LED BY JUDGE DREDD ARE FIGHTING BACK. AND NOW, IN THE CITY'S BROADCAST CONTROL BUILDING –
SHOOT TO WOUND, MEN. BUT IF YOU HAVE TO KILL – DON'T HESITATE !
ONLY GOT A HANDFUL OF MEN TO FIGHT CAL – AND MOST OF THEM ARE WOUNDED JUDGES WHO TEACH AT THE ACADEMY OF LAW !
DROKK! KEEP PUNCHING WITH THE RIGHT, BUT THE RIGHT AIN'T THERE !
DREDD KICKED THE STUDIO DOOR OPEN –
BUT IF WE TAKE BROADCAST CONTROL WE'LL HAVE AN ARMY OF 100 MILLION !
AAAHHHH!

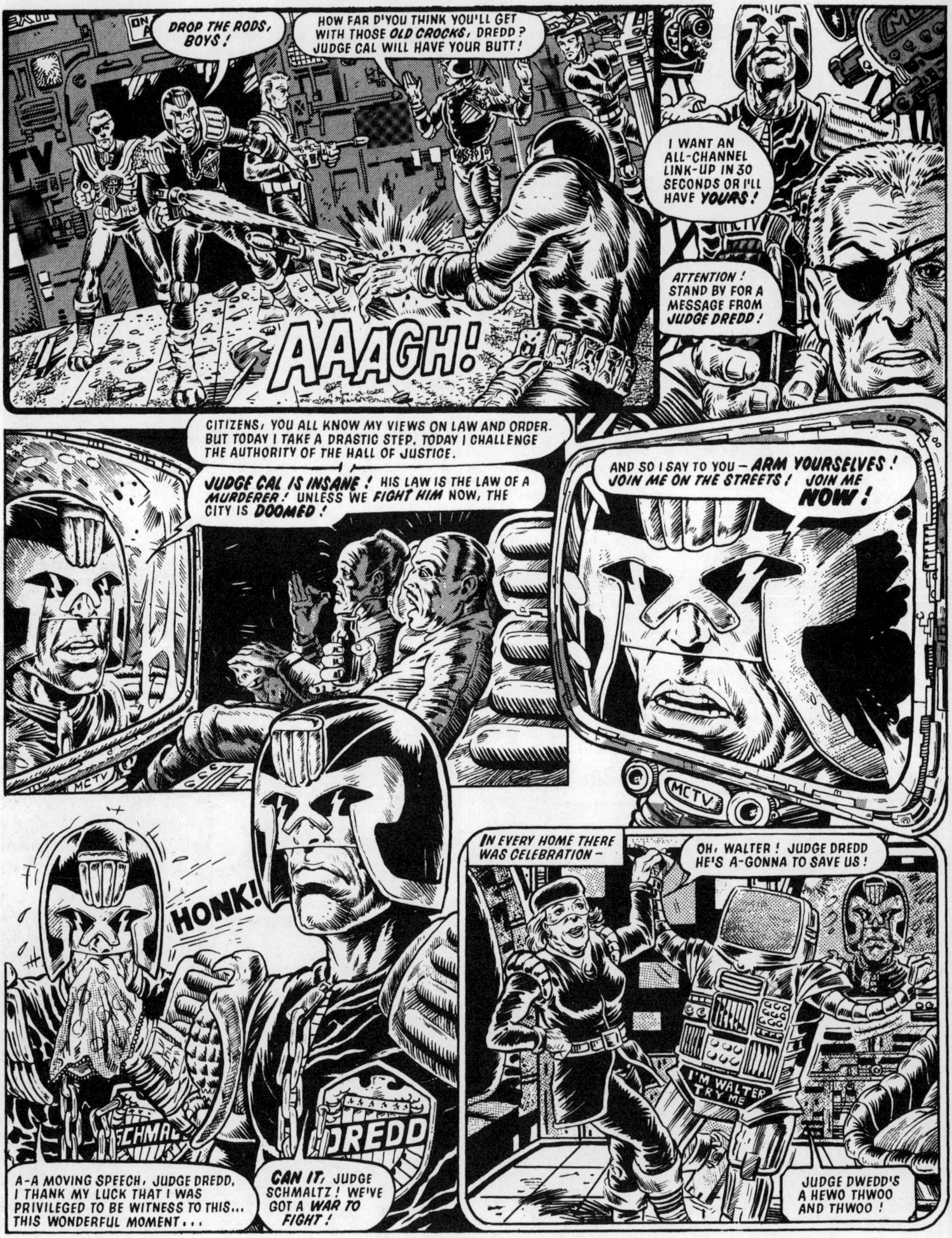
DROP THE RODS, BOYS!
HOW FAR D'YOU THINK YOU'LL GET WITH THOSE OLD CROCKS, DREDD? JUDGE CAL WILL HAVE YOUR BUTT!
AAAGH!
I WANT AN ALL-CHANNEL LINK-UP IN 30 SECONDS OR I'LL HAVE YOURS!
ATTENTION! STAND BY FOR A MESSAGE FROM JUDGE DREDD!
CITIZENS, YOU ALL KNOW MY VIEWS ON LAW AND ORDER. BUT TODAY I TAKE A DRASTIC STEP. TODAY I CHALLENGE THE AUTHORITY OF THE HALL OF JUSTICE.
JUDGE CAL IS INSANE! HIS LAW IS THE LAW OF A MURDERER! UNLESS WE FIGHT HIM NOW, THE CITY IS DOOMED!
AND SO I SAY TO YOU – ARM YOURSELVES! JOIN ME ON THE STREETS! JOIN ME NOW!
MCTV
MCTV
HONK!
DREDD
A-A MOVING SPEECH, JUDGE DREDD, I THANK MY LUCK THAT I WAS PRIVILEGED TO BE WITNESS TO THIS... THIS WONDERFUL MOMENT...
CAN IT, JUDGE SCHMALTZ! WE'VE GOT A WAR TO FIGHT!
IN EVERY HOME THERE WAS CELEBRATION –
OH, WALTER! JUDGE DREDD HE'S A-GONNA TO SAVE US!
I'M WALTER TRY ME
JUDGE DWEDD'S A HEWO THWOO AND THWOO!

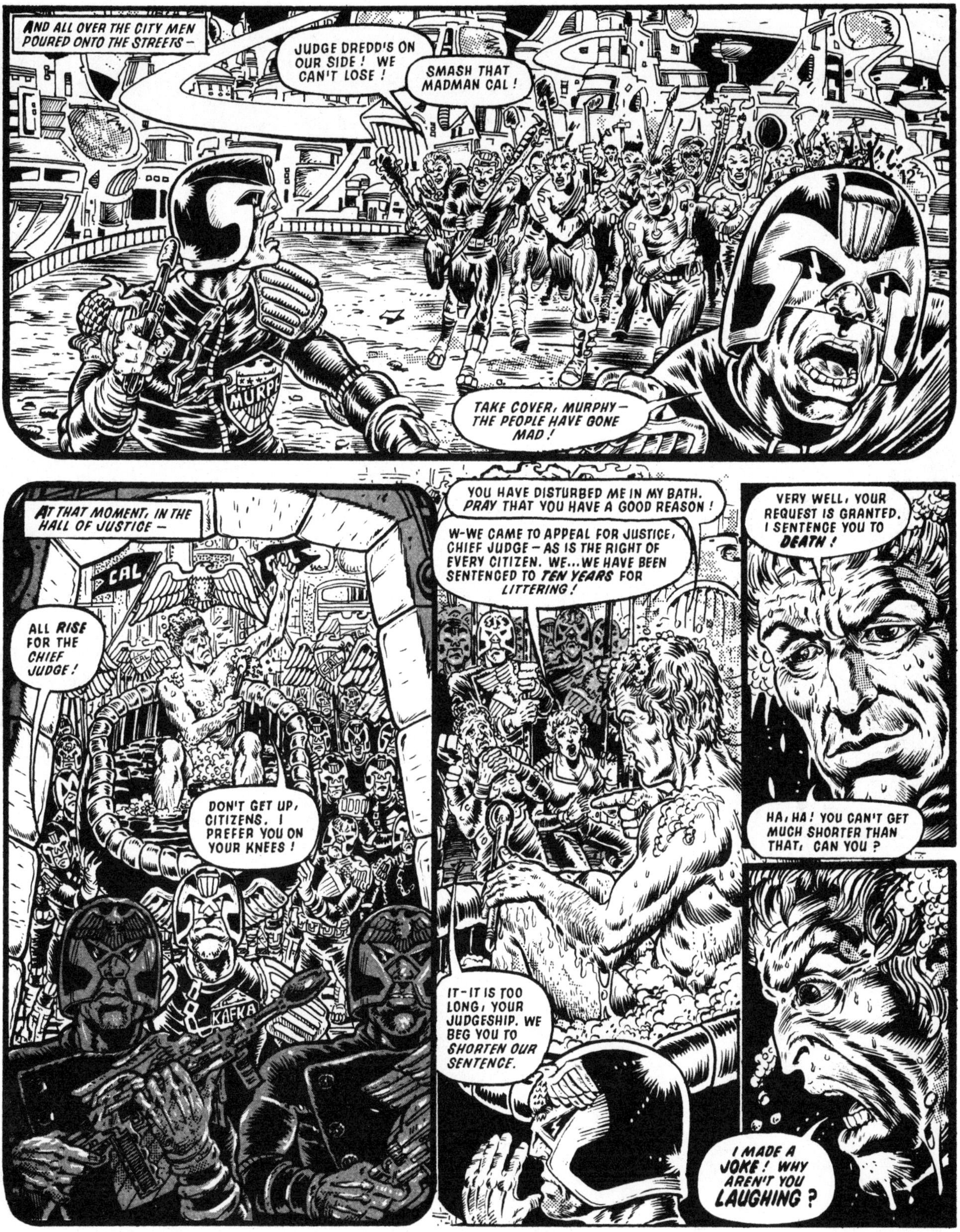
AND ALL OVER THE CITY MEN POURED ONTO THE STREETS –
JUDGE DREDD'S ON OUR SIDE! WE CAN'T LOSE!
SMASH THAT MADMAN CAL!
TAKE COVER, MURPHY – THE PEOPLE HAVE GONE MAD!
AT THAT MOMENT, IN THE HALL OF JUSTICE –
ALL RISE FOR THE CHIEF JUDGE!
DON'T GET UP, CITIZENS. I PREFER YOU ON YOUR KNEES!
YOU HAVE DISTURBED ME IN MY BATH. PRAY THAT YOU HAVE A GOOD REASON!
W-WE CAME TO APPEAL FOR JUSTICE, CHIEF JUDGE – AS IS THE RIGHT OF EVERY CITIZEN. WE... WE HAVE BEEN SENTENCED TO TEN YEARS FOR LITTERING!
IT-IT IS TOO LONG, YOUR JUDGESHIP. WE BEG YOU TO SHORTEN OUR SENTENCE.
VERY WELL, YOUR REQUEST IS GRANTED. I SENTENCE YOU TO DEATH!
HA, HA! YOU CAN'T GET MUCH SHORTER THAN THAT, CAN YOU?
I MADE A JOKE! WHY AREN'T YOU LAUGHING?

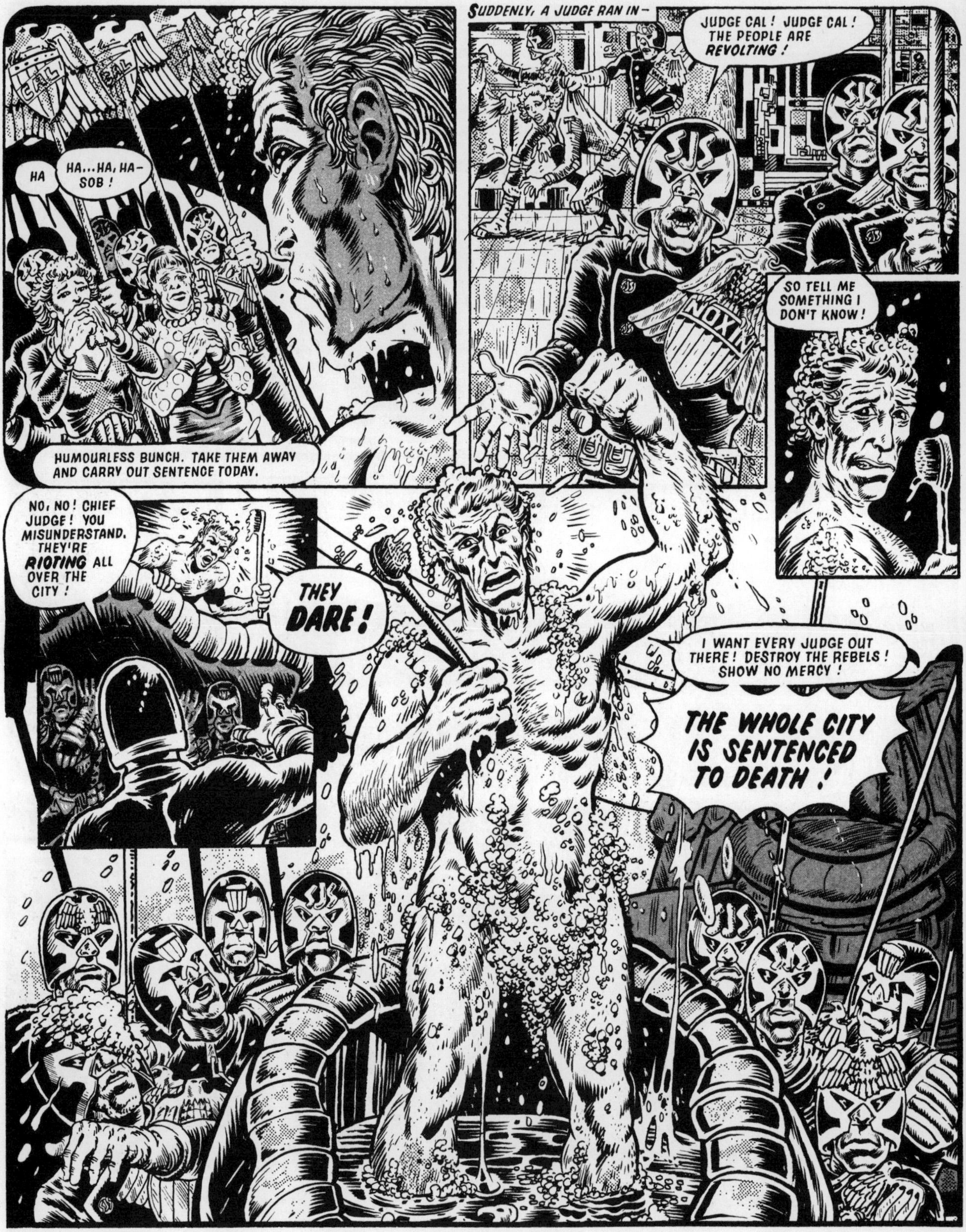
HA
HA...HA, HA-SOB!
HUMOURLESS BUNCH. TAKE THEM AWAY AND CARRY OUT SENTENCE TODAY.
SUDDENLY, A JUDGE RAN IN-
JUDGE CAL! JUDGE CAL! THE PEOPLE ARE REVOLTING!
SO TELL ME SOMETHING I DON'T KNOW!
NO, NO! CHIEF JUDGE! YOU MISUNDERSTAND. THEY'RE RIOTING ALL OVER THE CITY!
THEY DARE!
I WANT EVERY JUDGE OUT THERE! DESTROY THE REBELS! SHOW NO MERCY!
THE WHOLE CITY IS SENTENCED TO DEATH!

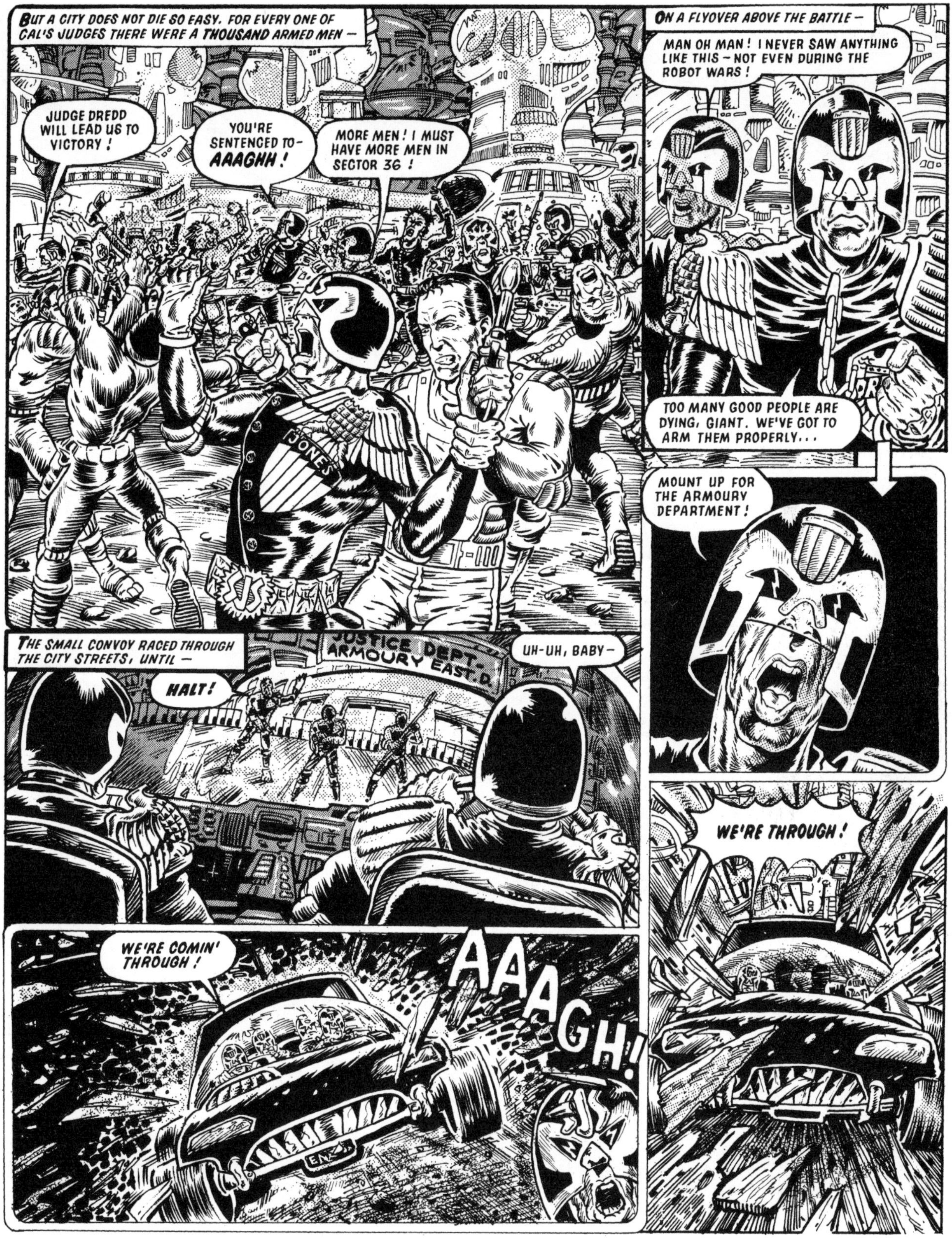

BUT A CITY DOES NOT DIE SO EASY. FOR EVERY ONE OF CAL'S JUDGES THERE WERE A THOUSAND ARMED MEN –
JUDGE DREDD WILL LEAD US TO VICTORY!
YOU'RE SENTENCED TO– AAAGHH!
MORE MEN! I MUST HAVE MORE MEN IN SECTOR 36!
JONES
ON A FLYOVER ABOVE THE BATTLE –
MAN OH MAN! I NEVER SAW ANYTHING LIKE THIS – NOT EVEN DURING THE ROBOT WARS!
TOO MANY GOOD PEOPLE ARE DYING, GIANT. WE'VE GOT TO ARM THEM PROPERLY...
MOUNT UP FOR THE ARMOURY DEPARTMENT!
THE SMALL CONVOY RACED THROUGH THE CITY STREETS, UNTIL –
JUSTICE DEPT. ARMOURY EAST.D.
HALT!
UH-UH, BABY–
WE'RE COMIN' THROUGH!
AAAAGH!
WE'RE THROUGH!

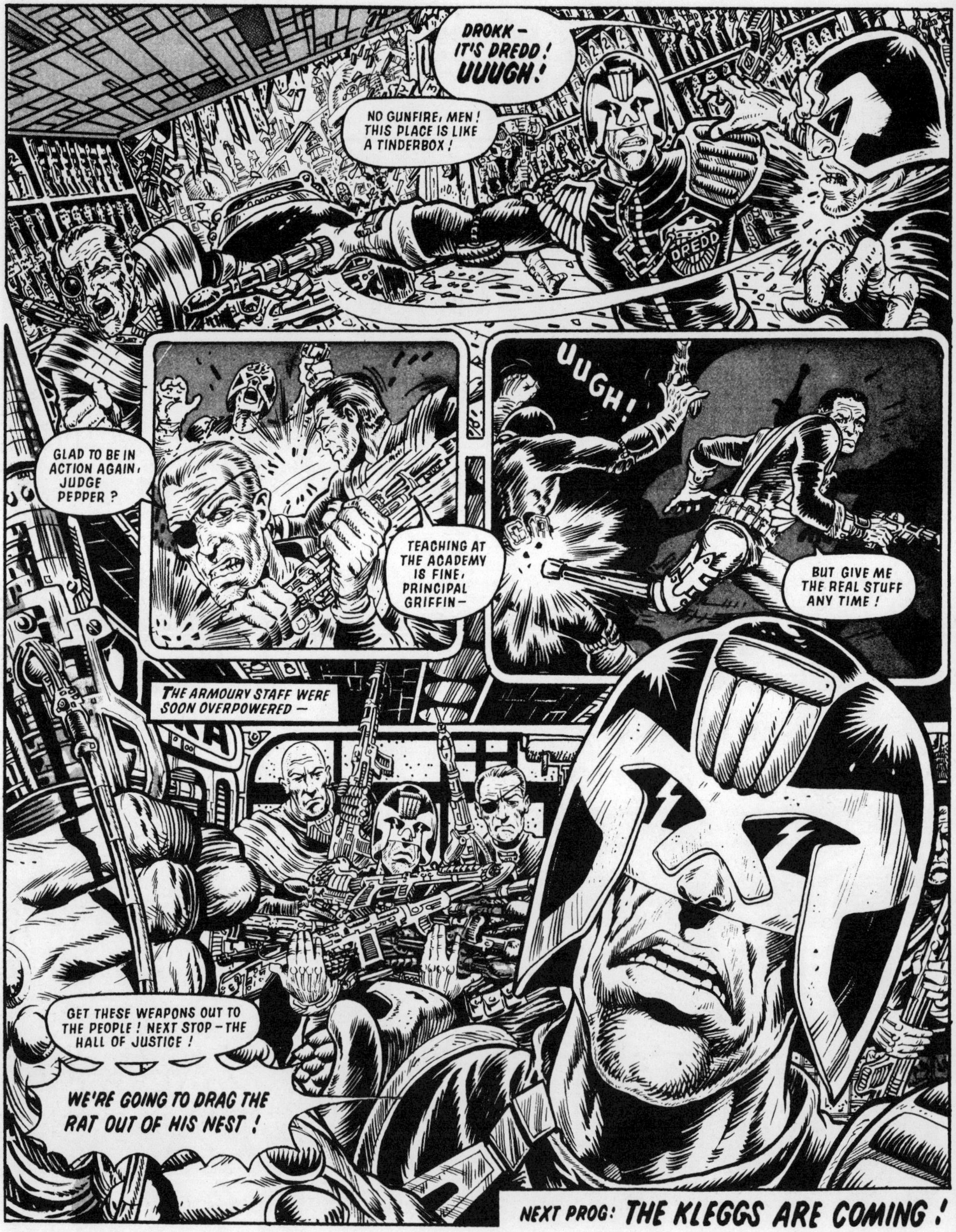
DROKK – IT'S DREDD! UUUGH!
NO GUNFIRE, MEN! THIS PLACE IS LIKE A TINDERBOX!
GLAD TO BE IN ACTION AGAIN, JUDGE PEPPER?
TEACHING AT THE ACADEMY IS FINE, PRINCIPAL GRIFFIN–
UUGH!
BUT GIVE ME THE REAL STUFF ANY TIME!
THE ARMOURY STAFF WERE SOON OVERPOWERED –
GET THESE WEAPONS OUT TO THE PEOPLE! NEXT STOP – THE HALL OF JUSTICE!
WE'RE GOING TO DRAG THE RAT OUT OF HIS NEST!
NEXT PROG: THE KLEGGS ARE COMING!

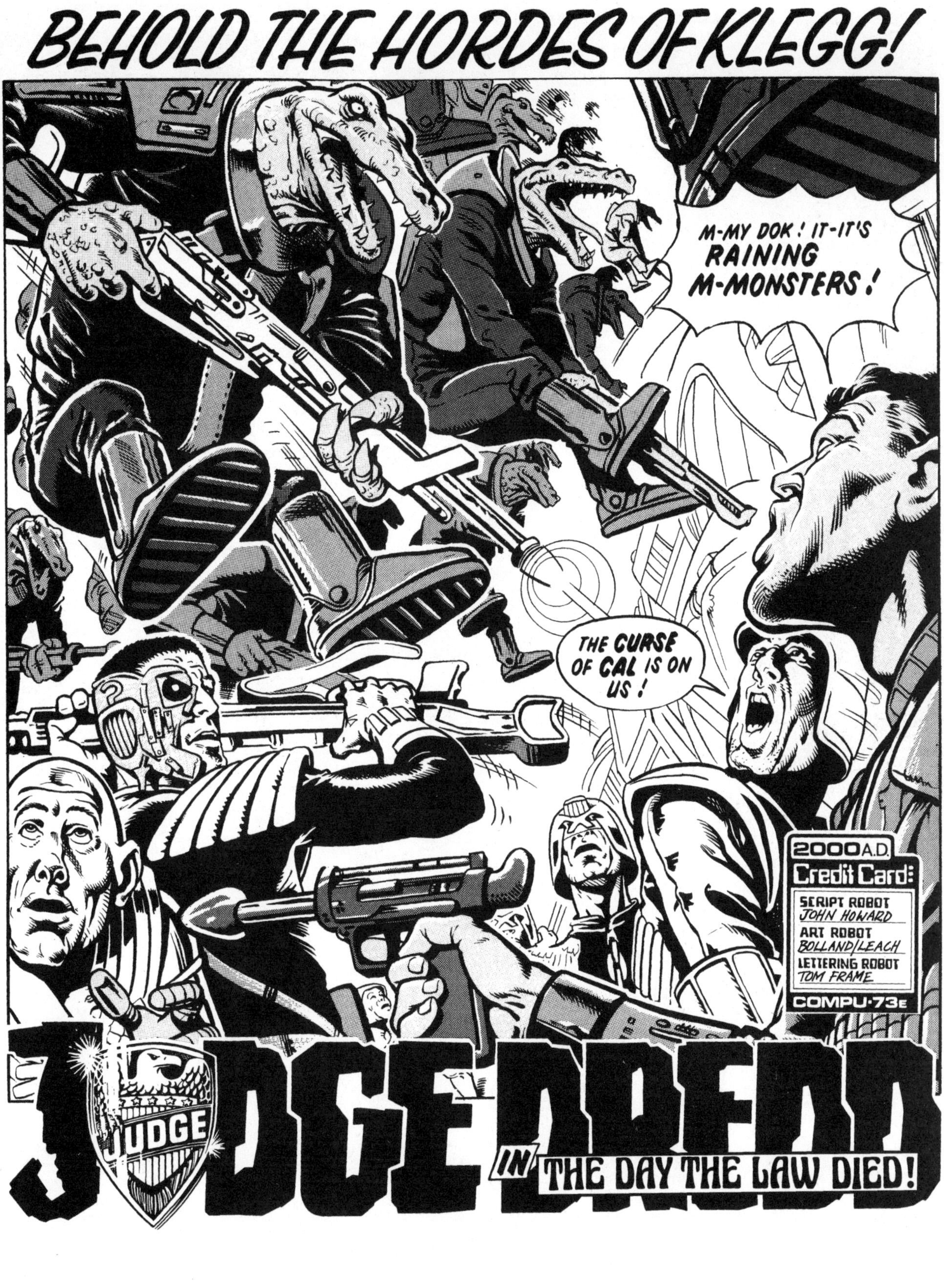
BEHOLD THE HORDES OF KLEGG!
M-MY DOK! IT-IT'S RAINING M-MONSTERS!
THE CURSE OF CAL IS ON US!
2000 A.D. Credit Card:
SCRIPT ROBOT JOHN HOWARD
ART ROBOT BOLLAND/LEACH
LETTERING ROBOT TOM FRAME
COMPU-73E
JUDGE DREDD IN THE DAY THE LAW DIED!

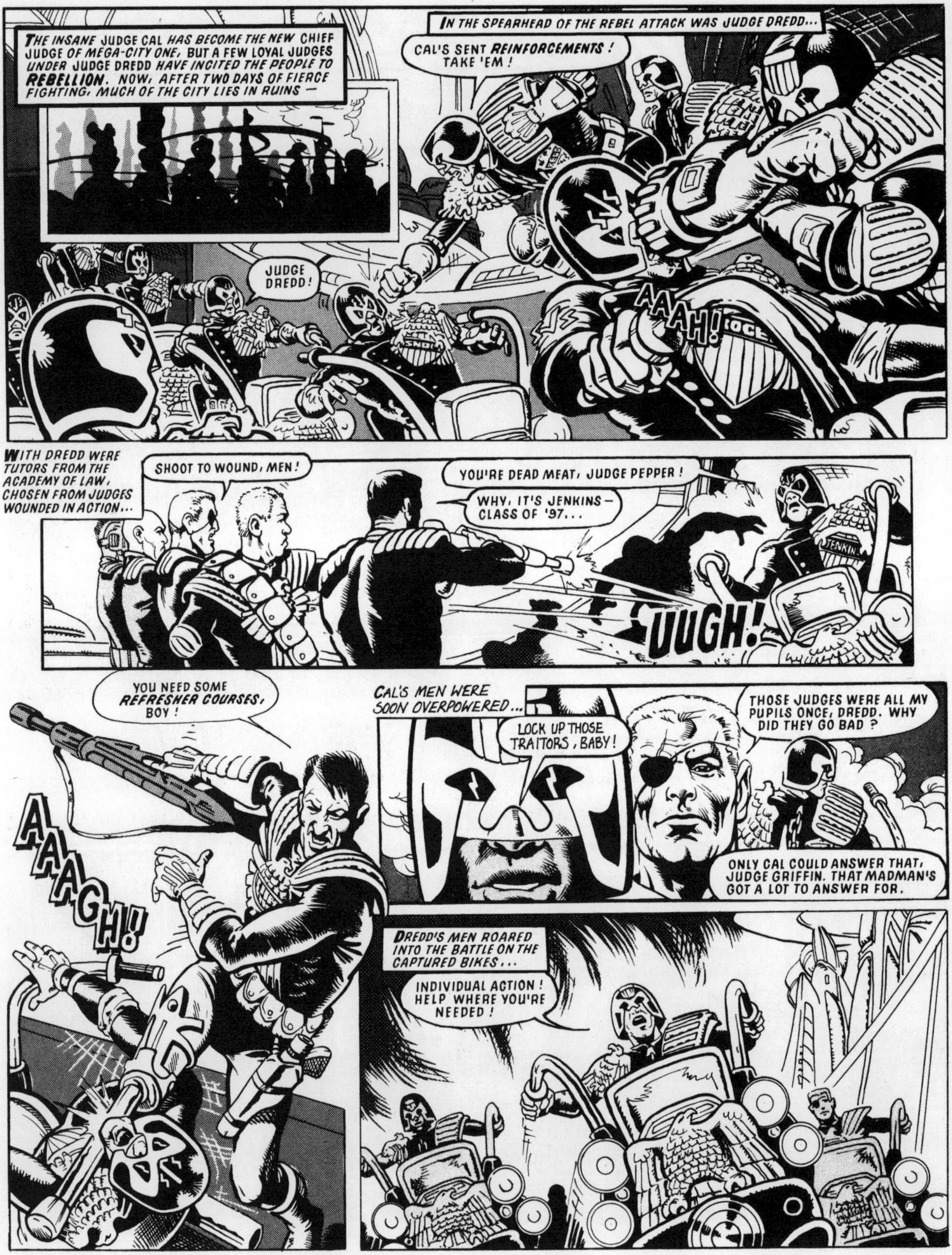
THE INSANE JUDGE CAL HAS BECOME THE NEW CHIEF JUDGE OF MEGA-CITY ONE, BUT A FEW LOYAL JUDGES UNDER JUDGE DREDD HAVE INCITED THE PEOPLE TO REBELLION. NOW, AFTER TWO DAYS OF FIERCE FIGHTING, MUCH OF THE CITY LIES IN RUINS —
IN THE SPEARHEAD OF THE REBEL ATTACK WAS JUDGE DREDD...
CAL'S SENT REINFORCEMENTS! TAKE 'EM!
JUDGE DREDD!
AAAH!
WITH DREDD WERE TUTORS FROM THE ACADEMY OF LAW, CHOSEN FROM JUDGES WOUNDED IN ACTION...
SHOOT TO WOUND, MEN!
YOU'RE DEAD MEAT, JUDGE PEPPER!
WHY, IT'S JENKINS — CLASS OF '97...
UUGH!
YOU NEED SOME REFRESHER COURSES, BOY!
AAAGH!
CAL'S MEN WERE SOON OVERPOWERED...
LOCK UP THOSE TRAITORS, BABY!
THOSE JUDGES WERE ALL MY PUPILS ONCE, DREDD. WHY DID THEY GO BAD?
ONLY CAL COULD ANSWER THAT, JUDGE GRIFFIN. THAT MADMAN'S GOT A LOT TO ANSWER FOR.
DREDD'S MEN ROARED INTO THE BATTLE ON THE CAPTURED BIKES...
INDIVIDUAL ACTION! HELP WHERE YOU'RE NEEDED!

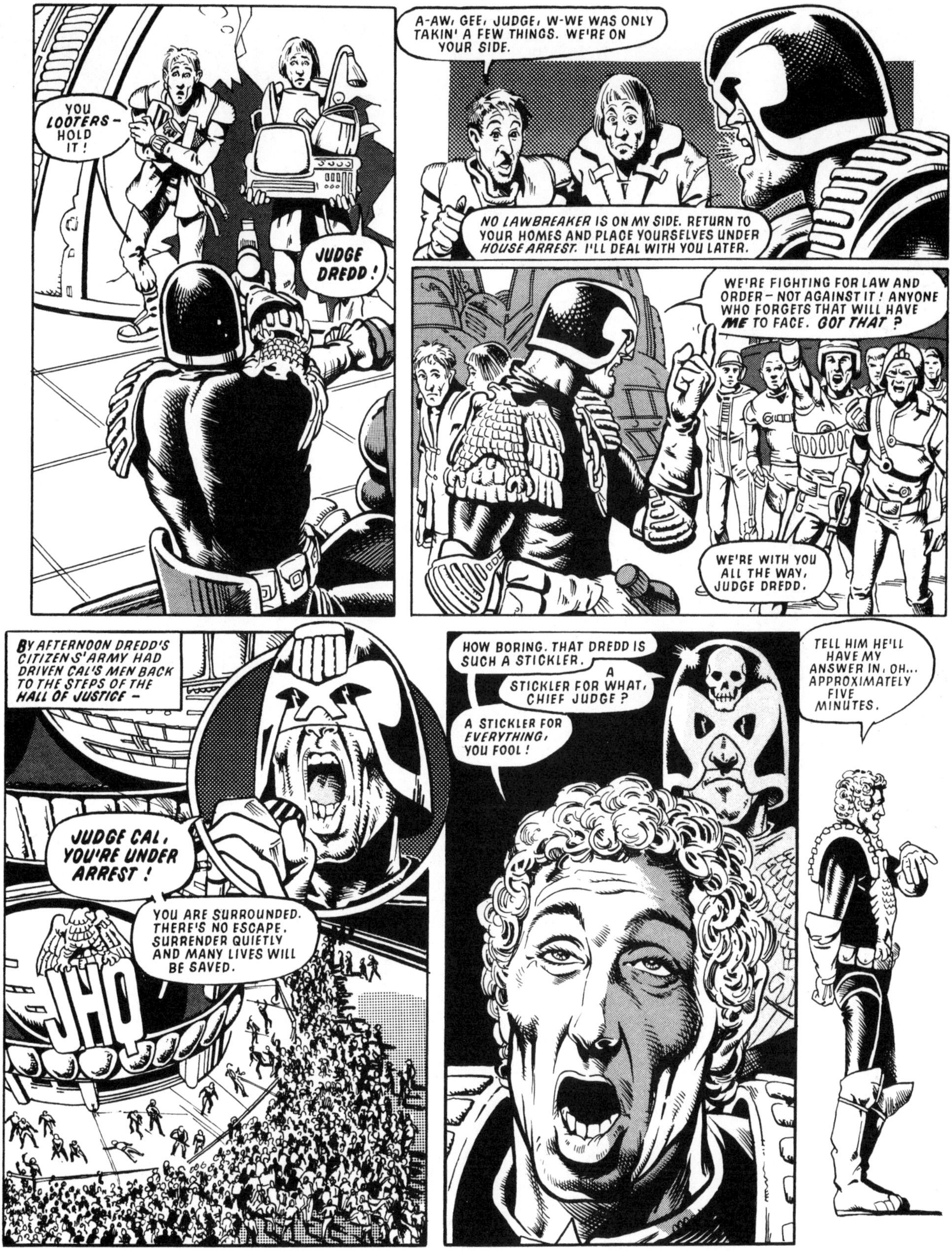
YOU LOOTERS - HOLD IT !
JUDGE DREDD !
A-AW, GEE, JUDGE, W-WE WAS ONLY TAKIN' A FEW THINGS. WE'RE ON YOUR SIDE.
NO LAWBREAKER IS ON MY SIDE. RETURN TO YOUR HOMES AND PLACE YOURSELVES UNDER HOUSE ARREST. I'LL DEAL WITH YOU LATER.
WE'RE FIGHTING FOR LAW AND ORDER - NOT AGAINST IT ! ANYONE WHO FORGETS THAT WILL HAVE ME TO FACE. GOT THAT ?
WE'RE WITH YOU ALL THE WAY, JUDGE DREDD.
BY AFTERNOON DREDD'S CITIZENS' ARMY HAD DRIVEN CAL'S MEN BACK TO THE STEPS OF THE HALL OF JUSTICE -
JUDGE CAL, YOU'RE UNDER ARREST !
YOU ARE SURROUNDED. THERE'S NO ESCAPE. SURRENDER QUIETLY AND MANY LIVES WILL BE SAVED.
JHQ
HOW BORING. THAT DREDD IS SUCH A STICKLER.
A STICKLER FOR WHAT, CHIEF JUDGE ?
A STICKLER FOR EVERYTHING, YOU FOOL !
TELL HIM HE'LL HAVE MY ANSWER IN, OH... APPROXIMATELY FIVE MINUTES.

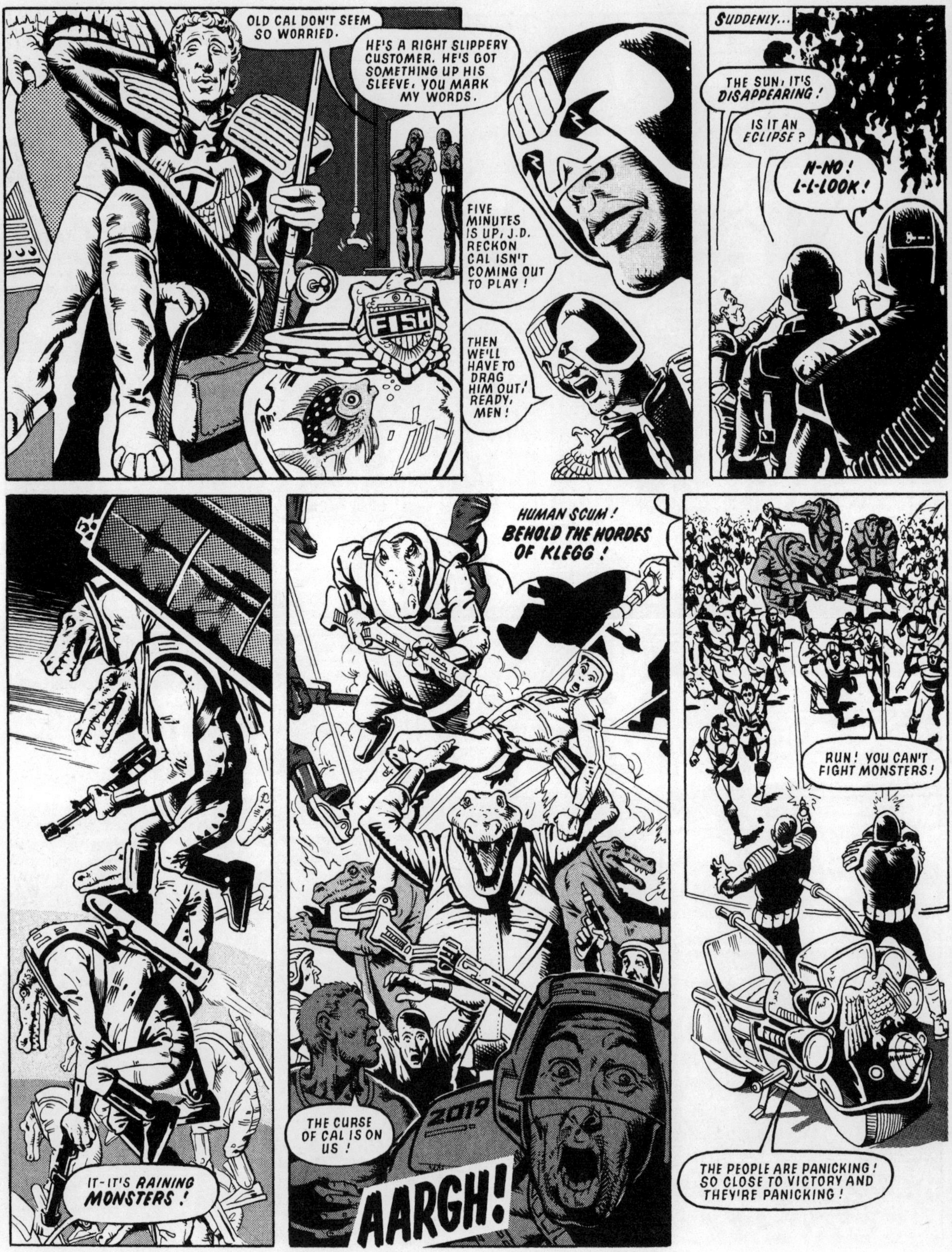
OLD CAL DON'T SEEM SO WORRIED.
HE'S A RIGHT SLIPPERY CUSTOMER. HE'S GOT SOMETHING UP HIS SLEEVE, YOU MARK MY WORDS.
FISH
FIVE MINUTES IS UP, J.D. RECKON CAL ISN'T COMING OUT TO PLAY!
THEN WE'LL HAVE TO DRAG HIM OUT! READY, MEN!
SUDDENLY...
THE SUN, IT'S DISAPPEARING!
IS IT AN ECLIPSE?
N-NO! L-L-LOOK!
IT-IT'S RAINING MONSTERS!
HUMAN SCUM! BEHOLD THE HORDES OF KLEGG!
THE CURSE OF CAL IS ON US!
2019
AARGH!
RUN! YOU CAN'T FIGHT MONSTERS!
THE PEOPLE ARE PANICKING! SO CLOSE TO VICTORY AND THEY'RE PANICKING!

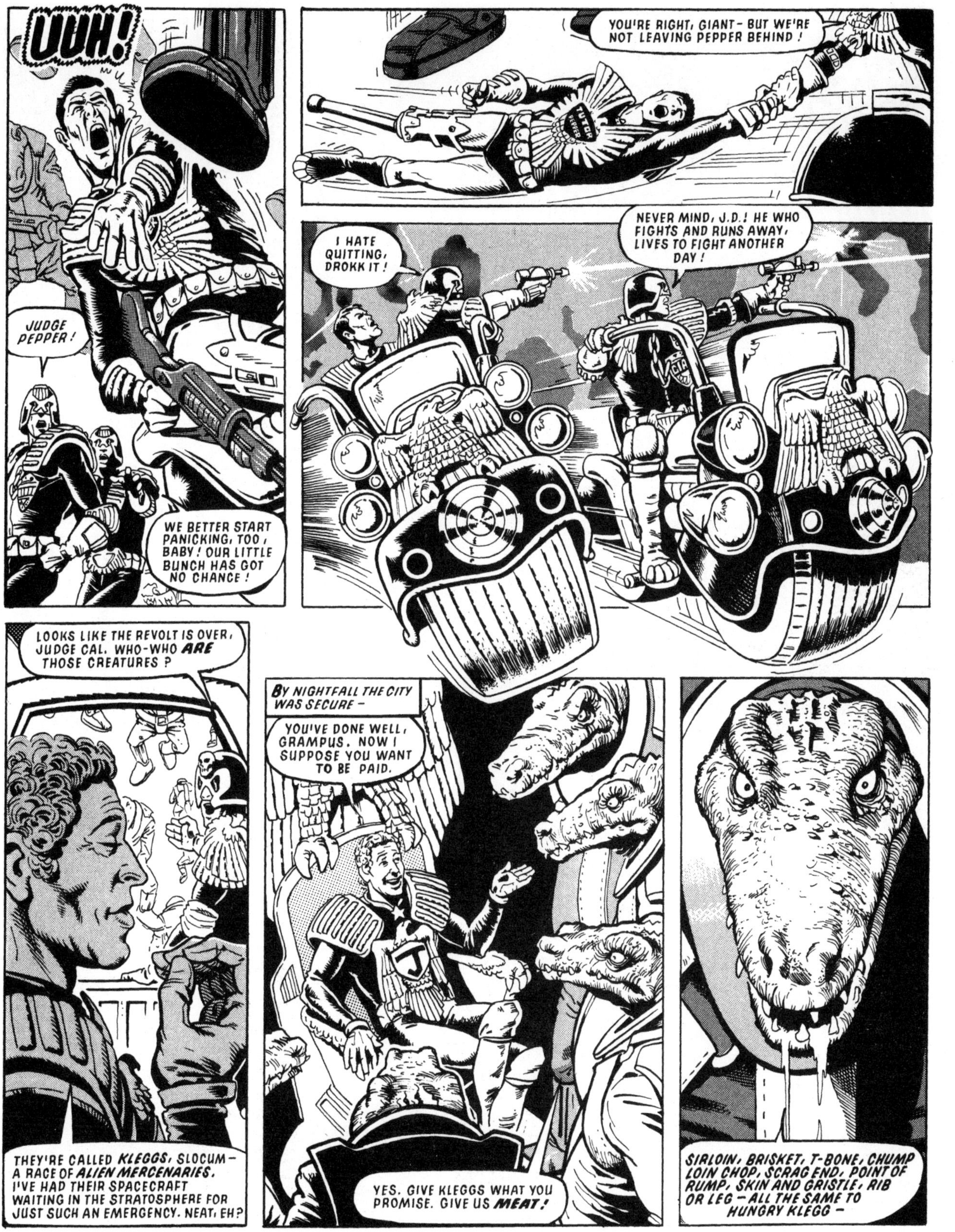
UUH!
JUDGE PEPPER!
WE BETTER START PANICKING, TOO, BABY! OUR LITTLE BUNCH HAS GOT NO CHANCE!
YOU'RE RIGHT, GIANT – BUT WE'RE NOT LEAVING PEPPER BEHIND!
I HATE QUITTING, DROKK IT!
NEVER MIND, J.D.! HE WHO FIGHTS AND RUNS AWAY, LIVES TO FIGHT ANOTHER DAY!
LOOKS LIKE THE REVOLT IS OVER, JUDGE CAL. WHO-WHO ARE THOSE CREATURES?
THEY'RE CALLED KLEGGS, SLOCUM – A RACE OF ALIEN MERCENARIES. I'VE HAD THEIR SPACECRAFT WAITING IN THE STRATOSPHERE FOR JUST SUCH AN EMERGENCY. NEAT, EH?
BY NIGHTFALL THE CITY WAS SECURE –
YOU'VE DONE WELL, GRAMPUS. NOW I SUPPOSE YOU WANT TO BE PAID.
YES. GIVE KLEGGS WHAT YOU PROMISE. GIVE US MEAT!
SIRLOIN, BRISKET, T-BONE, CHUMP LOIN CHOP, SCRAG END, POINT OF RUMP, SKIN AND GRISTLE, RIB OR LEG – ALL THE SAME TO HUNGRY KLEGG –

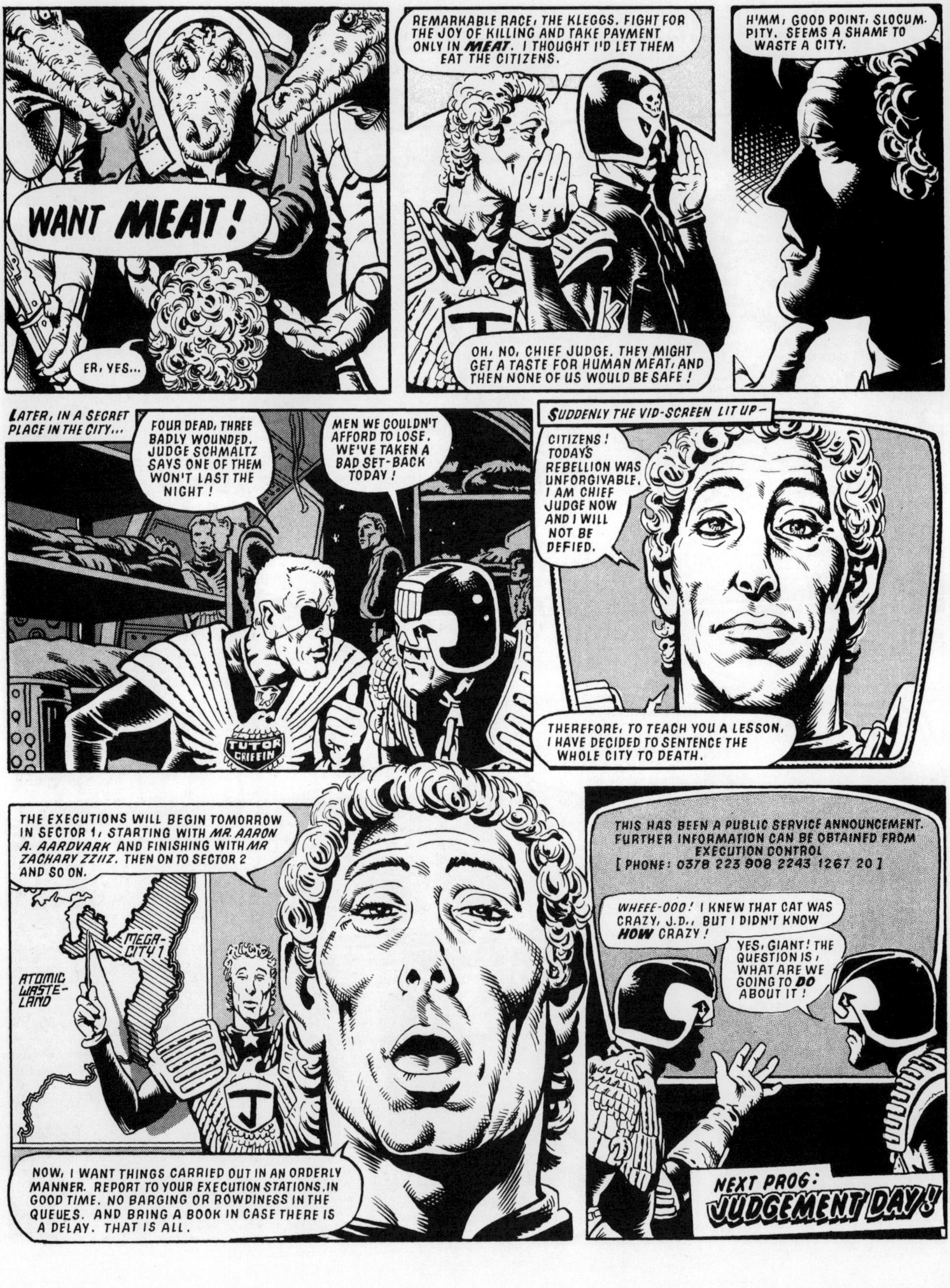
WANT MEAT!
ER, YES...
REMARKABLE RACE, THE KLEGGS. FIGHT FOR THE JOY OF KILLING AND TAKE PAYMENT ONLY IN MEAT. I THOUGHT I'D LET THEM EAT THE CITIZENS.
OH, NO, CHIEF JUDGE. THEY MIGHT GET A TASTE FOR HUMAN MEAT, AND THEN NONE OF US WOULD BE SAFE!
H'MM, GOOD POINT, SLOCUM. PITY. SEEMS A SHAME TO WASTE A CITY.
LATER, IN A SECRET PLACE IN THE CITY...
FOUR DEAD, THREE BADLY WOUNDED. JUDGE SCHMALTZ SAYS ONE OF THEM WON'T LAST THE NIGHT!
MEN WE COULDN'T AFFORD TO LOSE. WE'VE TAKEN A BAD SET-BACK TODAY!
TUTOR GRIFFIN
SUDDENLY THE VID-SCREEN LIT UP—
CITIZENS! TODAY'S REBELLION WAS UNFORGIVABLE. I AM CHIEF JUDGE NOW AND I WILL NOT BE DEFIED.
THEREFORE, TO TEACH YOU A LESSON, I HAVE DECIDED TO SENTENCE THE WHOLE CITY TO DEATH.
THE EXECUTIONS WILL BEGIN TOMORROW IN SECTOR 1, STARTING WITH MR. AARON A. AARDVARK AND FINISHING WITH MR ZACHARY ZZIIZ. THEN ON TO SECTOR 2 AND SO ON.
MEGA-CITY 1
ATOMIC WASTE-LAND
NOW, I WANT THINGS CARRIED OUT IN AN ORDERLY MANNER. REPORT TO YOUR EXECUTION STATIONS, IN GOOD TIME. NO BARGING OR ROWDINESS IN THE QUEUES. AND BRING A BOOK IN CASE THERE IS A DELAY. THAT IS ALL.
THIS HAS BEEN A PUBLIC SERVICE ANNOUNCEMENT. FURTHER INFORMATION CAN BE OBTAINED FROM EXECUTION CONTROL [PHONE: 0378 223 908 2243 1267 20]
WHEEE-DOO! I KNEW THAT CAT WAS CRAZY, J.D., BUT I DIDN'T KNOW HOW CRAZY!
YES, GIANT! THE QUESTION IS, WHAT ARE WE GOING TO DO ABOUT IT!
NEXT PROG:
JUDGEMENT DAY!

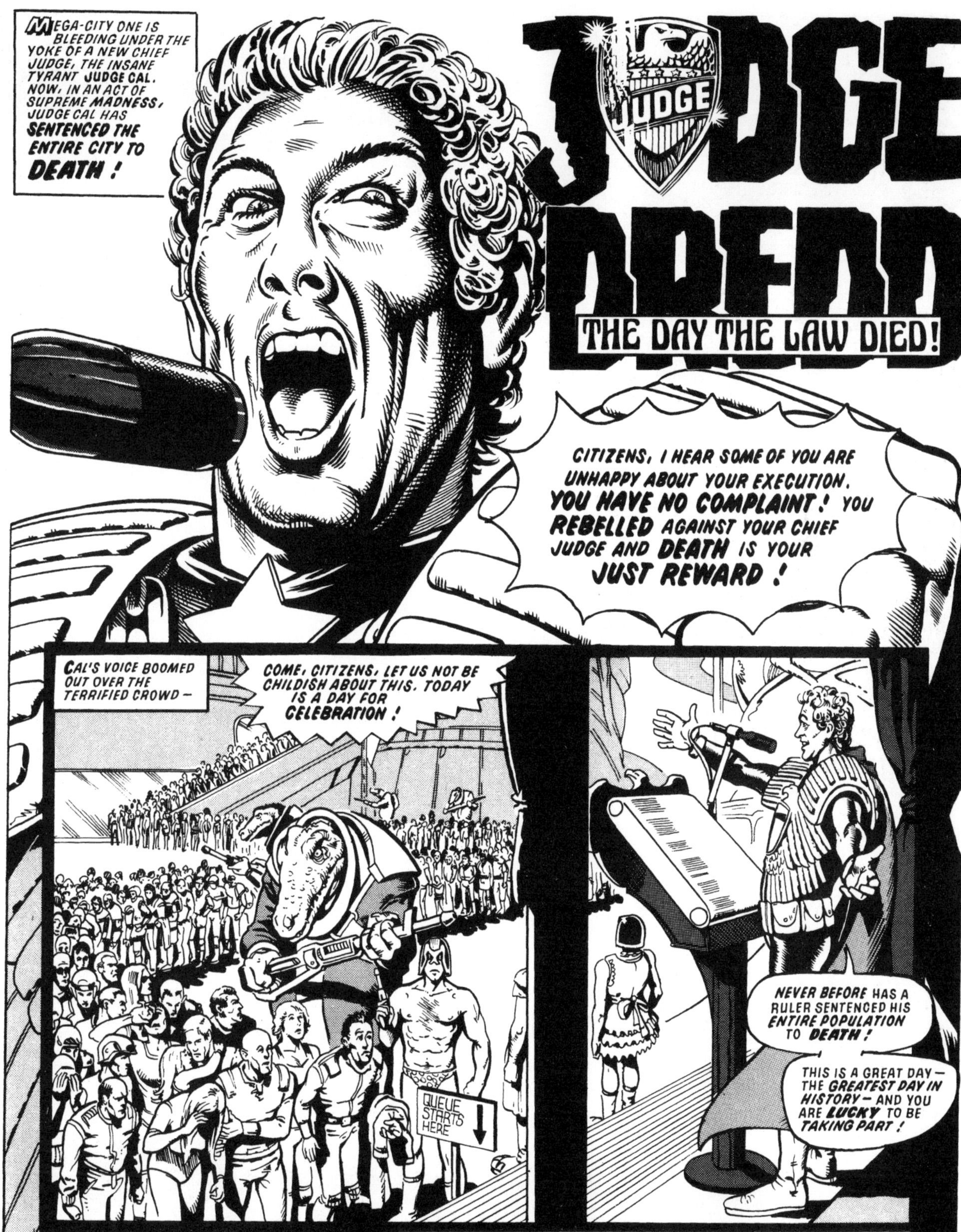
JUDGE DREDD
THE DAY THE LAW DIED!
MEGA-CITY ONE IS BLEEDING UNDER THE YOKE OF A NEW CHIEF JUDGE, THE INSANE TYRANT JUDGE CAL. NOW, IN AN ACT OF SUPREME MADNESS, JUDGE CAL HAS SENTENCED THE ENTIRE CITY TO DEATH!
CITIZENS, I HEAR SOME OF YOU ARE UNHAPPY ABOUT YOUR EXECUTION. YOU HAVE NO COMPLAINT! YOU REBELLED AGAINST YOUR CHIEF JUDGE AND DEATH IS YOUR JUST REWARD!
CAL'S VOICE BOOMED OUT OVER THE TERRIFIED CROWD —
COME, CITIZENS, LET US NOT BE CHILDISH ABOUT THIS. TODAY IS A DAY FOR CELEBRATION!
QUEUE STARTS HERE
NEVER BEFORE HAS A RULER SENTENCED HIS ENTIRE POPULATION TO DEATH!
THIS IS A GREAT DAY — THE GREATEST DAY IN HISTORY — AND YOU ARE LUCKY TO BE TAKING PART!

Credit Card: SCRIPT ROBOT JOHN HOWARD ART ROBOT BOLLAND/LEACH LETTERING ROBOT THOMAS

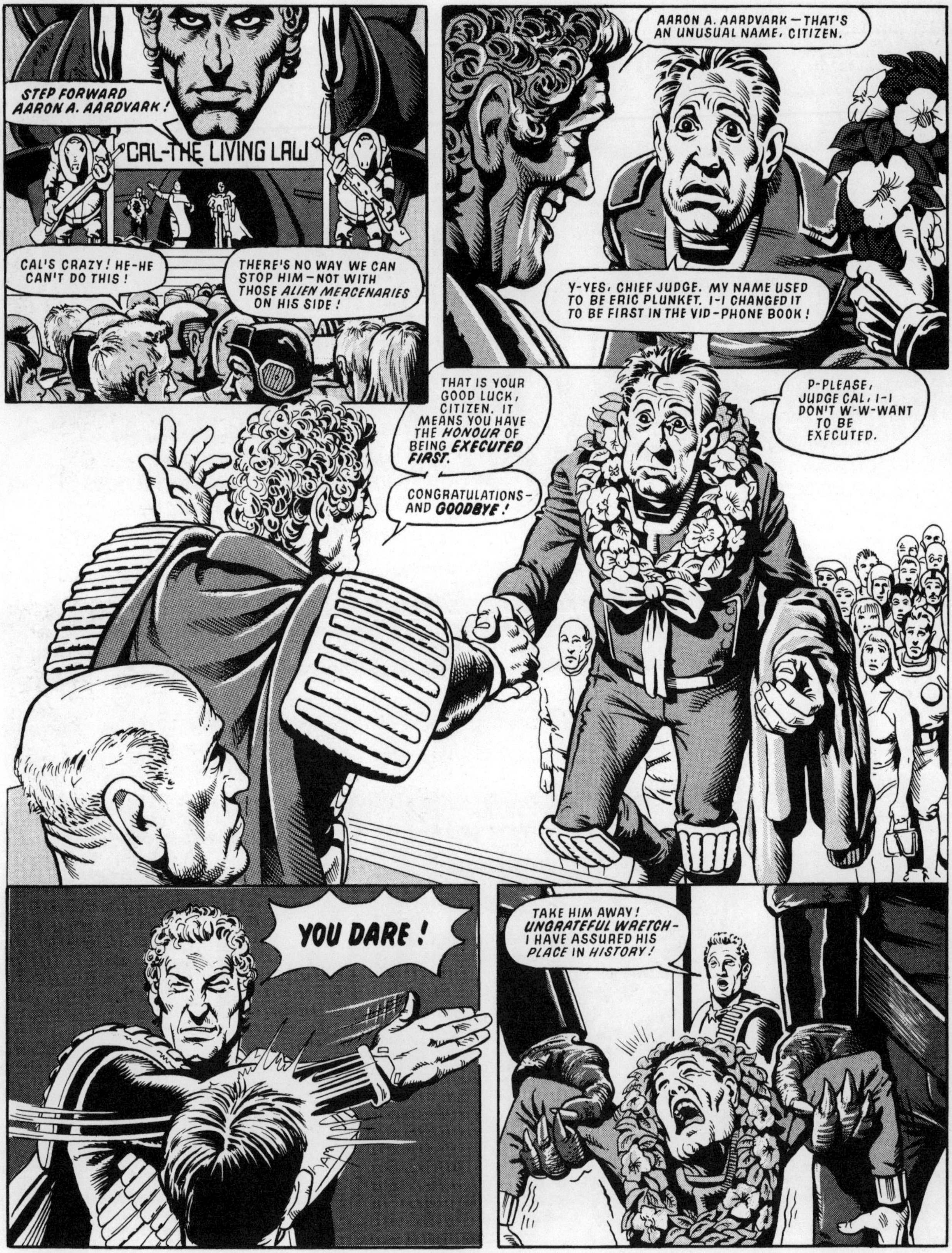
STEP FORWARD AARON A. AARDVARK!
CAL-THE LIVING LAW
CAL'S CRAZY! HE-HE CAN'T DO THIS!
THERE'S NO WAY WE CAN STOP HIM—NOT WITH THOSE ALIEN MERCENARIES ON HIS SIDE!
AARON A. AARDVARK—THAT'S AN UNUSUAL NAME, CITIZEN.
Y-YES, CHIEF JUDGE. MY NAME USED TO BE ERIC PLUNKET. I-I CHANGED IT TO BE FIRST IN THE VID-PHONE BOOK!
THAT IS YOUR GOOD LUCK, CITIZEN. IT MEANS YOU HAVE THE HONOUR OF BEING EXECUTED FIRST.
CONGRATULATIONS-AND GOODBYE!
P-PLEASE, JUDGE CAL, I-I DON'T W-W-WANT TO BE EXECUTED.
YOU DARE!
TAKE HIM AWAY! UNGRATEFUL WRETCH-I HAVE ASSURED HIS PLACE IN HISTORY!

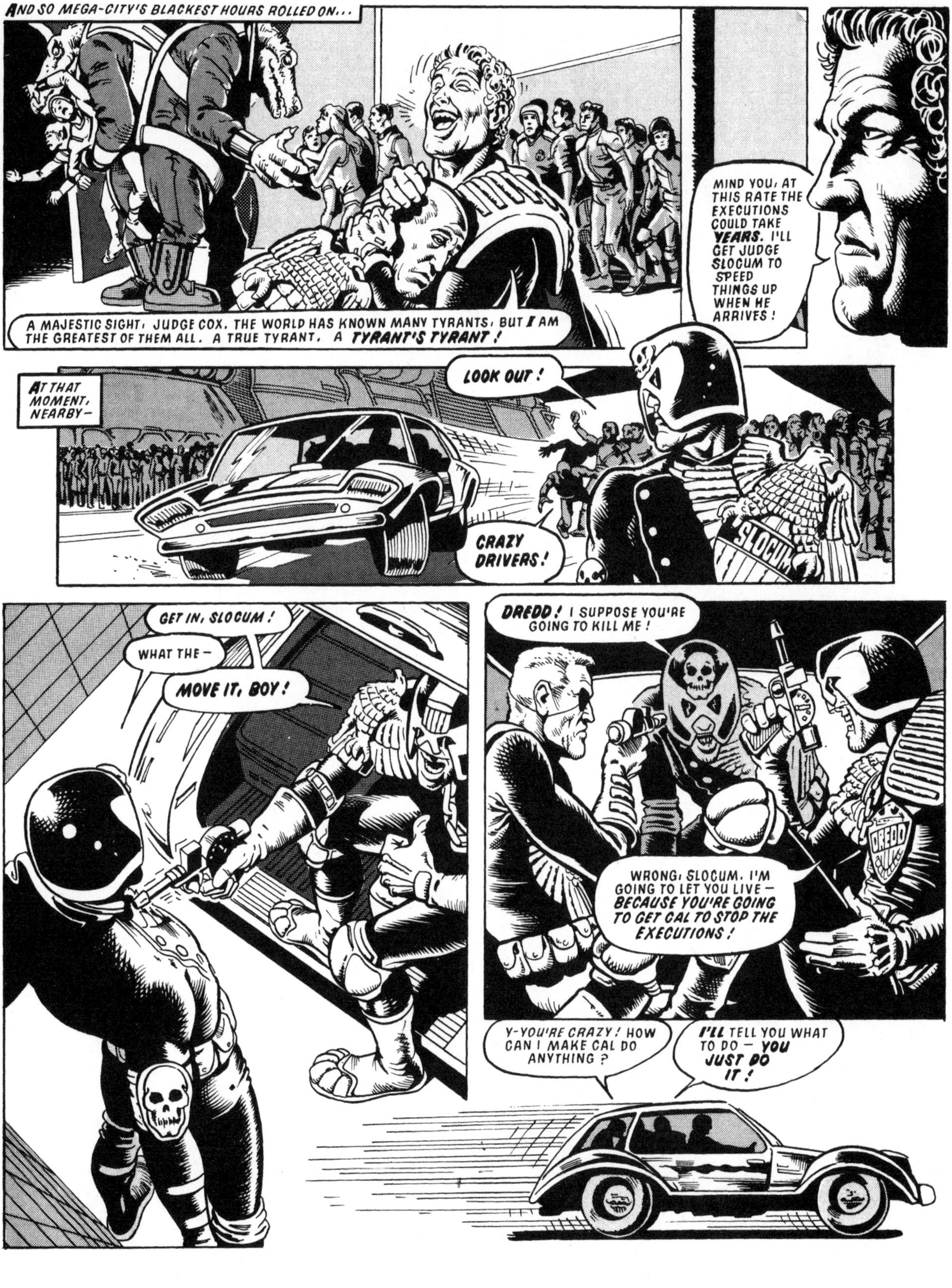

AND SO MEGA-CITY'S BLACKEST HOURS ROLLED ON...
A MAJESTIC SIGHT, JUDGE COX. THE WORLD HAS KNOWN MANY TYRANTS, BUT I AM THE GREATEST OF THEM ALL. A TRUE TYRANT. A TYRANT'S TYRANT!
MIND YOU, AT THIS RATE THE EXECUTIONS COULD TAKE YEARS. I'LL GET JUDGE SLOCUM TO SPEED THINGS UP WHEN HE ARRIVES!
AT THAT MOMENT, NEARBY—
LOOK OUT!
CRAZY DRIVERS!
SLOCUM
GET IN, SLOCUM!
WHAT THE—
MOVE IT, BOY!
DREDD! I SUPPOSE YOU'RE GOING TO KILL ME!
WRONG, SLOCUM. I'M GOING TO LET YOU LIVE— BECAUSE YOU'RE GOING TO GET CAL TO STOP THE EXECUTIONS!
DREDD
Y-YOU'RE CRAZY! HOW CAN I MAKE CAL DO ANYTHING?
I'LL TELL YOU WHAT TO DO — YOU JUST DO IT!

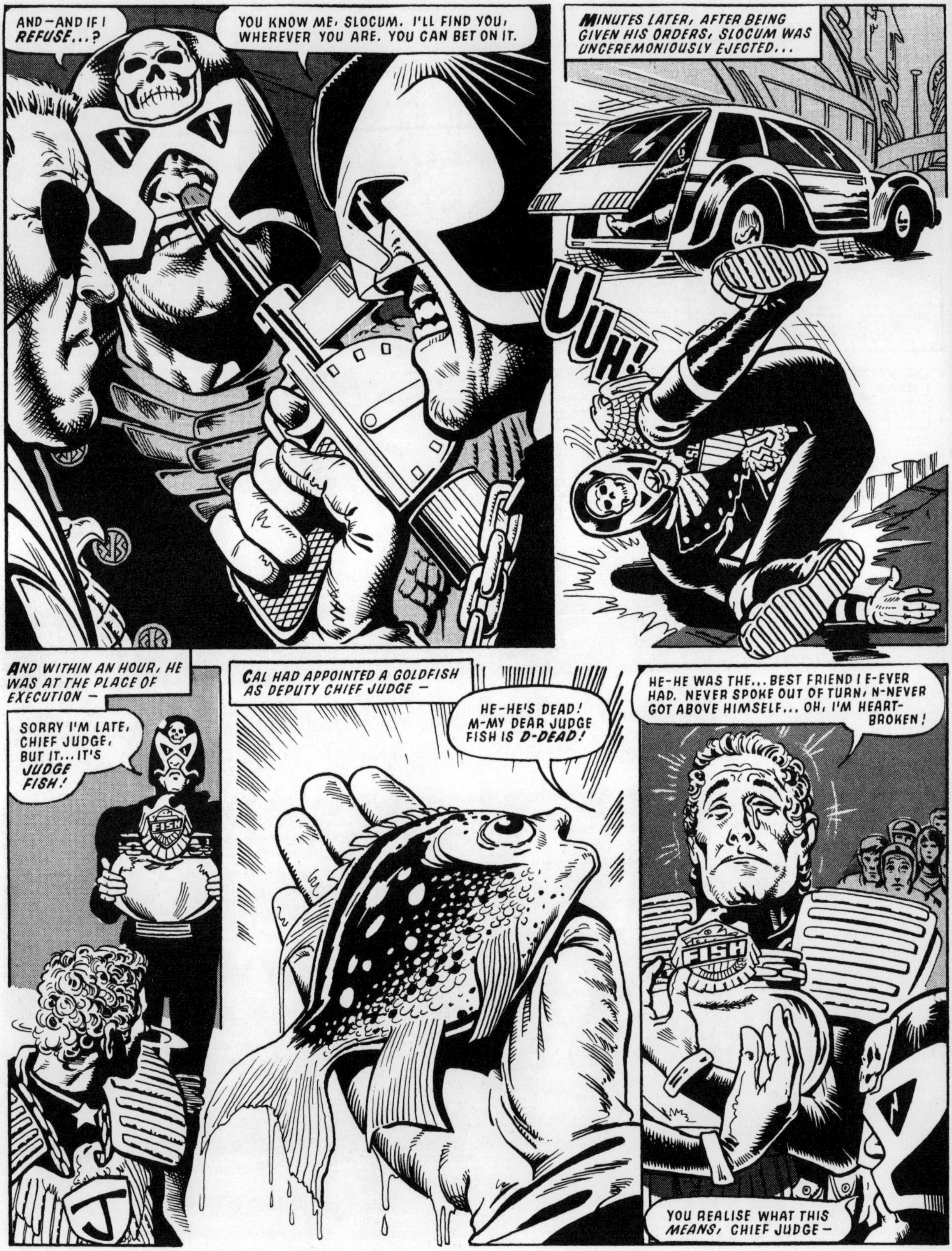
AND—AND IF I REFUSE...?
YOU KNOW ME, SLOCUM. I'LL FIND YOU, WHEREVER YOU ARE. YOU CAN BET ON IT.
MINUTES LATER, AFTER BEING GIVEN HIS ORDERS, SLOCUM WAS UNCEREMONIOUSLY EJECTED...
UUUH!
AND WITHIN AN HOUR, HE WAS AT THE PLACE OF EXECUTION—
SORRY I'M LATE, CHIEF JUDGE, BUT IT... IT'S JUDGE FISH!
FISH
CAL HAD APPOINTED A GOLDFISH AS DEPUTY CHIEF JUDGE—
HE-HE'S DEAD! M-MY DEAR JUDGE FISH IS D-DEAD!
HE-HE WAS THE... BEST FRIEND I E-EVER HAD. NEVER SPOKE OUT OF TURN, N-NEVER GOT ABOVE HIMSELF... OH, I'M HEART-BROKEN!
FISH
YOU REALISE WHAT THIS MEANS, CHIEF JUDGE—

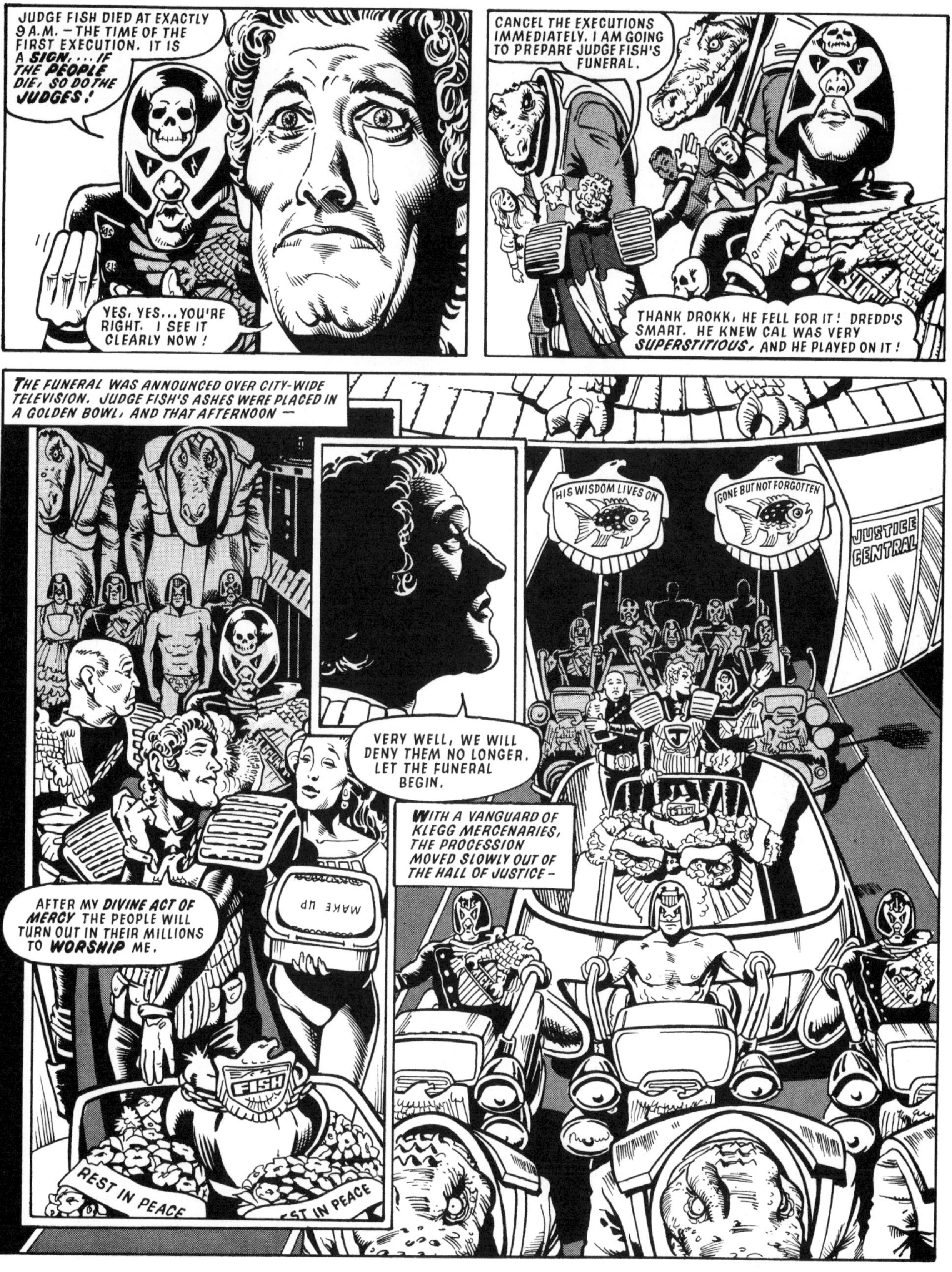
JUDGE FISH DIED AT EXACTLY 9 A.M. — THE TIME OF THE FIRST EXECUTION. IT IS A SIGN, ... IF THE PEOPLE DIE, SO DO THE JUDGES!
YES, YES... YOU'RE RIGHT. I SEE IT CLEARLY NOW!
CANCEL THE EXECUTIONS IMMEDIATELY. I AM GOING TO PREPARE JUDGE FISH'S FUNERAL.
THANK DROKK, HE FELL FOR IT! DREDD'S SMART. HE KNEW CAL WAS VERY SUPERSTITIOUS, AND HE PLAYED ON IT!
THE FUNERAL WAS ANNOUNCED OVER CITY-WIDE TELEVISION. JUDGE FISH'S ASHES WERE PLACED IN A GOLDEN BOWL, AND THAT AFTERNOON —
VERY WELL, WE WILL DENY THEM NO LONGER. LET THE FUNERAL BEGIN.
AFTER MY DIVINE ACT OF MERCY THE PEOPLE WILL TURN OUT IN THEIR MILLIONS TO WORSHIP ME.
MAKE UP
FISH
REST IN PEACE
REST IN PEACE
HIS WISDOM LIVES ON
GONE BUT NOT FORGOTTEN
JUSTICE CENTRAL
WITH A VANGUARD OF KLEGG MERCENARIES, THE PROCESSION MOVED SLOWLY OUT OF THE HALL OF JUSTICE —

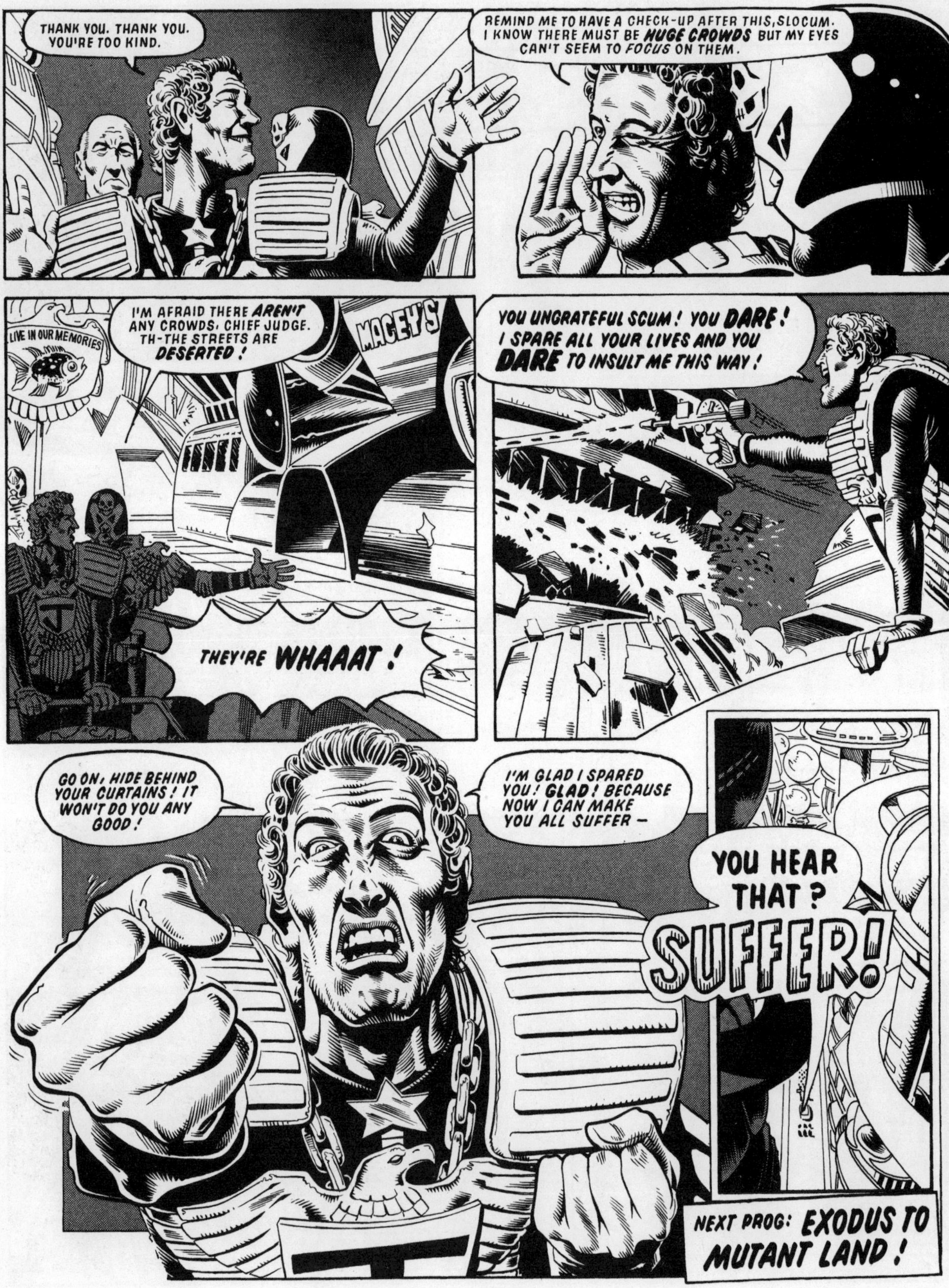
THANK YOU. THANK YOU. YOU'RE TOO KIND.
REMIND ME TO HAVE A CHECK-UP AFTER THIS, SLOCUM. I KNOW THERE MUST BE HUGE CROWDS BUT MY EYES CAN'T SEEM TO FOCUS ON THEM.
LIVE IN OUR MEMORIES
MACEY'S
I'M AFRAID THERE AREN'T ANY CROWDS, CHIEF JUDGE. TH-THE STREETS ARE DESERTED!
THEY'RE WHAAAT!
YOU UNGRATEFUL SCUM! YOU DARE! I SPARE ALL YOUR LIVES AND YOU DARE TO INSULT ME THIS WAY!
GO ON, HIDE BEHIND YOUR CURTAINS! IT WON'T DO YOU ANY GOOD!
I'M GLAD I SPARED YOU! GLAD! BECAUSE NOW I CAN MAKE YOU ALL SUFFER —
YOU HEAR THAT? SUFFER!
NEXT PROG: EXODUS TO MUTANT LAND!

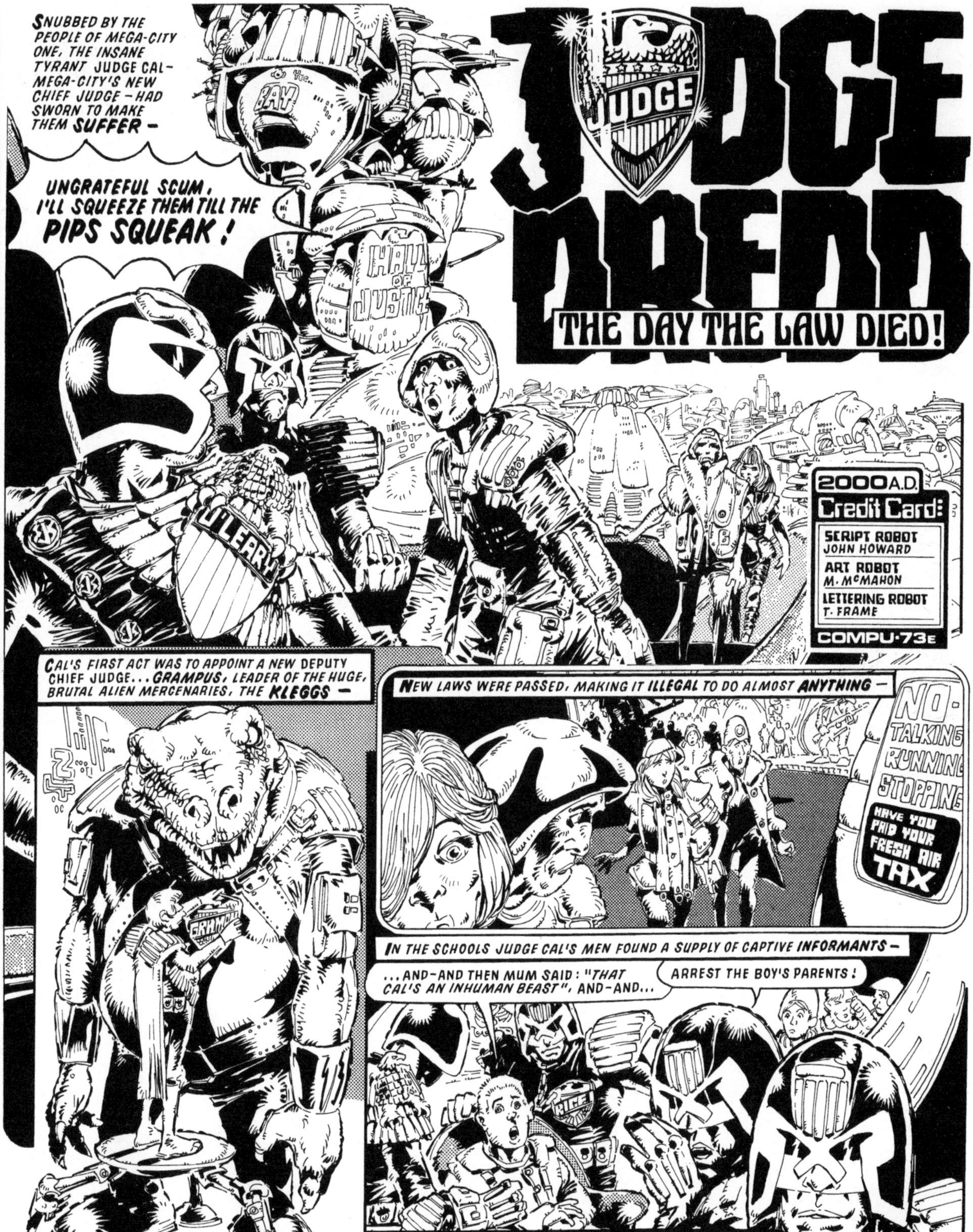
SNUBBED BY THE PEOPLE OF MEGA-CITY ONE, THE INSANE TYRANT JUDGE CAL–MEGA-CITY'S NEW CHIEF JUDGE–HAD SWORN TO MAKE THEM SUFFER–
UNGRATEFUL SCUM, I'LL SQUEEZE THEM TILL THE PIPS SQUEAK!
JUDGE
JUDGE DREDD
THE DAY THE LAW DIED!
HALL OF JUSTICE
O'LEARY
2000 A.D. Credit Card:
SCRIPT ROBOT JOHN HOWARD
ART ROBOT M. McMAHON
LETTERING ROBOT T. FRAME
COMPU-73E
CAL'S FIRST ACT WAS TO APPOINT A NEW DEPUTY CHIEF JUDGE... GRAMPUS, LEADER OF THE HUGE, BRUTAL ALIEN MERCENARIES, THE KLEGGS–
GRAMPUS
NEW LAWS WERE PASSED, MAKING IT ILLEGAL TO DO ALMOST ANYTHING–
NO– TALKING RUNNING STOPPING
HAVE YOU PAID YOUR FRESH AIR TAX
IN THE SCHOOLS JUDGE CAL'S MEN FOUND A SUPPLY OF CAPTIVE INFORMANTS–
...AND–AND THEN MUM SAID: "THAT CAL'S AN INHUMAN BEAST", AND–AND...
ARREST THE BOY'S PARENTS!
FINALLY, THE CITY COULD STAND NO MORE. FOR THE TORTURED PEOPLE THERE WAS ONLY ONE ESCAPE...

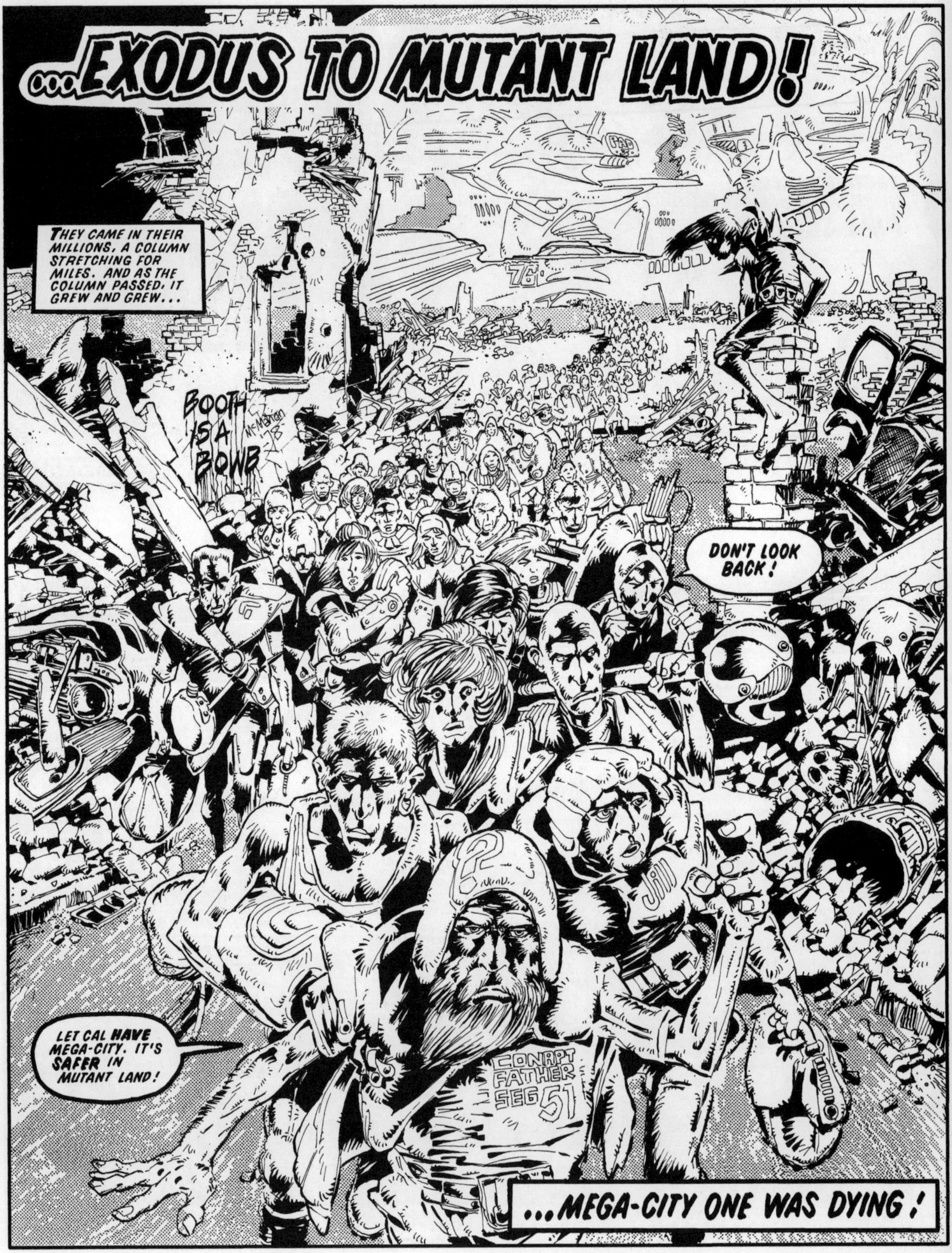
...EXODUS TO MUTANT LAND!
THEY CAME IN THEIR MILLIONS, A COLUMN STRETCHING FOR MILES. AND AS THE COLUMN PASSED, IT GREW AND GREW...
DON'T LOOK BACK!
LET CAL HAVE MEGA-CITY. IT'S SAFER IN MUTANT LAND!
...MEGA-CITY ONE WAS DYING!

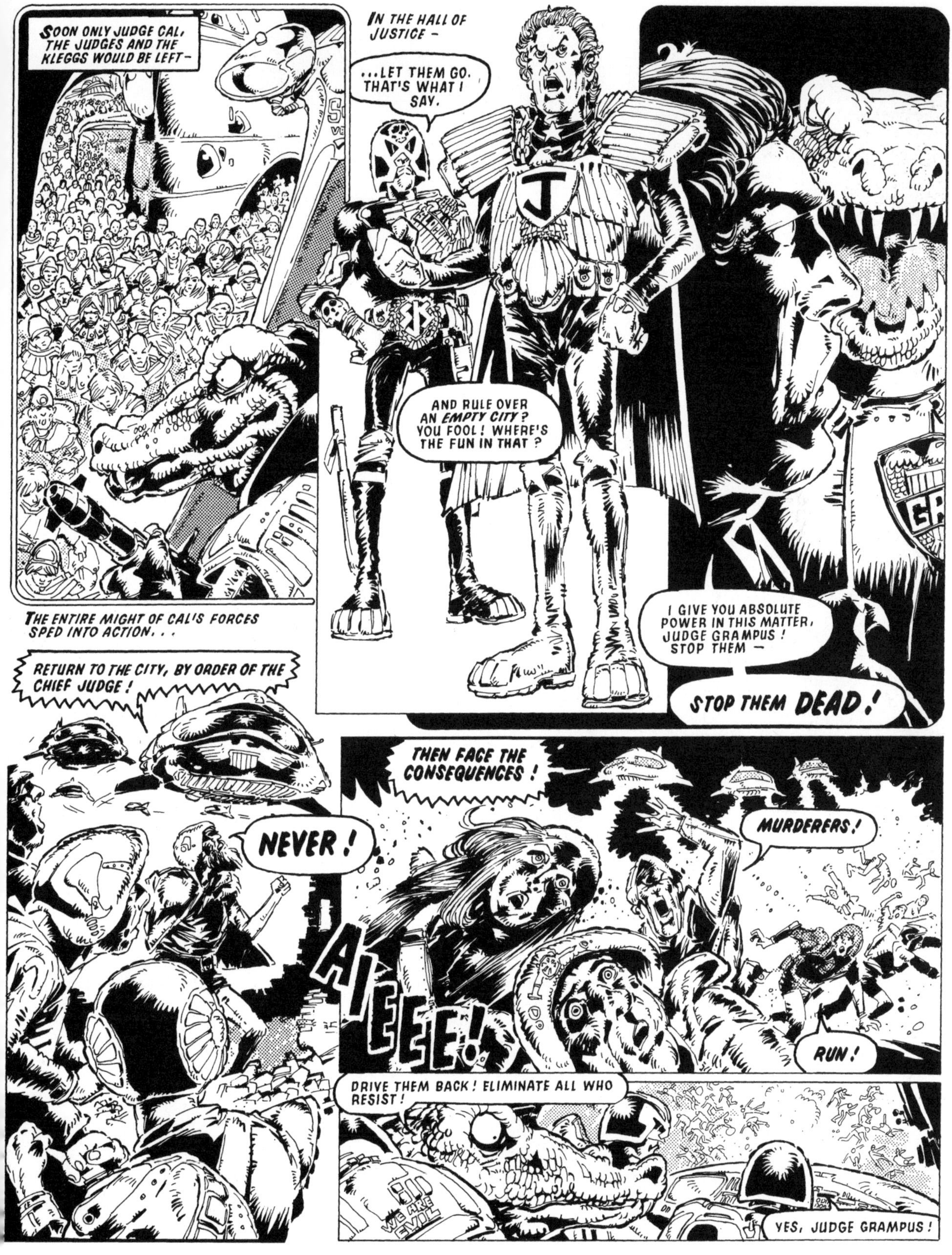
SOON ONLY JUDGE CAL, THE JUDGES AND THE KLEGGS WOULD BE LEFT –
IN THE HALL OF JUSTICE –
...LET THEM GO. THAT'S WHAT I SAY.
AND RULE OVER AN EMPTY CITY? YOU FOOL! WHERE'S THE FUN IN THAT?
I GIVE YOU ABSOLUTE POWER IN THIS MATTER, JUDGE GRAMPUS! STOP THEM –
STOP THEM DEAD!
THE ENTIRE MIGHT OF CAL'S FORCES SPED INTO ACTION...
RETURN TO THE CITY, BY ORDER OF THE CHIEF JUDGE!
NEVER!
THEN FACE THE CONSEQUENCES!
MURDERERS!
AIEEE!
RUN!
DRIVE THEM BACK! ELIMINATE ALL WHO RESIST!
WE ARE EVIL
YES, JUDGE GRAMPUS!

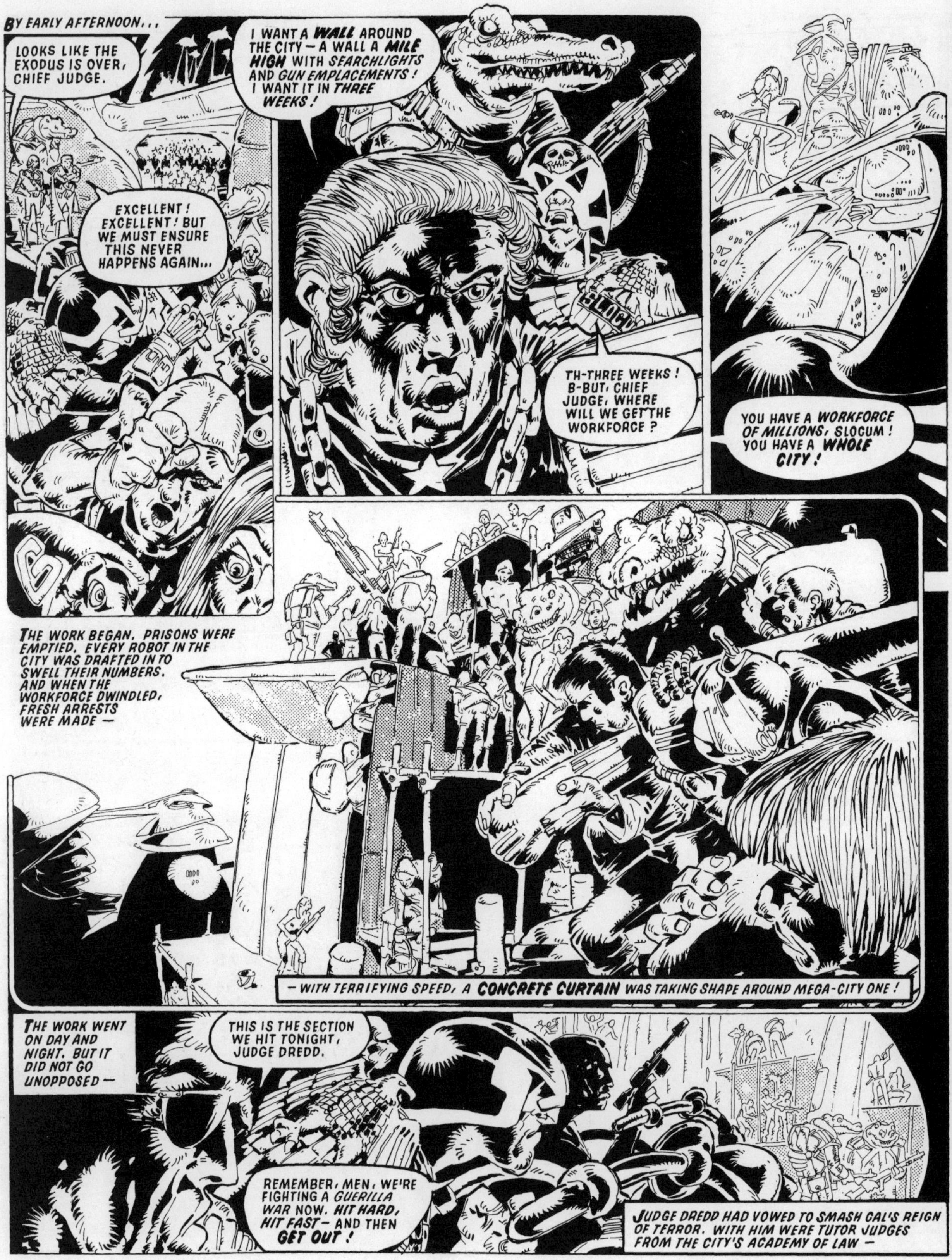
BY EARLY AFTERNOON...
LOOKS LIKE THE EXODUS IS OVER, CHIEF JUDGE.
EXCELLENT! EXCELLENT! BUT WE MUST ENSURE THIS NEVER HAPPENS AGAIN...
I WANT A WALL AROUND THE CITY — A WALL A MILE HIGH WITH SEARCHLIGHTS AND GUN EMPLACEMENTS! I WANT IT IN THREE WEEKS!
TH-THREE WEEKS! B-BUT, CHIEF JUDGE, WHERE WILL WE GET THE WORKFORCE?
YOU HAVE A WORKFORCE OF MILLIONS, SLOCUM! YOU HAVE A WHOLE CITY!
THE WORK BEGAN. PRISONS WERE EMPTIED. EVERY ROBOT IN THE CITY WAS DRAFTED IN TO SWELL THEIR NUMBERS. AND WHEN THE WORKFORCE DWINDLED, FRESH ARRESTS WERE MADE —
— WITH TERRIFYING SPEED, A CONCRETE CURTAIN WAS TAKING SHAPE AROUND MEGA-CITY ONE!
THE WORK WENT ON DAY AND NIGHT. BUT IT DID NOT GO UNOPPOSED —
THIS IS THE SECTION WE HIT TONIGHT, JUDGE DREDD.
REMEMBER, MEN, WE'RE FIGHTING A GUERILLA WAR NOW. HIT HARD, HIT FAST — AND THEN GET OUT!
JUDGE DREDD HAD VOWED TO SMASH CAL'S REIGN OF TERROR. WITH HIM WERE TUTOR JUDGES FROM THE CITY'S ACADEMY OF LAW —

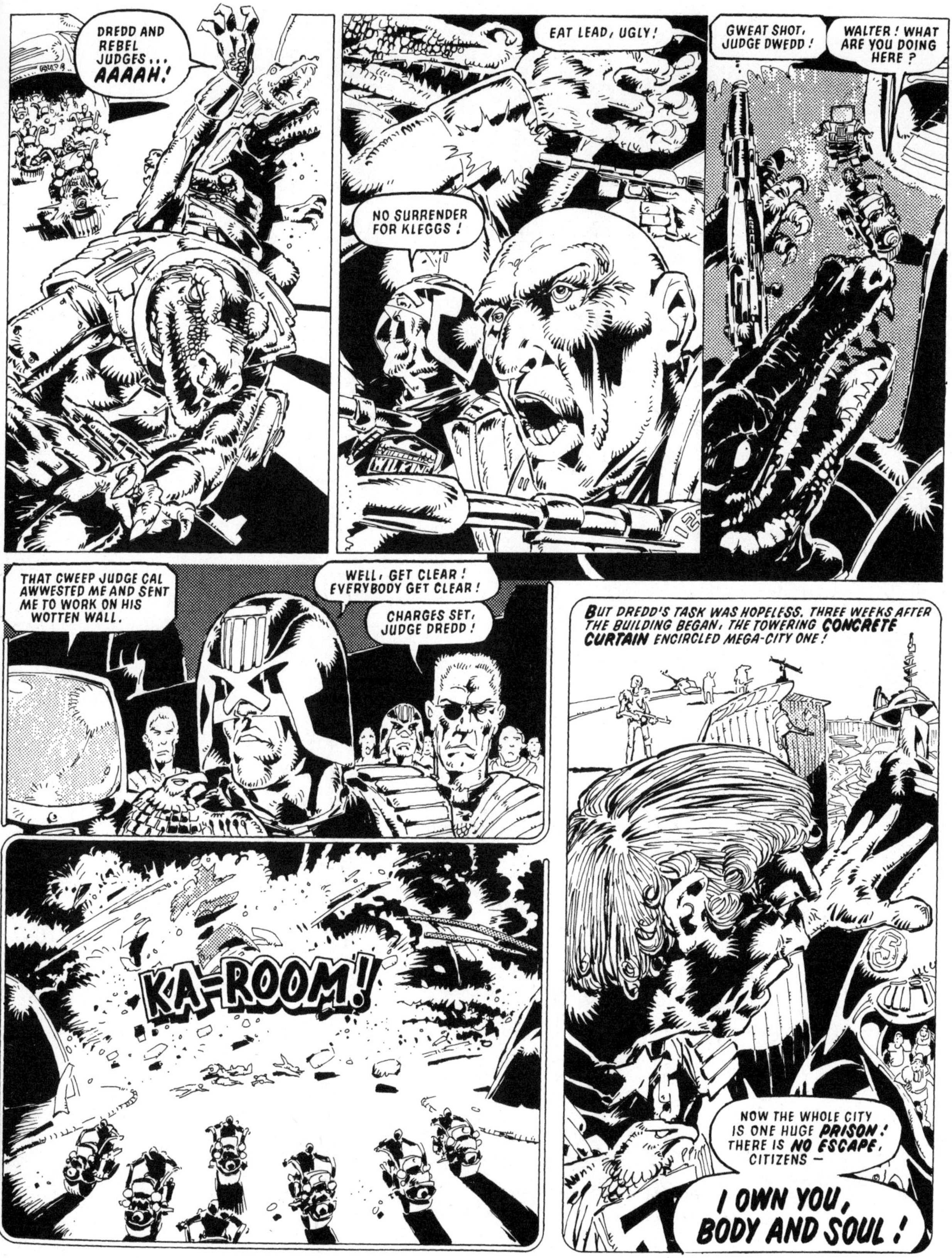

DREDD AND REBEL JUDGES... AAAAH!
EAT LEAD, UGLY!
NO SURRENDER FOR KLEGGS!
GWEAT SHOT, JUDGE DWEDD!
WALTER! WHAT ARE YOU DOING HERE?
THAT CWEEP JUDGE CAL AWWESTED ME AND SENT ME TO WORK ON HIS WOTTEN WALL.
WELL, GET CLEAR! EVERYBODY GET CLEAR!
CHARGES SET, JUDGE DREDD!
KA-ROOM!
BUT DREDD'S TASK WAS HOPELESS. THREE WEEKS AFTER THE BUILDING BEGAN, THE TOWERING CONCRETE CURTAIN ENCIRCLED MEGA-CITY ONE!
NOW THE WHOLE CITY IS ONE HUGE PRISON! THERE IS NO ESCAPE, CITIZENS —
I OWN YOU, BODY AND SOUL!

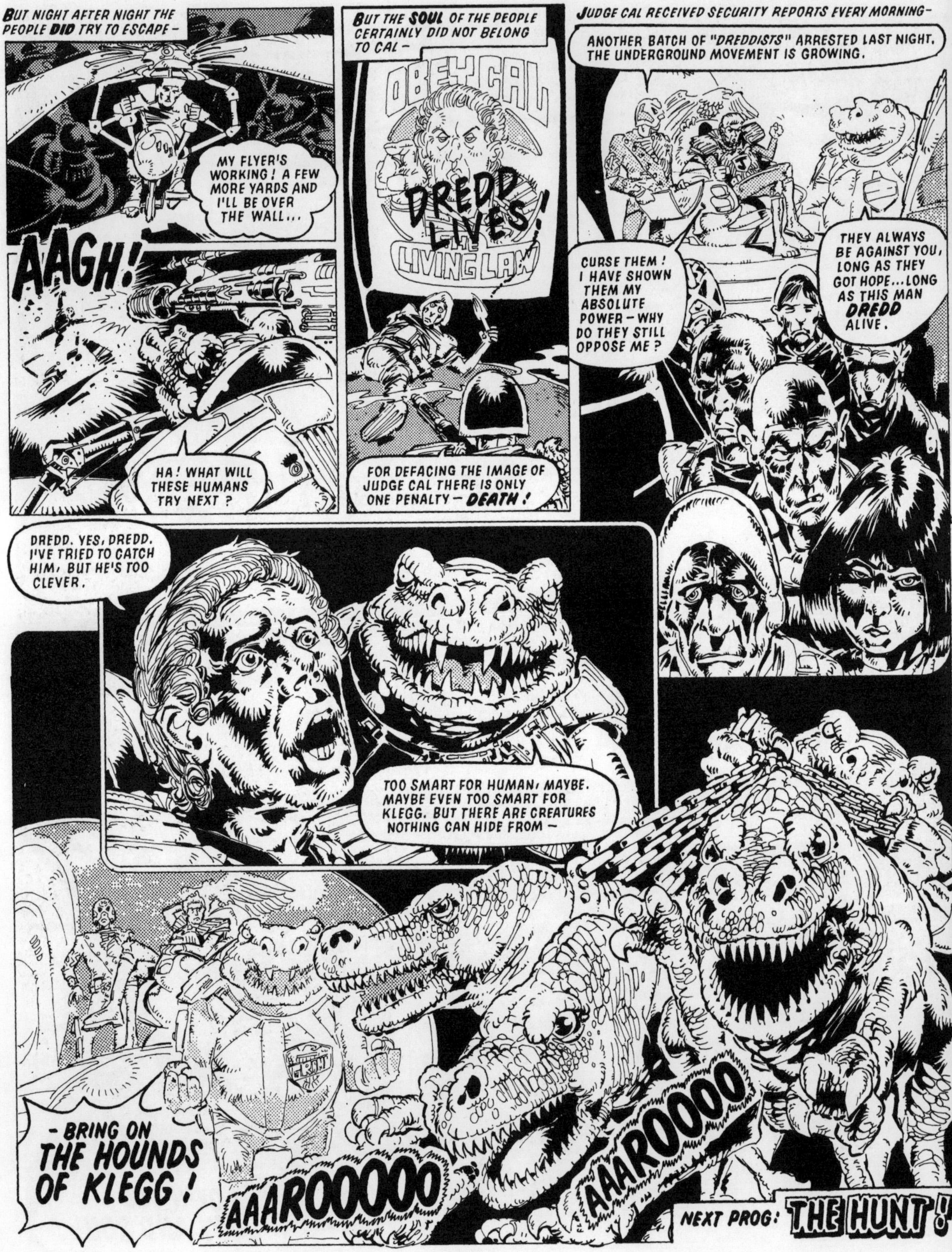

BUT NIGHT AFTER NIGHT THE PEOPLE DID TRY TO ESCAPE –
MY FLYER'S WORKING! A FEW MORE YARDS AND I'LL BE OVER THE WALL...
AAGH!
HA! WHAT WILL THESE HUMANS TRY NEXT?
BUT THE SOUL OF THE PEOPLE CERTAINLY DID NOT BELONG TO CAL –
OBEY CAL
DREDD LIVES!
THE LIVING LAW
FOR DEFACING THE IMAGE OF JUDGE CAL THERE IS ONLY ONE PENALTY – DEATH!
JUDGE CAL RECEIVED SECURITY REPORTS EVERY MORNING –
ANOTHER BATCH OF "DREDDISTS" ARRESTED LAST NIGHT. THE UNDERGROUND MOVEMENT IS GROWING.
CURSE THEM! I HAVE SHOWN THEM MY ABSOLUTE POWER – WHY DO THEY STILL OPPOSE ME?
THEY ALWAYS BE AGAINST YOU, LONG AS THEY GOT HOPE... LONG AS THIS MAN DREDD ALIVE.
DREDD. YES, DREDD. I'VE TRIED TO CATCH HIM, BUT HE'S TOO CLEVER.
TOO SMART FOR HUMAN, MAYBE. MAYBE EVEN TOO SMART FOR KLEGG. BUT THERE ARE CREATURES NOTHING CAN HIDE FROM –
– BRING ON THE HOUNDS OF KLEGG!
AAAROOOOOO
AAAROOOO
NEXT PROG: THE HUNT!

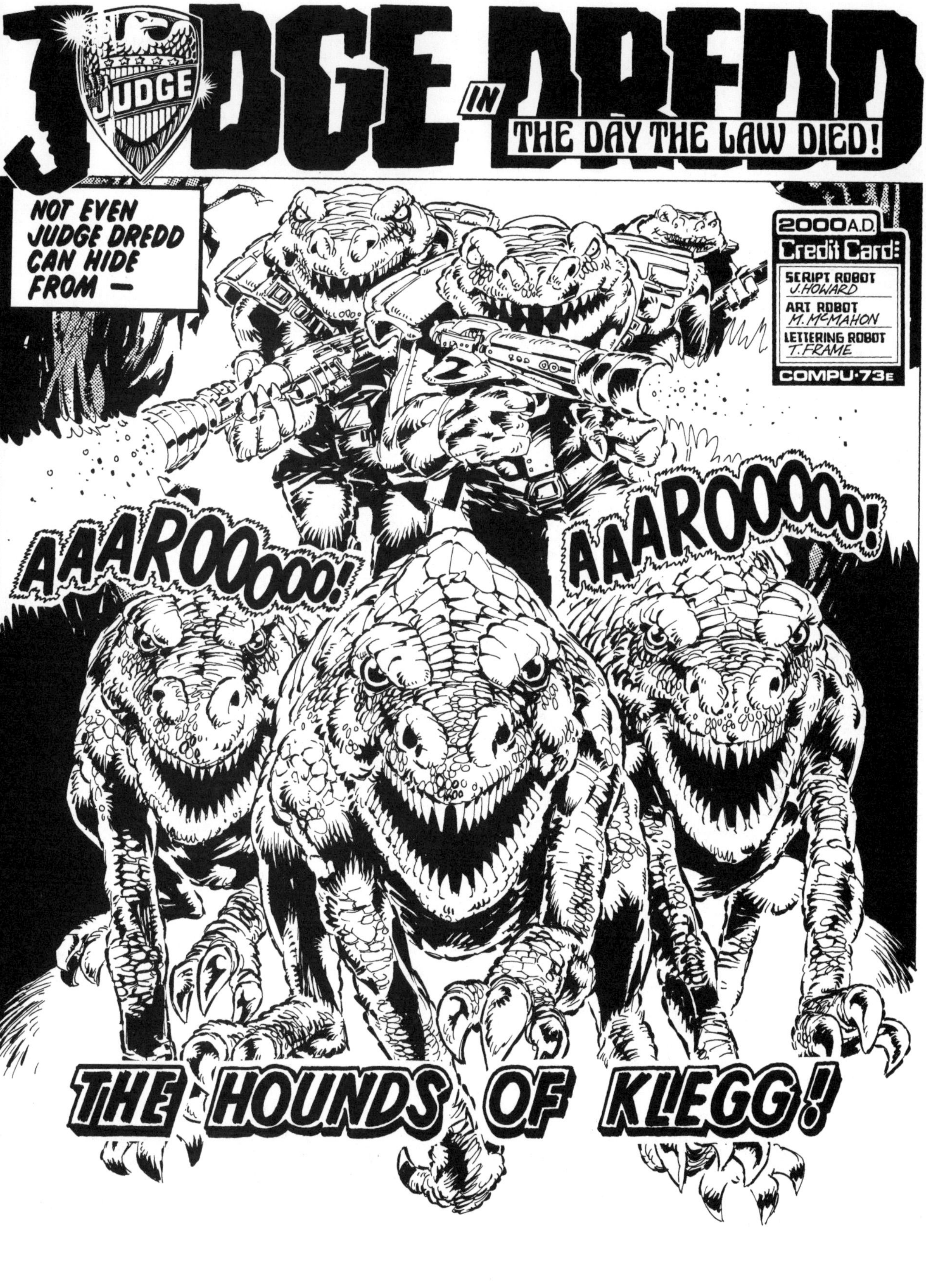

JUDGE DREDD
JUDGE
IN
THE DAY THE LAW DIED!
NOT EVEN JUDGE DREDD CAN HIDE FROM —
2000 A.D. Credit Card:
SCRIPT ROBOT J. HOWARD
ART ROBOT M. McMAHON
LETTERING ROBOT T. FRAME
COMPU-73E
AAAROOOOOO!
AAAROOOOOO!
THE HOUNDS OF KLEGG!

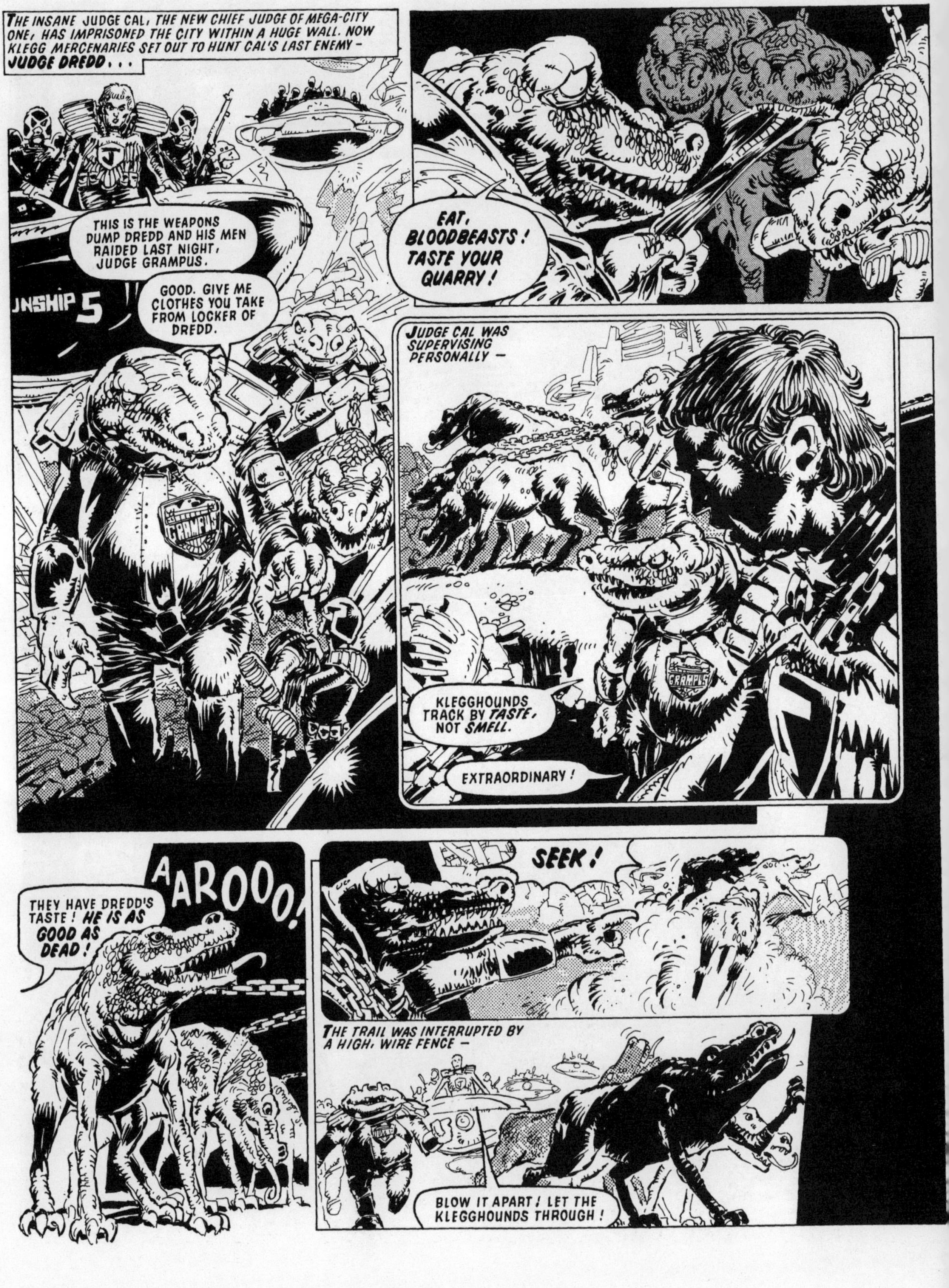
THE INSANE JUDGE CAL, THE NEW CHIEF JUDGE OF MEGA-CITY ONE, HAS IMPRISONED THE CITY WITHIN A HUGE WALL. NOW KLEGG MERCENARIES SET OUT TO HUNT CAL'S LAST ENEMY - JUDGE DREDD . . .
THIS IS THE WEAPONS DUMP DREDD AND HIS MEN RAIDED LAST NIGHT, JUDGE GRAMPUS.
GOOD. GIVE ME CLOTHES YOU TAKE FROM LOCKER OF DREDD.
UNSHIP 5
GRAMPUS
EAT, BLOODBEASTS! TASTE YOUR QUARRY!
JUDGE CAL WAS SUPERVISING PERSONALLY -
GRAMPUS
KLEGGHOUNDS TRACK BY TASTE, NOT SMELL.
EXTRAORDINARY!
AAROOO!
THEY HAVE DREDD'S TASTE! HE IS AS GOOD AS DEAD!
SEEK!
THE TRAIL WAS INTERRUPTED BY A HIGH, WIRE FENCE -
BLOW IT APART! LET THE KLEGGHOUNDS THROUGH!

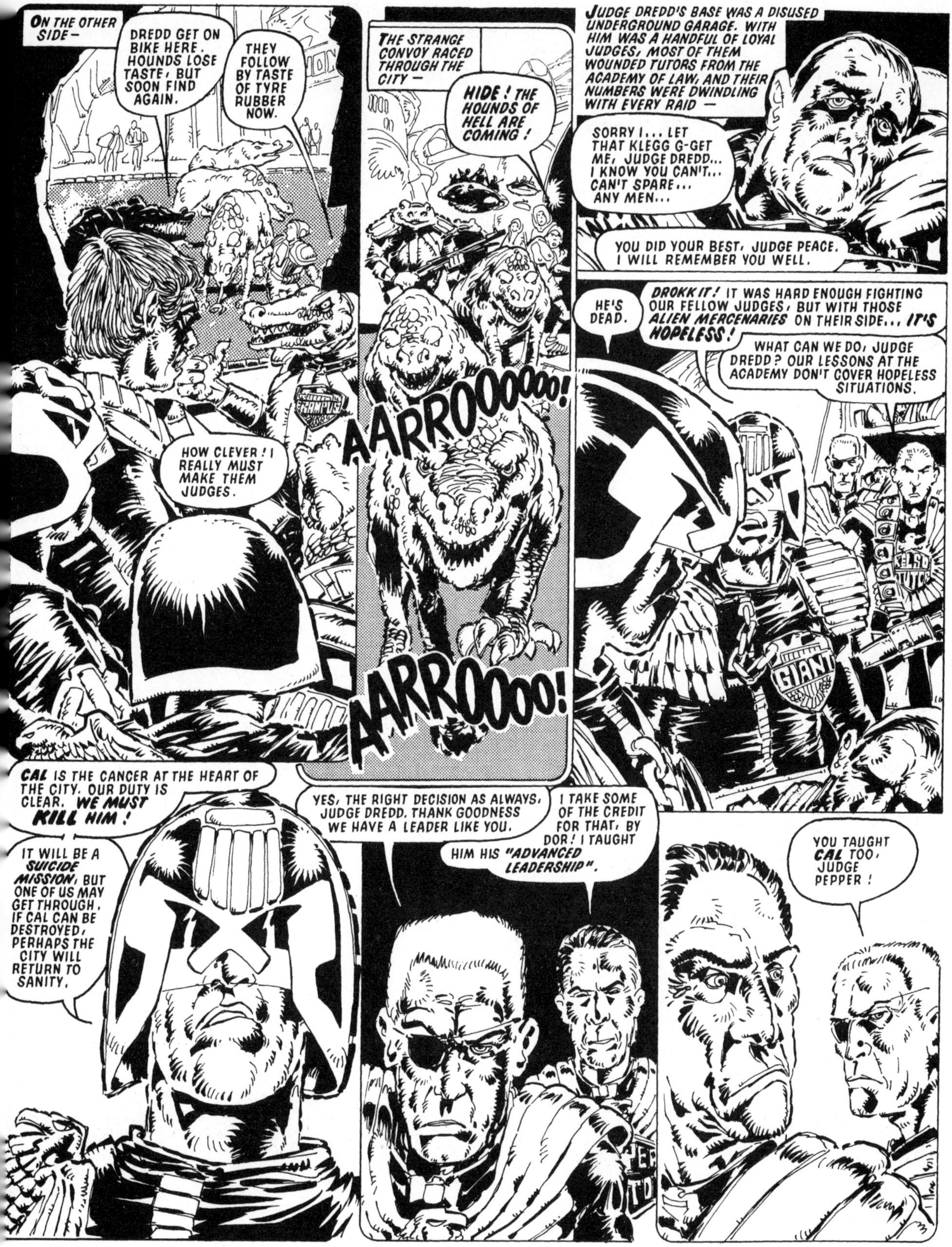

ON THE OTHER SIDE—
DREDD GET ON BIKE HERE. HOUNDS LOSE TASTE, BUT SOON FIND AGAIN.
THEY FOLLOW BY TASTE OF TYRE RUBBER NOW.
HOW CLEVER! I REALLY MUST MAKE THEM JUDGES.
THE STRANGE CONVOY RACED THROUGH THE CITY—
HIDE! THE HOUNDS OF HELL ARE COMING!
AARROOOOOO!
AARROOOO!
JUDGE DREDD'S BASE WAS A DISUSED UNDERGROUND GARAGE. WITH HIM WAS A HANDFUL OF LOYAL JUDGES, MOST OF THEM WOUNDED TUTORS FROM THE ACADEMY OF LAW, AND THEIR NUMBERS WERE DWINDLING WITH EVERY RAID—
SORRY I... LET THAT KLEGG G-GET ME, JUDGE DREDD... I KNOW YOU CAN'T... CAN'T SPARE... ANY MEN...
YOU DID YOUR BEST, JUDGE PEACE. I WILL REMEMBER YOU WELL.
HE'S DEAD.
DROKK IT! IT WAS HARD ENOUGH FIGHTING OUR FELLOW JUDGES, BUT WITH THOSE ALIEN MERCENARIES ON THEIR SIDE... IT'S HOPELESS!
WHAT CAN WE DO, JUDGE DREDD? OUR LESSONS AT THE ACADEMY DON'T COVER HOPELESS SITUATIONS.
GIANT
CAL IS THE CANCER AT THE HEART OF THE CITY. OUR DUTY IS CLEAR. WE MUST KILL HIM!
IT WILL BE A SUICIDE MISSION, BUT ONE OF US MAY GET THROUGH. IF CAL CAN BE DESTROYED, PERHAPS THE CITY WILL RETURN TO SANITY.
YES, THE RIGHT DECISION AS ALWAYS, JUDGE DREDD. THANK GOODNESS WE HAVE A LEADER LIKE YOU.
I TAKE SOME OF THE CREDIT FOR THAT, BY DOR! I TAUGHT HIM HIS "ADVANCED LEADERSHIP".
YOU TAUGHT CAL TOO, JUDGE PEPPER!

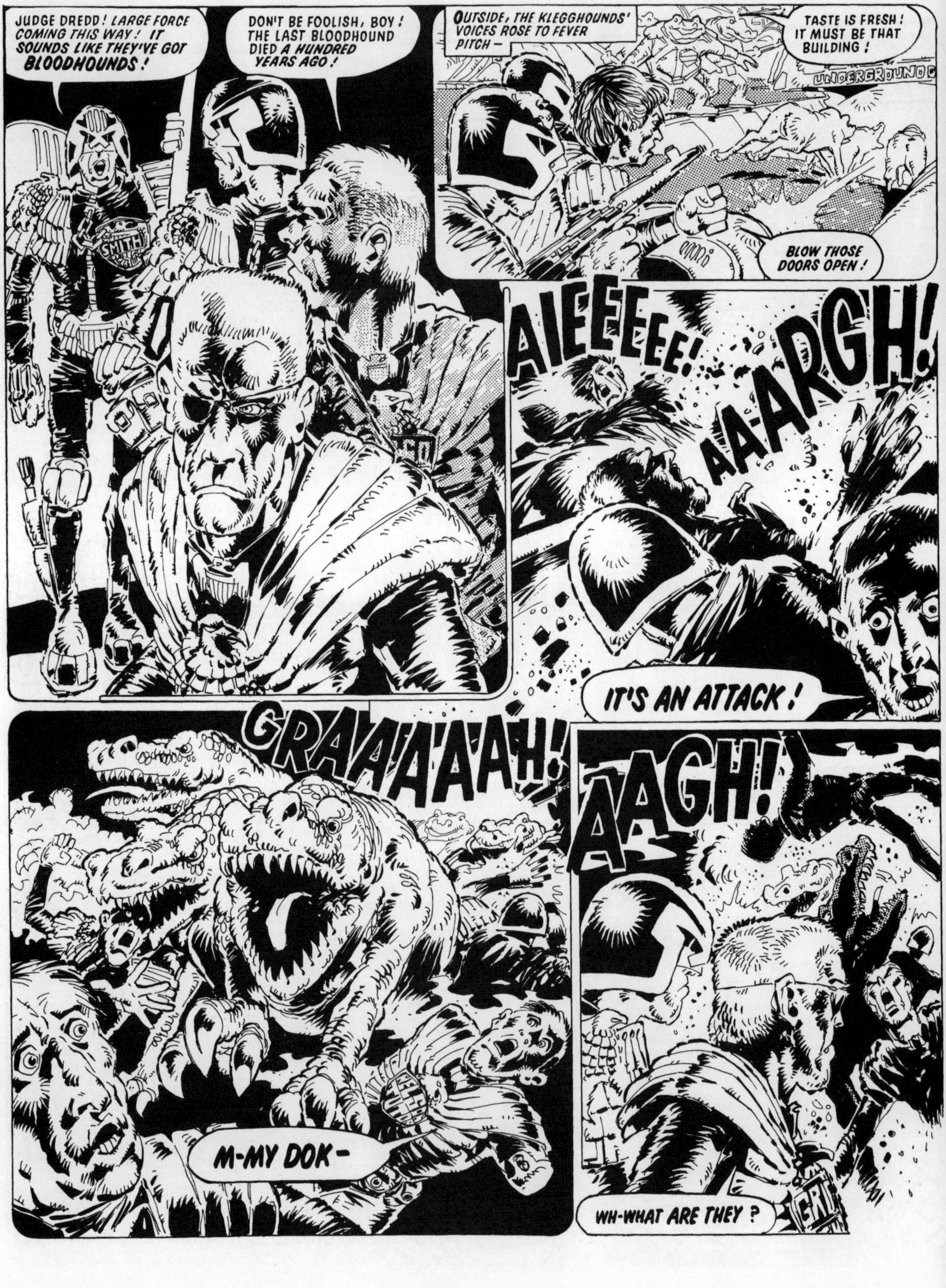

JUDGE DREDD! LARGE FORCE COMING THIS WAY! IT SOUNDS LIKE THEY'VE GOT BLOODHOUNDS!
DON'T BE FOOLISH, BOY! THE LAST BLOODHOUND DIED A HUNDRED YEARS AGO!
SMITH
OUTSIDE, THE KLEGGHOUNDS' VOICES ROSE TO FEVER PITCH –
TASTE IS FRESH! IT MUST BE THAT BUILDING!
UNDERGROUND
BLOW THOSE DOORS OPEN!
AIEEEEEE!
AAARGH!
IT'S AN ATTACK!
GRAAAAAAH!
M-MY DOK –
AAGH!
WH-WHAT ARE THEY?

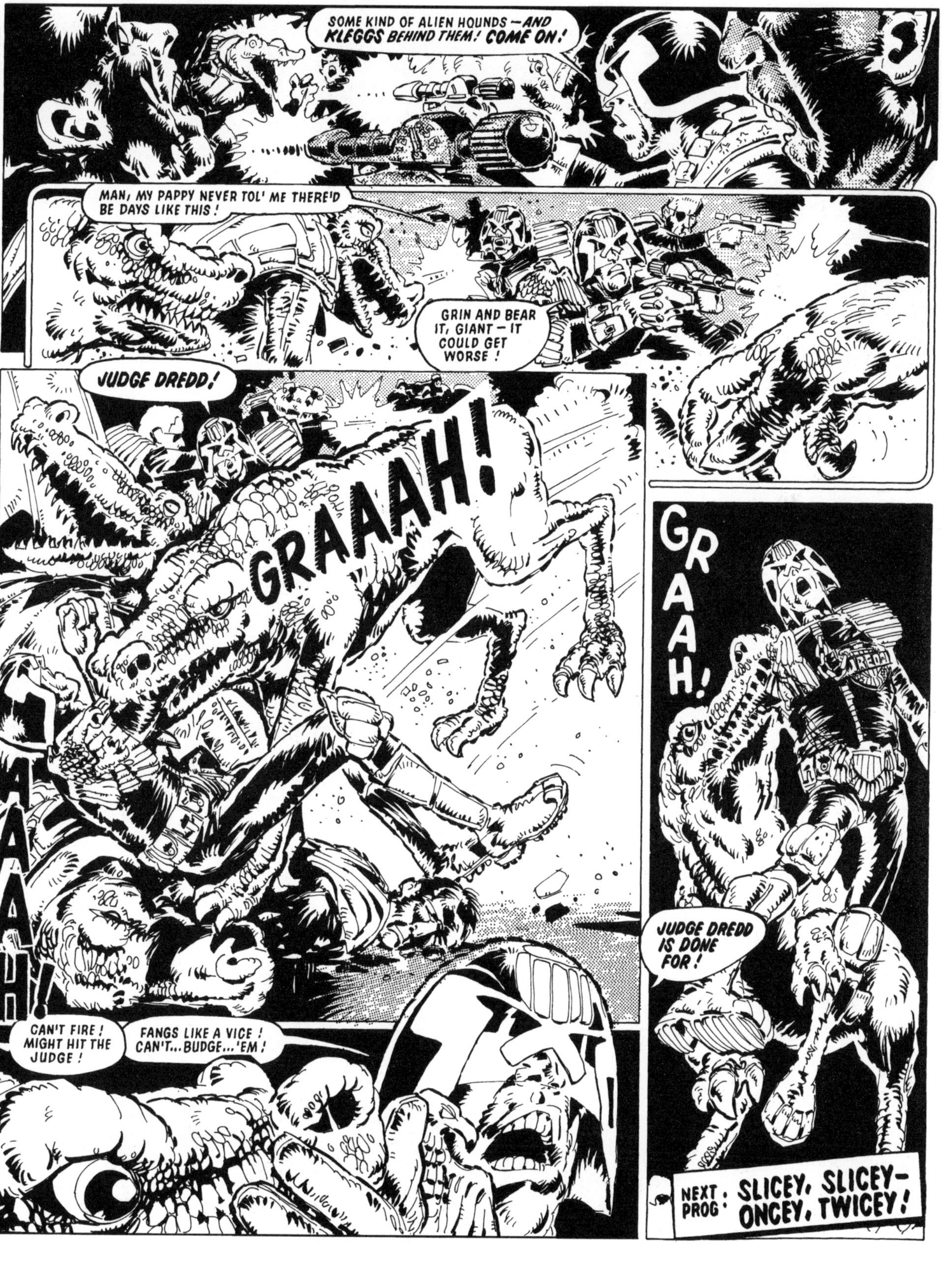

SOME KIND OF ALIEN HOUNDS — AND KLEGGS BEHIND THEM! COME ON!
MAN, MY PAPPY NEVER TOL' ME THERE'D BE DAYS LIKE THIS!
GRIN AND BEAR IT, GIANT — IT COULD GET WORSE!
JUDGE DREDD!
GRAAAH!
AAAAH!
CAN'T FIRE! MIGHT HIT THE JUDGE!
FANGS LIKE A VICE! CAN'T... BUDGE... 'EM!
GRAAH!
JUDGE DREDD IS DONE FOR!
NEXT PROG: SLICEY, SLICEY-ONCEY, TWICEY!

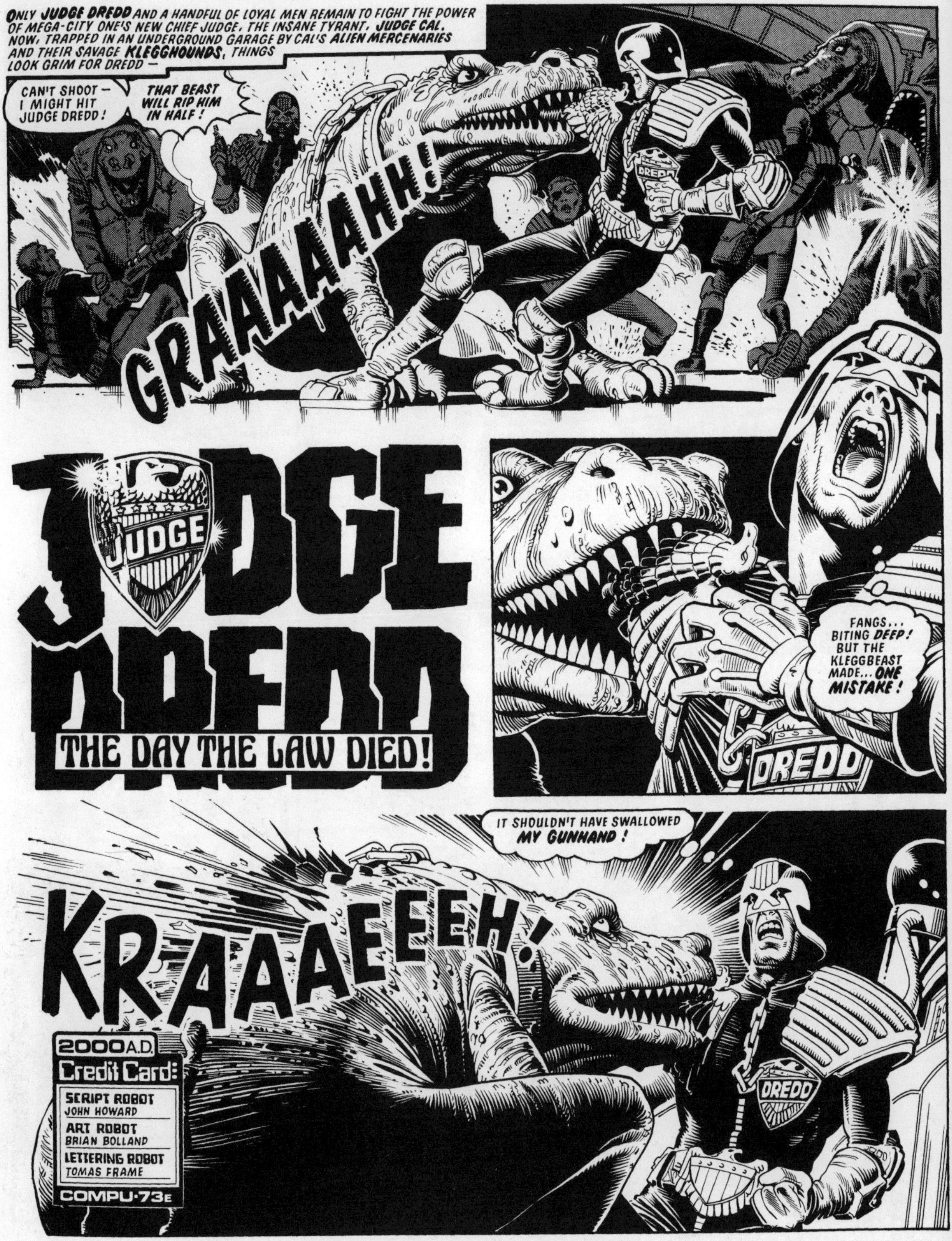

ONLY JUDGE DREDD AND A HANDFUL OF LOYAL MEN REMAIN TO FIGHT THE POWER OF MEGA-CITY ONE'S NEW CHIEF JUDGE, THE INSANE TYRANT, JUDGE CAL. NOW, TRAPPED IN AN UNDERGROUND GARAGE BY CAL'S ALIEN MERCENARIES AND THEIR SAVAGE KLEGGHOUNDS, THINGS LOOK GRIM FOR DREDD —
CAN'T SHOOT — I MIGHT HIT JUDGE DREDD!
THAT BEAST WILL RIP HIM IN HALF!
GRAAAAAAHH!
JUDGE DREDD
THE DAY THE LAW DIED!
FANGS... BITING DEEP! BUT THE KLEGGBEAST MADE... ONE MISTAKE!
IT SHOULDN'T HAVE SWALLOWED MY GUNHAND!
KRAAAEEEH!
2000 A.D. Credit Card:
SCRIPT ROBOT JOHN HOWARD
ART ROBOT BRIAN BOLLAND
LETTERING ROBOT TOMAS FRAME
COMPU-73E

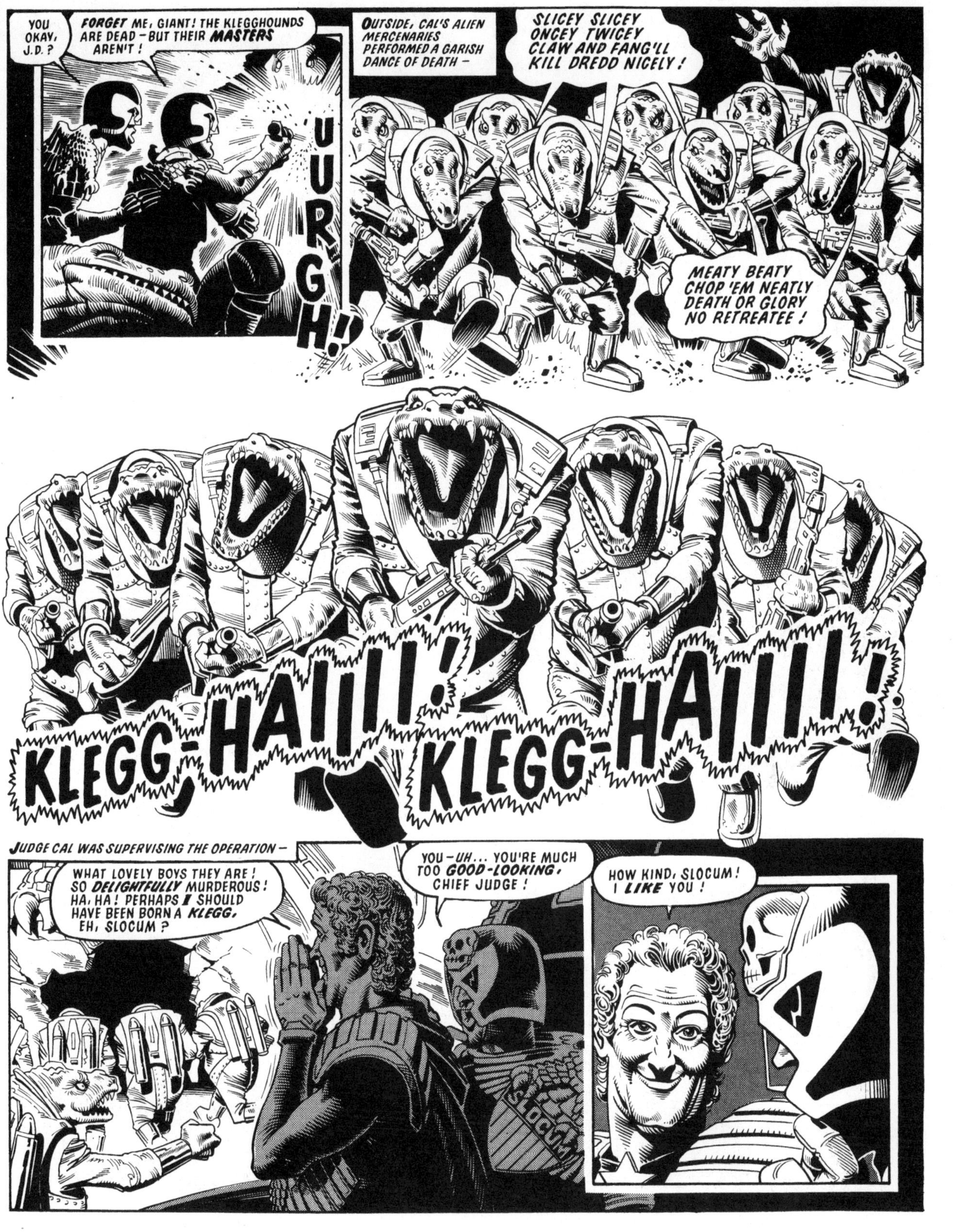

YOU OKAY, J.D.?
FORGET ME, GIANT! THE KLEGGHOUNDS ARE DEAD — BUT THEIR MASTERS AREN'T!
UURGH!
OUTSIDE, CAL'S ALIEN MERCENARIES PERFORMED A GARISH DANCE OF DEATH —
SLICEY SLICEY ONCEY TWICEY CLAW AND FANG'LL KILL DREDD NICELY!
MEATY BEATY CHOP 'EM NEATLY DEATH OR GLORY NO RETREATEE!
KLEGG-HAIIII! KLEGG-HAIIII!
JUDGE CAL WAS SUPERVISING THE OPERATION —
WHAT LOVELY BOYS THEY ARE! SO DELIGHTFULLY MURDEROUS! HA, HA! PERHAPS I SHOULD HAVE BEEN BORN A KLEGG, EH, SLOCUM?
YOU — UH... YOU'RE MUCH TOO GOOD-LOOKING, CHIEF JUDGE!
SLOCUM
HOW KIND, SLOCUM! I LIKE YOU!

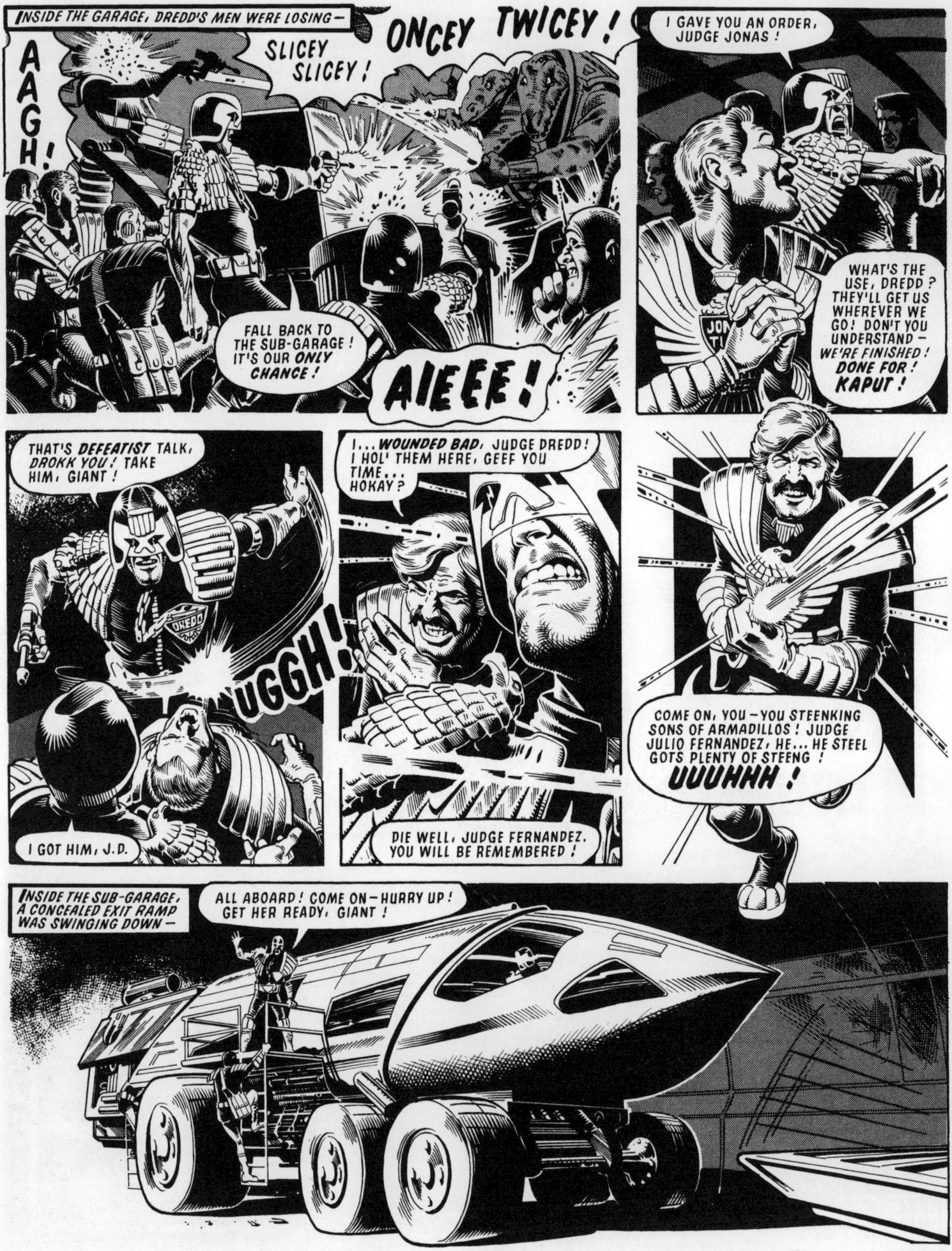
INSIDE THE GARAGE, DREDD'S MEN WERE LOSING—
AAGH!
SLICEY SLICEY!
ONCEY TWICEY!
FALL BACK TO THE SUB-GARAGE! IT'S OUR ONLY CHANCE!
AIEEE!
I GAVE YOU AN ORDER, JUDGE JONAS!
WHAT'S THE USE, DREDD? THEY'LL GET US WHEREVER WE GO! DON'T YOU UNDERSTAND— WE'RE FINISHED! DONE FOR! KAPUT!
THAT'S DEFEATIST TALK, DROKK YOU! TAKE HIM, GIANT!
UGGH!
I GOT HIM, J.D.
I... WOUNDED BAD, JUDGE DREDD! I HOL' THEM HERE, GEEF YOU TIME... HOKAY?
DIE WELL, JUDGE FERNANDEZ. YOU WILL BE REMEMBERED!
COME ON, YOU—YOU STEENKING SONS OF ARMADILLOS! JUDGE JULIO FERNANDEZ, HE... HE STEEL GOTS PLENTY OF STEENG!
UUUHHH!
INSIDE THE SUB-GARAGE, A CONCEALED EXIT RAMP WAS SWINGING DOWN—
ALL ABOARD! COME ON—HURRY UP! GET HER READY, GIANT!

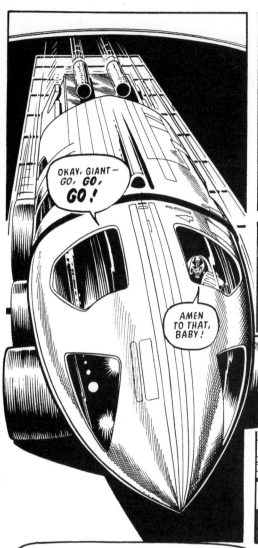

OKAY, GIANT— GO, GO, GO!

AMEN TO THAT, BABY!

CHIEF JUDGE—L-LOOK! TH-THEY'RE GETTING AWAY!

THEY WHAAAT? THEY DARE!

AS THE ROAD LINER SPED THROUGH THE CITY, A RED ALERT WENT OUT TO ALL JUSTICE DEPARTMENT UNITS! AND —

HOVER SHIP AHEAD!

I THINK I MADE THE TUNNEL BEFORE THEY SAW US!

I HOPE YOU'RE RIGHT, GIANT!

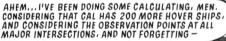

AHEM...I'VE BEEN DOING SOME CALCULATING, MEN. CONSIDERING THAT CAL HAS 200 MORE HOVER SHIPS, AND CONSIDERING THE OBSERVATION POINTS AT ALL MAJOR INTERSECTIONS, AND NOT FORGETTING —

YOU'RE NOT TEACHING CLASS NOW, KELSO! SKIP THE HOKUS-POKUS— JUST GIVE US THE FACTS!

MANY OF DREDD'S MEN WERE TUTORS FROM THE ACADEMY OF LAW —

HMMPH, THERE'S NO NEED TO BE SO RUDE, PEPPER. I WAS ONLY GOING TO SAY THAT OUR CHANCES OF SURVIVAL ARE A MILLION TO ONE —AGAINST!

THANKS, BABY... I NEEDED SOME CHEERING UP!

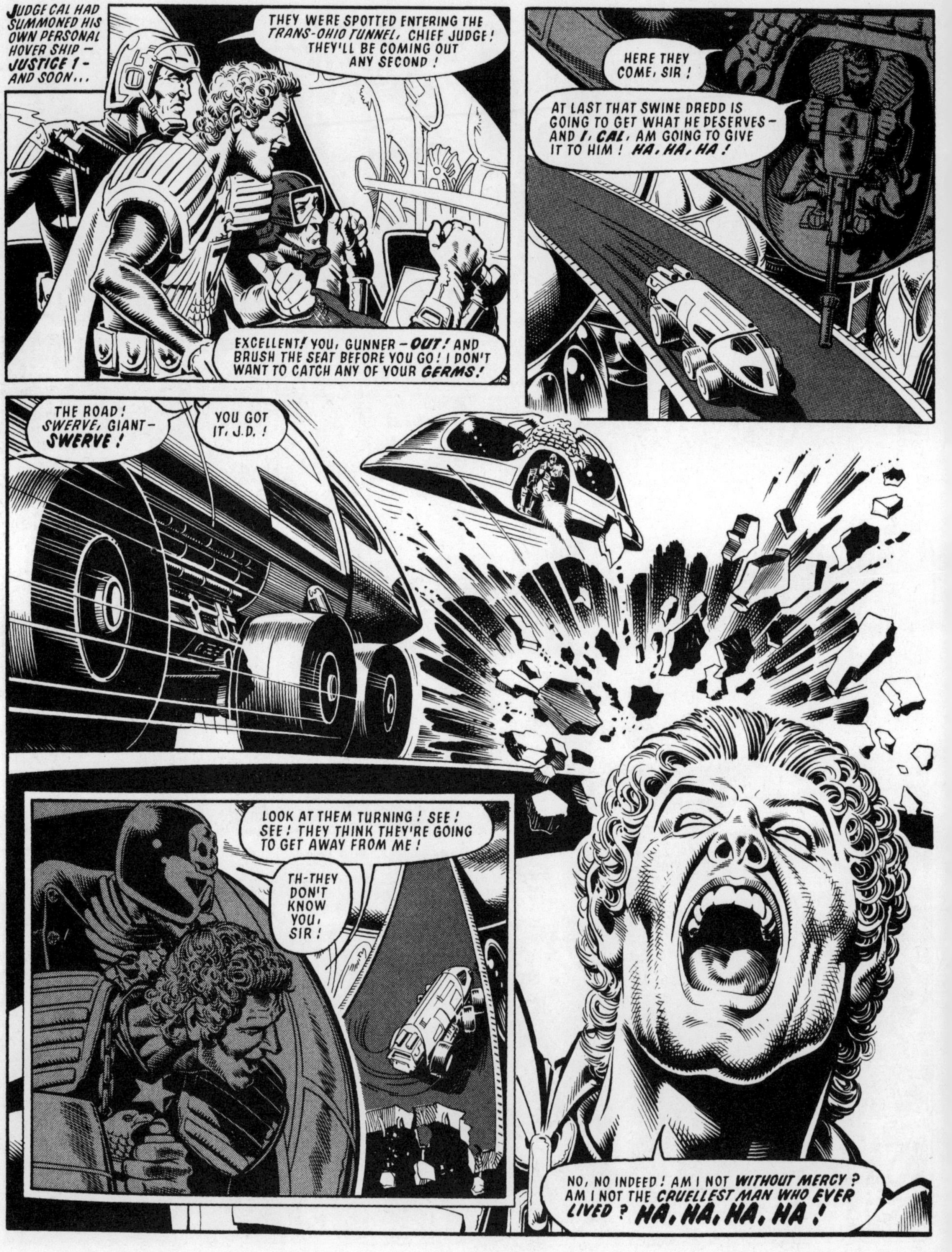

JUDGE CAL HAD SUMMONED HIS OWN PERSONAL HOVER SHIP — JUSTICE 1 — AND SOON...
THEY WERE SPOTTED ENTERING THE TRANS-OHIO TUNNEL, CHIEF JUDGE! THEY'LL BE COMING OUT ANY SECOND!
EXCELLENT! YOU, GUNNER — OUT! AND BRUSH THE SEAT BEFORE YOU GO! I DON'T WANT TO CATCH ANY OF YOUR GERMS!
HERE THEY COME, SIR!
AT LAST THAT SWINE DREDD IS GOING TO GET WHAT HE DESERVES — AND I, CAL, AM GOING TO GIVE IT TO HIM! HA, HA, HA!
THE ROAD! SWERVE, GIANT — SWERVE!
YOU GOT IT, J.D.!
LOOK AT THEM TURNING! SEE! SEE! THEY THINK THEY'RE GOING TO GET AWAY FROM ME!
TH-THEY DON'T KNOW YOU, SIR!
NO, NO INDEED! AM I NOT WITHOUT MERCY? AM I NOT THE CRUELLEST MAN WHO EVER LIVED? HA, HA, HA, HA!

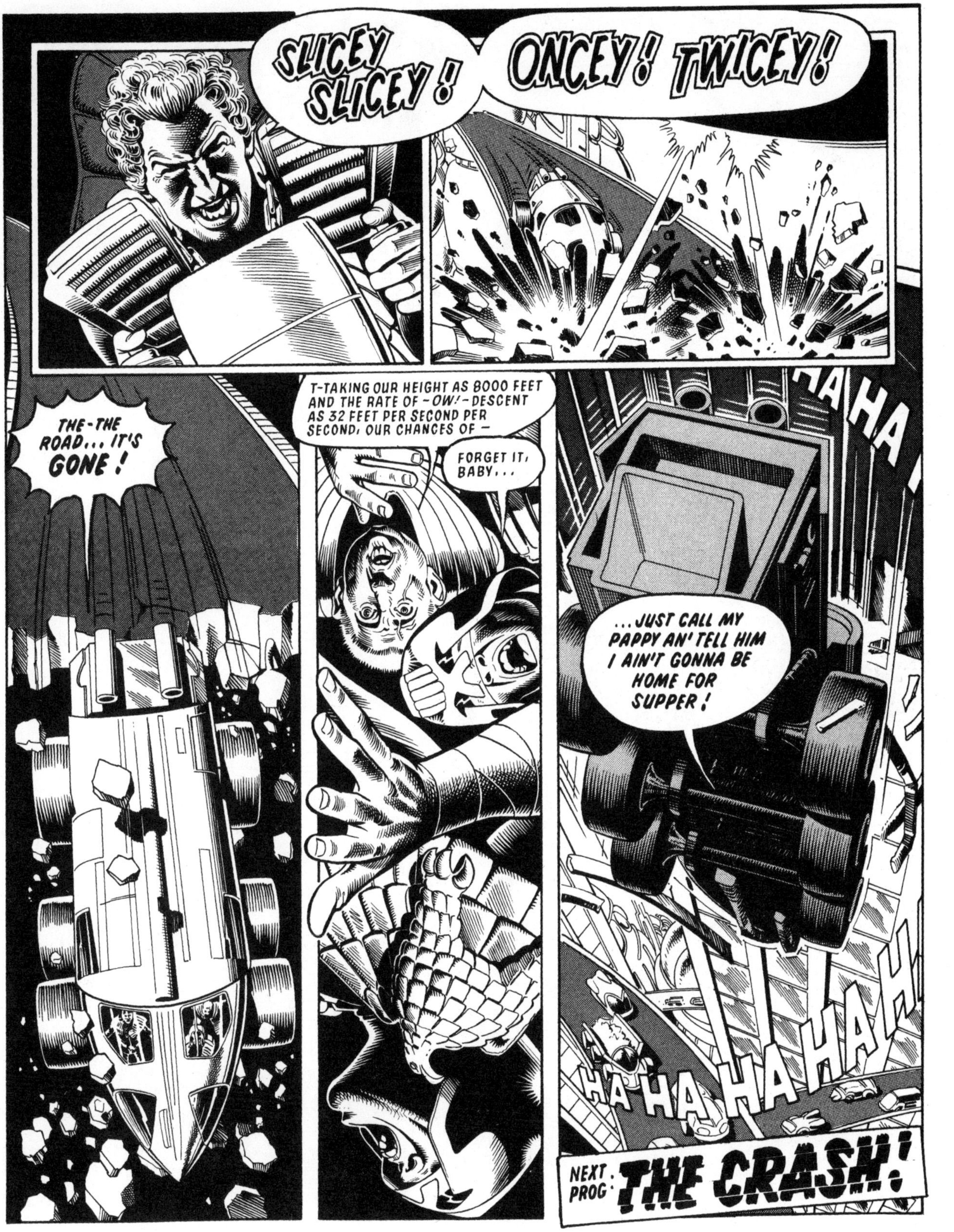
SLICEY SLICEY!
ONCEY! TWICEY!
THE-THE ROAD... IT'S GONE!
T-TAKING OUR HEIGHT AS 8000 FEET AND THE RATE OF -OW!- DESCENT AS 32 FEET PER SECOND PER SECOND, OUR CHANCES OF -
FORGET IT, BABY...
...JUST CALL MY PAPPY AN' TELL HIM I AIN'T GONNA BE HOME FOR SUPPER!
HA HA HA
HA HA HA HA HAH
NEXT PROG: THE CRASH!

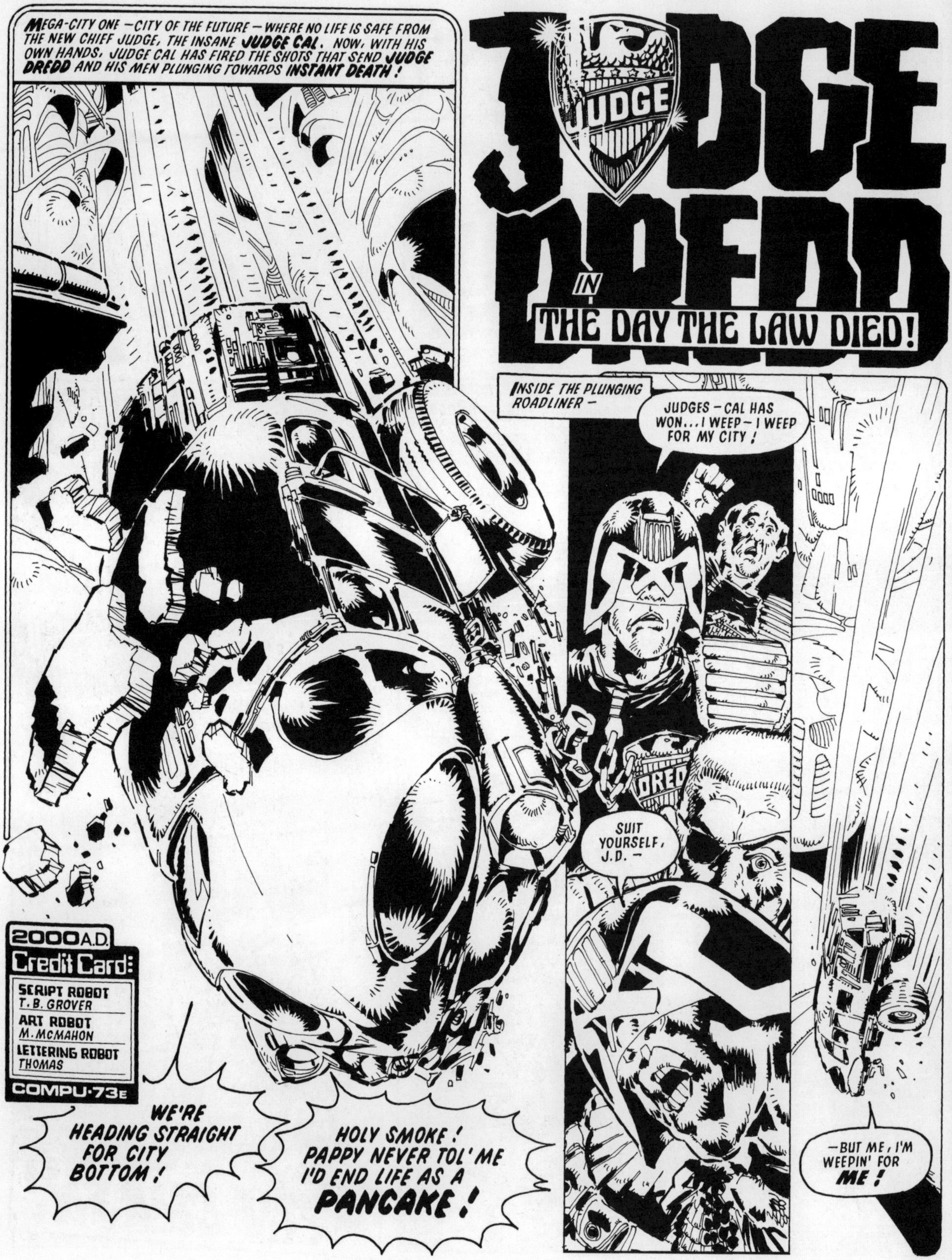
MEGA-CITY ONE — CITY OF THE FUTURE — WHERE NO LIFE IS SAFE FROM THE NEW CHIFF JUDGE, THE INSANE JUDGE CAL. NOW, WITH HIS OWN HANDS, JUDGE CAL HAS FIRED THE SHOTS THAT SEND JUDGE DREDD AND HIS MEN PLUNGING TOWARDS INSTANT DEATH!
JUDGE DREDD IN
THE DAY THE LAW DIED!
2000 A.D.
Credit Card:
SCRIPT ROBOT T. B. GROVER
ART ROBOT M. MCMAHON
LETTERING ROBOT THOMAS
COMPU-73E
WE'RE HEADING STRAIGHT FOR CITY BOTTOM!
HOLY SMOKE! PAPPY NEVER TOL' ME I'D END LIFE AS A PANCAKE!
INSIDE THE PLUNGING ROADLINER —
JUDGES — CAL HAS WON... I WEEP — I WEEP FOR MY CITY!
SUIT YOURSELF, J.D. —
—BUT ME, I'M WEEPIN' FOR ME!

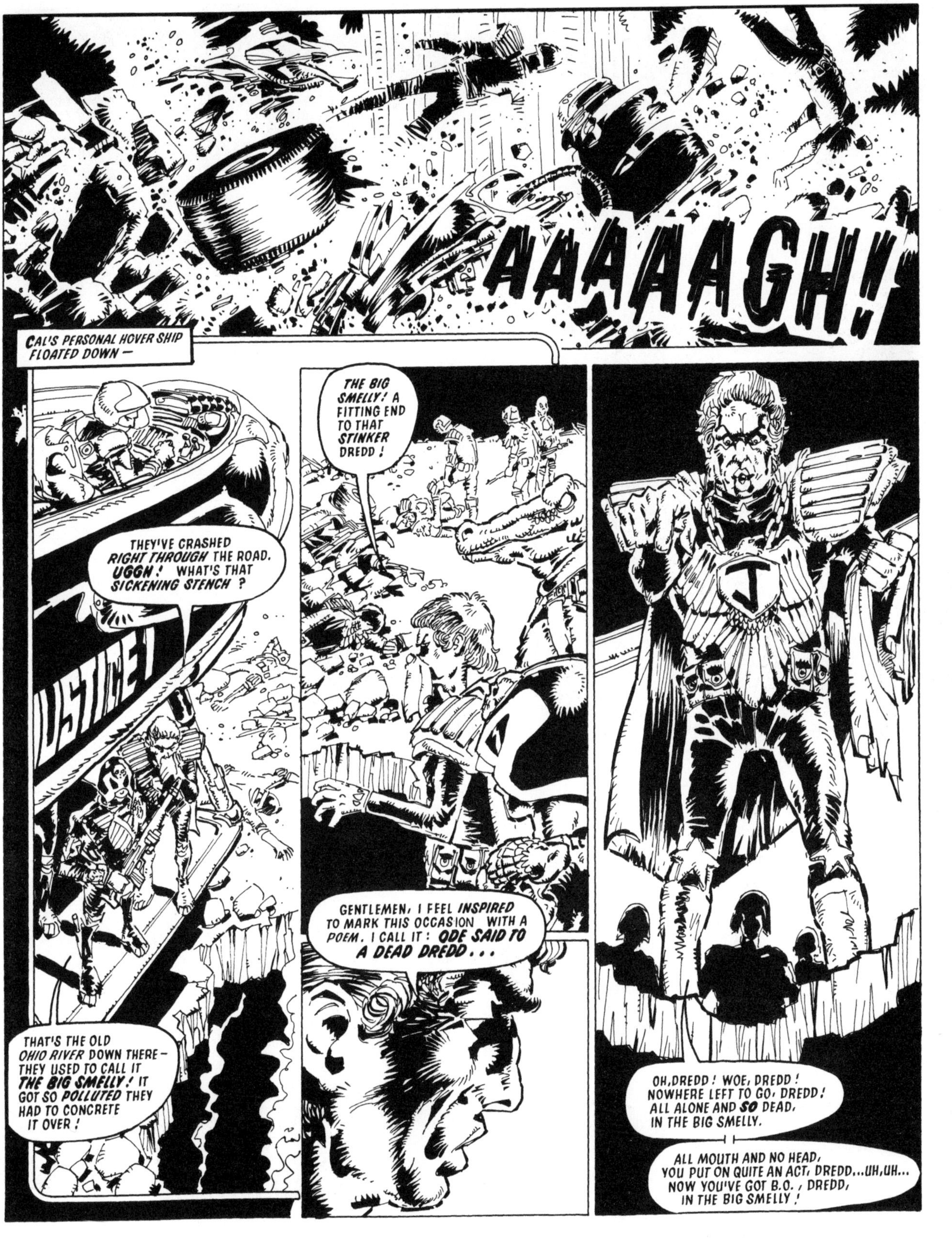
AAAAAAGH!!
CAL'S PERSONAL HOVER SHIP FLOATED DOWN —
THEY'VE CRASHED RIGHT THROUGH THE ROAD. UGGN! WHAT'S THAT SICKENING STENCH?
JUSTICE 1
THAT'S THE OLD OHIO RIVER DOWN THERE — THEY USED TO CALL IT THE BIG SMELLY! IT GOT SO POLLUTED THEY HAD TO CONCRETE IT OVER!
THE BIG SMELLY! A FITTING END TO THAT STINKER DREDD!
GENTLEMEN, I FEEL INSPIRED TO MARK THIS OCCASION WITH A POEM. I CALL IT: ODE SAID TO A DEAD DREDD...
OH, DREDD! WOE, DREDD! NOWHERE LEFT TO GO, DREDD! ALL ALONE AND SO DEAD, IN THE BIG SMELLY.
ALL MOUTH AND NO HEAD, YOU PUT ON QUITE AN ACT, DREDD... UH, UH... NOW YOU'VE GOT B.O., DREDD, IN THE BIG SMELLY!

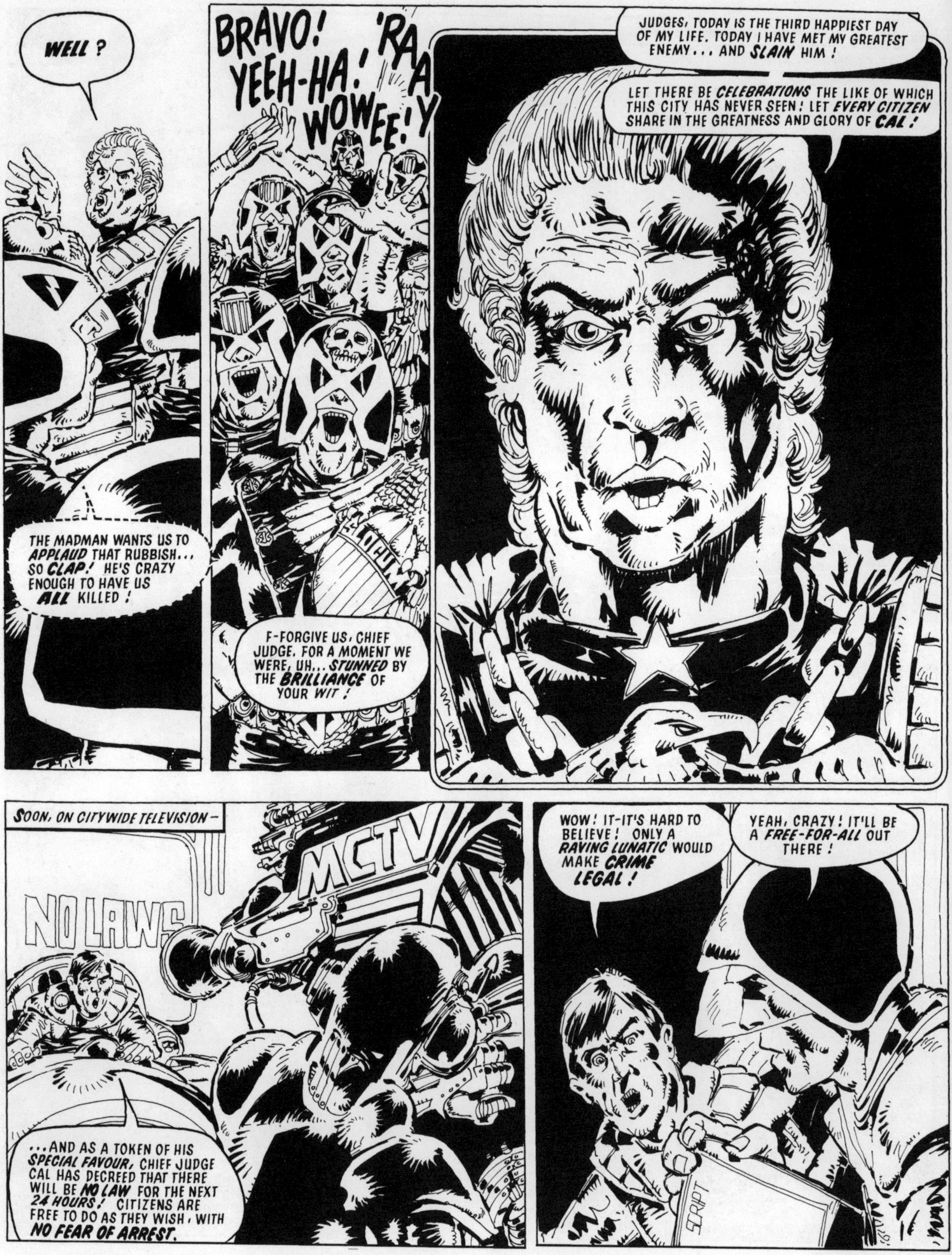
WELL ?
THE MADMAN WANTS US TO APPLAUD THAT RUBBISH... SO CLAP! HE'S CRAZY ENOUGH TO HAVE US ALL KILLED !
BRAVO! YEEH-HA! 'RAAAY WOWEE!
F-FORGIVE US, CHIEF JUDGE. FOR A MOMENT WE WERE, UH... STUNNED BY THE BRILLIANCE OF YOUR WIT !
JUDGES, TODAY IS THE THIRD HAPPIEST DAY OF MY LIFE. TODAY I HAVE MET MY GREATEST ENEMY... AND SLAIN HIM !
LET THERE BE CELEBRATIONS THE LIKE OF WHICH THIS CITY HAS NEVER SEEN! LET EVERY CITIZEN SHARE IN THE GREATNESS AND GLORY OF CAL !
SOON, ON CITYWIDE TELEVISION—
MCTV
NO LAWS
...AND AS A TOKEN OF HIS SPECIAL FAVOUR, CHIEF JUDGE CAL HAS DECREED THAT THERE WILL BE NO LAW FOR THE NEXT 24 HOURS! CITIZENS ARE FREE TO DO AS THEY WISH, WITH NO FEAR OF ARREST.
WOW! IT-IT'S HARD TO BELIEVE! ONLY A RAVING LUNATIC WOULD MAKE CRIME LEGAL !
YEAH, CRAZY! IT'LL BE A FREE-FOR-ALL OUT THERE !
SCRIPT

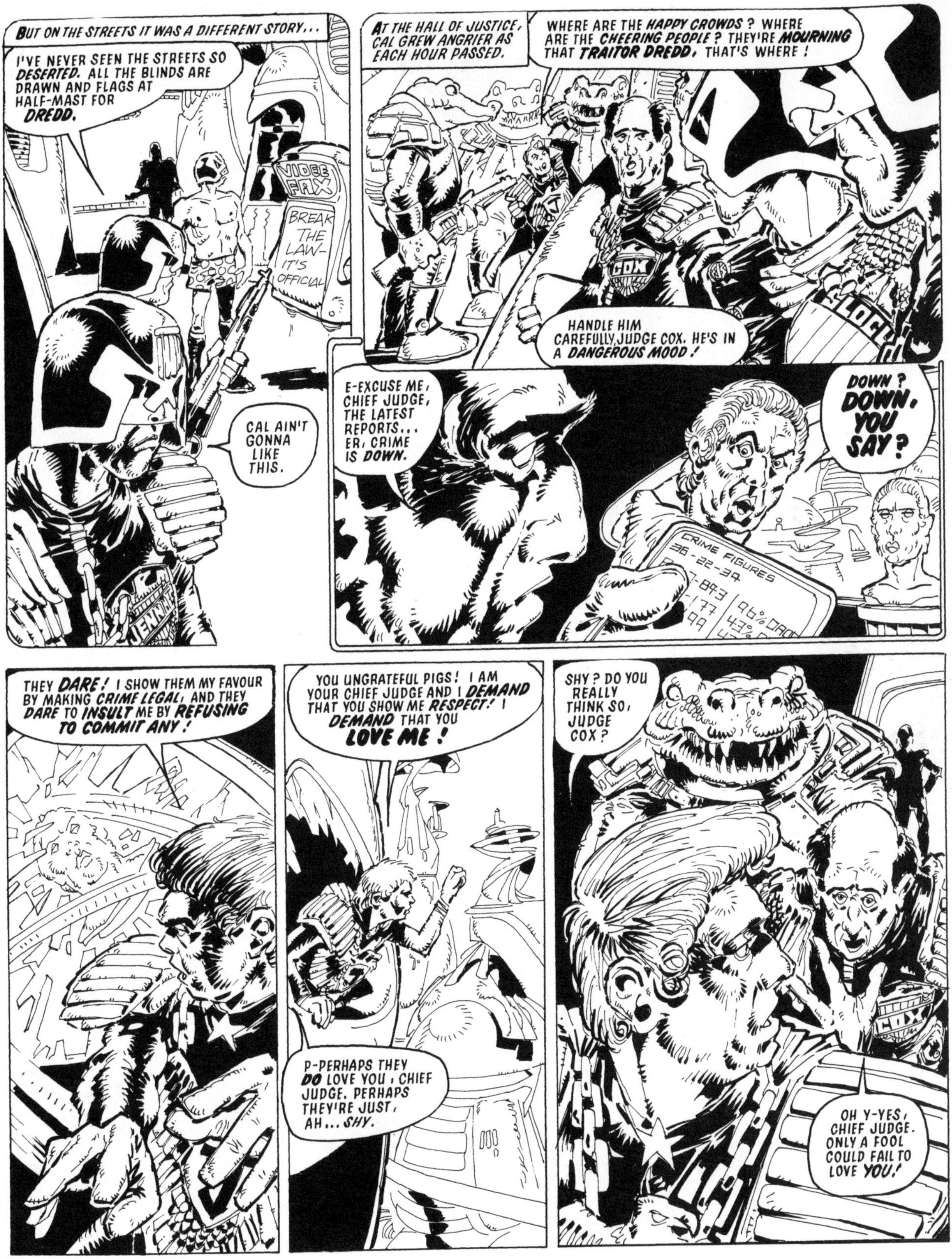
BUT ON THE STREETS IT WAS A DIFFERENT STORY...
I'VE NEVER SEEN THE STREETS SO DESERTED. ALL THE BLINDS ARE DRAWN AND FLAGS AT HALF-MAST FOR DREDD.
VIDEO FAX
BREAK THE LAW- IT'S OFFICIAL
CAL AIN'T GONNA LIKE THIS.
AT THE HALL OF JUSTICE, CAL GREW ANGRIER AS EACH HOUR PASSED.
WHERE ARE THE HAPPY CROWDS? WHERE ARE THE CHEERING PEOPLE? THEY'RE MOURNING THAT TRAITOR DREDD, THAT'S WHERE!
HANDLE HIM CAREFULLY, JUDGE COX. HE'S IN A DANGEROUS MOOD!
E-EXCUSE ME, CHIEF JUDGE, THE LATEST REPORTS... ER, CRIME IS DOWN.
DOWN? DOWN, YOU SAY?
CRIME FIGURES
THEY DARE! I SHOW THEM MY FAVOUR BY MAKING CRIME LEGAL, AND THEY DARE TO INSULT ME BY REFUSING TO COMMIT ANY!
YOU UNGRATEFUL PIGS! I AM YOUR CHIEF JUDGE AND I DEMAND THAT YOU SHOW ME RESPECT! I DEMAND THAT YOU LOVE ME!
P-PERHAPS THEY DO LOVE YOU, CHIEF JUDGE. PERHAPS THEY'RE JUST, AH... SHY.
SHY? DO YOU REALLY THINK SO, JUDGE COX?
OH Y-YES, CHIEF JUDGE. ONLY A FOOL COULD FAIL TO LOVE YOU!

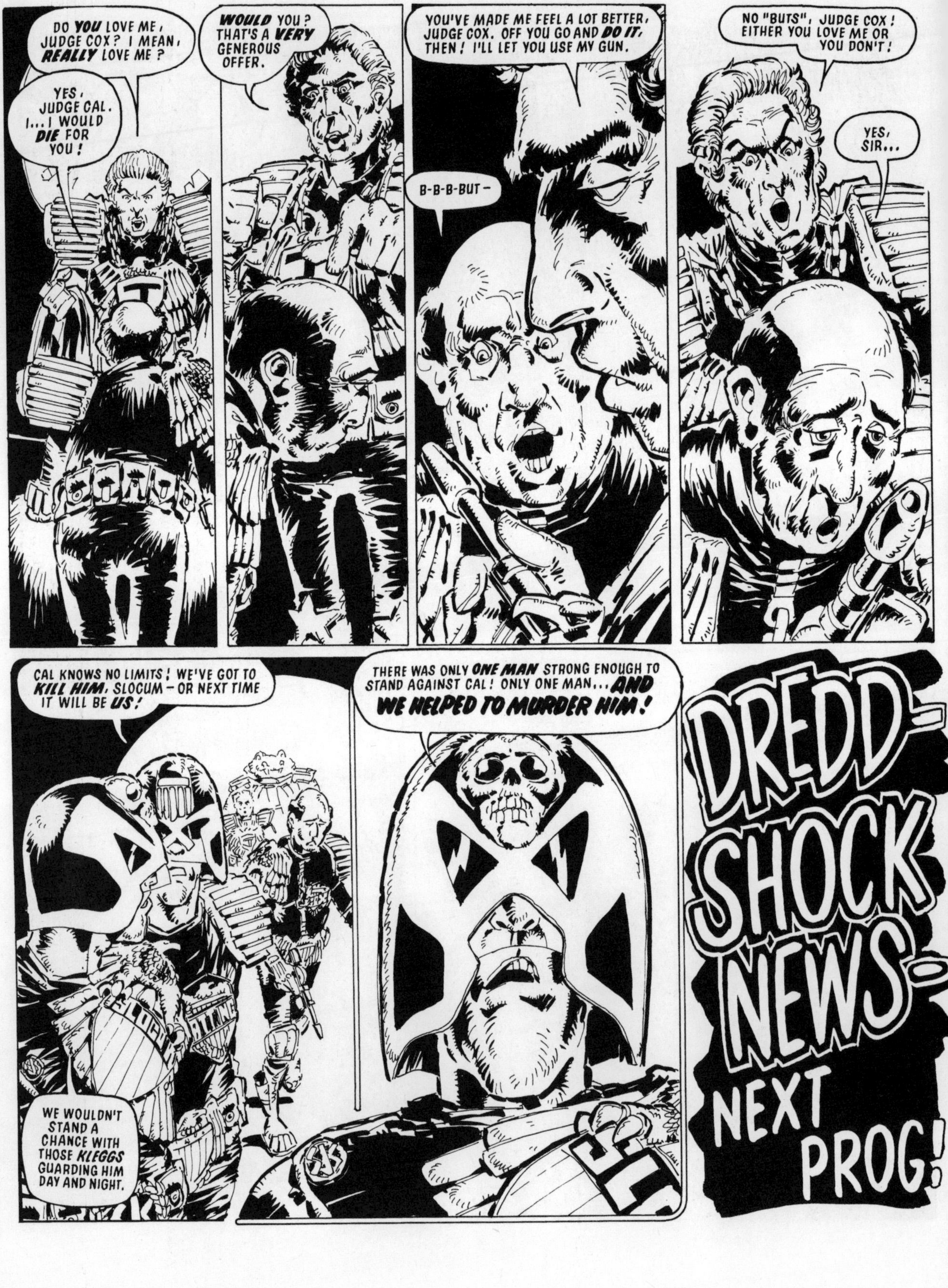
DO YOU LOVE ME, JUDGE COX? I MEAN, REALLY LOVE ME?
YES, JUDGE CAL. I... I WOULD DIE FOR YOU!
WOULD YOU? THAT'S A VERY GENEROUS OFFER.
YOU'VE MADE ME FEEL A LOT BETTER, JUDGE COX. OFF YOU GO AND DO IT, THEN! I'LL LET YOU USE MY GUN.
B-B-B-BUT–
NO "BUTS", JUDGE COX! EITHER YOU LOVE ME OR YOU DON'T!
YES, SIR...
CAL KNOWS NO LIMITS! WE'VE GOT TO KILL HIM, SLOCUM – OR NEXT TIME IT WILL BE US!
WE WOULDN'T STAND A CHANCE WITH THOSE KLEGGS GUARDING HIM DAY AND NIGHT.
THERE WAS ONLY ONE MAN STRONG ENOUGH TO STAND AGAINST CAL! ONLY ONE MAN... AND WE HELPED TO MURDER HIM!
DREDD-SHOCK NEWS-NEXT PROG!

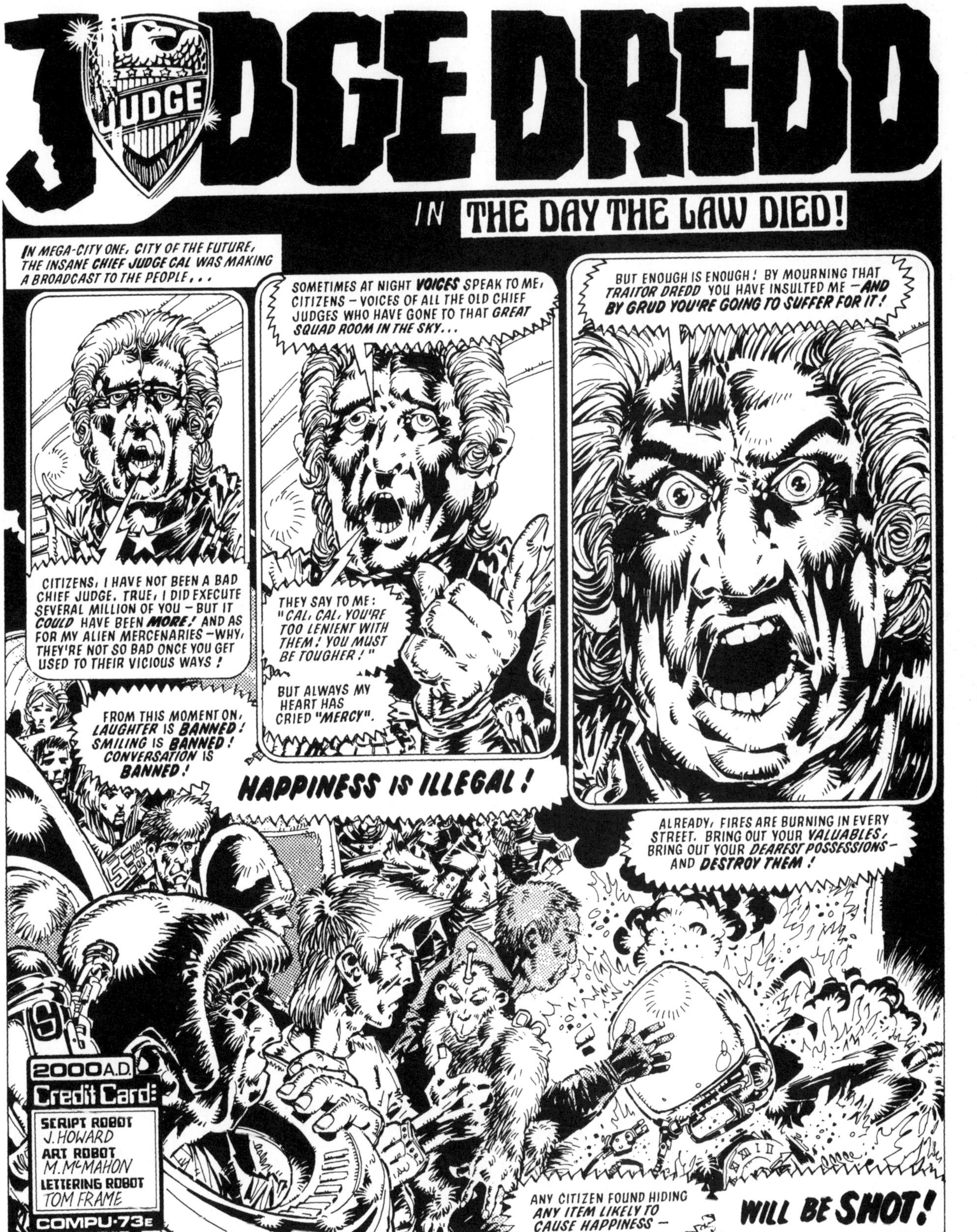

JUDGE DREDD
JUDGE
IN THE DAY THE LAW DIED!
IN MEGA-CITY ONE, CITY OF THE FUTURE, THE INSANE CHIEF JUDGE CAL WAS MAKING A BROADCAST TO THE PEOPLE...
CITIZENS, I HAVE NOT BEEN A BAD CHIEF JUDGE. TRUE, I DID EXECUTE SEVERAL MILLION OF YOU — BUT IT COULD HAVE BEEN MORE! AND AS FOR MY ALIEN MERCENARIES — WHY, THEY'RE NOT SO BAD ONCE YOU GET USED TO THEIR VICIOUS WAYS!
SOMETIMES AT NIGHT VOICES SPEAK TO ME, CITIZENS — VOICES OF ALL THE OLD CHIEF JUDGES WHO HAVE GONE TO THAT GREAT SQUAD ROOM IN THE SKY...
THEY SAY TO ME: "CAL, CAL, YOU'RE TOO LENIENT WITH THEM! YOU MUST BE TOUGHER!"
BUT ALWAYS MY HEART HAS CRIED "MERCY".
BUT ENOUGH IS ENOUGH! BY MOURNING THAT TRAITOR DREDD YOU HAVE INSULTED ME — AND BY GRUD YOU'RE GOING TO SUFFER FOR IT!
FROM THIS MOMENT ON, LAUGHTER IS BANNED! SMILING IS BANNED! CONVERSATION IS BANNED!
HAPPINESS IS ILLEGAL!
ALREADY, FIRES ARE BURNING IN EVERY STREET. BRING OUT YOUR VALUABLES, BRING OUT YOUR DEAREST POSSESSIONS — AND DESTROY THEM!
ANY CITIZEN FOUND HIDING ANY ITEM LIKELY TO CAUSE HAPPINESS —
WILL BE SHOT!
2000 A.D. Credit Card:
SCRIPT ROBOT J. HOWARD
ART ROBOT M. McMAHON
LETTERING ROBOT TOM FRAME
COMPU-73E

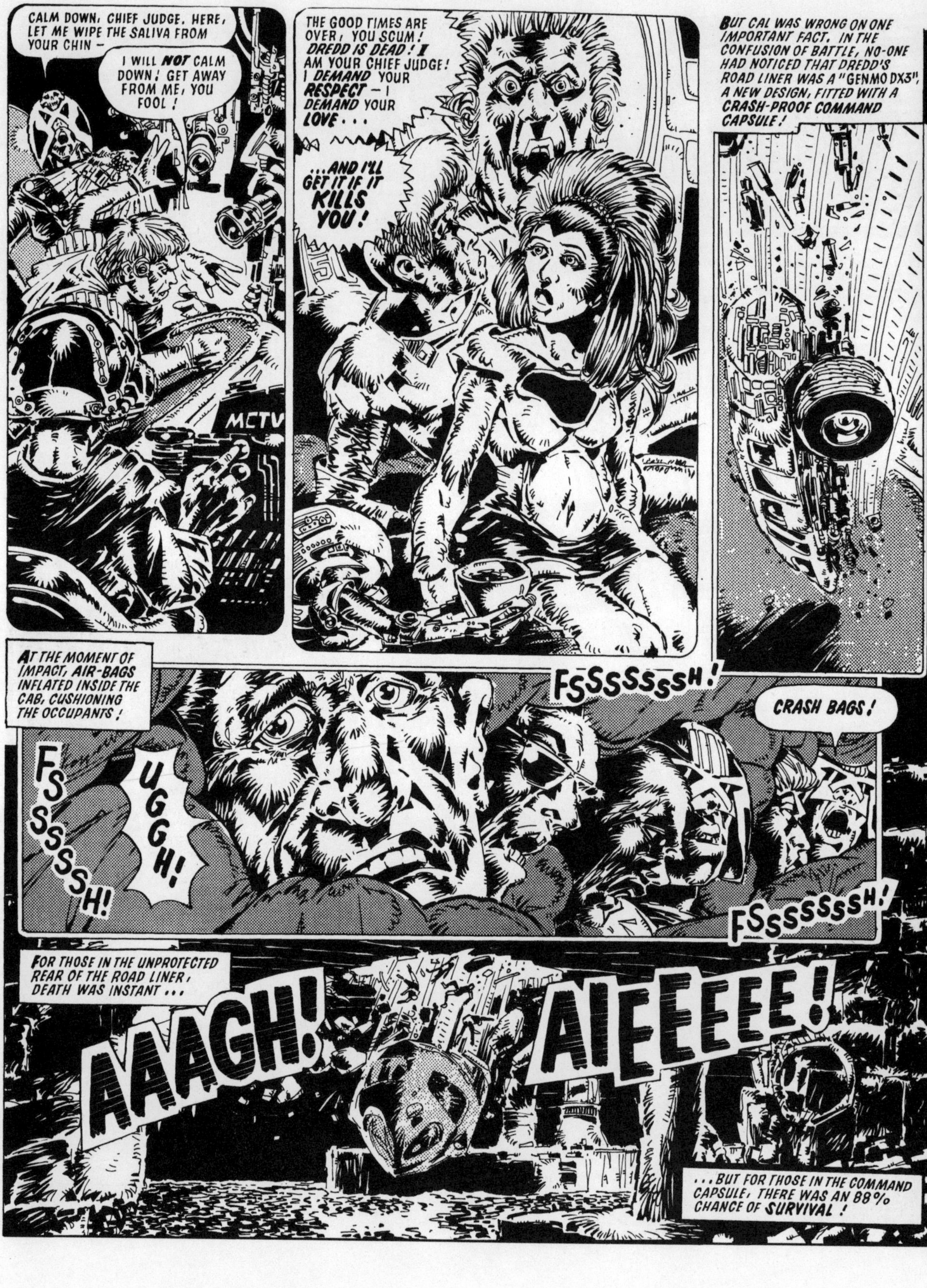
CALM DOWN, CHIEF JUDGE. HERE, LET ME WIPE THE SALIVA FROM YOUR CHIN –
I WILL NOT CALM DOWN! GET AWAY FROM ME, YOU FOOL!
MCTV
THE GOOD TIMES ARE OVER, YOU SCUM! DREDD IS DEAD! I AM YOUR CHIEF JUDGE! I DEMAND YOUR RESPECT – I DEMAND YOUR LOVE...
...AND I'LL GET IT IF IT KILLS YOU!
BUT CAL WAS WRONG ON ONE IMPORTANT FACT. IN THE CONFUSION OF BATTLE, NO-ONE HAD NOTICED THAT DREDD'S ROAD LINER WAS A "GENMO DX3", A NEW DESIGN, FITTED WITH A CRASH-PROOF COMMAND CAPSULE!
AT THE MOMENT OF IMPACT, AIR-BAGS INFLATED INSIDE THE CAB, CUSHIONING THE OCCUPANTS!
FSSSSSSSH!
CRASH BAGS!
FSSSSSSH!
UGGH!
FSSSSSSH!
FOR THOSE IN THE UNPROTECTED REAR OF THE ROAD LINER, DEATH WAS INSTANT...
AAAGH!
AIEEEEE!
...BUT FOR THOSE IN THE COMMAND CAPSULE, THERE WAS AN 88% CHANCE OF SURVIVAL!

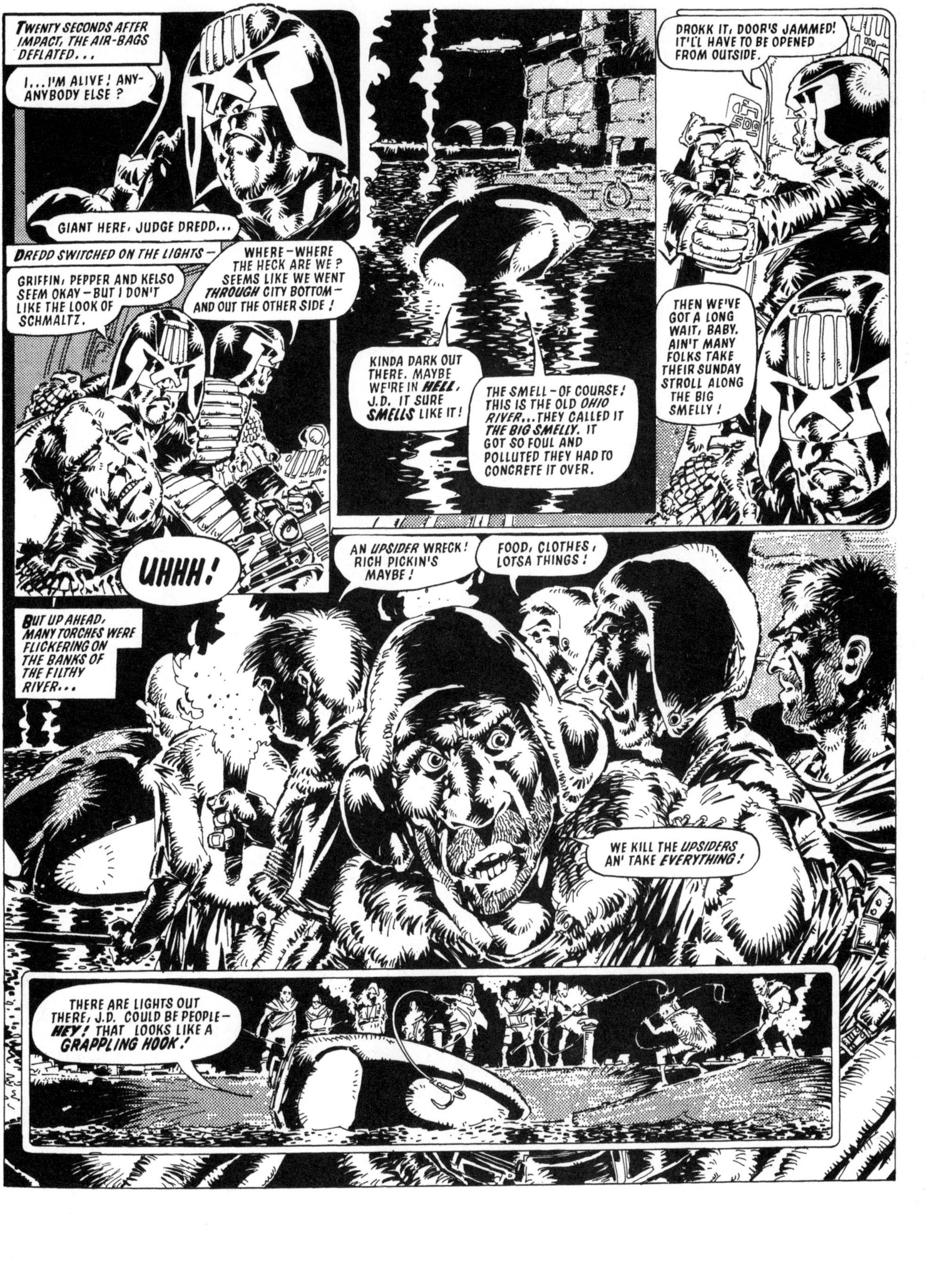

TWENTY SECONDS AFTER IMPACT, THE AIR-BAGS DEFLATED...
I...I'M ALIVE! ANY-ANYBODY ELSE?
GIANT HERE, JUDGE DREDD...
DREDD SWITCHED ON THE LIGHTS—
GRIFFIN, PEPPER AND KELSO SEEM OKAY—BUT I DON'T LIKE THE LOOK OF SCHMALTZ.
WHERE—WHERE THE HECK ARE WE? SEEMS LIKE WE WENT THROUGH CITY BOTTOM—AND OUT THE OTHER SIDE!
UHHH!
KINDA DARK OUT THERE. MAYBE WE'RE IN HELL, J.D. IT SURE SMELLS LIKE IT!
THE SMELL—OF COURSE! THIS IS THE OLD OHIO RIVER...THEY CALLED IT THE BIG SMELLY. IT GOT SO FOUL AND POLLUTED THEY HAD TO CONCRETE IT OVER.
DROKK IT, DOOR'S JAMMED! IT'LL HAVE TO BE OPENED FROM OUTSIDE.
THEN WE'VE GOT A LONG WAIT, BABY. AIN'T MANY FOLKS TAKE THEIR SUNDAY STROLL ALONG THE BIG SMELLY!
BUT UP AHEAD, MANY TORCHES WERE FLICKERING ON THE BANKS OF THE FILTHY RIVER...
AN UPSIDER WRECK! RICH PICKIN'S MAYBE!
FOOD, CLOTHES, LOTSA THINGS!
WE KILL THE UPSIDERS AN' TAKE EVERYTHING!
THERE ARE LIGHTS OUT THERE, J.D. COULD BE PEOPLE—HEY! THAT LOOKS LIKE A GRAPPLING HOOK!

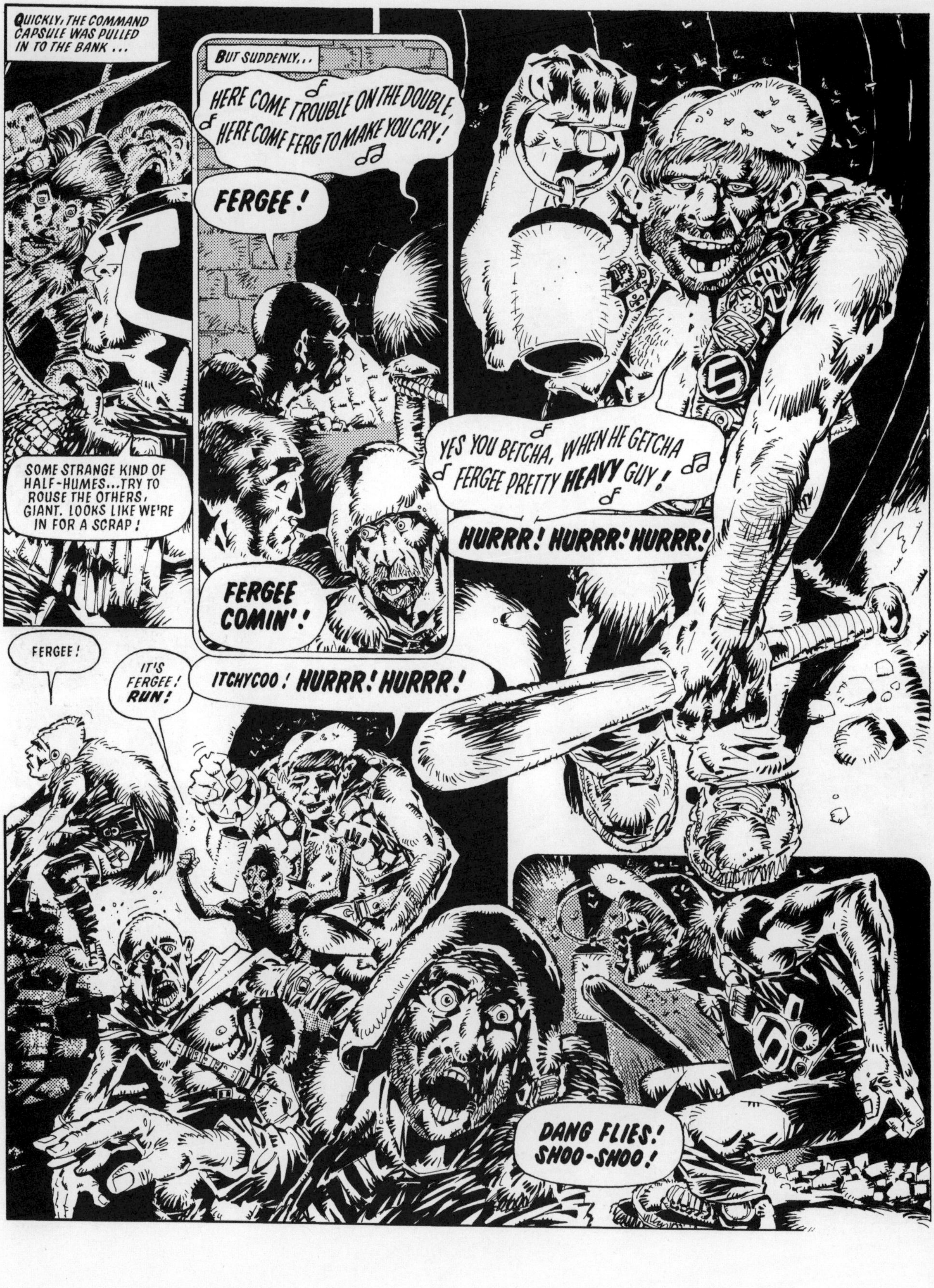
QUICKLY, THE COMMAND CAPSULE WAS PULLED IN TO THE BANK ...
SOME STRANGE KIND OF HALF-HUMES... TRY TO ROUSE THE OTHERS, GIANT. LOOKS LIKE WE'RE IN FOR A SCRAP!
BUT SUDDENLY...
HERE COME TROUBLE ON THE DOUBLE, HERE COME FERG TO MAKE YOU CRY!
FERGEE!
FERGEE COMIN'!
YES YOU BETCHA, WHEN HE GETCHA FERGEE PRETTY HEAVY GUY!
HURRR! HURRR! HURRR!
FERGEE!
IT'S FERGEE! RUN!
ITCHYCOO! HURRR! HURRR!
DANG FLIES! SHOO-SHOO!

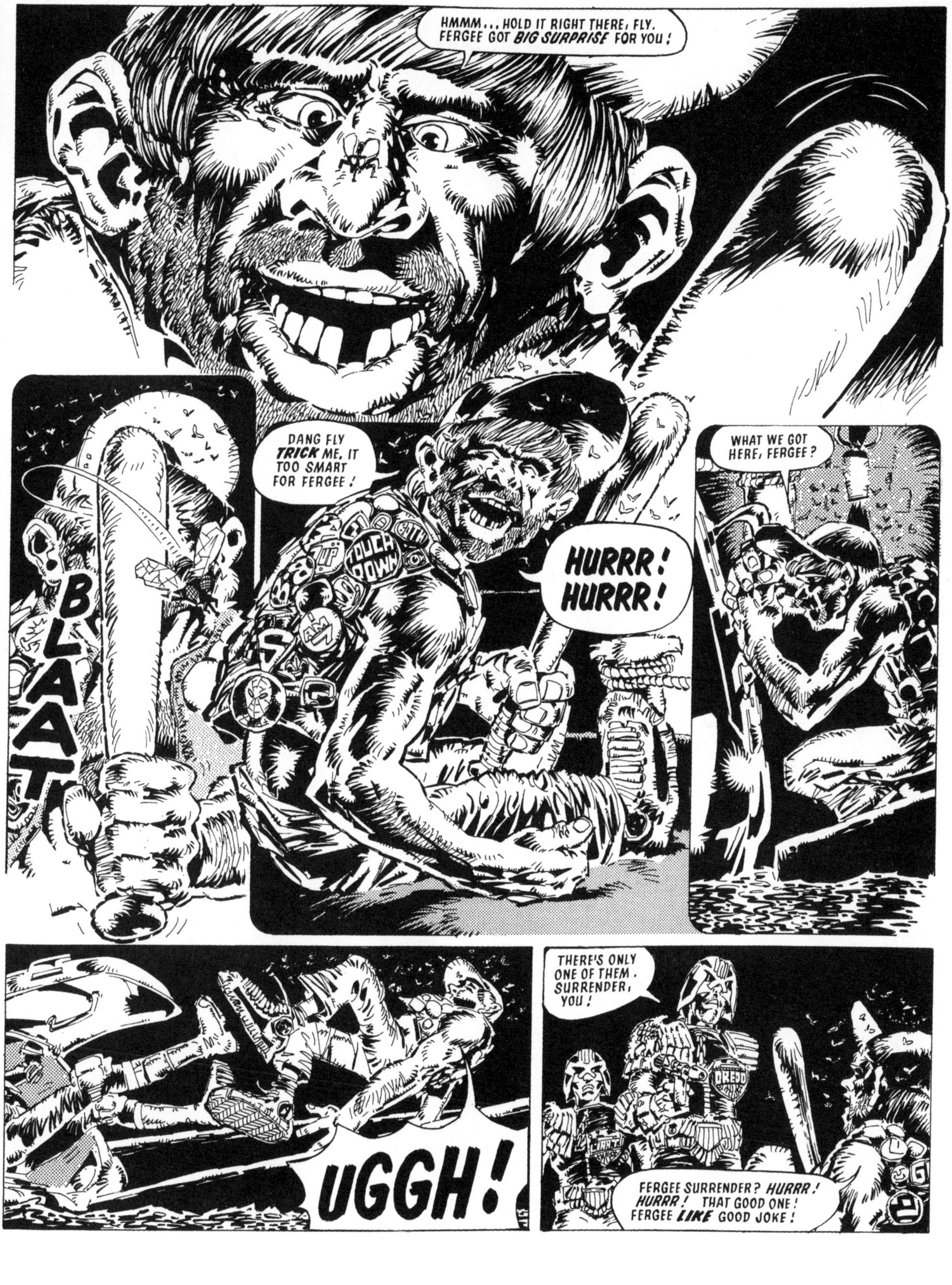
HMMM... HOLD IT RIGHT THERE, FLY. FERGEE GOT BIG SURPRISE FOR YOU!
BLAAT
DANG FLY TRICK ME. IT TOO SMART FOR FERGEE!
HURRR! HURRR!
WHAT WE GOT HERE, FERGEE?
UGGH!
THERE'S ONLY ONE OF THEM. SURRENDER, YOU!
FERGEE SURRENDER? HURRR! HURRR! THAT GOOD ONE! FERGEE LIKE GOOD JOKE!

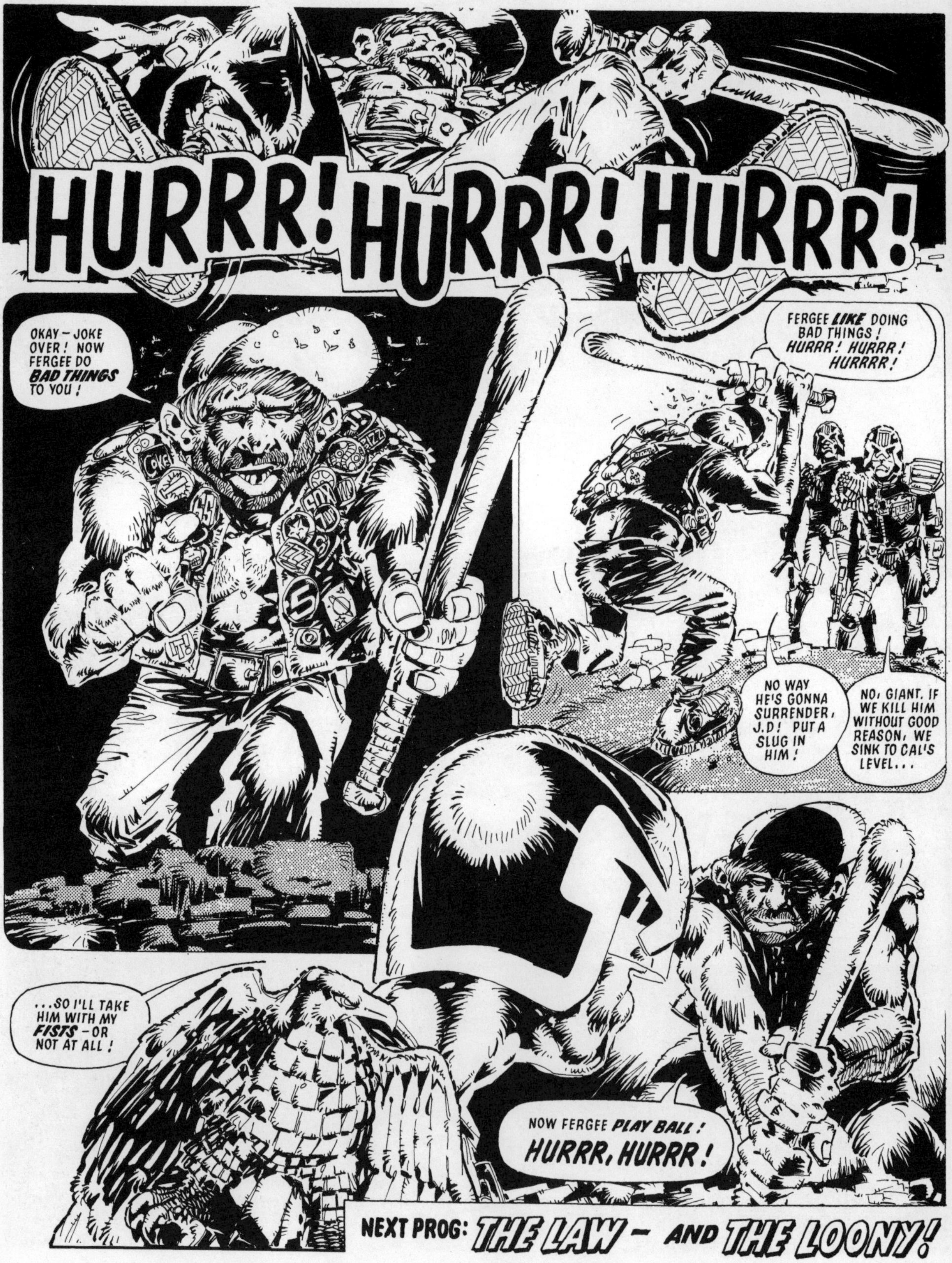
HURRR! HURRR! HURRR!
OKAY — JOKE OVER! NOW FERGEE DO BAD THINGS TO YOU!
FERGEE LIKE DOING BAD THINGS! HURRR! HURRR! HURRRR!
NO WAY HE'S GONNA SURRENDER, J.D! PUT A SLUG IN HIM!
NO, GIANT. IF WE KILL HIM WITHOUT GOOD REASON, WE SINK TO CAL'S LEVEL...
...SO I'LL TAKE HIM WITH MY FISTS — OR NOT AT ALL!
NOW FERGEE PLAY BALL! HURRR, HURRR!

NEXT PROG: THE LAW — AND THE LOONY!

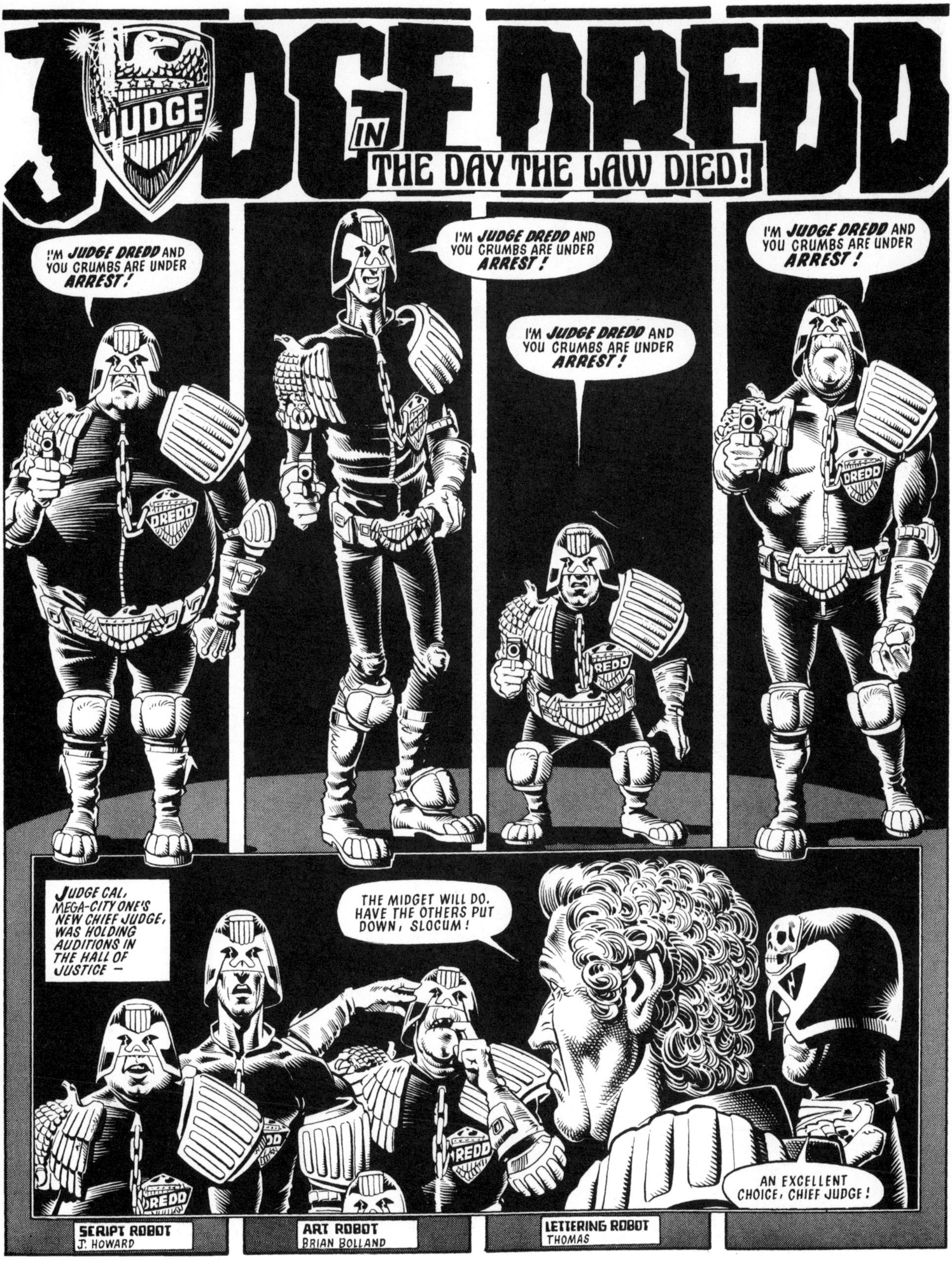

JUDGE DREDD
JUDGE
IN
THE DAY THE LAW DIED!
I'M JUDGE DREDD AND YOU CRUMBS ARE UNDER ARREST!
I'M JUDGE DREDD AND YOU CRUMBS ARE UNDER ARREST!
I'M JUDGE DREDD AND YOU CRUMBS ARE UNDER ARREST!
I'M JUDGE DREDD AND YOU CRUMBS ARE UNDER ARREST!
JUDGE CAL, MEGA-CITY ONE'S NEW CHIEF JUDGE, WAS HOLDING AUDITIONS IN THE HALL OF JUSTICE –
THE MIDGET WILL DO. HAVE THE OTHERS PUT DOWN, SLOCUM!
AN EXCELLENT CHOICE, CHIEF JUDGE!
SCRIPT ROBOT
J. HOWARD
ART ROBOT
BRIAN BOLLAND
LETTERING ROBOT
THOMAS

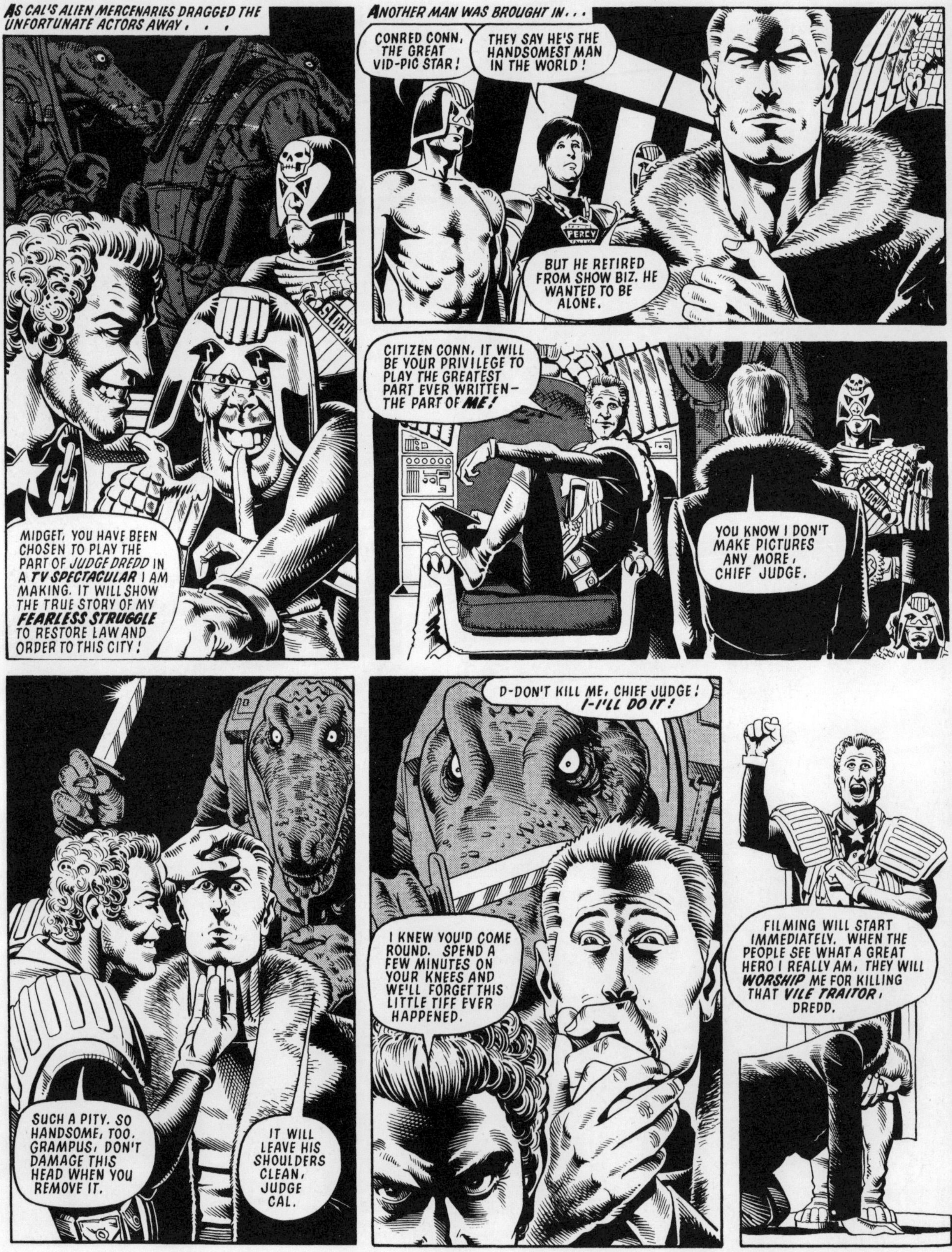
AS CAL'S ALIEN MERCENARIES DRAGGED THE UNFORTUNATE ACTORS AWAY . . .
MIDGET, YOU HAVE BEEN CHOSEN TO PLAY THE PART OF JUDGE DREDD IN A TV SPECTACULAR I AM MAKING. IT WILL SHOW THE TRUE STORY OF MY FEARLESS STRUGGLE TO RESTORE LAW AND ORDER TO THIS CITY!
ANOTHER MAN WAS BROUGHT IN . . .
CONRED CONN, THE GREAT VID-PIC STAR!
THEY SAY HE'S THE HANDSOMEST MAN IN THE WORLD!
BUT HE RETIRED FROM SHOW BIZ. HE WANTED TO BE ALONE.
PERCY
CITIZEN CONN, IT WILL BE YOUR PRIVILEGE TO PLAY THE GREATEST PART EVER WRITTEN— THE PART OF ME!
YOU KNOW I DON'T MAKE PICTURES ANY MORE, CHIEF JUDGE.
SUCH A PITY. SO HANDSOME, TOO. GRAMPUS, DON'T DAMAGE THIS HEAD WHEN YOU REMOVE IT.
IT WILL LEAVE HIS SHOULDERS CLEAN, JUDGE CAL.
D-DON'T KILL ME, CHIEF JUDGE! I-I'LL DO IT!
I KNEW YOU'D COME ROUND. SPEND A FEW MINUTES ON YOUR KNEES AND WE'LL FORGET THIS LITTLE TIFF EVER HAPPENED.
FILMING WILL START IMMEDIATELY. WHEN THE PEOPLE SEE WHAT A GREAT HERO I REALLY AM, THEY WILL WORSHIP ME FOR KILLING THAT VILE TRAITOR, DREDD.

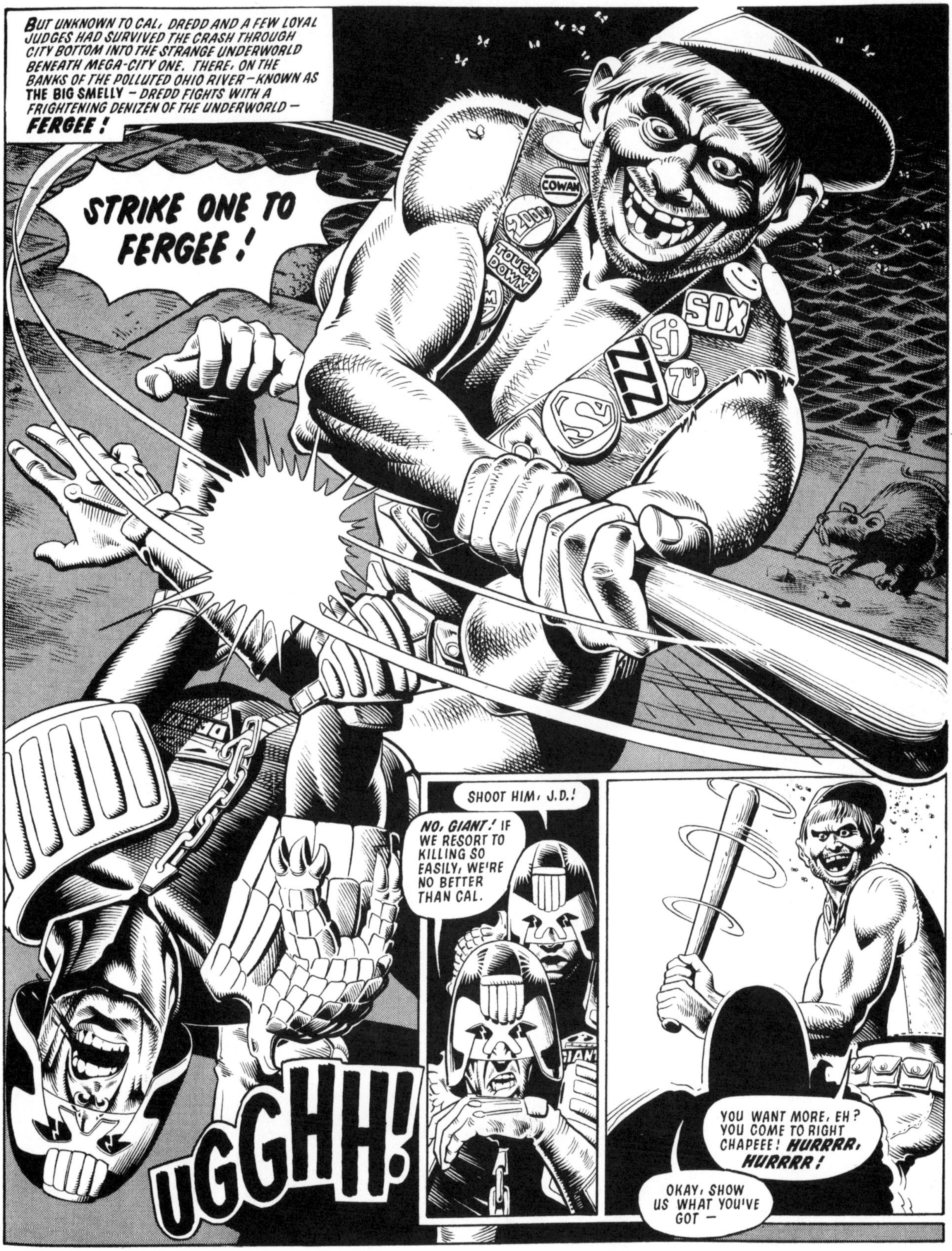
BUT UNKNOWN TO CAL, DREDD AND A FEW LOYAL JUDGES HAD SURVIVED THE CRASH THROUGH CITY BOTTOM INTO THE STRANGE UNDERWORLD BENEATH MEGA-CITY ONE. THERE, ON THE BANKS OF THE POLLUTED OHIO RIVER — KNOWN AS THE BIG SMELLY — DREDD FIGHTS WITH A FRIGHTENING DENIZEN OF THE UNDERWORLD — FERGEE!
STRIKE ONE TO FERGEE!
COWAN
2000
TOUCH DOWN
SOX
Si
ZZZ
7up
UGGHH!
SHOOT HIM, J.D.!
NO, GIANT! IF WE RESORT TO KILLING SO EASILY, WE'RE NO BETTER THAN CAL.
GIANT
YOU WANT MORE, EH? YOU COME TO RIGHT CHAPEEE! HURRRR, HURRRR!
OKAY, SHOW US WHAT YOU'VE GOT —

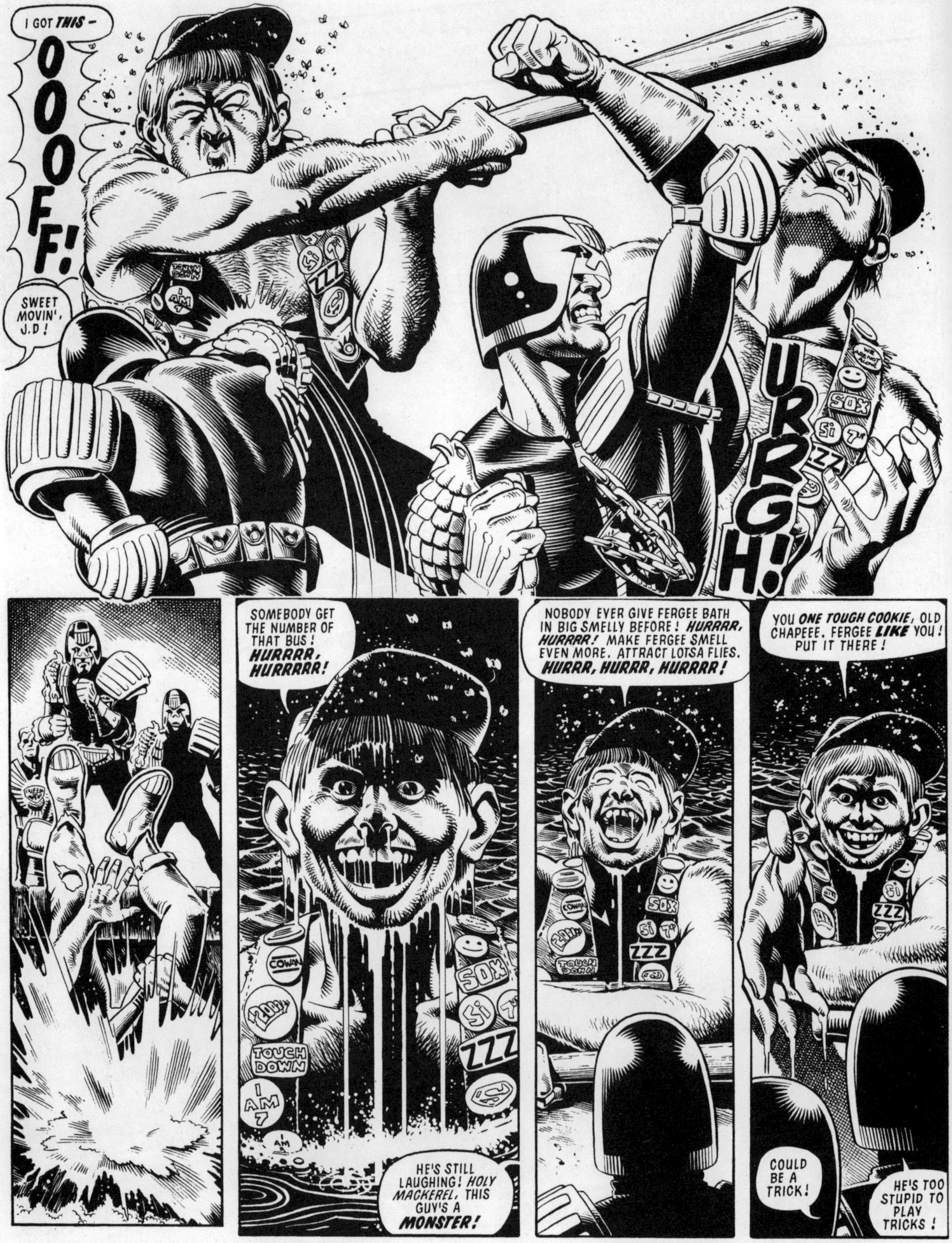

I GOT THIS –
OOOOFF!
SWEET MOVIN', J.D!
URRGH!
SOMEBODY GET THE NUMBER OF THAT BUS! HURRRR, HURRRRR!
HE'S STILL LAUGHING! HOLY MACKEREL, THIS GUY'S A MONSTER!
NOBODY EVER GIVE FERGEE BATH IN BIG SMELLY BEFORE! HURRRR, HURRRR! MAKE FERGEE SMELL EVEN MORE. ATTRACT LOTSA FLIES. HURRR, HURRR, HURRRR!
YOU ONE TOUGH COOKIE, OLD CHAPEEE. FERGEE LIKE YOU! PUT IT THERE!
COULD BE A TRICK!
HE'S TOO STUPID TO PLAY TRICKS!

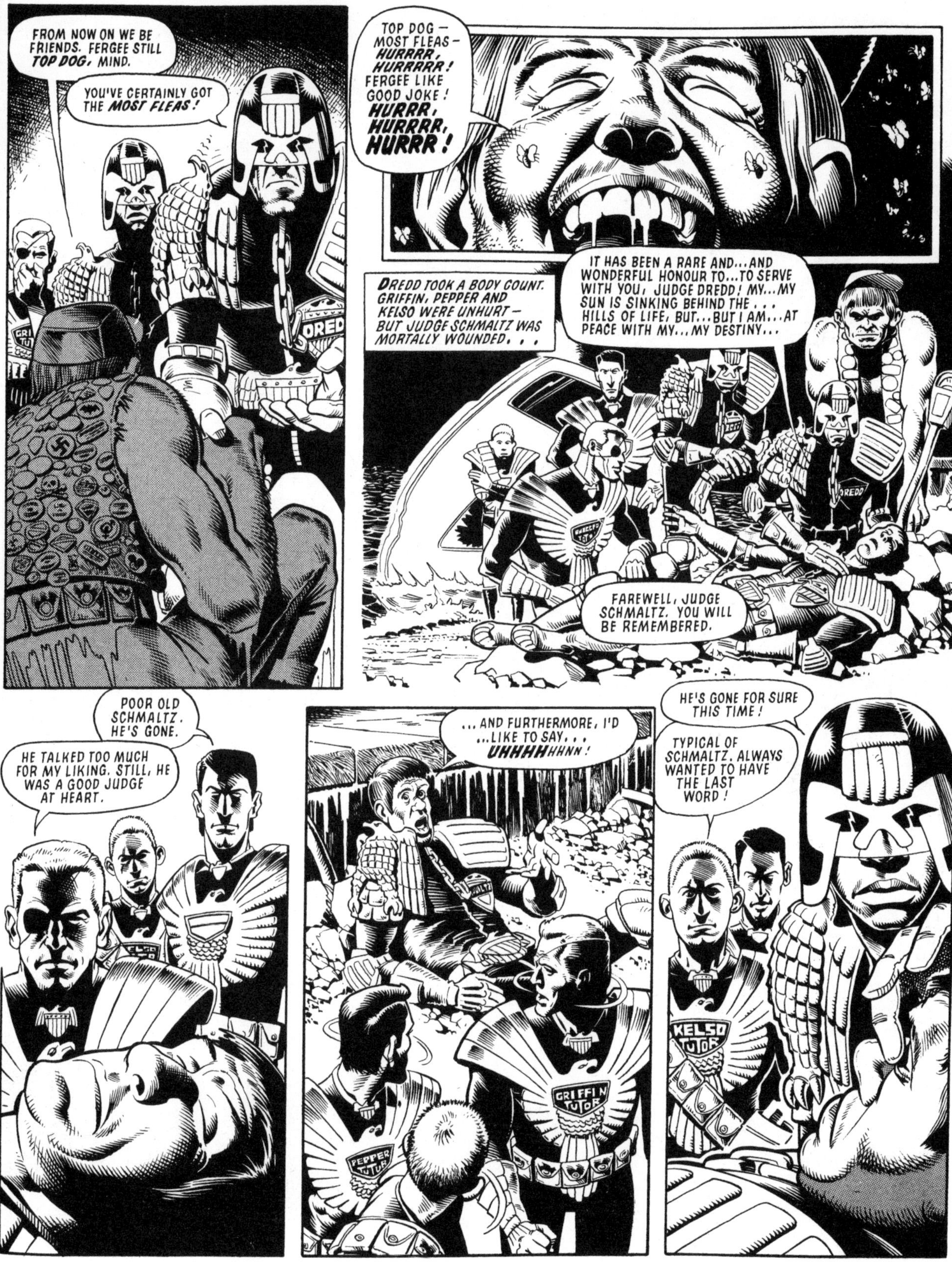

FROM NOW ON WE BE FRIENDS. FERGEE STILL TOP DOG, MIND.
YOU'VE CERTAINLY GOT THE MOST FLEAS!
TOP DOG — MOST FLEAS — HURRRR, HURRRRR! FERGEE LIKE GOOD JOKE! HURRR, HURRRR, HURRR!
DREDD TOOK A BODY COUNT. GRIFFIN, PEPPER AND KELSO WERE UNHURT — BUT JUDGE SCHMALTZ WAS MORTALLY WOUNDED...
IT HAS BEEN A RARE AND... AND WONDERFUL HONOUR TO... TO SERVE WITH YOU, JUDGE DREDD! MY... MY SUN IS SINKING BEHIND THE... HILLS OF LIFE, BUT... BUT I AM... AT PEACE WITH MY... MY DESTINY...
FAREWELL, JUDGE SCHMALTZ. YOU WILL BE REMEMBERED.
POOR OLD SCHMALTZ. HE'S GONE.
HE TALKED TOO MUCH FOR MY LIKING. STILL, HE WAS A GOOD JUDGE AT HEART.
... AND FURTHERMORE, I'D ...LIKE TO SAY... UHHHHHHNN!
HE'S GONE FOR SURE THIS TIME!
TYPICAL OF SCHMALTZ. ALWAYS WANTED TO HAVE THE LAST WORD!

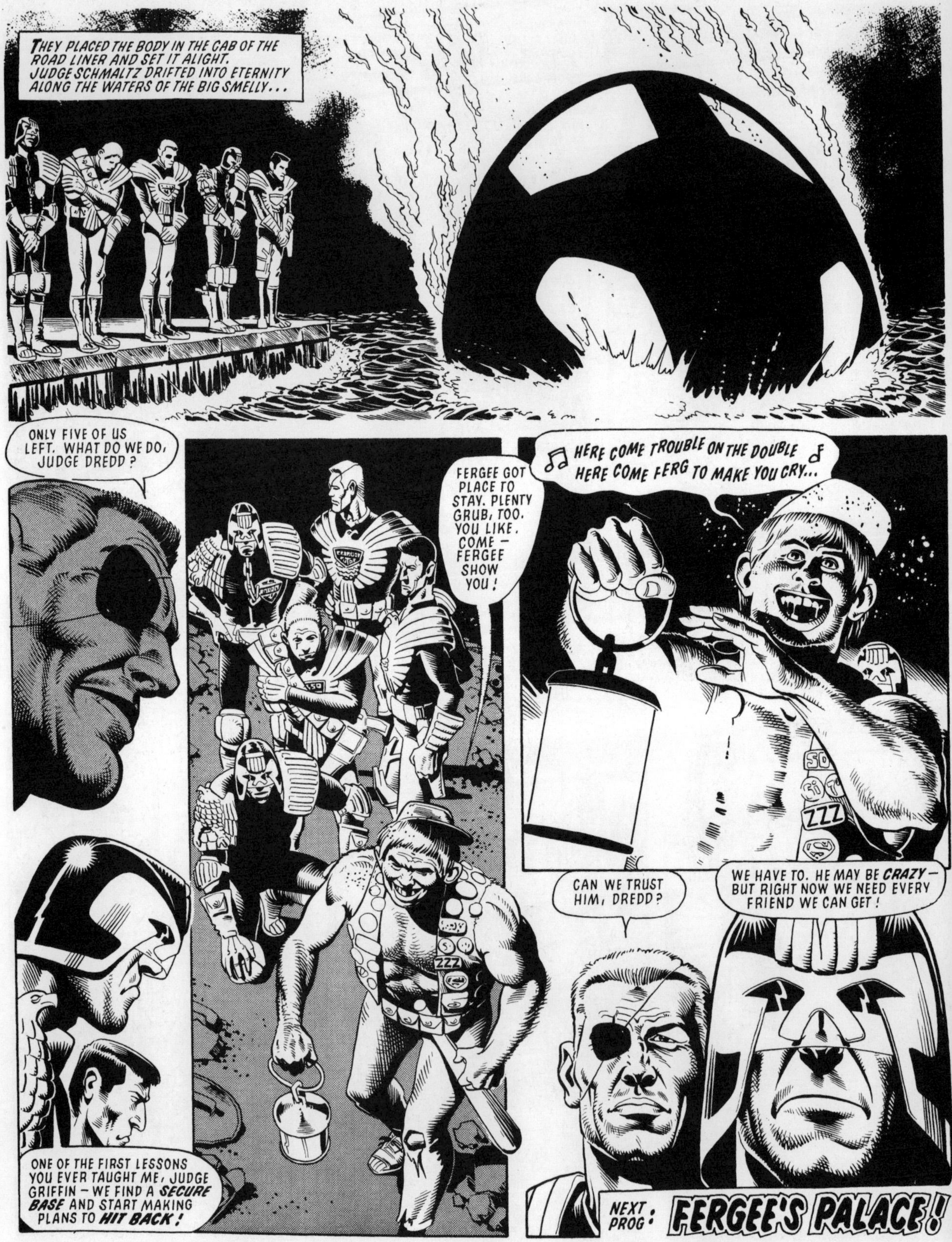
THEY PLACED THE BODY IN THE CAB OF THE ROAD LINER AND SET IT ALIGHT. JUDGE SCHMALTZ DRIFTED INTO ETERNITY ALONG THE WATERS OF THE BIG SMELLY...
ONLY FIVE OF US LEFT. WHAT DO WE DO, JUDGE DREDD?
ONE OF THE FIRST LESSONS YOU EVER TAUGHT ME, JUDGE GRIFFIN – WE FIND A SECURE BASE AND START MAKING PLANS TO HIT BACK!
FERGEE GOT PLACE TO STAY. PLENTY GRUB, TOO. YOU LIKE. COME – FERGEE SHOW YOU!
HERE COME TROUBLE ON THE DOUBLE HERE COME FERG TO MAKE YOU CRY...
ZZZ
CAN WE TRUST HIM, DREDD?
WE HAVE TO. HE MAY BE CRAZY – BUT RIGHT NOW WE NEED EVERY FRIEND WE CAN GET!
NEXT PROG: FERGEE'S PALACE!

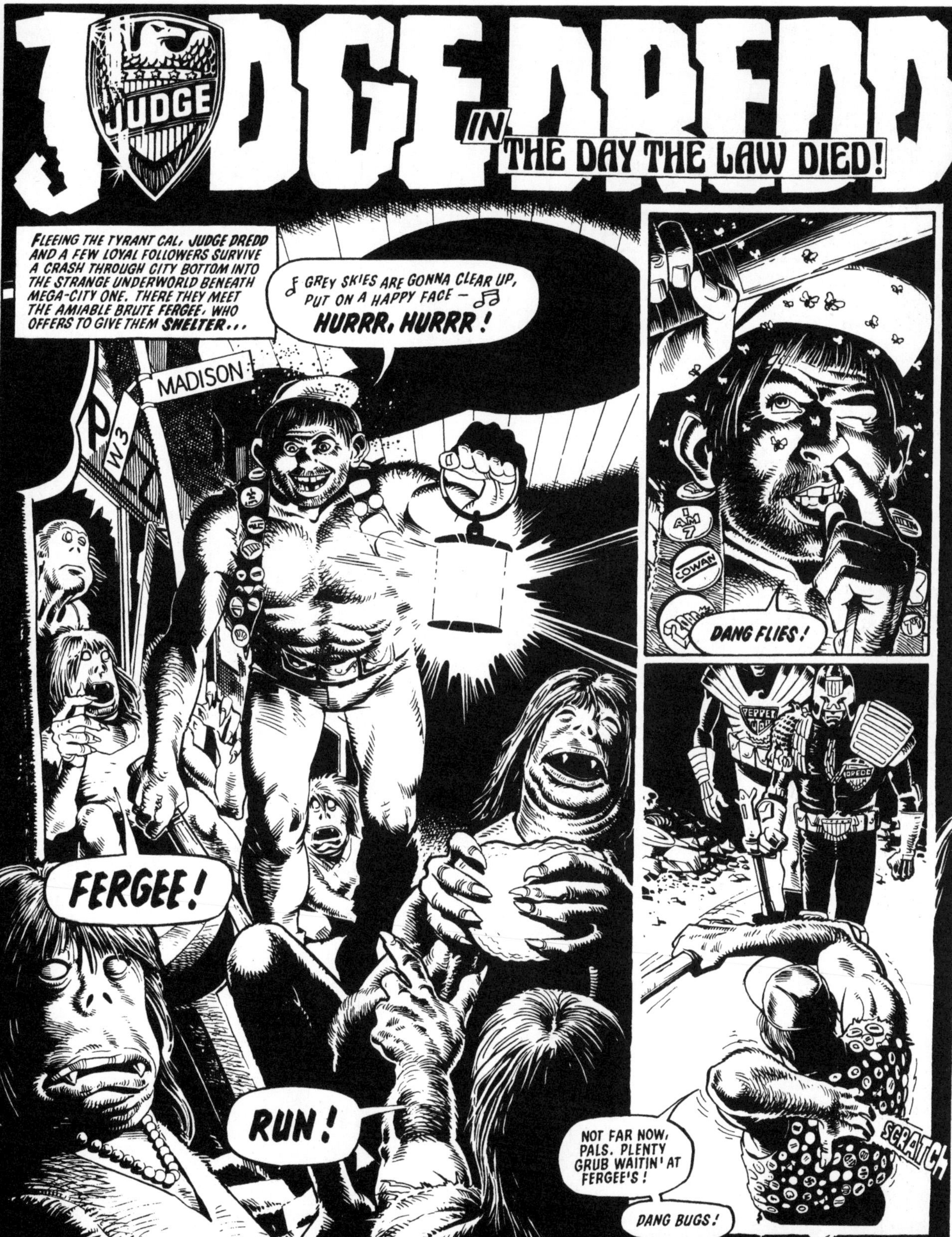

JUDGE DREDD
JUDGE
IN
THE DAY THE LAW DIED!
FLEEING THE TYRANT CAL, JUDGE DREDD AND A FEW LOYAL FOLLOWERS SURVIVE A CRASH THROUGH CITY BOTTOM INTO THE STRANGE UNDERWORLD BENEATH MEGA-CITY ONE. THERE THEY MEET THE AMIABLE BRUTE FERGEE, WHO OFFERS TO GIVE THEM SHELTER...
GREY SKIES ARE GONNA CLEAR UP, PUT ON A HAPPY FACE — HURRR, HURRR!
MADISON
P
W3
DANG FLIES!
I AM 7
COWAN
FERGEE!
RUN!
NOT FAR NOW, PALS. PLENTY GRUB WAITIN' AT FERGEE'S!
SCRATCH
DANG BUGS!

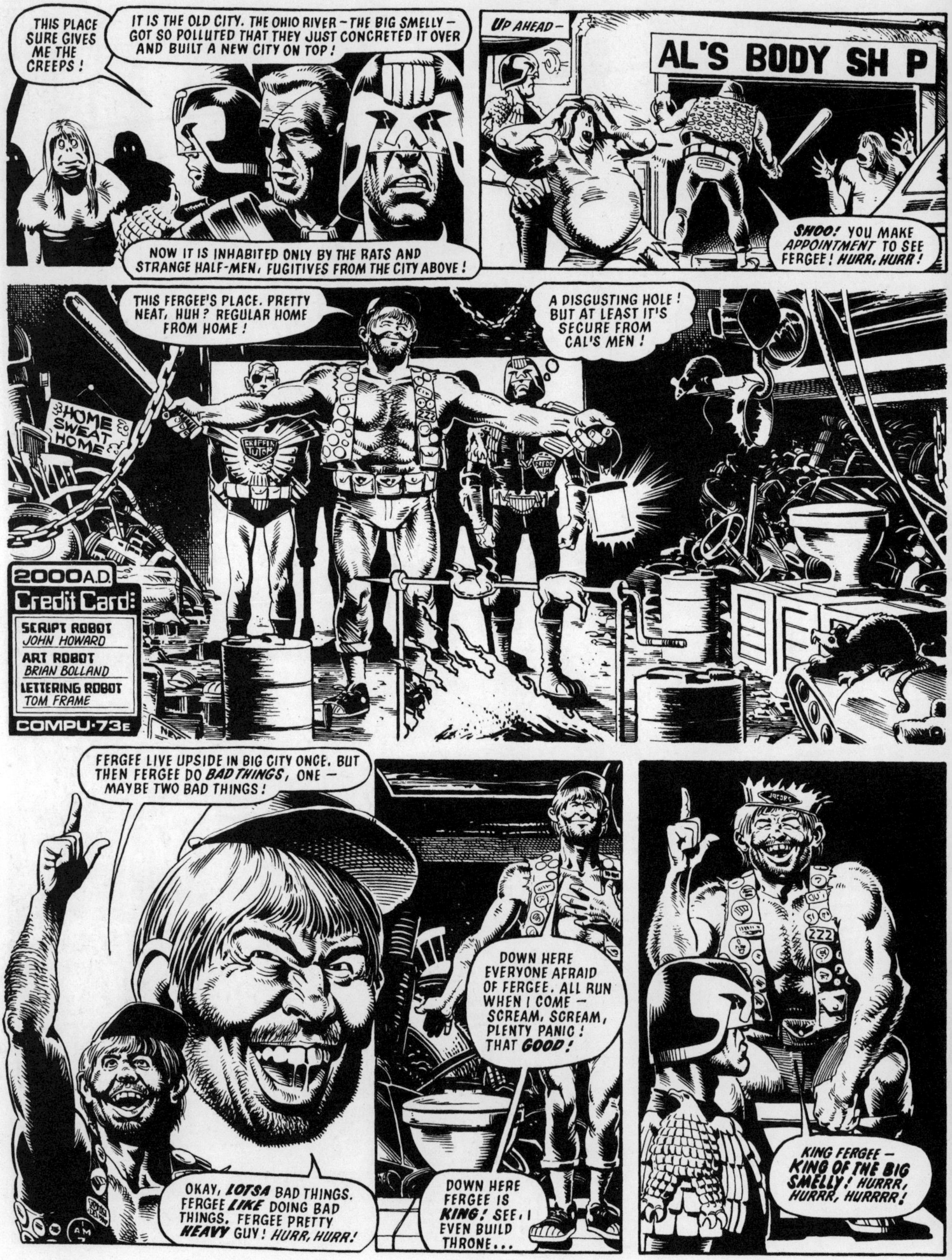
THIS PLACE SURE GIVES ME THE CREEPS!
IT IS THE OLD CITY. THE OHIO RIVER – THE BIG SMELLY – GOT SO POLLUTED THAT THEY JUST CONCRETED IT OVER AND BUILT A NEW CITY ON TOP!
NOW IT IS INHABITED ONLY BY THE RATS AND STRANGE HALF-MEN, FUGITIVES FROM THE CITY ABOVE!
UP AHEAD–
AL'S BODY SH P
SHOO! YOU MAKE APPOINTMENT TO SEE FERGEE! HURR, HURR!
THIS FERGEE'S PLACE. PRETTY NEAT, HUH? REGULAR HOME FROM HOME!
A DISGUSTING HOLE! BUT AT LEAST IT'S SECURE FROM CAL'S MEN!
HOME SWEAT HOME
2000 A.D.
Credit Card:
SCRIPT ROBOT JOHN HOWARD
ART ROBOT BRIAN BOLLAND
LETTERING ROBOT TOM FRAME
COMPU·73E
FERGEE LIVE UPSIDE IN BIG CITY ONCE. BUT THEN FERGEE DO BAD THINGS, ONE – MAYBE TWO BAD THINGS!
OKAY, LOTSA BAD THINGS. FERGEE LIKE DOING BAD THINGS. FERGEE PRETTY HEAVY GUY! HURR, HURR!
DOWN HERE EVERYONE AFRAID OF FERGEE. ALL RUN WHEN I COME – SCREAM, SCREAM, PLENTY PANIC! THAT GOOD!
DOWN HERE FERGEE IS KING! SEE, I EVEN BUILD THRONE...
KING FERGEE – KING OF THE BIG SMELLY! HURRR, HURRR, HURRRR!

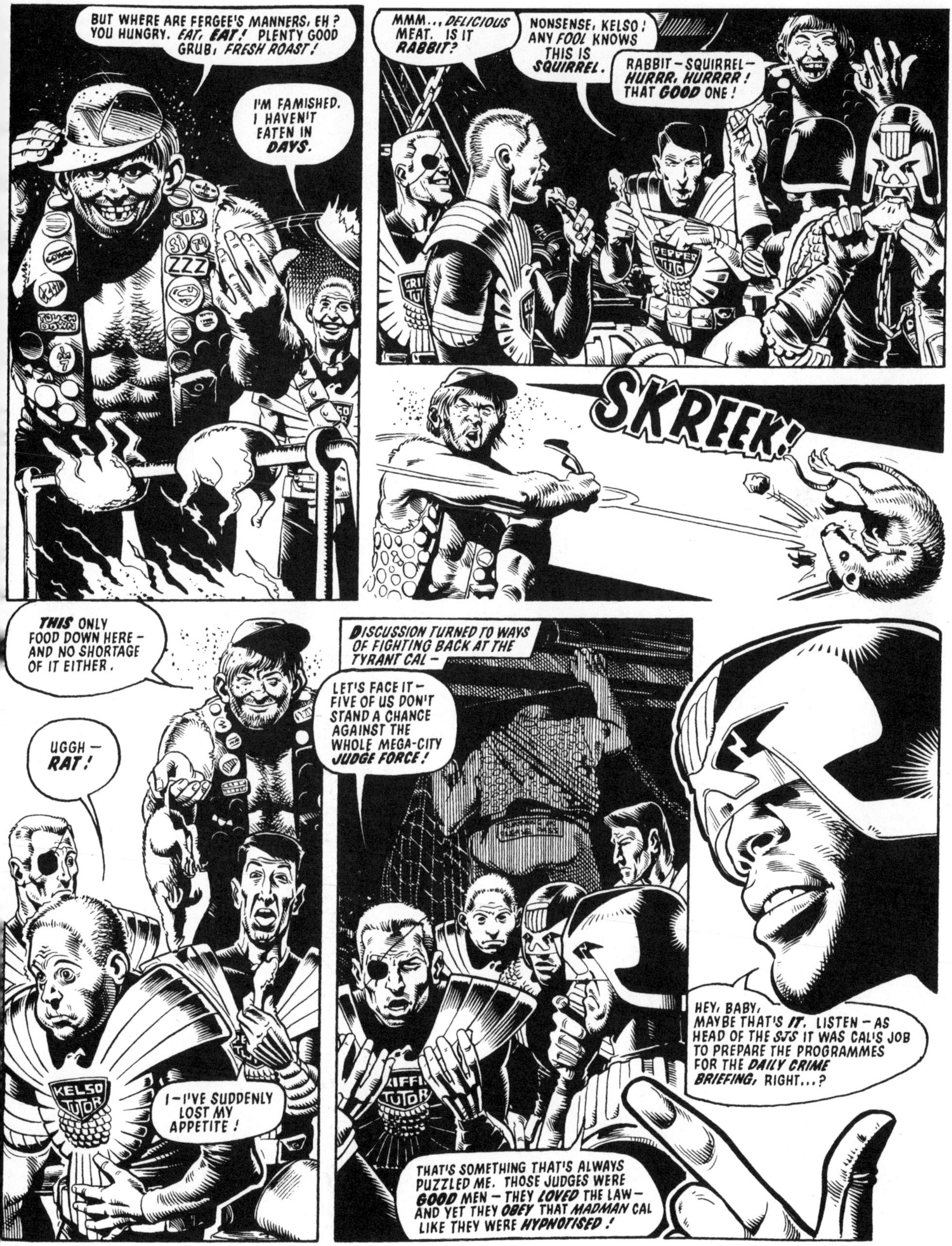
BUT WHERE ARE FERGEE'S MANNERS, EH ? YOU HUNGRY. EAT, EAT! PLENTY GOOD GRUB, FRESH ROAST!
I'M FAMISHED. I HAVEN'T EATEN IN DAYS.
MMM... DELICIOUS MEAT. IS IT RABBIT?
NONSENSE, KELSO! ANY FOOL KNOWS THIS IS SQUIRREL.
RABBIT — SQUIRREL — HURRR, HURRRR! THAT GOOD ONE!
SKREEK!
THIS ONLY FOOD DOWN HERE — AND NO SHORTAGE OF IT EITHER.
UGGH — RAT!
I — I'VE SUDDENLY LOST MY APPETITE!
DISCUSSION TURNED TO WAYS OF FIGHTING BACK AT THE TYRANT CAL —
LET'S FACE IT — FIVE OF US DON'T STAND A CHANCE AGAINST THE WHOLE MEGA-CITY JUDGE FORCE!
THAT'S SOMETHING THAT'S ALWAYS PUZZLED ME. THOSE JUDGES WERE GOOD MEN — THEY LOVED THE LAW — AND YET THEY OBEY THAT MADMAN CAL LIKE THEY WERE HYPNOTISED!
HEY, BABY, MAYBE THAT'S IT. LISTEN — AS HEAD OF THE SJS IT WAS CAL'S JOB TO PREPARE THE PROGRAMMES FOR THE DAILY CRIME BRIEFING, RIGHT...?

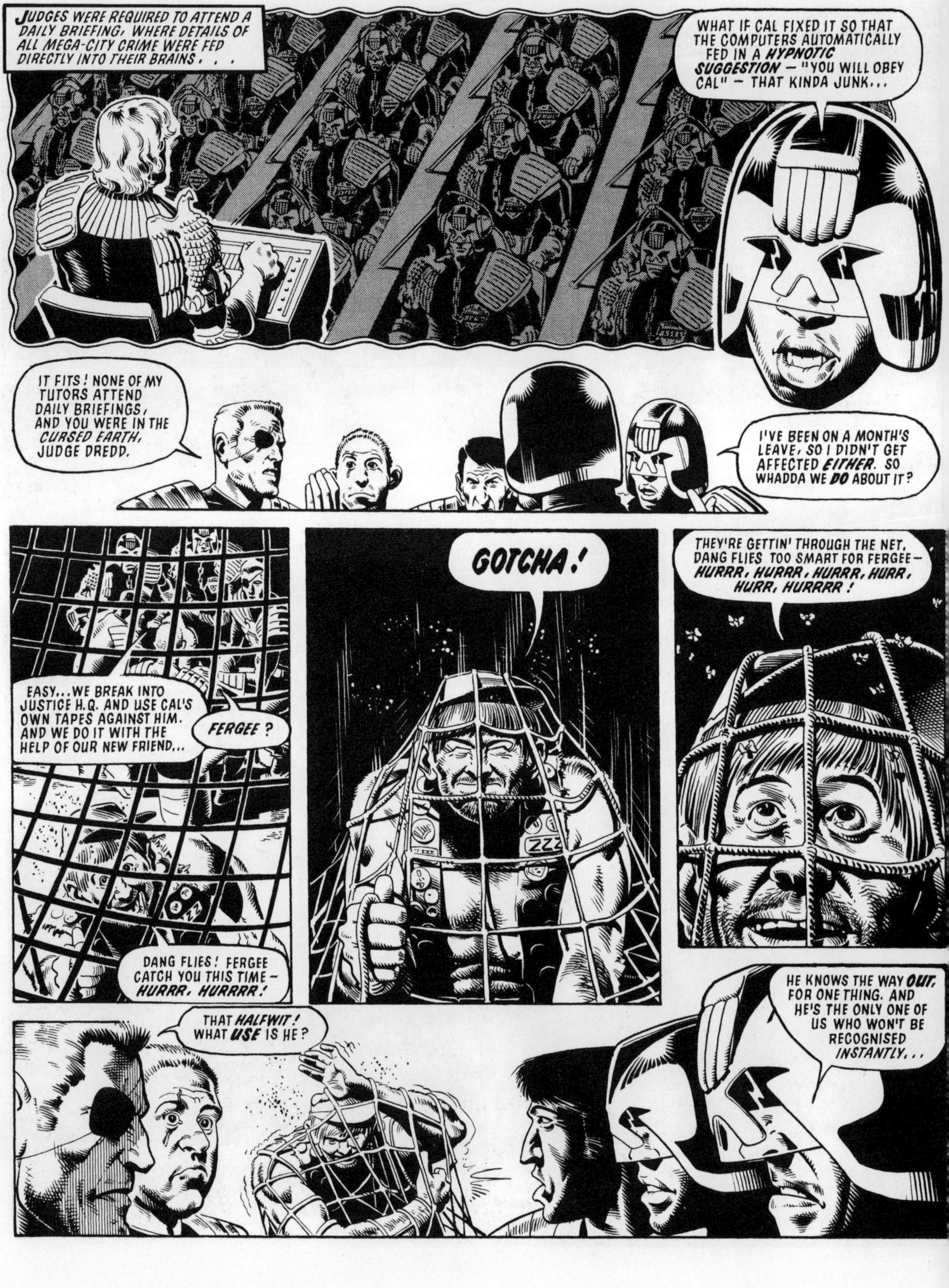
JUDGES WERE REQUIRED TO ATTEND A DAILY BRIEFING, WHERE DETAILS OF ALL MEGA-CITY CRIME WERE FED DIRECTLY INTO THEIR BRAINS . . .
WHAT IF CAL FIXED IT SO THAT THE COMPUTERS AUTOMATICALLY FED IN A HYPNOTIC SUGGESTION — "YOU WILL OBEY CAL" — THAT KINDA JUNK...
IT FITS! NONE OF MY TUTORS ATTEND DAILY BRIEFINGS, AND YOU WERE IN THE CURSED EARTH, JUDGE DREDD.
I'VE BEEN ON A MONTH'S LEAVE, SO I DIDN'T GET AFFECTED EITHER. SO WHADDA WE DO ABOUT IT?
EASY...WE BREAK INTO JUSTICE H.Q. AND USE CAL'S OWN TAPES AGAINST HIM. AND WE DO IT WITH THE HELP OF OUR NEW FRIEND...
FERGEE ?
DANG FLIES! FERGEE CATCH YOU THIS TIME — HURRR, HURRRR!
GOTCHA!
THEY'RE GETTIN' THROUGH THE NET, DANG FLIES TOO SMART FOR FERGEE — HURRR, HURRR, HURRR, HURR, HURR, HURRRR!
THAT HALFWIT! WHAT USE IS HE?
HE KNOWS THE WAY OUT, FOR ONE THING. AND HE'S THE ONLY ONE OF US WHO WON'T BE RECOGNISED INSTANTLY...

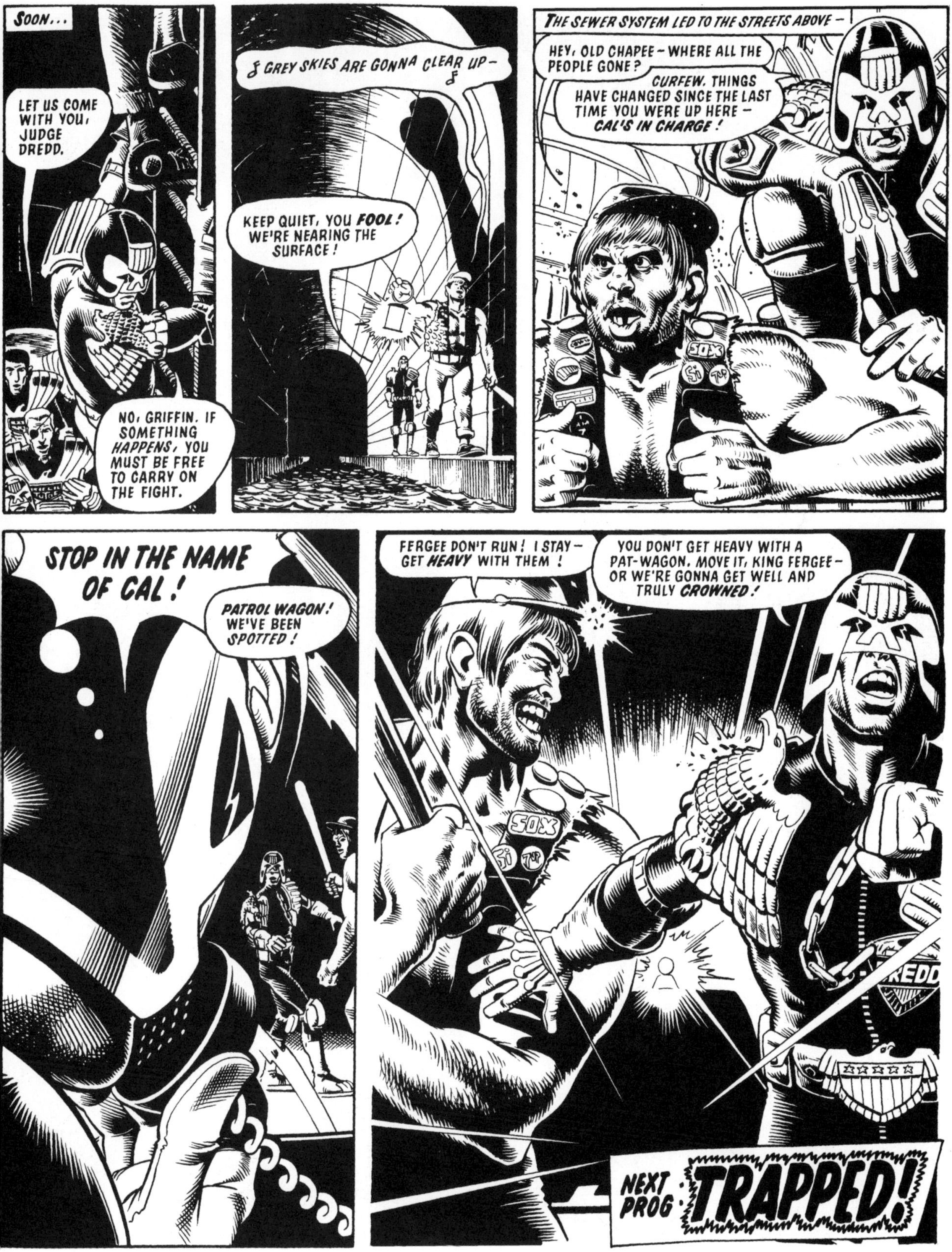

SOON...
LET US COME WITH YOU, JUDGE DREDD.
NO, GRIFFIN. IF SOMETHING HAPPENS, YOU MUST BE FREE TO CARRY ON THE FIGHT.
GREY SKIES ARE GONNA CLEAR UP–
KEEP QUIET, YOU FOOL! WE'RE NEARING THE SURFACE!
THE SEWER SYSTEM LED TO THE STREETS ABOVE–
HEY, OLD CHAPEE – WHERE ALL THE PEOPLE GONE?
CURFEW. THINGS HAVE CHANGED SINCE THE LAST TIME YOU WERE UP HERE – CAL'S IN CHARGE!
STOP IN THE NAME OF CAL!
PATROL WAGON! WE'VE BEEN SPOTTED!
FERGEE DON'T RUN! I STAY– GET HEAVY WITH THEM!
YOU DON'T GET HEAVY WITH A PAT-WAGON. MOVE IT, KING FERGEE– OR WE'RE GONNA GET WELL AND TRULY CROWNED!
NEXT PROG: TRAPPED!

JUDGE DREDD in THE DAY THE LAW DIED!

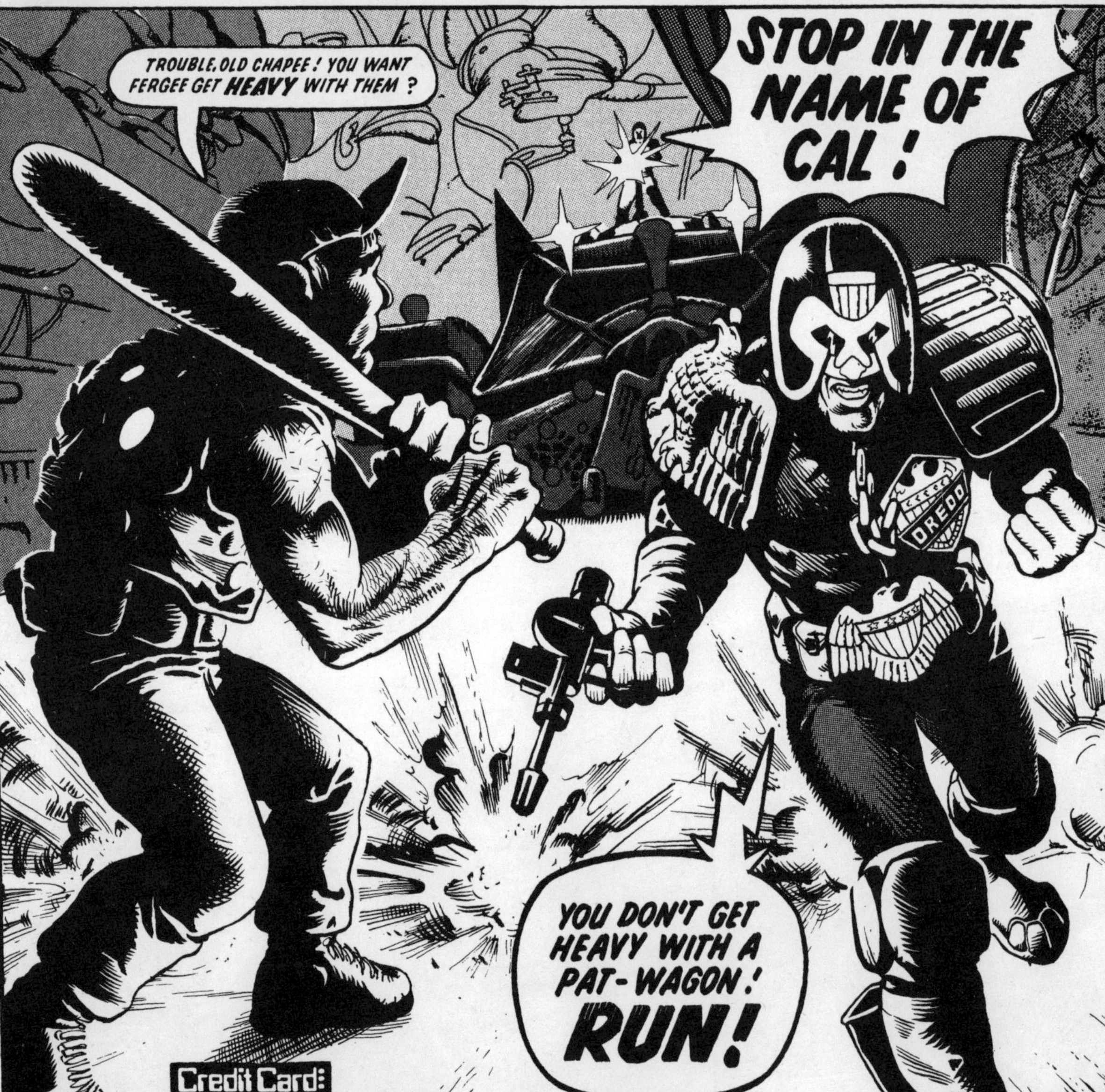
TROUBLE, OLD CHAPEE! YOU WANT FERGEE GET HEAVY WITH THEM?
STOP IN THE NAME OF CAL!
YOU DON'T GET HEAVY WITH A PAT-WAGON! RUN!
Credit Card:
SCRIPT ROBOT JOHN HOWARD
ART ROBOT GARY LEACH
LETTERING ROBOT THOMAS
COMPU-73E

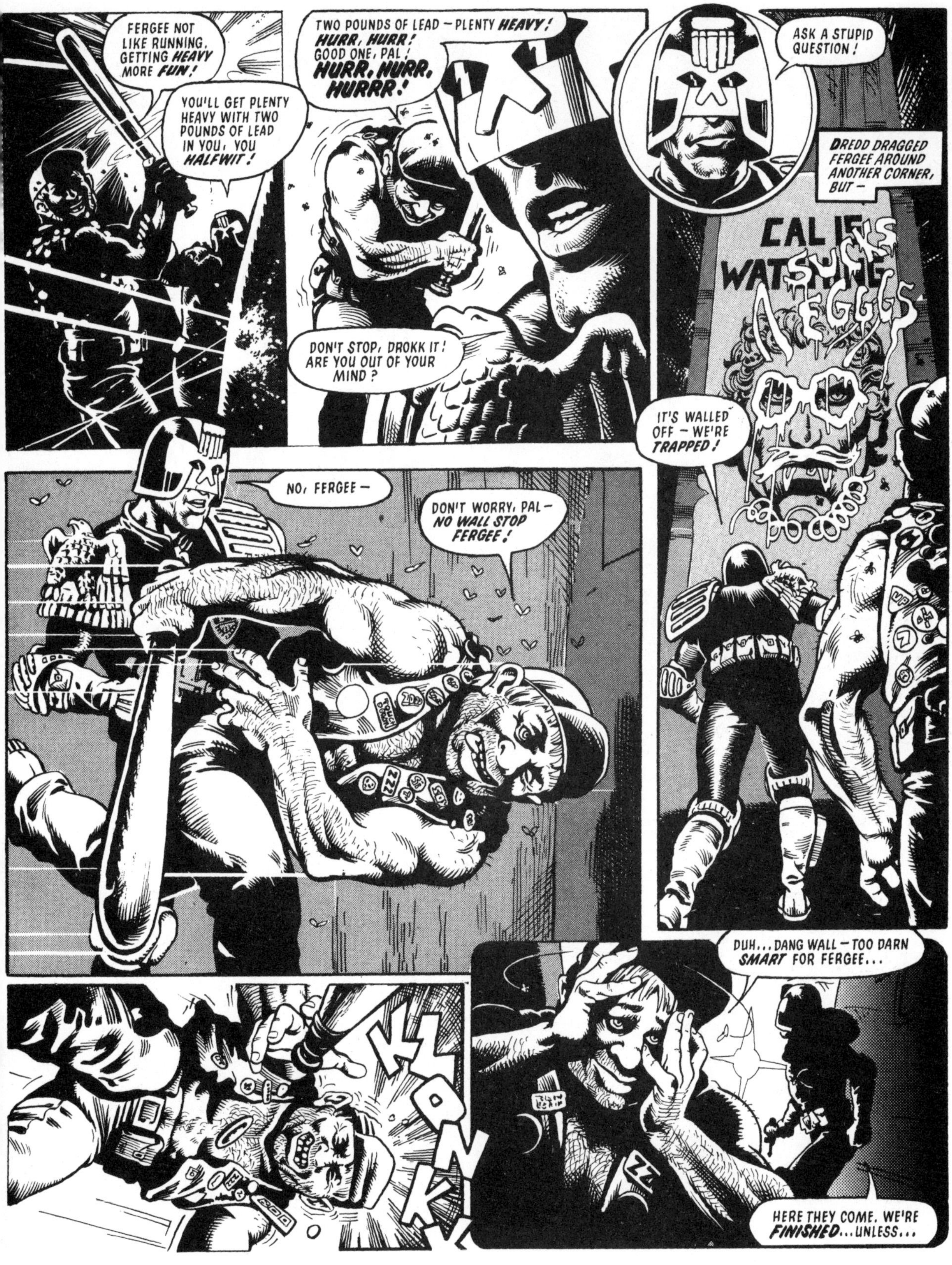
FERGEE NOT LIKE RUNNING, GETTING HEAVY MORE FUN!
YOU'LL GET PLENTY HEAVY WITH TWO POUNDS OF LEAD IN YOU, YOU HALFWIT!
TWO POUNDS OF LEAD — PLENTY HEAVY! HURR, HURR! GOOD ONE, PAL! HURR, HURR, HURRR!
DON'T STOP, DROKK IT! ARE YOU OUT OF YOUR MIND?
ASK A STUPID QUESTION!
DREDD DRAGGED FERGEE AROUND ANOTHER CORNER, BUT —
CAL IS WATSUCKS EGGS
IT'S WALLED OFF — WE'RE TRAPPED!
NO, FERGEE —
DON'T WORRY, PAL — NO WALL STOP FERGEE!
KLONK
DUH... DANG WALL — TOO DARN SMART FOR FERGEE...
HERE THEY COME. WE'RE FINISHED... UNLESS...

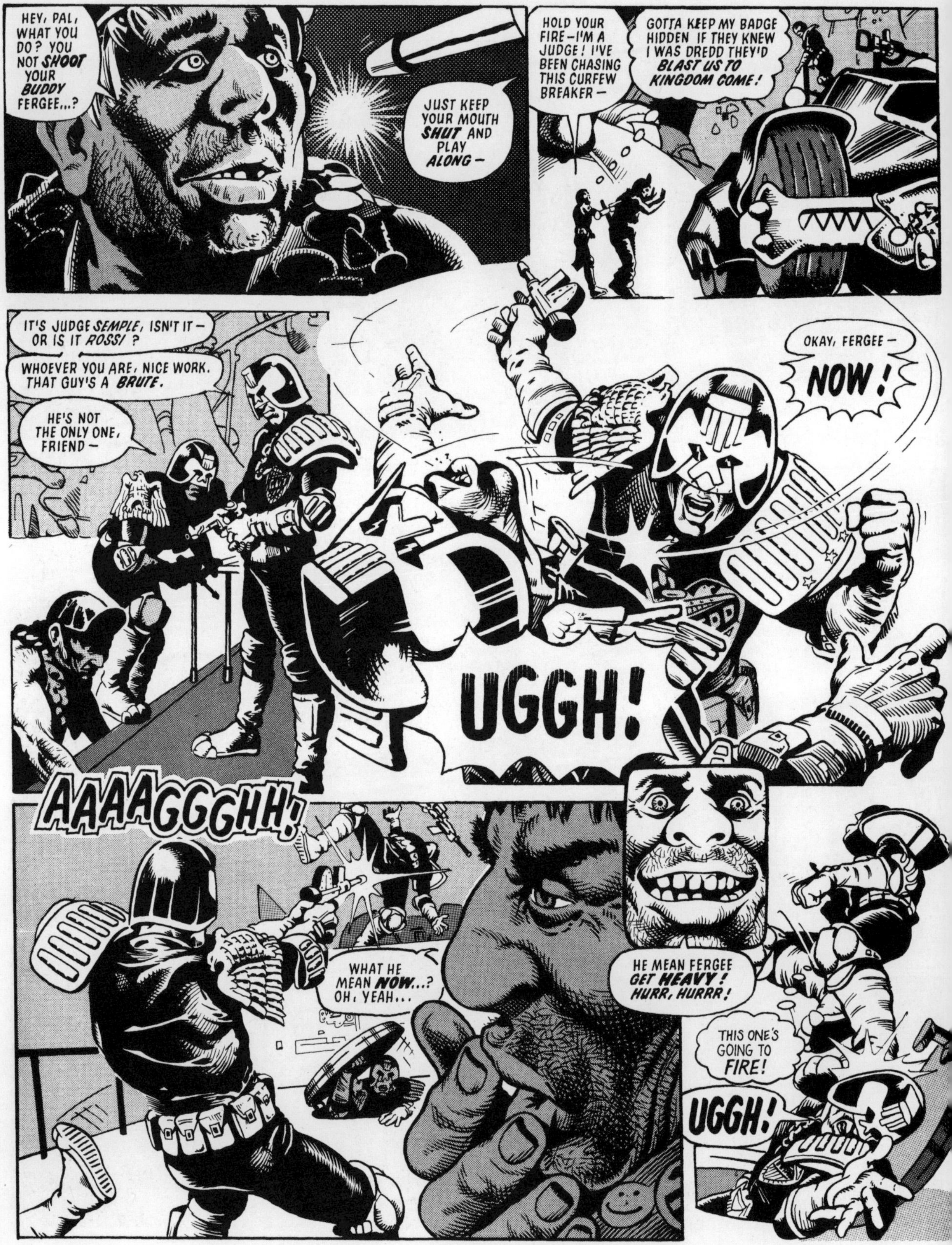

HEY, PAL, WHAT YOU DO? YOU NOT SHOOT YOUR BUDDY FERGEE...?
JUST KEEP YOUR MOUTH SHUT AND PLAY ALONG –
HOLD YOUR FIRE – I'M A JUDGE! I'VE BEEN CHASING THIS CURFEW BREAKER –
GOTTA KEEP MY BADGE HIDDEN IF THEY KNEW I WAS DREDD THEY'D BLAST US TO KINGDOM COME!
IT'S JUDGE SEMPLE, ISN'T IT – OR IS IT ROSSI?
WHOEVER YOU ARE, NICE WORK. THAT GUY'S A BRUTE.
HE'S NOT THE ONLY ONE, FRIEND –
OKAY, FERGEE – NOW!
UGGH!
AAAAGGGHH!
WHAT HE MEAN NOW...? OH, YEAH...
HE MEAN FERGEE GET HEAVY! HURR, HURRR!
THIS ONE'S GOING TO FIRE!
UGGH!

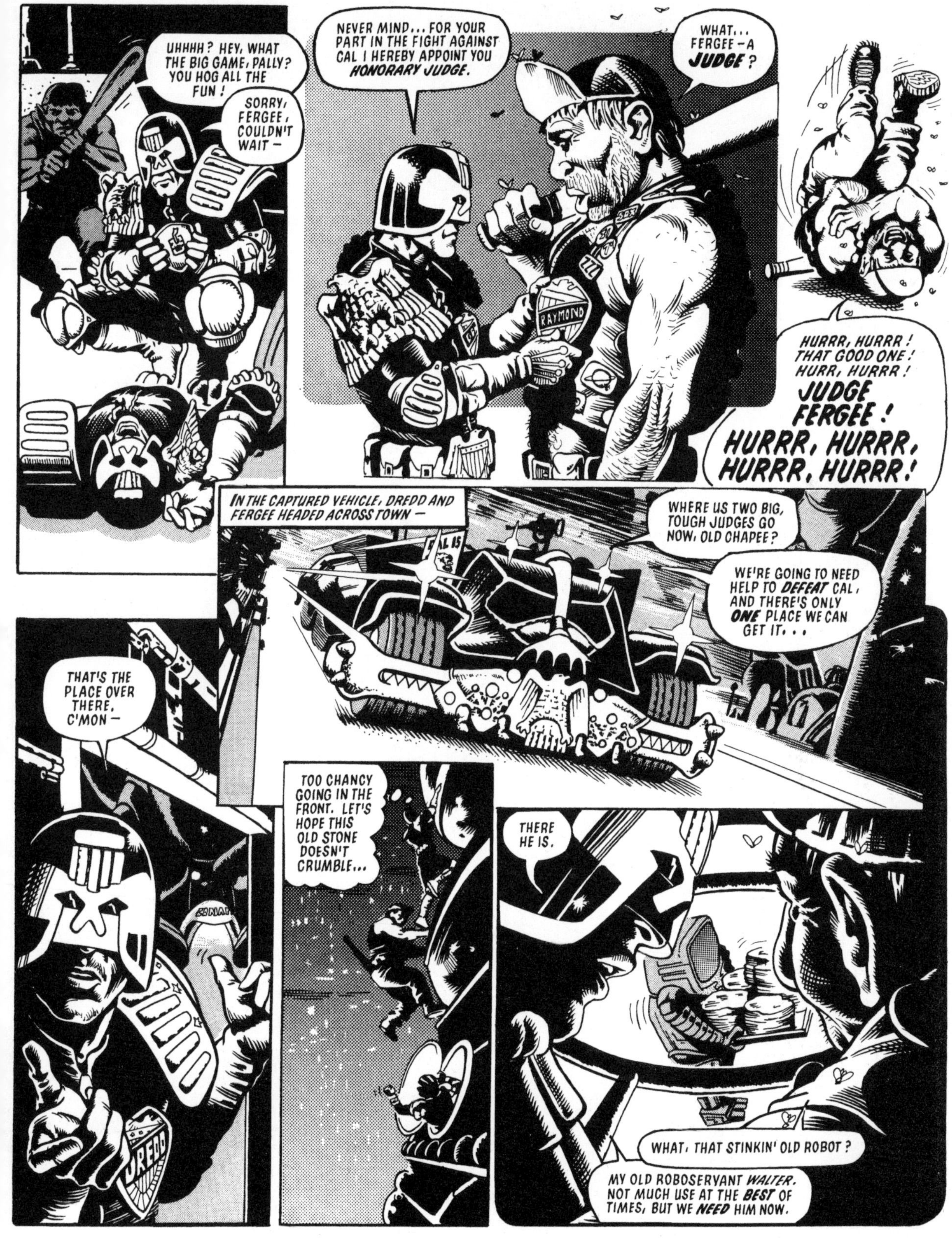
UHHHH? HEY, WHAT THE BIG GAME, PALLY? YOU HOG ALL THE FUN!
SORRY, FERGEE, COULDN'T WAIT –
NEVER MIND... FOR YOUR PART IN THE FIGHT AGAINST CAL I HEREBY APPOINT YOU HONORARY JUDGE.
WHAT... FERGEE – A JUDGE?
RAYMOND
HURRR, HURRR! THAT GOOD ONE! HURR, HURRR! JUDGE FERGEE! HURRR, HURRR, HURRR, HURRR!
IN THE CAPTURED VEHICLE, DREDD AND FERGEE HEADED ACROSS TOWN –
WHERE US TWO BIG, TOUGH JUDGES GO NOW, OLD CHAPEE?
WE'RE GOING TO NEED HELP TO DEFEAT CAL, AND THERE'S ONLY ONE PLACE WE CAN GET IT...
THAT'S THE PLACE OVER THERE. C'MON –
TOO CHANCY GOING IN THE FRONT. LET'S HOPE THIS OLD STONE DOESN'T CRUMBLE...
THERE HE IS.
WHAT, THAT STINKIN' OLD ROBOT?
MY OLD ROBOSERVANT WALTER. NOT MUCH USE AT THE BEST OF TIMES, BUT WE NEED HIM NOW.

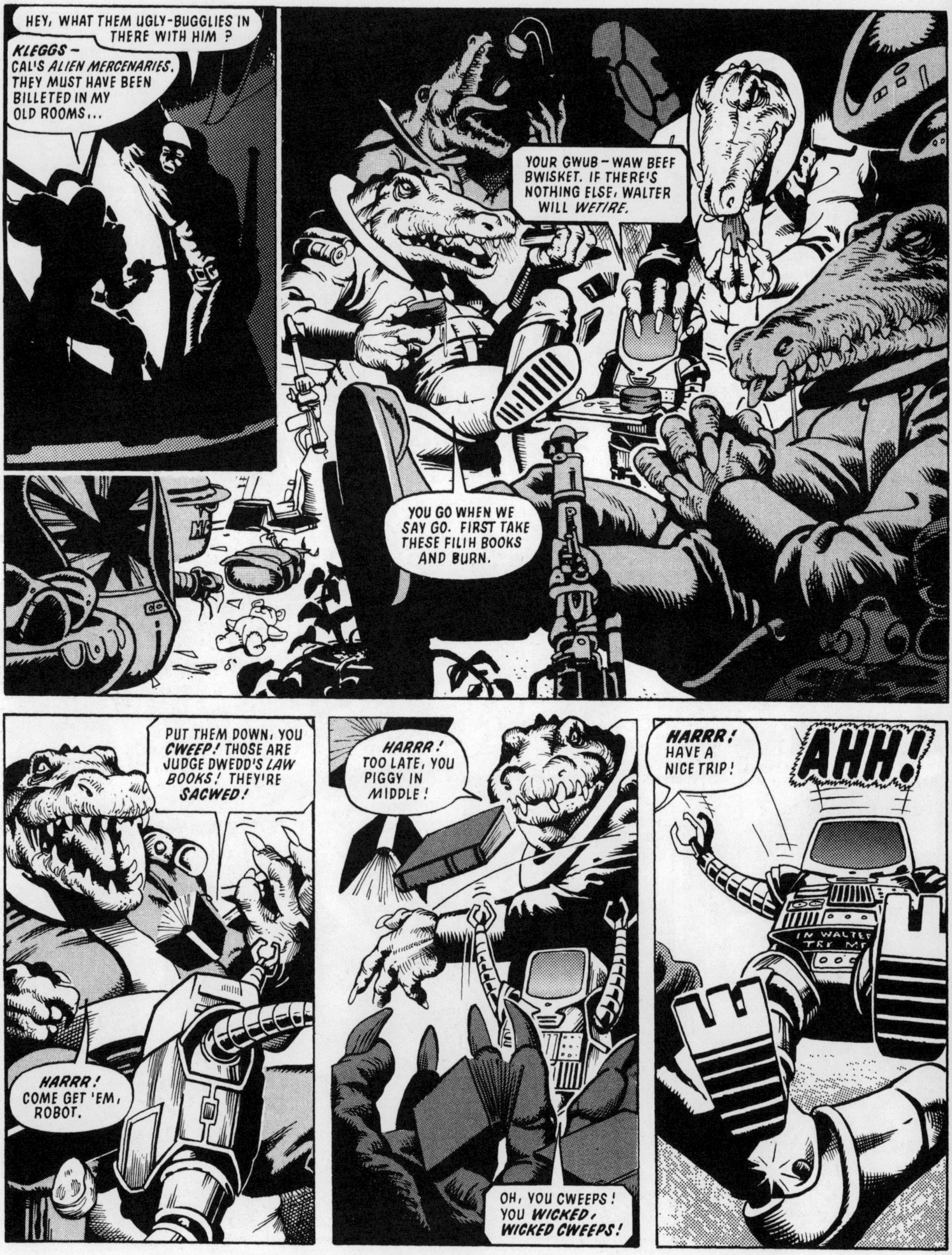

HEY, WHAT THEM UGLY-BUGGLIES IN THERE WITH HIM ?
KLEGGS – CAL'S ALIEN MERCENARIES. THEY MUST HAVE BEEN BILLETED IN MY OLD ROOMS...
YOUR GWUB – WAW BEEF BWISKET. IF THERE'S NOTHING ELSE, WALTER WILL WETIRE.
YOU GO WHEN WE SAY GO. FIRST TAKE THESE FILIH BOOKS AND BURN.
PUT THEM DOWN, YOU CWEEP! THOSE ARE JUDGE DWEDD'S LAW BOOKS! THEY'RE SACWED!
HARRR! COME GET 'EM, ROBOT.
HARRR! TOO LATE, YOU PIGGY IN MIDDLE!
OH, YOU CWEEPS! YOU WICKED, WICKED CWEEPS!
HARRR! HAVE A NICE TRIP!
AHH!

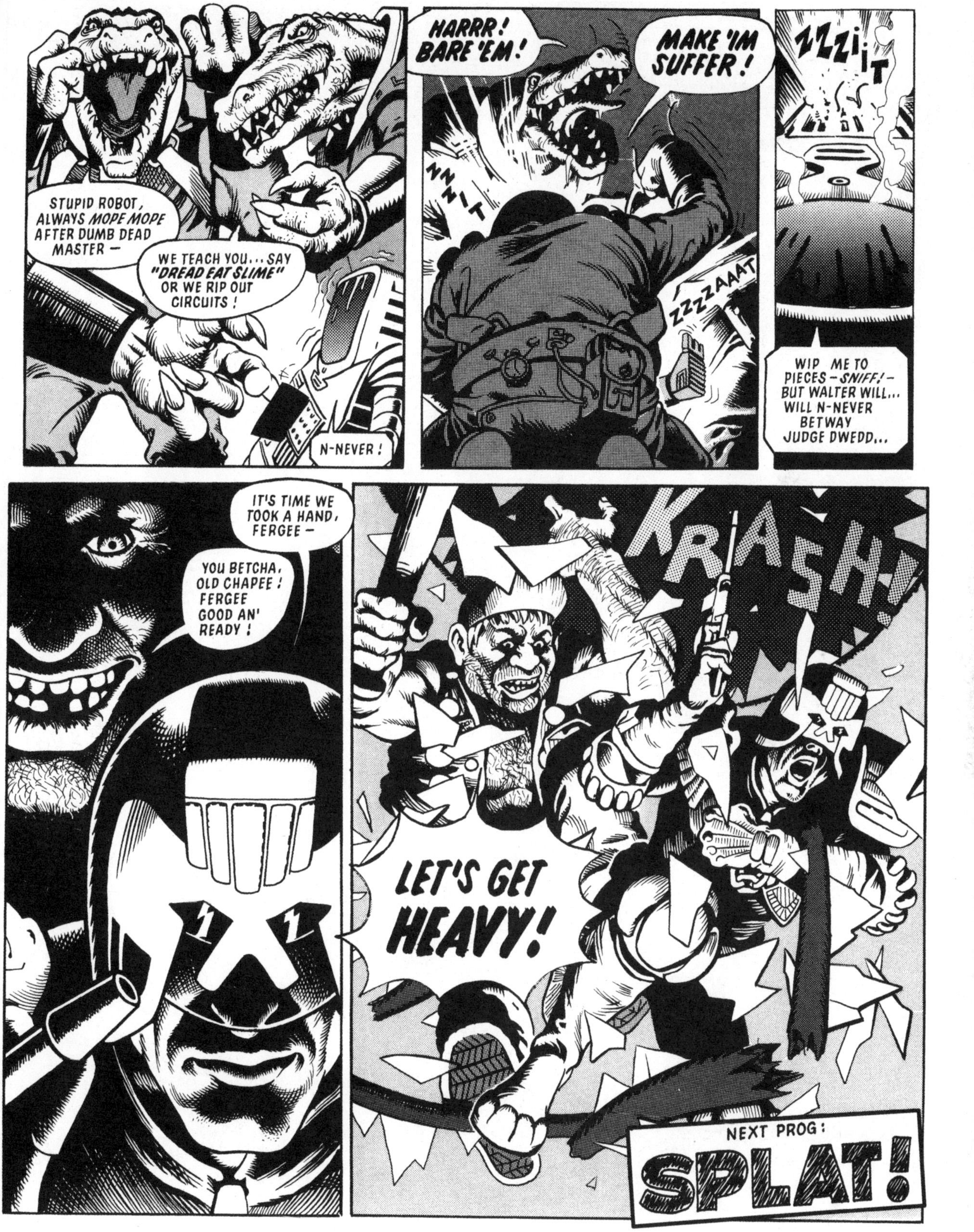

STUPID ROBOT, ALWAYS MOPE MOPE AFTER DUMB DEAD MASTER –
WE TEACH YOU... SAY "DREAD EAT SLIME" OR WE RIP OUT CIRCUITS!
N-NEVER!
HARRR! BARE 'EM!
MAKE 'IM SUFFER!
NNNIT
ZZZZAAAT
ZZZIIT
WIP ME TO PIECES – SNIFF! – BUT WALTER WILL... WILL N-NEVER BETWAY JUDGE DWEDD...
IT'S TIME WE TOOK A HAND, FERGEE –
YOU BETCHA, OLD CHAPEE! FERGEE GOOD AN' READY!
KRASH!
LET'S GET HEAVY!
NEXT PROG:
SPLAT!

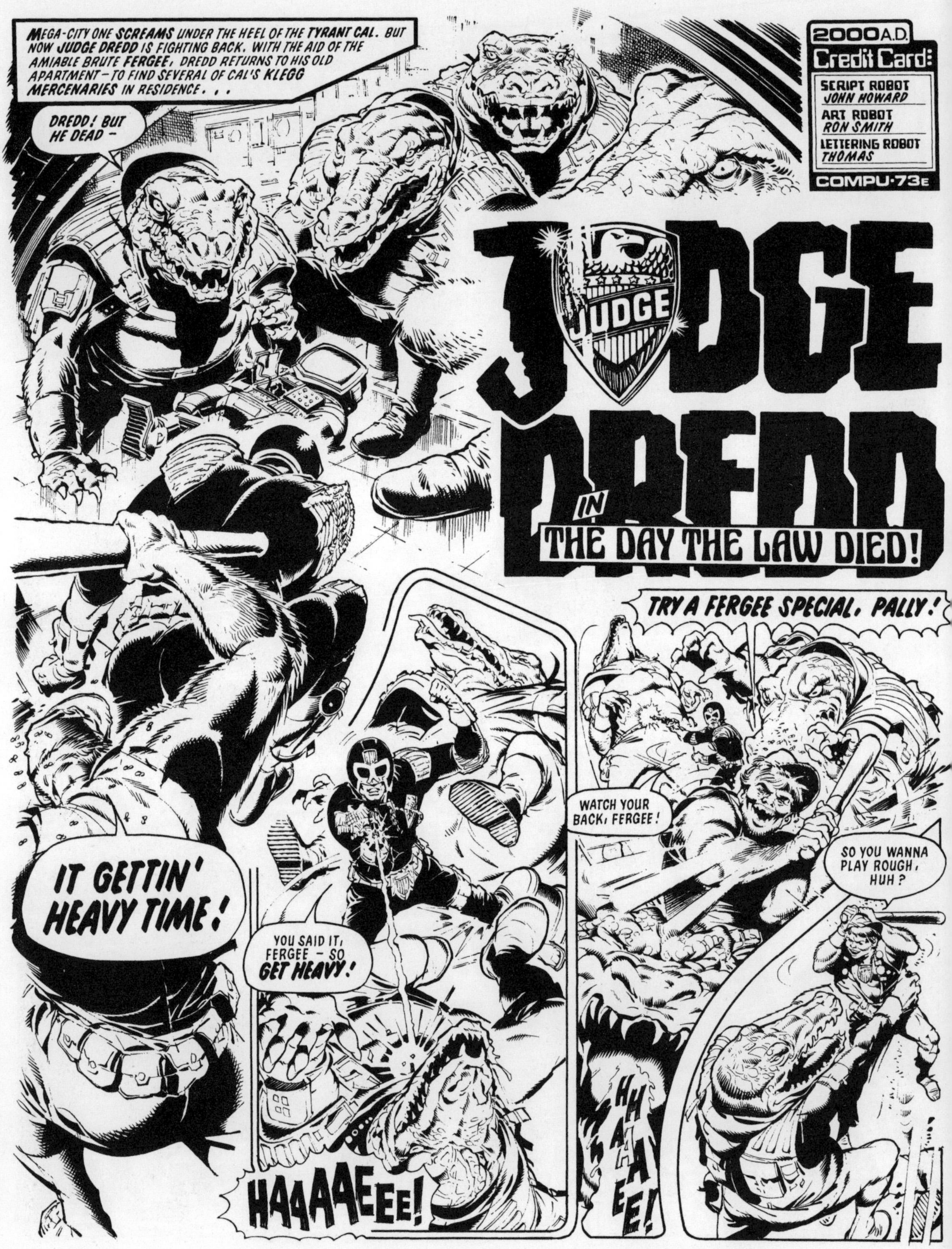
MEGA-CITY ONE SCREAMS UNDER THE HEEL OF THE TYRANT CAL. BUT NOW JUDGE DREDD IS FIGHTING BACK. WITH THE AID OF THE AMIABLE BRUTE FERGEE, DREDD RETURNS TO HIS OLD APARTMENT – TO FIND SEVERAL OF CAL'S KLEGG MERCENARIES IN RESIDENCE . . .
2000 A.D. Credit Card:
SCRIPT ROBOT JOHN HOWARD
ART ROBOT RON SMITH
LETTERING ROBOT THOMAS
COMPU-73E
JUDGE DREDD IN
THE DAY THE LAW DIED!
DREDD! BUT HE DEAD –
IT GETTIN' HEAVY TIME!
YOU SAID IT, FERGEE – SO GET HEAVY!
HAAAAEEEE!
TRY A FERGEE SPECIAL, PALLY!
WATCH YOUR BACK, FERGEE!
SO YOU WANNA PLAY ROUGH, HUH?
HHAAAEE!

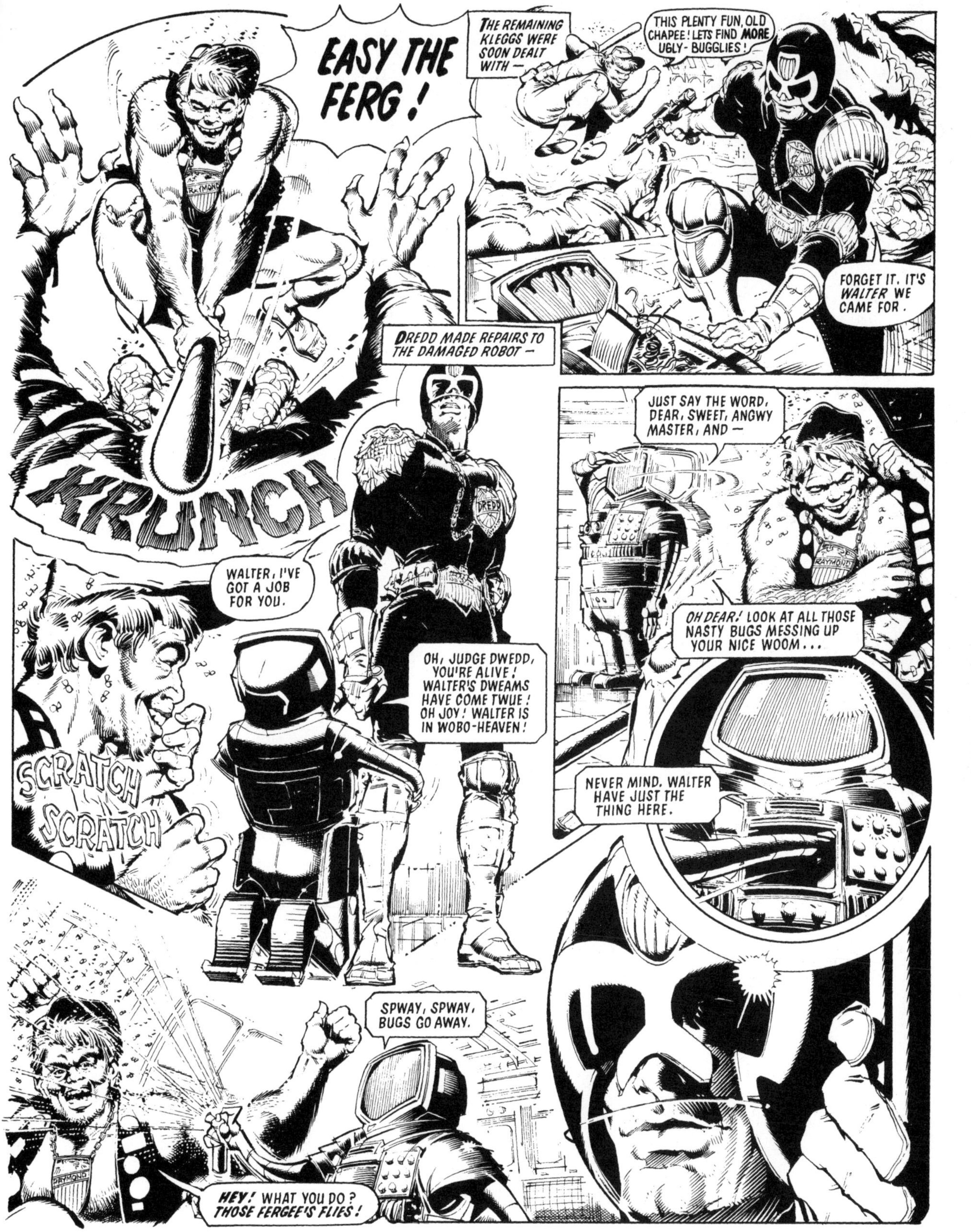
EASY THE FERG!
KRUNCH
THE REMAINING KLEGGS WERE SOON DEALT WITH —
THIS PLENTY FUN, OLD CHAPEE! LETS FIND MORE UGLY-BUGGLIES!
FORGET IT. IT'S WALTER WE CAME FOR.
DREDD MADE REPAIRS TO THE DAMAGED ROBOT —
WALTER, I'VE GOT A JOB FOR YOU.
OH, JUDGE DWEDD, YOU'RE ALIVE! WALTER'S DWEAMS HAVE COME TWUE! OH JOY! WALTER IS IN WOBO-HEAVEN!
SCRATCH SCRATCH
JUST SAY THE WORD, DEAR, SWEET, ANGWY MASTER, AND —
OH DEAR! LOOK AT ALL THOSE NASTY BUGS MESSING UP YOUR NICE WOOM...
NEVER MIND. WALTER HAVE JUST THE THING HERE.
SPWAY, SPWAY, BUGS GO AWAY.
HEY! WHAT YOU DO? THOSE FERGEE'S FLIES!

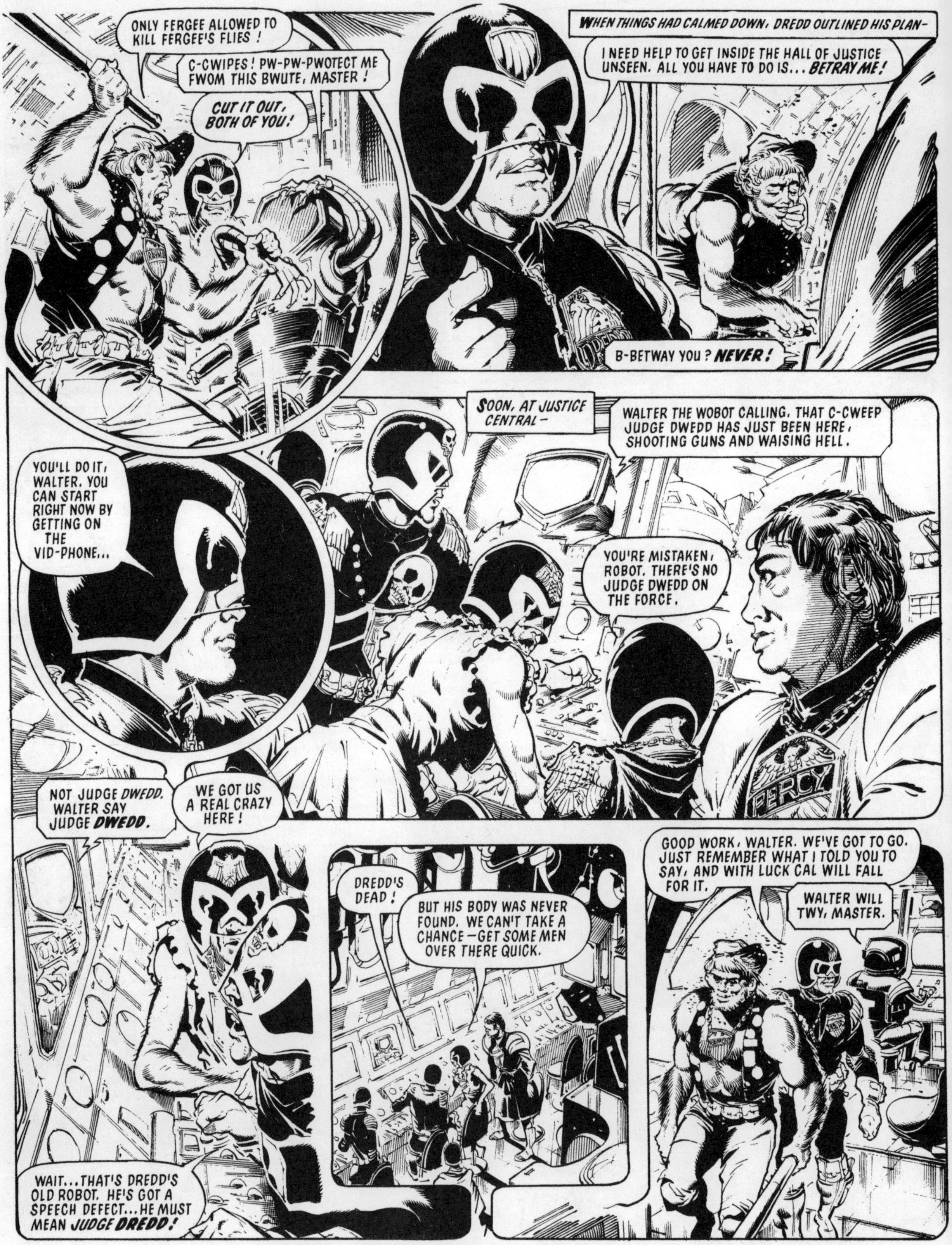

ONLY FERGEE ALLOWED TO KILL FERGEE'S FLIES!
C-CWIPES! PW-PW-PWOTECT ME FWOM THIS BWUTE, MASTER!
CUT IT OUT, BOTH OF YOU!
WHEN THINGS HAD CALMED DOWN, DREDD OUTLINED HIS PLAN–
I NEED HELP TO GET INSIDE THE HALL OF JUSTICE UNSEEN. ALL YOU HAVE TO DO IS... BETRAY ME!
B-BETWAY YOU? NEVER!
YOU'LL DO IT, WALTER. YOU CAN START RIGHT NOW BY GETTING ON THE VID-PHONE...
SOON, AT JUSTICE CENTRAL–
WALTER THE WOBOT CALLING. THAT C-CWEEP JUDGE DWEDD HAS JUST BEEN HERE, SHOOTING GUNS AND WAISING HELL.
YOU'RE MISTAKEN, ROBOT. THERE'S NO JUDGE DWEDD ON THE FORCE.
PERCY
NOT JUDGE DWEDD. WALTER SAY JUDGE DWEDD.
WE GOT US A REAL CRAZY HERE!
WAIT... THAT'S DREDD'S OLD ROBOT. HE'S GOT A SPEECH DEFECT... HE MUST MEAN JUDGE DREDD!
DREDD'S DEAD!
BUT HIS BODY WAS NEVER FOUND. WE CAN'T TAKE A CHANCE—GET SOME MEN OVER THERE QUICK.
GOOD WORK, WALTER. WE'VE GOT TO GO. JUST REMEMBER WHAT I TOLD YOU TO SAY, AND WITH LUCK CAL WILL FALL FOR IT.
WALTER WILL TWY, MASTER.

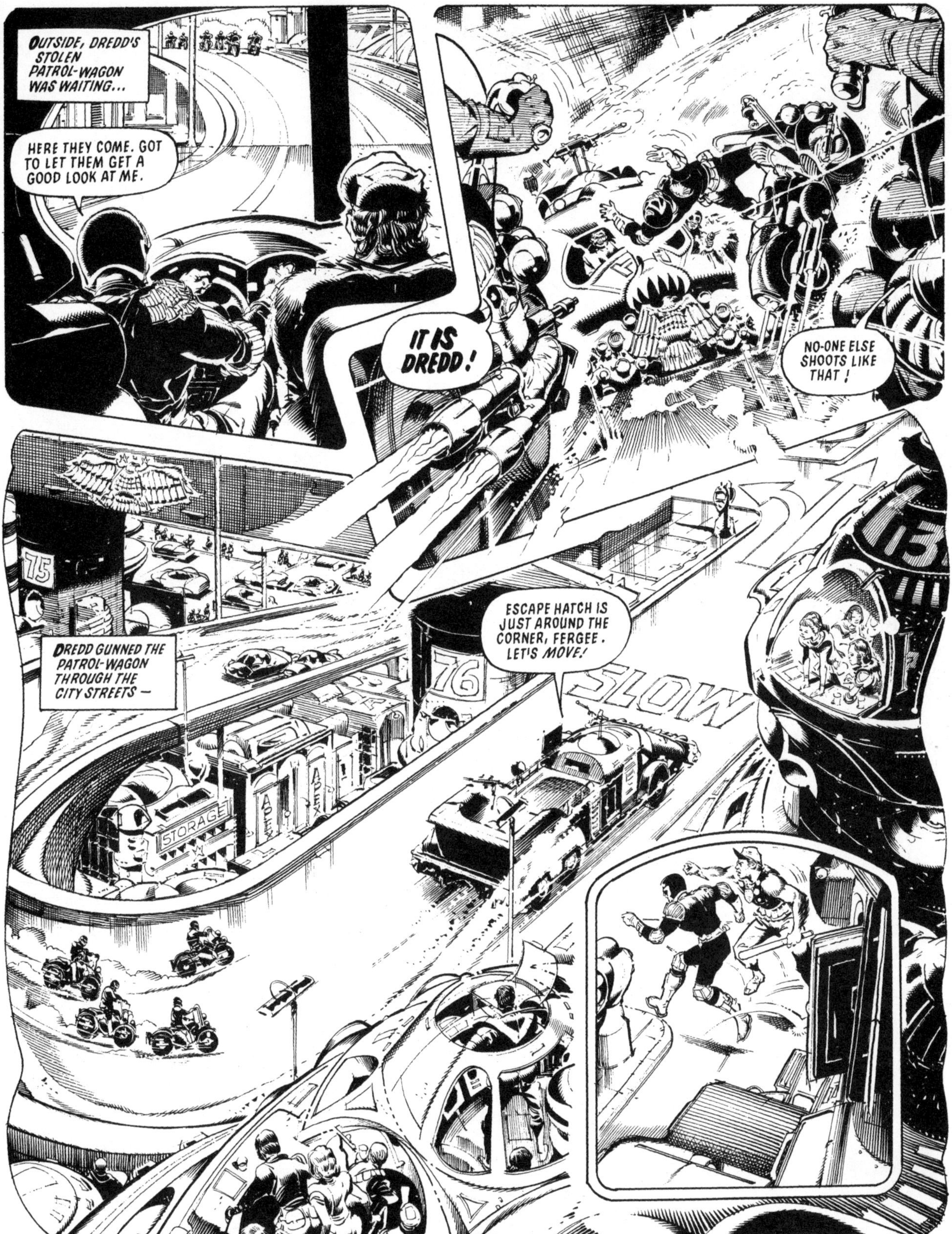
OUTSIDE, DREDD'S STOLEN PATROL-WAGON WAS WAITING...
HERE THEY COME. GOT TO LET THEM GET A GOOD LOOK AT ME.
IT IS DREDD!
NO-ONE ELSE SHOOTS LIKE THAT!
DREDD GUNNED THE PATROL-WAGON THROUGH THE CITY STREETS —
ESCAPE HATCH IS JUST AROUND THE CORNER, FERGEE. LET'S MOVE!
SLOW
75
76
STORAGE
APEX
APEX

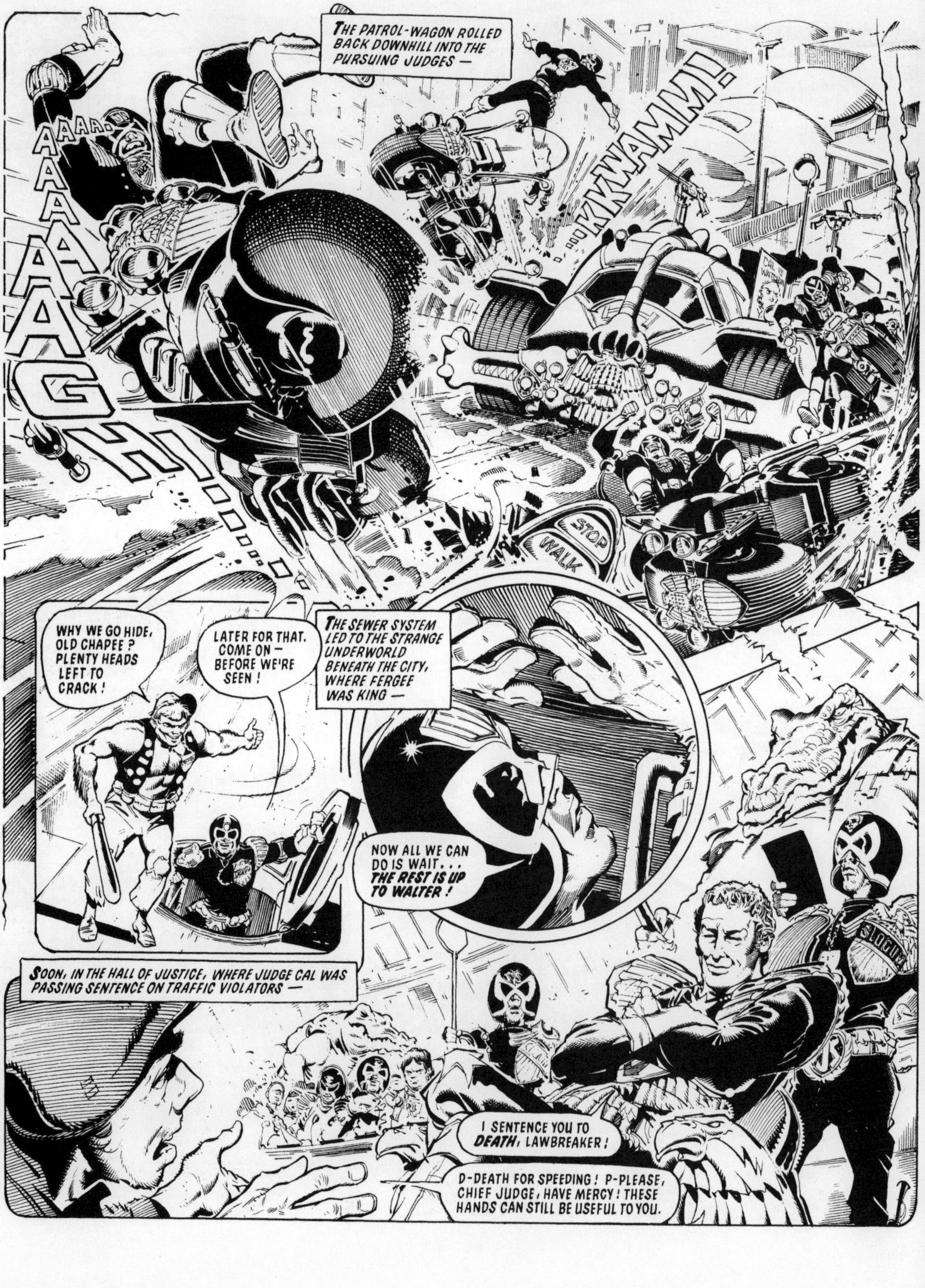
THE PATROL-WAGON ROLLED BACK DOWNHILL INTO THE PURSUING JUDGES —
AAAAAAAAAAGH!
KKWAMM!
STOP
WALK
CAL IS WATCHIN
WHY WE GO HIDE, OLD CHAPEE? PLENTY HEADS LEFT TO CRACK!
LATER FOR THAT. COME ON — BEFORE WE'RE SEEN!
THE SEWER SYSTEM LED TO THE STRANGE UNDERWORLD BENEATH THE CITY, WHERE FERGEE WAS KING —
NOW ALL WE CAN DO IS WAIT... THE REST IS UP TO WALTER!
SOON, IN THE HALL OF JUSTICE, WHERE JUDGE CAL WAS PASSING SENTENCE ON TRAFFIC VIOLATORS —
I SENTENCE YOU TO DEATH, LAWBREAKER!
D-DEATH FOR SPEEDING! P-PLEASE, CHIEF JUDGE, HAVE MERCY! THESE HANDS CAN STILL BE USEFUL TO YOU.

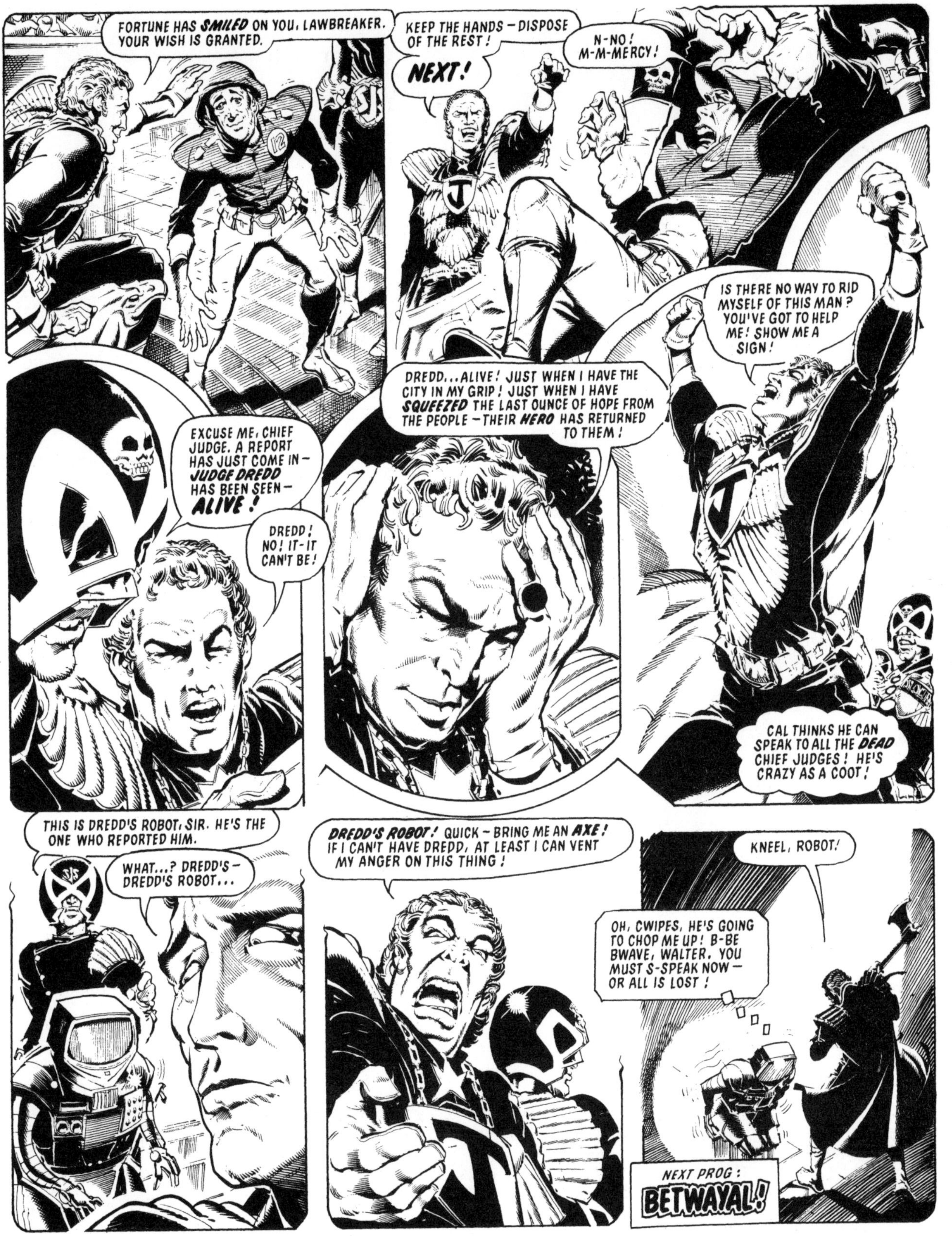
FORTUNE HAS SMILED ON YOU, LAWBREAKER. YOUR WISH IS GRANTED.
KEEP THE HANDS – DISPOSE OF THE REST!
NEXT!
N-NO! M-M-MERCY!
IS THERE NO WAY TO RID MYSELF OF THIS MAN? YOU'VE GOT TO HELP ME! SHOW ME A SIGN!
EXCUSE ME, CHIEF JUDGE. A REPORT HAS JUST COME IN – JUDGE DREDD HAS BEEN SEEN – ALIVE!
DREDD! NO! IT-IT CAN'T BE!
DREDD...ALIVE! JUST WHEN I HAVE THE CITY IN MY GRIP! JUST WHEN I HAVE SQUEEZED THE LAST OUNCE OF HOPE FROM THE PEOPLE – THEIR HERO HAS RETURNED TO THEM!
CAL THINKS HE CAN SPEAK TO ALL THE DEAD CHIEF JUDGES! HE'S CRAZY AS A COOT!
THIS IS DREDD'S ROBOT, SIR. HE'S THE ONE WHO REPORTED HIM.
WHAT...? DREDD'S – DREDD'S ROBOT...
DREDD'S ROBOT! QUICK – BRING ME AN AXE! IF I CAN'T HAVE DREDD, AT LEAST I CAN VENT MY ANGER ON THIS THING!
KNEEL, ROBOT!
OH, CWIPES, HE'S GOING TO CHOP ME UP! B-BE BWAVE, WALTER, YOU MUST S-SPEAK NOW – OR ALL IS LOST!
NEXT PROG:
BETWAYAL!

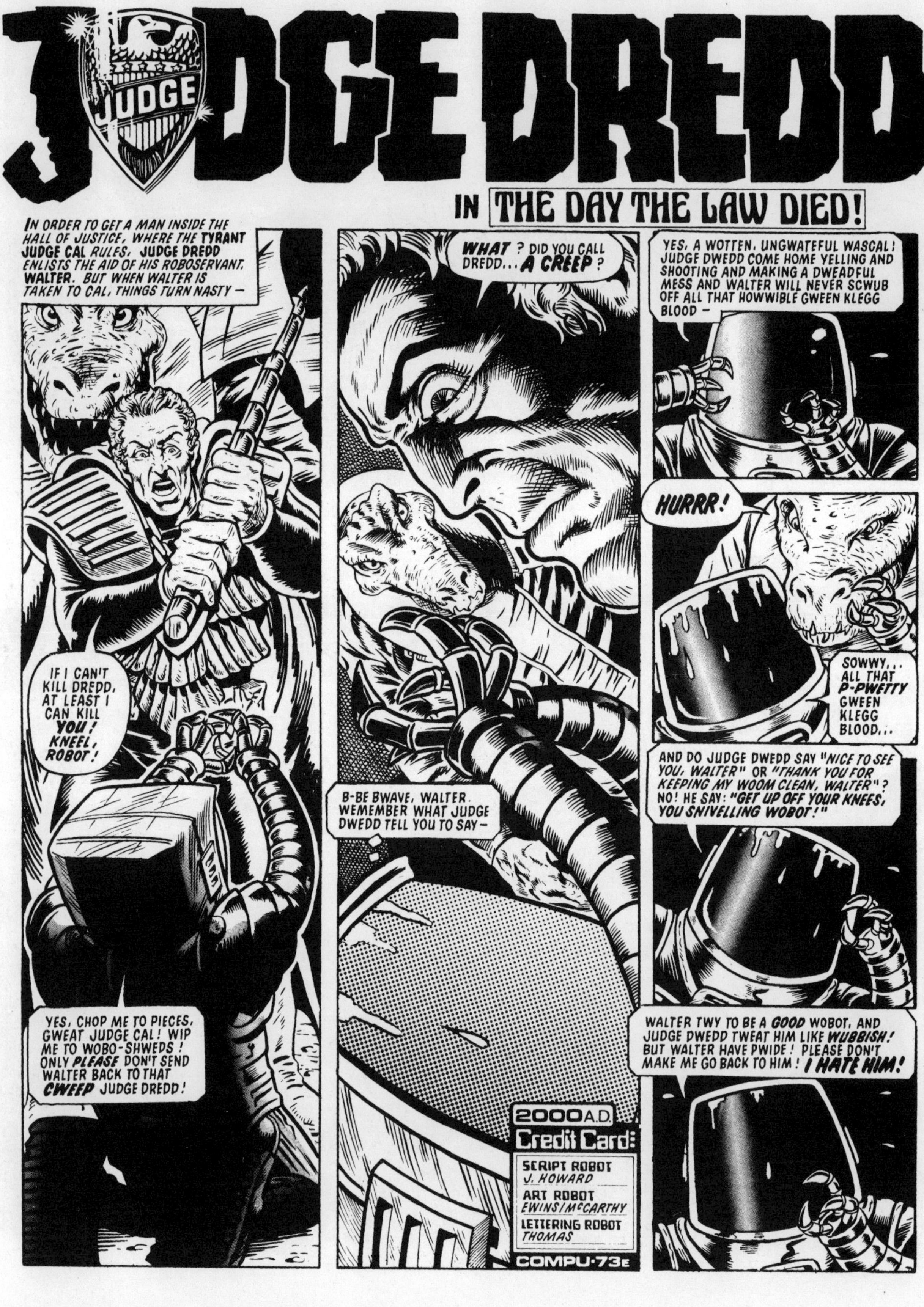
JUDGE
JUDGE DREDD
IN THE DAY THE LAW DIED!
IN ORDER TO GET A MAN INSIDE THE HALL OF JUSTICE, WHERE THE TYRANT JUDGE CAL RULES, JUDGE DREDD ENLISTS THE AID OF HIS ROBOSERVANT, WALTER. BUT WHEN WALTER IS TAKEN TO CAL, THINGS TURN NASTY –
IF I CAN'T KILL DREDD, AT LEAST I CAN KILL YOU! KNEEL, ROBOT!
YES, CHOP ME TO PIECES, GWEAT JUDGE CAL! WIP ME TO WOBO-SHWEDS! ONLY PLEASE DON'T SEND WALTER BACK TO THAT CWEEP JUDGE DREDD!
WHAT? DID YOU CALL DREDD... A CREEP?
B-BE BWAVE, WALTER. WEMEMBER WHAT JUDGE DWEDD TELL YOU TO SAY –
YES, A WOTTEN, UNGWATEFUL WASCAL! JUDGE DWEDD COME HOME YELLING AND SHOOTING AND MAKING A DWEADFUL MESS AND WALTER WILL NEVER SCWUB OFF ALL THAT HOWWIBLE GWEEN KLEGG BLOOD –
HURRR!
SOWWY... ALL THAT P-PWETTY GWEEN KLEGG BLOOD...
AND DO JUDGE DWEDD SAY "NICE TO SEE YOU, WALTER" OR "THANK YOU FOR KEEPING MY WOOM CLEAN, WALTER"? NO! HE SAY: "GET UP OFF YOUR KNEES, YOU SNIVELLING WOBOT!"
WALTER TWY TO BE A GOOD WOBOT, AND JUDGE DWEDD TWEAT HIM LIKE WUBBISH! BUT WALTER HAVE PWIDE! PLEASE DON'T MAKE ME GO BACK TO HIM! I HATE HIM!
2000 A.D.
Credit Card:
SCRIPT ROBOT J. HOWARD
ART ROBOT EWINS/McCARTHY
LETTERING ROBOT THOMAS
COMPU-73E

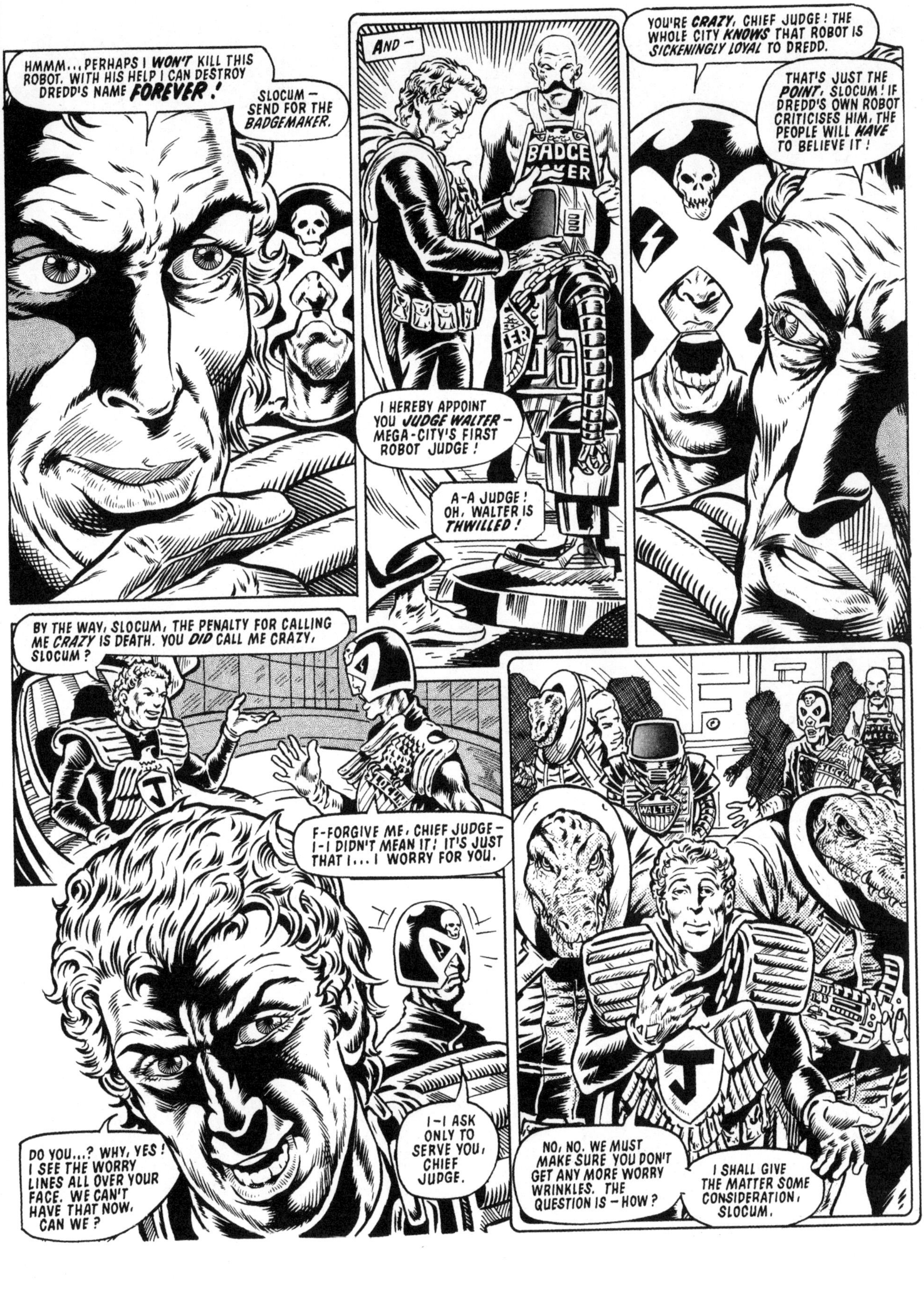
HMMM... PERHAPS I WON'T KILL THIS ROBOT. WITH HIS HELP I CAN DESTROY DREDD'S NAME FOREVER!
SLOCUM — SEND FOR THE BADGEMAKER.
AND —
BADGE MAKER
I HEREBY APPOINT YOU JUDGE WALTER — MEGA-CITY'S FIRST ROBOT JUDGE!
A-A JUDGE! OH, WALTER IS THWILLED!
YOU'RE CRAZY, CHIEF JUDGE! THE WHOLE CITY KNOWS THAT ROBOT IS SICKENINGLY LOYAL TO DREDD.
THAT'S JUST THE POINT, SLOCUM! IF DREDD'S OWN ROBOT CRITICISES HIM, THE PEOPLE WILL HAVE TO BELIEVE IT!
BY THE WAY, SLOCUM, THE PENALTY FOR CALLING ME CRAZY IS DEATH. YOU DID CALL ME CRAZY, SLOCUM?
F-FORGIVE ME, CHIEF JUDGE — I-I DIDN'T MEAN IT! IT'S JUST THAT I... I WORRY FOR YOU.
DO YOU...? WHY, YES! I SEE THE WORRY LINES ALL OVER YOUR FACE. WE CAN'T HAVE THAT NOW, CAN WE?
I-I ASK ONLY TO SERVE YOU, CHIEF JUDGE.
WALTER
NO, NO. WE MUST MAKE SURE YOU DON'T GET ANY MORE WORRY WRINKLES. THE QUESTION IS — HOW?
I SHALL GIVE THE MATTER SOME CONSIDERATION, SLOCUM.

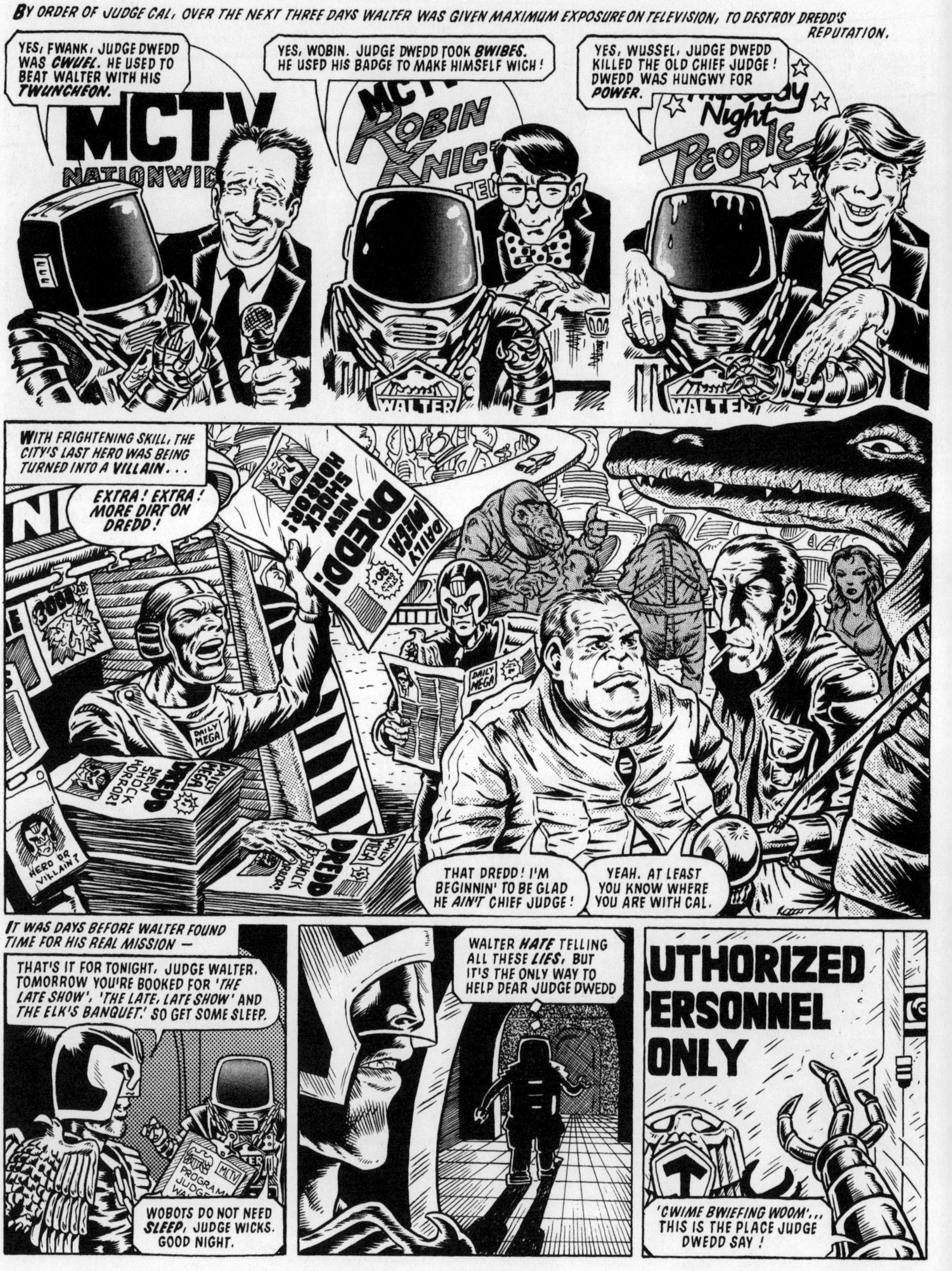
BY ORDER OF JUDGE CAL, OVER THE NEXT THREE DAYS WALTER WAS GIVEN MAXIMUM EXPOSURE ON TELEVISION, TO DESTROY DREDD'S REPUTATION.
YES, FWANK, JUDGE DWEDD WAS CWUEL. HE USED TO BEAT WALTER WITH HIS TWUNCHEON.
MCTV
YES, WOBIN. JUDGE DWEDD TOOK BWIBES. HE USED HIS BADGE TO MAKE HIMSELF WICH!
YES, WUSSEL, JUDGE DWEDD KILLED THE OLD CHIEF JUDGE! DWEDD WAS HUNGWY FOR POWER.
WALTER
WITH FRIGHTENING SKILL, THE CITY'S LAST HERO WAS BEING TURNED INTO A VILLAIN...
EXTRA! EXTRA! MORE DIRT ON DREDD!
DAILY MEGA
DREDD! NEW SHOCK HORROR!
HERO OR VILLAIN?
THAT DREDD! I'M BEGINNIN' TO BE GLAD HE AIN'T CHIEF JUDGE!
YEAH. AT LEAST YOU KNOW WHERE YOU ARE WITH CAL.
IT WAS DAYS BEFORE WALTER FOUND TIME FOR HIS REAL MISSION —
THAT'S IT FOR TONIGHT, JUDGE WALTER. TOMORROW YOU'RE BOOKED FOR 'THE LATE SHOW', 'THE LATE, LATE SHOW' AND THE ELK'S BANQUET.' SO GET SOME SLEEP.
WOBOTS DO NOT NEED SLEEP, JUDGE WICKS. GOOD NIGHT.
WALTER HATE TELLING ALL THESE LIES, BUT IT'S THE ONLY WAY TO HELP DEAR JUDGE DWEDD
UTHORIZED PERSONNEL ONLY
'CWIME BWIEFING WOOM'... THIS IS THE PLACE JUDGE DWEDD SAY!

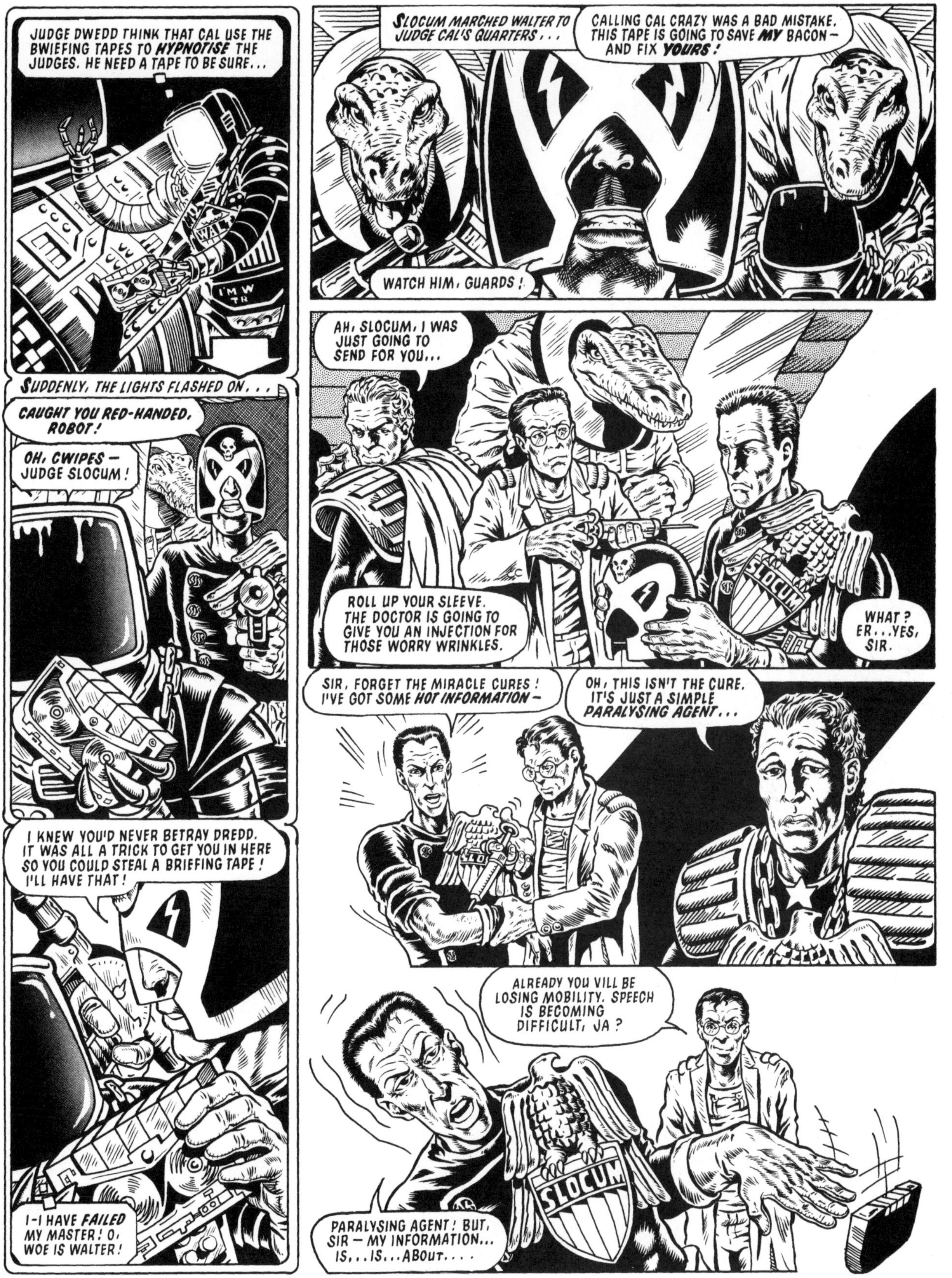
JUDGE DWEDD THINK THAT CAL USE THE BWIEFING TAPES TO HYPNOTISE THE JUDGES. HE NEED A TAPE TO BE SURE...
SUDDENLY, THE LIGHTS FLASHED ON...
CAUGHT YOU RED-HANDED, ROBOT!
OH, CWIPES – JUDGE SLOCUM!
I KNEW YOU'D NEVER BETRAY DREDD. IT WAS ALL A TRICK TO GET YOU IN HERE SO YOU COULD STEAL A BRIEFING TAPE! I'LL HAVE THAT!
I-I HAVE FAILED MY MASTER! O, WOE IS WALTER!
SLOCUM MARCHED WALTER TO JUDGE CAL'S QUARTERS...
CALLING CAL CRAZY WAS A BAD MISTAKE. THIS TAPE IS GOING TO SAVE MY BACON – AND FIX YOURS!
WATCH HIM, GUARDS!
AH, SLOCUM, I WAS JUST GOING TO SEND FOR YOU...
ROLL UP YOUR SLEEVE. THE DOCTOR IS GOING TO GIVE YOU AN INJECTION FOR THOSE WORRY WRINKLES.
WHAT? ER...YES, SIR.
SIR, FORGET THE MIRACLE CURES! I'VE GOT SOME HOT INFORMATION –
OH, THIS ISN'T THE CURE. IT'S JUST A SIMPLE PARALYSING AGENT...
ALREADY YOU VILL BE LOSING MOBILITY. SPEECH IS BECOMING DIFFICULT, JA?
PARALYSING AGENT! BUT, SIR – MY INFORMATION... IS...IS...ABOUT....

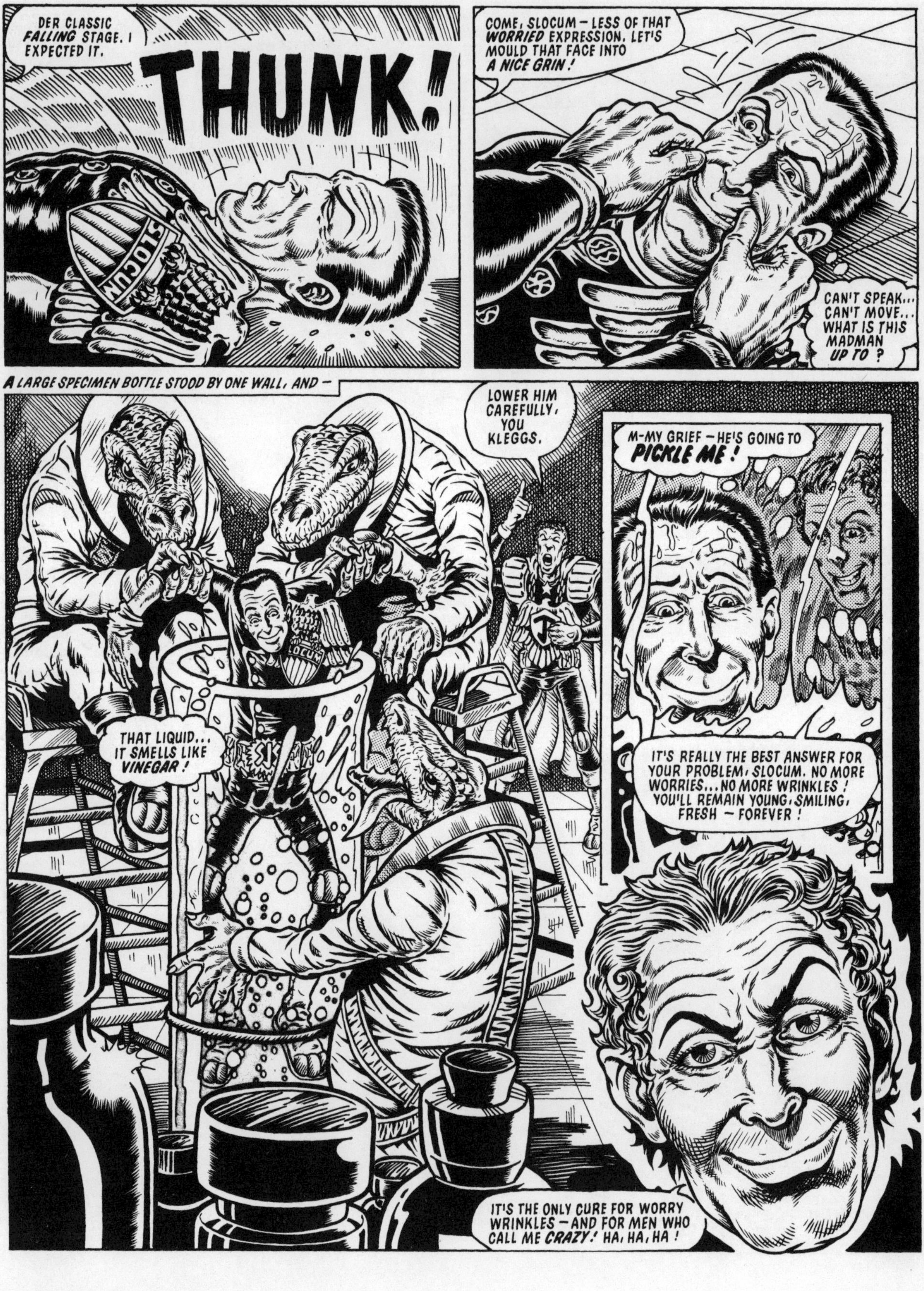
DER CLASSIC FALLING STAGE. I EXPECTED IT.
THUNK!
SLOCUM
COME, SLOCUM – LESS OF THAT WORRIED EXPRESSION. LET'S MOULD THAT FACE INTO A NICE GRIN!
CAN'T SPEAK... CAN'T MOVE... WHAT IS THIS MADMAN UP TO?
A LARGE SPECIMEN BOTTLE STOOD BY ONE WALL, AND –
LOWER HIM CAREFULLY, YOU KLEGGS.
M-MY GRIEF – HE'S GOING TO PICKLE ME!
THAT LIQUID... IT SMELLS LIKE VINEGAR!
IT'S REALLY THE BEST ANSWER FOR YOUR PROBLEM, SLOCUM. NO MORE WORRIES... NO MORE WRINKLES! YOU'LL REMAIN YOUNG, SMILING, FRESH – FOREVER!
IT'S THE ONLY CURE FOR WORRY WRINKLES – AND FOR MEN WHO CALL ME CRAZY! HA, HA, HA!

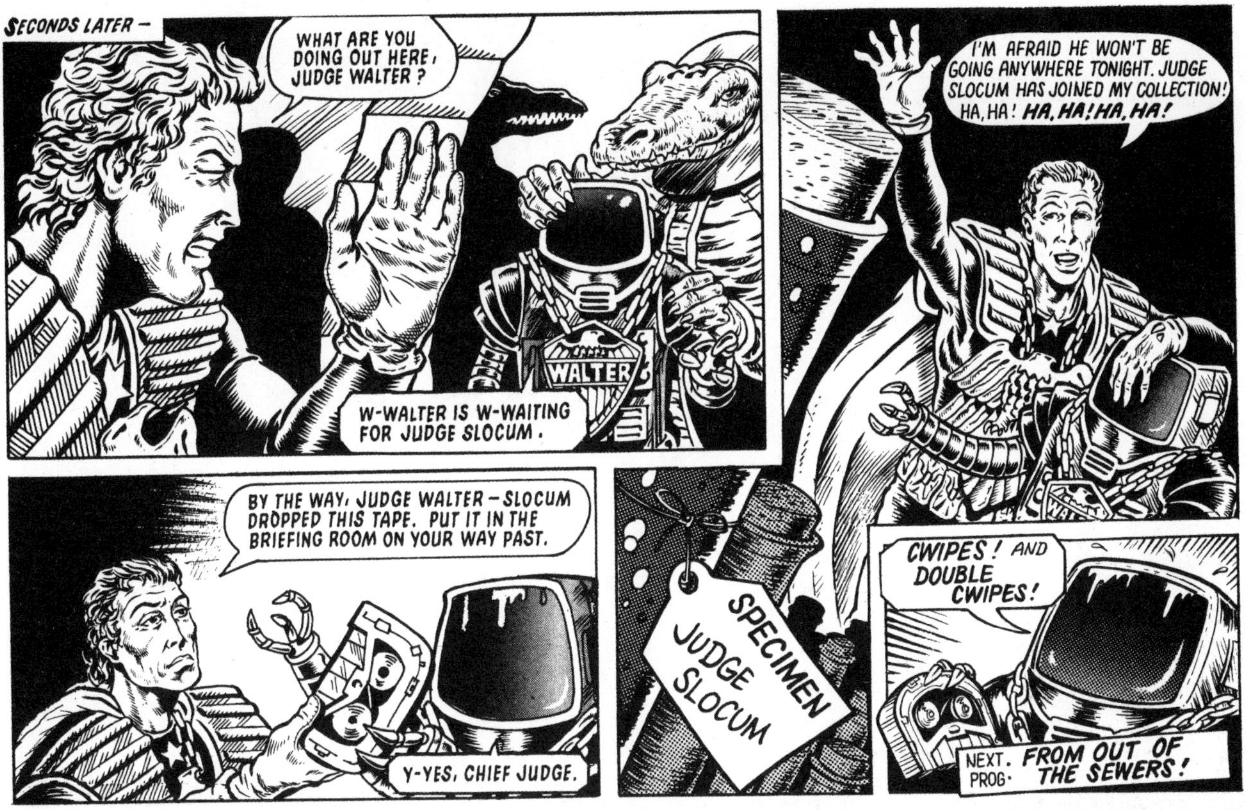
SECONDS LATER —
WHAT ARE YOU DOING OUT HERE, JUDGE WALTER ?
W-WALTER IS W-WAITING FOR JUDGE SLOCUM.
WALTER
I'M AFRAID HE WON'T BE GOING ANYWHERE TONIGHT. JUDGE SLOCUM HAS JOINED MY COLLECTION! HA, HA! HA, HA! HA, HA!
BY THE WAY, JUDGE WALTER — SLOCUM DROPPED THIS TAPE. PUT IT IN THE BRIEFING ROOM ON YOUR WAY PAST.
Y-YES, CHIEF JUDGE.
SPECIMEN JUDGE SLOCUM
CWIPES! AND DOUBLE CWIPES!
NEXT. PROG. FROM OUT OF THE SEWERS!

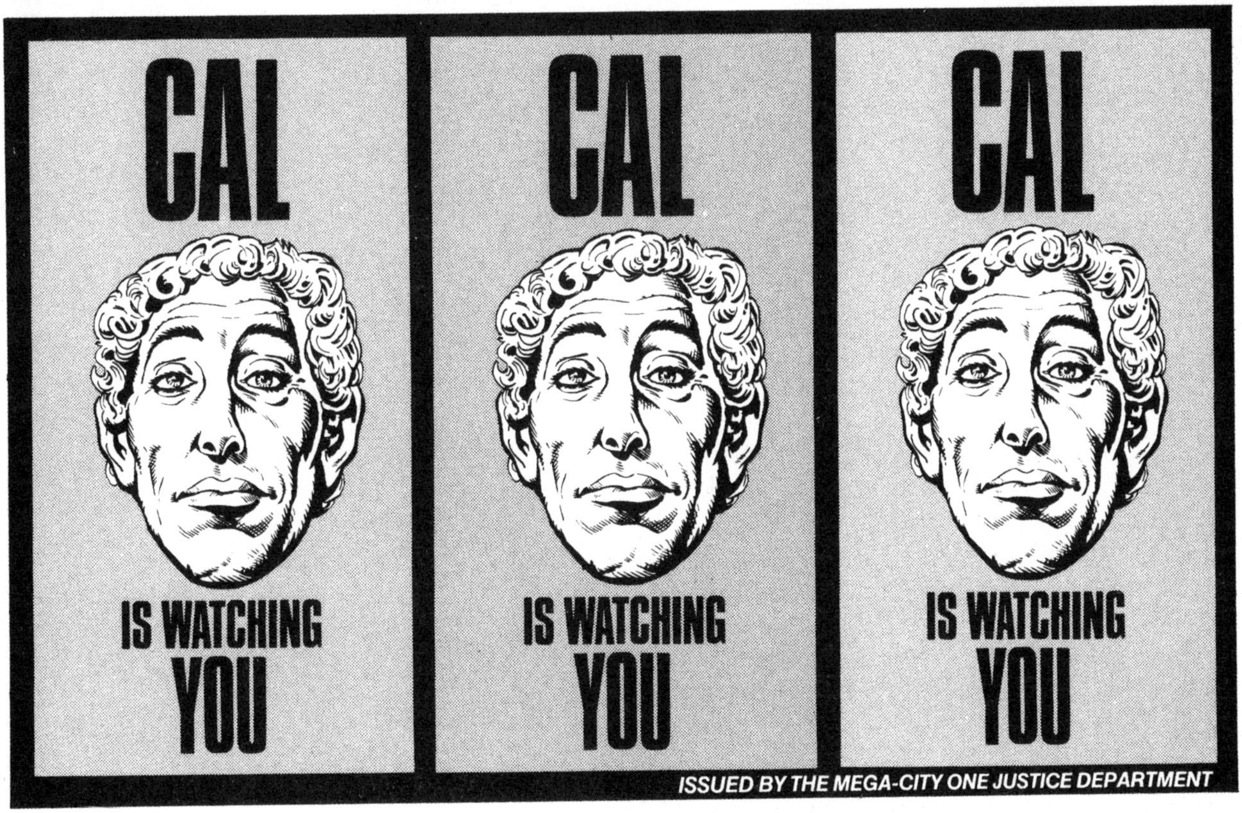
CAL
IS WATCHING YOU
CAL
IS WATCHING YOU
CAL
IS WATCHING YOU
ISSUED BY THE MEGA-CITY ONE JUSTICE DEPARTMENT

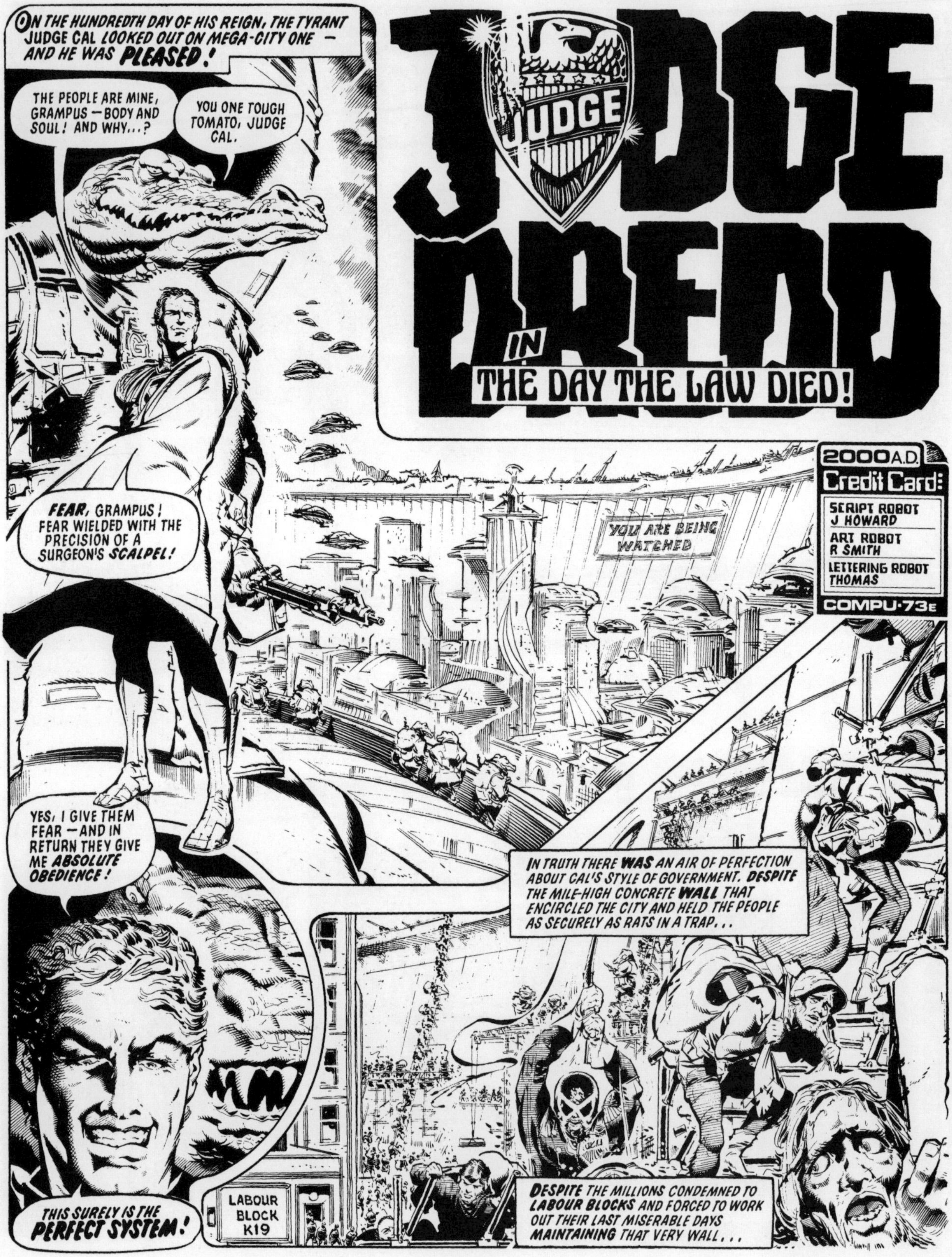

ON THE HUNDREDTH DAY OF HIS REIGN, THE TYRANT JUDGE CAL LOOKED OUT ON MEGA-CITY ONE — AND HE WAS PLEASED!
JUDGE DREDD
JUDGE
IN
THE DAY THE LAW DIED!
THE PEOPLE ARE MINE, GRAMPUS — BODY AND SOUL! AND WHY...?
YOU ONE TOUGH TOMATO, JUDGE CAL.
2000 A.D. Credit Card:
SCRIPT ROBOT J HOWARD
ART ROBOT R SMITH
LETTERING ROBOT THOMAS
COMPU-73E
YOU ARE BEING WATCHED
FEAR, GRAMPUS! FEAR WIELDED WITH THE PRECISION OF A SURGEON'S SCALPEL!
YES, I GIVE THEM FEAR — AND IN RETURN THEY GIVE ME ABSOLUTE OBEDIENCE!
IN TRUTH THERE WAS AN AIR OF PERFECTION ABOUT CAL'S STYLE OF GOVERNMENT. DESPITE THE MILE-HIGH CONCRETE WALL THAT ENCIRCLED THE CITY AND HELD THE PEOPLE AS SECURELY AS RATS IN A TRAP...
THIS SURELY IS THE PERFECT SYSTEM!
LABOUR BLOCK K19
DESPITE THE MILLIONS CONDEMNED TO LABOUR BLOCKS AND FORCED TO WORK OUT THEIR LAST MISERABLE DAYS MAINTAINING THAT VERY WALL...

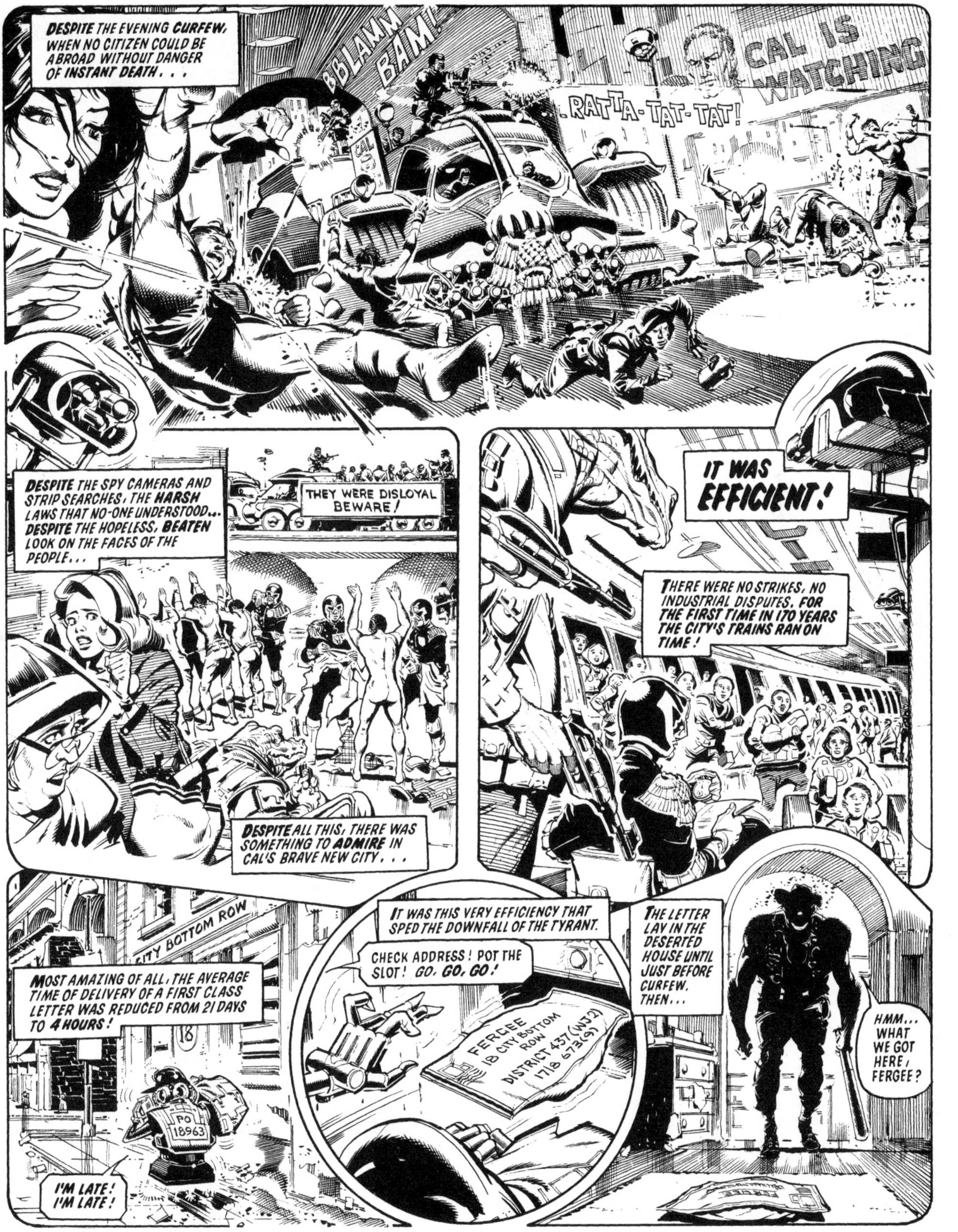

DESPITE THE EVENING CURFEW, WHEN NO CITIZEN COULD BE ABROAD WITHOUT DANGER OF INSTANT DEATH . . .
BBLAMM
BAM!
CAL IS WATCHING
RATTA-TAT-TAT!
DESPITE THE SPY CAMERAS AND STRIP SEARCHES, THE HARSH LAWS THAT NO-ONE UNDERSTOOD... DESPITE THE HOPELESS, BEATEN LOOK ON THE FACES OF THE PEOPLE...
THEY WERE DISLOYAL BEWARE!
DESPITE ALL THIS, THERE WAS SOMETHING TO ADMIRE IN CAL'S BRAVE NEW CITY . . .
IT WAS EFFICIENT!
THERE WERE NO STRIKES, NO INDUSTRIAL DISPUTES. FOR THE FIRST TIME IN 170 YEARS THE CITY'S TRAINS RAN ON TIME!
CITY BOTTOM ROW
MOST AMAZING OF ALL, THE AVERAGE TIME OF DELIVERY OF A FIRST CLASS LETTER WAS REDUCED FROM 21 DAYS TO 4 HOURS!
18
PO 18963
I'M LATE! I'M LATE!
IT WAS THIS VERY EFFICIENCY THAT SPED THE DOWNFALL OF THE TYRANT.
CHECK ADDRESS! POT THE SLOT! GO, GO, GO!
FERGEE 18 CITY BOTTOM ROW DISTRICT 437 (WJ2) 1718 673(9)
THE LETTER LAY IN THE DESERTED HOUSE UNTIL JUST BEFORE CURFEW. THEN...
HMM... WHAT WE GOT HERE, FERGEE?

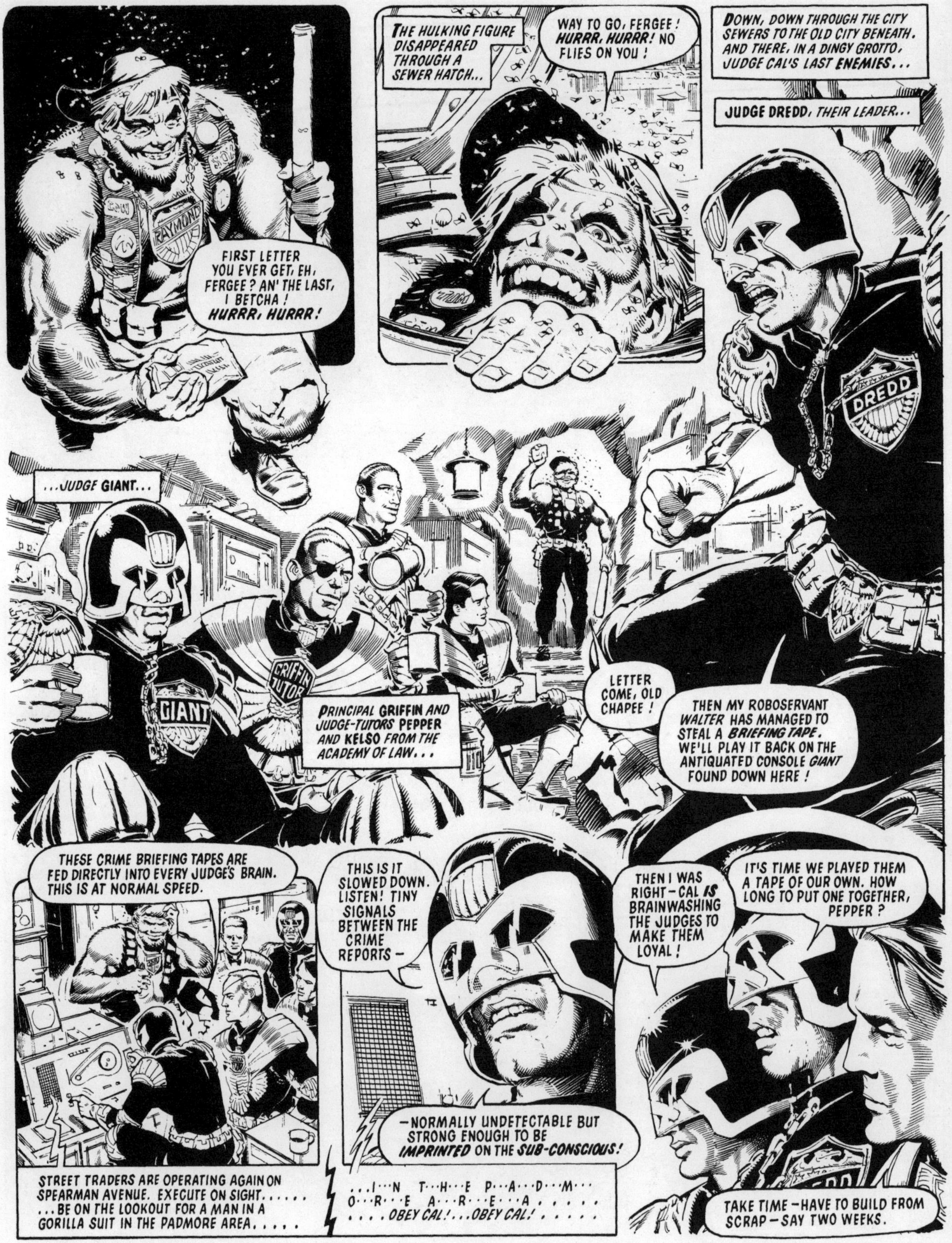
FIRST LETTER YOU EVER GET, EH, FERGEE ? AN' THE LAST, I BETCHA ! HURRR, HURRR!
THE HULKING FIGURE DISAPPEARED THROUGH A SEWER HATCH...
WAY TO GO, FERGEE ! HURRR, HURRR! NO FLIES ON YOU !
DOWN, DOWN THROUGH THE CITY SEWERS TO THE OLD CITY BENEATH. AND THERE, IN A DINGY GROTTO, JUDGE CAL'S LAST ENEMIES...
JUDGE DREDD, THEIR LEADER...
DREDD
...JUDGE GIANT...
GIANT
GRIFFIN TUTOR
PRINCIPAL GRIFFIN AND JUDGE-TUTORS PEPPER AND KELSO FROM THE ACADEMY OF LAW...
LETTER COME, OLD CHAPEE !
THEN MY ROBOSERVANT WALTER HAS MANAGED TO STEAL A BRIEFING TAPE. WE'LL PLAY IT BACK ON THE ANTIQUATED CONSOLE GIANT FOUND DOWN HERE !
THESE CRIME BRIEFING TAPES ARE FED DIRECTLY INTO EVERY JUDGE'S BRAIN. THIS IS AT NORMAL SPEED.
STREET TRADERS ARE OPERATING AGAIN ON SPEARMAN AVENUE. EXECUTE ON SIGHT...... ...BE ON THE LOOKOUT FOR A MAN IN A GORILLA SUIT IN THE PADMORE AREA.....
THIS IS IT SLOWED DOWN. LISTEN! TINY SIGNALS BETWEEN THE CRIME REPORTS –
–NORMALLY UNDETECTABLE BUT STRONG ENOUGH TO BE IMPRINTED ON THE SUB-CONSCIOUS!
...I·N·T·H·E·P·A·D·M··· O·R·E·A·R·E·A······ ....OBEY CAL!...OBEY CAL!.....
THEN I WAS RIGHT – CAL IS BRAINWASHING THE JUDGES TO MAKE THEM LOYAL !
IT'S TIME WE PLAYED THEM A TAPE OF OUR OWN. HOW LONG TO PUT ONE TOGETHER, PEPPER ?
TAKE TIME – HAVE TO BUILD FROM SCRAP – SAY TWO WEEKS.

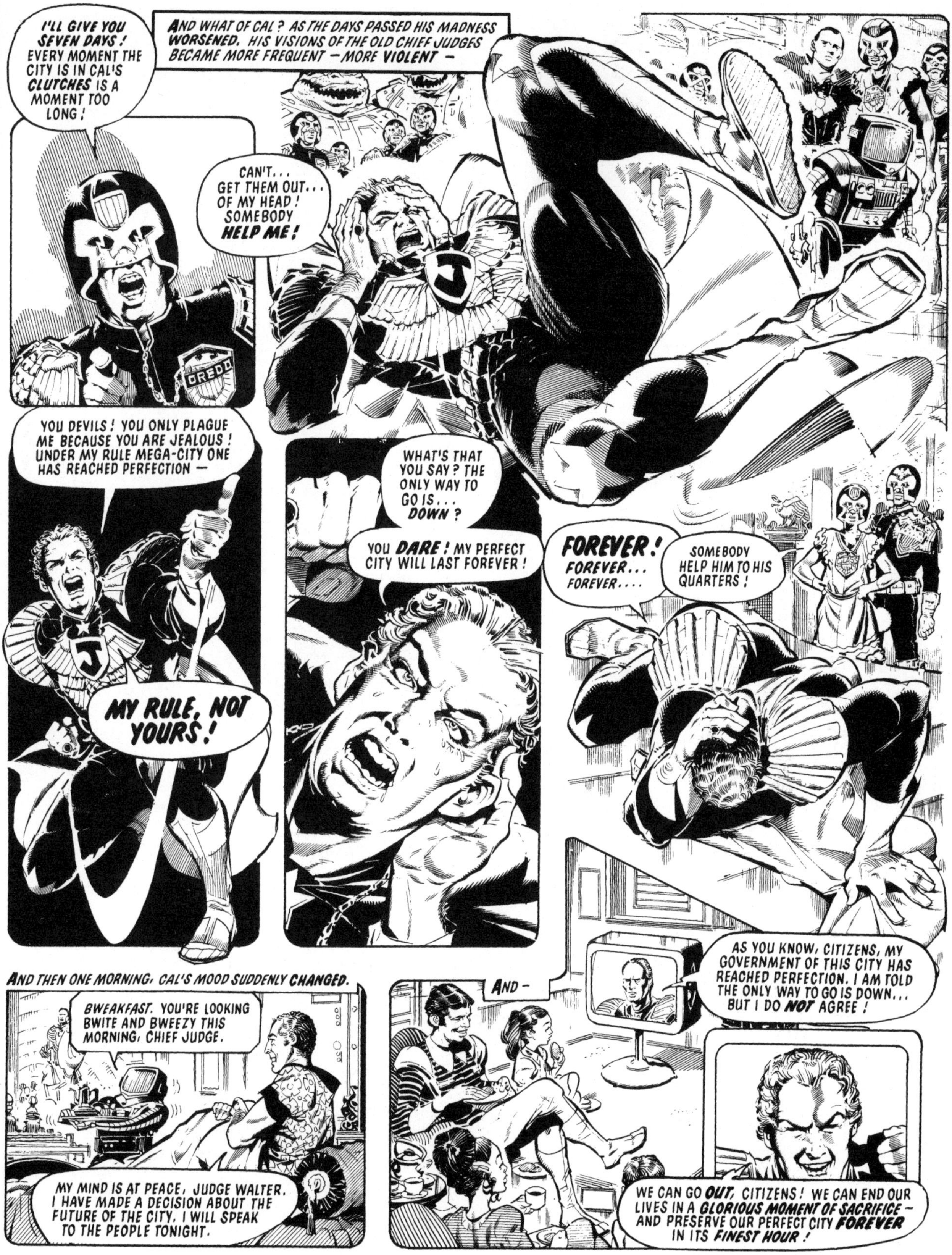
I'LL GIVE YOU SEVEN DAYS! EVERY MOMENT THE CITY IS IN CAL'S CLUTCHES IS A MOMENT TOO LONG!
AND WHAT OF CAL? AS THE DAYS PASSED HIS MADNESS WORSENED. HIS VISIONS OF THE OLD CHIEF JUDGES BECAME MORE FREQUENT — MORE VIOLENT —
CAN'T... GET THEM OUT... OF MY HEAD! SOMEBODY HELP ME!
YOU DEVILS! YOU ONLY PLAGUE ME BECAUSE YOU ARE JEALOUS! UNDER MY RULE MEGA-CITY ONE HAS REACHED PERFECTION —
MY RULE, NOT YOURS!
WHAT'S THAT YOU SAY? THE ONLY WAY TO GO IS... DOWN?
YOU DARE! MY PERFECT CITY WILL LAST FOREVER!
FOREVER! FOREVER... FOREVER....
SOMEBODY HELP HIM TO HIS QUARTERS!
AND THEN ONE MORNING, CAL'S MOOD SUDDENLY CHANGED.
BWEAKFAST. YOU'RE LOOKING BWITE AND BWEEZY THIS MORNING, CHIEF JUDGE.
MY MIND IS AT PEACE, JUDGE WALTER. I HAVE MADE A DECISION ABOUT THE FUTURE OF THE CITY. I WILL SPEAK TO THE PEOPLE TONIGHT.
AND—
AS YOU KNOW, CITIZENS, MY GOVERNMENT OF THIS CITY HAS REACHED PERFECTION. I AM TOLD THE ONLY WAY TO GO IS DOWN... BUT I DO NOT AGREE!
WE CAN GO OUT, CITIZENS! WE CAN END OUR LIVES IN A GLORIOUS MOMENT OF SACRIFICE — AND PRESERVE OUR PERFECT CITY FOREVER IN ITS FINEST HOUR!

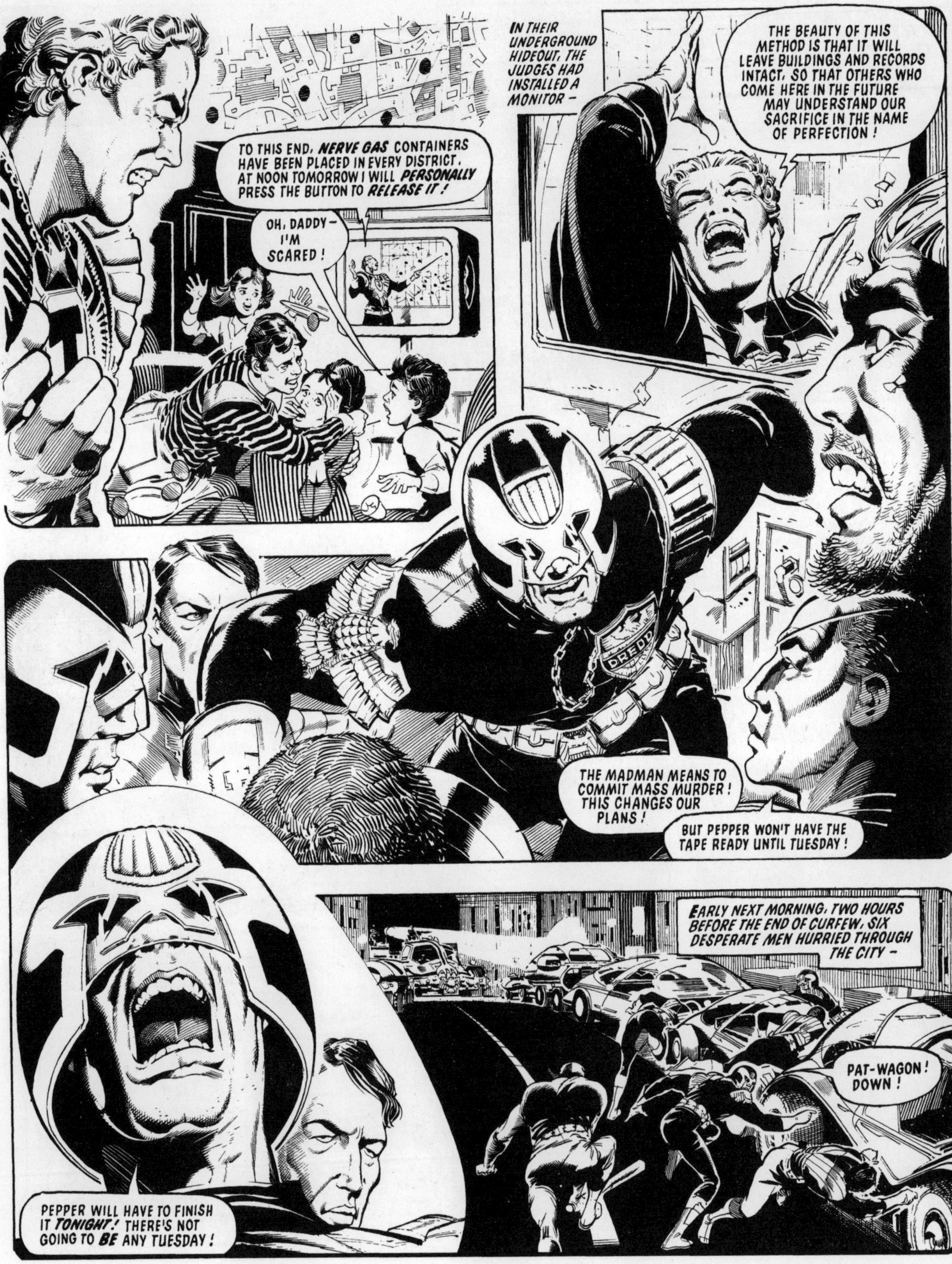
TO THIS END, NERVE GAS CONTAINERS HAVE BEEN PLACED IN EVERY DISTRICT. AT NOON TOMORROW I WILL PERSONALLY PRESS THE BUTTON TO RELEASE IT!
OH, DADDY – I'M SCARED!
IN THEIR UNDERGROUND HIDEOUT, THE JUDGES HAD INSTALLED A MONITOR –
THE BEAUTY OF THIS METHOD IS THAT IT WILL LEAVE BUILDINGS AND RECORDS INTACT, SO THAT OTHERS WHO COME HERE IN THE FUTURE MAY UNDERSTAND OUR SACRIFICE IN THE NAME OF PERFECTION!
DREDD
THE MADMAN MEANS TO COMMIT MASS MURDER! THIS CHANGES OUR PLANS!
BUT PEPPER WON'T HAVE THE TAPE READY UNTIL TUESDAY!
PEPPER WILL HAVE TO FINISH IT TONIGHT! THERE'S NOT GOING TO BE ANY TUESDAY!
EARLY NEXT MORNING, TWO HOURS BEFORE THE END OF CURFEW, SIX DESPERATE MEN HURRIED THROUGH THE CITY –
PAT-WAGON! DOWN!

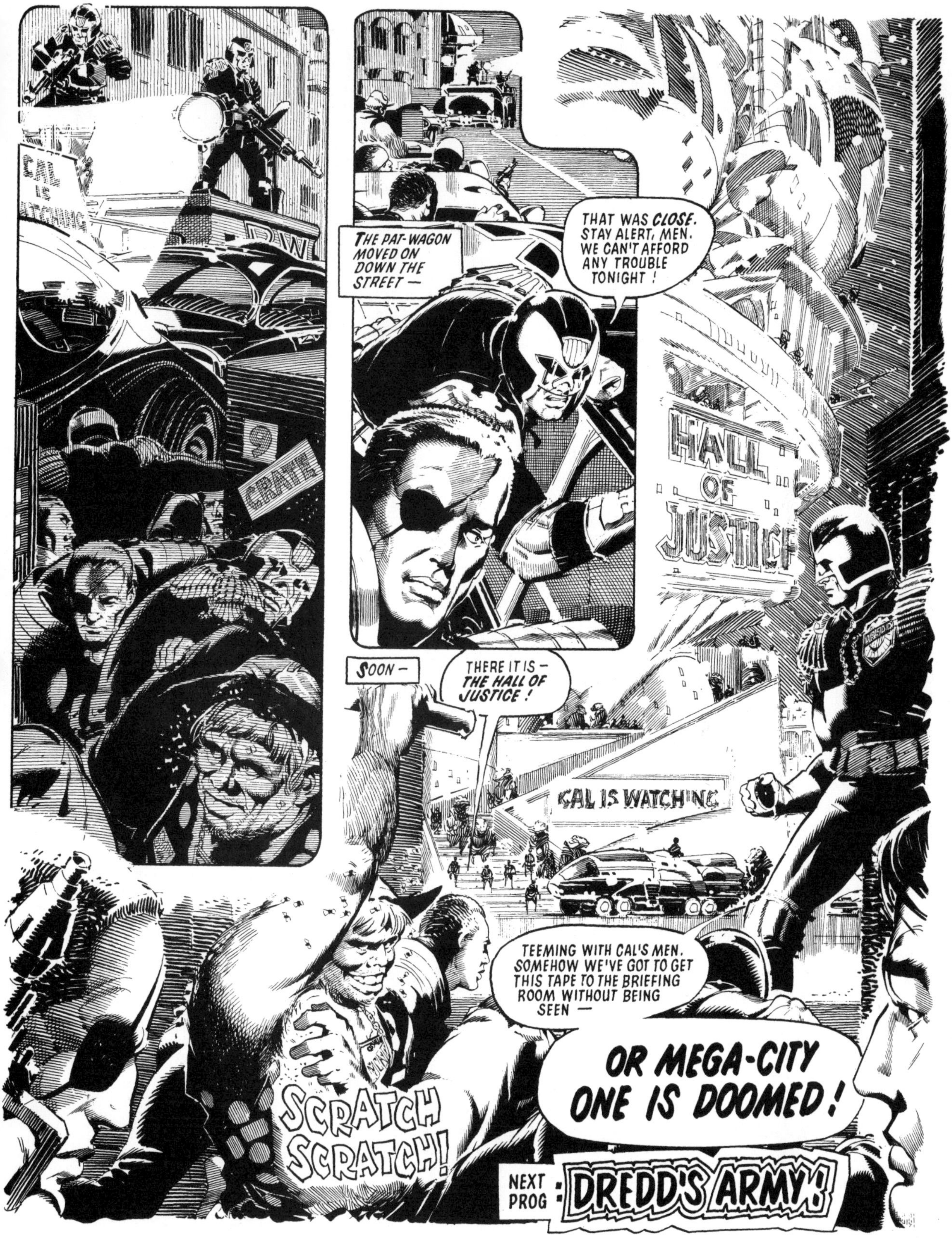
CAL IS WATCHING
RW
9
CRATE
THE PAT-WAGON MOVED ON DOWN THE STREET —
THAT WAS CLOSE. STAY ALERT, MEN. WE CAN'T AFFORD ANY TROUBLE TONIGHT!
HALL OF JUSTICE
SOON —
THERE IT IS — THE HALL OF JUSTICE!
CAL IS WATCHING
TEEMING WITH CAL'S MEN. SOMEHOW WE'VE GOT TO GET THIS TAPE TO THE BRIEFING ROOM WITHOUT BEING SEEN —
OR MEGA-CITY ONE IS DOOMED!
SCRATCH SCRATCH!
NEXT PROG: DREDD'S ARMY!

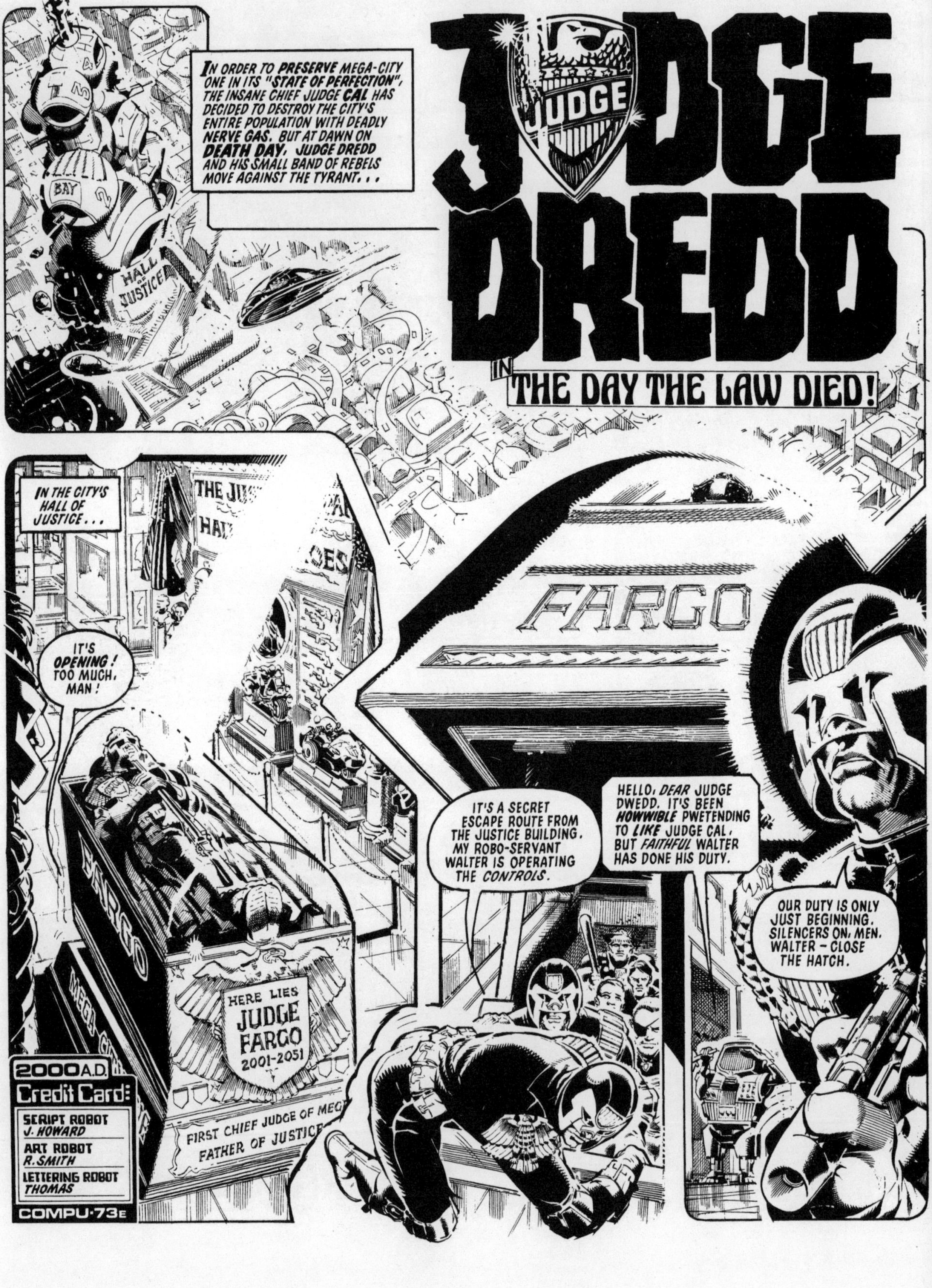
IN ORDER TO PRESERVE MEGA-CITY ONE IN ITS "STATE OF PERFECTION", THE INSANE CHIEF JUDGE CAL HAS DECIDED TO DESTROY THE CITY'S ENTIRE POPULATION WITH DEADLY NERVE GAS. BUT AT DAWN ON DEATH DAY, JUDGE DREDD AND HIS SMALL BAND OF REBELS MOVE AGAINST THE TYRANT. . .
JUDGE DREDD
IN THE DAY THE LAW DIED!
HALL OF JUSTICE
IN THE CITY'S HALL OF JUSTICE . . .
IT'S OPENING! TOO MUCH, MAN!
FARGO
HERE LIES JUDGE FARGO 2001-2051
FIRST CHIEF JUDGE OF MEG
FATHER OF JUSTICE
IT'S A SECRET ESCAPE ROUTE FROM THE JUSTICE BUILDING. MY ROBO-SERVANT WALTER IS OPERATING THE CONTROLS.
HELLO, DEAR JUDGE DWEDD. IT'S BEEN HOWWIBLE PWETENDING TO LIKE JUDGE CAL, BUT FAITHFUL WALTER HAS DONE HIS DUTY.
OUR DUTY IS ONLY JUST BEGINNING. SILENCERS ON, MEN. WALTER – CLOSE THE HATCH.
2000 A.D. Credit Card:
SCRIPT ROBOT J. HOWARD
ART ROBOT R. SMITH
LETTERING ROBOT THOMAS
COMPU-73E

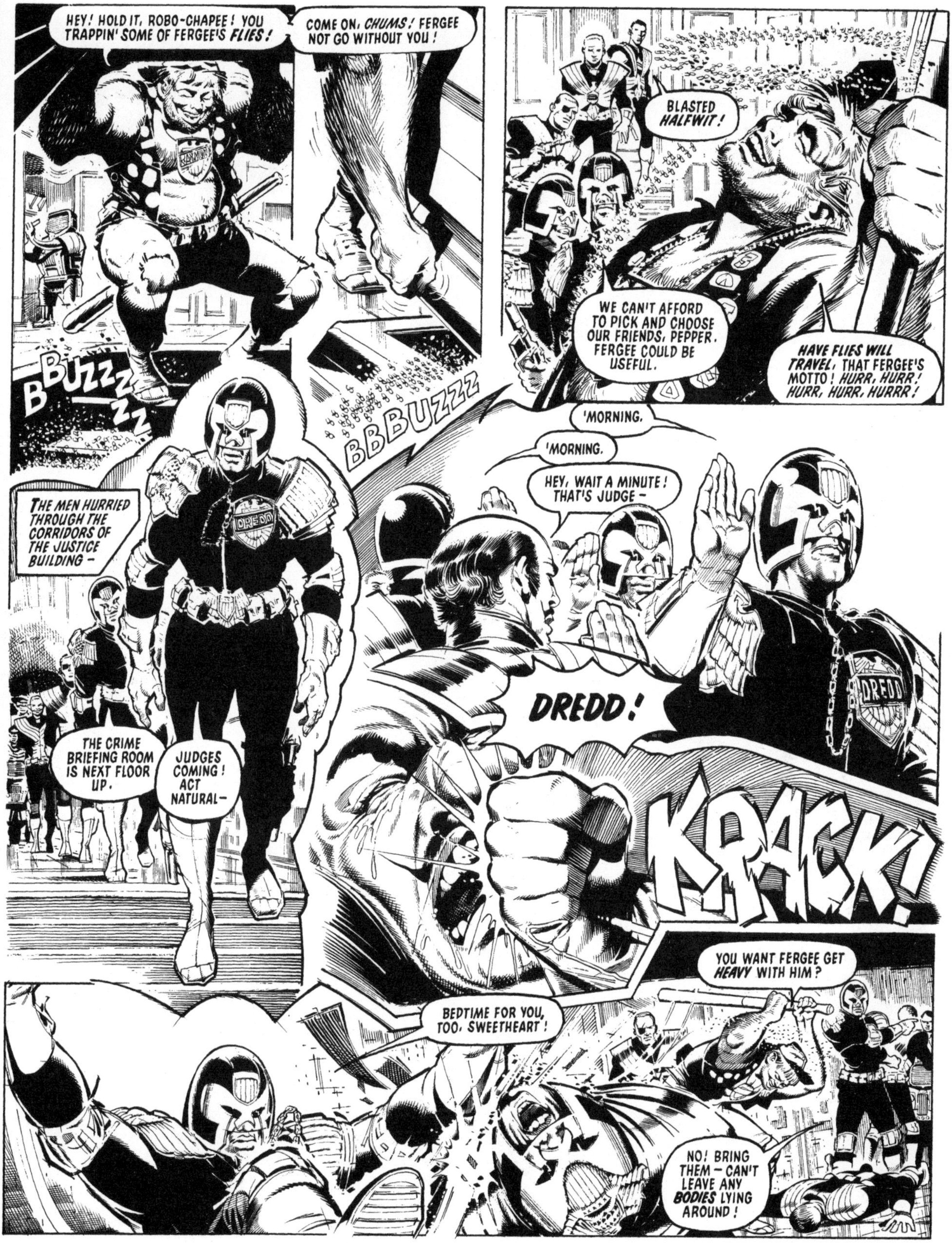
HEY! HOLD IT, ROBO-CHAPEE! YOU TRAPPIN' SOME OF FERGEE'S FLIES!
COME ON, CHUMS! FERGEE NOT GO WITHOUT YOU!
BLASTED HALFWIT!
WE CAN'T AFFORD TO PICK AND CHOOSE OUR FRIENDS, PEPPER. FERGEE COULD BE USEFUL.
HAVE FLIES WILL TRAVEL, THAT FERGEE'S MOTTO! HURR, HURR! HURR, HURR, HURRR!
BBUZZZZZ
BBBUZZZ
THE MEN HURRIED THROUGH THE CORRIDORS OF THE JUSTICE BUILDING—
THE CRIME BRIEFING ROOM IS NEXT FLOOR UP.
JUDGES COMING! ACT NATURAL—
'MORNING.
'MORNING.
HEY, WAIT A MINUTE! THAT'S JUDGE—
DREDD!
KRACK!
BEDTIME FOR YOU, TOO, SWEETHEART!
YOU WANT FERGEE GET HEAVY WITH HIM?
NO! BRING THEM — CAN'T LEAVE ANY BODIES LYING AROUND!

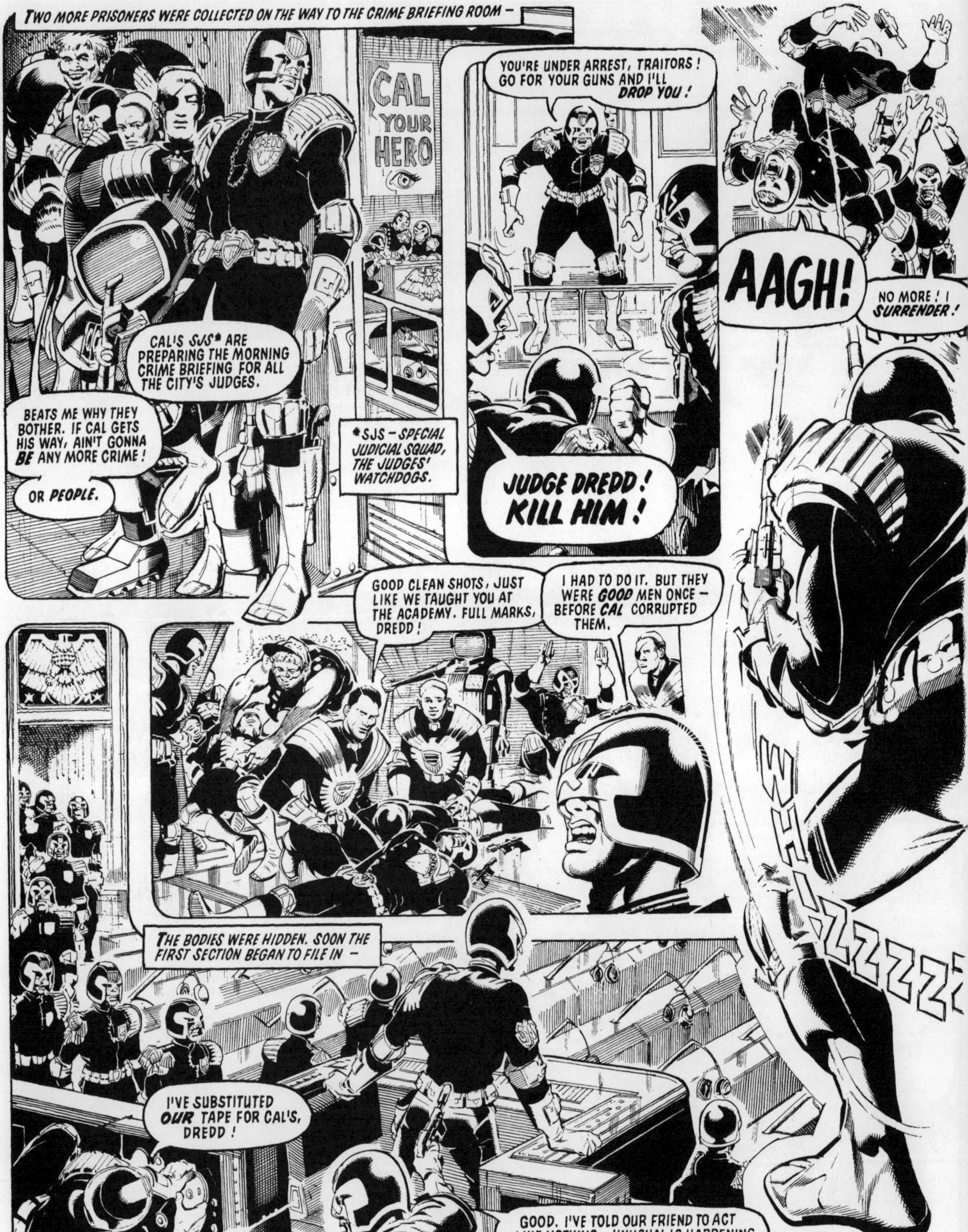

TWO MORE PRISONERS WERE COLLECTED ON THE WAY TO THE CRIME BRIEFING ROOM –
CAL YOUR HERO
CAL'S SJS* ARE PREPARING THE MORNING CRIME BRIEFING FOR ALL THE CITY'S JUDGES.
BEATS ME WHY THEY BOTHER. IF CAL GETS HIS WAY, AIN'T GONNA BE ANY MORE CRIME!
OR PEOPLE.
*SJS – SPECIAL JUDICIAL SQUAD, THE JUDGES' WATCHDOGS.
YOU'RE UNDER ARREST, TRAITORS! GO FOR YOUR GUNS AND I'LL DROP YOU!
JUDGE DREDD! KILL HIM!
AAGH!
NO MORE! I SURRENDER!
WHIZZZZZ
GOOD CLEAN SHOTS, JUST LIKE WE TAUGHT YOU AT THE ACADEMY. FULL MARKS, DREDD!
I HAD TO DO IT. BUT THEY WERE GOOD MEN ONCE – BEFORE CAL CORRUPTED THEM.
THE BODIES WERE HIDDEN. SOON THE FIRST SECTION BEGAN TO FILE IN –
I'VE SUBSTITUTED OUR TAPE FOR CAL'S, DREDD!
GOOD. I'VE TOLD OUR FRIEND TO ACT LIKE NOTHING UNUSUAL IS HAPPENING AND HE'LL STAY HEALTHY.

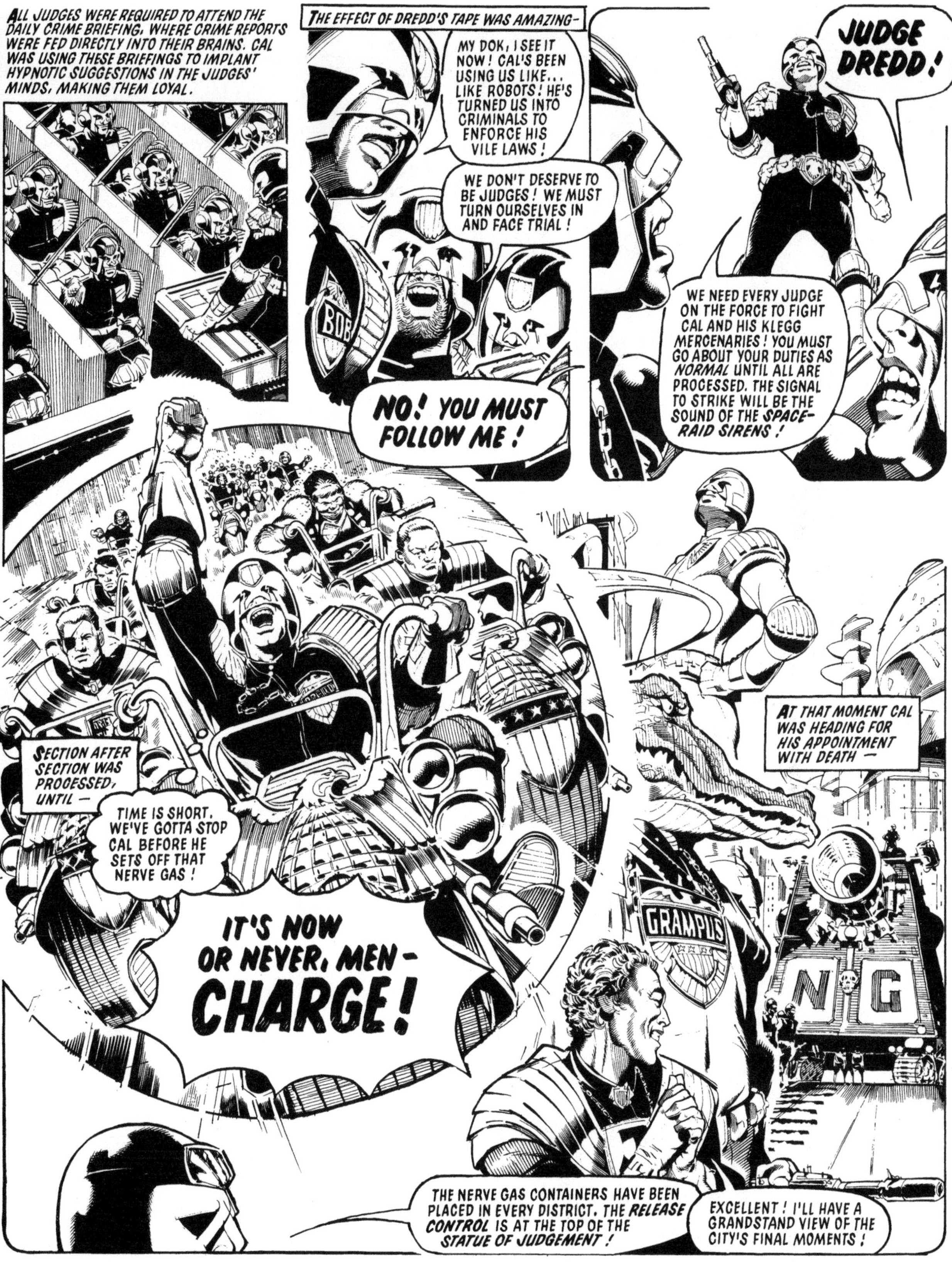

ALL JUDGES WERE REQUIRED TO ATTEND THE DAILY CRIME BRIEFING, WHERE CRIME REPORTS WERE FED DIRECTLY INTO THEIR BRAINS. CAL WAS USING THESE BRIEFINGS TO IMPLANT HYPNOTIC SUGGESTIONS IN THE JUDGES' MINDS, MAKING THEM LOYAL.
THE EFFECT OF DREDD'S TAPE WAS AMAZING–
MY DOK, I SEE IT NOW! CAL'S BEEN USING US LIKE... LIKE ROBOTS! HE'S TURNED US INTO CRIMINALS TO ENFORCE HIS VILE LAWS!
WE DON'T DESERVE TO BE JUDGES! WE MUST TURN OURSELVES IN AND FACE TRIAL!
BOB
NO! YOU MUST FOLLOW ME!
JUDGE DREDD!
WE NEED EVERY JUDGE ON THE FORCE TO FIGHT CAL AND HIS KLEGG MERCENARIES! YOU MUST GO ABOUT YOUR DUTIES AS NORMAL UNTIL ALL ARE PROCESSED. THE SIGNAL TO STRIKE WILL BE THE SOUND OF THE SPACE-RAID SIRENS!
SECTION AFTER SECTION WAS PROCESSED, UNTIL–
TIME IS SHORT. WE'VE GOTTA STOP CAL BEFORE HE SETS OFF THAT NERVE GAS!
IT'S NOW OR NEVER, MEN– CHARGE!
AT THAT MOMENT CAL WAS HEADING FOR HIS APPOINTMENT WITH DEATH–
GRAMPUS
N G
THE NERVE GAS CONTAINERS HAVE BEEN PLACED IN EVERY DISTRICT. THE RELEASE CONTROL IS AT THE TOP OF THE STATUE OF JUDGEMENT!
EXCELLENT! I'LL HAVE A GRANDSTAND VIEW OF THE CITY'S FINAL MOMENTS!

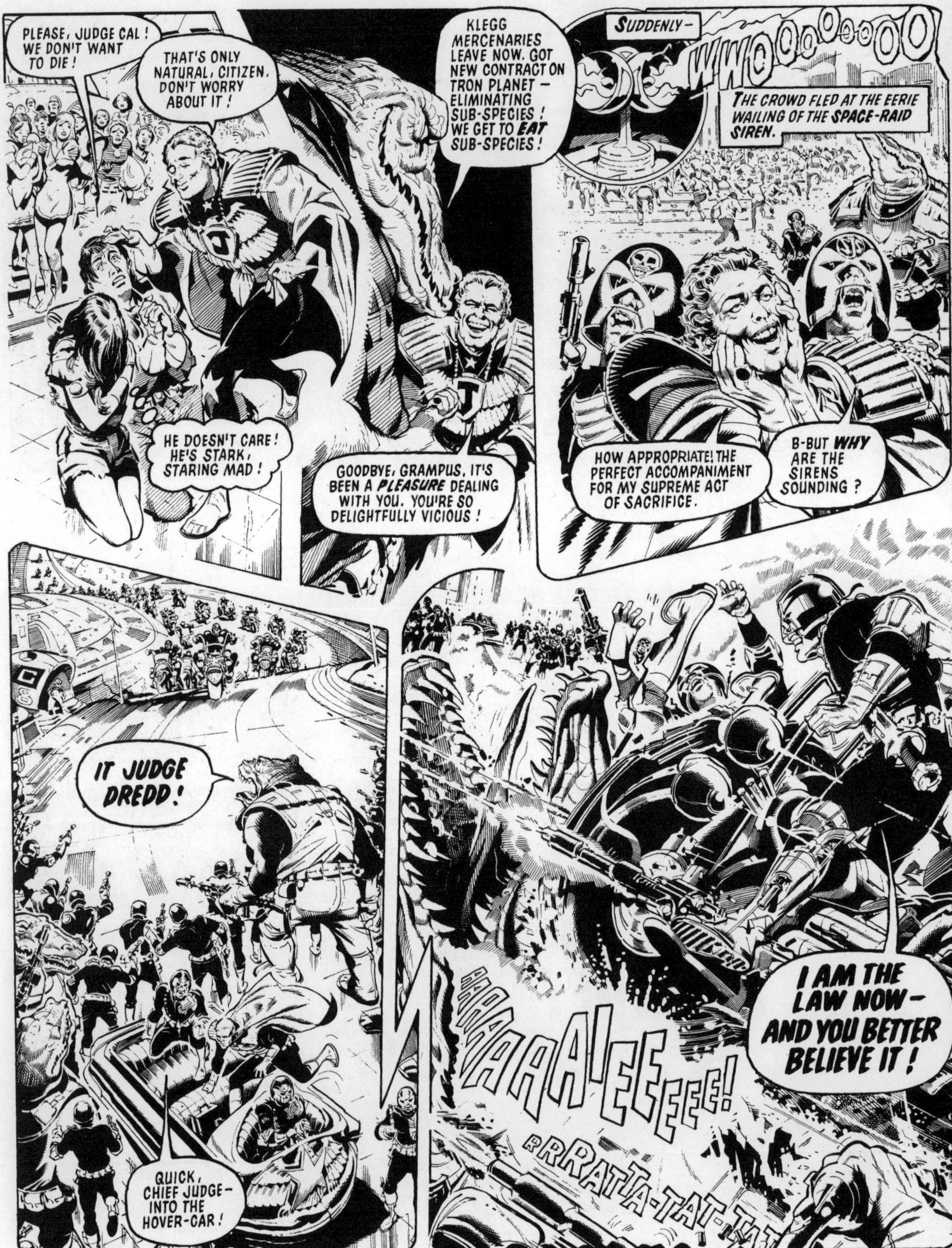
PLEASE, JUDGE CAL! WE DON'T WANT TO DIE!
THAT'S ONLY NATURAL, CITIZEN. DON'T WORRY ABOUT IT!
HE DOESN'T CARE! HE'S STARK, STARING MAD!
KLEGG MERCENARIES LEAVE NOW. GOT NEW CONTRACT ON TRON PLANET — ELIMINATING SUB-SPECIES! WE GET TO EAT SUB-SPECIES!
GOODBYE, GRAMPUS. IT'S BEEN A PLEASURE DEALING WITH YOU. YOU'RE SO DELIGHTFULLY VICIOUS!
SUDDENLY—
WWOOOOOOOOO
THE CROWD FLED AT THE EERIE WAILING OF THE SPACE-RAID SIREN.
HOW APPROPRIATE! THE PERFECT ACCOMPANIMENT FOR MY SUPREME ACT OF SACRIFICE.
B-BUT WHY ARE THE SIRENS SOUNDING?
IT JUDGE DREDD!
QUICK, CHIEF JUDGE — INTO THE HOVER-CAR!
AAAAAAAIEEEEEE!
RRRATTA-TAT-TAT
I AM THE LAW NOW — AND YOU BETTER BELIEVE IT!

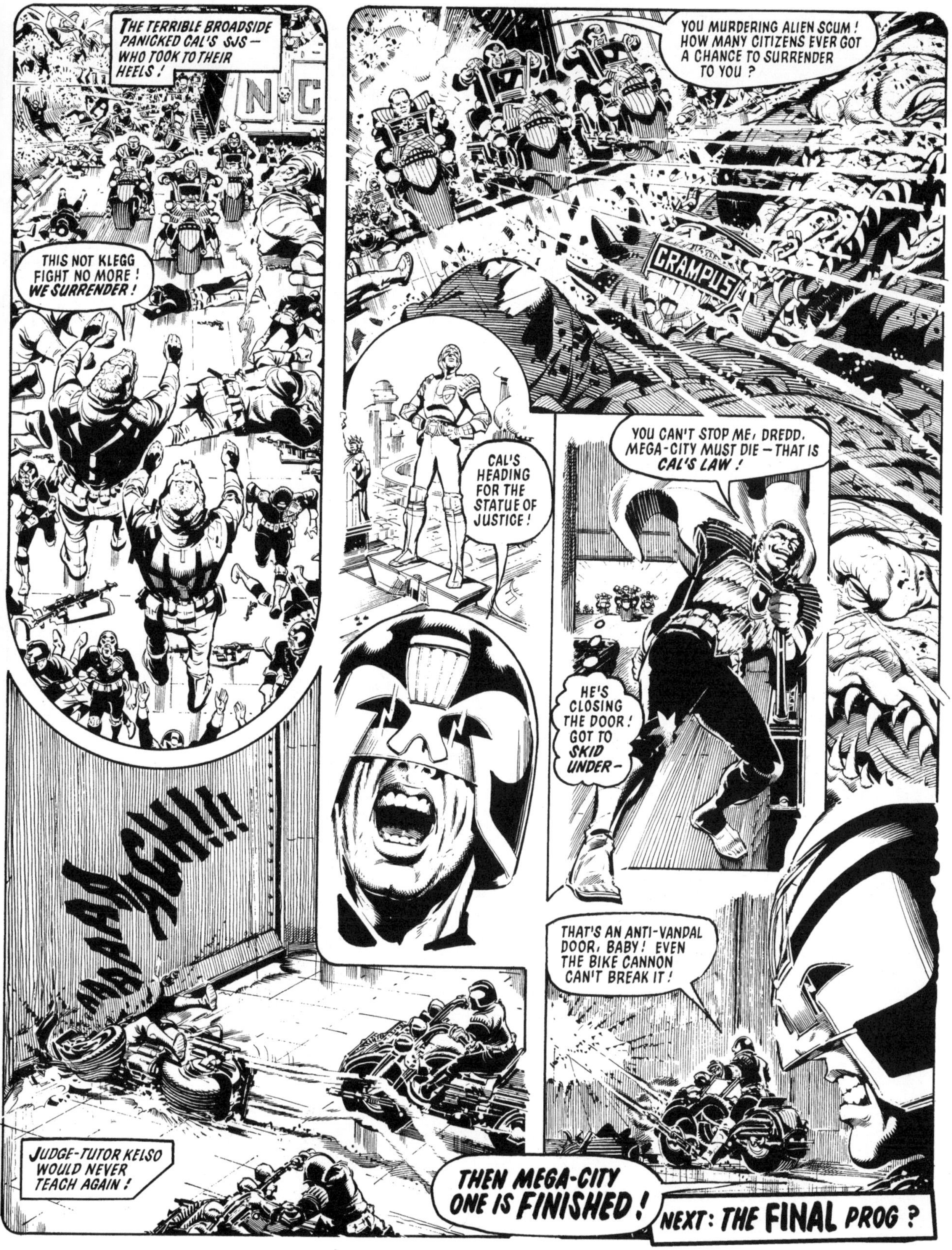
THE TERRIBLE BROADSIDE PANICKED CAL'S SJS — WHO TOOK TO THEIR HEELS!
THIS NOT KLEGG FIGHT NO MORE! WE SURRENDER!
YOU MURDERING ALIEN SCUM! HOW MANY CITIZENS EVER GOT A CHANCE TO SURRENDER TO YOU?
CRAMPUS
CAL'S HEADING FOR THE STATUE OF JUSTICE!
YOU CAN'T STOP ME, DREDD. MEGA-CITY MUST DIE — THAT IS CAL'S LAW!
HE'S CLOSING THE DOOR! GOT TO SKID UNDER—
AAAAAAYAGH!!!
THAT'S AN ANTI-VANDAL DOOR, BABY! EVEN THE BIKE CANNON CAN'T BREAK IT!
JUDGE-TUTOR KELSO WOULD NEVER TEACH AGAIN!
THEN MEGA-CITY ONE IS FINISHED!
NEXT: THE FINAL PROG?

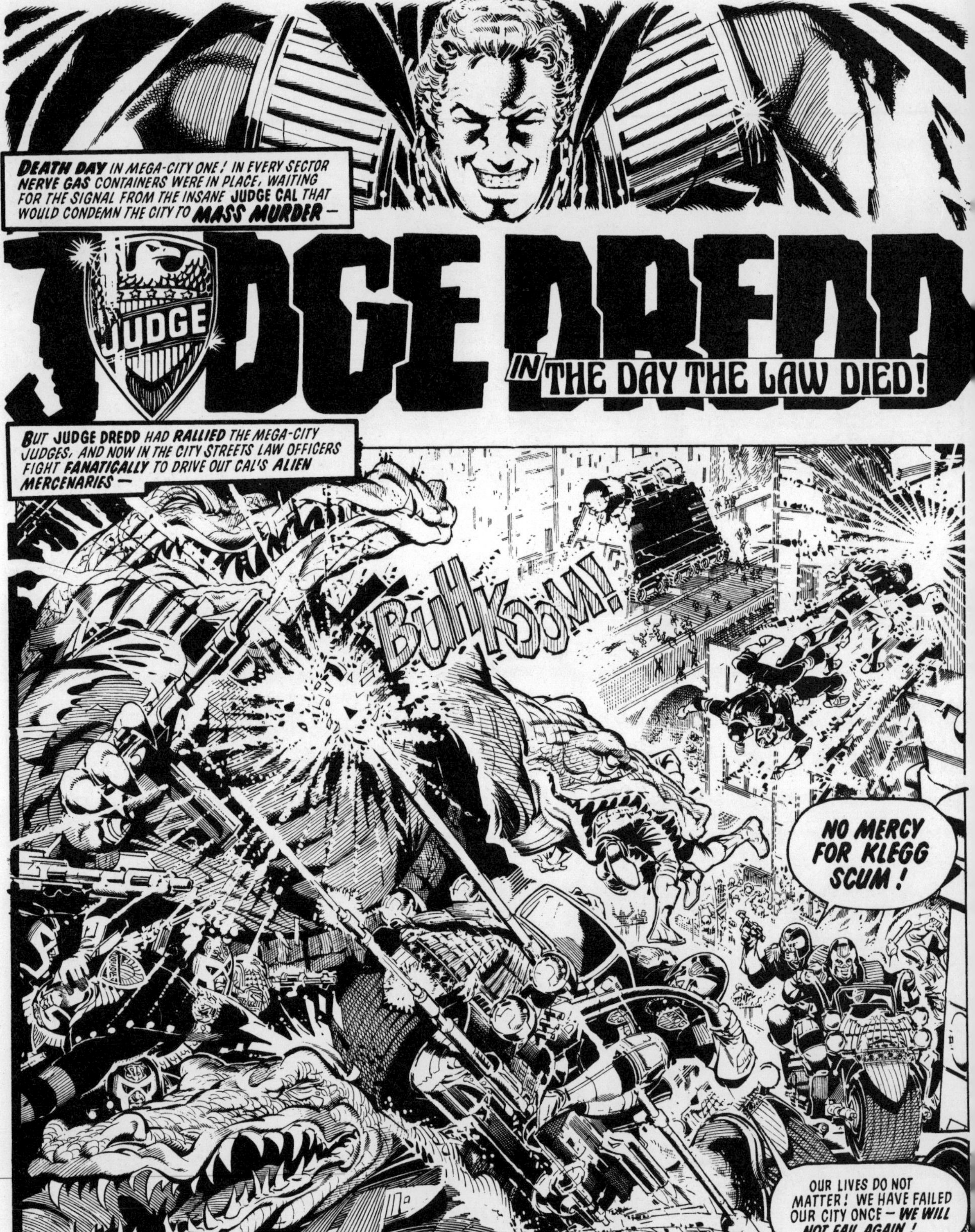
DEATH DAY IN MEGA-CITY ONE! IN EVERY SECTOR NERVE GAS CONTAINERS WERE IN PLACE, WAITING FOR THE SIGNAL FROM THE INSANE JUDGE CAL THAT WOULD CONDEMN THE CITY TO MASS MURDER—
JUDGE DREDD
JUDGE
IN THE DAY THE LAW DIED!
BUT JUDGE DREDD HAD RALLIED THE MEGA-CITY JUDGES, AND NOW IN THE CITY STREETS LAW OFFICERS FIGHT FANATICALLY TO DRIVE OUT CAL'S ALIEN MERCENARIES—
BUHKOOM!
NO MERCY FOR KLEGG SCUM!
OUR LIVES DO NOT MATTER! WE HAVE FAILED OUR CITY ONCE — WE WILL NOT FAIL AGAIN!

ON THE EAST SIDE OF THE CITY, THE BATTLE FOR LIFE ITSELF WAS BEING FOUGHT—

B BLAST!

CAL'S LOCKED HIMSELF IN THE *STATUE OF JUDGEMENT!*

EVEN BIKE CANNON CAN'T CRACK THE ANTI-VANDAL DOOR!

BUT THIS TRUCK MIGHT! GET OUT OF THE WAY, JUDGE GRIFFIN!

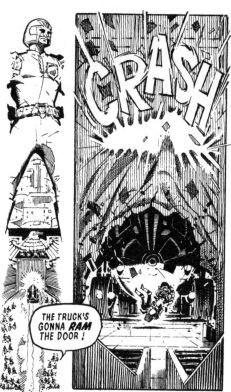

CRASH

THE TRUCK'S GONNA *RAM* THE DOOR!

DREDD AND THE OTHERS RACED IN PAST THE BODY OF JUDGE KELSO, KILLED TRYING TO SQUEEZE UNDER THE DOOR—

JUDGE KELSO... MY OLD FRIEND AND COLLEAGUE...

TIME TO MOURN LATER, PEPPER! IN FIVE MINUTES THE NERVE GAS RELEASE CONTROL BECOMES *ACTIVE!*

PRETTY SOON FERGEE GET *HEAVY*, EH, OLD CHAPEE? FERGEE *LIKE* GETTIN' HEAVY!

YOU CAN GET AS HEAVY AS YOU LIKE, PAL—*IF* WE MAKE IT IN TIME!

DREDD

ON TOP OF THE STATUE OF JUDGEMENT, CAL WAITED FOR *ZERO HOUR* WITH TWO SJS* BODYGUARDS—

MEGA-CITY ONE'S GREATEST MOMENT APPROACHES! THE MOMENT OF *SUPREME SACRIFICE!*

FOOTSTEPS POUNDING UP THE STAIRS— DREDD'S COMING!

WE CAN STOP THIS MADMAN NOW AND WIN A PARDON FOR OUR OWN ACTIONS. WE'LL BE *HEROES!*

*SJS - SPECIAL JUDICIAL SQUAD.

SOON ALL WILL BE DEAD — HEE, HEE — AND MEGA-CITY ONE WILL STAND FOREVER AS A MONUMENT TO PERFECT GOVERNMENT! *MY* GOVERNMENT!

COME, GENTLEMEN, DRINK WITH ME TO MARK THIS HISTORIC MOMENT. I HAVE SAVED A BOTTLE OF *ICI '89* - A RARE VINTAGE.

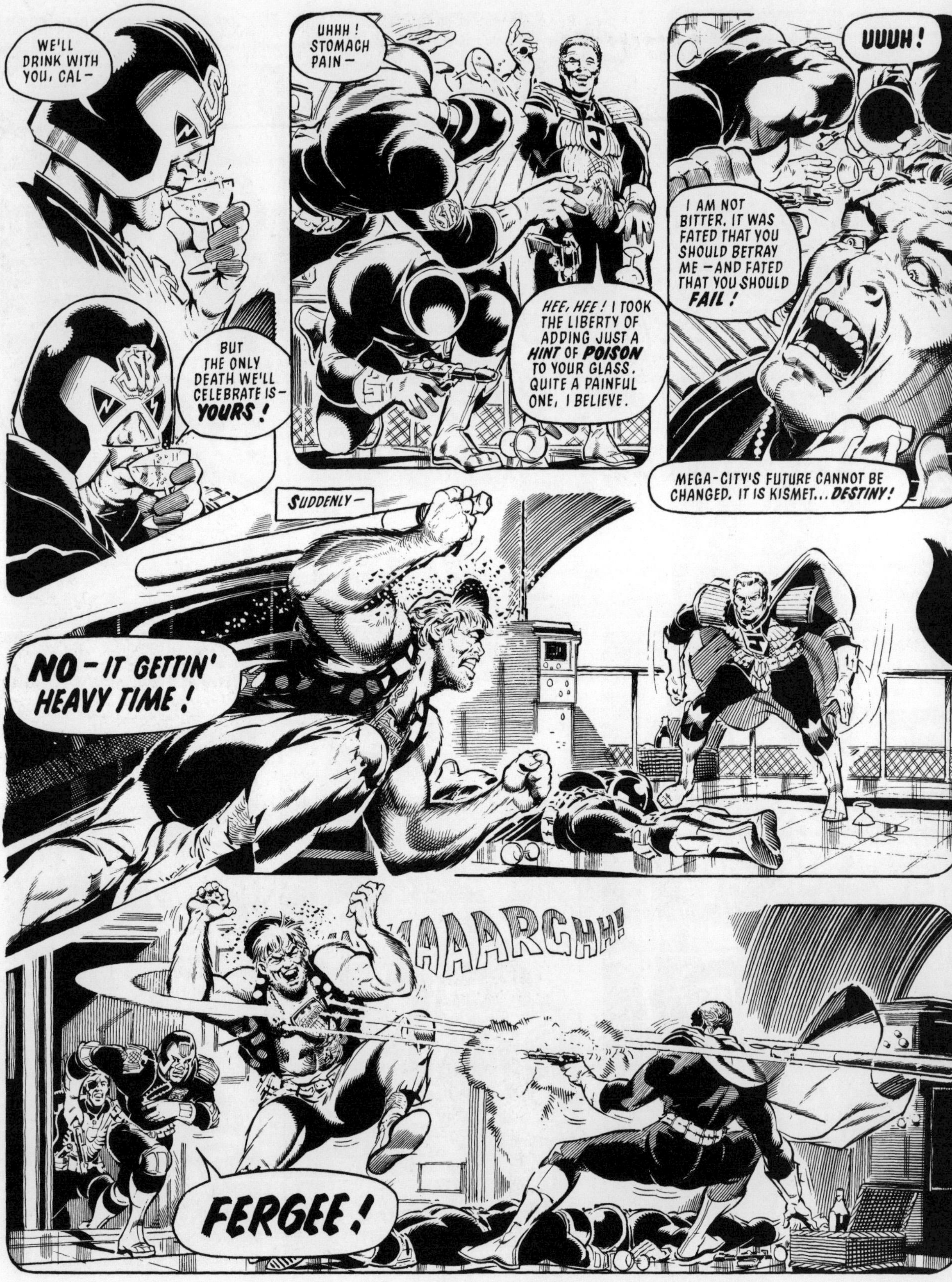
WE'LL DRINK WITH YOU, CAL-
BUT THE ONLY DEATH WE'LL CELEBRATE IS- YOURS!
UHHH! STOMACH PAIN-
HEE, HEE! I TOOK THE LIBERTY OF ADDING JUST A HINT OF POISON TO YOUR GLASS. QUITE A PAINFUL ONE, I BELIEVE.
UUUH!
I AM NOT BITTER. IT WAS FATED THAT YOU SHOULD BETRAY ME — AND FATED THAT YOU SHOULD FAIL!
MEGA-CITY'S FUTURE CANNOT BE CHANGED. IT IS KISMET... DESTINY!
SUDDENLY-
NO - IT GETTIN' HEAVY TIME!
AAAARGHH!
FERGEE!

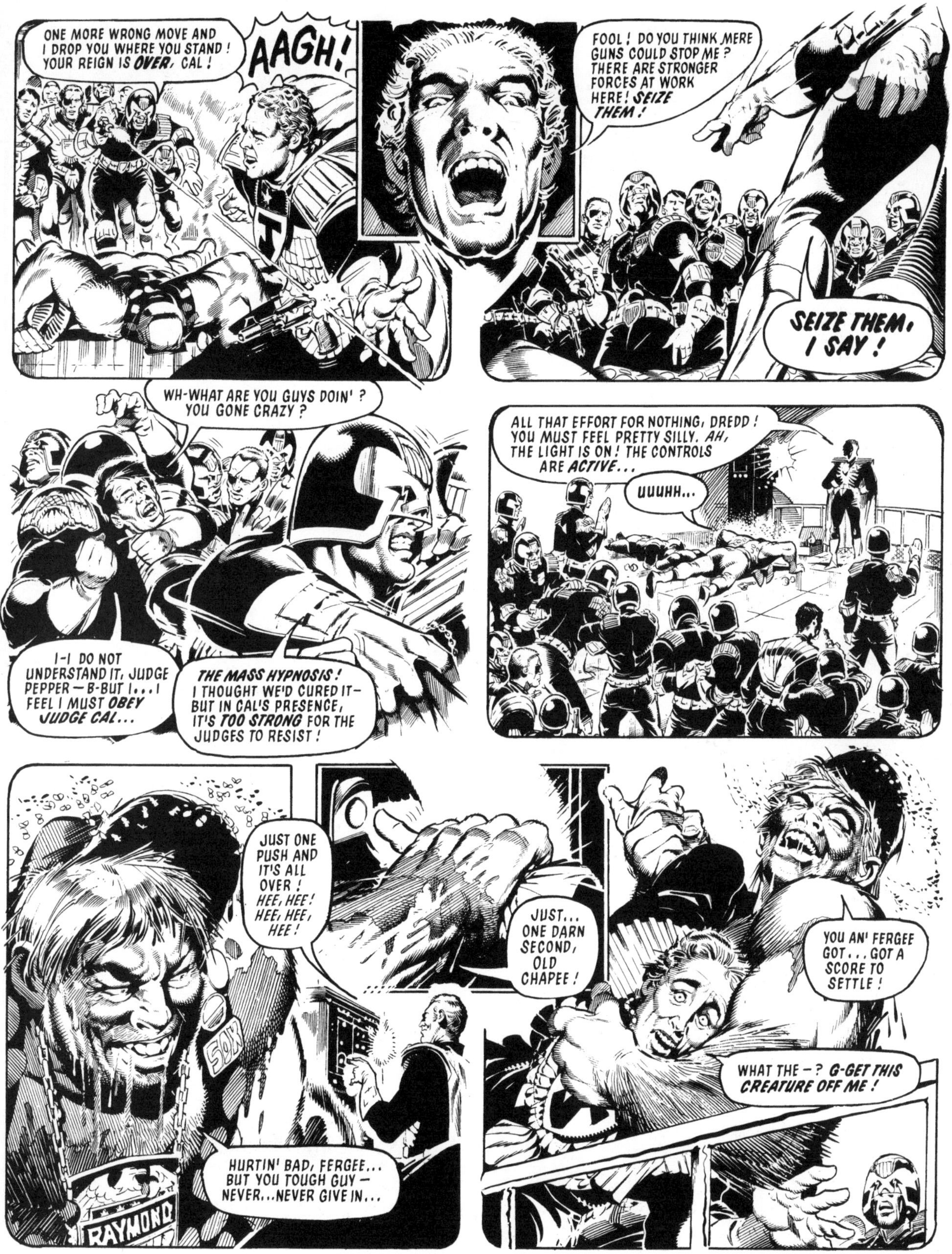
ONE MORE WRONG MOVE AND I DROP YOU WHERE YOU STAND! YOUR REIGN IS OVER, CAL!
AAGH!
FOOL! DO YOU THINK MERE GUNS COULD STOP ME? THERE ARE STRONGER FORCES AT WORK HERE! SEIZE THEM!
SEIZE THEM, I SAY!
WH-WHAT ARE YOU GUYS DOIN'? YOU GONE CRAZY?
I-I DO NOT UNDERSTAND IT, JUDGE PEPPER — B-BUT I...I FEEL I MUST OBEY JUDGE CAL...
THE MASS HYPNOSIS! I THOUGHT WE'D CURED IT — BUT IN CAL'S PRESENCE, IT'S TOO STRONG FOR THE JUDGES TO RESIST!
ALL THAT EFFORT FOR NOTHING, DREDD! YOU MUST FEEL PRETTY SILLY. AH, THE LIGHT IS ON! THE CONTROLS ARE ACTIVE...
UUUHH...
JUST ONE PUSH AND IT'S ALL OVER! HEE, HEE! HEE, HEE, HEE!
HURTIN' BAD, FERGEE... BUT YOU TOUGH GUY — NEVER...NEVER GIVE IN...
RAYMOND
50K
JUST... ONE DARN SECOND, OLD CHAPEE!
YOU AN' FERGEE GOT...GOT A SCORE TO SETTLE!
WHAT THE —? G-GET THIS CREATURE OFF ME!

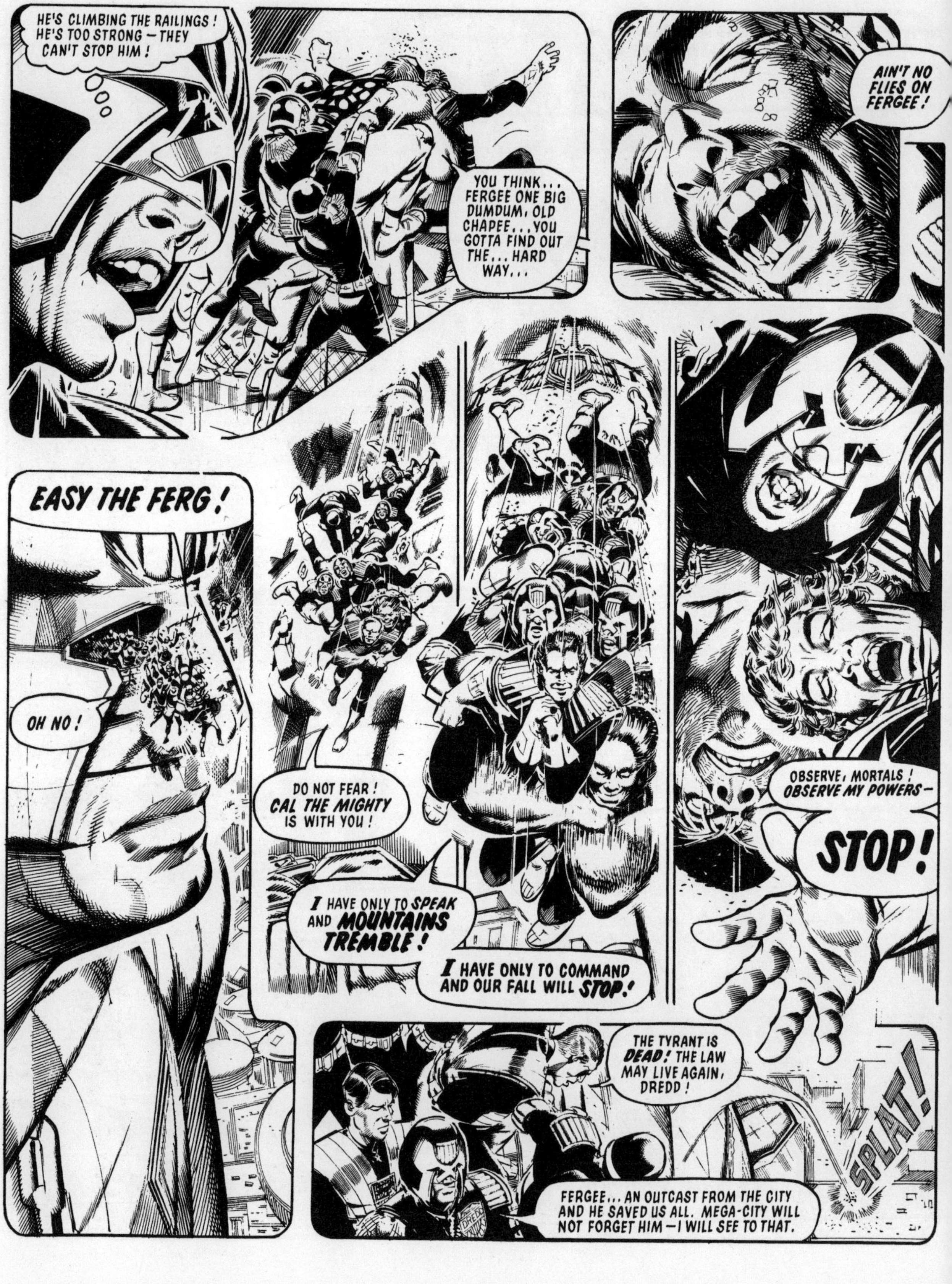

HE'S CLIMBING THE RAILINGS! HE'S TOO STRONG — THEY CAN'T STOP HIM!
YOU THINK... FERGEE ONE BIG DUMDUM, OLD CHAPEE... YOU GOTTA FIND OUT THE... HARD WAY...
AIN'T NO FLIES ON FERGEE!
EASY THE FERG!
OH NO!
DO NOT FEAR! CAL THE MIGHTY IS WITH YOU!
I HAVE ONLY TO SPEAK AND MOUNTAINS TREMBLE!
I HAVE ONLY TO COMMAND AND OUR FALL WILL STOP!
OBSERVE, MORTALS! OBSERVE MY POWERS—
STOP!
SPLAT!
THE TYRANT IS DEAD! THE LAW MAY LIVE AGAIN, DREDD!
FERGEE... AN OUTCAST FROM THE CITY AND HE SAVED US ALL. MEGA-CITY WILL NOT FORGET HIM — I WILL SEE TO THAT.

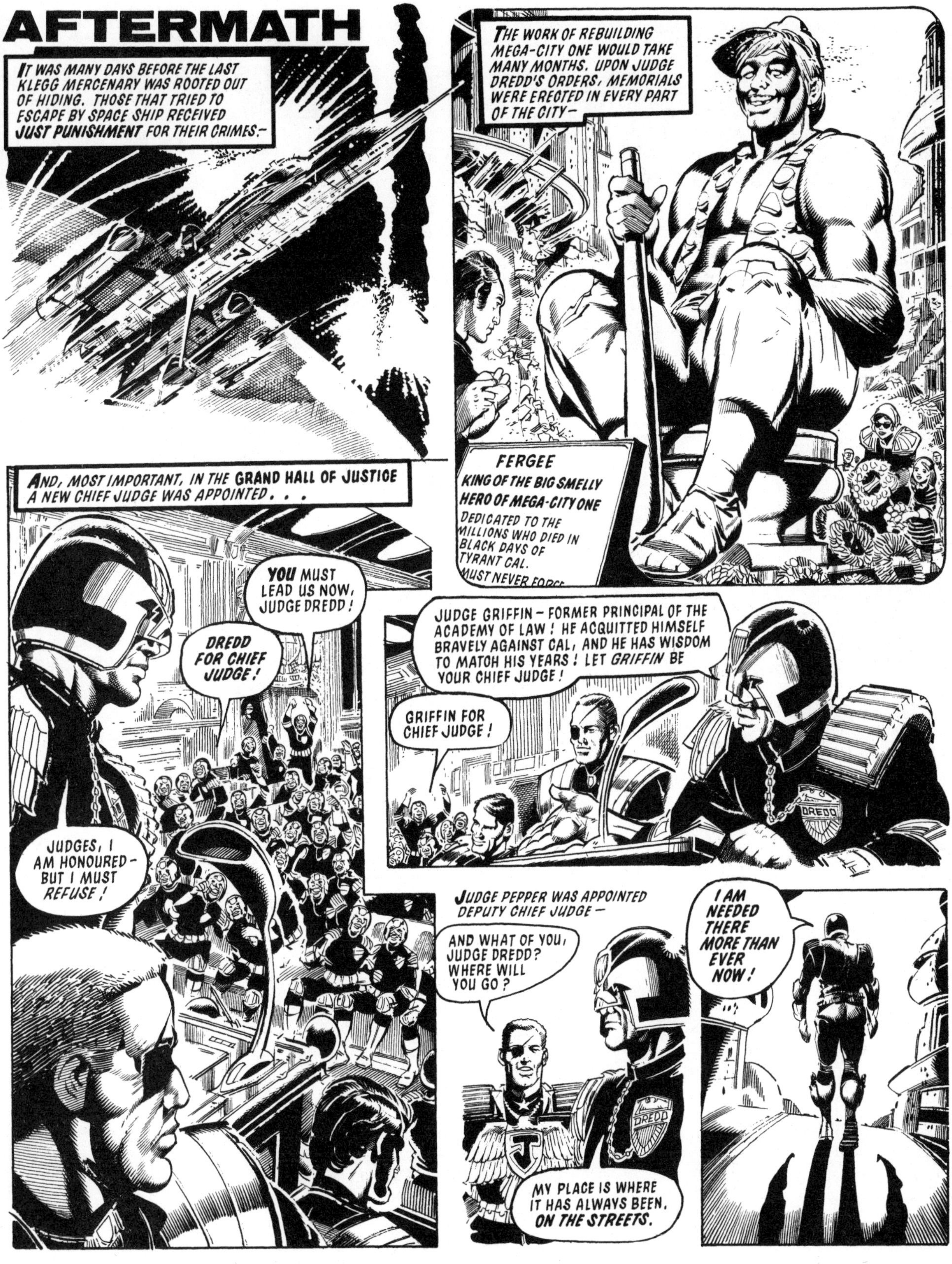

AFTERMATH
IT WAS MANY DAYS BEFORE THE LAST KLEGG MERCENARY WAS ROOTED OUT OF HIDING. THOSE THAT TRIED TO ESCAPE BY SPACE SHIP RECEIVED JUST PUNISHMENT FOR THEIR CRIMES.–
THE WORK OF REBUILDING MEGA-CITY ONE WOULD TAKE MANY MONTHS. UPON JUDGE DREDD'S ORDERS, MEMORIALS WERE ERECTED IN EVERY PART OF THE CITY–
FERGEE
KING OF THE BIG SMELLY
HERO OF MEGA-CITY ONE
DEDICATED TO THE MILLIONS WHO DIED IN BLACK DAYS OF TYRANT CAL.
MUST NEVER
AND, MOST IMPORTANT, IN THE GRAND HALL OF JUSTICE A NEW CHIEF JUDGE WAS APPOINTED . . .
YOU MUST LEAD US NOW, JUDGE DREDD!
DREDD FOR CHIEF JUDGE!
JUDGES, I AM HONOURED– BUT I MUST REFUSE!
JUDGE GRIFFIN – FORMER PRINCIPAL OF THE ACADEMY OF LAW! HE ACQUITTED HIMSELF BRAVELY AGAINST CAL, AND HE HAS WISDOM TO MATCH HIS YEARS! LET GRIFFIN BE YOUR CHIEF JUDGE!
GRIFFIN FOR CHIEF JUDGE!
DREDD
JUDGE PEPPER WAS APPOINTED DEPUTY CHIEF JUDGE–
AND WHAT OF YOU, JUDGE DREDD? WHERE WILL YOU GO?
DREDD
MY PLACE IS WHERE IT HAS ALWAYS BEEN. ON THE STREETS.
I AM NEEDED THERE MORE THAN EVER NOW!

FOLLOWING THE DEATH OF THE TYRANT CAL, MEGA-CITY ONE SLOWLY BEGAN TO RETURN TO NORMAL. BUT THERE WERE SOME PLACES IN THE CITY WHERE LAW AND ORDER HAD BROKEN DOWN TOO FAR... PLACES WHERE EVEN JUDGES WERE NOT SAFE TO VENTURE!

JUDGE DREDD

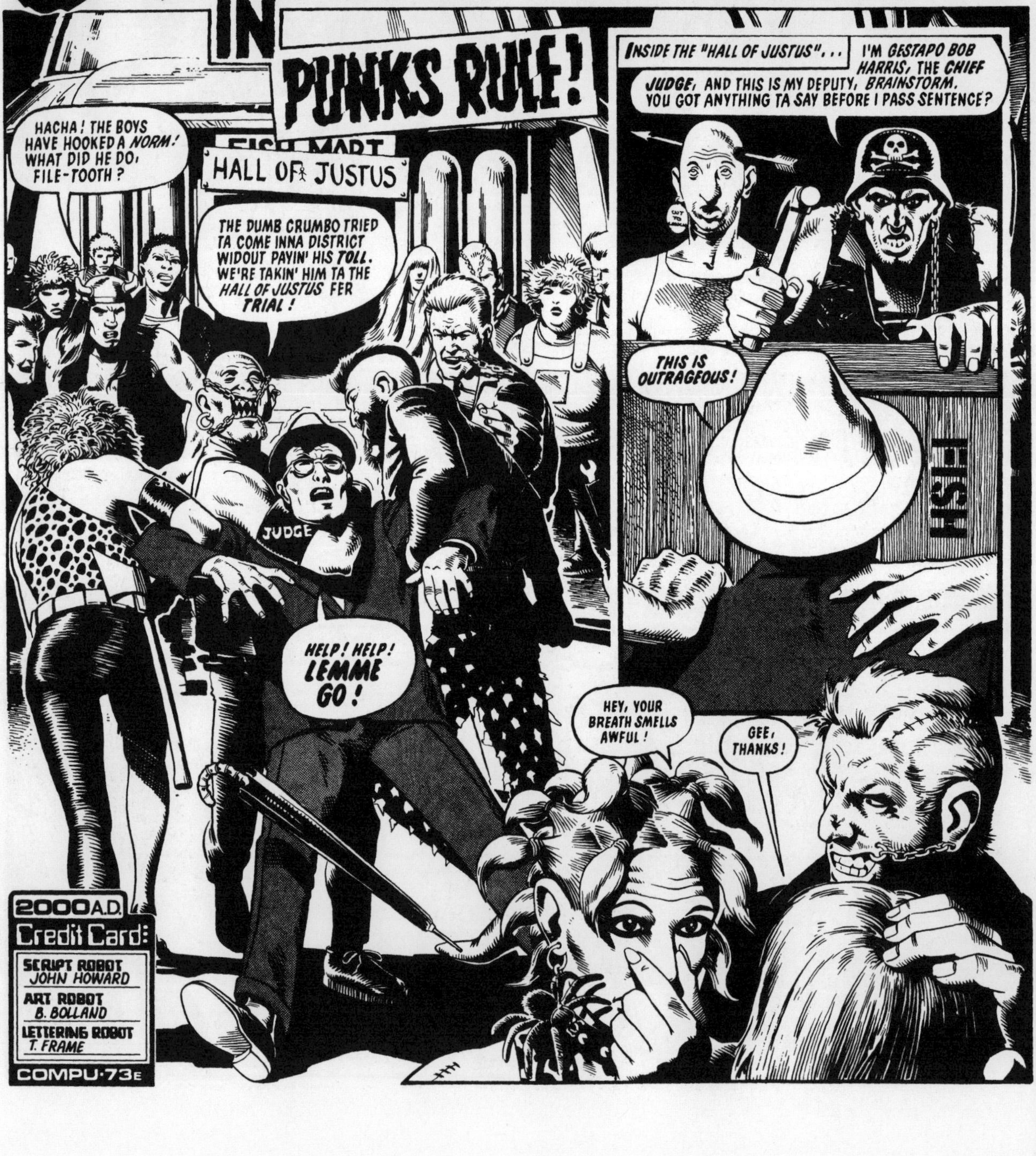

IN
PUNKS RULE!
FISH MART
HALL OF JUSTUS
HACHA! THE BOYS HAVE HOOKED A NORM! WHAT DID HE DO, FILE-TOOTH?
THE DUMB CRUMBO TRIED TA COME INNA DISTRICT WIDOUT PAYIN' HIS TOLL. WE'RE TAKIN' HIM TA THE HALL OF JUSTUS FER TRIAL!
JUDGE
HELP! HELP! LEMME GO!
INSIDE THE "HALL OF JUSTUS"...
I'M GESTAPO BOB HARRIS, THE CHIFF JUDGE, AND THIS IS MY DEPUTY, BRAINSTORM. YOU GOT ANYTHING TA SAY BEFORE I PASS SENTENCE?
THIS IS OUTRAGEOUS!
FISH
HEY, YOUR BREATH SMELLS AWFUL!
GEE, THANKS!
2000 A.D.
Credit Card:
SCRIPT ROBOT JOHN HOWARD
ART ROBOT B. BOLLAND
LETTERING ROBOT T. FRAME
COMPU·73E

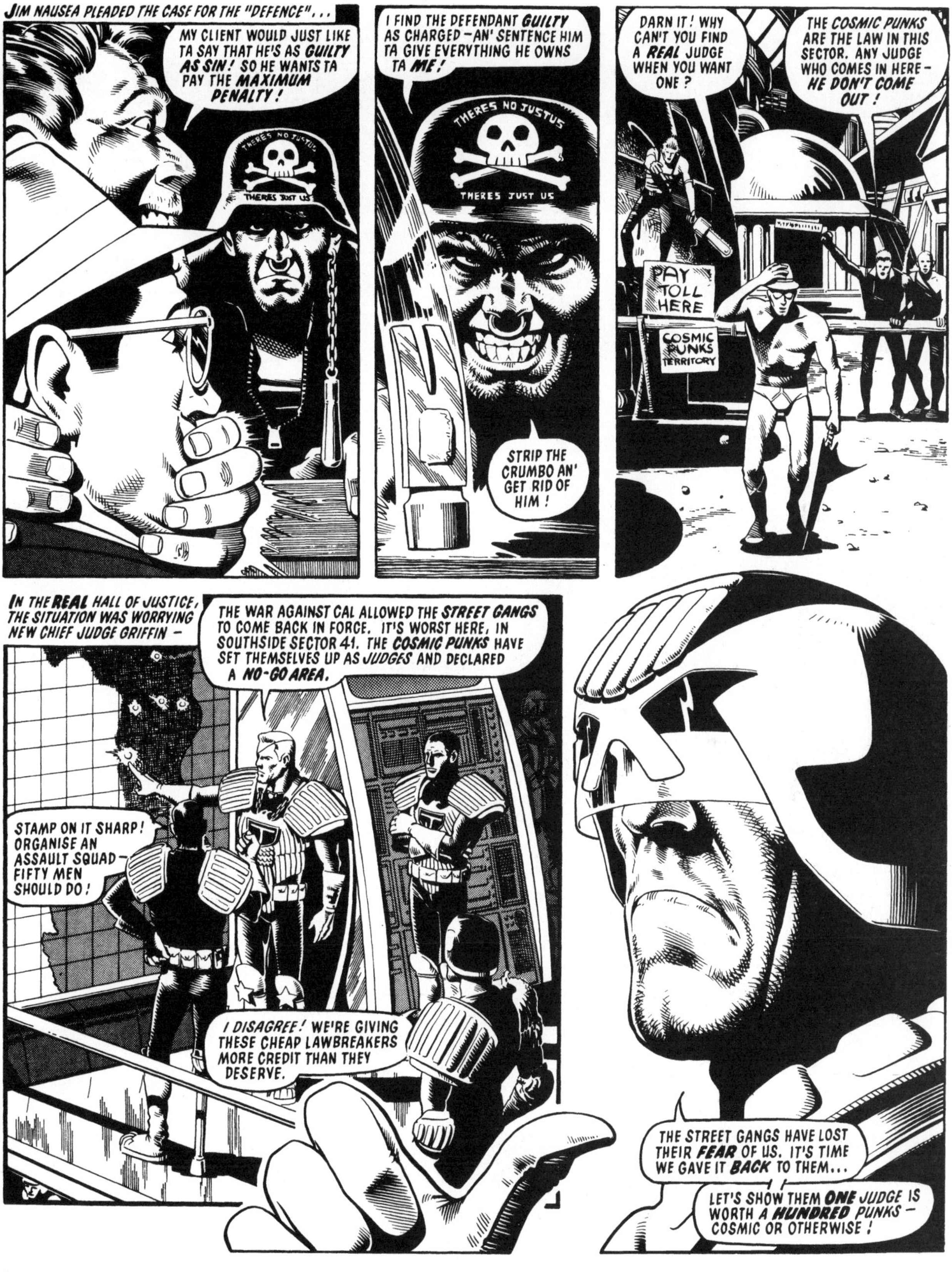

JIM NAUSEA PLEADED THE CASE FOR THE "DEFENCE"...
MY CLIENT WOULD JUST LIKE TA SAY THAT HE'S AS GUILTY AS SIN! SO HE WANTS TA PAY THE MAXIMUM PENALTY!
THERES NO JUSTUS
THERES JUST US
I FIND THE DEFENDANT GUILTY AS CHARGED — AN' SENTENCE HIM TA GIVE EVERYTHING HE OWNS TA ME!
THERES NO JUSTUS
THERES JUST US
STRIP THE CRUMBO AN' GET RID OF HIM!
DARN IT! WHY CAN'T YOU FIND A REAL JUDGE WHEN YOU WANT ONE?
THE COSMIC PUNKS ARE THE LAW IN THIS SECTOR. ANY JUDGE WHO COMES IN HERE — HE DON'T COME OUT!
PAY TOLL HERE
COSMIC PUNKS TERRITORY
IN THE REAL HALL OF JUSTICE, THE SITUATION WAS WORRYING NEW CHIEF JUDGE GRIFFIN —
THE WAR AGAINST CAL ALLOWED THE STREET GANGS TO COME BACK IN FORCE. IT'S WORST HERE, IN SOUTHSIDE SECTOR 41. THE COSMIC PUNKS HAVE SET THEMSELVES UP AS JUDGES AND DECLARED A NO-GO AREA.
STAMP ON IT SHARP! ORGANISE AN ASSAULT SQUAD — FIFTY MEN SHOULD DO!
I DISAGREE! WE'RE GIVING THESE CHEAP LAWBREAKERS MORE CREDIT THAN THEY DESERVE.
THE STREET GANGS HAVE LOST THEIR FEAR OF US. IT'S TIME WE GAVE IT BACK TO THEM...
LET'S SHOW THEM ONE JUDGE IS WORTH A HUNDRED PUNKS — COSMIC OR OTHERWISE!

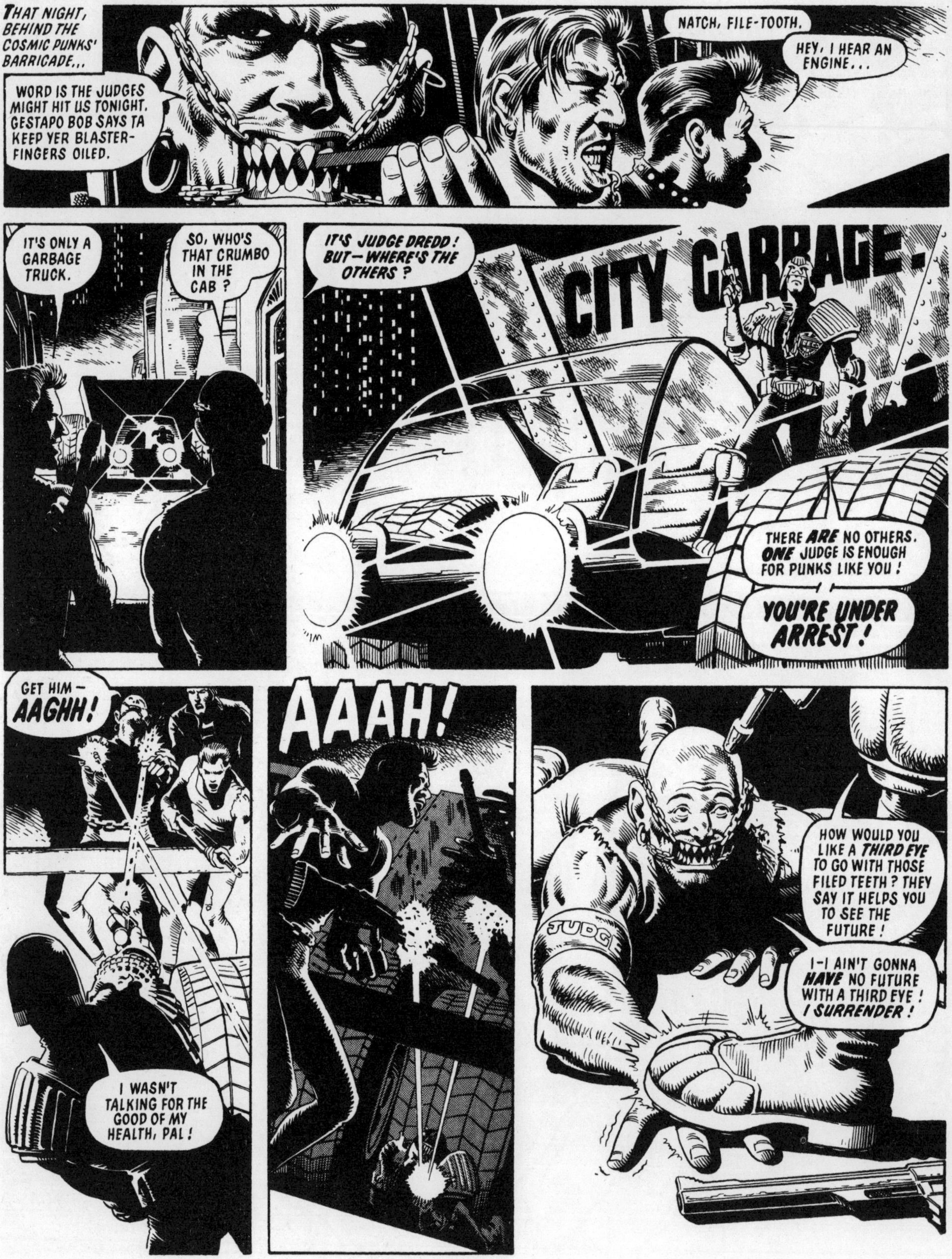
THAT NIGHT, BEHIND THE COSMIC PUNKS' BARRICADE...
WORD IS THE JUDGES MIGHT HIT US TONIGHT. GESTAPO BOB SAYS TA KEEP YER BLASTER-FINGERS OILED.
NATCH, FILE-TOOTH.
HEY, I HEAR AN ENGINE...
IT'S ONLY A GARBAGE TRUCK.
SO, WHO'S THAT CRUMBO IN THE CAB ?
IT'S JUDGE DREDD ! BUT—WHERE'S THE OTHERS ?
CITY GARBAGE.
THERE ARE NO OTHERS. ONE JUDGE IS ENOUGH FOR PUNKS LIKE YOU !
YOU'RE UNDER ARREST !
GET HIM— AAGHH!
I WASN'T TALKING FOR THE GOOD OF MY HEALTH, PAL !
AAAH!
HOW WOULD YOU LIKE A THIRD EYE TO GO WITH THOSE FILED TEETH ? THEY SAY IT HELPS YOU TO SEE THE FUTURE !
I-I AIN'T GONNA HAVE NO FUTURE WITH A THIRD EYE ! I SURRENDER !

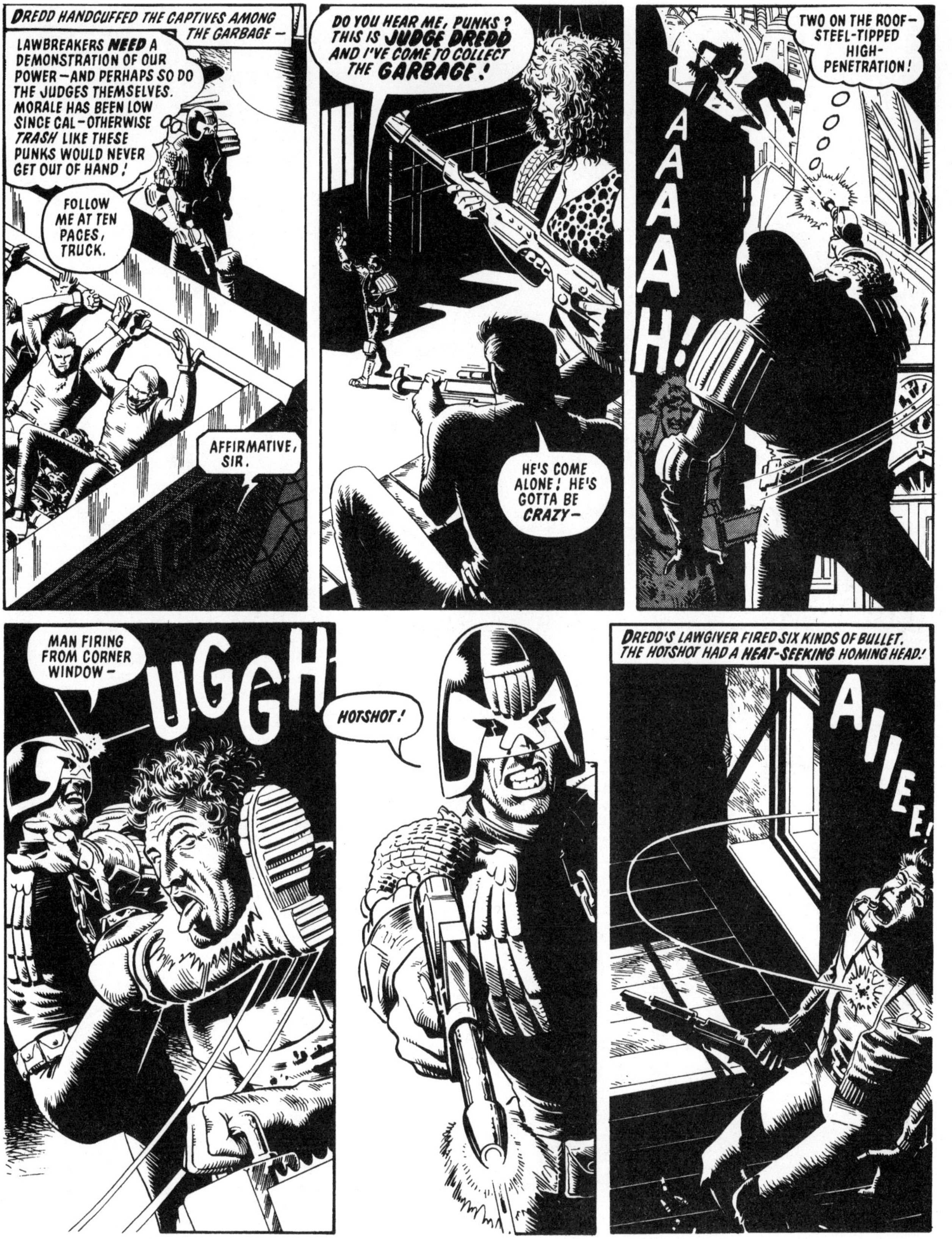
DREDD HANDCUFFED THE CAPTIVES AMONG THE GARBAGE –
LAWBREAKERS NEED A DEMONSTRATION OF OUR POWER – AND PERHAPS SO DO THE JUDGES THEMSELVES. MORALE HAS BEEN LOW SINCE CAL – OTHERWISE TRASH LIKE THESE PUNKS WOULD NEVER GET OUT OF HAND!
FOLLOW ME AT TEN PACES, TRUCK.
AFFIRMATIVE, SIR.
DO YOU HEAR ME, PUNKS? THIS IS JUDGE DREDD AND I'VE COME TO COLLECT THE GARBAGE!
HE'S COME ALONE! HE'S GOTTA BE CRAZY –
TWO ON THE ROOF – STEEL-TIPPED HIGH-PENETRATION!
AAAAAH!
MAN FIRING FROM CORNER WINDOW –
UGGH
HOTSHOT!
DREDD'S LAWGIVER FIRED SIX KINDS OF BULLET. THE HOTSHOT HAD A HEAT-SEEKING HOMING HEAD!
AIIEEE!

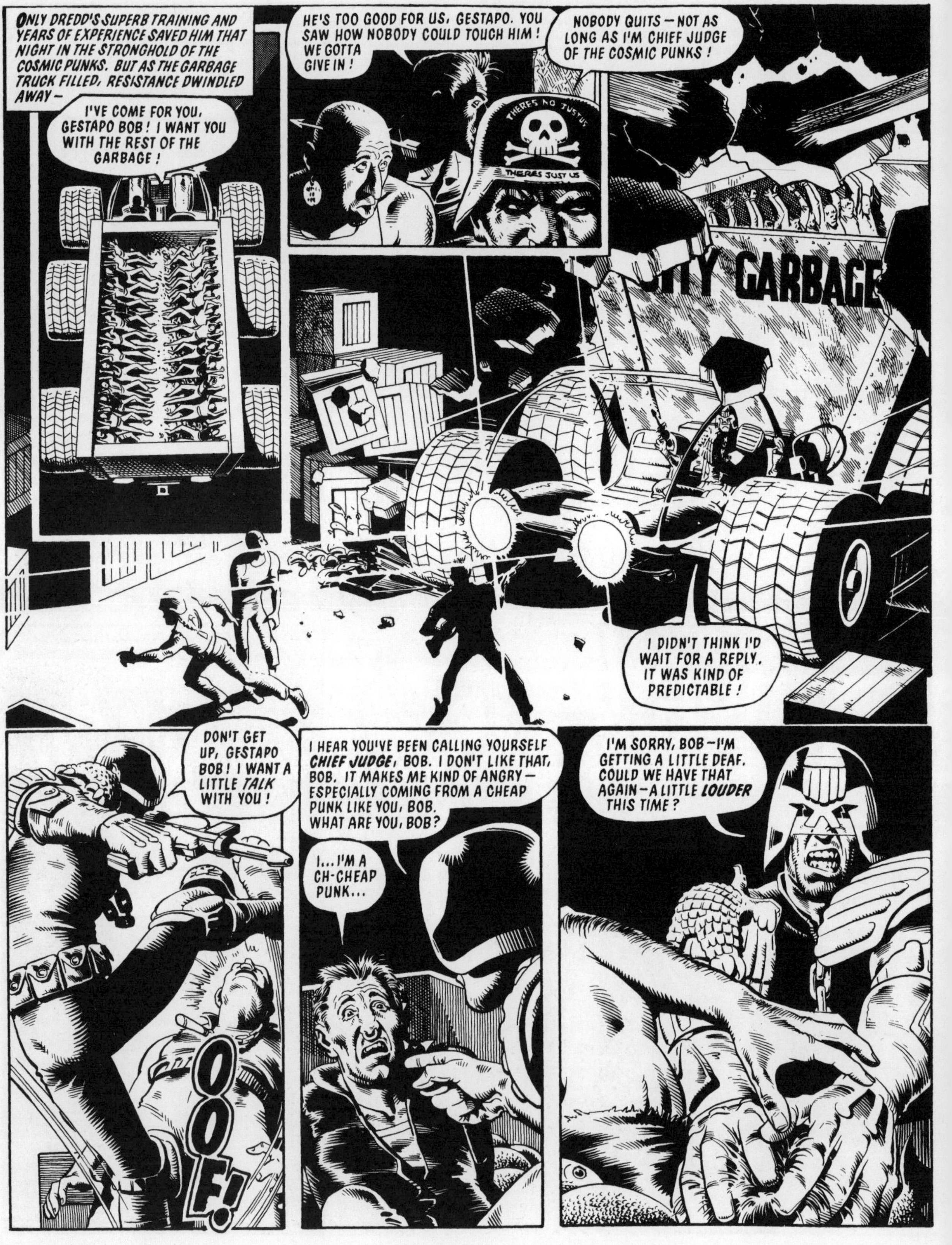
ONLY DREDD'S SUPERB TRAINING AND YEARS OF EXPERIENCE SAVED HIM THAT NIGHT IN THE STRONGHOLD OF THE COSMIC PUNKS. BUT AS THE GARBAGE TRUCK FILLED, RESISTANCE DWINDLED AWAY—
I'VE COME FOR YOU, GESTAPO BOB! I WANT YOU WITH THE REST OF THE GARBAGE!
HE'S TOO GOOD FOR US, GESTAPO. YOU SAW HOW NOBODY COULD TOUCH HIM! WE GOTTA GIVE IN!
THERES NO JUSTUS
THERES JUST US
NOBODY QUITS — NOT AS LONG AS I'M CHIEF JUDGE OF THE COSMIC PUNKS!
CITY GARBAGE
I DIDN'T THINK I'D WAIT FOR A REPLY. IT WAS KIND OF PREDICTABLE!
DON'T GET UP, GESTAPO BOB! I WANT A LITTLE TALK WITH YOU!
OOOF!
I HEAR YOU'VE BEEN CALLING YOURSELF CHIEF JUDGE, BOB. I DON'T LIKE THAT, BOB. IT MAKES ME KIND OF ANGRY — ESPECIALLY COMING FROM A CHEAP PUNK LIKE YOU, BOB. WHAT ARE YOU, BOB?
I...I'M A CH-CHEAP PUNK...
I'M SORRY, BOB — I'M GETTING A LITTLE DEAF. COULD WE HAVE THAT AGAIN — A LITTLE LOUDER THIS TIME?

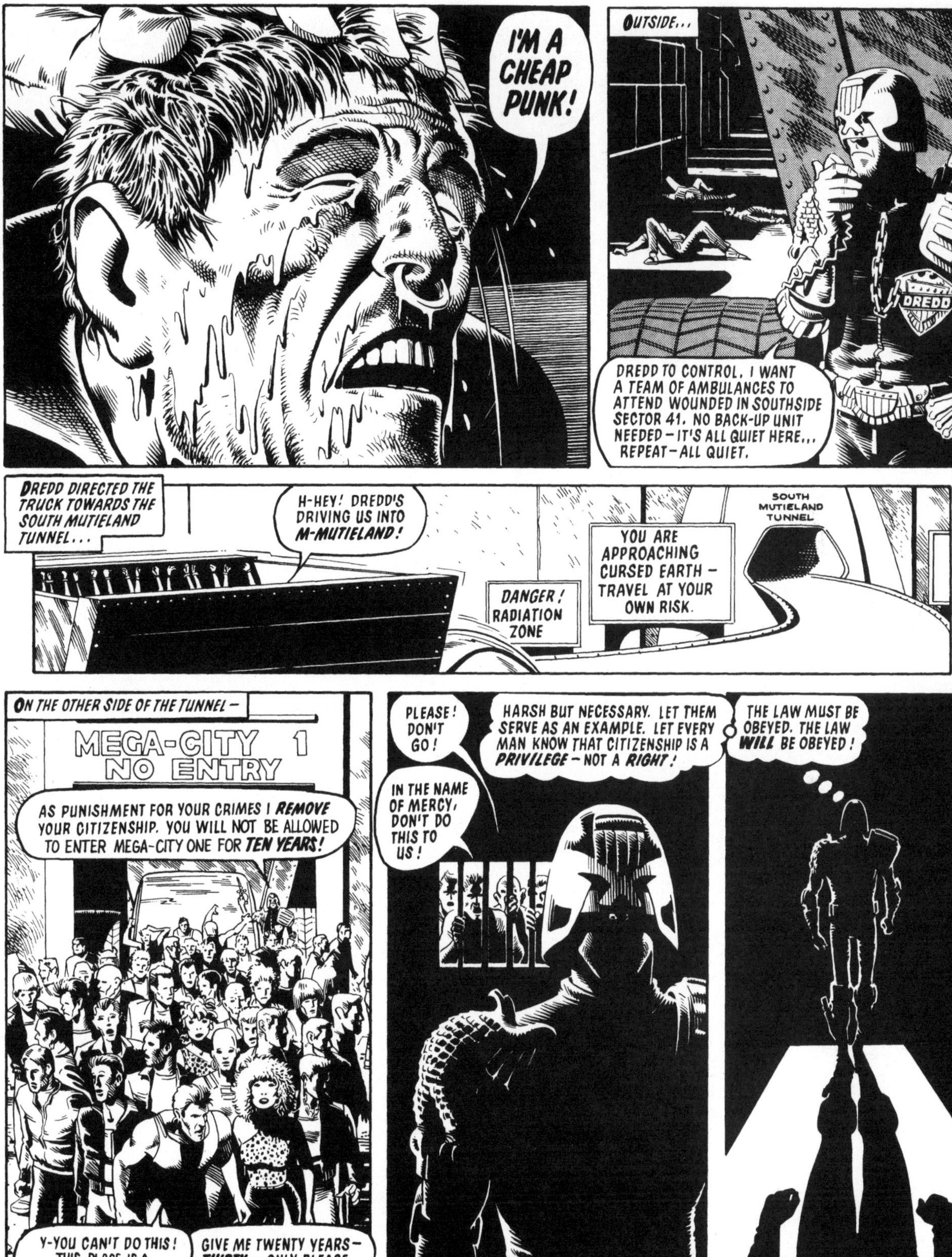
I'M A CHEAP PUNK!
OUTSIDE...
DREDD TO CONTROL. I WANT A TEAM OF AMBULANCES TO ATTEND WOUNDED IN SOUTHSIDE SECTOR 41. NO BACK-UP UNIT NEEDED — IT'S ALL QUIET HERE... REPEAT — ALL QUIET.
DREDD
DREDD DIRECTED THE TRUCK TOWARDS THE SOUTH MUTIELAND TUNNEL...
H-HEY! DREDD'S DRIVING US INTO M-MUTIELAND!
SOUTH MUTIELAND TUNNEL
YOU ARE APPROACHING CURSED EARTH — TRAVEL AT YOUR OWN RISK.
DANGER! RADIATION ZONE
ON THE OTHER SIDE OF THE TUNNEL —
MEGA-CITY 1 NO ENTRY
AS PUNISHMENT FOR YOUR CRIMES I REMOVE YOUR CITIZENSHIP. YOU WILL NOT BE ALLOWED TO ENTER MEGA-CITY ONE FOR TEN YEARS!
Y-YOU CAN'T DO THIS! THIS PLACE IS A HELL ON EARTH!
GIVE ME TWENTY YEARS — THIRTY — ONLY PLEASE DON'T BANISH ME!
PLEASE! DON'T GO!
IN THE NAME OF MERCY, DON'T DO THIS TO US!
HARSH BUT NECESSARY. LET THEM SERVE AS AN EXAMPLE. LET EVERY MAN KNOW THAT CITIZENSHIP IS A PRIVILEGE — NOT A RIGHT!
THE LAW MUST BE OBEYED. THE LAW WILL BE OBEYED!

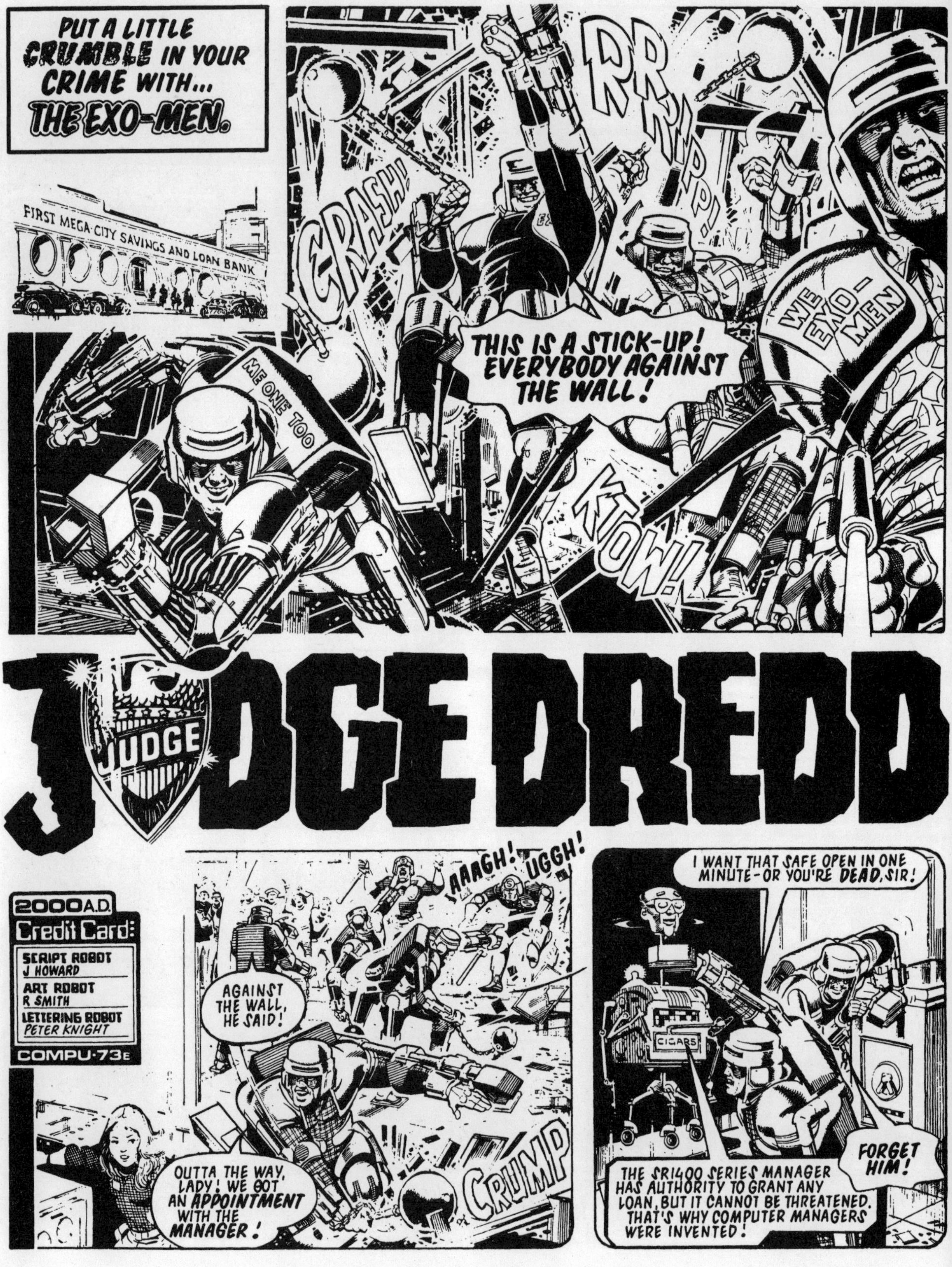
PUT A LITTLE CRUMBLE IN YOUR CRIME WITH... THE EXO-MEN.
FIRST MEGA-CITY SAVINGS AND LOAN BANK
CRASH!
RRRIPP!
WE EXO-MEN
ME ONE TOO
THIS IS A STICK-UP! EVERYBODY AGAINST THE WALL!
KTOW!
JUDGE
JUDGE DREDD
2000 A.D. Credit Card:
SCRIPT ROBOT J HOWARD
ART ROBOT R SMITH
LETTERING ROBOT PETER KNIGHT
COMPU-73E
AAAGH!
UGGH!
AGAINST THE WALL, HE SAID!
OUTTA THE WAY, LADY! WE GOT AN APPOINTMENT WITH THE MANAGER!
CRUMP
I WANT THAT SAFE OPEN IN ONE MINUTE-OR YOU'RE DEAD, SIR!
CIGARS
FORGET HIM!
THE SR1400 SERIES MANAGER HAS AUTHORITY TO GRANT ANY LOAN, BUT IT CANNOT BE THREATENED. THAT'S WHY COMPUTER MANAGERS WERE INVENTED!

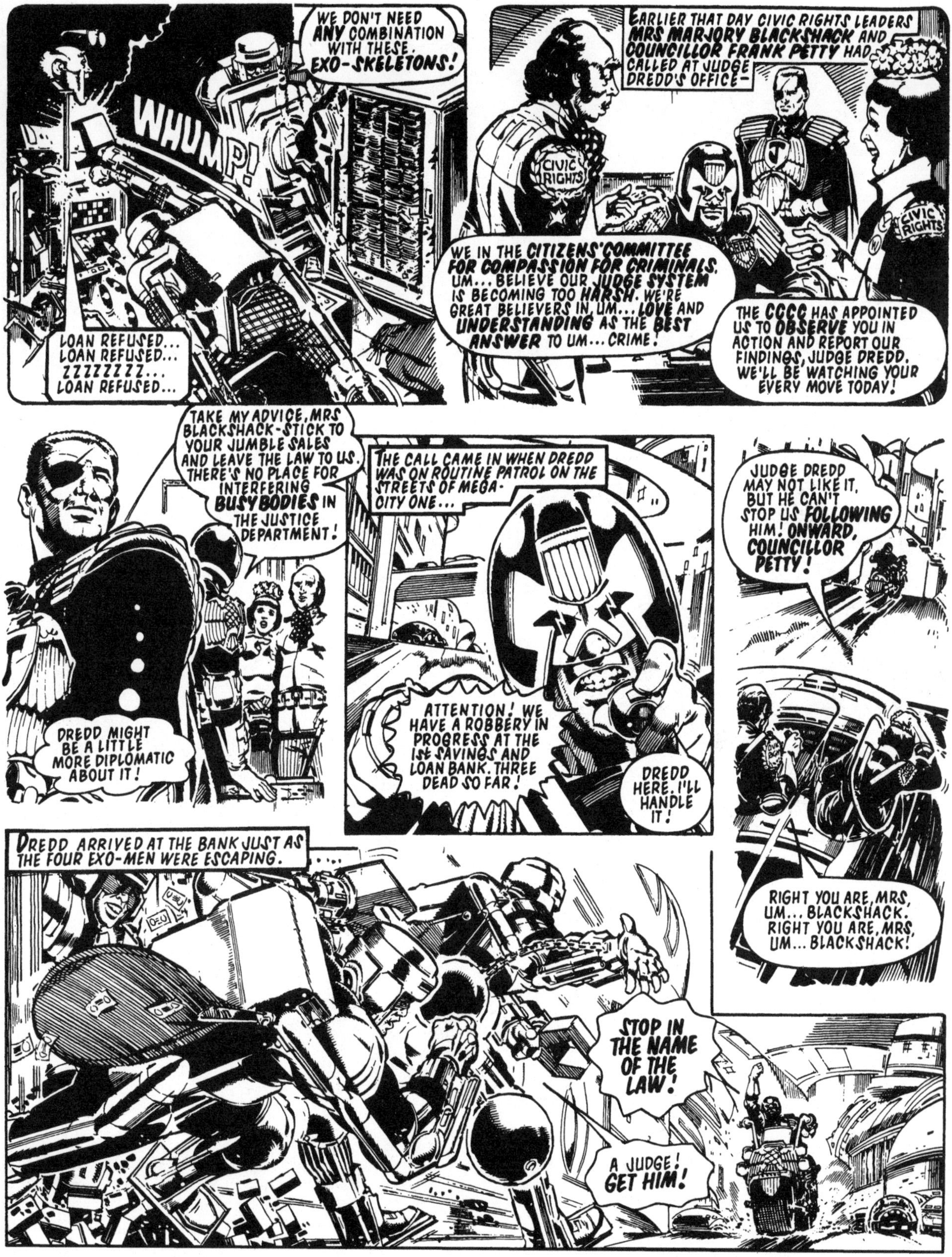
WE DON'T NEED ANY COMBINATION WITH THESE. EXO-SKELETONS!
WHUMP!
LOAN REFUSED... LOAN REFUSED... ZZZZZZZZ... LOAN REFUSED...
EARLIER THAT DAY CIVIC RIGHTS LEADERS MRS MARJORY BLACKSHACK AND COUNCILLOR FRANK PETTY HAD CALLED AT JUDGE DREDD'S OFFICE–
CIVIC RIGHTS
WE IN THE CITIZENS' COMMITTEE FOR COMPASSION FOR CRIMINALS, UM... BELIEVE OUR JUDGE SYSTEM IS BECOMING TOO HARSH. WE'RE GREAT BELIEVERS IN, UM... LOVE AND UNDERSTANDING AS THE BEST ANSWER TO UM... CRIME!
THE CCCC HAS APPOINTED US TO OBSERVE YOU IN ACTION AND REPORT OUR FINDINGS, JUDGE DREDD. WE'LL BE WATCHING YOUR EVERY MOVE TODAY!
TAKE MY ADVICE, MRS BLACKSHACK-STICK TO YOUR JUMBLE SALES AND LEAVE THE LAW TO US. THERE'S NO PLACE FOR INTERFERING BUSYBODIES IN THE JUSTICE DEPARTMENT!
DREDD MIGHT BE A LITTLE MORE DIPLOMATIC ABOUT IT!
THE CALL CAME IN WHEN DREDD WAS ON ROUTINE PATROL ON THE STREETS OF MEGA-CITY ONE...
ATTENTION! WE HAVE A ROBBERY IN PROGRESS AT THE 1st SAVINGS AND LOAN BANK. THREE DEAD SO FAR!
DREDD HERE. I'LL HANDLE IT!
JUDGE DREDD MAY NOT LIKE IT, BUT HE CAN'T STOP US FOLLOWING HIM! ONWARD, COUNCILLOR PETTY!
RIGHT YOU ARE, MRS, UM... BLACKSHACK. RIGHT YOU ARE, MRS, UM... BLACKSHACK!
DREDD ARRIVED AT THE BANK JUST AS THE FOUR EXO-MEN WERE ESCAPING.
STOP IN THE NAME OF THE LAW!
A JUDGE! GET HIM!

FFIZZZZZ
AAAGH!
MRS BLACKSHACK- ARE YOU UM... ALL RIGHT?
YOU SAW IT, COUNCILLOR PETTY! IT WAS JUDGE DREDD'S FAULT! HE PROVOKED THOSE MEN INTO FIRING!
AAAAGH!
THEY'RE WEARING DEMOLITION WORKERS' EXO-SKELETONS- POWERED SUITS! THE CRIMINAL MIND NEVER CEASES TO AMAZE ME!
KRACCK
JUST OUR LUCK TO GET JUDGE DREDD HIMSELF! GOTTA GET THROUGH THIS WALL AND OUT OF HERE!
YOU SAID IT!
AAAAA
ONE MAN WAS DEAD, THE OTHER ONLY DAZED...
YOU GET TWENTY YEARS FOR YOUR TROUBLE, CRUMB. WAIT HERE WHILE I ROUND UP YOUR PALS!
TWENTY YEARS! HOW SIMPLY MONSTROUS! MAKE A NOTE, COUNCILLOR PETTY!
YES, IT DOES SEEM, UM... EXCESSIVE FOR SUCH A TEENSY-WEENSY ROBBERY...
TELL ME, YOUNG MAN, WAS YOUR MOTHER, UM... CRUEL TO YOU?

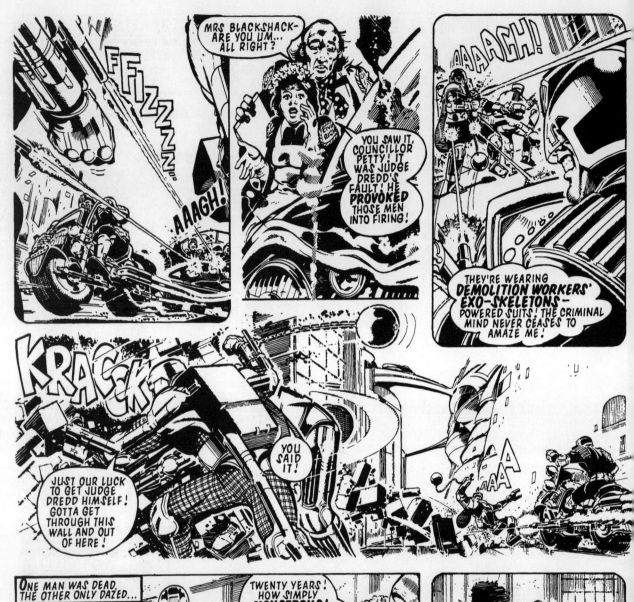

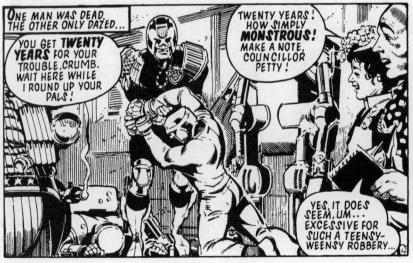

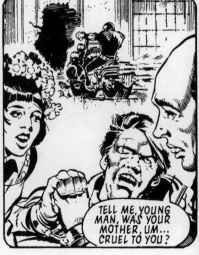

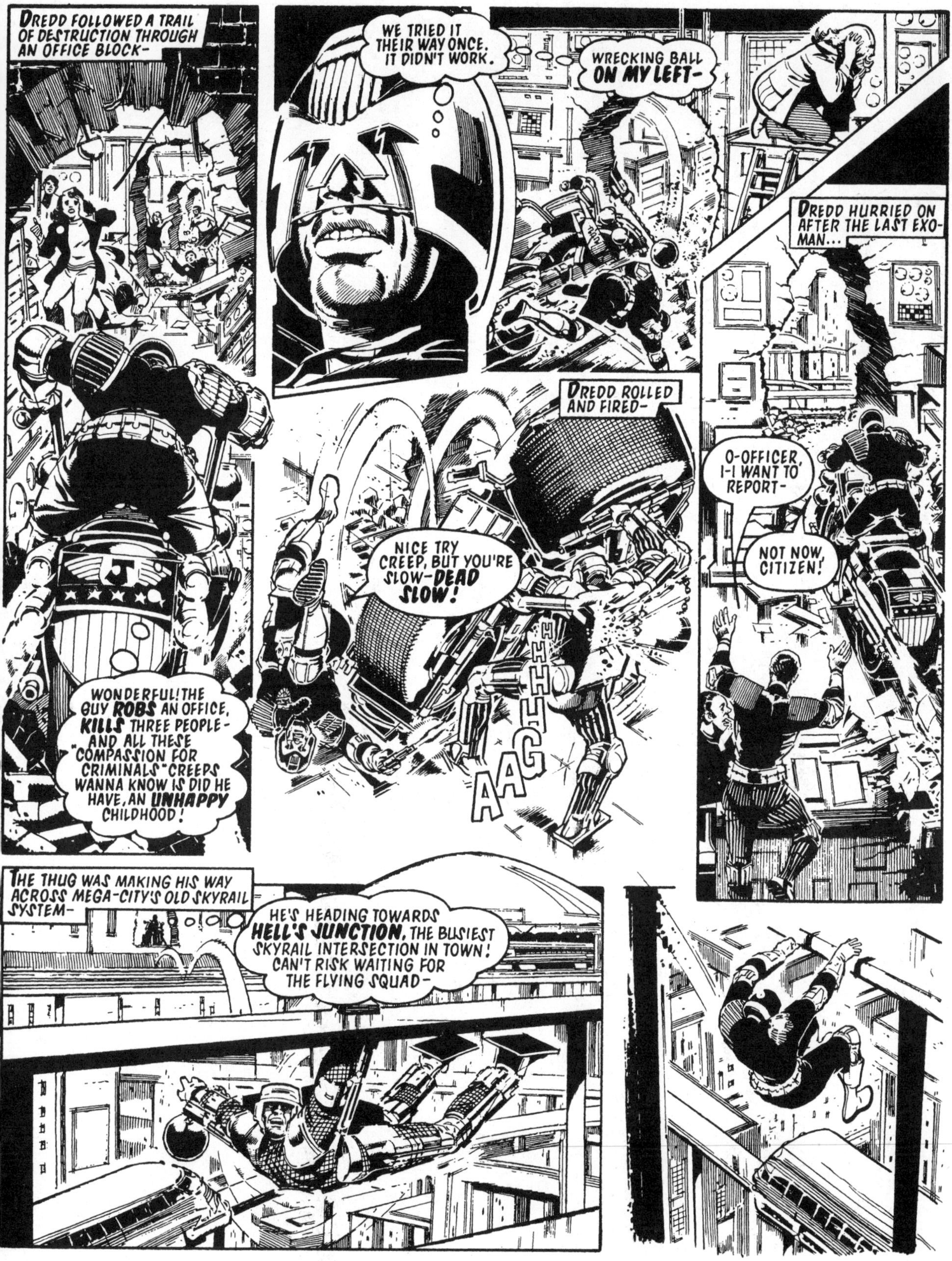
DREDD FOLLOWED A TRAIL OF DESTRUCTION THROUGH AN OFFICE BLOCK-
WONDERFUL! THE GUY ROBS AN OFFICE, KILLS THREE PEOPLE- AND ALL THESE "COMPASSION FOR CRIMINALS" CREEPS WANNA KNOW IS DID HE HAVE AN UNHAPPY CHILDHOOD!
WE TRIED IT THEIR WAY ONCE. IT DIDN'T WORK.
WRECKING BALL ON MY LEFT-
DREDD ROLLED AND FIRED-
NICE TRY CREEP, BUT YOU'RE SLOW-DEAD SLOW!
AAGHHHHH
DREDD HURRIED ON AFTER THE LAST EXO-MAN...
O-OFFICER, I-I WANT TO REPORT-
NOT NOW, CITIZEN!
THE THUG WAS MAKING HIS WAY ACROSS MEGA-CITY'S OLD SKYRAIL SYSTEM-
HE'S HEADING TOWARDS HELL'S JUNCTION, THE BUSIEST SKYRAIL INTERSECTION IN TOWN! CAN'T RISK WAITING FOR THE FLYING SQUAD-

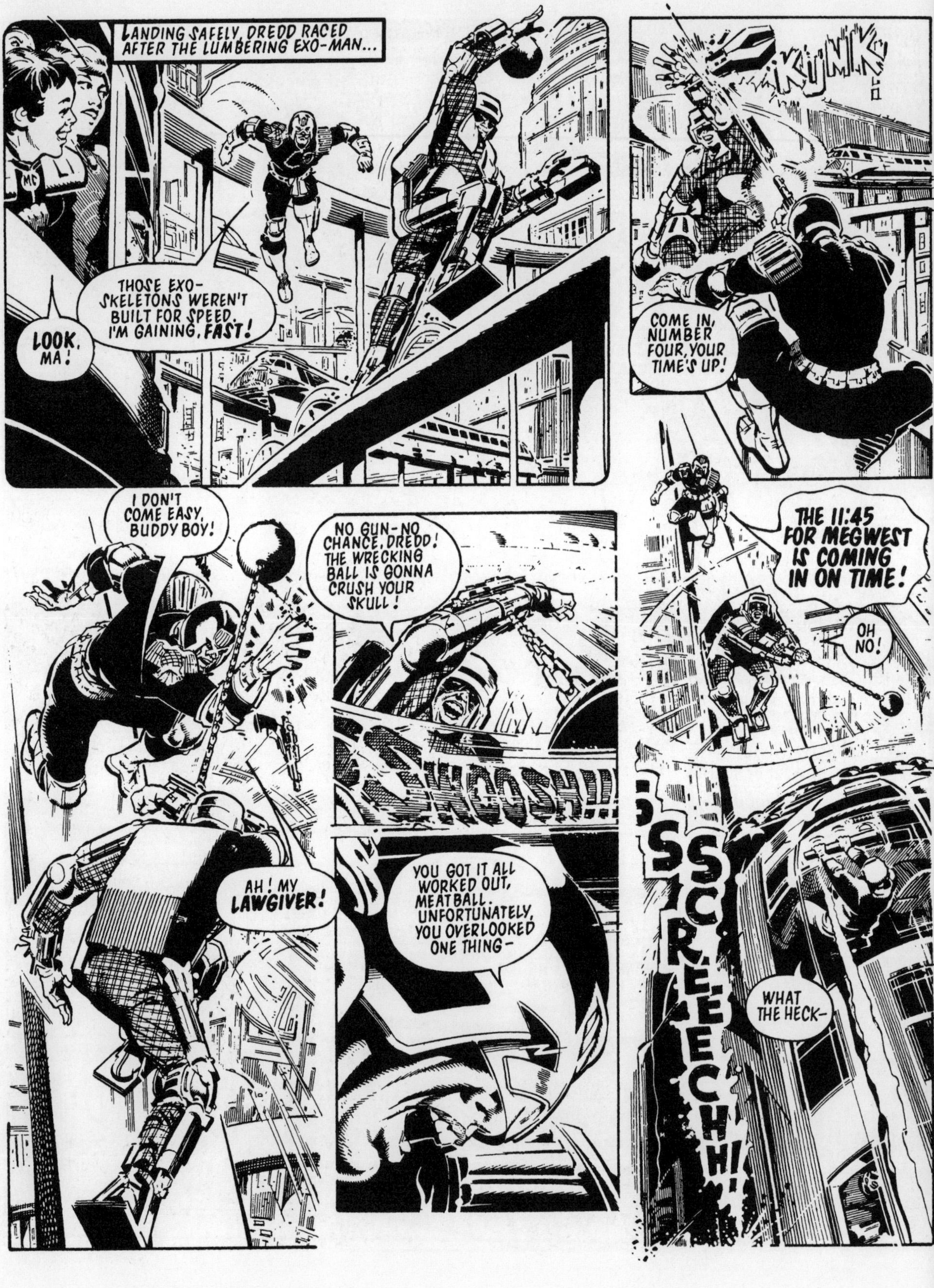
LANDING SAFELY, DREDD RACED AFTER THE LUMBERING EXO-MAN...
THOSE EXO-SKELETONS WEREN'T BUILT FOR SPEED. I'M GAINING, FAST!
LOOK, MA!
KUNK
COME IN, NUMBER FOUR, YOUR TIME'S UP!
I DON'T COME EASY, BUDDY BOY!
AH! MY LAWGIVER!
NO GUN-NO CHANCE, DREDD! THE WRECKING BALL IS GONNA CRUSH YOUR SKULL!
SWOOSH!!!
YOU GOT IT ALL WORKED OUT, MEATBALL. UNFORTUNATELY, YOU OVERLOOKED ONE THING-
THE 11:45 FOR MEGWEST IS COMING IN ON TIME!
OH NO!
SSSCREEECHH!
WHAT THE HECK-

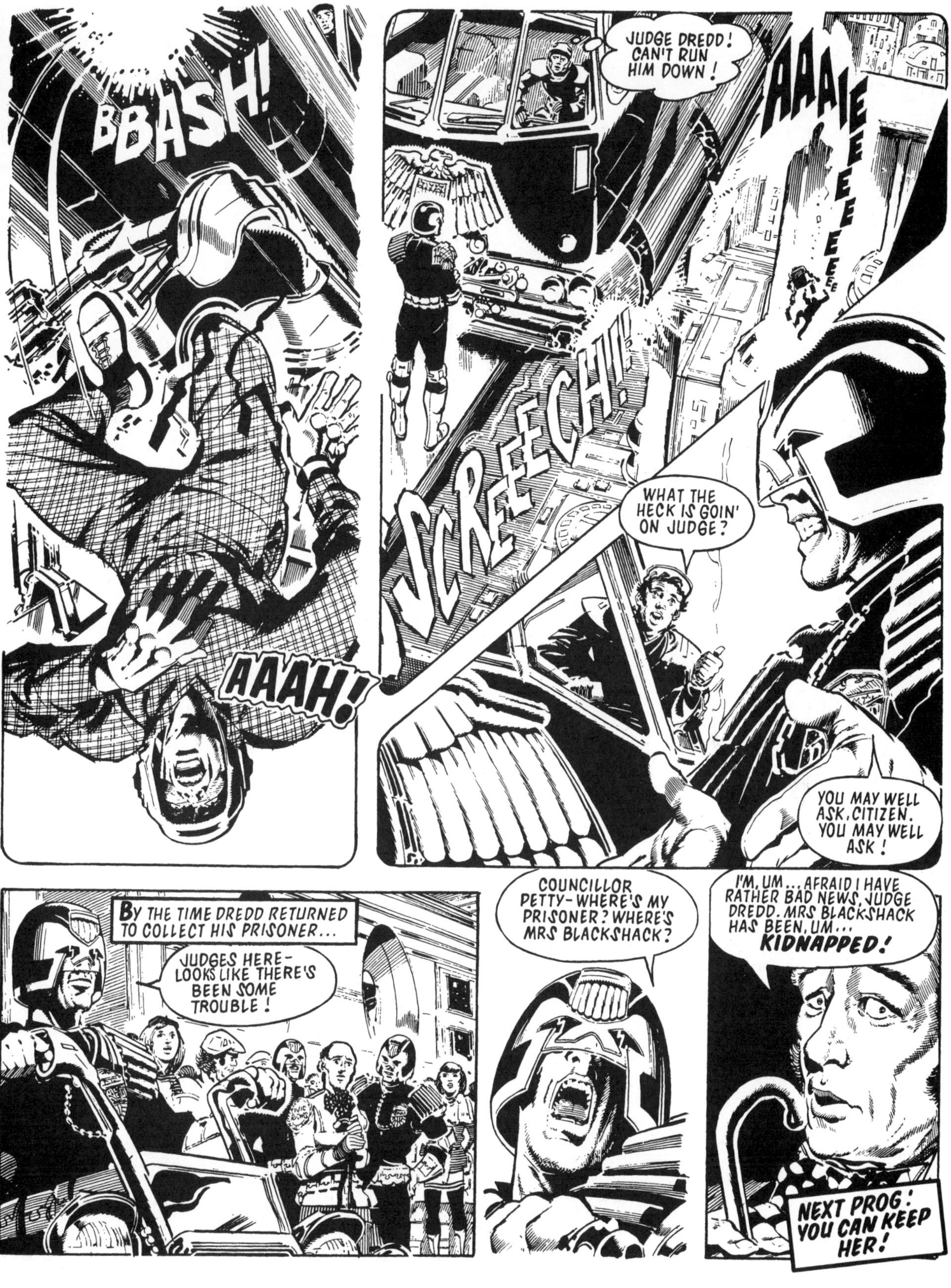
BBASH!
AAAH!
JUDGE DREDD! CAN'T RUN HIM DOWN!
AAAIEEEEEEEE
SCREEECH!!
WHAT THE HECK IS GOIN' ON JUDGE?
YOU MAY WELL ASK, CITIZEN. YOU MAY WELL ASK!
BY THE TIME DREDD RETURNED TO COLLECT HIS PRISONER...
JUDGES HERE- LOOKS LIKE THERE'S BEEN SOME TROUBLE!
COUNCILLOR PETTY- WHERE'S MY PRISONER? WHERE'S MRS BLACKSHACK?
I'M, UM... AFRAID I HAVE RATHER BAD NEWS, JUDGE DREDD. MRS BLACKSHACK HAS BEEN, UM... KIDNAPPED!
NEXT PROG: YOU CAN KEEP HER!

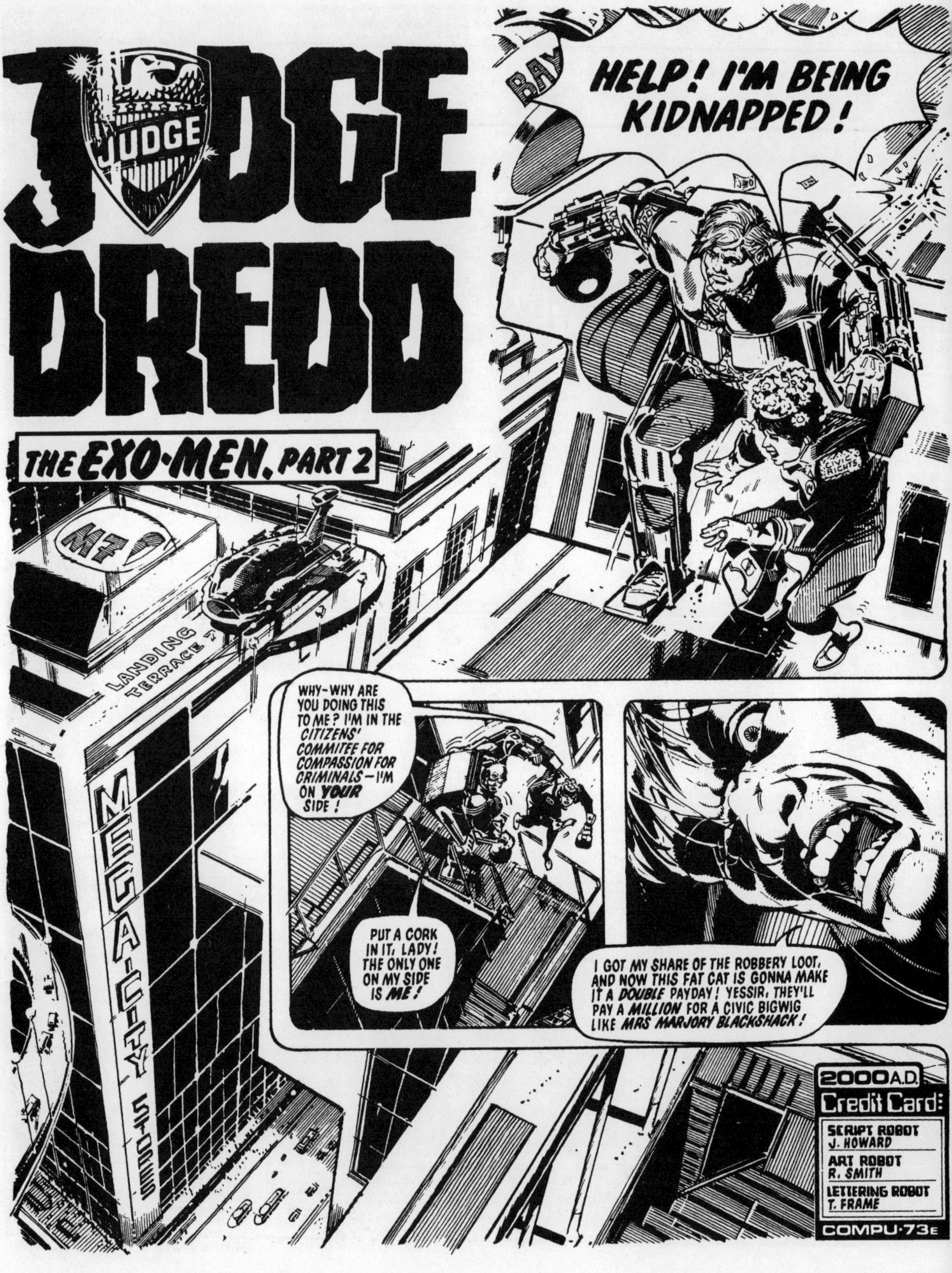
JUDGE DREDD
THE EXO-MEN. PART 2
HELP! I'M BEING KIDNAPPED!
WHY-WHY ARE YOU DOING THIS TO ME? I'M IN THE CITIZENS' COMMITEE FOR COMPASSION FOR CRIMINALS—I'M ON YOUR SIDE!
PUT A CORK IN IT, LADY! THE ONLY ONE ON MY SIDE IS ME!
I GOT MY SHARE OF THE ROBBERY LOOT, AND NOW THIS FAT CAT IS GONNA MAKE IT A DOUBLE PAYDAY! YESSIR, THEY'LL PAY A MILLION FOR A CIVIC BIGWIG LIKE MRS MARJORY BLACKSHACK!
LANDING TERRACE
MEGA-CITY STORES
2000 A.D. Credit Card:
SCRIPT ROBOT J. HOWARD
ART ROBOT R. SMITH
LETTERING ROBOT T. FRAME
COMPU-73E

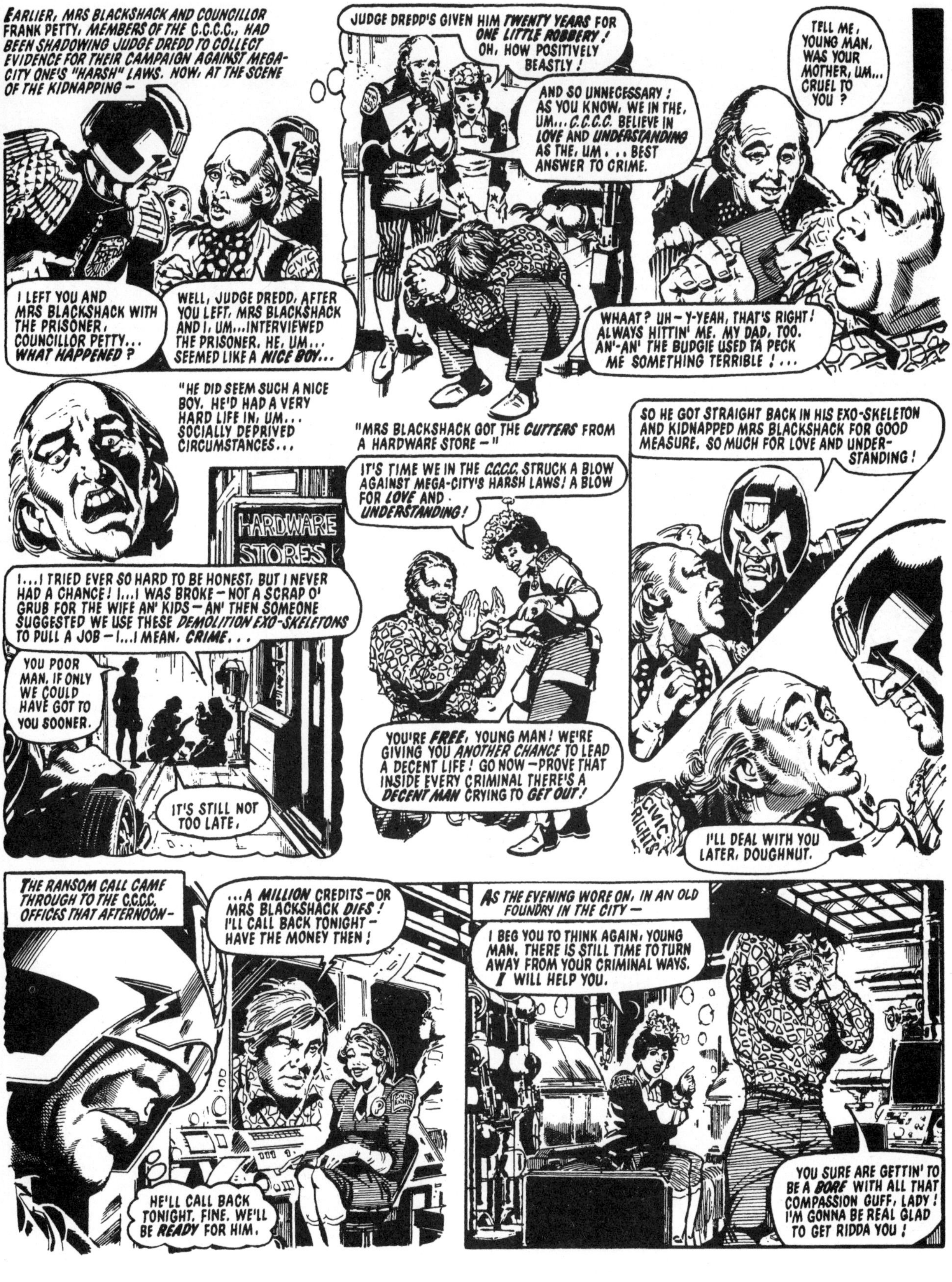

EARLIER, MRS BLACKSHACK AND COUNCILLOR FRANK PETTY, MEMBERS OF THE C.C.C.C., HAD BEEN SHADOWING JUDGE DREDD TO COLLECT EVIDENCE FOR THEIR CAMPAIGN AGAINST MEGA-CITY ONE'S "HARSH" LAWS. NOW, AT THE SCENE OF THE KIDNAPPING –
I LEFT YOU AND MRS BLACKSHACK WITH THE PRISONER, COUNCILLOR PETTY... WHAT HAPPENED ?
WELL, JUDGE DREDD, AFTER YOU LEFT, MRS BLACKSHACK AND I, UM...INTERVIEWED THE PRISONER. HE, UM... SEEMED LIKE A NICE BOY...
JUDGE DREDD'S GIVEN HIM TWENTY YEARS FOR ONE LITTLE ROBBERY ! OH, HOW POSITIVELY BEASTLY !
AND SO UNNECESSARY ! AS YOU KNOW, WE IN THE, UM... C.C.C.C. BELIEVE IN LOVE AND UNDERSTANDING AS THE, UM . . . BEST ANSWER TO CRIME.
TELL ME, YOUNG MAN, WAS YOUR MOTHER, UM... CRUEL TO YOU ?
WHAAT? UH – Y-YEAH, THAT'S RIGHT! ALWAYS HITTIN' ME. MY DAD, TOO. AN'-AN' THE BUDGIE USED TA PECK ME SOMETHING TERRIBLE ! ...
"HE DID SEEM SUCH A NICE BOY. HE'D HAD A VERY HARD LIFE IN, UM... SOCIALLY DEPRIVED CIRCUMSTANCES...
HARDWARE STORES
I...I TRIED EVER SO HARD TO BE HONEST, BUT I NEVER HAD A CHANCE! I...I WAS BROKE – NOT A SCRAP O' GRUB FOR THE WIFE AN' KIDS – AN' THEN SOMEONE SUGGESTED WE USE THESE DEMOLITION EXO-SKELETONS TO PULL A JOB – I...I MEAN, CRIME...
YOU POOR MAN. IF ONLY WE COULD HAVE GOT TO YOU SOONER.
IT'S STILL NOT TOO LATE.
"MRS BLACKSHACK GOT THE CUTTERS FROM A HARDWARE STORE –"
IT'S TIME WE IN THE C.C.C.C. STRUCK A BLOW AGAINST MEGA-CITY'S HARSH LAWS! A BLOW FOR LOVE AND UNDERSTANDING !
YOU'RE FREE, YOUNG MAN ! WE'RE GIVING YOU ANOTHER CHANCE TO LEAD A DECENT LIFE ! GO NOW – PROVE THAT INSIDE EVERY CRIMINAL THERE'S A DECENT MAN CRYING TO GET OUT !
SO HE GOT STRAIGHT BACK IN HIS EXO-SKELETON AND KIDNAPPED MRS BLACKSHACK FOR GOOD MEASURE. SO MUCH FOR LOVE AND UNDERSTANDING !
CIVIC RIGHTS
I'LL DEAL WITH YOU LATER, DOUGHNUT.
THE RANSOM CALL CAME THROUGH TO THE C.C.C.C. OFFICES THAT AFTERNOON –
...A MILLION CREDITS – OR MRS BLACKSHACK DIES ! I'LL CALL BACK TONIGHT – HAVE THE MONEY THEN !
HE'LL CALL BACK TONIGHT. FINE. WE'LL BE READY FOR HIM.
AS THE EVENING WORE ON, IN AN OLD FOUNDRY IN THE CITY –
I BEG YOU TO THINK AGAIN, YOUNG MAN. THERE IS STILL TIME TO TURN AWAY FROM YOUR CRIMINAL WAYS. I WILL HELP YOU.
YOU SURE ARE GETTIN' TO BE A BORE WITH ALL THAT COMPASSION GUFF, LADY ! I'M GONNA BE REAL GLAD TO GET RIDDA YOU !

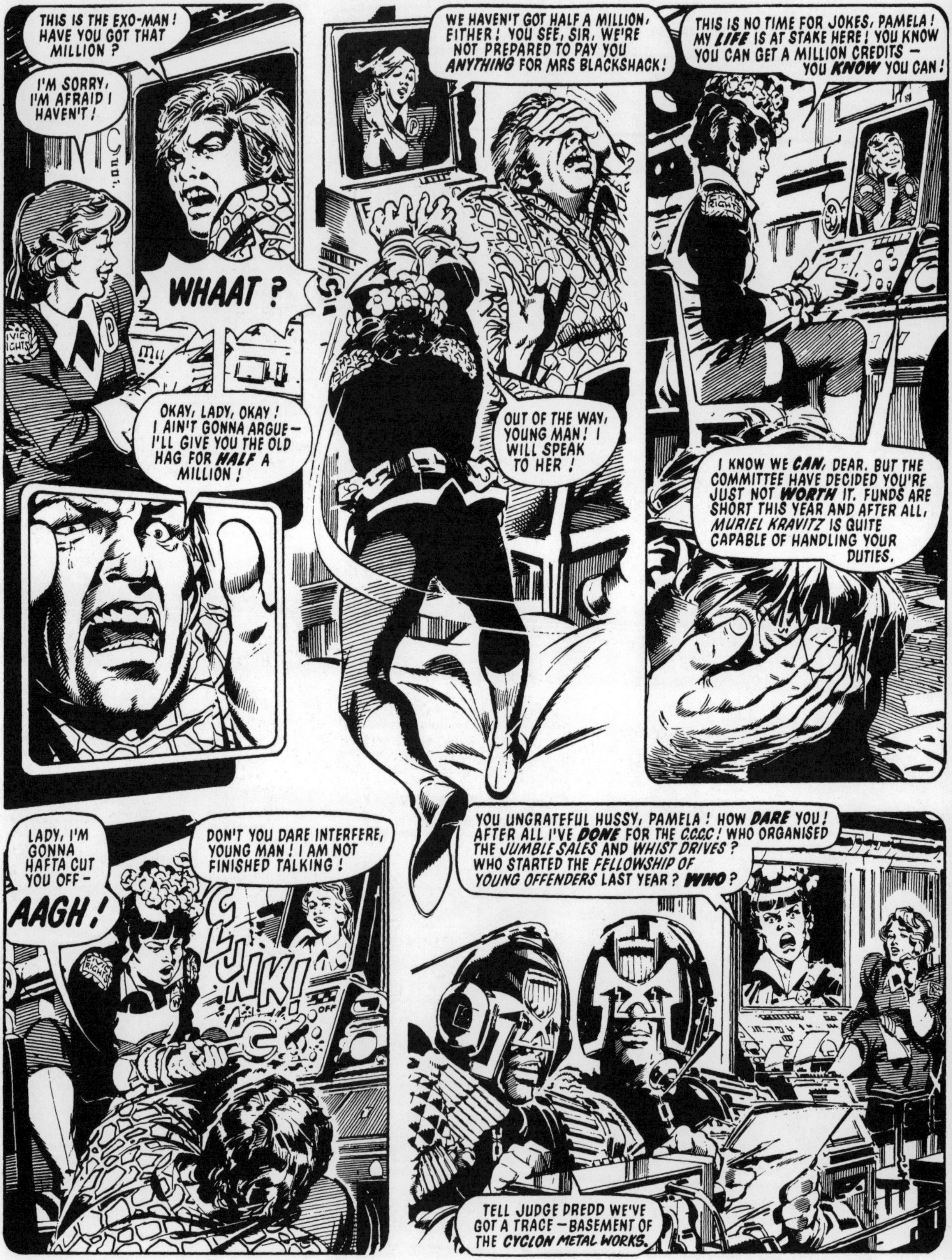
THIS IS THE EXO-MAN! HAVE YOU GOT THAT MILLION?
I'M SORRY, I'M AFRAID I HAVEN'T!
WHAAT?
OKAY, LADY, OKAY! I AIN'T GONNA ARGUE– I'LL GIVE YOU THE OLD HAG FOR HALF A MILLION!
WE HAVEN'T GOT HALF A MILLION, EITHER! YOU SEE, SIR, WE'RE NOT PREPARED TO PAY YOU ANYTHING FOR MRS BLACKSHACK!
OUT OF THE WAY, YOUNG MAN! I WILL SPEAK TO HER!
THIS IS NO TIME FOR JOKES, PAMELA! MY LIFE IS AT STAKE HERE! YOU KNOW YOU CAN GET A MILLION CREDITS – YOU KNOW YOU CAN!
I KNOW WE CAN, DEAR. BUT THE COMMITTEE HAVE DECIDED YOU'RE JUST NOT WORTH IT. FUNDS ARE SHORT THIS YEAR AND AFTER ALL, MURIEL KRAVITZ IS QUITE CAPABLE OF HANDLING YOUR DUTIES.
LADY, I'M GONNA HAFTA CUT YOU OFF–
AAGH!
DON'T YOU DARE INTERFERE, YOUNG MAN! I AM NOT FINISHED TALKING!
CLUNK!
YOU UNGRATEFUL HUSSY, PAMELA! HOW DARE YOU! AFTER ALL I'VE DONE FOR THE C.C.C.C! WHO ORGANISED THE JUMBLE SALES AND WHIST DRIVES? WHO STARTED THE FELLOWSHIP OF YOUNG OFFENDERS LAST YEAR? WHO?
TELL JUDGE DREDD WE'VE GOT A TRACE – BASEMENT OF THE CYCLON METAL WORKS.

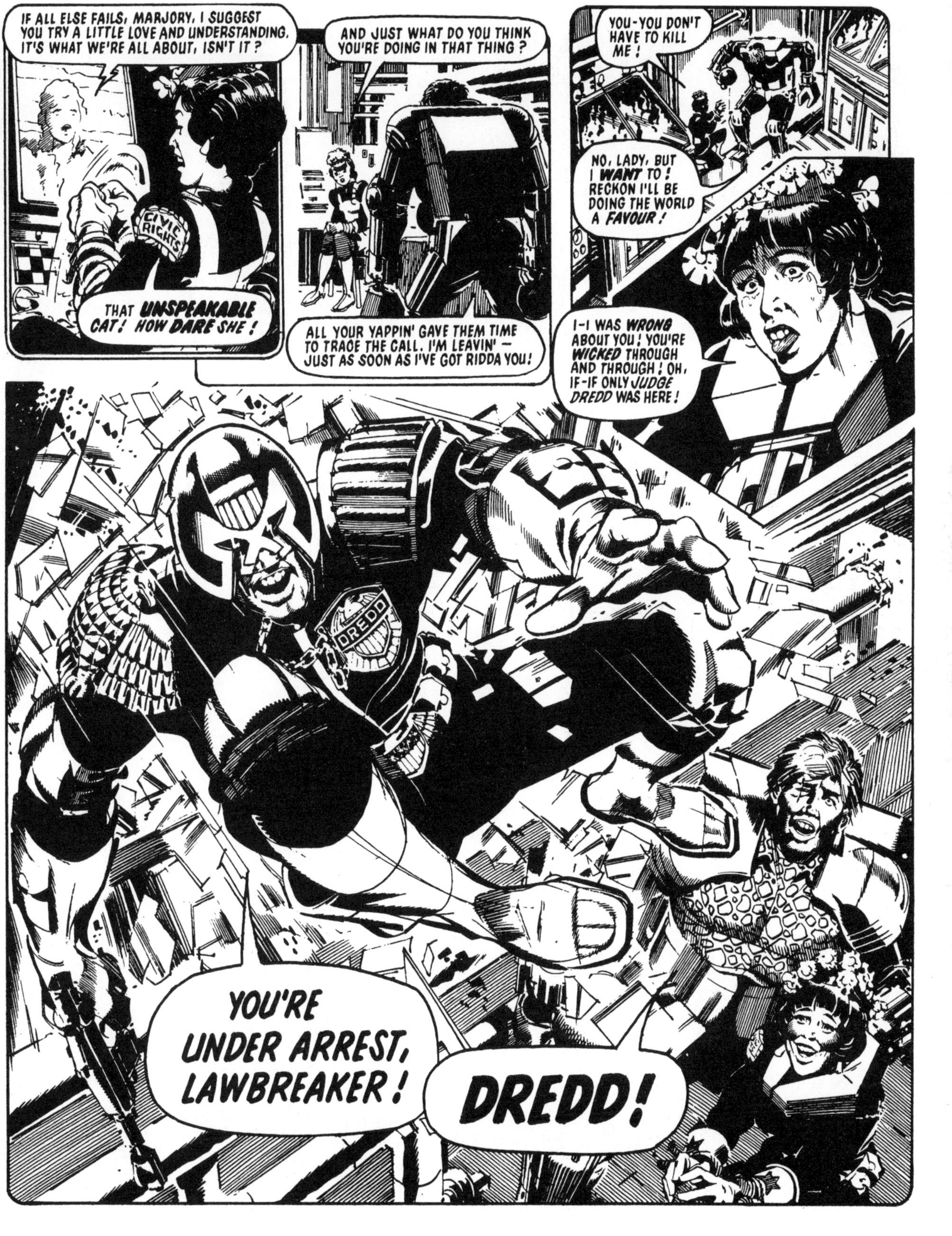
IF ALL ELSE FAILS, MARJORY, I SUGGEST YOU TRY A LITTLE LOVE AND UNDERSTANDING. IT'S WHAT WE'RE ALL ABOUT, ISN'T IT ?
CIVIC RIGHTS
THAT UNSPEAKABLE CAT! HOW DARE SHE !
AND JUST WHAT DO YOU THINK YOU'RE DOING IN THAT THING ?
ALL YOUR YAPPIN' GAVE THEM TIME TO TRACE THE CALL. I'M LEAVIN' — JUST AS SOON AS I'VE GOT RIDDA YOU!
YOU-YOU DON'T HAVE TO KILL ME !
NO, LADY, BUT I WANT TO ! RECKON I'LL BE DOING THE WORLD A FAVOUR !
I-I WAS WRONG ABOUT YOU ! YOU'RE WICKED THROUGH AND THROUGH ! OH, IF-IF ONLY JUDGE DREDD WAS HERE !
DREDD
YOU'RE UNDER ARREST, LAWBREAKER !
DREDD!

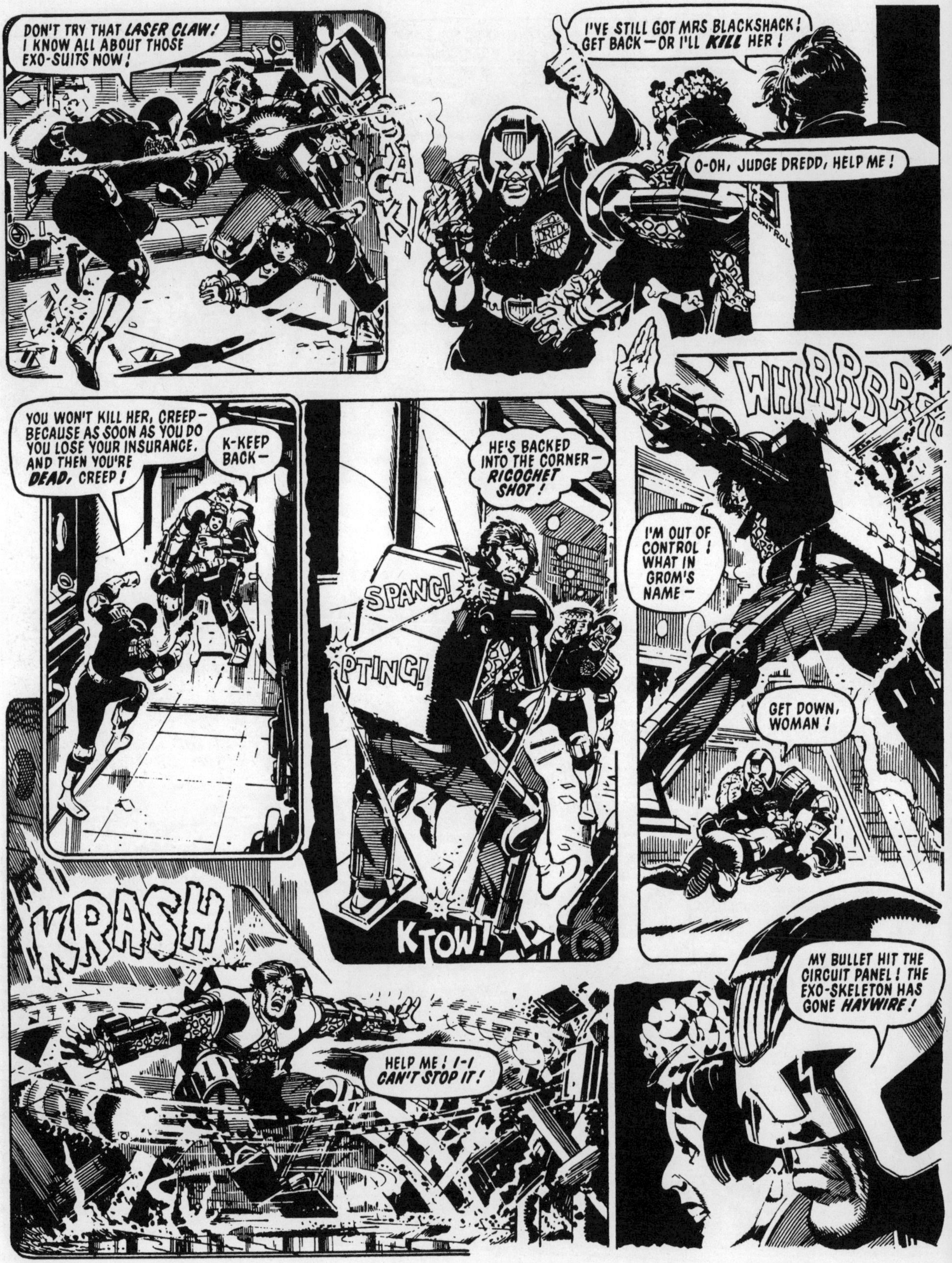
DON'T TRY THAT LASER CLAW! I KNOW ALL ABOUT THOSE EXO-SUITS NOW!
KRACK!
I'VE STILL GOT MRS BLACKSHACK! GET BACK—OR I'LL KILL HER!
O-OH, JUDGE DREDD, HELP ME!
YOU WON'T KILL HER, CREEP—BECAUSE AS SOON AS YOU DO YOU LOSE YOUR INSURANCE. AND THEN YOU'RE DEAD, CREEP!
K-KEEP BACK—
HE'S BACKED INTO THE CORNER—RICOCHET SHOT!
SPANG!
PTING!
KTOW!
WHIRRRRR
I'M OUT OF CONTROL! WHAT IN GROM'S NAME—
GET DOWN, WOMAN!
KRASH
HELP ME! I-I CAN'T STOP IT!
MY BULLET HIT THE CIRCUIT PANEL! THE EXO-SKELETON HAS GONE HAYWIRE!

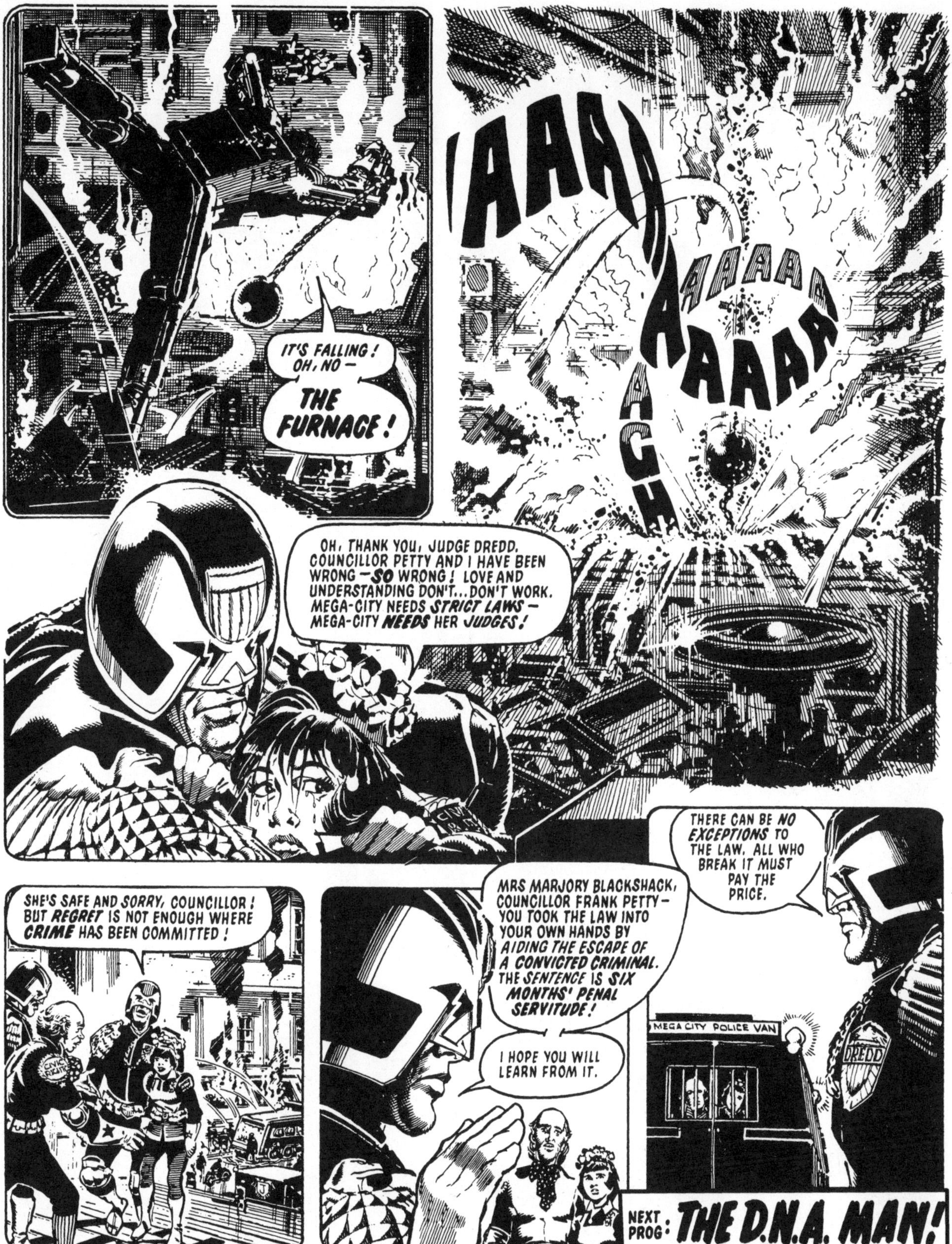
IT'S FALLING! OH, NO — THE FURNACE!
AAAAAAAAAAAAAAACH
OH, THANK YOU, JUDGE DREDD. COUNCILLOR PETTY AND I HAVE BEEN WRONG — SO WRONG! LOVE AND UNDERSTANDING DON'T... DON'T WORK. MEGA-CITY NEEDS STRICT LAWS — MEGA-CITY NEEDS HER JUDGES!
SHE'S SAFE AND SORRY, COUNCILLOR! BUT REGRET IS NOT ENOUGH WHERE CRIME HAS BEEN COMMITTED!
MRS MARJORY BLACKSHACK, COUNCILLOR FRANK PETTY — YOU TOOK THE LAW INTO YOUR OWN HANDS BY AIDING THE ESCAPE OF A CONVICTED CRIMINAL. THE SENTENCE IS SIX MONTHS' PENAL SERVITUDE!
I HOPE YOU WILL LEARN FROM IT.
THERE CAN BE NO EXCEPTIONS TO THE LAW. ALL WHO BREAK IT MUST PAY THE PRICE.
MEGA CITY POLICE VAN
DREDD
NEXT PROG: THE D.N.A. MAN!

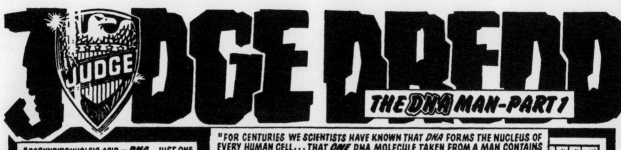

JUDGE DREDD

THE DNA MAN — PART 1

"DEOXYRIBONUCLEIC ACID — *DNA*. JUST ONE MOLECULE TAKEN FROM *MY BLOOD*... BUT IN IT IS THE *ESSENCE OF LIFE!*"

"FOR CENTURIES WE SCIENTISTS HAVE KNOWN THAT *DNA* FORMS THE NUCLEUS OF EVERY HUMAN CELL... THAT *ONE* DNA MOLECULE TAKEN FROM A MAN CONTAINS THE *CHEMICAL BLUEPRINT* NECESSARY TO *RECREATE* THAT MAN!"

TO RE-CREATE *ME*, BEAKER!

Y-YOU'RE *MAD*, PROFESSOR!

THE LINE BETWEEN *MADNESS* AND *GENIUS* IS A FINE ONE. ASSIST ME WITH MY EXPERIMENT — AND YOU MAY DECIDE WHICH I AM!

2000 A.D.
Credit Card:

SCRIPT ROBOT
J. HOWARD

ART ROBOT
B. EWINS

LETTERING ROBOT
T. FRAME

COMPU-73e

THE DNA MOLECULE WAS SUSPENDED IN A GLASS FORMATION CYLINDER. A FLICK OF A SWITCH, AND THE CYLINDER BEGAN TO FLOOD WITH ELECTRO-STATICALLY CHARGED CHEMICALS —

M-MY LIFE — THERE'S SOMETHING...SOMETHING *GROWING* IN THERE! GROWING FAST!

CHEMICAL *SOUP*, BEAKER — MY OWN RECIPE! THIS IS WHERE I HAVE SUCCEEDED WHERE OTHERS HAVE *FAILED*. ONLY *I* HAVE FOUND THE CORRECT BLEND OF CHEMICAL AND ELECTRO-STIMULATION NECESSARY TO PROMOTE *GROWTH*.

YOU ARE WATCHING A WONDER OF CREATION, BEAKER! *30 YEARS OF LIFE* CRAMMED INTO A BRIEF *30 MINUTES!*

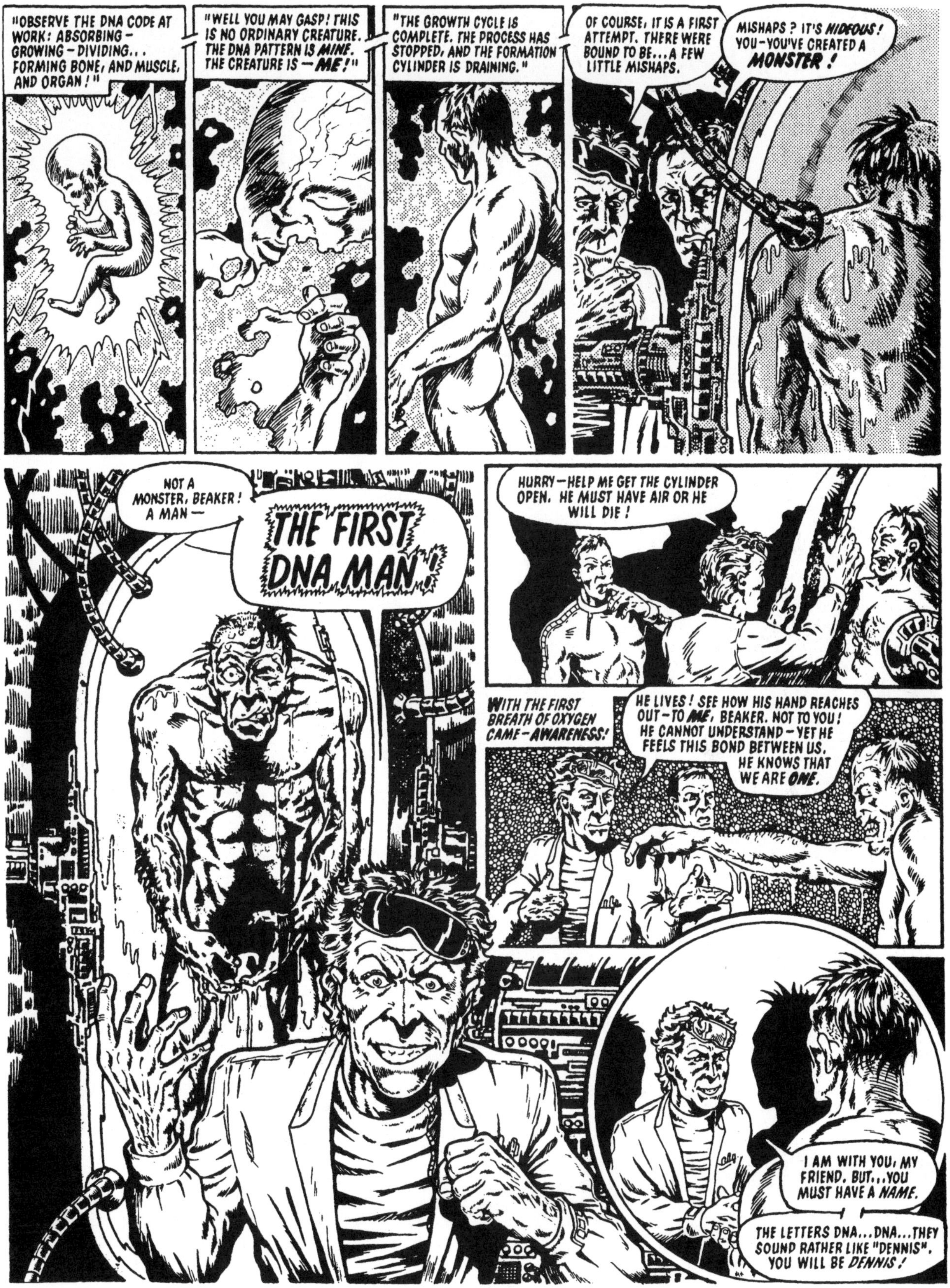
"OBSERVE THE DNA CODE AT WORK: ABSORBING - GROWING - DIVIDING... FORMING BONE, AND MUSCLE, AND ORGAN!"
"WELL YOU MAY GASP! THIS IS NO ORDINARY CREATURE. THE DNA PATTERN IS MINE. THE CREATURE IS - ME!"
"THE GROWTH CYCLE IS COMPLETE. THE PROCESS HAS STOPPED, AND THE FORMATION CYLINDER IS DRAINING."
OF COURSE, IT IS A FIRST ATTEMPT. THERE WERE BOUND TO BE... A FEW LITTLE MISHAPS.
MISHAPS? IT'S HIDEOUS! YOU - YOU'VE CREATED A MONSTER!
NOT A MONSTER, BEAKER! A MAN -
THE FIRST DNA MAN!
HURRY - HELP ME GET THE CYLINDER OPEN. HE MUST HAVE AIR OR HE WILL DIE!
WITH THE FIRST BREATH OF OXYGEN CAME - AWARENESS!
HE LIVES! SEE HOW HIS HAND REACHES OUT - TO ME, BEAKER. NOT TO YOU! HE CANNOT UNDERSTAND - YET HE FEELS THIS BOND BETWEEN US. HE KNOWS THAT WE ARE ONE.
I AM WITH YOU, MY FRIEND. BUT... YOU MUST HAVE A NAME.
THE LETTERS DNA... DNA... THEY SOUND RATHER LIKE "DENNIS". YOU WILL BE DENNIS!

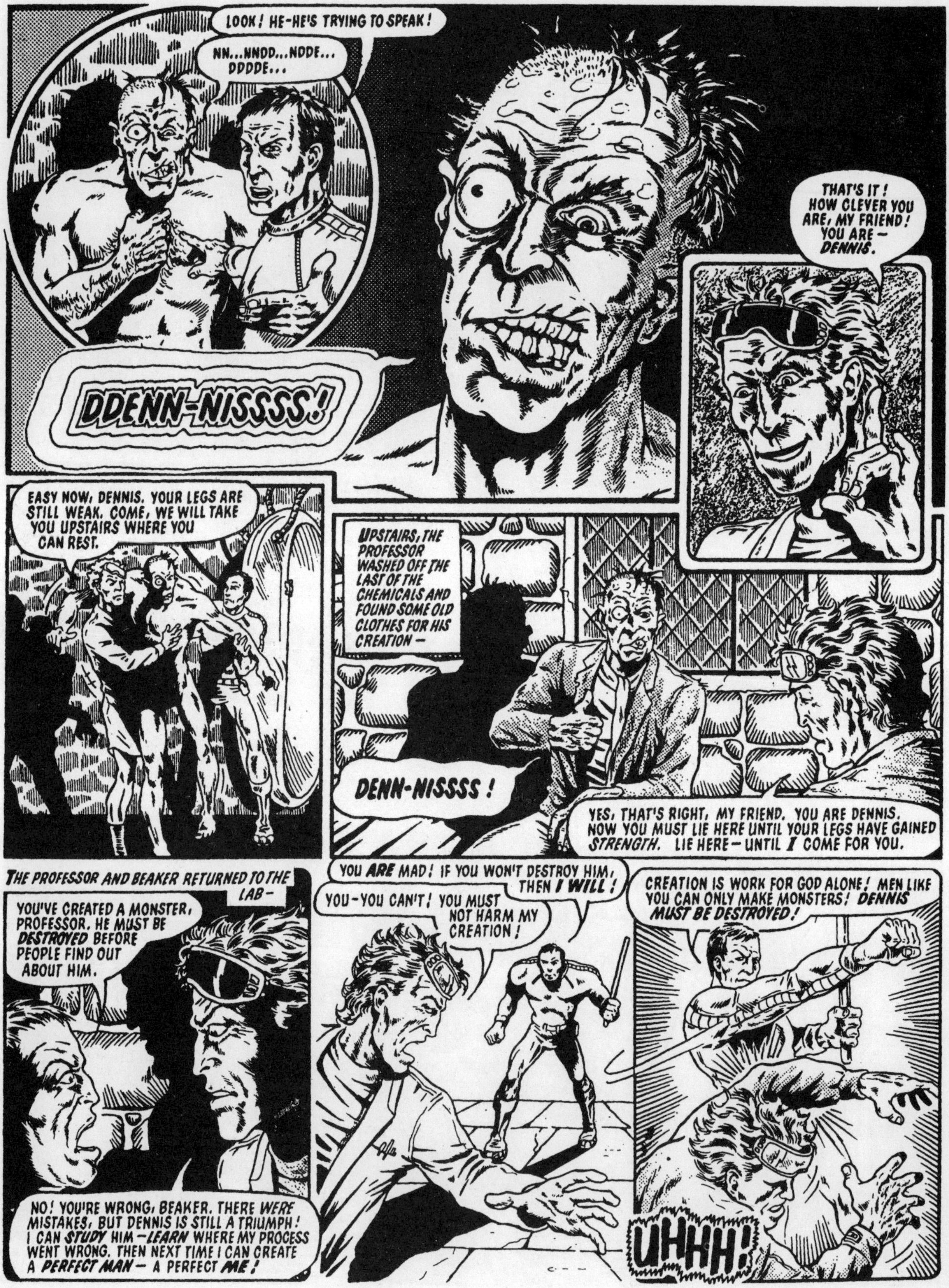
LOOK! HE-HE'S TRYING TO SPEAK!
NN...NNDD...NODE... DDDDE...
DDENN-NISSSSS!
THAT'S IT! HOW CLEVER YOU ARE, MY FRIEND! YOU ARE - DENNIS.
EASY NOW, DENNIS. YOUR LEGS ARE STILL WEAK. COME, WE WILL TAKE YOU UPSTAIRS WHERE YOU CAN REST.
UPSTAIRS, THE PROFESSOR WASHED OFF THE LAST OF THE CHEMICALS AND FOUND SOME OLD CLOTHES FOR HIS CREATION -
DENN-NISSSS!
YES, THAT'S RIGHT, MY FRIEND. YOU ARE DENNIS. NOW YOU MUST LIE HERE UNTIL YOUR LEGS HAVE GAINED STRENGTH. LIE HERE - UNTIL I COME FOR YOU.
THE PROFESSOR AND BEAKER RETURNED TO THE LAB -
YOU'VE CREATED A MONSTER, PROFESSOR. HE MUST BE DESTROYED BEFORE PEOPLE FIND OUT ABOUT HIM.
NO! YOU'RE WRONG, BEAKER. THERE WERE MISTAKES, BUT DENNIS IS STILL A TRIUMPH! I CAN STUDY HIM - LEARN WHERE MY PROCESS WENT WRONG. THEN NEXT TIME I CAN CREATE A PERFECT MAN - A PERFECT ME!
YOU ARE MAD! IF YOU WON'T DESTROY HIM, THEN I WILL!
YOU-YOU CAN'T! YOU MUST NOT HARM MY CREATION!
CREATION IS WORK FOR GOD ALONE! MEN LIKE YOU CAN ONLY MAKE MONSTERS! DENNIS MUST BE DESTROYED!
UHHH!

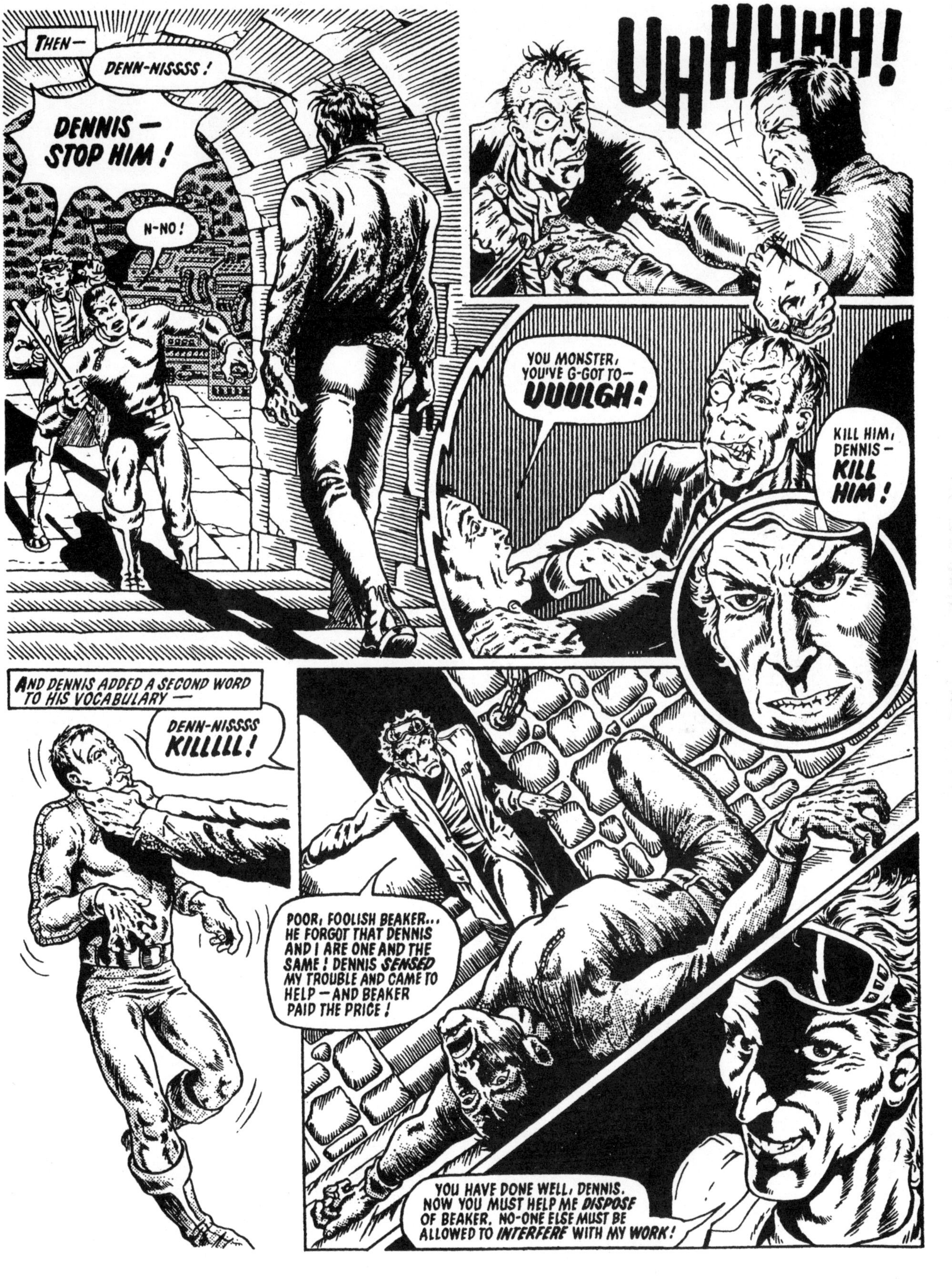
THEN—
DENN-NISSSS!
DENNIS — STOP HIM!
N-NO!
UHHHHHH!
YOU MONSTER, YOU'VE G-GOT TO— UUULGH!
KILL HIM, DENNIS— KILL HIM!
AND DENNIS ADDED A SECOND WORD TO HIS VOCABULARY —
DENN-NISSSS KILLLLL!
POOR, FOOLISH BEAKER... HE FORGOT THAT DENNIS AND I ARE ONE AND THE SAME! DENNIS SENSED MY TROUBLE AND CAME TO HELP — AND BEAKER PAID THE PRICE!
YOU HAVE DONE WELL, DENNIS. NOW YOU MUST HELP ME DISPOSE OF BEAKER. NO-ONE ELSE MUST BE ALLOWED TO INTERFERE WITH MY WORK!

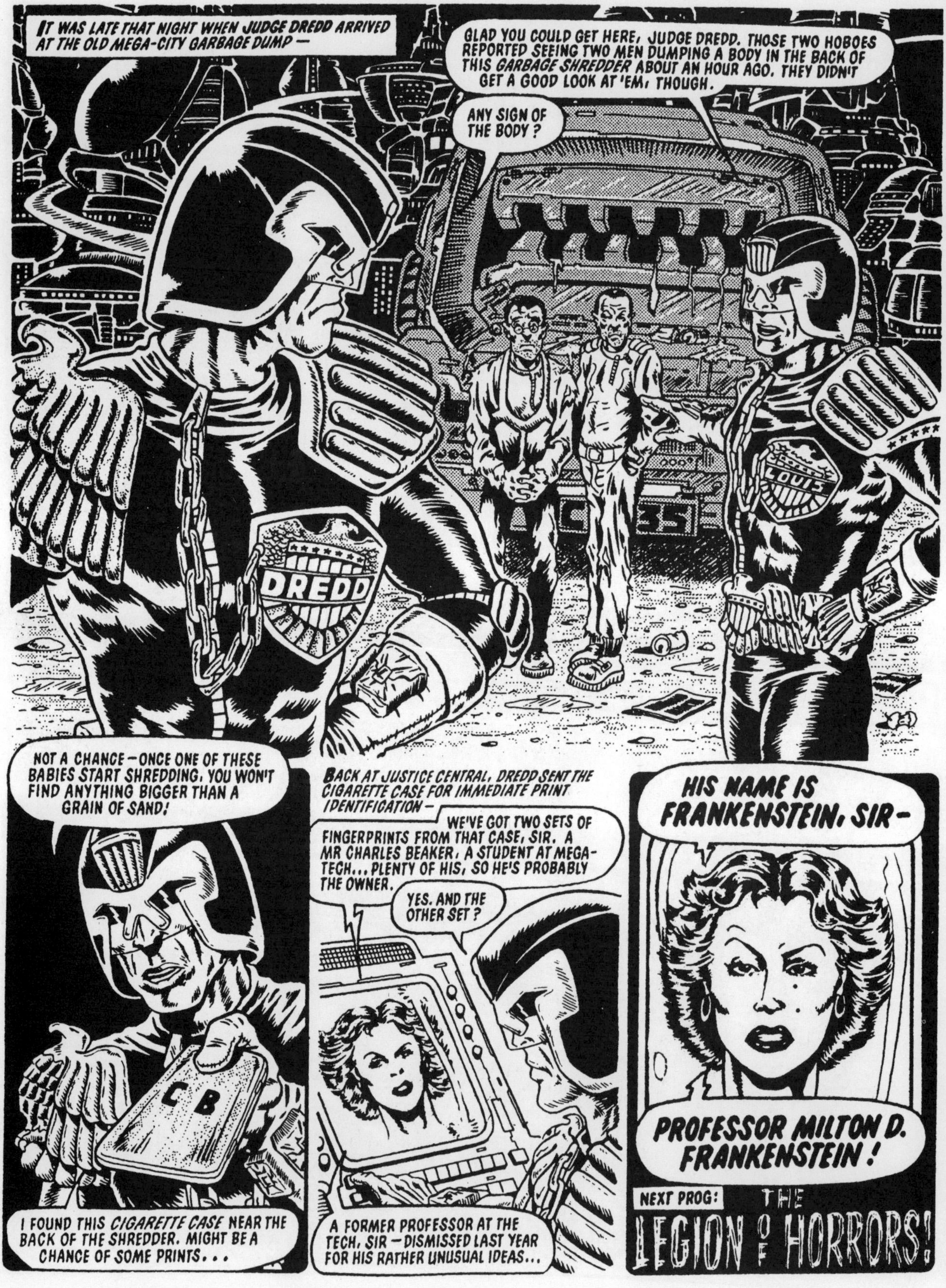

IT WAS LATE THAT NIGHT WHEN JUDGE DREDD ARRIVED AT THE OLD MEGA-CITY GARBAGE DUMP —
GLAD YOU COULD GET HERE, JUDGE DREDD. THOSE TWO HOBOES REPORTED SEEING TWO MEN DUMPING A BODY IN THE BACK OF THIS GARBAGE SHREDDER ABOUT AN HOUR AGO. THEY DIDN'T GET A GOOD LOOK AT 'EM, THOUGH.
ANY SIGN OF THE BODY ?
DREDD
LOUIS
NOT A CHANCE — ONCE ONE OF THESE BABIES START SHREDDING, YOU WON'T FIND ANYTHING BIGGER THAN A GRAIN OF SAND!
CB
I FOUND THIS CIGARETTE CASE NEAR THE BACK OF THE SHREDDER. MIGHT BE A CHANCE OF SOME PRINTS. . .
BACK AT JUSTICE CENTRAL, DREDD SENT THE CIGARETTE CASE FOR IMMEDIATE PRINT IDENTIFICATION —
WE'VE GOT TWO SETS OF FINGERPRINTS FROM THAT CASE, SIR. A MR CHARLES BEAKER, A STUDENT AT MEGA-TECH. . . PLENTY OF HIS, SO HE'S PROBABLY THE OWNER.
YES. AND THE OTHER SET ?
A FORMER PROFESSOR AT THE TECH, SIR — DISMISSED LAST YEAR FOR HIS RATHER UNUSUAL IDEAS. . .
HIS NAME IS FRANKENSTEIN, SIR —
PROFESSOR MILTON D. FRANKENSTEIN !
NEXT PROG: THE LEGION OF HORRORS!

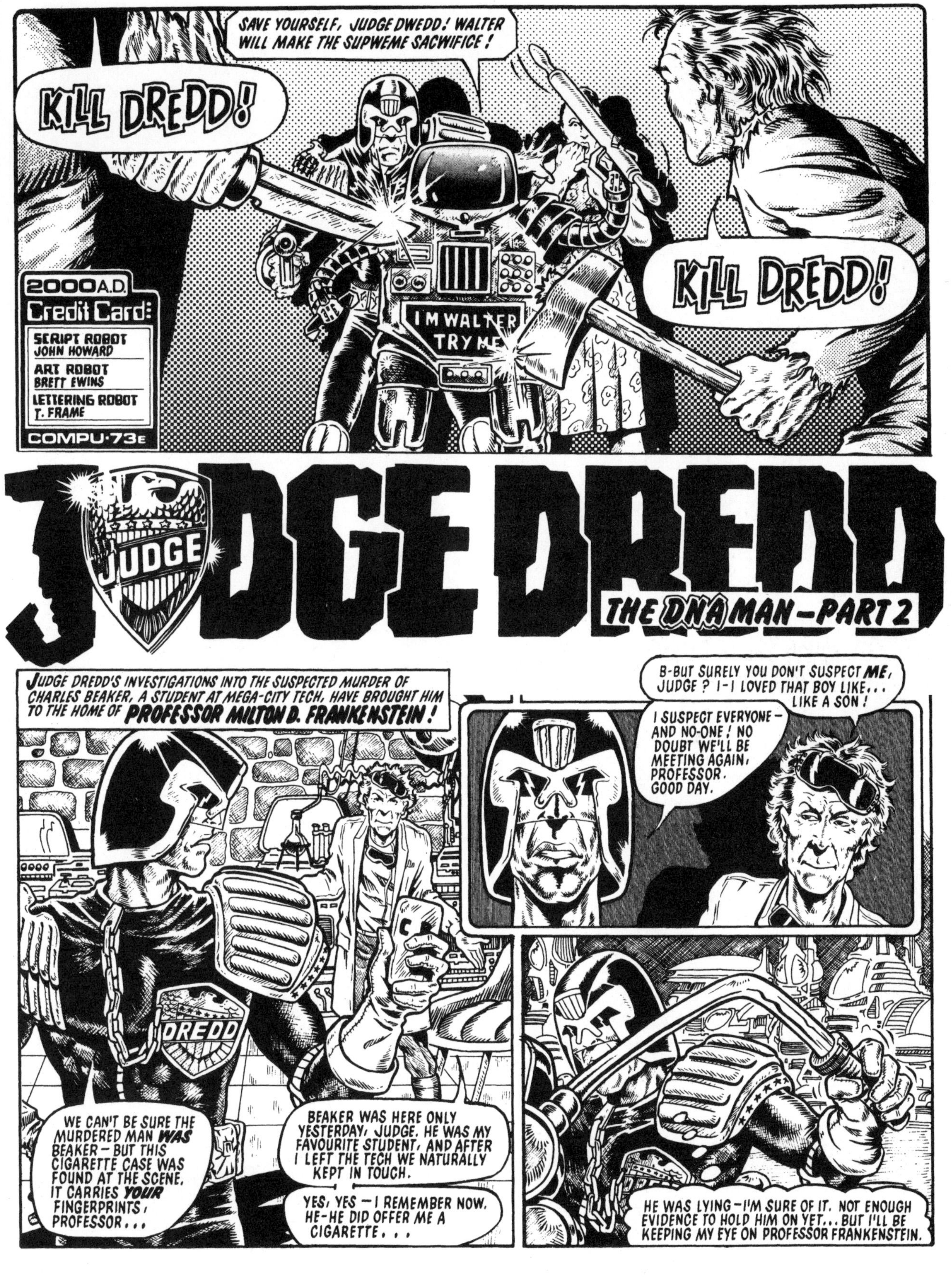
SAVE YOURSELF, JUDGE DWEDD! WALTER WILL MAKE THE SUPWEME SACWIFICE!
KILL DREDD!
KILL DREDD!
I'M WALTER TRY ME
2000 A.D. Credit Card:
SCRIPT ROBOT JOHN HOWARD
ART ROBOT BRETT EWINS
LETTERING ROBOT T. FRAME
COMPU-73E
JUDGE DREDD
THE DNA MAN – PART 2
JUDGE DREDD'S INVESTIGATIONS INTO THE SUSPECTED MURDER OF CHARLES BEAKER, A STUDENT AT MEGA-CITY TECH, HAVE BROUGHT HIM TO THE HOME OF PROFESSOR MILTON D. FRANKENSTEIN!
DREDD
WE CAN'T BE SURE THE MURDERED MAN WAS BEAKER – BUT THIS CIGARETTE CASE WAS FOUND AT THE SCENE. IT CARRIES YOUR FINGERPRINTS, PROFESSOR...
BEAKER WAS HERE ONLY YESTERDAY, JUDGE. HE WAS MY FAVOURITE STUDENT, AND AFTER I LEFT THE TECH WE NATURALLY KEPT IN TOUCH.
YES, YES – I REMEMBER NOW. HE-HE DID OFFER ME A CIGARETTE...
B-BUT SURELY YOU DON'T SUSPECT ME, JUDGE? I-I LOVED THAT BOY LIKE... LIKE A SON!
I SUSPECT EVERYONE – AND NO-ONE! NO DOUBT WE'LL BE MEETING AGAIN, PROFESSOR. GOOD DAY.
HE WAS LYING – I'M SURE OF IT. NOT ENOUGH EVIDENCE TO HOLD HIM ON YET... BUT I'LL BE KEEPING MY EYE ON PROFESSOR FRANKENSTEIN.

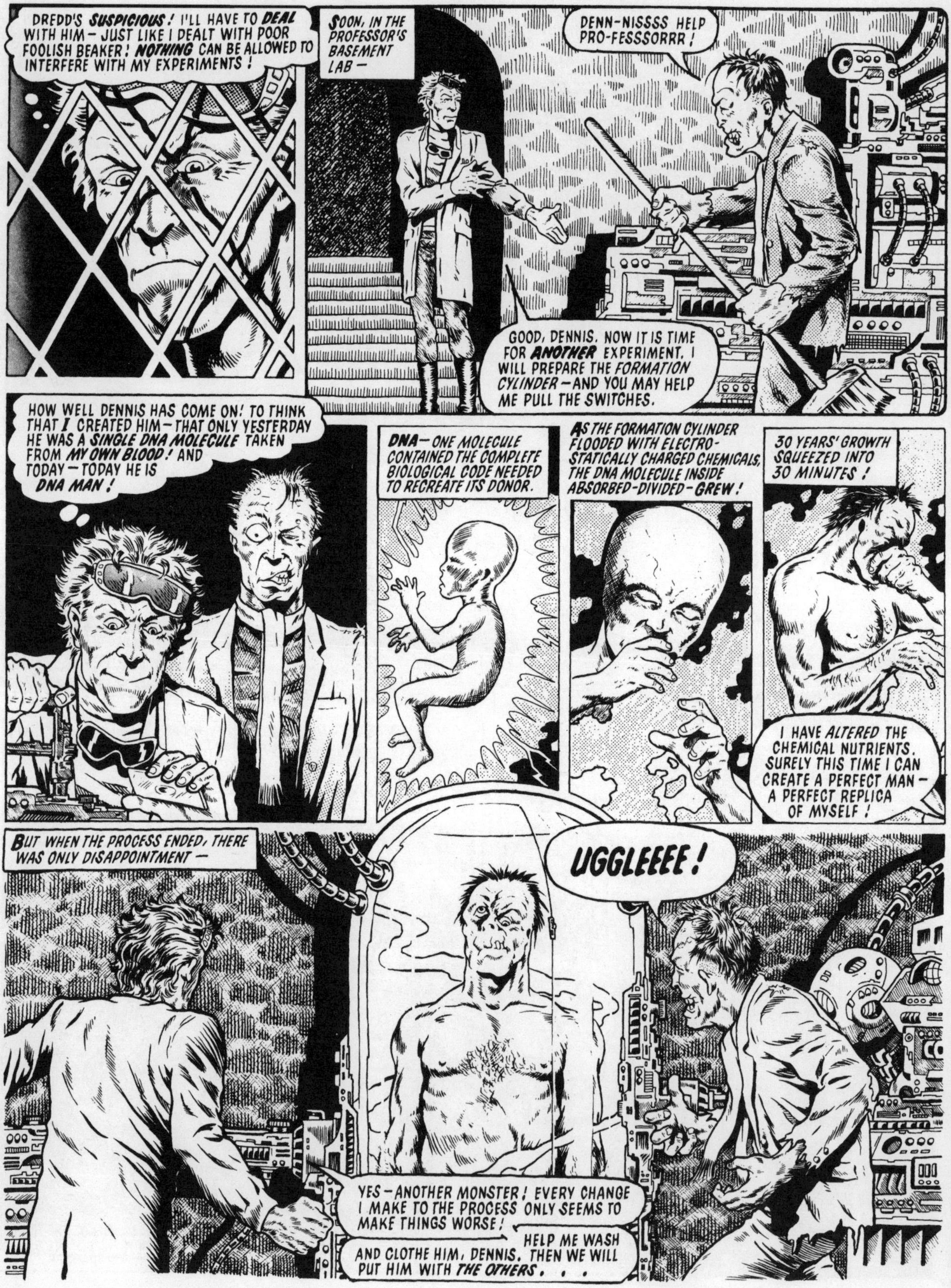
DREDD'S SUSPICIOUS! I'LL HAVE TO DEAL WITH HIM — JUST LIKE I DEALT WITH POOR FOOLISH BEAKER! NOTHING CAN BE ALLOWED TO INTERFERE WITH MY EXPERIMENTS!
SOON, IN THE PROFESSOR'S BASEMENT LAB —
DENN-NISSSS HELP PRO-FESSSORRR!
GOOD, DENNIS. NOW IT IS TIME FOR ANOTHER EXPERIMENT. I WILL PREPARE THE FORMATION CYLINDER — AND YOU MAY HELP ME PULL THE SWITCHES.
HOW WELL DENNIS HAS COME ON! TO THINK THAT I CREATED HIM — THAT ONLY YESTERDAY HE WAS A SINGLE DNA MOLECULE TAKEN FROM MY OWN BLOOD! AND TODAY — TODAY HE IS DNA MAN!
DNA — ONE MOLECULE CONTAINED THE COMPLETE BIOLOGICAL CODE NEEDED TO RECREATE ITS DONOR.
AS THE FORMATION CYLINDER FLOODED WITH ELECTRO-STATICALLY CHARGED CHEMICALS, THE DNA MOLECULE INSIDE ABSORBED-DIVIDED-GREW!
30 YEARS' GROWTH SQUEEZED INTO 30 MINUTES!
I HAVE ALTERED THE CHEMICAL NUTRIENTS. SURELY THIS TIME I CAN CREATE A PERFECT MAN — A PERFECT REPLICA OF MYSELF!
BUT WHEN THE PROCESS ENDED, THERE WAS ONLY DISAPPOINTMENT —
UGGLEEEE!
YES — ANOTHER MONSTER! EVERY CHANGE I MAKE TO THE PROCESS ONLY SEEMS TO MAKE THINGS WORSE!
HELP ME WASH AND CLOTHE HIM, DENNIS. THEN WE WILL PUT HIM WITH THE OTHERS . . .

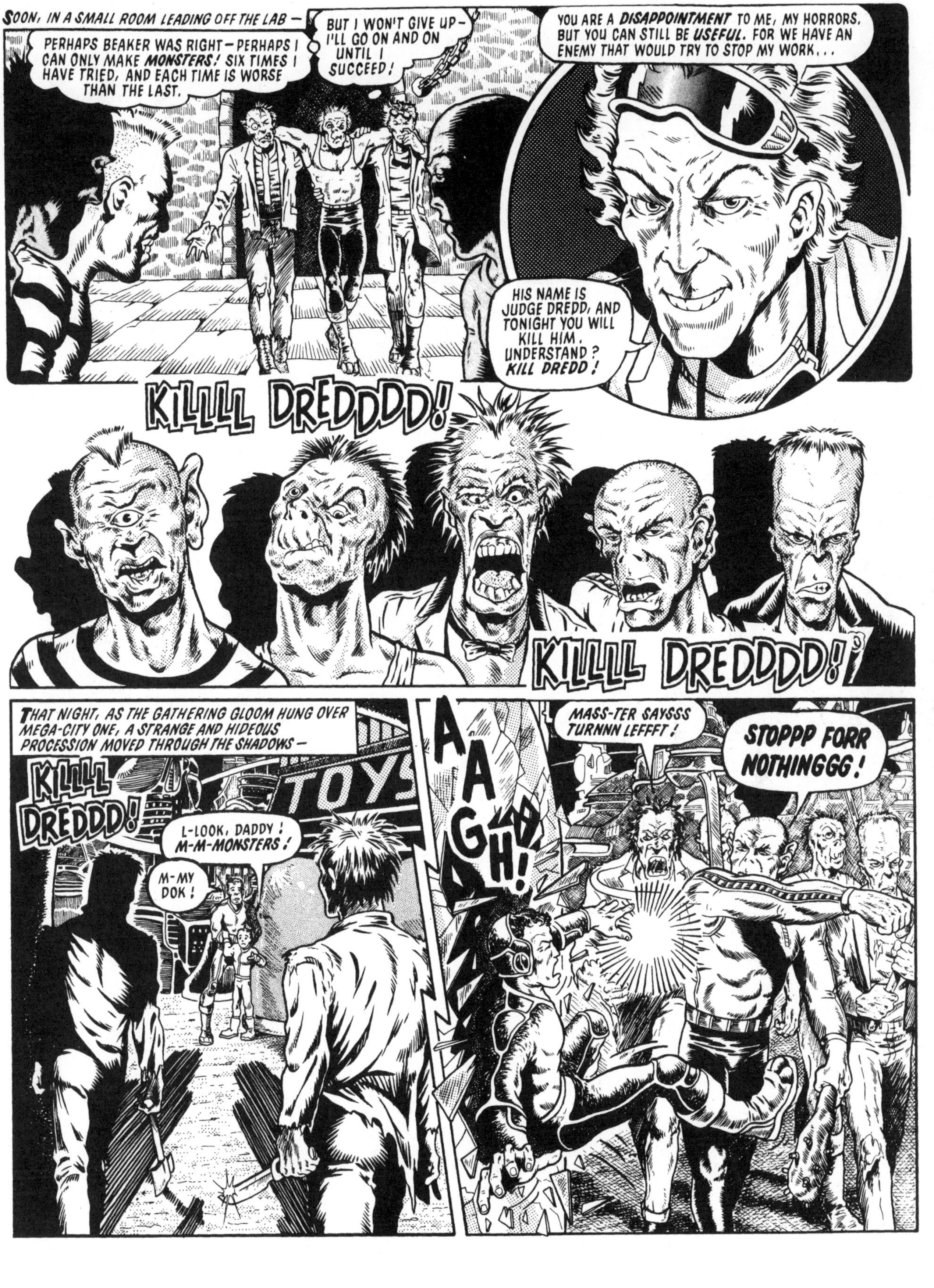
SOON, IN A SMALL ROOM LEADING OFF THE LAB —
PERHAPS BEAKER WAS RIGHT — PERHAPS I CAN ONLY MAKE MONSTERS! SIX TIMES I HAVE TRIED, AND EACH TIME IS WORSE THAN THE LAST.
BUT I WON'T GIVE UP — I'LL GO ON AND ON UNTIL I SUCCEED!
YOU ARE A DISAPPOINTMENT TO ME, MY HORRORS. BUT YOU CAN STILL BE USEFUL. FOR WE HAVE AN ENEMY THAT WOULD TRY TO STOP MY WORK...
HIS NAME IS JUDGE DREDD, AND TONIGHT YOU WILL KILL HIM. UNDERSTAND? KILL DREDD!
KILLLLL DREDDDD!
KILLLLL DREDDDD!
THAT NIGHT, AS THE GATHERING GLOOM HUNG OVER MEGA-CITY ONE, A STRANGE AND HIDEOUS PROCESSION MOVED THROUGH THE SHADOWS —
KILLLL DREDDD!
TOYS
L-LOOK, DADDY! M-M-MONSTERS!
M-MY DOK!
AAGH!
MASS-TER SAYSSS TURNNN LEFFFT!
STOPPP FORR NOTHINGGG!

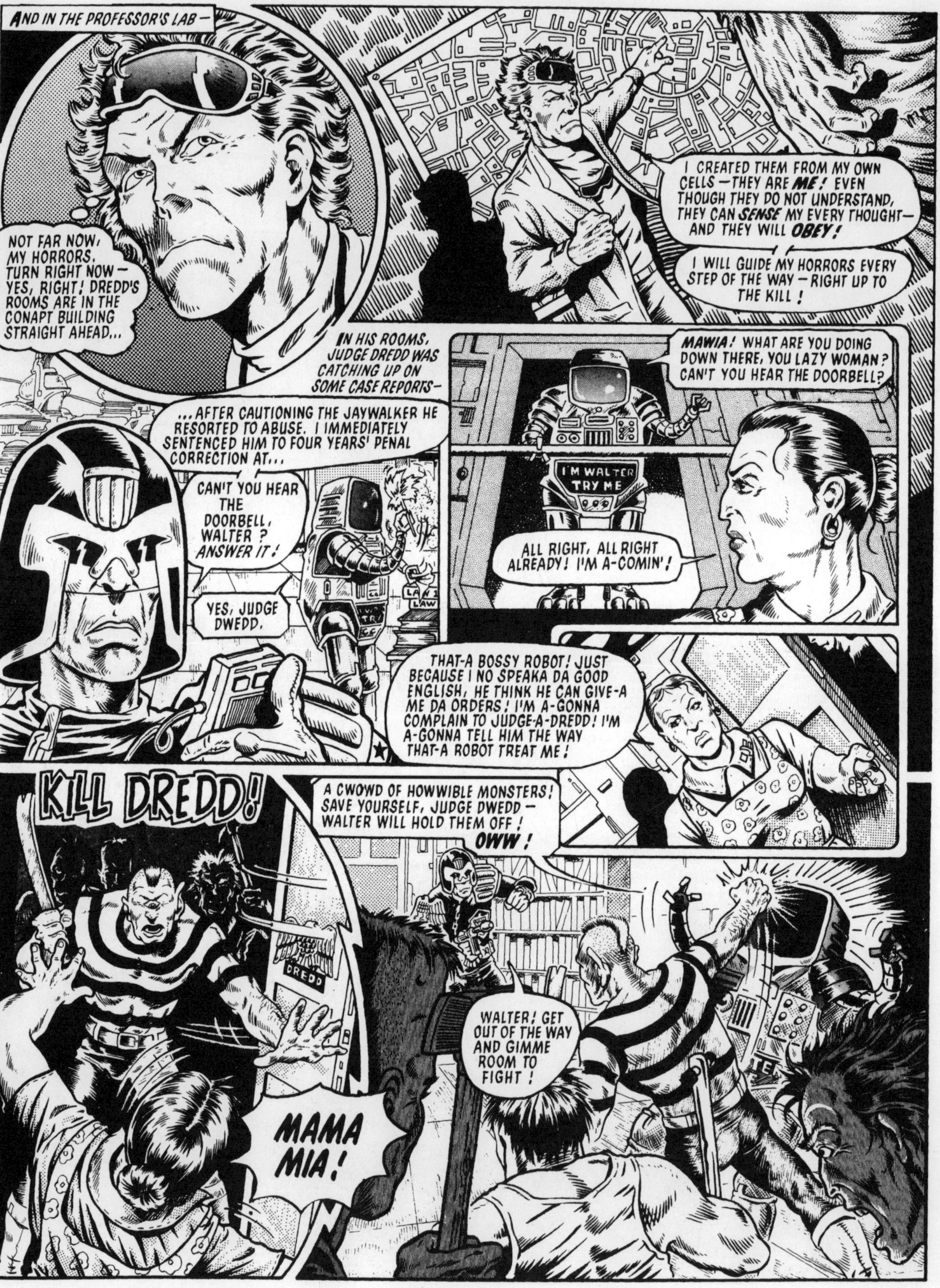
AND IN THE PROFESSOR'S LAB—
NOT FAR NOW, MY HORRORS. TURN RIGHT NOW—YES, RIGHT! DREDD'S ROOMS ARE IN THE CONAPT BUILDING STRAIGHT AHEAD...
I CREATED THEM FROM MY OWN CELLS—THEY ARE ME! EVEN THOUGH THEY DO NOT UNDERSTAND, THEY CAN SENSE MY EVERY THOUGHT—AND THEY WILL OBEY!
I WILL GUIDE MY HORRORS EVERY STEP OF THE WAY—RIGHT UP TO THE KILL!
IN HIS ROOMS, JUDGE DREDD WAS CATCHING UP ON SOME CASE REPORTS—
...AFTER CAUTIONING THE JAYWALKER HE RESORTED TO ABUSE. I IMMEDIATELY SENTENCED HIM TO FOUR YEARS' PENAL CORRECTION AT...
CAN'T YOU HEAR THE DOORBELL, WALTER? ANSWER IT!
YES, JUDGE DWEDD.
MAWIA! WHAT ARE YOU DOING DOWN THERE, YOU LAZY WOMAN? CAN'T YOU HEAR THE DOORBELL?
I'M WALTER TRY ME
ALL RIGHT, ALL RIGHT ALREADY! I'M A-COMIN'!
THAT-A BOSSY ROBOT! JUST BECAUSE I NO SPEAKA DA GOOD ENGLISH, HE THINK HE CAN GIVE-A ME DA ORDERS! I'M A-GONNA COMPLAIN TO JUDGE-A-DREDD! I'M A-GONNA TELL HIM THE WAY THAT-A ROBOT TREAT ME!
KILL DREDD!
A CWOWD OF HOWWIBLE MONSTERS! SAVE YOURSELF, JUDGE DWEDD—WALTER WILL HOLD THEM OFF!
OWW!
DREDD
WALTER! GET OUT OF THE WAY AND GIMME ROOM TO FIGHT!
MAMA MIA!

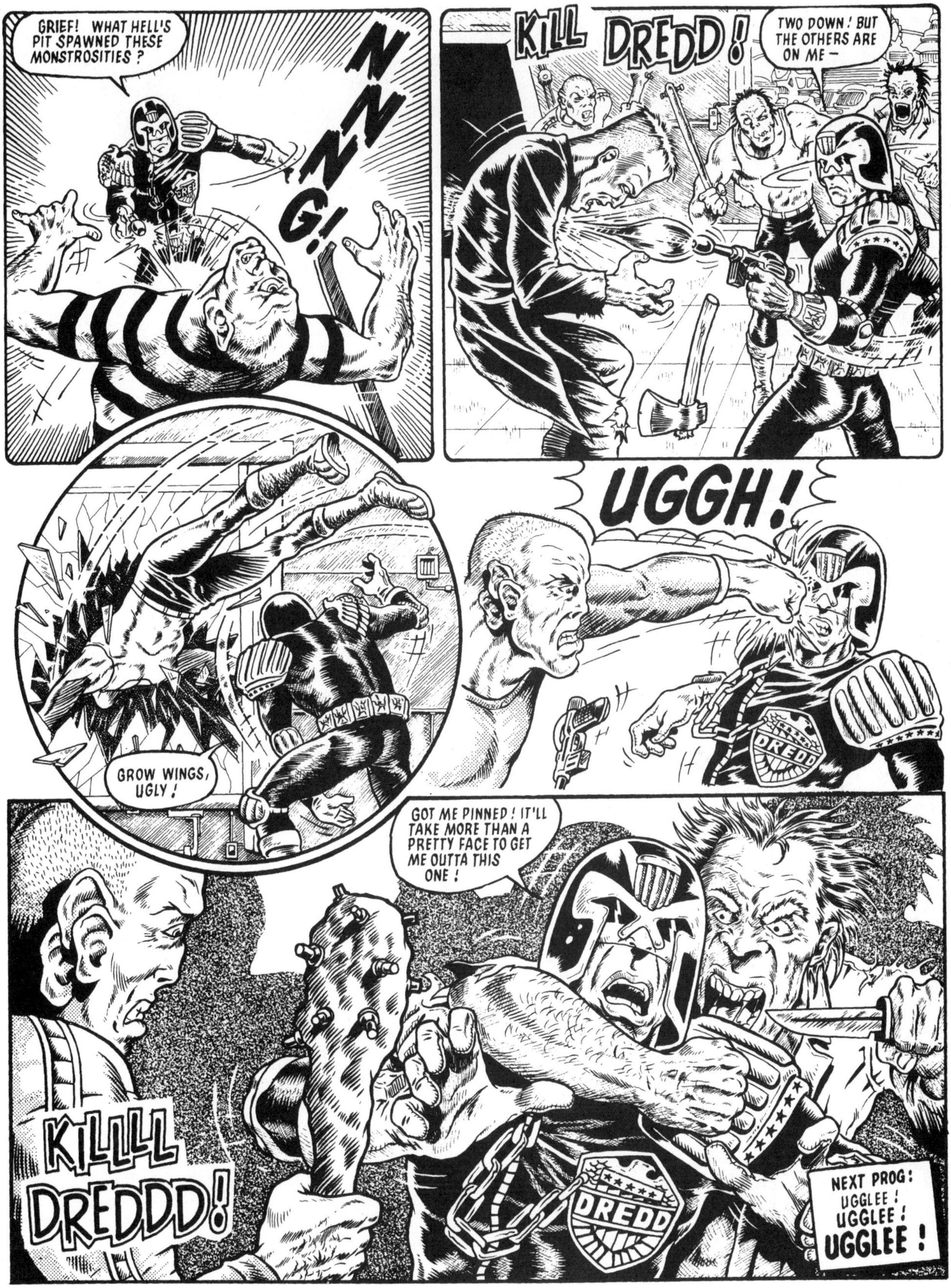

GRIEF! WHAT HELL'S PIT SPAWNED THESE MONSTROSITIES ?
NNNG!
KILL DREDD!
TWO DOWN! BUT THE OTHERS ARE ON ME –
GROW WINGS, UGLY!
UGGH!
GOT ME PINNED! IT'LL TAKE MORE THAN A PRETTY FACE TO GET ME OUTTA THIS ONE!
KILLLLL DREDDD!
NEXT PROG: UGGLEE! UGGLEE! UGGLEE!

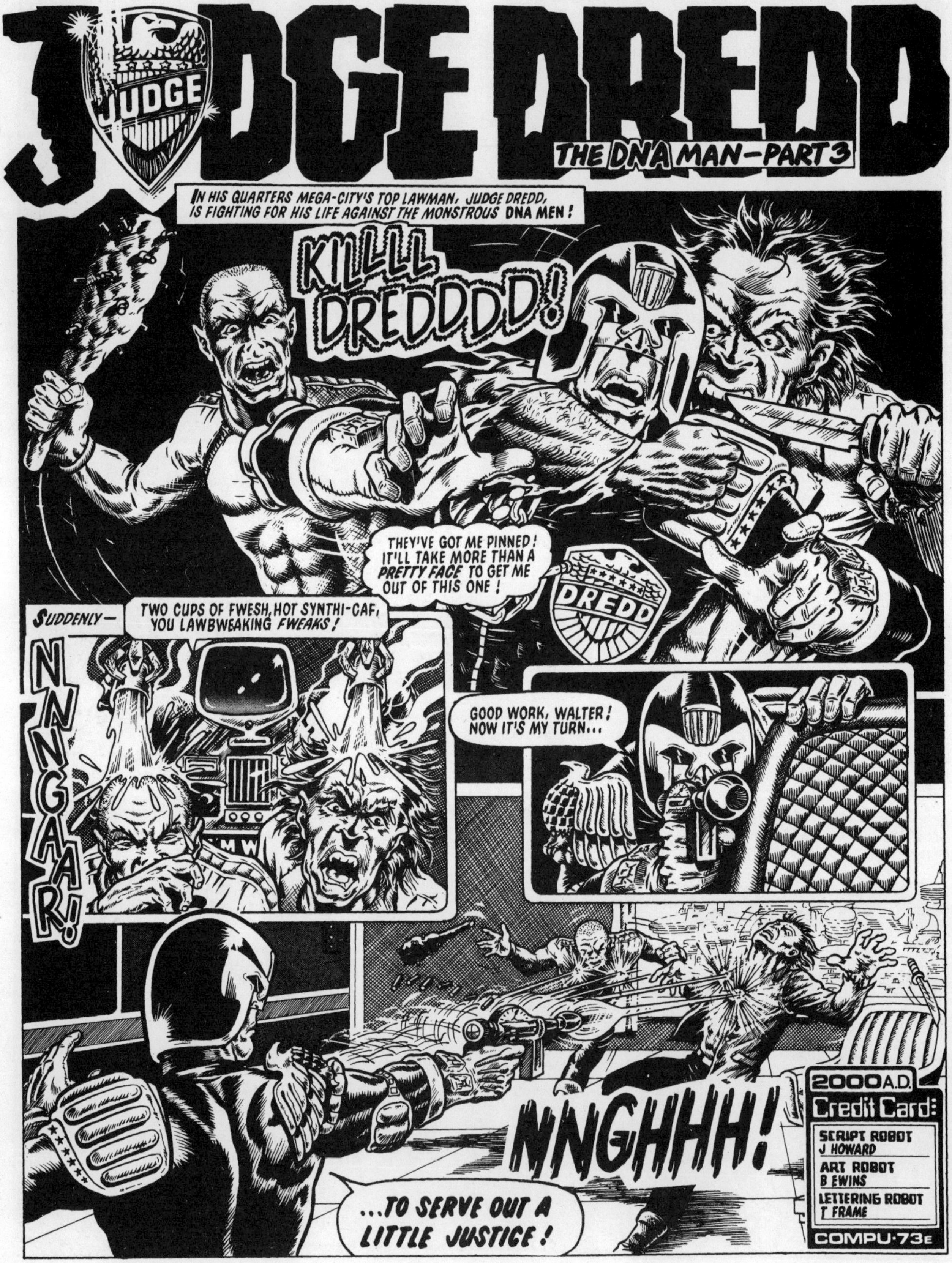
JUDGE DREDD
JUDGE
THE DNA MAN—PART 3
IN HIS QUARTERS MEGA-CITY'S TOP LAWMAN, JUDGE DREDD, IS FIGHTING FOR HIS LIFE AGAINST THE MONSTROUS DNA MEN!
KILLLL DREDDDD!
THEY'VE GOT ME PINNED! IT'LL TAKE MORE THAN A PRETTY FACE TO GET ME OUT OF THIS ONE!
DREDD
SUDDENLY—
TWO CUPS OF FWESH, HOT SYNTHI-CAF, YOU LAWBWEAKING FWEAKS!
NNNGAAR!
GOOD WORK, WALTER! NOW IT'S MY TURN...
NNGHHH!
...TO SERVE OUT A LITTLE JUSTICE!
2000 A.D.
Credit Card:
SCRIPT ROBOT
J HOWARD
ART ROBOT
B EWINS
LETTERING ROBOT
T FRAME
COMPU·73E

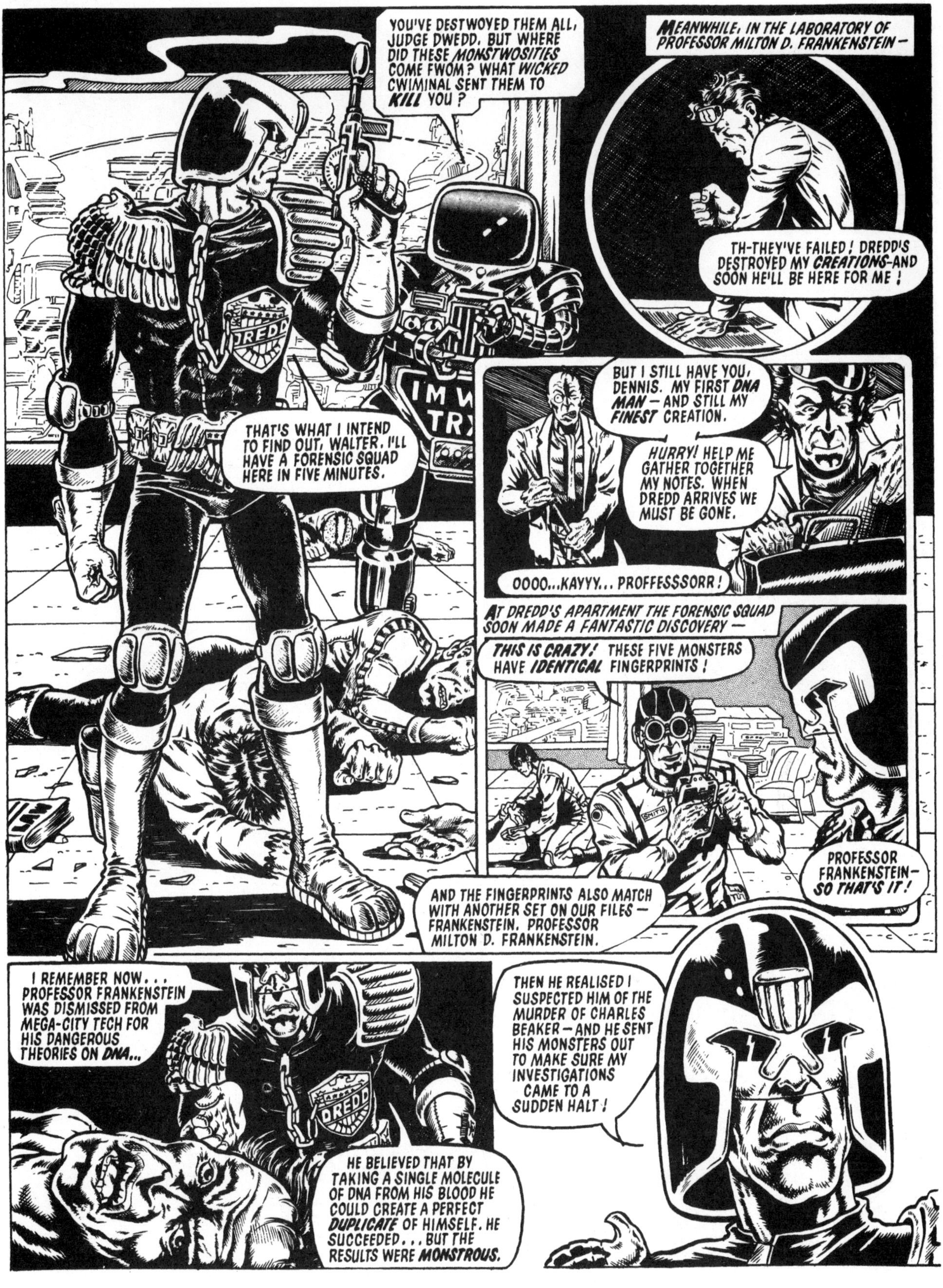
YOU'VE DESTWOYED THEM ALL, JUDGE DWEDD. BUT WHERE DID THESE MONSTWOSITIES COME FWOM? WHAT WICKED CWIMINAL SENT THEM TO KILL YOU?
THAT'S WHAT I INTEND TO FIND OUT, WALTER. I'LL HAVE A FORENSIC SQUAD HERE IN FIVE MINUTES.
MEANWHILE, IN THE LABORATORY OF PROFESSOR MILTON D. FRANKENSTEIN —
TH-THEY'VE FAILED! DREDD'S DESTROYED MY CREATIONS — AND SOON HE'LL BE HERE FOR ME!
BUT I STILL HAVE YOU, DENNIS. MY FIRST DNA MAN — AND STILL MY FINEST CREATION.
HURRY! HELP ME GATHER TOGETHER MY NOTES. WHEN DREDD ARRIVES WE MUST BE GONE.
OOOO...KAYYY... PROFFESSSORR!
AT DREDD'S APARTMENT THE FORENSIC SQUAD SOON MADE A FANTASTIC DISCOVERY —
THIS IS CRAZY! THESE FIVE MONSTERS HAVE IDENTICAL FINGERPRINTS!
SMITH
AND THE FINGERPRINTS ALSO MATCH WITH ANOTHER SET ON OUR FILES — FRANKENSTEIN. PROFESSOR MILTON D. FRANKENSTEIN.
PROFESSOR FRANKENSTEIN — SO THAT'S IT!
I REMEMBER NOW... PROFESSOR FRANKENSTEIN WAS DISMISSED FROM MEGA-CITY TECH FOR HIS DANGEROUS THEORIES ON DNA...
HE BELIEVED THAT BY TAKING A SINGLE MOLECULE OF DNA FROM HIS BLOOD HE COULD CREATE A PERFECT DUPLICATE OF HIMSELF. HE SUCCEEDED... BUT THE RESULTS WERE MONSTROUS.
THEN HE REALISED I SUSPECTED HIM OF THE MURDER OF CHARLES BEAKER — AND HE SENT HIS MONSTERS OUT TO MAKE SURE MY INVESTIGATIONS CAME TO A SUDDEN HALT!

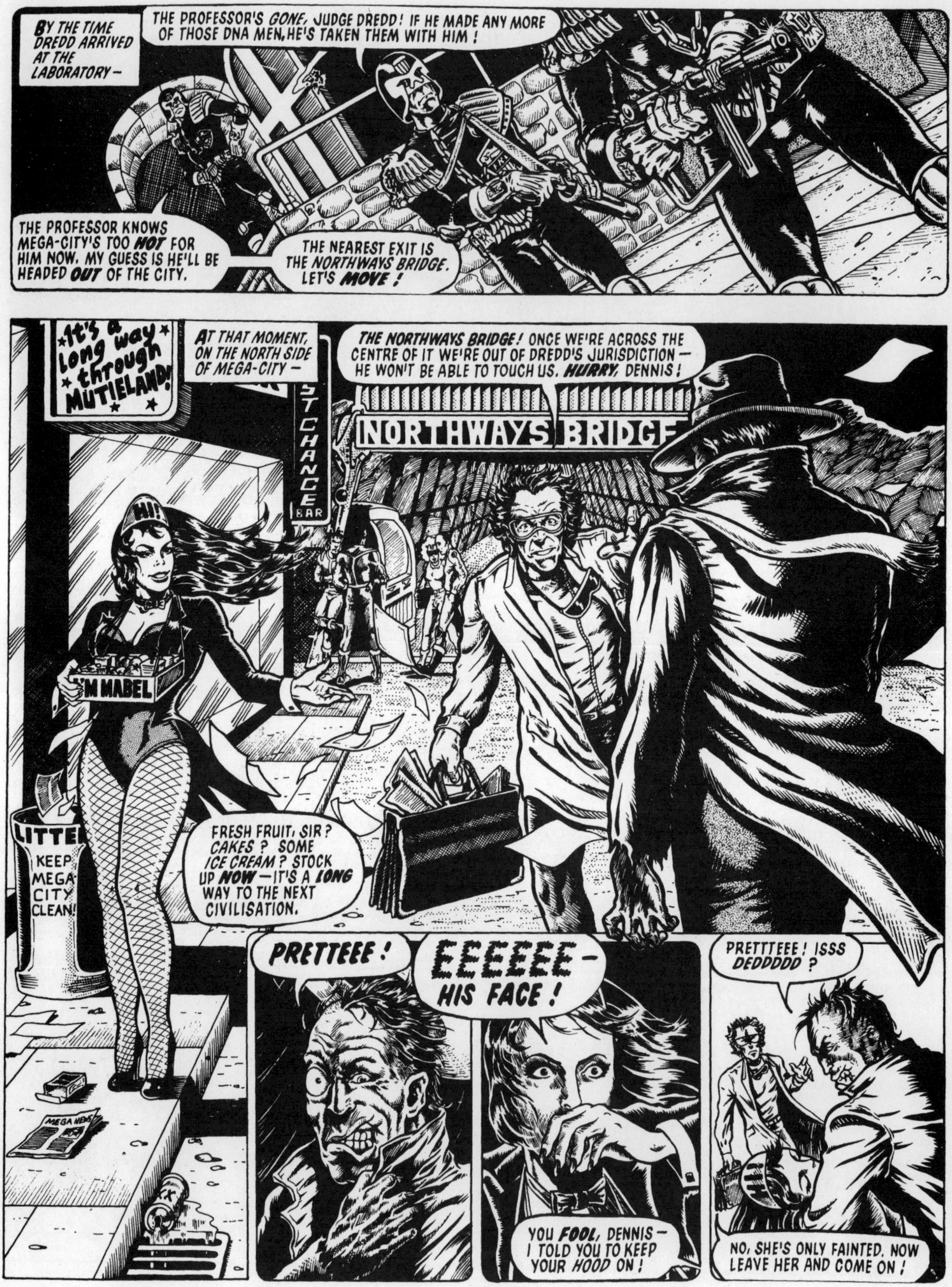
BY THE TIME DREDD ARRIVED AT THE LABORATORY —
THE PROFESSOR'S GONE, JUDGE DREDD! IF HE MADE ANY MORE OF THOSE DNA MEN, HE'S TAKEN THEM WITH HIM!
THE PROFESSOR KNOWS MEGA-CITY'S TOO HOT FOR HIM NOW. MY GUESS IS HE'LL BE HEADED OUT OF THE CITY.
THE NEAREST EXIT IS THE NORTHWAYS BRIDGE. LET'S MOVE!
It's a long way through MUTIELAND!
AT THAT MOMENT, ON THE NORTH SIDE OF MEGA-CITY —
THE NORTHWAYS BRIDGE! ONCE WE'RE ACROSS THE CENTRE OF IT WE'RE OUT OF DREDD'S JURISDICTION — HE WON'T BE ABLE TO TOUCH US. HURRY, DENNIS!
NORTHWAYS BRIDGE
ST CHANCE BAR
HI!
I'M MABEL
LITTER KEEP MEGA-CITY CLEAN!
FRESH FRUIT, SIR? CAKES? SOME ICE CREAM? STOCK UP NOW — IT'S A LONG WAY TO THE NEXT CIVILISATION.
MEGA NEWS
PRETTEEE!
EEEEEE — HIS FACE!
YOU FOOL, DENNIS — I TOLD YOU TO KEEP YOUR HOOD ON!
PRETTTEEE! ISSS DEDDDDD?
NO, SHE'S ONLY FAINTED. NOW LEAVE HER AND COME ON!

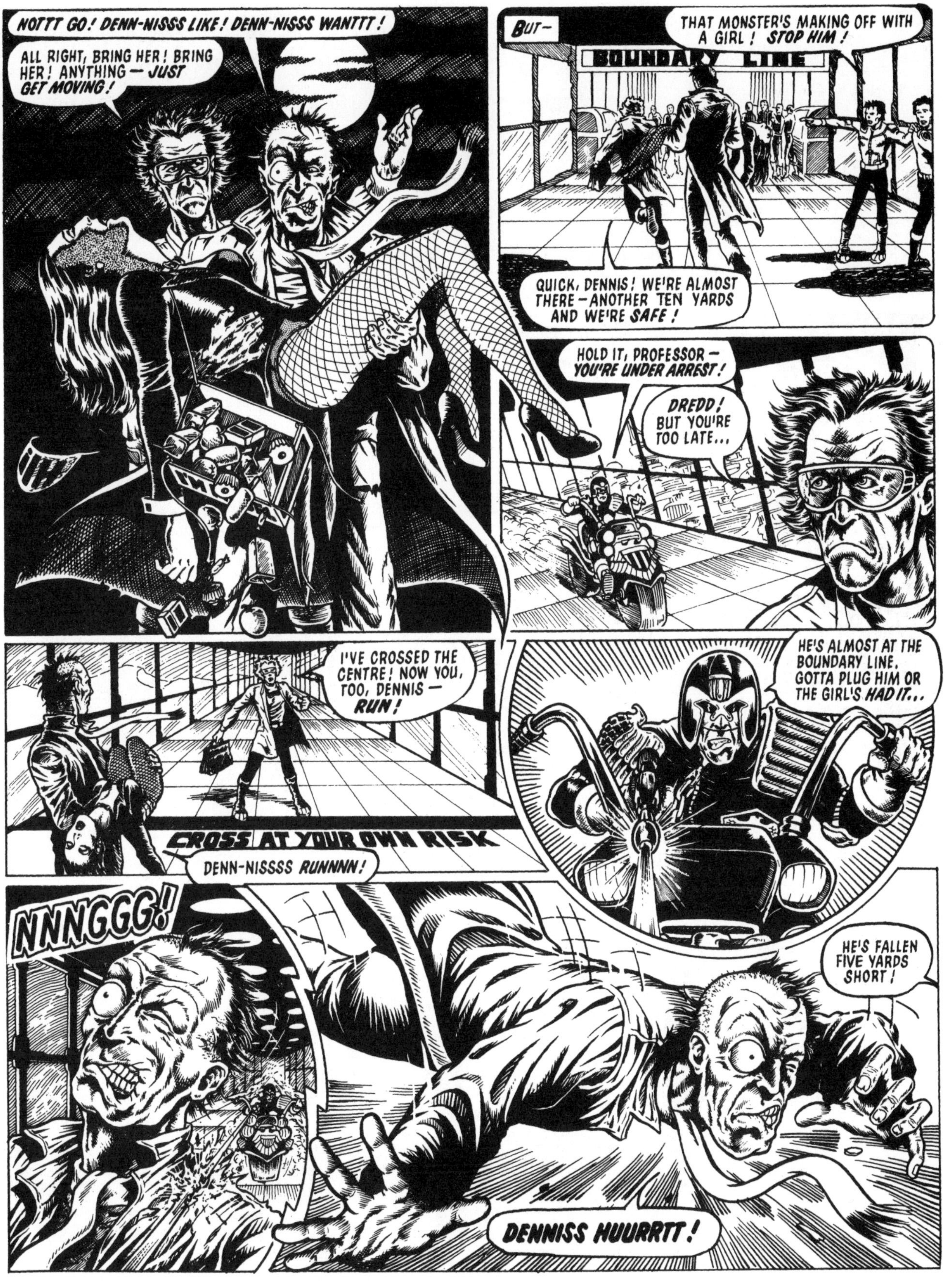
NOTTT GO! DENN-NISSS LIKE! DENN-NISSS WANTTT!
ALL RIGHT, BRING HER! BRING HER! ANYTHING — JUST GET MOVING!
BUT—
THAT MONSTER'S MAKING OFF WITH A GIRL! STOP HIM!
BOUNDARY LINE
QUICK, DENNIS! WE'RE ALMOST THERE — ANOTHER TEN YARDS AND WE'RE SAFE!
HOLD IT, PROFESSOR — YOU'RE UNDER ARREST!
DREDD! BUT YOU'RE TOO LATE...
I'VE CROSSED THE CENTRE! NOW YOU, TOO, DENNIS — RUN!
CROSS AT YOUR OWN RISK
DENN-NISSSS RUNNNN!
HE'S ALMOST AT THE BOUNDARY LINE. GOTTA PLUG HIM OR THE GIRL'S HAD IT...
NNNGGG!
HE'S FALLEN FIVE YARDS SHORT!
DENNISS HUURRTT!

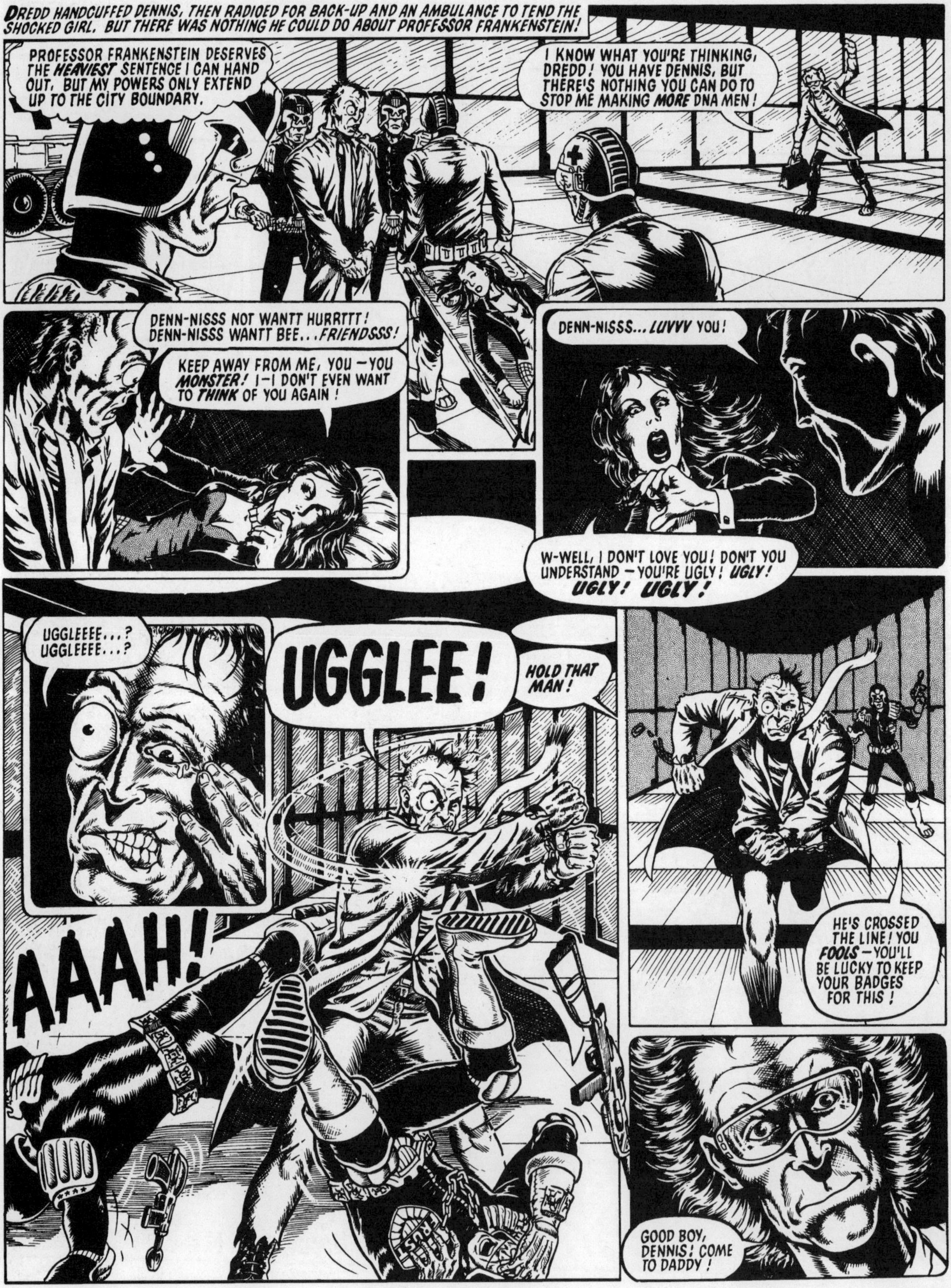
DREDD HANDCUFFED DENNIS, THEN RADIOED FOR BACK-UP AND AN AMBULANCE TO TEND THE SHOCKED GIRL. BUT THERE WAS NOTHING HE COULD DO ABOUT PROFESSOR FRANKENSTEIN!
PROFESSOR FRANKENSTEIN DESERVES THE HEAVIEST SENTENCE I CAN HAND OUT. BUT MY POWERS ONLY EXTEND UP TO THE CITY BOUNDARY.
I KNOW WHAT YOU'RE THINKING, DREDD! YOU HAVE DENNIS, BUT THERE'S NOTHING YOU CAN DO TO STOP ME MAKING MORE DNA MEN!
DENN-NISSS NOT WANTT HURRTTT! DENN-NISSS WANTT BEE... FRIENDSSS!
KEEP AWAY FROM ME, YOU — YOU MONSTER! I-I DON'T EVEN WANT TO THINK OF YOU AGAIN!
DENN-NISSS... LUVVV YOU!
W-WELL, I DON'T LOVE YOU! DON'T YOU UNDERSTAND — YOU'RE UGLY! UGLY! UGLY! UGLY!
UGGLEEEE...? UGGLEEEE...?
UGGLEE!
HOLD THAT MAN!
AAAH!
HE'S CROSSED THE LINE! YOU FOOLS — YOU'LL BE LUCKY TO KEEP YOUR BADGES FOR THIS!
GOOD BOY, DENNIS! COME TO DADDY!

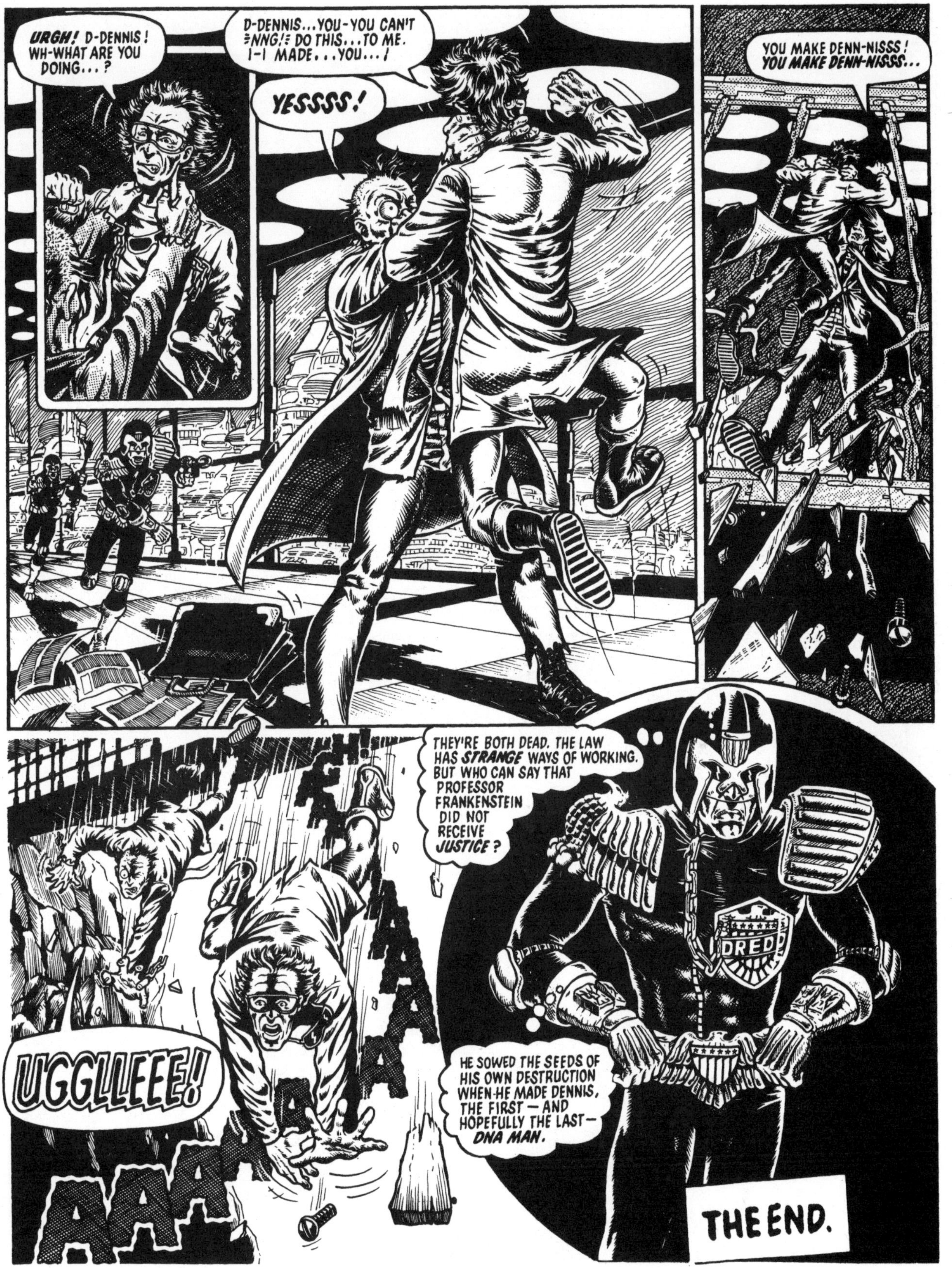
URGH! D-DENNIS! WH-WHAT ARE YOU DOING...?
D-DENNIS...YOU-YOU CAN'T NNG! DO THIS...TO ME. I-I MADE...YOU...!
YESSSS!
YOU MAKE DENN-NISSS! YOU MAKE DENN-NISSS...
UGGLLEEE!
AAAAAAAAH!
THEY'RE BOTH DEAD. THE LAW HAS STRANGE WAYS OF WORKING. BUT WHO CAN SAY THAT PROFESSOR FRANKENSTEIN DID NOT RECEIVE JUSTICE?
HE SOWED THE SEEDS OF HIS OWN DESTRUCTION WHEN HE MADE DENNIS, THE FIRST — AND HOPEFULLY THE LAST — DNA MAN.
DRED
THE END.

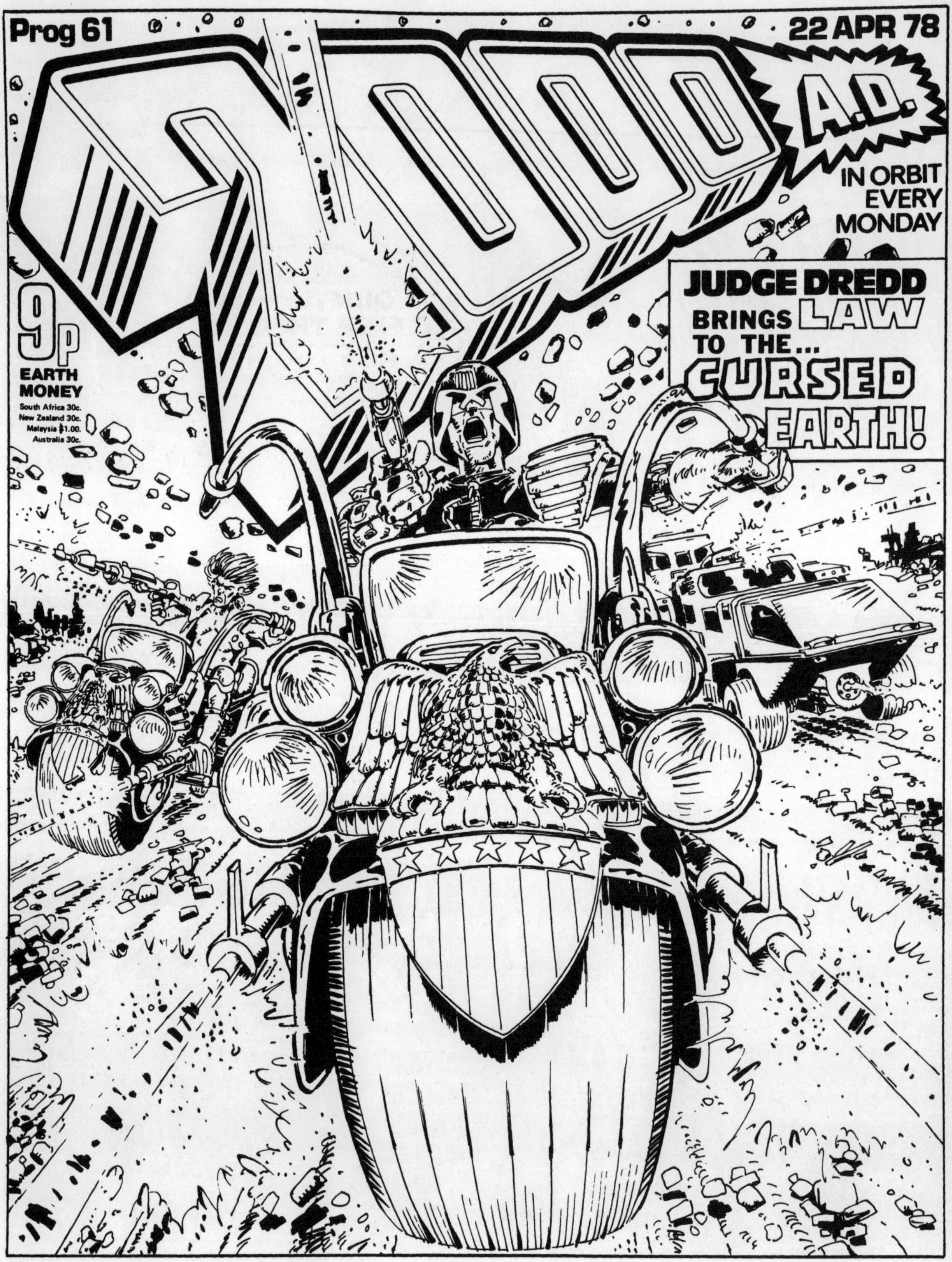
Prog 61
22 APR 78
2000 A.D.
IN ORBIT EVERY MONDAY
9p
EARTH MONEY
South Africa 30c.
New Zealand 30c.
Malaysia $1.00.
Australia 30c.
JUDGE DREDD BRINGS LAW TO THE... CURSED EARTH!

2000 AD Prog 61: Cover by **Mike McMahon**

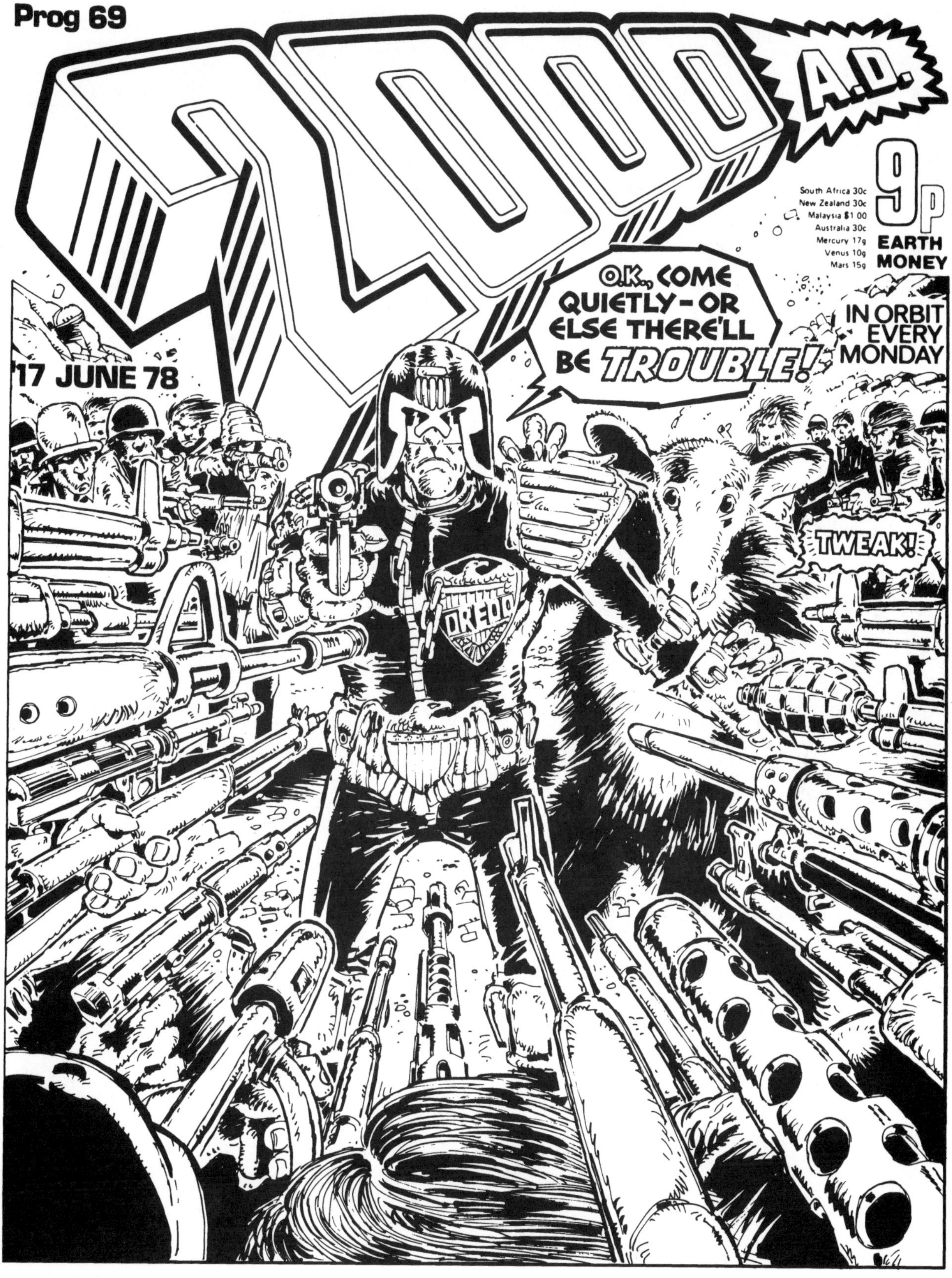

Prog 69
2000 A.D.
9p
South Africa 30c
New Zealand 30c
Malaysia $1 00
Australia 30c
Mercury 17g
Venus 10g
Mars 15g
EARTH MONEY
O.K., COME QUIETLY – OR ELSE THERE'LL BE TROUBLE!
IN ORBIT EVERY MONDAY
17 JUNE 78
DREDD
TWEAK!

2000 AD Prog 69: Cover by **Mike McMahon**

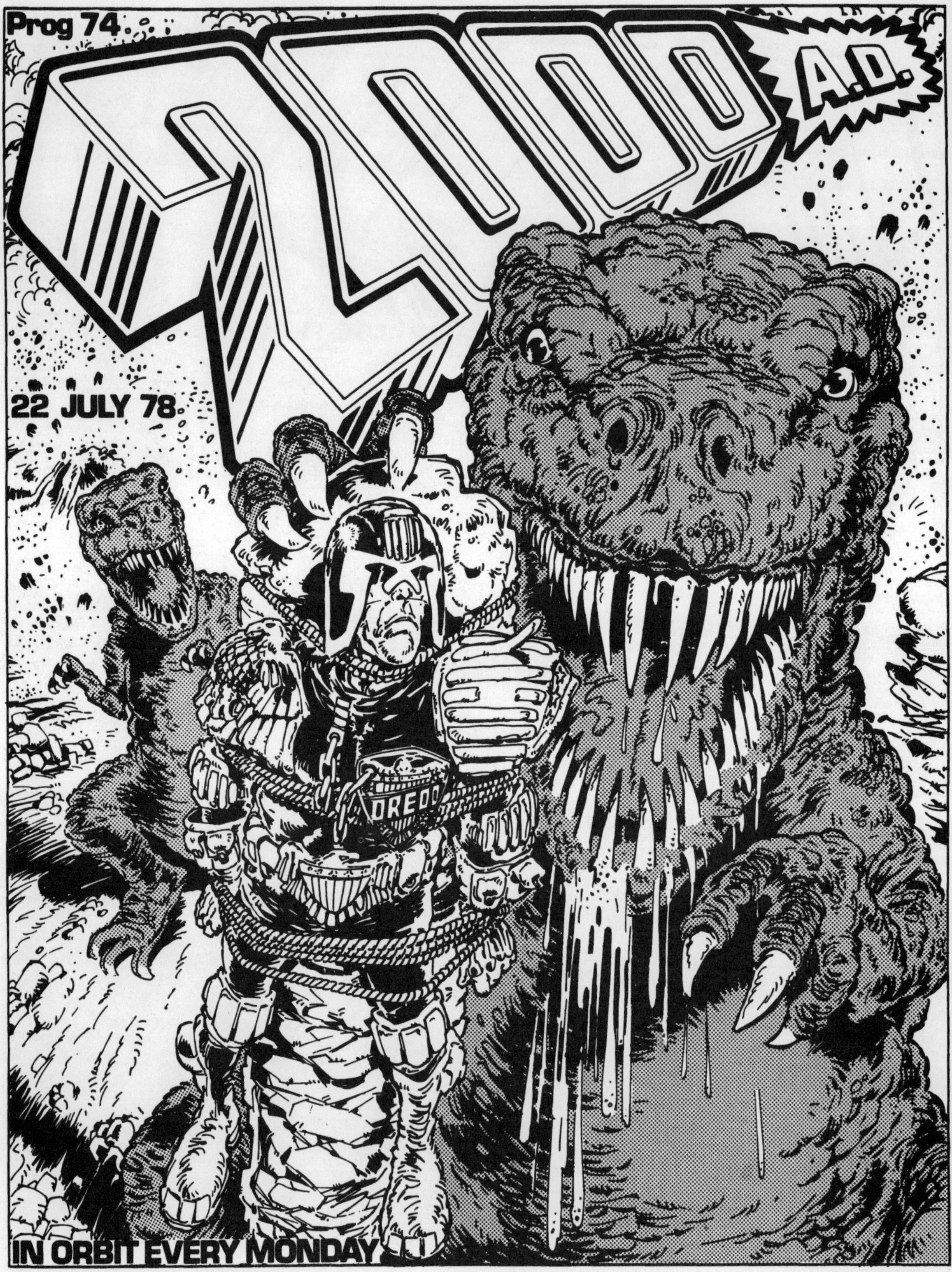

Prog 74
2000 A.D.
22 JULY 78
DREDD
IN ORBIT EVERY MONDAY

2000 AD Prog 74: Cover by **Mike McMahon**

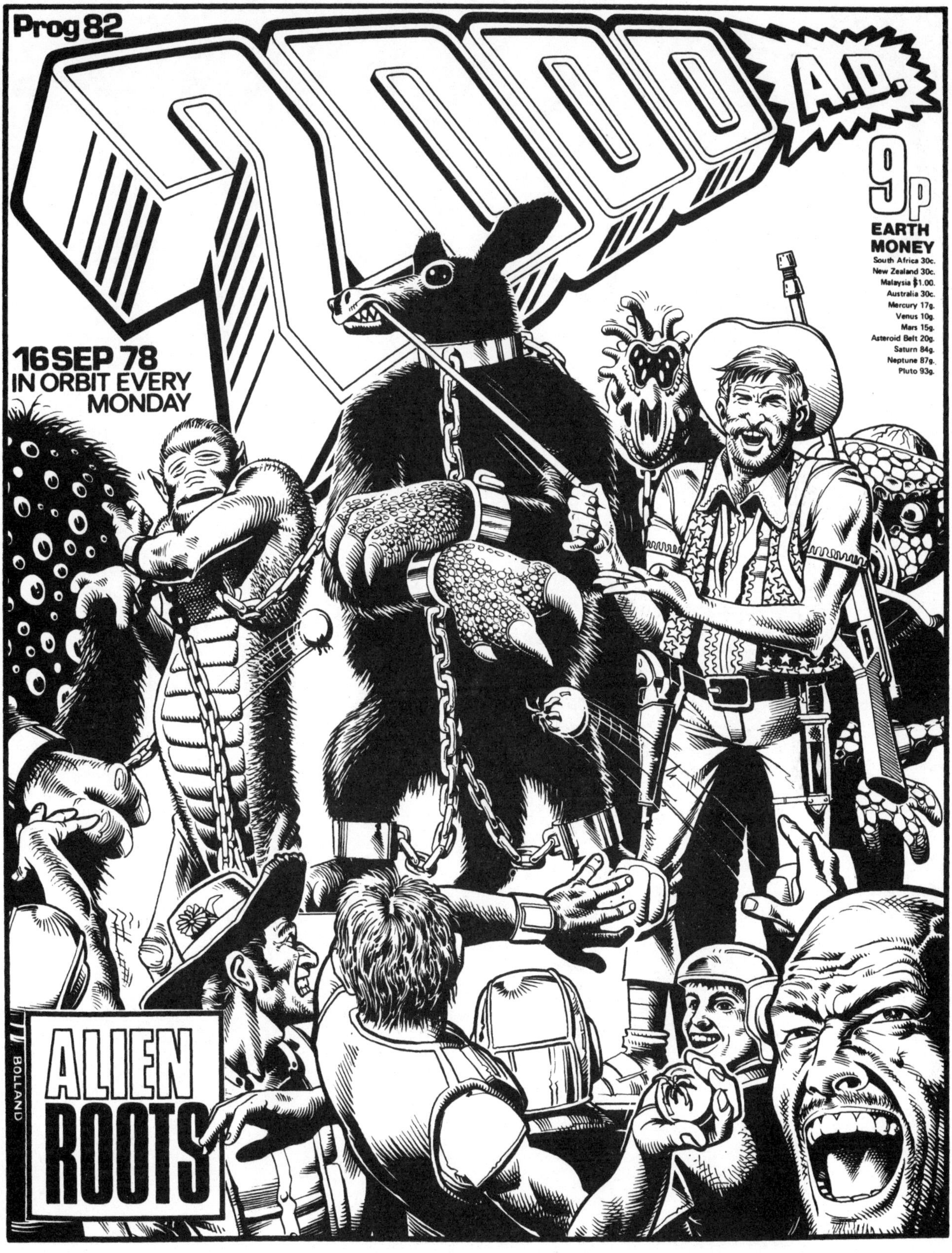
Prog 82
2000 A.D.
9p
EARTH MONEY
South Africa 30c.
New Zealand 30c.
Malaysia $1.00.
Australia 30c.
Mercury 17g.
Venus 10g.
Mars 15g.
Asteroid Belt 20g.
Saturn 84g.
Neptune 87g.
Pluto 93g.
16 SEP 78
IN ORBIT EVERY MONDAY
ALIEN ROOTS
BOLLAND

2000 AD Prog 82: Cover by **Brian Bolland**

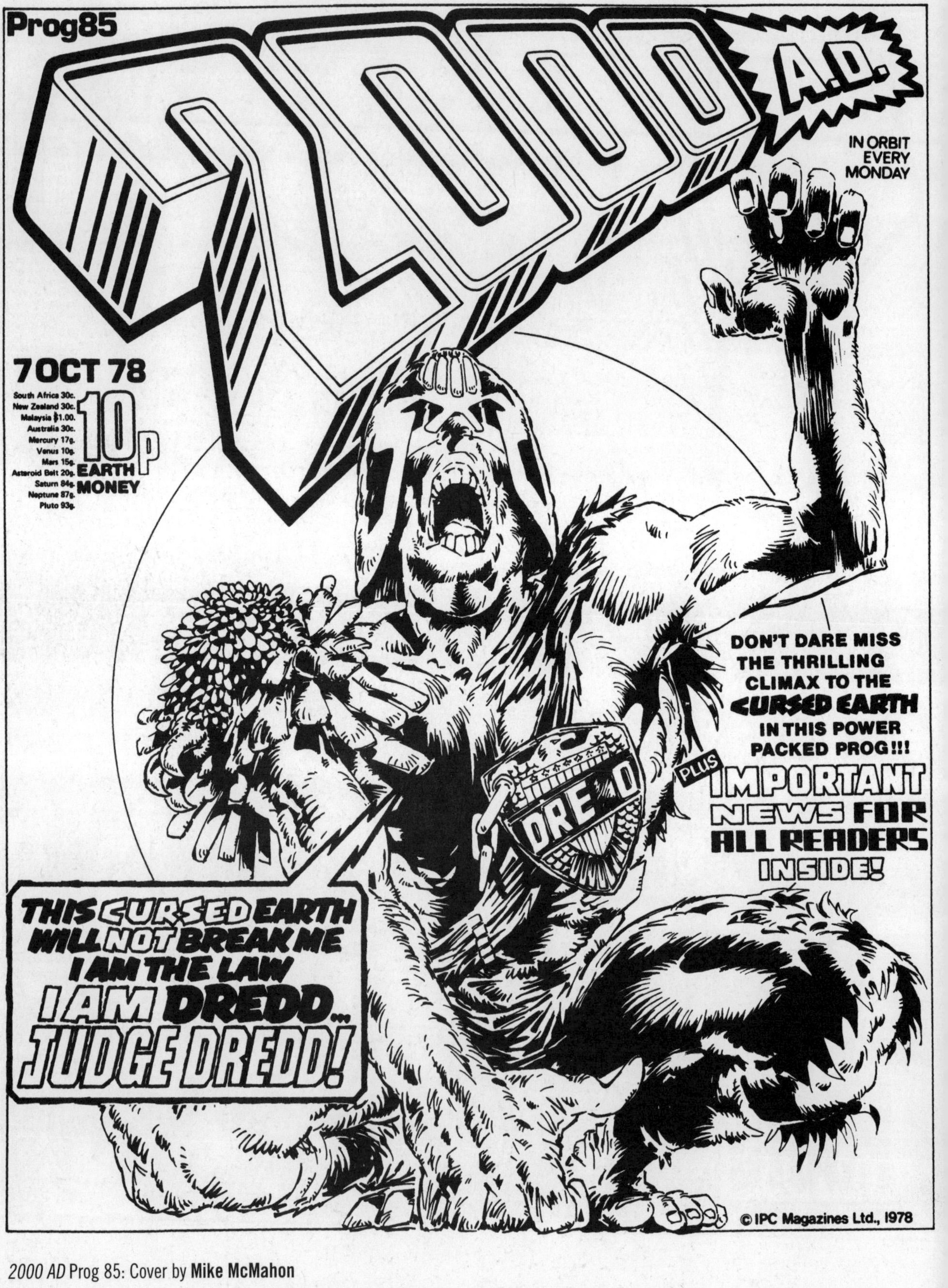
Prog85
2000 A.D.
IN ORBIT EVERY MONDAY
7 OCT 78
South Africa 30c.
New Zealand 30c.
Malaysia $1.00.
Australia 30c.
Mercury 17g.
Venus 10g.
Mars 15g.
Asteroid Belt 20g.
Saturn 84g.
Neptune 87g.
Pluto 93g.
10p EARTH MONEY
DON'T DARE MISS THE THRILLING CLIMAX TO THE CURSED EARTH IN THIS POWER PACKED PROG!!!
PLUS IMPORTANT NEWS FOR ALL READERS INSIDE!
DREDD
THIS CURSED EARTH WILL NOT BREAK ME I AM THE LAW I AM DREDD... JUDGE DREDD!
© IPC Magazines Ltd., 1978

2000 AD Prog 85: Cover by **Mike McMahon**

WRITERS

Pat Mills is the creator and first editor of *2000 AD*. For the Galaxy's Greatest Comic, he is the writer and co-creator of *ABC Warriors, Finn, Flesh, Nemesis the Warlock, Sláine, M.A.C.H 1, Harlem Heroes* and Savage. He also developed Judge Dredd and wrote one of the early Dredd serials, The Cursed Earth. He wrote Third World War for *Crisis!*, a politically charged spin-off from *2000 AD*, and *Black Siddha* for the *Judge Dredd Megazine*. Outside *2000 AD* he is the writer and co-creator of the long-running classic anti-war story *Charley's War,* as well as *Marshal Law*. He has also written for the *Batman, Star Wars* and *Zombie World* series for the US market. Currently Mills is writing the bestselling series *Requiem - Vampire Knight* for Editions Nickel of France with artist Olivier Ledroit and a spin-off series *Claudia - Vampire* with artist Frank Tacito. He is also completing the graphic novel version of *American Reaper* co-created with Clint Langley, based on his screenplay for Xingu Films.

John Wagner has been scripting for *2000 AD* for more years than he cares to remember. His creations include *Judge Dredd, Strontium Dog, Ace Trucking, Al's Baby, Button Man* and *Mean Machine*. Outside of *2000 AD* his credits include *Star Wars, Lobo, The Punisher* and the critically acclaimed *A History of Violence*.

Chris Lowder has contributed to various *2000AD* series including *Judge Dredd, Dan Dare, Tharg's Future Shocks* and *Time Twisters*.

ARTISTS

Perhaps the most popular *2000 AD* artist of all time, **Brian Bolland**'s clean-line style and meticulous attention to detail ensure that his artwork on strips including *Dan Dare, Future Shocks, Judge Dredd* and *Walter the Wobot* looks as fresh today as it did when first published. Co-creator of both *Judge Anderson* and *The Kleggs*, Bolland's highly detailed style unfortunately precluded him from doing many sequential strips — although he found the time to pencil both *Camelot 3000* and *Batman: The Killing Joke* for DC Comics.

Although **Mike McMahon** may not have illustrated as many strips as other *2000 AD* creators, his importance to the comic cannot be overstated. It was McMahon who co-created perennial classics *A.B.C. Warriors* and *The V.C.'s*, and it was also *McMahon* who gave *Judge Dredd* his classic, defining, "*big boots*" look. McMahon has also illustrated *One-Offs, Ro-Busters*, and provided a classic run on *Sláine*. Outside of the Galaxy's Greatest Comic, he has pencilled *Batman: Legends of the Dark Knight* and *The Last American*, which he co-created with *John Wagner*.

Dave Gibbons is one of *2000 AD*'s most popular artists, having created *Harlem Heroes* and *Rogue Trooper*. He has also pencilled *A.B.C. Warriors, Dan Dare, Judge Dredd, Mega-City One, Ro-Busters, Tharg the Mighty, Tharg's Future Shocks* and *Time Twisters*, as well as having scripted several *Rogue Trooper* stories — making Gibbons one of the few *2000 AD* creators to have served as writer, artist and letterer!
Beyond *2000 AD*, Gibbons is unquestionably best known for his work on the award-winning classic *Watchmen* (with Alan Moore), but he has also pencilled *A1, Batman, Doctor Who, Give Me Liberty, Green Lantern, Superman, Star Wars* and *War Story*. His graphic novel *The Originals* won an Eisner award in 2005.

Brendan McCarthy was a key early artist for *2000 AD*, and designed *Zenith* with Grant Morrison, and many of the perennially popular *A.B.C. Warriors* with Pat Mills (and others). He also illustrated *Judge Dredd, Strontium Dog,* and *Tharg's Future Shocks.*
McCarthy's non-*2000 AD* work includes *Skin* in *Crisis, Strange Days, Paradox!, Freakwave* in *Vanguard* Illustrated and work for *Revolver.*

Since his Future Shock debut in Prog 37, **Brett Ewins** has been one of the Galaxy's Greatest Comic's most beloved artists. Co-creator of the classic *Bad Company*, Ewins has also contributed to *A.B.C. Warriors, Daily Star Dredd, Judge Anderson, Judge Dredd, Kelly, Mega-City One, Rogue Trooper, Ro-Jaws, Robo-Tales* and *Universal Soldier.*
Beyond *2000 AD*, Ewins was a co-founding editor of Deadline magazine, and co-pencilled and inked the hugely acclaimed *Skreemer* series, which he co-created with writer Peter Milligan. He also created *Johnny Nemo*, which has enjoyed great success in the US with Cyberosia Publishing.

Garry Leach is a highly-respected artist who has pencilled *Dan Dare, Judge Dredd, Tharg's Future Shocks* and *The V.C.'s.* His career beyond *2000 AD* is highly notable for his work on the legendary *Miracleman*, which he effectively co-created with Alan Moore, but also includes *Axel Pressbutton, Deadline* and *Global Frequency.*

Ron Smith drew many *2000 AD* stories including some of the epic *Judge Dredd* tale 'The Day The Law Died.' His other work for *2000 AD* includes *Chronos Carnival* and *Tales of The Doghouse.*